This is a FLAME TREE Book

Publisher & Creative Director: Nick Wells
Project Editor: Gillian Whitaker
Editorial Board: Gillian Whitaker, Catherine Taylor, Jocelyn Pontes,
Jemma North and Simran Aulakh

Publisher's Note: Due to the historical nature of the classic text, we're aware that there may be some language used which has the potential to cause offence to the modern reader. However, wishing overall to preserve the integrity of the text, rather than imposing contemporary sensibilities, we have left it unaltered.

FLAME TREE PUBLISHING
6 Melbray Mews, Fulham,
London SW6 3NS, United Kingdom
www.flametreepublishing.com

First published 2025

Copyright © 2025 Flame Tree Publishing Ltd

Stories by modern authors are subject to international copyright law, and are licensed for publication in this volume.

25 27 29 28 26
1 3 5 7 9 10 8 6 4 2

ISBN: 978-1-83562-265-0
Special ISBN: 978-1-83562-639-9

All rights reserved. No part of this publication may be reproduced, stored in a retrieval system, or transmitted in any form or by any means, electronic, mechanical, photocopying, recording or otherwise, without the prior written permission of the publisher.

The cover image is created by Flame Tree Studio based on artwork courtesy of Shutterstock.com and Denis Andricic Obsidian Fantasy Studio, Slava Gerj and Gabor Ruszkai.

A copy of the CIP data for this book is available from the British Library.

Printed and bound in China

Contents

Foreword by Dr. Karen E. Macfarlane 10

Publisher's Note 11

The Iron Wolf 14
    Cossack Folktale

The Werewolf Howls 16
    Clifford Ball

The Cull 21
    Richard Beauchamp

The Camp of the Dog 28
    Algernon Blackwood

Moonskin 68
    Charlotte Bond

The Claws Come Out 75
    B.A. Booher

The White Wolf of Kostopchin 82
    Gilbert Edward Campbell

The Change 99
    Ramsey Campbell

The Thing in the Forest 106
    Bernard Capes

CONTENTS

Dance, Mephisto 108
Catherine Cavendish

The Lay of the Were-Wolf 115
French Medieval Romance by Marie de France

Rougarou Moon 119
E.C. Dorgan

A Pastoral Horror 126
Arthur Conan Doyle

The Werewolf 136
Eugene Field

We Are Not the Wolf 140
Roy Graham

Margaery the Wolf 147
Maria Haskins

The Were-Wolf 154
Clemence Housman

In the Forest of Villeféré 177
Robert E. Howard

Morraha 180
Celtic Fairy Tale

When It Happens 187
Rebecca Jones-Howe

Boy Beautiful, the Golden Apples, and the Were-Wolf 197
Romanian Fairy Tale

How William of Palermo Was Carried Off by the Werwolf..................202
Medieval Romance

The White Wolf..................211
Andrew Lang

The Son of the Wolf Chief..................215
From Tlingit Mythology

The Feelings of Sheep..................218
Andrew Lyall

When Sleeping Wolves Lie..................224
Mark Patrick Lynch

The Gray Wolf..................232
George MacDonald

Skin Traders..................236
Clara MacGauffin

Madame Bisclavret..................242
Natasha Marshall

Hugues the Wer-Wolf..................247
Sutherland Menzies

Arthur and Gorlagon..................259
From Arthurian Legend

Sigmund, Sinfjotli and the Wolf Pelts..................267
translated by William Morris & Eiríkur Magnússon

The Cage in the Forest..................268
Jim Moss

CONTENTS

Fangs Fur Love **275**
James Musgrave

Bran, the Wolf-Dog **284**
Jane Pentzer Myers

Happy Dancing Rejects **288**
Plangdi Neple

Danger from Wolves and Young Men **296**
Aggie Novak

Starved **301**
Rachel Nussbaum

Loke's Wolf **308**
From Norse Mythology

Solange, the Wolf-Girl **312**
Antoinette Ogden, from the French of Marcel Prévost

Wagner, the Wehr-Wolf: Chapters I-XII **316**
George W.M. Reynolds

The She-Wolf **357**
Saki

Curse of the Bayou **361**
Natalie Shea

The White Dog **368**
Fyodor Sologub

The Other Side **372**
Eric Stenbock

The Werewolf **379**
Swedish Fairy Tale

The Eyes of Sebastien **385**
Alan Sullivan

No Eye-Witnesses **394**
Henry S. Whitehead

He Who Would Chase the Sun **400**
M.M. Williams

Mouths **407**
Zez Wyatt

Worse than a Wolf **414**
Wen Wen Yang

Biographies & Sources **420**

Foreword: Were Wolf Short Stories

MONSTERS do important cultural work: They embody anxieties, disturb categories and disrupt conventions, and it is the werewolf that fulfils these roles more effectively than any other monster. If vampires and zombies can be said to transgress apparently stable boundaries and definitions (such as life/death, human/beast, civilised/uncivilised), werewolves embody boundaries. They are borderline creatures: not human one minute and animal the next, but always simultaneously both. Their transformation is temporary but it enacts fundamental questions about the nature of humanity and destabilises the distinction between the human and the animal.

The fact that it is the figure of the wolf that has been blurring these definitions is significant. The relation between humans and wolves goes back to the earliest times of human community, when wolves circled spectrally around campfires, competed with our ancestors for game and, later, became opportunistic poachers of our livestock. But even as wolves served as a sort of wild villain to humanity's civilisation, they were also, oddly, familiar. Like humans, they were and are cooperative hunters, have deep family bonds and a strong sense of territory. In this sense, the wolf has always been intimately connected with the evolution of human communities and as such, has a central place in our mythologies.

This centrality can be seen in the uncanny blending of the two species in the werewolf. Werewolves have appeared in the European narratives since Antiquity. But the imaginative threat that they posed became horrifyingly real during the werewolf trials that started in the mid-fifteenth century. Running parallel and often directly connected with the more famous witch trials, werewolf trials sought to expose and eliminate the disturbing, potentially destructive forces and impulses that lived, unrecognised, in the heart of human communities and in maybe humanity itself. But as the figure moved back into the realm of the imagination in later centuries, the werewolf took on a more metaphorical role and became a body onto which a variety of cultural contradictions, anxieties and inconsistencies could be projected.

The werewolf's metaphorical meanings have shifted over time and continue to change along with our desires and fears about cultural and social relations. While the majority of werewolf figures from the fifteenth to the eighteenth centuries tended to be male, it is interesting to note that in the late nineteenth century most fictional werewolves were women. In stories like Gilbert Campbell's 'The White Wolf of Kostopchin' (1889), the protagonist's powerful sexual attraction to the woman/wolf at the centre of the story dramatises the potentially destructive power of women as the head of an ancient family both figuratively and, ultimately, literally, as he agrees to 'give his heart' to his werewolf bride. This, and similar stories, posit the female werewolf as a threat to the power of masculine lineage at a time when women were threatening to social order by agitating for the vote, lobbying for legal rights, property, and education. In later incarnations, writers made the logical connection between the female werewolf and the cycles of the moon, explicit in films like *Ginger Snaps* (2000), where both sexual voraciousness and powerful violence combine to challenge the carefully regulated world of suburban North America.

More conventionally, though, the werewolf is male and embodies a wider range of metaphorical meanings. Not simply human *or* wolf, it is human *and* wolf, and the one is never fully rid of the other in spite of what his metamorphosing body might suggest. The shift from human to werewolf in these stories becomes an almost unimaginable, unrepresentable destabilisation of what lies at the very core of our sense of selves: our bodies. The werewolf's body, and the dangers posed by that body and the need to control it, is a place through which these narratives expose complex concerns about differences such as race, class, gender, sexuality, identity and ability. The body that seems knowable and stable but which transforms terrifyingly into an almost unrecognisable creature can be thought of as a metaphor for adolescence, for example, in films like *Teen Wolf* (1985, 2023). But its existence at the heart of human community can also reflect on the horrors of intimate partner violence, where the volatile nature of the wolf represents the contradictory nature of a love/violence trajectory. Werewolves' shifting bodies and unstable behaviour questions what we think we know about social relationships and about the very nature of being human.

Werewolf stories get to the heart of how we think about ourselves. They allow us to work through the layers of concerns about humanity, difference, appetite, contagion, and violence that have stalked us since we first noticed the uncannily familiar but alien glint of eyes beyond the deceptively safe circle of our campfire.

Dr. Karen E. Macfarlane
Mount Saint Vincent University

Publisher's Note

THE WEREWOLF is prevalent in horror and gothic fiction, immediately recognizable and thrilling for its uncanny drawing together of human and animal. Its usage in storytelling around the world goes much further back, though, as a mythological or legendary creature associated with the moon, or more simply as a shapeshifter from the wilderness, at odds with society. We have sought to reflect this history on the classic side of this anthology, featuring some early myths, folklore and fairy tales from a variety of cultures. Veles, Slavic god of the underworld, is found in the shape of a wolf in the Cossack folktale 'The Iron Wolf' included here, and the infamous Fenrir of Norse myth can be found in these pages too, among werewolves from Canada, Romania, Sweden, Ireland and more. As well as these, we were keen to include the medieval English folktales, Arthurian legend and old French romances that present werewolves in yet another light, as well as classic gothic tales from authors like Algernon Blackwood and Clemence Housman.

Our submission calls are always met with an enthusiastic response and this latest was no exception. We were delighted with the huge range of stories submitted for consideration, making the selection a difficult yet rewarding task. The final line-up is one in which we hope the reader, too, can marvel at the werewolf's role in tales of horror, romance, power and identity. Modern issues and settings provide a fascinating look at what the werewolf – and other were-creatures – can mean in today's world: the freedom of the wolf form, but also its isolation and curse. Together in conjunction with the older tales, we are pleased to feature these newer stories that connect back to myth, folklore, and classic gothic horror while reinventing the werewolf for the present era.

The Iron Wolf

Cossack Folktale

THERE WAS ONCE UPON A TIME a parson who had a servant, and when this servant had served him faithfully for twelve years and upward, he came to the parson and said, "Let us now settle our accounts, master, and pay me what thou owest me. I have now served long enough, and would fain have a little place in the wide world all to myself."

"Good!" said the parson. "I'll tell thee now what wage I'll give thee for thy faithful service. I'll give thee this egg. Take it home, and when thou gettest there, make to thyself a cattle-pen, and make it strong; then break the egg in the middle of thy cattle-pen, and thou shalt see something. But whatever thou doest, don't break it on thy way home, or all thy luck will leave thee."

So the servant departed on his homeward way. He went on and on, and at last he thought to himself, "Come now, I'll see what is inside this egg of mine!" So he broke it, and out of it came all sorts of cattle in such numbers that the open steppe became like a fair. The servant stood there in amazement, and he thought to himself, "However in God's world shall I be able to drive all these cattle back again?"

He had scarcely uttered the words when the Iron Wolf came running up, and said to him, "I'll collect and drive back all these cattle into the egg again, and I'll patch the egg up so that it will become quite whole. But in return for that," continued the Iron Wolf, "whenever thou dost sit down on the bridal bench, I'll come and eat thee."

"Well," thought the servant to himself, "a lot of things may happen before I sit down on the bridal bench and he comes to eat me, and in the meantime I shall get all these cattle."

"Agreed, then," said he. So the Iron Wolf immediately collected all the cattle, and drove them back into the egg, and patched up the egg and made it whole just as it was before.

The servant went home to the village where he lived, made him a cattle-pen stronger than strong, went inside it and broke the egg, and immediately that cattle-pen was as full of cattle as it could hold. Then he took to farming and cattle-breeding, and he became so rich that in the whole wide world there was none richer than he. He kept to himself, and his goods increased and multiplied exceedingly; the only thing wanting to his happiness was a wife, but a wife he was afraid to take.

Now near to where he lived was a General who had a lovely daughter, and this daughter fell in love with the rich man. So the General went and said to him, "Come, why don't you marry? I'll give you my daughter and lots of money with her."

"How is it possible for me to marry?" replied the man. "As soon as ever I sit down on the bridal bench, the Iron Wolf will come and eat me up." And he told the General all that had happened.

"Oh, nonsense!" said the General. "Don't be afraid. I have a mighty host, and when the time comes for you to sit down on the bridal bench, we'll surround your house with three strong rows of soldiers, and *they* won't let the Iron Wolf get at you, I can tell you."

So they talked the matter over till he let himself be persuaded, and then they began to make great preparations for the bridal banquet. Everything went off excellently well, and they made merry till the time came when bride and bridegroom were to sit down together on the bridal bench. Then the General placed his men in three strong rows all round the house so as not to let the Iron Wolf get in;

and no sooner had the young people sat down upon the bridal bench than, sure enough, the Iron Wolf came running up. He saw the host standing round the house in three strong rows, but through all three rows he leaped and made straight for the house. But the man, as soon as he saw the Iron Wolf, leaped out of the window, mounted his horse, and galloped off with the wolf after him.

Away and away he galloped, and after him came the wolf, but try as it would, it could not catch him up anyhow.

At last, toward evening, the man stopped and looked about him, and saw that he was in a lone forest, and before him stood a hut. He went up to this hut and saw an old man and an old woman sitting in front of it, and said to them, "Would you let me rest a little while with you, good people?"

"By all means!" said they.

"There is one thing, however, good people!" said he. "Don't let the Iron Wolf catch me while I am resting with you."

"Have no fear of that!" replied the old couple. "We have a dog called Chutko, who can hear a wolf coming a mile off, and he'll be sure to let us know."

So he laid him down to sleep, and was just dropping off when Chutko began to bark. Then the old people awoke him and said, "Be off! be off! for the Iron Wolf is coming." And they gave him the dog, and a wheaten hearth-cake as provision by the way.

So he went on and on, and the dog followed after him till it began to grow dark, and then he perceived another hut in another forest. He went up to that hut, and in front of it were sitting an old man and an old woman.

He asked them for a night's lodging. "Only," said he, "take care that the Iron Wolf doesn't catch me!"

"Have no fear of that," said they. "We have a dog here called Vazhko, who can hear a wolf nine miles off."

So he laid him down and slept. Just before dawn Vazhko began to bark. Immediately they awoke him.

"Run!" cried they, "the Iron Wolf is coming!" And they gave him the dog, and a barley hearth-cake as provision by the way. So he took the hearth-cake, sat him on his horse, and off he went, and his two dogs followed after him.

He went on and on. On and on he went till evening, when again he stopped and looked about him, and he saw that he was in another forest, and another little hut stood before him. He went into the hut, and there were sitting an old man and an old woman.

"Will you let me pass the night here, good people?" said he. "Only take care that the Iron Wolf does not get hold of me!"

"Have no fear!" said they, "we have a dog called Bary, who can hear a wolf coming twelve miles off. He'll let us know." So he lay down to sleep, and early in the morning Bary let them know that the Iron Wolf was drawing nigh.

Immediately they awoke him. "'Tis high time for you to be off!" said they. Then they gave him the dog, and a buckwheat hearth-cake as provision by the way. He took the hearth-cake, sat him on his horse, and off he went. So now he had three dogs, and they all three followed him.

He went on and on, and toward evening he found himself in front of another hut. He went into it, and there was nobody there. He went and lay down, and his dogs lay down also, Chutko on the threshold of the room door, Vazhko at the threshold of the house door, and Bary at the threshold of the outer gate. Presently the Iron Wolf came trotting up. Immediately Chutko gave the alarm, Vazhko nailed him to the earth, and Bary tore him to pieces.

Then the man gathered his faithful dogs around him, mounted his horse, and went back to his own home.

The Werewolf Howls
Clifford Ball

TWILIGHT HAD COME upon the slopes of the vineyards, and a gentle, caressing breeze drifted through the open casement to stir into further disorder the papers upon the desk where Monsieur Etienne Delacroix was diligently applying himself. He raised his leonine head, the hair of which had in his later years turned to gray, and stared vacantly from beneath bushy brows at the formation of a wind-driven cloud as if he thought that the passive elements of the heavens could, if they so desired, aid him in some momentous decision.

There was a light but firm tap on the door which led to the hall of the château. Monsieur Delacroix blinked as his thoughts were dispersed and, in some haste, gathered various documents together and thrust them into the maw of a large envelope before bidding the knocker to enter.

Pierre, his eldest son, came quietly into the room. The father felt a touch of the pride he could never quite subdue when Pierre approached, for he had a great faith in his son's probity, as well as an admiration for the straight carriage and clear eye he, at his own age, could no longer achieve. Of late he had been resting a great many matters pertaining to the management of the Château Doré and the business of its vineyards, which supported the estate, on the broad shoulders poised before him.

But Etienne Delacroix had been born in a strict household and his habits fashioned in a stern school, and was the lineal descendant of ancestors who had planted their peasant's feet, reverently but independently, deep into the soil of France; so visible emotions were to him a betrayal of weakness. There was no trace of the deep regard he felt for his son evident when he addressed the younger man.

"Where are your brothers? Did I not ask you to return with them?"

"They are here, Father. I entered first, to be certain that you were ready to receive us."

"Bid them enter."

Jacques and François came in to stand with their elder brother and were careful to remain a few inches in his rear; he was the acknowledged spokesman. Their greetings were spoken simultaneously; Jacques' voice breaking off on a high note which caused him obvious embarrassment, for he was adolescent. Together, thought Monsieur Delacroix, they represented three important steps in his life, three payments on account to posterity. He was glad his issue had all been males; since the early death of his wife he had neither cared for any woman nor taken interest in anything feminine.

"I have here, my son, some papers of importance," he announced, addressing Pierre. "As you observe, I am placing them here where you may easily obtain them in the event of my absence." Suiting the action to the word, he removed the bulky envelope to a drawer in the desk and turned its key, allowing the tiny piece of metal to remain in its lock. "I am growing older" – his fierce, challenging eyes swept the trio as if he dared a possible contradiction – "and it is best that you are aware of these accounts, which are relative to the business of the château."

"*Non, non!*" chorused all three. "You are as young as ever, papa!"

"*Sacre bleu!* Do you name me a liar, my children? Attend, Pierre!"

"Yes, papa."

"I have work for you this night."

The elder son's forehead wrinkled. "But the work, it is over. Our tasks are completed. The workers have been checked, the last cart is in the shed—"

"This is a special task, one which requires the utmost diligence of you all. It is of the wolf."

"*The werewolf!*" exclaimed Jacques, crossing himself.

The other brothers remained silent, but mingled expressions of wonder and dislike passed across their features. Ever since the coming of the wolf the topic of its depredations had been an unwelcome one in the household of the Château Doré.

"*Mon Dieu*, Jacques!" exploded the head of the house. "Have you, too, been listening to the old wives' tales? Must you be such an imbecile, and I your father? Rubbish! There can be no werewolves; has not the most excellent Father Cromecq flouted such stories ten thousand times? It is a common wolf, a large one, true, but nevertheless a common mongrel, a beast from the distant mountain. Of its ferocity we are unfortunately well aware; so it must be dispatched with the utmost alacrity."

"But, the workers say, papa, that there have been no wolves in the fields for more than a hundred—"

"*Peste!* The ever verbose workers! The animal is patently a vagrant, a stray beast driven from the mountains by the lash of its hunger. And I, Etienne Delacroix, have pronounced that it must die!"

The father passed a heavy hand across his forehead, for he was weary from his unaccustomed labor over the accounts. His hands trembled slightly, the result of an old nervous disorder. The fingers were thick, and blunt from the hardy toil of earlier years; the blue veins were still corded from the strength which he had once possessed.

"It is well," said Pierre in his own level tones. "Since the wolf came upon and destroyed poor little Marguerite D'Estourie, tearing her throat to shreds, and the gendarmes who almost cornered it were unable to slap it because they could not shoot straight, and it persists in—"

"It slashed the shoulder of old Gavroche who is so feeble he cannot walk without two canes!" interrupted François, excitedly.

"—ravaging our ewes," concluded the single-minded Pierre, who was not to be side-tracked once he had chosen his way, whether in speech or action. "The damage to our flocks has been great, papa. It is just that we should take action, since the police have failed. I have thought this wolf strange, too, although I place no faith in demons. If it but seeks food, why must it slay so wantonly and feed so little? It is indeed like a great, gray demon in appearance. Twice have I viewed it, leaping across the meadows in the moonlight, its long, gray legs hurling it an unbelievable distance at every bound. And Marie Polydore, of the kitchens, found its tracks only yesterday at the very gates of the château!"

"I have been told," revealed Jacques, flinging his hands about in adolescent earnestness, "that the wolf is the beast-soul of one who has been stricken by the moon-demons. By day he is as other men, but by night, though he has the qualities of a saint he cannot help himself. Perhaps he is one with whom we walk and talk, little guessing his dreadful affliction."

"Silence!" roared Monsieur Delacroix. One of his clenched fists struck the desk a powerful blow and the sons were immediately quieted. "Must I listen to the ranting and raving and driveling of fools and imbeciles? Am I not still the master of the Château Doré? I will tend to the accursed matter as I have always, will I not? I have always seen to the welfare of the dwellers in the shadow of the Château Doré! And with the help of the good God I shall continue to do so, until the last drop of my blood has dried away from my bones. You comprehend?"

In a quieter tone, after the enforced silence, he continued: "I have given orders to both the foreman and Monsieur the mayor that this night, the night of the full moon by which we may detect the marauder, all the people of the vineyards and of the town beyond must remain behind locked windows and barred doors. If they have obeyed my orders – and may the good God look after those who have not – they are even now secure in the safety of their respective homes. Let me discover but one demented idiot peeking from behind his shutter and I promise you he shall have cause to remember his disobedience!"

Pierre nodded without speaking, knowing he was being instructed to punish a possible, but improbable, offender.

"Now, we are four intelligent men, I trust," said Monsieur Delacroix, pretending not to notice the glow of pleasure which suffused Jacques' features at being included in their number. "We are the Delacroix's, which is sufficient. And as leaders we must, from time to time, grant certain concessions to the inferior mentalities of the unfortunate who dwell in ignorance; so I have this day promised the good foremen, who petitioned me regarding the activities of this wolf, to perform certain things. They firmly believe the gray wolf is a demon, an inhuman atrocity visited upon us by the Evil One. And also, according to their ancient but childish witch-lore, that it may only be destroyed by a silver weapon."

Monsieur Delacroix reached beneath his chair and drew forth a small, but apparently heavy, sack. Upending it on the surface of the desk, he scattered in every direction a double dozen glittering cylindrical objects.

"Bullets!" exclaimed Jacques.

"*Silver* bullets!" amended Pierre.

"Yes, my son. Bullets of silver which I molded myself in the cellars, and which I have shown to the men, with the promise that they will be put to use."

"Expensive weapons," commented the thrifty François.

"It is the poor peasant's belief. If we slew tills wolf with mere lead or iron they would still be frightened of their own shadows and consequently worthless at their work, as they have been for the past month. Here are the guns. Tonight you will go forth, my sons, and slay this fabulous werewolf, and cast its carcass upon the cart-load of dry wood I have had piled by the vineyard road, and burn it until there is nothing left but the ash, for all to see and know."

"Yes, papa," Assented Pierre and François as one, but the boy Jacques cried: "What? So fine a skin? I would like it for the wall of my room! These who have seen the wolf say its pelt is like silver shaded into gray—"

"Jacques!" Etienne Delacroix's anger flooded his face with a great surge of red and bulging veins, and Pierre and François were stricken with awe at the sight of their father's wrath.

"If you do not burn this beast as I say, immediately after slaying it, I will forget you are my son, and almost a man! I will—"

His own temper choked him into incoherency.

"I crave your pardon, father," begged Jacques, humbled and alarmed. "I forgot myself."

"We will obey, papa, as always," said François, quickly, and Pierre gravely nodded.

"The moon will soon be up," said Monsieur Delacroix, after a short silence. The room had grown dark while they talked; receiving a wordless signal from his father, Pierre struck a match and lit the blackened lamp on the desk. With the startling transition, as light leaped forth to dispel the murky shadows of the room, Pierre came near to exclaiming aloud at sight of the haggard lines in his father's face. For the first time in his life he realized that what his parent had said earlier in the evening about aging was not spoken jocularly, not the repeated jest Monsieur Delacroix had always allowed himself, but the truth. His father was old.

"You had better go," said Etienne Delacroix, as his keen eyes caught the fleeting expression on his son's face. His fingers drummed a muffled tattoo upon the fine edge of his desk, the only sign of his nervous condition that he could not entirely control. "Monsieur the Mayor's opinion is that the wolf is stronger when the moon is full. But it is mine that tonight it will be easier to discover."

The three turned to the door, but as they reached the threshold Monsieur Delacroix beckoned to the eldest. "An instant, Pierre. I speak to you alone."

The young man closed the door on his brothers' backs and returned to the desk, his steady eyes directed at his father.

Monsieur Delacroix, for the moment, seemed to have forgotten what he intended to say. His head was bowed on his chest and the long locks of his ashen hair had fallen forward over his brow. Suddenly he sat erect, as if it took an immense effort of his will to perform the simple action, and again Pierre was startled to perceive the emotions which twisted his father's features.

It was the first time he had ever seen tenderness there, or beheld love in the eyes he had sometimes, in secret, thought a little cruel.

"Have you a pocket crucifix, my son?"

"In my room."

"Take it with you tonight. And – you will stay close to Jacques, will you not?" His voice was hoarse with unaccustomed anxiety. "He is young, confident, and – careless. I would not wish to endanger your good mother's last child."

Pierre was amazed. It had been fifteen years since he had last heard his father mention his mother.

"You have been a good son, Pierre. Obey me now. Do not let the three of you separate, for I hear this beast is a savage one and unafraid even of armed men. Take care of yourself, and see to your brothers."

"Will you remain in the château for safety, papa? You are not armed."

"I am armed by my faith in the good God and the walls of Château Doré. When you have lit the fire under the wolf's body – I will be there."

He lowered the leonine head once more, and Pierre, not without another curious look, departed.

For a long while Monsieur Delacroix sat immobile, his elbows resting on the padded arras of the chair, the palms of his hands pressing into his cheeks. Then he abruptly arose and, approaching the open casement, drew the curtains wide. Outside, the long, rolling slopes fell away toward a dim horizon already blanketed by the dragons of night, whose tiny, flickering eyes were winking into view one by one in the dark void above. Hurrying cloudlets scurried in little groups across the sky.

Lamps were being lit in the jumble of cottages that were the abodes of Monsieur Delacroix's workmen, but at the moment the sky was illuminated better than the earth; for the gathering darkness seemed to cling like an animate thing to the fields and meadows, and stretch ebony claws across the ribbon of the roadway.

It was time for the moon to rise.

Monsieur Delacroix turned away from the casement and with swift, certain steps went to the door, opening it. The hall was still, but from the direction of the dining room there came a clatter of dishes as the servants cleared the table. Quickly, with an unusual alacrity for a man of his years, he silently traversed the floor of the huge hall and passed through its outer portals. A narrow gravel lane led him along the side of the château until he reached the building's extreme corner, where he abandoned it to strike off across the closely clipped sward in the direction of a small clump of beech trees.

The night was warm and peaceful, with no threat of rain. A teasing zephyr tugged at the thick locks on his uncovered head; from somewhere near his feet came the chirp of a cricket.

In the grove it was darker until he came to its center, wending through and past the entangled thickets like one who had traveled the same path many times, and found the small glade that opened beneath the stars. Here there was more light again but no breeze at all. In the center of the glade was an oblong, grassy mound, and at one end of it a white stone, and on the stone the name of his wife.

Monsieur Delacroix stood for an instant beside the grave with lowered head, and then he sank to his knees and began to pray.

In the east the sky began to brighten as though some torch-bearing giant drew near, walking with great strides beyond the edge of the earth. The stars struggled feebly against the superior illumination, but their strength diminished as a narrow band of encroaching yellow fire appeared on the rim of the world.

With its arrival the low monotone of prayer was checked, to continue afterward with what seemed to be some difficulty. Monsieur Delacroix's throat was choked, either with grief for the unchangeable past or an indefinable apprehension for the inevitable future. His breath came in struggling gasps and tiny beads of perspiration formed on his face and hands. His prayers became mumbled, jerky utterances, holding no recognizable phrases of speech. Whispers, and they ceased altogether.

A small dark cloud danced across a far-off mountain-top, slid furtively over the border of the land, and for a minute erased the yellow gleam from the horizon. Then, as if in terror, shaken by its own temerity, it fled frantically into oblivion, and the great golden platter of the full moon issued from behind the darkness it had left to deluge the landscape with a ceaseless shower of illusive atoms; tiny motes that danced the pathways of space.

Monsieur Delacroix gave a low cry like a child in pain. His agonized eyes were fixed on the backs of his two hands as he held them pressed against the dew-dampened sward. His fingers had begun to stiffen and curl at their tips; he could see the long, coarse hairs sprouting from the pores of his flesh – as he had many times within the past month since the night he had fallen asleep by the grave of his wife and slept throughout the night under the baleful beams of the moon.

He flung back his head, whimpering because of the terrible pressure he could feel upon his skull, and its shape appeared to alter so that it seemed curiously elongated. His eyes were bloodshot, and as they sank into their sockets his lips began to twitch over the fangs in his mouth.

The three brothers, crouching nervously in the shadows of the vineyards, started violently.

Jacques, the younger, almost lost his grasp on the gun with the silver bullets which his father had given him.

From somewhere nearby there had arisen a great volume of sound, swirling and twisting and climbing to shatter itself into a hundred echoes against the vault of the heavens, rushing and dipping and sinking into the cores of all living hearts and the very souls of men – the hunting-cry of the werewolf.

The Cull

Richard Beauchamp

JERRICA WATCHED THEM file in one by one. When the bells of their church tolled, she was always the first one to Ma Lizbeth's deep, deceptively inviting porch. The official meeting place of their little enclave, Seven Cedars. Many a heavy decision had been deliberated under those slat roof shingles, with the exposed cedar support beams and handmade wicker chairs, and the big black potbelly stove which was always roaring with a cord of seasoned Poplar.

One couldn't help but feel welcome under that cozy, rustic enclosure. But this was a place where fates were decided, where lives were forfeited under the accordance of laws and ways of Luna, their one true god, or so the old woman claimed. And she being Ma Lizbeth's closest neighbor in this knob-studded valley, Jerrica was always first to heed the call of the bells, and warm one of those stiff, knotty chairs. By the time the rest of the Seven Cedars families started showing up, she'd already smoked down the last of her home-rolled cigarillos.

"Mornin' Lyle, Able," she said to the two rawboned men who ambled down from the steep footpath that led up to their cabin on top of Cedar Knob, the highest point in the county. Given Ma Lizbeth lived in the deepest part of the valley below, the two men's journey was a harrowing one compared to the ways other folks had to come in. But Jerrica always thought it was worth the journey. She'd been up to the married men's cabin before to trade, and she was always envious of the way they could see the whole vast swathe of verdant hills and stubby knobs for miles.

"Mornin', Jerr. I see the fools haven't shown themselves yet," Able, the more mercurial of the two, grumbled.

"It's too damn early to be makin' a fuss, honey." Lyle put a soothing hand to his bristling husband's shoulder. Able shrugged it off, whirled on the man.

"Yeah, I know it's up to the gods, but shit, Lyle, why not just send out the ones who tipped the scales? What if it's *me* the gods choose this time, huh? What if *you're* the one who Luna chooses?"

"Then that would be Her will, and we will obey it," came a stony voice from the dense copse of shortleaf pine that clustered around Lizbeth's demesne.

A moment later, Aric Lasalle came trundling through the clearing, a cup of coffee steaming from a hand-carved cedar mug. The man sported a huge silver-bladed buck knife housed in a leather sheath on his hip, which may as well be a sheriff's gold star. He was the closest semblance to a lawman Seven Cedars had.

"Hope you can keep that man of yours on a leash, Lyle. I'm too tired for this bullshit," Aric said, then nodded curtly to Jerrica, a bit of silent communication passing between them. Once upon a time, the big red-haired man shared a bed with Jerrica. He'd even cut his palm one night and got down on his knees to initiate the sacred marriage covenant. But Jericca had denied him. She refused to take a chance with upsetting the balance. She refused to have to be the one to send her own kin off to be fodder for the beasts in the surrounding counties. She didn't dare tell him her true thoughts on the cull, on this pact with the monsters. So, she left him instead.

As Ma Lizbeth's big old rooster, Buster, serenaded the rising sun, the families started to file in by twos and threes. Within thirty minutes of that sonorous, low tolling of stained brass, the entirety of

Seven Cedars was clustered around the porch, including 'the fools', Arnold and Daisy Boswell, and their little girl, Luna. Named after the goddess herself, as if that might curry some favor with the benevolent celestial forces who apparently oversaw this lottery.

The Boswells stood a few feet apart from the rest of the families. Jerrica could sense the growing animosity, even if what had happened was just the natural order of things. A new pup would come along sooner or later. Not everyone was smart like Lyle and Able. Jerrica didn't share their animosity. She pitied these folks. Most of them were too young to remember how it was before. They didn't question this ceremony.

Jerrica was the second oldest of their tribe, with Ma Lizbeth being the official den elder. Twenty-three families, with a population of fifty, until recently, that was. Now it was fifty-one, and the bells had gonged to announce this upset of the status quo, demanding rectification. Used to be, the bells rung in celebration of new life.

Jericca, like Ma Lizbeth, was old enough to remember a time before the culling. A time when the residents of Seven Cedars were free to rut, to hunt, and to roam without fear of slaughter. Back when they were a self-sufficient mountain enclave, a hidden secret nestled between the viridian bosom of these ancient karst peaks, with their own religion and ways of life. Before the world changed profoundly around them. Before the diaspora of the beasts with their ignorance and weapons and technology infested this land. Before Luna, Askas, and the other gods of the fang started demanding tributes to appease those that now outnumbered them, their very existence inimical to the ways of Luna's proselytizers.

Ma Lizbeth, as per her usual way, opened the door of the cabin and showed her old self only when everyone else was present and accounted for. Ancient though she was, she stood straight and her shoulders and arms were corded with lean muscle. Only her crepe skin and liver spots, and the insipient cloudiness of cataracts belied her many epochs upon this land.

"You all know why we're here. No point in dragging this out." The old woman's voice was a mix between a bullfrog and a door hinge thirsty for oiling. Equal parts regal and grating. "Let us pray the Psalm of Gratitude before we begin," she said, bowing her head.

Soon harsh syllables filled the chilly November air in great puffs of steam. The language was an old one, proto-Germanic, betraying the origin of the Seven Cedars residents. Jerrica joined in, even if it felt like a mockery, saying the prayers now.

They thanked God and Goddess alike, but Luna especially for their earthen bounty. May the elk, the hare, the squirrel and the bear be blessed with virility and fertility. May these hills forever teem with their life. May their hunts always be fruitful. May the scales always be balanced.

When the prayer was done, the head of each family stepped forward, the small wooden talisman clutched in each hand unique in its design and appearance. Jerrica, having no family, as well as the lawman, stepped forward with their own wooden effigies, symbols of their stunted bloodlines. Jerrica looked down at hers. She'd picked it up this morning, where it sat collecting dust on her shelf. Something seemed off about it. It'd been years since she'd last put eyes upon it, but she'd hand-carved the crest herself from a fallen oak tree. It felt lighter... and, wrong, somehow.

Ma Lizbeth held out the bear-skin sorting bag and kept a blank expression as one by one the head of each family, sometimes men, sometimes women, deposited their wooden crests. There was a brief, heavy silence in the meadow as the last of the heirlooms were dropped in, before the wooden clacking of all those fates intermingling broke it.

While the elder agitated the bag, ensuring a thorough mixing of bloodlines, everyone except Jerrica cast a reproachful glance at the Boswells, who clutched their daughter protectively between them, as if that might ward off Luna's casting of the stone for their lot. It was obvious they all wished for the Boswell clan to be the ones chosen. Jerrica just wished for another cigarette. Unfortunately, she'd smoked her last one.

She had a strong feeling she knew how this was going to go. If her intuition proved right, a trip to Gunther's general store was due. It would be her last.

Since the covenant with the beasts was made, each child born in Seven Cedars was instilled at birth with a strict set of rules to follow, rule number one being no fraternization between themselves and the beasts of the outlying counties. They were taught that the world outside of Seven Cedars was a hostile one, and that the things who called themselves men but who were not of the Lunar blood were things to be feared and reviled. Things that hunted for pure sport and pleasure, which broke rule number two of their sacred tenets: Honor the life of that which you destroy. Their hunts were purely for sustenance, even when the wild blood was upon them. Not a single sinew or scrap of gristle was ever to be wasted, lest you insult Her.

Still, being one of the old ones had its privileges. While it was true most of the men in the surrounding counties would kill any Seven Cedars folk seen wandering outside the county line on sight, there were those who forewent the ancient blood feud in pursuit of commerce. Gunther Kirkwell was one such specimen.

The rattling of wood on wood stopped, and Ma Lizbeth opened the drawstring bag. There was that thick silence again as she cast her eyes upwards, asking Luna to stay her hand. The old woman reached blindly into the bag. All eyes were on her now. Jerrica held her breath. She'd survived three culls, and now she was wise to the ways of this false prophet.

Ma Lizbeth held up the selected sigil. Eyes widened. Gasps of relief were heard. Eyes flitted to Jerrica.

Her suspicions had been right after all.

"Jerrica Louis Lorimer, you have been bestowed the gift of sacrifice. Luna, mother of stars and ward of our earth, has chosen your blood as succor, and a pound of your flesh to balance the scales."

* * *

The walk to the general store was four miles over two steep valleys. Seven Cedars did not have roads or even designated walking trails as per the truce with the beasts. Jerrica did not mind the journey, however. Walking among the short pine and huge pink boulders that jutted from the earth like Luna's gums was a comfort to her. The dense forests that hemmed the small village in on all sides had been her life since the pact, and this place became a prison. She'd hunted and rutted and worshipped in these woods, knew each individual tree and stone she passed. She savored that familiarity, for soon she would be in the killing fields, a place she'd only heard of.

Those who Luna's gaze fell upon were given three days to sort their affairs and for the beasts to prepare for the hunt. Though she was a hermit among her village and did not take a mate, she still had unsettled business to tend to, and she was going to enjoy her one vice while she could.

The general store was a whitewashed wooden shack that leaned like an old man with a bad leg, the signs all hand-painted. Out front were two of those stinky metal monoliths that the beasts used to feed their huge metal carriages, and she gave these a wide berth. She stood under the awning, slipping on her rarely worn moccasins to heed the rules of service posted outside the general store: SHOES ON, SHIRTS ON, GUNS UNLOADED.

A bell chimed as she entered the store, and the three men who stood conversing around the counter abruptly shut their mouths when she entered. Seven Cedars folks were easily marked by their homespun clothes and generally wild demeanor, the women especially. The beasts kept their bitches strangled in strange, tight-fitting contraptions that shrunk the waists, and forced them to shear their natural coat, scant though it was, to make them appear perpetually pre-pubescent. It was one of the stranger rituals she'd observed of these creatures.

The two men talking to Gunther quickly made a beeline for the door, scowling at Jerrica as they went.

"Fuckin' mongrel. Don't know why we don't just go in there and wipe your kind out for good," one of them said. Jerrica playfully snarled at them, showing her teeth. The one who didn't speak went as pale as fish belly and almost ran into the door on his way out.

"Go on now, get your sundries and don't dally. I get enough shit as it is letting you folks in here," the old man with a three foot-beard said.

Jerrica nodded and made haste, finding the cherry tobacco she liked so much among hand-carved pipes, bags of chaw and snuff. Next, she plucked the extra-large rolling papers. She ignored the various foodstuffs lining the shelves. How the beasts lived on their overly salty, oily vittles baffled her. The smells they produced were almost worse than the smoke that belched from their noisy carriages. She reached into the pocket of her deerskin smock and counted out the ancient iron and brass men that she'd stolen off one of the dead beasts long ago. One who'd violated the pact, and had come onto their land outside of culling season. No one need know she'd spilled blood for this money.

"Hear there's gonna be another cullin'," Gunther said as he held out a trembling hand for the coins. He flinched as each one was deposited into his gnarled appendage.

"You heard right." Jerrica noted how the man wouldn't meet her eyes. Gunther may be more tolerant than the rest, but that didn't mean he viewed her as an equal.

"You folks, uh, do your little ceremony? Got somebody lined up?"

"That we do. Take care, sir. Thank you, for not being like the others," Jerrica said as she took her goods and promptly departed. As soon as she was back outside, she kicked off the moccasins and left them in the gravel lot. She wouldn't be needing them anymore. Once she was past the tree line and out of sight, she shed her deerskin coverings as well, opting to spend the rest of her days as Luna intended.

* * *

That night, she sat atop Askas bluff, the limestone shelf cool and welcoming against her bare flesh. Blue smoke reamed her head in a misty corona as she waited for Aric to answer her summons. Just as Luna was showing herself above the distant mountain peaks, the lawman came and sat down next to her. He sighed.

"I'm sorry, Jerrica. I'm—"

"Shhh. Luna is watching. Honor her with me, one last time."

His confusion didn't last as she promptly undressed him. Soon those old, animalistic urges took heed.

The rutting was fierce, desperate, purposeful. By the time Luna was red and swollen in the sky, she had pulled their true selves out, and the coupling became even more bestial. This time, when she sensed his nearing climax, she did not spurn him off as before. This time she drove him deeper, allowing total submission as his teeth sunk into her scruff, drawing blood, just as a pulsing warmth blossomed deep within her. Together, they shuddered and panted as they rode the tide as one being, bathed in Her vermillion light. The light of fertility. Rarely did the seed find root in their kind. It was why the culling was always a once-in-a-decade event. Still, it was only now, facing the inevitability of death, that she allowed herself to experience that most visceral of primal pleasures. She knew deep in her marrow this seed would be viable.

Afterwards, they lay nude upon the stone face, the speckled night sky vast and vivid before them, Luna retreating to show Her children, the stars.

"The branding is tomorrow… I don't—" Aric gestured towards the knife, which sat atop his discarded clothes a few feet away. "I… don't know if I can. I know it's my job, but—"

Jerrica reached up, forced her eyes to meet his.

"Do you remember before? When we were free?" she asked. Aric was not as old as she, but he was no pup either. He looked at her, confused.

"Of course I do, but I don't—"

"So why did we let the beasts dictate how we lived? Ma Lizbeth claims it is Luna's will, but you and I know it isn't. We made a truce with those… *things*. To keep us from being wiped out. Luna has nothing to do with this shit."

Aric stared at the deepening shadows of the steep gorge below them.

"What're you proposing, Jerr?"

"They outnumber us. And they have weapons that can strike from afar. But we're faster. Smarter. Stronger. And surely, this isn't the only enclave out there with Luna's blood. What if we fight back? And win? Find others like us?"

Aric didn't speak for a long time.

* * *

It was the final day. What their church called the Eve of Reckoning. On this day, a crescent moon was carved into the chosen one's forehead, done with silver so the wound would be etched in permanence. Letting the beasts know who the target was. The knife wavered in Ma Lizbeth's hands. Unsheathed, the knife's silver tang was an affront to the senses. She was unused to handling the blade. But given Aric's feelings for Jerrica (one-sided though they may be), Ma Lizbeth took up the blade in his stead. She approached Jerrica, who sat in the woman's old foyer. Very few residents had seen the inside of the ancient woman's cabin. There were secrets stored away whose revelations were fit only for those who've been wizened by age and perspective.

"You know, after the conversations we've had before, young lady, I was surprised you didn't try to spark a mutiny when it was your turn. I'm glad you've come around." The blade's quivering tip inched towards her forehead. Jerrica could feel the alchemical heat of it. Jerrica looked at Aric, who stood in the corner, his face pale. *Do not betray me, lawman. Your seed burns in my belly*, she thought harshly as their eyes met, and she blinked twice at him, her signal.

Just as Ma Lizbeth touched the blade to her forehead, Jerrica grasped the thin wrist in her hand. Their eyes met.

"I was not chosen by Luna. I was chosen by you. You didn't think I wouldn't notice the balsa replica of my crest? Make it lighter than the others so it would stay on top?"

Jerrica and Aric moved as one. Old though she was, Ma Lizbeth was not weak. She could change faster than any of them, an ability that only came to the old ones. The pups needed Luna to bring about the change, but with age comes bodily autonomy.

Jerrica was wrestling for the knife just as the dewlaps of flesh and liver spots were erased by gray fur and black gums.

"Fool! They'll kill you all!" came a voice that started frail but concluded monstrous. Just as the half paw, half hand lost its grip on the knife, Jerrica felt a muzzle bite into her shoulder. As she held the woman-wolf chimera away from her, Aric came up with the knife.

"Luna forgive me!" he yelled as he plunged that wicked silver deep into the side of a thick furred neck. Golden eyes met Jerrica's blue ones, and she was not moved by the betrayal she saw in them.

Blood hot and syrupy pumped against Jerrica's face, the rivers of her own life-water mixing with the elder's.

"I did it... to protect... us. Fool." It was Ma Lizbeth's final words.

As the elder slumped to the floor of her cabin, reverting back to her usual self, Aric came to Jerrica's side, a nourishing strip of venison ready. Jerrica inhaled the tough meat without even tasting it. A second later the crescent valleys of gore carved into her shoulder were but pink lines of scar tissue.

"By Luna, we did it. Shit..." Aric stumbled back, staring at the blood on his hands. They'd broken one of the most sacred of tenets: Never attack another member of the pack. Even knowing this was the right thing to do, the gravity of their actions made Jerrica's limbs and soul heavy. "What do we do now?"

"We tell the others, quickly. We have the night to prepare for an offensive," Jerrica said as she knelt down and picked up the knife, its aura nauseating. She turned it upon herself.

"Jerrica, what are you—"

"This is no longer... a symbol of death. It will be... a... symbol of power. Of defiance." Jerrica screamed through gritted teeth as she branded herself with Luna's face. It was the worst pain she had ever felt, and yet, her body thrummed with an invigorating euphoria at this profound act of liberation.

* * *

The designated hunting grounds was an adjoining valley in the next county over, on *their* land. The chosen were to make their way to the grounds at sun up, appearing in their true form to honor Luna in battle. And they would wait for the whistles to blow. Then the hounds would come, those poor cousins of Luna corrupted by the will of the beasts. The chosen would then fight to the death. Never running. To die a coward was the ultimate offense.

Just as the sun crested the valley wall to her back, Jerrica sauntered up the small hill in the middle of the prairie, her huge vulpine form barely seen above the tall grass. She rose up on her hind legs and howled, baring herself to the hidden scopes and the eyes that sought her in their cross hairs. She made sure they saw the jagged crescent on her forehead, which still seeped blood from a wound that would not heal.

The whistles blew. The hounds bayed. The scent of silver hung thick in the air. Behind her, keeping low and spread out, the entirety of Seven Cedars stalked. They had snuck out into the killing fields at night, disarming the silver traps and tripwires, another violation of the cull, and set their own traps as further defiance.

Jerrica charged headlong into those guns and their silver bullets. She was destined to die today, and if it was truly Luna's choice, she would honor it. But not before letting the blood of the enemy.

Her true form flowed over the land like a stream over a creek bed. She could smell the men and their fear and their silver. She found one high up in a tree, saw the small black eye of his rifle as it trained on her. Jerrica leapt and dug her claws in, propelling herself up the tall white oak just as the man fired, a silver meteor grazing her flank.

The pain was breathtaking, but so was the gush of arterial blood that exploded into her mouth, and the pathetic gurgling sounds of death.

There were shouts of alarm as the beasts saw more of them coming. Hounds cried and yipped in pain and fear. Men shot wildly, screaming, *It's a trap, it's a trap!*

Some stayed, stood their ground, determined to die with honor in service of their own false gods, but most fled. But those on four legs were faster. Limping down from the tree and feeling that dichotomous sensation of itching and burning as her body struggled to heal the lethal silver wound, Jerrica watched with pride as one by one the men in their useless camouflage and huge bore rifles fertilized the soil with their blood.

That night they feasted with ravenous abandon, tasting the most forbidden of fruits and finding it ambrosial. They howled for those that fell in today's battle and for all those who were marched to this field to appease a most heinous perversion of their religion.

That night they marched beyond the fences and traps lining the perimeter of their prison. Luna had cast her stone, and it was not for one of her own.

They had their own cull to see to.

The Camp of the Dog

Algernon Blackwood

Chapter I

ISLANDS of all shapes and sizes troop northward from Stockholm by the hundred, and the little steamer that threads their intricate mazes in summer leaves the traveller in a somewhat bewildered state as regards the points of the compass when it reaches the end of its journey at Waxholm. But it is only after Waxholm that the true islands begin, so to speak, to run wild, and start up the coast on their tangled course of a hundred miles of deserted loveliness, and it was in the very heart of this delightful confusion that we pitched our tents for a summer holiday. A veritable wilderness of islands lay about us: from the mere round button of a rock that bore a single fir, to the mountainous stretch of a square mile, densely wooded, and bounded by precipitous cliffs; so close together often that a strip of water ran between no wider than a country lane, or, again, so far that an expanse stretched like the open sea for miles.

Although the larger islands boasted farms and fishing stations, the majority were uninhabited. Carpeted with moss and heather, their coast-lines showed a series of ravines and clefts and little sandy bays, with a growth of splendid pine-woods that came down to the water's edge and led the eye through unknown depths of shadow and mystery into the very heart of primitive forest.

The particular islands to which we had camping rights by virtue of paying a nominal sum to a Stockholm merchant lay together in a picturesque group far beyond the reach of the steamer, one being a mere reef with a fringe of fairy-like birches, and two others, cliff-bound monsters rising with wooded heads out of the sea. The fourth, which we selected because it enclosed a little lagoon suitable for anchorage, bathing, night-lines, and what-not, shall have what description is necessary as the story proceeds; but, so far as paying rent was concerned, we might equally well have pitched our tents on any one of a hundred others that clustered about us as thickly as a swarm of bees.

It was in the blaze of an evening in July, the air clear as crystal, the sea a cobalt blue, when we left the steamer on the borders of civilisation and sailed away with maps, compasses, and provisions for the little group of dots in the Skägård that were to be our home for the next two months. The dinghy and my Canadian canoe trailed behind us, with tents and dunnage carefully piled aboard, and when the point of cliff intervened to hide the steamer and the Waxholm hotel we realised for the first time that the horror of trains and houses was far behind us, the fever of men and cities, the weariness of streets and confined spaces. The wilderness opened up on all sides into endless blue reaches, and the map and compasses were so frequently called into requisition that we went astray more often than not and progress was enchantingly slow. It took us, for instance, two whole days to find our crescent-shaped home, and the camps we made on the way were so fascinating that we left them with difficulty and regret, for each island seemed more desirable than the one before it, and over all lay the spell of haunting peace, remoteness from the turmoil of the world, and the freedom of open and desolate spaces.

And so many of these spots of world-beauty have I sought out and dwelt in, that in my mind remains only a composite memory of their faces, a true map of heaven, as it were, from which this particular one stands forth with unusual sharpness because of the strange things that happened there, and also, I think, because anything in which John Silence played a part has a habit of fixing itself in the mind with a living and lasting quality of vividness.

For the moment, however, Dr. Silence was not of the party. Some private case in the interior of Hungary claimed his attention, and it was not till later – the 15th of August, to be exact – that I had arranged to meet him in Berlin and then return to London together for our harvest of winter work. All the members of our party, however, were known to him more or less well, and on this third day as we sailed through the narrow opening into the lagoon and saw the circular ridge of trees in a gold and crimson sunset before us, his last words to me when we parted in London for some unaccountable reason came back very sharply to my memory, and recalled the curious impression of prophecy with which I had first heard them:

"Enjoy your holiday and store up all the force you can," he had said as the train slipped out of Victoria; "and we will meet in Berlin on the 15th – unless you should send for me sooner."

And now suddenly the words returned to me so clearly that it seemed I almost heard his voice in my ear: "Unless you should send for me sooner"; and returned, moreover, with a significance I was wholly at a loss to understand that touched somewhere in the depths of my mind a vague sense of apprehension that they had all along been intended in the nature of a prophecy.

In the lagoon, then, the wind failed us this July evening, as was only natural behind the shelter of the belt of woods, and we took to the oars, all breathless with the beauty of this first sight of our island home, yet all talking in somewhat hushed voices of the best place to land, the depth of water, the safest place to anchor, to put up the tents in, the most sheltered spot for the camp-fires, and a dozen things of importance that crop up when a home in the wilderness has actually to be made.

And during this busy sunset hour of unloading before the dark, the souls of my companions adopted the trick of presenting themselves very vividly anew before my mind, and introducing themselves afresh.

In reality, I suppose, our party was in no sense singular. In the conventional life at home they certainly seemed ordinary enough, but suddenly, as we passed through these gates of the wilderness, I saw them more sharply than before, with characters stripped of the atmosphere of men and cities. A complete change of setting often furnishes a startlingly new view of people hitherto held for well-known; they present another facet of their personalities. I seemed to see my own party almost as new people – people I had not known properly hitherto, people who would drop all disguises and henceforth reveal themselves as they really were. And each one seemed to say: "Now you will see me as I am. You will see me here in this primitive life of the wilderness without clothes. All my masks and veils I have left behind in the abodes of men. So, look out for surprises!"

The Reverend Timothy Maloney helped me to put up the tents, long practice making the process easy, and while he drove in pegs and tightened ropes, his coat off, his flannel collar flying open without a tie, it was impossible to avoid the conclusion that he was cut out for the life of a pioneer rather than the church. He was fifty years of age, muscular, blue-eyed and hearty, and he took his share of the work, and more, without shirking. The way he handled the axe in cutting down saplings for the tent-poles was a delight to see, and his eye in judging the level was unfailing.

Bullied as a young man into a lucrative family living, he had in turn bullied his mind into some semblance of orthodox beliefs, doing the honours of the little country church with an energy that made one think of a coal-heaver tending china; and it was only in the past few years that he had resigned the living and taken instead to cramming young men for their examinations. This suited him better. It enabled him, too, to indulge his passion for spells of 'wild life', and to spend the summer months of most years under canvas in one part of the world or another where he could take his young men with him and combine 'reading' with open air.

His wife usually accompanied him, and there was no doubt she enjoyed the trips, for she possessed, though in less degree, the same joy of the wilderness that was his own distinguishing characteristic. The only difference was that while he regarded it as the real life, she regarded it as an interlude. While he camped out with his heart and mind, she played at camping out with her clothes and body. None the less, she made a splendid companion, and to watch her busy cooking dinner over the fire we had built among the stones was to understand that her heart was in the business for the moment and that she was happy even with the detail.

Mrs. Maloney at home, knitting in the sun and believing that the world was made in six days, was one woman; but Mrs. Maloney, standing with bare arms over the smoke of a wood fire under the pine trees, was another; and Peter Sangree, the Canadian pupil, with his pale skin, and his loose, though not ungainly figure, stood beside her in very unfavourable contrast as he scraped potatoes and sliced bacon with slender white fingers that seemed better suited to hold a pen than a knife. She ordered him about like a slave, and he obeyed, too, with willing pleasure, for in spite of his general appearance of debility he was as happy to be in camp as any of them.

But more than any other member of the party, Joan Maloney, the daughter, was the one who seemed a natural and genuine part of the landscape, who belonged to it all just in the same way that the trees and the moss and the grey rocks running out into the water belonged to it. For she was obviously in her right and natural setting, a creature of the wilds, a gipsy in her own home.

To any one with a discerning eye this would have been more or less apparent, but to me, who had known her during all the twenty-two years of her life and was familiar with the ins and outs of her primitive, utterly un-modern type, it was strikingly clear. To see her there made it impossible to imagine her again in civilisation. I lost all recollection of how she looked in a town. The memory somehow evaporated. This slim creature before me, flitting to and fro with the grace of the woodland life, swift, supple, adroit, on her knees blowing the fire, or stirring the frying-pan through a veil of smoke, suddenly seemed the only way I had ever really seen her. Here she was at home; in London she became someone concealed by clothes, an artificial doll overdressed and moving by clockwork, only a portion of her alive. Here she was alive all over.

I forget altogether how she was dressed, just as I forget how any particular tree was dressed, or how the markings ran on any one of the boulders that lay about the Camp. She looked just as wild and natural and untamed as everything else that went to make up the scene, and more than that I cannot say.

Pretty, she was decidedly not. She was thin, skinny, dark-haired, and possessed of great physical strength in the form of endurance. She had, too, something of the force and vigorous purpose of a man, tempestuous sometimes and wild to passionate, frightening her mother, and puzzling her easy-going father with her storms of waywardness, while at the same time she stirred his admiration by her violence. A pagan of the pagans she was besides, and with some haunting suggestion of old-world pagan beauty about her dark face and eyes. Altogether an odd and difficult character, but with a generosity and high courage that made her very lovable.

In town life she always seemed to me to feel cramped, bored, a devil in a cage, in her eyes a hunted expression as though any moment she dreaded to be caught. But up in these spacious solitudes all this disappeared. Away from the limitations that plagued and stung her, she would show at her best, and as I watched her moving about the Camp I repeatedly found myself thinking of a wild creature that had just obtained its freedom and was trying its muscles.

Peter Sangree, of course, at once went down before her. But she was so obviously beyond his reach, and besides so well able to take care of herself, that I think her parents gave the matter but little thought, and he himself worshipped at a respectful distance, keeping admirable control of his passion in all respects save one; for at his age the eyes are difficult to master, and the yearning, almost the devouring, expression often visible in them was probably there unknown even to himself. He, better than anyone else, understood that he had fallen in love with something most hard of attainment, something that drew him to the very edge of life, and almost beyond it. It, no doubt, was a secret and terrible joy to him, this passionate worship from afar; only I think he suffered more than anyone guessed, and that his want of vitality was due in large measure to the constant stream of unsatisfied yearning that poured for ever from his soul and body. Moreover, it seemed to me, who now saw them for the first time together, that there was an unnamable something – an elusive quality of some kind – that marked them as belonging to the same world, and that although the girl ignored him she was secretly, and perhaps unknown to herself, drawn by some attribute very deep in her own nature to some quality equally deep in his.

This, then, was the party when we first settled down into our two months' camp on the island in the Baltic Sea. Other figures flitted from time to time across the scene, and sometimes one reading man, sometimes another, came to join us and spend his four hours a day in the clergyman's tent, but they came for short periods only, and they went without leaving much trace in my memory, and certainly they played no important part in what subsequently happened.

The weather favoured us that night, so that by sunset the tents were up, the boats unloaded, a store of wood collected and chopped into lengths, and the candle-lanterns hung round ready for lighting on the trees. Sangree, too, had picked deep mattresses of balsam boughs for the women's beds, and had cleared little paths of brushwood from their tents to the central fireplace. All was prepared for bad weather. It was a cosy supper and a well-cooked one that we sat down to and ate under the stars, and, according to the clergyman, the only meal fit to eat we had seen since we left London a week before.

The deep stillness, after that roar of steamers, trains, and tourists, held something that thrilled, for as we lay round the fire there was no sound but the faint sighing of the pines and the soft lapping of the waves along the shore and against the sides of the boat in the lagoon. The ghostly outline of her white sails was just visible through the trees, idly rocking to and fro in her calm anchorage, her sheets flapping gently against the mast. Beyond lay the dim blue shapes of other islands floating in the night, and from all the great spaces about us came the murmur of the sea and the soft breathing of great woods. The odours of the wilderness – smells of wind and earth, of trees and water, clean, vigorous, and mighty – were the true odours of a virgin world unspoilt by men, more penetrating and more subtly intoxicating than any other perfume in the whole world. Oh! – and dangerously strong, too, no doubt, for some natures!

"Ahhh!" breathed out the clergyman after supper, with an indescribable gesture of satisfaction and relief. "Here there is freedom, and room for body and mind to turn in. Here one can work and rest and play. Here one can be alive and absorb something of the earth-forces that never get within touching distance in the cities. By George, I shall make a permanent camp here and come when it is time to die!"

The good man was merely giving vent to his delight at being under canvas. He said the same thing every year, and he said it often. But it more or less expressed the superficial feelings of us all. And when, a little later, he turned to compliment his wife on the fried potatoes, and discovered that she was snoring, with her back against a tree, he grunted with content at the sight and put a ground-sheet over her feet, as if it were the most natural thing in the world for her to fall asleep after dinner, and then moved back to his own corner, smoking his pipe with great satisfaction.

And I, smoking mine too, lay and fought against the most delicious sleep imaginable, while my eyes wandered from the fire to the stars peeping through the branches, and then back again to the group about me. The Rev. Timothy soon let his pipe go out, and succumbed as his wife had done, for he had worked hard and eaten well. Sangree, also smoking, leaned against a tree with his gaze fixed on the girl, a depth of yearning in his face that he could not hide, and that really distressed me for him. And Joan herself, with wide staring eyes, alert, full of the new forces of the place, evidently keyed up by the magic of finding herself among all the things her soul recognised as 'home', sat rigid by the fire, her thoughts roaming through the spaces, the blood stirring about her heart. She was as unconscious of the Canadian's gaze as she was that her parents both slept. She looked to me more like a tree, or something that had grown out of the island, than a living girl of the century; and when I spoke across to her in a whisper and suggested a tour of investigation, she started and looked up at me as though she heard a voice in her dreams.

Sangree leaped up and joined us, and without waking the others we three went over the ridge of the island and made our way down to the shore behind. The water lay like a lake before us still coloured by the sunset. The air was keen and scented, wafting the smell of the wooded islands that hung about us in the darkening air. Very small waves tumbled softly on the sand. The sea was sown with stars, and everywhere breathed and pulsed the beauty of the northern summer night. I confess I speedily lost consciousness of the human presences beside me, and I have little doubt Joan did too. Only Sangree felt otherwise, I suppose, for presently we heard him sighing; and I can well imagine that he absorbed the whole wonder and passion of the scene into his aching heart, to swell the pain there that was more searching even than the pain at the sight of such matchless and incomprehensible beauty.

The splash of a fish jumping broke the spell.

"I wish we had the canoe now," remarked Joan; "we could paddle out to the other islands."

"Of course," I said; "wait here and I'll go across for it," and was turning to feel my way back through the darkness when she stopped me in a voice that meant what it said.

"No; Mr. Sangree will get it. We will wait here and cooee to guide him."

The Canadian was off in a moment, for she had only to hint of her wishes and he obeyed.

"Keep out from shore in case of rocks," I cried out as he went, "and turn to the right out of the lagoon. That's the shortest way round by the map."

My voice travelled across the still waters and woke echoes in the distant islands that came back to us like people calling out of space. It was only thirty or forty yards over the ridge and down the other side to the lagoon where the boats lay, but it was a good mile to coast round the shore in the dark to where we stood and waited. We heard him stumbling away among the boulders, and then the sounds suddenly ceased as he topped the ridge and went down past the fire on the other side.

"I didn't want to be left alone with him," the girl said presently in a low voice. "I'm always afraid he's going to say or do something—" She hesitated a moment, looking quickly over her shoulder towards the ridge where he had just disappeared – "something that might lead to unpleasantness."

She stopped abruptly.

"*You* frightened, Joan!" I exclaimed, with genuine surprise. "This is a new light on your wicked character. I thought the human being who could frighten you did not exist." Then I suddenly realised she was talking seriously – looking to me for help of some kind – and at once I dropped the teasing attitude.

"He's very far gone, I think, Joan," I added gravely. "You must be kind to him, whatever else you may feel. He's exceedingly fond of you."

"I know, but I can't help it," she whispered, lest her voice should carry in the stillness; "there's something about him that – that makes me feel creepy and half afraid."

"But, poor man, it's not his fault if he is delicate and sometimes looks like death," I laughed gently, by way of defending what I felt to be a very innocent member of my sex.

"Oh, but it's not that I mean," she answered quickly; "it's something I feel about him, something in his soul, something he hardly knows himself, but that may come out if we are much together. It draws me, I feel, tremendously. It stirs what is wild in me – deep down – oh, very deep down – yet at the same time makes me feel afraid."

"I suppose his thoughts are always playing about you," I said, "but he's nice-minded and—"

"Yes, yes," she interrupted impatiently, "I can trust myself absolutely with him. He's gentle and singularly pure-minded. But there's something else that—" She stopped again sharply to listen. Then she came up close beside me in the darkness, whispering –

"You know, Mr. Hubbard, sometimes my intuitions warn me a little too strongly to be ignored. Oh, yes, you needn't tell me again that it's difficult to distinguish between fancy and intuition. I know all that. But I also know that there's something deep down in that man's soul that calls to something deep down in mine. And at present it frightens me. Because I cannot make out what it is; and I know, I *know*, he'll do something some day that – that will shake my life to the very bottom." She laughed a little at the strangeness of her own description.

I turned to look at her more closely, but the darkness was too great to show her face. There was an intensity, almost of suppressed passion, in her voice that took me completely by surprise.

"Nonsense, Joan," I said, a little severely; "you know him well. He's been with your father for months now."

"But that was in London; and up here it's different – I mean, I feel that it may be different. Life in a place like this blows away the restraints of the artificial life at home. I know, oh, I know what I'm saying. I feel all untied in a place like this; the rigidity of one's nature begins to melt and flow. Surely *you* must understand what I mean!"

"Of course I understand," I replied, yet not wishing to encourage her in her present line of thought, "and it's a grand experience – for a short time. But you're overtired tonight, Joan, like the rest of us. A few days in this air will set you above all fears of the kind you mention."

Then, after a moment's silence, I added, feeling I should estrange her confidence altogether if I blundered any more and treated her like a child –

"I think, perhaps, the true explanation is that you pity him for loving you, and at the same time you feel the repulsion of the healthy, vigorous animal for what is weak and timid. If he came up boldly and took you by the throat and shouted that he would force you to love him – well, then you would feel no fear at all. You would know exactly how to deal with him. Isn't it, perhaps, something of that kind?"

The girl made no reply, and when I took her hand I felt that it trembled a little and was cold.

"It's not his love that I'm afraid of," she said hurriedly, for at this moment we heard the dip of a paddle in the water, "it's something in his very soul that terrifies me in a way I have never been terrified before – yet fascinates me. In town I was hardly conscious of his presence. But the moment we got away from civilisation, it began to come. He seems so – so *real* up here. I dread being alone with him. It makes me feel that something must burst and tear its way out – that he would do something – or I should do something – I don't know exactly what I mean, probably – but that I should let myself go and scream—"

"Joan!"

"Don't be alarmed," she laughed shortly; "I shan't do anything silly, but I wanted to tell you my feelings in case I needed your help. When I have intuitions as strong as this they are never wrong, only I don't know yet what it means exactly."

"You must hold out for the month, at any rate," I said in as matter-of-fact a voice as I could manage, for her manner had somehow changed my surprise to a subtle sense of alarm. "Sangree only stays the month, you know. And, anyhow, you are such an odd creature yourself that you should feel generously towards other odd creatures," I ended lamely, with a forced laugh.

She gave my hand a sudden pressure. "I'm glad I've told you at any rate," she said quickly under her breath, for the canoe was now gliding up silently like a ghost to our feet, "and I'm glad you're here, too," she added as we moved down towards the water to meet it.

I made Sangree change into the bows and got into the steering seat myself, putting the girl between us so that I could watch them both by keeping their outlines against the sea and stars. For the intuitions of certain folk – women and children usually, I confess – I have always felt a great respect that has more often than not been justified by experience; and now the curious emotion stirred in me by the girl's words remained somewhat vividly in my consciousness. I explained it in some measure by the fact that the girl, tired out by the fatigue of many days' travel, had suffered a vigorous reaction of some kind from the strong, desolate scenery, and further, perhaps, that she had been treated to my own experience of seeing the members of the party in a new light – the Canadian, being partly a stranger, more vividly than the rest of us. But, at the same time, I felt it was quite possible that she had sensed some subtle link between his personality and her own, some quality that she had hitherto ignored and that the routine of town life had kept buried out of sight. The only thing that seemed difficult to explain was the fear she had spoken of, and this I hoped the wholesome effects of camp-life and exercise would sweep away naturally in the course of time.

We made the tour of the island without speaking. It was all too beautiful for speech. The trees crowded down to the shore to hear us pass. We saw their fine dark heads, bowed low with splendid dignity to watch us, forgetting for a moment that the stars were caught in the needled network of their hair. Against the sky in the west, where still lingered the sunset gold, we saw the wild toss of the horizon, shaggy with forest and cliff, gripping the heart like the motive in a symphony, and sending the sense of beauty all a-shiver through the mind – all these surrounding islands standing above the water like low clouds, and like them seeming to post along silently into the engulfing night. We heard the musical drip-drip of the paddle, and the little wash of our waves on the shore, and then suddenly we found ourselves at the opening of the lagoon again, having made the complete circuit of our home.

The Reverend Timothy had awakened from sleep and was singing to himself; and the sound of his voice as we glided down the fifty yards of enclosed water was pleasant to hear and undeniably wholesome. We saw the glow of the fire up among the trees on the ridge, and his shadow moving about as he threw on more wood.

"There you are!" he called aloud. "Good again! Been setting the night-lines, eh? Capital! And your mother's still fast asleep, Joan."

His cheery laugh floated across the water; he had not been in the least disturbed by our absence, for old campers are not easily alarmed.

"Now, remember," he went on, after we had told our little tale of travel by the fire, and Mrs. Maloney had asked for the fourth time exactly where her tent was and whether the door faced east or south, "everyone takes their turn at cooking breakfast, and one of the men is always out at sunrise to catch it first. Hubbard, I'll toss you which you do in the morning and which I do!" He lost the toss. "Then I'll catch it," I said, laughing at his discomfiture, for I knew he loathed stirring porridge. "And mind you don't burn it as you did every blessed time last year on the Volga," I added by way of reminder.

Mrs. Maloney's fifth interruption about the door of her tent, and her further pointed observation that it was past nine o'clock, set us lighting lanterns and putting the fire out for safety.

But before we separated for the night the clergyman had a time-honoured little ritual of his own to go through that no one had the heart to deny him. He always did this. It was a relic of his pulpit habits. He glanced briefly from one to the other of us, his face grave and earnest, his hands lifted to the stars and his eyes all closed and puckered up beneath a momentary frown. Then he offered up a short, almost inaudible prayer, thanking Heaven for our safe arrival, begging for good weather, no illness or accidents, plenty of fish, and strong sailing winds.

And then, unexpectedly – no one knew why exactly – he ended up with an abrupt request that nothing from the kingdom of darkness should be allowed to afflict our peace, and no evil thing come near to disturb us in the night-time.

And while he uttered these last surprising words, so strangely unlike his usual ending, it chanced that I looked up and let my eyes wander round the group assembled about the dying fire. And it certainly seemed to me that Sangree's face underwent a sudden and visible alteration. He was staring at Joan, and as he stared the change ran over it like a shadow and was gone. I started in spite of myself, for something oddly concentrated, potent, collected, had come into the expression usually so scattered and feeble. But it was all swift as a passing meteor, and when I looked a second time his face was normal and he was looking among the trees.

And Joan, luckily, had not observed him, her head being bowed and her eyes tightly closed while her father prayed.

"The girl has a vivid imagination indeed," I thought, half laughing, as I lit the lanterns, "if her thoughts can put a glamour upon mine in this way"; and yet somehow, when we said good-night, I took occasion to give her a few vigorous words of encouragement, and went to her tent to make sure I could find it quickly in the night in case anything happened. In her quick way the girl understood and thanked me, and the last thing I heard as I moved off to the men's quarters was Mrs. Maloney crying that there were beetles in her tent, and Joan's laughter as she went to help her turn them out.

Half an hour later the island was silent as the grave, but for the mournful voices of the wind as it sighed up from the sea. Like white sentries stood the three tents of the men on one side of the ridge, and on the other side, half hidden by some birches, whose leaves just shivered as the breeze caught them, the women's tents, patches of ghostly grey, gathered more closely together for mutual shelter and protection. Something like fifty yards of broken ground, grey rock, moss and lichen, lay between, and over all lay the curtain of the night and the great whispering winds from the forests of Scandinavia.

And the very last thing, just before floating away on that mighty wave that carries one so softly off into the deeps of forgetfulness, I again heard the voice of John Silence as the train moved out of Victoria Station; and by some subtle connection that met me on the very threshold of consciousness there rose in my mind simultaneously the memory of the girl's half-given confidence, and of her distress. As by some wizardry of approaching dreams they seemed in that instant to be related; but before I could analyse the why and the wherefore, both sank away out of sight again, and I was off beyond recall.

"Unless you should send for me sooner."

Chapter II

WHETHER Mrs. Maloney's tent door opened south or east I think she never discovered, for it is quite certain she always slept with the flap tightly fastened; I only know that my own little 'five by seven, all silk' faced due east, because next morning the sun, pouring in as only the wilderness sun knows how to pour, woke me early, and a moment later, with a short run over soft moss and a flying dive from the granite ledge, I was swimming in the most sparkling water imaginable.

It was barely four o'clock, and the sun came down a long vista of blue islands that led out to the open sea and Finland. Nearer by rose the wooded domes of our own property, still capped and wreathed with smoky trails of fast-melting mist, and looking as fresh as though it was the morning of Mrs. Maloney's Sixth Day and they had just issued, clean and brilliant, from the hands of the great Architect.

In the open spaces the ground was drenched with dew, and from the sea a cool salt wind stole in among the trees and set the branches trembling in an atmosphere of shimmering silver. The tents shone white where the sun caught them in patches. Below lay the lagoon, still dreaming of the summer night; in the open the fish were jumping busily, sending musical ripples towards the shore; and in the air hung the magic of dawn – silent, incommunicable.

I lit the fire, so that an hour later the clergyman should find good ashes to stir his porridge over, and then set forth upon an examination of the island, but hardly had I gone a dozen yards when I saw a figure standing a little in front of me where the sunlight fell in a pool among the trees.

It was Joan. She had already been up an hour, she told me, and had bathed before the last stars had left the sky. I saw at once that the new spirit of this solitary region had entered into her, banishing the fears of the night, for her face was like the face of a happy denizen of the wilderness, and her eyes stainless and shining. Her feet were bare, and drops of dew she had shaken from the branches hung in her loose-flying hair. Obviously she had come into her own.

"I've been all over the island," she announced laughingly, "and there are two things wanting."

"You're a good judge, Joan. What are they?"

"There's no animal life, and there's no – water."

"They go together," I said. "Animals don't bother with a rock like this unless there's a spring on it."

And as she led me from place to place, happy and excited, leaping adroitly from rock to rock, I was glad to note that my first impressions were correct. She made no reference to our conversation of the night before. The new spirit had driven out the old. There was no room in her heart for fear or anxiety, and Nature had everything her own way.

The island, we found, was some three-quarters of a mile from point to point, built in a circle, or wide horseshoe, with an opening of twenty feet at the mouth of the lagoon. Pine-trees grew thickly all over, but here and there were patches of silver birch, scrub oak, and considerable colonies of wild raspberry and gooseberry bushes. The two ends of the horseshoe formed bare slabs of smooth granite running into the sea and forming dangerous reefs just below the surface, but the rest of the island rose in a forty-foot ridge and sloped down steeply to the sea on either side, being nowhere more than a hundred yards wide.

The outer shore-line was much indented with numberless coves and bays and sandy beaches, with here and there caves and precipitous little cliffs against which the sea broke in spray and thunder. But the inner shore, the shore of the lagoon, was low and regular, and so well protected by the wall of trees along the ridge that no storm could ever send more than a passing ripple along its sandy marges. Eternal shelter reigned there.

On one of the other islands, a few hundred yards away – for the rest of the party slept late this first morning, and we took to the canoe – we discovered a spring of fresh water untainted by the brackish flavour of the Baltic, and having thus solved the most important problem of the Camp, we next proceeded to deal with the second – fish. And in half an hour we reeled in and turned homewards, for we had no means of storage, and to clean more fish than may be stored or eaten in a day is no wise occupation for experienced campers.

And as we landed towards six o'clock we heard the clergyman singing as usual and saw his wife and Sangree shaking out their blankets in the sun, and dressed in a fashion that finally dispelled all memories of streets and civilisation.

"The Little People lit the fire for me," cried Maloney, looking natural and at home in his ancient flannel suit and breaking off in the middle of his singing, "so I've got the porridge going – and this time it's *not* burnt."

We reported the discovery of water and held up the fish.

"Good! Good again!" he cried. "We'll have the first decent breakfast we've had this year. Sangree'll clean 'em in no time, and the Bo'sun's Mate—"

"Will fry them to a turn," laughed the voice of Mrs. Maloney, appearing on the scene in a tight blue jersey and sandals, and catching up the frying-pan. Her husband always called her the Bo'sun's Mate in Camp, because it was her duty, among others, to pipe all hands to meals.

"And as for you, Joan," went on the happy man, "you look like the spirit of the island, with moss in your hair and wind in your eyes, and sun and stars mixed in your face." He looked at her with delighted admiration. "Here, Sangree, take these twelve, there's a good fellow, they're the biggest; and we'll have 'em in butter in less time than you can say Baltic island!"

I watched the Canadian as he slowly moved off to the cleaning pail. His eyes were drinking in the girl's beauty, and a wave of passionate, almost feverish, joy passed over his face, expressive of the ecstasy of true worship more than anything else. Perhaps he was thinking that he still had three weeks to come with that vision always before his eyes; perhaps he was thinking of his dreams in the night. I cannot say. But I noticed the curious mingling of yearning and happiness in his eyes, and the strength of the impression touched my curiosity. Something in his face held my gaze for a second, something to do with its intensity. That so timid, so gentle a personality should conceal so virile a passion almost seemed to require explanation.

But the impression was momentary, for that first breakfast in Camp permitted no divided attentions, and I dare swear that the porridge, the tea, the Swedish 'flatbread', and the fried fish flavoured with points of frizzled bacon, were better than any meal eaten elsewhere that day in the whole world.

The first clear day in a new camp is always a furiously busy one, and we soon dropped into the routine upon which in large measure the real comfort of everyone depends. About the cooking-fire, greatly improved with stones from the shore, we built a high stockade consisting of upright poles thickly twined with branches, the roof lined with moss and lichen and weighted with rocks, and round the interior we made low wooden seats so that we could lie round the fire even in rain and eat our meals in peace. Paths, too, outlined themselves from tent to tent, from the bathing places and the landing stage, and a fair division of the island was decided upon between the quarters of the men and the women. Wood was stacked, awkward trees and boulders removed, hammocks slung, and tents strengthened. In a word, Camp was established, and duties were assigned and accepted as though we expected to live on this Baltic island for years to come and the smallest detail of the Community life was important.

Moreover, as the Camp came into being, this sense of a community developed, proving that we were a definite whole, and not merely separate human beings living for a while in tents upon a desert island. Each fell willingly into the routine. Sangree, as by natural selection, took upon himself the cleaning of the fish and the cutting of the wood into lengths sufficient for a day's use. And he did it well. The pan of water was never without a fish, cleaned and scaled, ready to fry for whoever was hungry; the nightly fire never died down for lack of material to throw on without going farther afield to search.

And Timothy, once reverend, caught the fish and chopped down the trees. He also assumed responsibility for the condition of the boat, and did it so thoroughly that nothing in the little cutter was ever found wanting. And when, for any reason, his presence was in demand, the first place to look for him was – in the boat, and there, too, he was usually found, tinkering away with sheets, sails, or rudder and singing as he tinkered.

Nor was the 'reading' neglected; for most mornings there came a sound of droning voices form the white tent by the raspberry bushes, which signified that Sangree, the tutor, and whatever other man chanced to be in the party at the time, were hard at it with history or the classics.

And while Mrs. Maloney, also by natural selection, took charge of the larder and the kitchen, the mending and general supervision of the rough comforts, she also made herself peculiarly mistress of the megaphone which summoned to meals and carried her voice easily from one end of the island to the other; and in her hours of leisure she daubed the surrounding scenery on to a sketching block with all the honesty and devotion of her determined but unreceptive soul.

Joan, meanwhile, Joan, elusive creature of the wilds, became I know not exactly what. She did plenty of work in the Camp, yet seemed to have no very precise duties. She was everywhere and anywhere. Sometimes she slept in her tent, sometimes under the stars with a blanket. She knew every inch of the island and kept turning up in places where she was least expected – for ever wandering about, reading her books in sheltered corners, making little fires on sunless days to "worship by to the gods", as she put it, ever finding new pools to dive and bathe in, and swimming day and night in the warm and waveless lagoon like a fish in a huge tank. She went bare-legged and bare-footed, with her hair down and her skirts caught up to the knees, and if ever a human being turned into a jolly savage within the compass of a single week, Joan Maloney was certainly that human being. She ran wild.

So completely, too, was she possessed by the strong spirit of the place that the little human fear she had yielded to so strangely on our arrival seemed to have been utterly dispossessed. As I hoped and expected, she made no reference to our conversation of the first evening. Sangree bothered her with no special attentions, and after all they were very little together. His behaviour was perfect in that respect, and I, for my part, hardly gave the matter another thought. Joan was ever a prey to vivid fancies of one kind or another, and this was one of them. Mercifully for the happiness of all concerned, it had melted away before the spirit of busy, active life and deep content that reigned over the island. Everyone was intensely alive, and peace was upon all.

* * *

Meanwhile the effect of the camp-life began to tell. Always a searching test of character, its results, sooner or later, are infallible, for it acts upon the soul as swiftly and surely as the hypo bath upon the negative of a photograph. A readjustment of the personal forces takes place quickly; some parts of the personality go to sleep, others wake up: but the first sweeping change that the primitive life brings about is that the artificial portions of the character shed themselves one after another like dead skins. Attitudes and poses that seemed genuine in the city drop away. The mind, like the body, grows quickly hard, simple, uncomplex. And in a camp as primitive and close to nature as ours was, these effects became speedily visible.

Some folk, of course, who talk glibly about the simple life when it is safely out of reach, betray themselves in camp by for ever peering about for the artificial excitements of civilisation which they miss. Some get bored at once; some grow slovenly; some reveal the animal in most unexpected fashion; and some, the select few, find themselves in very short order and are happy.

And, in our little party, we could flatter ourselves that we all belonged to the last category, so far as the general effect was concerned. Only there were certain other changes as well, varying with each individual, and all interesting to note.

It was only after the first week or two that these changes became marked, although this is the proper place, I think, to speak of them. For, having myself no other duty than to enjoy a well-earned holiday, I used to load my canoe with blankets and provisions and journey forth on exploration trips among the islands of several days together; and it was on my return from the first of these – when I rediscovered the party, so to speak – that these changes first presented themselves vividly to me, and in one particular instance produced a rather curious impression.

In a word, then, while everyone had grown wilder, naturally wilder, Sangree, it seemed to me, had grown much wilder, and what I can only call unnaturally wilder. He made me think of a savage.

To begin with, he had changed immensely in mere physical appearance, and the full brown cheeks, the brighter eyes of absolute health, and the general air of vigour and robustness that had come to replace his customary lassitude and timidity, had worked such an improvement that I hardly knew him for the same man. His voice, too, was deeper and his manner bespoke for the first time a greater measure of confidence in himself. He now had some claims to be called nice-looking, or at least to a certain air of virility that would not lessen his value in the eyes of the opposite sex.

All this, of course, was natural enough, and most welcome. But, altogether apart from this physical change, which no doubt had also been going forward in the rest of us, there was a subtle note in his personality that came to me with a degree of surprise that almost amounted to shock.

And two things – as he came down to welcome me and pull up the canoe – leaped up in my mind unbidden, as though connected in some way I could not at the moment divine – first, the curious judgment formed of him by Joan; and secondly, that fugitive expression I had caught in his face while Maloney was offering up his strange prayer for special protection from Heaven.

The delicacy of manner and feature – to call it by no milder term – which had always been a distinguishing characteristic of the man, had been replaced by something far more vigorous and decided, that yet utterly eluded analysis. The change which impressed me so oddly was not easy to name. The others – singing Maloney, the bustling Bo'sun's Mate, and Joan, that fascinating half-breed of undine and salamander – all showed the effects of a life so close to nature; but in their case the change was perfectly natural and what was to be expected, whereas with Peter Sangree, the Canadian, it was something unusual and unexpected.

It is impossible to explain how he managed gradually to convey to my mind the impression that something in him had turned savage, yet this, more or less, is the impression that he did convey. It was not that he seemed really less civilised, or that his character had undergone any definite alteration, but rather that something in him, hitherto dormant, had awakened to life. Some quality, latent till now – so far, at least, as we were concerned, who, after all, knew him but slightly – had stirred into activity and risen to the surface of his being.

And while, for the moment, this seemed as far as I could get, it was but natural that my mind should continue the intuitive process and acknowledge that John Silence, owing to his peculiar faculties, and the girl, owing to her singularly receptive temperament, might each in a different way have divined this latent quality in his soul, and feared its manifestation later.

On looking back to this painful adventure, too, it now seems equally natural that the same process, carried to its logical conclusion, should have wakened some deep instinct in me that, wholly without direction from my will, set itself sharply and persistently upon the watch from that very moment. Thenceforward the personality of Sangree was never far from my thoughts, and I was for ever analysing and searching for the explanation that took so long in coming.

"I declare, Hubbard, you're tanned like an aboriginal, and you look like one, too," laughed Maloney.

"And I can return the compliment," was my reply, as we all gathered round a brew of tea to exchange news and compare notes.

And later, at supper, it amused me to observe that the distinguished tutor, once clergyman, did not eat his food quite as 'nicely' as he did at home – he devoured it; that Mrs. Maloney ate more, and, to say the least, with less delay, than was her custom in the select atmosphere of her English dining-room; and that while Joan attacked her tin plateful with genuine avidity, Sangree, the Canadian, bit and gnawed at his, laughing and talking and complimenting the cook all the while, and making me think with secret amusement of a starved animal at its first meal. While, from their remarks about myself, I judged that I had changed and grown wild as much as the rest of them.

In this and in a hundred other little ways the change showed, ways difficult to define in detail, but all proving – not the coarsening effect of leading the primitive life, but, let us say, the more direct and unvarnished methods that became prevalent. For all day long we were in the bath of the elements – wind, water, sun – and just as the body became insensible to cold and shed unnecessary clothing, the mind grew straightforward and shed many of the disguises required by the conventions of civilisation.

And in each, according to temperament and character, there stirred the life-instincts that were natural, untamed, and, in a sense – savage.

Chapter III

SO IT came about that I stayed with our island party, putting off my second exploring trip from day to day, and I think that this far-fetched instinct to watch Sangree was really the cause of my postponement.

For another ten days the life of the Camp pursued its even and delightful way, blessed by perfect summer weather, a good harvest of fish, fine winds for sailing, and calm, starry nights. Maloney's selfish prayer had been favourably received. Nothing came to disturb or perplex. There was not even the prowling of night animals to vex the rest of Mrs. Maloney; for in previous camps it had often been her peculiar affliction that she heard the porcupines scratching against the canvas, or the squirrels dropping fir-cones in the early morning with a sound of miniature thunder upon the roof of her tent. But on this island there was not even a squirrel or a mouse. I think two toads and a small and harmless snake were the only living creatures that had been discovered during the whole of the first fortnight. And these two toads in all probability were not two toads, but one toad.

Then, suddenly, came the terror that changed the whole aspect of the place – the devastating terror.

It came, at first, gently, but from the very start it made me realise the unpleasant loneliness of our situation, our remote isolation in this wilderness of sea and rock, and how the islands in this tideless Baltic ocean lay about us like the advance guard of a vast besieging army. Its entry, as I say, was gentle, hardly noticeable, in fact, to most of us: singularly undramatic it certainly was. But, then, in actual life this is often the way the dreadful climaxes move upon us, leaving the heart undisturbed almost to the last minute, and then overwhelming it with a sudden rush of horror. For it was the custom at breakfast to listen patiently while each in turn related the trivial adventures of the night – how they slept, whether the wind shook their tent, whether the spider on the ridge pole had moved, whether they had heard the toad, and so forth – and on this particular morning Joan, in the middle of a little pause, made a truly novel announcement:

"In the night I heard the howling of a dog," she said, and then flushed up to the roots of her hair when we burst out laughing. For the idea of there being a dog on this forsaken island that was only able to support a snake and two toads was distinctly ludicrous, and I remember Maloney, half-way through his burnt porridge, capping the announcement by declaring that he had heard a 'Baltic turtle' in the lagoon, and his wife's expression of frantic alarm before the laughter undeceived her.

But the next morning Joan repeated the story with additional and convincing detail.

"Sounds of whining and growling woke me," she said, "and I distinctly heard sniffing under my tent, and the scratching of paws."

"Oh, Timothy! Can it be a porcupine?" exclaimed the Bo'sun's Mate with distress, forgetting that Sweden was not Canada.

But the girl's voice had sounded to me in quite another key, and looking up I saw that her father and Sangree were staring at her hard. They, too, understood that she was in earnest, and had been struck by the serious note in her voice.

"Rubbish, Joan! You are always dreaming something or other wild," her father said a little impatiently.

"There's not an animal of any size on the whole island," added Sangree with a puzzled expression. He never took his eyes from her face.

"But there's nothing to prevent one swimming over," I put in briskly, for somehow a sense of uneasiness that was not pleasant had woven itself into the talk and pauses. "A deer, for instance, might easily land in the night and take a look round—"

"Or a bear!" gasped the Bo'sun's Mate, with a look so portentous that we all welcomed the laugh.

But Joan did not laugh. Instead, she sprang up and called to us to follow.

"There," she said, pointing to the ground by her tent on the side farthest from her mother's; "there are the marks close to my head. You can see for yourselves."

We saw plainly. The moss and lichen – for earth there was hardly any – had been scratched up by paws. An animal about the size of a large dog it must have been, to judge by the marks. We stood and stared in a row.

"Close to my head," repeated the girl, looking round at us. Her face, I noticed, was very pale, and her lip seemed to quiver for an instant. Then she gave a sudden gulp – and burst into a flood of tears.

The whole thing had come about in the brief space of a few minutes, and with a curious sense of inevitableness, moreover, as though it had all been carefully planned from all time and nothing could have stopped it. It had all been rehearsed before – had actually happened before, as the strange feeling sometimes has it; it seemed like the opening movement in some ominous drama, and that I knew exactly what would happen next. Something of great moment was impending.

For this sinister sensation of coming disaster made itself felt from the very beginning, and an atmosphere of gloom and dismay pervaded the entire Camp from that moment forward.

I drew Sangree to one side and moved away, while Maloney took the distressed girl into her tent, and his wife followed them, energetic and greatly flustered.

For thus, in undramatic fashion, it was that the terror I have spoken of first attempted the invasion of our Camp, and, trivial and unimportant though it seemed, every little detail of this opening scene is photographed upon my mind with merciless accuracy and precision. It happened exactly as described. This was exactly the language used. I see it written before me in black and white. I see, too, the faces of all concerned with the sudden ugly signature of alarm where before had been peace. The terror had stretched out, so to speak, a first tentative feeler toward us and had touched the hearts of each with a horrid directness. And from this moment the Camp changed.

Sangree in particular was visibly upset. He could not bear to see the girl distressed, and to hear her actually cry was almost more than he could stand. The feeling that he had no right to protect her hurt him keenly, and I could see that he was itching to do something to help, and liked him for it. His expression said plainly that he would tear in a thousand pieces anything that dared to injure a hair of her head.

We lit our pipes and strolled over in silence to the men's quarters, and it was his odd Canadian expression "Gee whiz!" that drew my attention to a further discovery.

"The brute's been scratching round my tent too," he cried, as he pointed to similar marks by the door and I stooped down to examine them. We both stared in amazement for several minutes without speaking.

"Only I sleep like the dead," he added, straightening up again, "and so heard nothing, I suppose."

We traced the paw-marks from the mouth of his tent in a direct line across to the girl's, but nowhere else about the Camp was there a sign of the strange visitor. The deer, dog, or whatever it was that had twice favoured us with a visit in the night, had confined its attentions to these two tents. And, after all, there was really nothing out of the way about these visits of an unknown animal, for although our own island was destitute of life, we were in the heart of a wilderness, and the mainland and larger islands must be swarming with all kinds of four-footed creatures, and no very prolonged swimming was necessary to reach us. In any other country it would not have caused a moment's interest – interest of the kind we felt, that is. In our Canadian camps the bears were for ever grunting about among the provision bags at night, porcupines scratching unceasingly, and chipmunks scuttling over everything.

"My daughter is overtired, and that's the truth of it," explained Maloney presently when he rejoined us and had examined in turn the other paw-marks. "She's been overdoing it lately, and camp-life, you know, always means a great excitement to her. It's natural enough, if we take no notice she'll be all right." He paused to borrow my tobacco pouch and fill his pipe, and the blundering way he filled it and spilled the precious weed on the ground visibly belied the calm of his easy language. "You might take her out for a bit of fishing, Hubbard, like a good chap; she's hardly up to the long day in the cutter. Show her some of the other islands in your canoe, perhaps. Eh?"

And by lunch-time the cloud had passed away as suddenly, and as suspiciously, as it had come.

But in the canoe, on our way home, having till then purposely ignored the subject uppermost in our minds, she suddenly spoke to me in a way that again touched the note of sinister alarm – the note that kept on sounding and sounding until finally John Silence came with his great vibrating presence and relieved it; yes, and even after he came, too, for a while.

"I'm ashamed to ask it," she said abruptly, as she steered me home, her sleeves rolled up, her hair blowing in the wind, "and ashamed of my silly tears too, because I really can't make out what caused them; but, Mr. Hubbard, I want you to promise me not to go off for your long expeditions – just yet. I beg it of you." She was so in earnest that she forgot the canoe, and the wind caught it sideways and made us roll dangerously. "I have tried hard not to ask this," she added, bringing the canoe round again, "but I simply can't help myself."

It was a good deal to ask, and I suppose my hesitation was plain; for she went on before I could reply, and her beseeching expression and intensity of manner impressed me very forcibly.

"For another two weeks only—"

"Mr. Sangree leaves in a fortnight," I said, seeing at once what she was driving at, but wondering if it was best to encourage her or not.

"If I knew you were to be on the island till then," she said, her face alternately pale and blushing, and her voice trembling a little, "I should feel so much happier."

I looked at her steadily, waiting for her to finish.

"And safer," she added almost in a whisper; "especially – at night, I mean."

"Safer, Joan?" I repeated, thinking I had never seen her eyes so soft and tender. She nodded her head, keeping her gaze fixed on my face.

It was really difficult to refuse, whatever my thoughts and judgment may have been, and somehow I understood that she spoke with good reason, though for the life of me I could not have put it into words.

"Happier – and safer," she said gravely, the canoe giving a dangerous lurch as she leaned forward in her seat to catch my answer. Perhaps, after all, the wisest way was to grant her request and make light of it, easing her anxiety without too much encouraging its cause.

"All right, Joan, you queer creature; I promise," and the instant look of relief in her face, and the smile that came back like sunlight to her eyes, made me feel that, unknown to myself and the world, I was capable of considerable sacrifice after all.

"But, you know, there's nothing to be afraid of," I added sharply; and she looked up in my face with the smile women use when they know we are talking idly, yet do not wish to tell us so.

"*You* don't feel afraid, I know," she observed quietly.

"Of course not; why should I?"

"So, if you will just humour me this once I – I will never ask anything foolish of you again as long as I live," she said gratefully.

"You have my promise," was all I could find to say.

She headed the nose of the canoe for the lagoon lying a quarter of a mile ahead, and paddled swiftly; but a minute or two later she paused again and stared hard at me with the dripping paddle across the thwarts.

"You've not heard anything at night yourself, have you?" she asked.

"I never hear anything at night," I replied shortly, "from the moment I lie down till the moment I get up."

"That dismal howling, for instance," she went on, determined to get it out, "far away at first and then getting closer, and stopping just outside the Camp?"

"Certainly not."

"Because, sometimes I think I almost dreamed it."

"Most likely you did," was my unsympathetic response.

"And you don't think father has heard it either, then?"

"No. He would have told me if he had."

This seemed to relieve her mind a little. "I know mother hasn't," she added, as if speaking to herself, "for she hears nothing – ever."

* * *

It was two nights after this conversation that I woke out of deep sleep and heard sounds of screaming. The voice was really horrible, breaking the peace and silence with its shrill clamour. In less than ten seconds I was half dressed and out of my tent. The screaming had stopped abruptly, but I knew the general direction, and ran as fast as the darkness would allow over to the women's quarters, and on getting close I heard sounds of suppressed weeping. It was Joan's voice. And just as I came up I saw Mrs. Maloney, marvellously attired, fumbling with a lantern. Other voices became audible in the same moment behind me, and Timothy Maloney arrived, breathless, less than half dressed, and carrying another lantern that had gone out on the way from being banged against a tree. Dawn was just breaking, and a chill wind blew in from the sea. Heavy black clouds drove low overhead.

The scene of confusion may be better imagined than described. Questions in frightened voices filled the air against this background of suppressed weeping. Briefly – Joan's silk tent had been torn, and the girl was in a state bordering upon hysterics. Somewhat reassured by our noisy presence, however – for she was plucky at heart – she pulled herself together and tried to explain what had happened; and her broken words, told there on the edge of night and morning upon this wild island ridge, were oddly thrilling and distressingly convincing.

"Something touched me and I woke," she said simply, but in a voice still hushed and broken with the terror of it, "something pushing against the tent; I felt it through the canvas. There was the same sniffing and scratching as before, and I felt the tent give a little as when wind shakes it. I heard breathing – very loud, very heavy breathing – and then came a sudden great tearing blow, and the canvas ripped open close to my face."

She had instantly dashed out through the open flap and screamed at the top of her voice, thinking the creature had actually got into the tent. But nothing was visible, she declared, and she heard not the faintest sound of an animal making off under cover of the darkness. The brief account seemed to exercise a paralysing effect upon us all as we listened to it. I can see the dishevelled group to this day, the wind blowing the women's hair, and Maloney craning his head forward to listen, and his wife, open-mouthed and gasping, leaning against a pine tree.

"Come over to the stockade and we'll get the fire going," I said; "that's the first thing," for we were all shaking with the cold in our scanty garments. And at that moment Sangree arrived wrapped in a blanket and carrying his gun; he was still drunken with sleep.

"The dog again," Maloney explained briefly, forestalling his questions; "been at Joan's tent. Torn it, by Gad! this time. It's time we did something." He went on mumbling confusedly to himself.

Sangree gripped his gun and looked about swiftly in the darkness. I saw his eyes aflame in the glare of the flickering lanterns. He made a movement as though to start out and hunt – and kill. Then his glance fell on the girl crouching on the ground, her face hidden in her hands, and there leaped into his features an expression of savage anger that transformed them. He could have faced a dozen lions with a walking stick at that moment, and again I liked him for the strength of his anger, his self-control, and his hopeless devotion.

But I stopped him going off on a blind and useless chase.

"Come and help me start the fire, Sangree," I said, anxious also to relieve the girl of our presence; and a few minutes later the ashes, still growing from the night's fire, had kindled the fresh wood, and there was a blaze that warmed us well while it also lit up the surrounding trees within a radius of twenty yards.

"I heard nothing," he whispered; "what in the world do you think it is? It surely can't be only a dog!"

"We'll find that out later," I said, as the others came up to the grateful warmth; "the first thing is to make as big a fire as we can."

Joan was calmer now, and her mother had put on some warmer, and less miraculous, garments. And while they stood talking in low voices Maloney and I slipped off to examine the tent. There was little enough to see, but that little was unmistakable. Some animal had scratched up the ground at the head of the tent, and with a great blow of a powerful paw – a paw clearly provided with good claws – had struck the silk and torn it open. There was a hole large enough to pass a fist and arm through.

"It can't be far away," Maloney said excitedly. "We'll organise a hunt at once; this very minute."

We hurried back to the fire, Maloney talking boisterously about his proposed hunt. "There's nothing like prompt action to dispel alarm," he whispered in my ear; and then turned to the rest of us.

"We'll hunt the island from end to end at once," he said, with excitement; "that's what we'll do. The beast can't be far away. And the Bo'sun's Mate and Joan must come too, because they can't be left alone. Hubbard, you take the right shore, and you, Sangree, the left, and I'll go in the middle with the women. In this way we can stretch clean across the ridge, and nothing bigger than a rabbit can possibly escape us." He was extraordinarily excited, I thought. Anything affecting Joan, of course, stirred him prodigiously. "Get your guns and we'll start the drive at once," he cried. He lit another lantern and handed one each to his wife and Joan, and while I ran to fetch my gun I heard him singing to himself with the excitement of it all.

Meanwhile the dawn had come on quickly. It made the flickering lanterns look pale. The wind, too, was rising, and I heard the trees moaning overhead and the waves breaking with increasing clamour on the shore. In the lagoon the boat dipped and splashed, and the sparks from the fire were carried aloft in a stream and scattered far and wide.

We made our way to the extreme end of the island, measured our distances carefully, and then began to advance. None of us spoke. Sangree and I, with cocked guns, watched the shore lines, and all within easy touch and speaking distance. It was a slow and blundering drive, and there were many false alarms, but after the best part of half an hour we stood on the farther end, having made the complete tour, and without putting up so much as a squirrel. Certainly there was no living creature on that island but ourselves.

"I know what it is!" cried Maloney, looking out over the dim expanse of grey sea, and speaking with the air of a man making a discovery; "it's a dog from one of the farms on the larger islands" – he pointed seawards where the archipelago thickened – "and it's escaped and turned wild. Our fires and voices attracted it, and it's probably half starved as well as savage, poor brute!"

No one said anything in reply, and he began to sing again very low to himself.

The point where we stood – a huddled, shivering group – faced the wider channels that led to the open sea and Finland. The grey dawn had broken in earnest at last, and we could see the racing waves with their angry crests of white. The surrounding islands showed up as dark masses in the distance, and in the east, almost as Maloney spoke, the sun came up with a rush in a stormy and magnificent sky of red and gold. Against this splashed and gorgeous background black clouds, shaped like fantastic and legendary animals, filed past swiftly in a tearing stream, and to this day I have only to close my eyes to see again that vivid and hurrying procession in the air. All about us the pines made black splashes against the sky. It was an angry sunrise. Rain, indeed, had already begun to fall in big drops.

We turned, as by a common instinct, and, without speech, made our way back slowly to the stockade, Maloney humming snatches of his songs, Sangree in front with his gun, prepared to shoot at a moment's notice, and the women floundering in the rear with myself and the extinguished lanterns.

Yet it was only a dog!

Really, it was most singular when one came to reflect soberly upon it all. Events, say the occultists, have souls, or at least that agglomerate life due to the emotions and thoughts of all concerned in them, so that cities, and even whole countries, have great astral shapes which may become visible to the eye of vision; and certainly here, the soul of this drive – this vain, blundering, futile drive – stood somewhere between ourselves and – laughed.

All of us heard that laugh, and all of us tried hard to smother the sound, or at least to ignore it. Everyone talked at once, loudly, and with exaggerated decision, obviously trying to say something plausible against heavy odds, striving to explain naturally that an animal might so easily conceal itself from us, or swim away before we had time to light upon its trail. For we all spoke of that 'trail' as though it really existed, and we had more to go upon than the mere marks of paws about the tents of Joan and the Canadian. Indeed, but for these, and the torn tent, I think it would, of course, have been possible to ignore the existence of this beast intruder altogether.

And it was here, under this angry dawn, as we stood in the shelter of the stockade from the pouring rain, weary yet so strangely excited – it was here, out of this confusion of voices and explanations, that – very stealthily – the ghost of something horrible slipped in and stood among us. It made all our explanations seem childish and untrue; the false relation was instantly exposed. Eyes exchanged quick, anxious glances, questioning, expressive of dismay. There was a sense of wonder, of poignant distress, and of trepidation. Alarm stood waiting at our elbows. We shivered.

Then, suddenly, as we looked into each other's faces, came the long, unwelcome pause in which this new arrival established itself in our hearts.

And, without further speech, or attempt at explanation, Maloney moved off abruptly to mix the porridge for an early breakfast; Sangree to clean the fish; myself to chop wood and tend the fire; Joan and her mother to change their wet garments; and, most significant of all, to prepare her mother's tent for its future complement of two.

Each went to his duty, but hurriedly, awkwardly, silently; and this new arrival, this shape of terror and distress stalked, viewless, by the side of each.

"If only I could have traced that dog," I think was the thought in the minds of all.

But in Camp, where everyone realises how important the individual contribution is to the comfort and well-being of all, the mind speedily recovers tone and pulls itself together.

During the day, a day of heavy and ceaseless rain, we kept more or less to our tents, and though there were signs of mysterious conferences between the three members of the Maloney family, I think that most of us slept a good deal and stayed alone with his thoughts. Certainly, I did, because when Maloney came to say that his wife invited us all to a special 'tea' in her tent, he had to shake me awake before I realised that he was there at all.

And by supper-time we were more or less even-minded again, and almost jolly. I only noticed that there was an undercurrent of what is best described as 'jumpiness', and that the merest snapping of a twig, or plop of a fish in the lagoon, was sufficient to make us start and look over our shoulders. Pauses were rare in our talk, and the fire was never for one instant allowed to get low. The wind and rain had ceased, but the dripping of the branches still kept up an excellent imitation of a downpour. In particular, Maloney was vigilant and alert, telling us a series of tales in which the wholesome humorous element was especially strong. He lingered, too, behind with me after Sangree had gone to bed, and while I mixed myself a glass of hot Swedish punch, he did a thing I had never known him do before – he mixed one for himself, and then asked me to light him over to his tent. We said nothing on the way, but I felt that he was glad of my companionship.

I returned alone to the stockade, and for a long time after that kept the fire blazing, and sat up smoking and thinking. I hardly knew why; but sleep was far from me for one thing, and for another, an idea was taking form in my mind that required the comfort of tobacco and a bright fire for its growth. I lay against a corner of the stockade seat, listening to the wind whispering and to the ceaseless drip-drip of the trees. The night, otherwise, was very still, and the sea quiet as a lake. I remember that I was conscious, peculiarly conscious, of this host of desolate islands crowding about us in the darkness, and that we were the one little spot of humanity in a rather wonderful kind of wilderness.

But this, I think, was the only symptom that came to warn me of highly strung nerves, and it certainly was not sufficiently alarming to destroy my peace of mind. One thing, however, did come to disturb my peace, for just as I finally made ready to go, and had kicked the embers of the fire into a last effort, I fancied I saw, peering at me round the farther end of the stockade wall, a dark and shadowy mass that might have been – that strongly resembled, in fact – the body of a large animal. Two glowing eyes shone for an instant in the middle of it. But the next second I saw that it was merely a projecting mass of moss and lichen in the wall of our stockade, and the eyes were a couple of wandering sparks from the dying ashes I had kicked. It was easy enough, too, to imagine I saw an animal moving here and there between the trees, as I picked my way stealthily to my tent. Of course, the shadows tricked me.

And though it was after one o'clock, Maloney's light was still burning, for I saw his tent shining white among the pines.

It was, however, in the short space between consciousness and sleep – that time when the body is low and the voices of the submerged region tell sometimes true – that the idea which had been all this while maturing reached the point of an actual decision, and I suddenly realised that I had resolved to send word to Dr. Silence. For, with a sudden wonder that I had hitherto been so blind, the unwelcome conviction dawned upon me all at once that some dreadful thing was lurking about us on this island, and that the safety of at least one of us was threatened by something monstrous and unclean that was too horrible to contemplate. And, again remembering those last words of his as the train moved out of the platform, I understood that Dr. Silence would hold himself in readiness to come.

"Unless you should send for me sooner," he had said.

* * *

I found myself suddenly wide awake. It is impossible to say what woke me, but it was no gradual process, seeing that I jumped from deep sleep to absolute alertness in a single instant. I had evidently slept for an hour and more, for the night had cleared, stars crowded the sky, and a pallid half-moon just sinking into the sea threw a spectral light between the trees.

I went outside to sniff the air, and stood upright. A curious impression that something was astir in the Camp came over me, and when I glanced across at Sangree's tent, some twenty feet away, I saw that it was moving. He too, then, was awake and restless, for I saw the canvas sides bulge this way and that as he moved within.

The flap pushed forward. He was coming out, like myself, to sniff the air; and I was not surprised, for its sweetness after the rain was intoxicating. And he came on all fours, just as I had done. I saw a head thrust round the edge of the tent.

And then I saw that it was not Sangree at all. It was an animal. And the same instant I realised something else too – it was *the* animal; and its whole presentment for some unaccountable reason was unutterably malefic.

A cry I was quite unable to suppress escaped me, and the creature turned on the instant and stared at me with baleful eyes. I could have dropped on the spot, for the strength all ran out of my body with a rush. Something about it touched in me the living terror that grips and paralyses. If the mind requires but the tenth of a second to form an impression, I must have stood there stockstill for several seconds while I seized the ropes for support and stared. Many and vivid impressions flashed through my mind, but not one of them resulted in action, because I was in instant dread that the beast any moment would leap in my direction and be upon me. Instead, however, after what seemed a vast period, it slowly turned its eyes from my face, uttered a low whining sound, and came out altogether into the open.

Then, for the first time, I saw it in its entirety and noted two things: it was about the size of a large dog, but at the same time it was utterly unlike any animal that I had ever seen. Also, that the quality that had impressed me first as being malefic was really only its singular and original strangeness. Foolish as it may sound, and impossible as it is for me to adduce proof, I can only say that the animal seemed to me then to be – not real.

But all this passed through my mind in a flash, almost subconsciously, and before I had time to check my impressions, or even properly verify them, I made an involuntary movement, catching the tight rope in my hand so that it twanged like a banjo string, and in that instant the creature turned the corner of Sangree's tent and was gone into the darkness.

Then, of course, my senses in some measure returned to me, and I realised only one thing: it had been inside his tent!

I dashed out, reached the door in half a dozen strides, and looked in. The Canadian, thank God! lay upon his bed of branches. His arm was stretched outside, across the blankets, the fist tightly clenched, and the body had an appearance of unusual rigidity that was alarming. On his face there was an expression of effort, almost of painful effort, so far as the uncertain light permitted me to see, and his sleep seemed to be very profound. He looked, I thought, so stiff, so unnaturally stiff, and in some indefinable way, too, he looked smaller – shrunken.

I called to him to wake, but called many times in vain. Then I decided to shake him, and had already moved forward to do so vigorously when there came a sound of footsteps padding softly behind me, and I felt a stream of hot breath burn my neck as I stooped. I turned sharply. The tent door was darkened and something silently swept in. I felt a rough and shaggy body push past me, and knew that the animal had returned. It seemed to leap forward between me and Sangree – in fact, to leap upon Sangree, for its dark body hid him momentarily from view, and in that moment my soul turned sick and coward with a horror that rose from the very dregs and depths of life, and gripped my existence at its central source.

The creature seemed somehow to melt away into him, almost as though it belonged to him and were a part of himself, but in the same instant – that instant of extraordinary confusion and terror in my mind – it seemed to pass over and behind him, and, in some utterly unaccountable fashion, it was gone. And the Canadian woke and sat up with a start.

"Quick! You fool!" I cried, in my excitement, "the beast has been in your tent, here at your very throat while you sleep like the dead. Up, man! Get your gun! Only this second it disappeared over there behind your head. Quick! or Joan—!"

And somehow the fact that he was there, wide-awake now, to corroborate me, brought the additional conviction to my own mind that this was no animal, but some perplexing and dreadful form of life that drew upon my deeper knowledge, that much reading had perhaps assented to, but that had never yet come within actual range of my senses.

He was up in a flash, and out. He was trembling, and very white. We searched hurriedly, feverishly, but found only the traces of paw-marks passing from the door of his own tent across the moss to the women's. And the sight of the tracks about Mrs. Maloney's tent, where Joan now slept, set him in a perfect fury.

"Do you know what it is, Hubbard, this beast?" he hissed under his breath at me; "it's a damned wolf, that's what it is – a wolf lost among the islands, and starving to death – desperate. So help me God, I believe it's that!"

He talked a lot of rubbish in his excitement. He declared he would sleep by day and sit up every night until he killed it. Again his rage touched my admiration; but I got him away before he made enough noise to wake the whole Camp.

"I have a better plan than that," I said, watching his face closely. "I don't think this is anything we can deal with. I'm going to send for the only man I know who can help. We'll go to Waxholm this very morning and get a telegram through."

Sangree stared at me with a curious expression as the fury died out of his face and a new look of alarm took its place.

"John Silence," I said, "will know—"

"You think it's something – of that sort?" he stammered.

"I am sure of it."

There was a moment's pause. "That's worse, far worse than anything material," he said, turning visibly paler. He looked from my face to the sky, and then added with sudden resolution, "Come; the wind's rising. Let's get off at once. From there you can telephone to Stockholm and get a telegram sent without delay."

I sent him down to get the boat ready, and seized the opportunity myself to run and wake Maloney. He was sleeping very lightly, and sprang up the moment I put my head inside his tent. I told him briefly what I had seen, and he showed so little surprise that I caught myself wondering for the first time whether he himself had seen more going on than he had deemed wise to communicate to the rest of us.

He agreed to my plan without a moment's hesitation, and my last words to him were to let his wife and daughter think that the great psychic doctor was coming merely as a chance visitor, and not with any professional interest.

So, with frying-pan, provisions, and blankets aboard, Sangree and I sailed out of the lagoon fifteen minutes later, and headed with a good breeze for the direction of Waxholm and the borders of civilisation.

Chapter IV

ALTHOUGH nothing John Silence did ever took me, properly speaking, by surprise, it was certainly unexpected to find a letter from Stockholm waiting for me. "I have finished my Hungary business," he wrote, "and am here for ten days. Do not hesitate to send if you need me. If you telephone any morning from Waxholm I can catch the afternoon steamer."

My years of intercourse with him were full of 'coincidences' of this description, and although he never sought to explain them by claiming any magical system of communication with my mind, I have never doubted that there actually existed some secret telepathic method by which he knew my circumstances and gauged the degree of my need. And that this power was independent of time in the sense that it saw into the future, always seemed to me equally apparent.

Sangree was as much relieved as I was, and within an hour of sunset that very evening we met him on the arrival of the little coasting steamer, and carried him off in the dinghy to the camp we had prepared on a neighbouring island, meaning to start for home early next morning.

"Now," he said, when supper was over and we were smoking round the fire, "let me hear your story." He glanced from one to the other, smiling.

"You tell it, Mr. Hubbard," Sangree interrupted abruptly, and went off a little way to wash the dishes, yet not so far as to be out of earshot. And while he splashed with the hot water, and scraped the tin plates with sand and moss, my voice, unbroken by a single question from Dr. Silence, ran on for the next half-hour with the best account I could give of what had happened.

My listener lay on the other side of the fire, his face half hidden by a big sombrero; sometimes he glanced up questioningly when a point needed elaboration, but he uttered no single word till I had reached the end, and his manner all through the recital was grave and attentive. Overhead, the wash of the wind in the pine branches filled in the pauses; the darkness settled down over the sea, and the stars came out in thousands, and by the time I finished the moon had risen to flood the scene with silver. Yet, by his face and eyes, I knew quite well that the doctor was listening to something he had expected to hear, even if he had not actually anticipated all the details.

"You did well to send for me," he said very low, with a significant glance at me when I finished; "very well," – and for one swift second his eye took in Sangree – "for what we have to deal with here is nothing more than a werewolf – rare enough, I am glad to say, but often very sad, and sometimes very terrible."

I jumped as though I had been shot, but the next second was heartily ashamed of my want of control; for this brief remark, confirming as it did my own worst suspicions, did more to convince me of the gravity of the adventure than any number of questions or explanations. It seemed to draw close the circle about us, shutting a door somewhere that locked us in with the animal and the horror, and turning the key. Whatever it was had now to be faced and dealt with.

"No one has been actually injured so far?" he asked aloud, but in a matter-of-fact tone that lent reality to grim possibilities.

"Good heavens, no!" cried the Canadian, throwing down his dishcloths and coming forward into the circle of firelight. "Surely there can be no question of this poor starved beast injuring anybody, can there?"

His hair straggled untidily over his forehead, and there was a gleam in his eyes that was not all reflection from the fire. His words made me turn sharply. We all laughed a little short, forced laugh.

"I trust not, indeed," Dr. Silence said quietly. "But what makes you think the creature is starved?" He asked the question with his eyes straight on the other's face. The prompt question explained to me why I had started, and I waited with just a tremor of excitement for the reply.

Sangree hesitated a moment, as though the question took him by surprise. But he met the doctor's gaze unflinchingly across the fire, and with complete honesty.

"Really," he faltered, with a little shrug of the shoulders, "I can hardly tell you. The phrase seemed to come out of its own accord. I have felt from the beginning that it was in pain and – starved, though why I felt this never occurred to me till you asked."

"You really know very little about it, then?" said the other, with a sudden gentleness in his voice.

"No more than that," Sangree replied, looking at him with a puzzled expression that was unmistakably genuine. "In fact, nothing at all, really," he added, by way of further explanation.

"I am glad of that," I heard the doctor murmur under his breath, but so low that I only just caught the words, and Sangree missed them altogether, as evidently he was meant to do.

"And now," he cried, getting on his feet and shaking himself with a characteristic gesture, as though to shake out the horror and the mystery, "let us leave the problem till tomorrow and enjoy this wind and sea and stars. I've been living lately in the atmosphere of many people, and feel that I want to wash and be clean. I propose a swim and then bed. Who'll second me?" And two minutes later we were all diving from the boat into cool, deep water, that reflected a thousand moons as the waves broke away from us in countless ripples.

We slept in blankets under the open sky, Sangree and I taking the outside places, and were up before sunrise to catch the dawn wind. Helped by this early start we were half-way home by noon, and then the wind shifted to a few points behind us so that we fairly ran. In and out among a thousand islands, down narrow channels where we lost the wind, out into open spaces where we had to take in a reef, racing along under a hot and cloudless sky, we flew through the very heart of the bewildering and lonely scenery.

"A real wilderness," cried Dr. Silence from his seat in the bows where he held the jib sheet. His hat was off, his hair tumbled in the wind, and his lean brown face gave him the touch of an Oriental. Presently he changed places with Sangree, and came down to talk with me by the tiller.

"A wonderful region, all this world of islands," he said, waving his hand to the scenery rushing past us, "but doesn't it strike you there's something lacking?"

"It's – hard," I answered, after a moment's reflection. "It has a superficial, glittering prettiness, without—" I hesitated to find the word I wanted.

John Silence nodded his head with approval.

"Exactly," he said. "The picturesqueness of stage scenery that is not real, not alive. It's like a landscape by a clever painter, yet without true imagination. Soulless – that's the word you wanted."

"Something like that," I answered, watching the gusts of wind on the sails. "Not dead so much, as without soul. That's it."

"Of course," he went on, in a voice calculated, it seemed to me, not to reach our companion in the bows, "to live long in a place like this – long and alone – might bring about a strange result in some men."

I suddenly realised he was talking with a purpose and pricked up my ears.

"There's no life here. These islands are mere dead rocks pushed up from below the sea – not living land; and there's nothing really alive on them. Even the sea, this tideless, brackish sea, neither salt water nor fresh, is dead. It's all a pretty image of life without the real heart and soul of life. To a man with too strong desires who came here and lived close to nature, strange things might happen."

"Let her out a bit," I shouted to Sangree, who was coming aft. "The wind's gusty and we've got hardly any ballast."

He went back to the bows, and Dr. Silence continued –

"Here, I mean, a long sojourn would lead to deterioration, to degeneration. The place is utterly unsoftened by human influences, by any humanising associations of history, good or bad. This landscape has never awakened into life; it's still dreaming in its primitive sleep."

"In time," I put in, "you mean a man living here might become brutal?"

"The passions would run wild, selfishness become supreme, the instincts coarsen and turn savage probably."

"But—"

"In other places just as wild, parts of Italy for instance, where there are other moderating influences, it could not happen. The character might grow wild, savage too in a sense, but with a human wildness one could understand and deal with. But here, in a hard place like this, it might be otherwise." He spoke slowly, weighing his words carefully.

I looked at him with many questions in my eyes, and a precautionary cry to Sangree to stay in the fore part of the boat, out of earshot.

"First of all there would come callousness to pain, and indifference to the rights of others. Then the soul would turn savage, not from passionate human causes, or with enthusiasm, but by deadening down into a kind of cold, primitive, emotionless savagery – by turning, like the landscape, soulless."

"And a man with strong desires, you say, might change?"

"Without being aware of it, yes; he might turn savage, his instincts and desires turn animal. And if" – he lowered his voice and turned for a moment towards the bows, and then continued in his most weighty manner – "owing to delicate health or other predisposing causes, his Double – you know what I mean, of course – his etheric Body of Desire, or astral body, as some term it – that part in which the emotions, passions and desires reside – if this, I say, were for some constitutional reason loosely joined to his physical organism, there might well take place an occasional projection—"

Sangree came aft with a sudden rush, his face aflame, but whether with wind or sun, or with what he had heard, I cannot say. In my surprise I let the tiller slip and the cutter gave a great plunge as she came sharply into the wind and flung us all together in a heap on the bottom. Sangree said nothing, but while he scrambled up and made the jib sheet fast my companion found a moment to add to his unfinished sentence the words, too low for any ear but mine –

"Entirely unknown to himself, however."

We righted the boat and laughed, and then Sangree produced the map and explained exactly where we were. Far away on the horizon, across an open stretch of water, lay a blue cluster of islands with our crescent-shaped home among them and the safe anchorage of the lagoon. An hour with this wind would get us there comfortably, and while Dr. Silence and Sangree fell into conversation, I sat and pondered over the strange suggestions that had just been put into my mind concerning the 'Double', and the possible form it might assume when dissociated temporarily from the physical body.

The whole way home these two chatted, and John Silence was as gentle and sympathetic as a woman. I did not hear much of their talk, for the wind grew occasionally to the force of a hurricane and the sails and tiller absorbed my attention; but I could see that Sangree was pleased and happy, and was pouring out intimate revelations to his companion in the way that most people did – when John Silence wished them to do so.

But it was quite suddenly, while I sat all intent upon wind and sails, that the true meaning of Sangree's remark about the animal flared up in me with its full import. For his admission that he knew it was in pain and starved was in reality nothing more or less than a revelation of his deeper self. It was in the nature of a confession. He was speaking of something that he knew positively, something that was beyond question or argument, something that had to do directly with himself. 'Poor starved beast' he had called it in words that had 'come out of their own accord', and there had not been the slightest evidence of any desire to conceal or explain away. He had spoken instinctively – from his heart, and as though about his own self.

And half an hour before sunset we raced through the narrow opening of the lagoon and saw the smoke of the dinner-fire blowing here and there among the trees, and the figures of Joan and the Bo'sun's Mate running down to meet us at the landing-stage.

Chapter V

EVERYTHING changed from the moment John Silence set foot on that island; it was like the effect produced by calling in some big doctor, some great arbiter of life and death, for consultation. The sense of gravity increased a hundredfold. Even inanimate objects took upon themselves a subtle alteration, for the setting of the adventure – this deserted bit of sea with its hundreds of uninhabited islands – somehow turned sombre. An element that was mysterious, and in a sense disheartening, crept unbidden into the severity of grey rock and dark pine forest and took the sparkle from the sunshine and the sea.

I, at least, was keenly aware of the change, for my whole being shifted, as it were, a degree higher, becoming keyed up and alert. The figures from the background of the stage moved forward a little into the light – nearer to the inevitable action. In a word this man's arrival intensified the whole affair.

And, looking back down the years to the time when all this happened, it is clear to me that he had a pretty sharp idea of the meaning of it from the very beginning. How much he knew beforehand by his strange divining powers, it is impossible to say, but from the moment he came upon the scene and caught within himself the note of what was going on amongst us, he undoubtedly held the true solution of the puzzle and had no need to ask questions. And this certitude it was that set him in such an atmosphere of power and made us all look to him instinctively; for he took no tentative steps, made no false moves, and while the rest of us floundered he moved straight to the climax. He was indeed a true diviner of souls.

I can now read into his behaviour a good deal that puzzled me at the time, for though I had dimly guessed the solution, I had no idea how he would deal with it. And the conversations I can reproduce almost verbatim, for, according to my invariable habit, I kept full notes of all he said.

To Mrs. Maloney, foolish and dazed; to Joan, alarmed, yet plucky; and to the clergyman, moved by his daughter's distress below his usual shallow emotions, he gave the best possible treatment in the best possible way, yet all so easily and simply as to make it appear naturally spontaneous. For he dominated the Bo'sun's Mate, taking the measure of her ignorance with infinite patience; he keyed up Joan, stirring her courage and interest to the highest point for her own safety; and the Reverend Timothy he soothed and comforted, while obtaining his implicit obedience, by taking him into his confidence, and leading him gradually to a comprehension of the issue that was bound to follow.

And Sangree – here his wisdom was most wisely calculated – he neglected outwardly because inwardly he was the object of his unceasing and most concentrated attention. Under the guise of apparent indifference his mind kept the Canadian under constant observation.

There was a restless feeling in the Camp that evening and none of us lingered round the fire after supper as usual. Sangree and I busied ourselves with patching up the torn tent for our guest and with finding heavy stones to hold the ropes, for Dr. Silence insisted on having it pitched on the highest point of the island ridge, just where it was most rocky and there was no earth for pegs. The place, moreover, was midway between the men's and women's tents, and, of course, commanded the most comprehensive view of the Camp.

"So that if your dog comes," he said simply, "I may be able to catch him as he passes across."

The wind had gone down with the sun and an unusual warmth lay over the island that made sleep heavy, and in the morning we assembled at a late breakfast, rubbing our eyes and yawning. The cool north wind had given way to the warm southern air that sometimes came up with haze and moisture across the Baltic, bringing with it the relaxing sensations that produced enervation and listlessness.

And this may have been the reason why at first I failed to notice that anything unusual was about, and why I was less alert than normally; for it was not till after breakfast that the silence of our little party struck me and I discovered that Joan had not yet put in an appearance. And then, in a flash, the last heaviness of sleep vanished and I saw that Maloney was white and troubled and his wife could not hold a plate without trembling.

A desire to ask questions was stopped in me by a swift glance from Dr. Silence, and I suddenly understood in some vague way that they were waiting till Sangree should have gone. How this idea came to me I cannot determine, but the soundness of the intuition was soon proved, for the moment he moved off to his tent, Maloney looked up at me and began to speak in a low voice.

"You slept through it all," he half whispered.

"Through what?" I asked, suddenly thrilled with the knowledge that something dreadful had happened.

"We didn't wake you for fear of getting the whole Camp up," he went on, meaning, by the Camp, I supposed, Sangree. "It was just before dawn when the screams woke me."

"The dog again?" I asked, with a curious sinking of the heart.

"Got right into the tent," he went on, speaking passionately but very low, "and woke my wife by scrambling all over her. Then she realised that Joan was struggling beside her. And, by God! the beast had torn her arm; scratched all down the arm she was, and bleeding."

"Joan injured?" I gasped.

"Merely scratched – this time," put in John Silence, speaking for the first time; "suffering more from shock and fright than actual wounds."

"Isn't it a mercy the doctor was here?" said Mrs. Maloney, looking as if she would never know calmness again. "I think we should both have been killed."

"It has been a most merciful escape," Maloney said, his pulpit voice struggling with his emotion. "But, of course, we cannot risk another – we must strike Camp and get away at once—"

"Only poor Mr. Sangree must not know what has happened. He is so attached to Joan and would be so terribly upset," added the Bo'sun's Mate distractedly, looking all about in her terror.

"It is perhaps advisable that Mr. Sangree should not know what has occurred," Dr. Silence said with quiet authority, "but I think, for the safety of all concerned, it will be better not to leave the island just now." He spoke with great decision and Maloney looked up and followed his words closely.

"If you will agree to stay here a few days longer, I have no doubt we can put an end to the attentions of your strange visitor, and incidentally have the opportunity of observing a most singular and interesting phenomenon—"

"What!" gasped Mrs. Maloney, "a phenomenon? – you mean that you know what it is?"

"I am quite certain I know what it is," he replied very low, for we heard the footsteps of Sangree approaching, "though I am not so certain yet as to the best means of dealing with it. But in any case it is not wise to leave precipitately—"

"Oh, Timothy, does he think it's a devil—?" cried the Bo'sun's Mate in a voice that even the Canadian must have heard.

"In my opinion," continued John Silence, looking across at me and the clergyman, "it is a case of modern lycanthropy with other complications that may—" He left the sentence unfinished, for Mrs. Maloney got up with a jump and fled to her tent fearful she might hear a worse thing, and at that moment Sangree turned the corner of the stockade and came into view.

"There are footmarks all round the mouth of my tent," he said with excitement. "The animal has been here again in the night. Dr. Silence, you really must come and see them for yourself. They're as plain on the moss as tracks in snow."

But later in the day, while Sangree went off in the canoe to fish the pools near the larger islands, and Joan still lay, bandaged and resting, in her tent, Dr. Silence called me and the tutor and proposed a walk to the granite slabs at the far end. Mrs. Maloney sat on a stump near her daughter, and busied herself energetically with alternate nursing and painting.

"We'll leave you in charge," the doctor said with a smile that was meant to be encouraging, "and when you want us for lunch, or anything, the megaphone will always bring us back in time."

For, though the very air was charged with strange emotions, everyone talked quietly and naturally as with a definite desire to counteract unnecessary excitement.

"I'll keep watch," said the plucky Bo'sun's Mate, "and meanwhile I find comfort in my work." She was busy with the sketch she had begun on the day after our arrival. "For even a tree," she added proudly, pointing to her little easel, "is a symbol of the divine, and the thought makes me feel safer."

We glanced for a moment at a daub which was more like the symptom of a disease than a symbol of the divine – and then took the path round the lagoon.

At the far end we made a little fire and lay round it in the shadow of a big boulder. Maloney stopped his humming suddenly and turned to his companion.

"And what do you make of it all?" he asked abruptly.

"In the first place," replied John Silence, making himself comfortable against the rock, "it is of human origin, this animal; it is undoubted lycanthropy."

His words had the effect precisely of a bombshell. Maloney listened as though he had been struck.

"You puzzle me utterly," he said, sitting up closer and staring at him.

"Perhaps," replied the other, "but if you'll listen to me for a few moments you may be less puzzled at the end – or more. It depends how much you know. Let me go further and say that you have underestimated, or miscalculated, the effect of this primitive wild life upon all of you."

"In what way?" asked the clergyman, bristling a trifle.

"It is strong medicine for any town-dweller, and for some of you it has been too strong. One of you has gone wild." He uttered these last words with great emphasis.

"Gone savage," he added, looking from one to the other.

Neither of us found anything to reply.

"To say that the brute has awakened in a man is not a mere metaphor always," he went on presently.

"Of course not!"

"But, in the sense I mean, may have a very literal and terrible significance," pursued Dr. Silence. "Ancient instincts that no one dreamed of, least of all their possessor, may leap forth—"

"Atavism can hardly explain a roaming animal with teeth and claws and sanguinary instincts," interrupted Maloney with impatience.

"The term is of your own choice," continued the doctor equably, "not mine, and it is a good example of a word that indicates a result while it conceals the process; but the explanation of this beast that haunts your island and attacks your daughter is of far deeper significance than mere atavistic tendencies, or throwing back to animal origin, which I suppose is the thought in your mind."

"You spoke just now of lycanthropy," said Maloney, looking bewildered and anxious to keep to plain facts evidently; "I think I have come across the word, but really – really – it can have no actual significance today, can it? These superstitions of medieval times can hardly—"

He looked round at me with his jolly red face, and the expression of astonishment and dismay on it would have made me shout with laughter at any other time. Laughter, however, was never farther from my mind than at this moment when I listened to Dr. Silence as he carefully suggested to the clergyman the very explanation that had gradually been forcing itself upon my own mind.

"However medieval ideas may have exaggerated the idea is not of much importance to us now," he said quietly, "when we are face to face with a modern example of what, I take it, has always been a profound fact. For the moment let us leave the name of any one in particular out of the matter and consider certain possibilities."

We all agreed with that at any rate. There was no need to speak of Sangree, or of any one else, until we knew a little more.

"The fundamental fact in this most curious case," he went on, "is that the 'Double' of a man—"

"You mean the astral body? I've heard of that, of course," broke in Maloney with a snort of triumph.

"No doubt," said the other, smiling, "no doubt you have; – that this Double, or fluidic body of a man, as I was saying, has the power under certain conditions of projecting itself and becoming visible to others. Certain training will accomplish this, and certain drugs likewise; illnesses, too, that ravage the body may produce temporarily the result that death produces permanently, and let loose this counterpart of a human being and render it visible to the sight of others.

"Everyone, of course, knows this more or less today; but it is not so generally known, and probably believed by none who have not witnessed it, that this fluidic body can, under certain conditions, assume other forms than human, and that such other forms may be determined by the dominating thought and wish of the owner. For this Double, or astral body as you call it, is really the seat of the passions, emotions and desires in the psychical economy. It is the Passion Body; and, in projecting itself, it can often assume a form that gives expression to the overmastering desire that moulds it; for it is composed of such tenuous matter that it lends itself readily to the moulding by thought and wish."

"I follow you perfectly," said Maloney, looking as if he would much rather be chopping firewood elsewhere and singing.

"And there are some persons so constituted," the doctor went on with increasing seriousness, "that the fluid body in them is but loosely associated with the physical, persons of poor health as a rule, yet often of strong desires and passions; and in these persons it is easy for the Double to dissociate itself during deep sleep from their system, and, driven forth by some consuming desire, to assume an animal form and seek the fulfilment of that desire."

There, in broad daylight, I saw Maloney deliberately creep closer to the fire and heap the wood on. We gathered in to the heat, and to each other, and listened to Dr. Silence's voice as it mingled with the swish and whirr of the wind about us, and the falling of the little waves.

"For instance, to take a concrete example," he resumed; "suppose some young man, with the delicate constitution I have spoken of, forms an overpowering attachment to a young woman, yet perceives that it is not welcomed, and is man enough to repress its outward manifestations. In such a case, supposing his Double be easily projected, the very repression of his love in the daytime would add to the intense force of his desire when released in deep sleep from the control of his will, and his fluidic body might issue forth in monstrous or animal shape and become actually visible to others. And, if his devotion were dog-like in its fidelity, yet concealing the fires of a fierce passion beneath, it might well assume the form of a creature that seemed to be half dog, half wolf—"

"A werewolf, you mean?" cried Maloney, pale to the lips as he listened.

John Silence held up a restraining hand. "A werewolf," he said, "is a true psychical fact of profound significance, however absurdly it may have been exaggerated by the imaginations of a superstitious peasantry in the days of unenlightenment, for a werewolf is nothing but the savage, and possibly sanguinary, instincts of a passionate man scouring the world in his fluidic body, his passion body, his body of desire. As in the case at hand, he may not know it—"

"It is not necessarily deliberate, then?" Maloney put in quickly, with relief.

" – It is hardly ever deliberate. It is the desires released in sleep from the control of the will finding a vent. In all savage races it has been recognised and dreaded, this phenomenon styled 'Wehr Wolf', but today it is rare. And it is becoming rarer still, for the world grows tame and civilised, emotions have become refined, desires lukewarm, and few men have savagery enough left in them to generate impulses of such intense force, and certainly not to project them in animal form."

"By Gad!" exclaimed the clergyman breathlessly, and with increasing excitement, "then I feel I must tell you – what has been given to me in confidence – that Sangree has in him an admixture of savage blood – of Red Indian ancestry—"

"Let us stick to our supposition of a man as described," the doctor stopped him calmly, "and let us imagine that he has in him this admixture of savage blood; and further, that he is wholly unaware of his dreadful physical and psychical infirmity; and that he suddenly finds himself leading the primitive life together with the object of his desires; with the result that the strain of the untamed wild-man in his blood—"

"Red Indian, for instance," from Maloney.

"Red Indian, perfectly," agreed the doctor; "the result, I say, that this savage strain in him is awakened and leaps into passionate life. What then?"

He looked hard at Timothy Maloney, and the clergyman looked hard at him.

"The wild life such as you lead here on this island, for instance, might quickly awaken his savage instincts – his buried instincts – and with profoundly disquieting results."

"You mean his Subtle Body, as you call it, might issue forth automatically in deep sleep and seek the object of its desire?" I said, coming to Maloney's aid, who was finding it more and more difficult to get words.

"Precisely; – yet the desire of the man remaining utterly unmalefic – pure and wholesome in every sense—"

"Ah!" I heard the clergyman gasp.

"The lover's desire for union run wild, run savage, tearing its way out in primitive, untamed fashion, I mean," continued the doctor, striving to make himself clear to a mind bounded by conventional thought and knowledge; "for the desire to possess, remember, may easily become importunate, and, embodied in this animal form of the Subtle Body which acts as its vehicle, may go forth to tear in pieces all that obstructs, to reach to the very heart of the loved object and seize it. *Au fond*, it is nothing more than the aspiration for union, as I said – the splendid and perfectly clean desire to absorb utterly into itself—"

He paused a moment and looked into Maloney's eyes.

"To bathe in the very heart's blood of the one desired," he added with grave emphasis.

The fire spurted and crackled and made me start, but Maloney found relief in a genuine shudder, and I saw him turn his head and look about him from the sea to the trees. The wind dropped just at that moment and the doctor's words rang sharply through the stillness.

"Then it might even kill?" stammered the clergyman presently in a hushed voice, and with a little forced laugh by way of protest that sounded quite ghastly.

"In the last resort it might kill," repeated Dr. Silence. Then, after another pause, during which he was clearly debating how much or how little it was wise to give to his audience, he continued: "And if the Double does not succeed in getting back to its physical body, that physical body would wake an imbecile – an idiot – or perhaps never wake at all."

Maloney sat up and found his tongue.

"You mean that if this fluid animal thing, or whatever it is, should be prevented getting back, the man might never wake again?" he asked, with shaking voice.

"He might be dead," replied the other calmly. The tremor of a positive sensation shivered in the air about us.

"Then isn't that the best way to cure the fool – the brute—?" thundered the clergyman, half rising to his feet.

"Certainly it would be an easy and undiscoverable form of murder," was the stern reply, spoken as calmly as though it were a remark about the weather.

Maloney collapsed visibly, and I gathered the wood over the fire and coaxed up a blaze.

"The greater part of the man's life – of his vital forces – goes out with this Double," Dr. Silence resumed, after a moment's consideration, "and a considerable portion of the actual material of his physical body. So the physical body that remains behind is depleted, not only of force, but of matter. You would see it small, shrunken, dropped together, just like the body of a materialising medium at a seance. Moreover, any mark or injury inflicted upon this Double will be found exactly reproduced by the phenomenon of repercussion upon the shrunken physical body lying in its trance—"

"An injury inflicted upon the one you say would be reproduced also on the other?" repeated Maloney, his excitement growing again.

"Undoubtedly," replied the other quietly; "for there exists all the time a continuous connection between the physical body and the Double – a connection of matter, though of exceedingly attenuated, possibly of etheric, matter. The wound *travels*, so to speak, from one to the other, and if this connection were broken the result would be death."

"Death," repeated Maloney to himself, "death!" He looked anxiously at our faces, his thoughts evidently beginning to clear.

"And this solidity?" he asked presently, after a general pause; "this tearing of tents and flesh; this howling, and the marks of paws? You mean that the Double—?"

"Has sufficient material drawn from the depleted body to produce physical results? Certainly!" the doctor took him up. "Although to explain at this moment such problems as the passage of matter through matter would be as difficult as to explain how the thought of a mother can actually break the bones of the child unborn."

Dr. Silence pointed out to sea, and Maloney, looking wildly about him, turned with a violent start. I saw a canoe, with Sangree in the stern-seat, slowly coming into view round the farther point. His hat was off, and his tanned face for the first time appeared to me – to us all, I think – as though it were the face of someone else. He looked like a wild man. Then he stood up in the canoe to make a cast with the rod, and he looked for all the world like an Indian. I recalled the expression of his face as I had seen it once or twice, notably on that occasion of the evening prayer, and an involuntary shudder ran down my spine.

At that very instant he turned and saw us where we lay, and his face broke into a smile, so that his teeth showed white in the sun. He looked in his element, and exceedingly attractive. He called out something about his fish, and soon after passed out of sight into the lagoon.

For a time none of us said a word.

"And the cure?" ventured Maloney at length.

"Is not to quench this savage force," replied Dr. Silence, "but to steer it better, and to provide other outlets. This is the solution of all these problems of accumulated force, for this force is the raw material of usefulness, and should be increased and cherished, not by separating it from the body by death, but by raising it to higher channels. The best and quickest cure of all," he went on, speaking very gently and with a hand upon the clergyman's arm, "is to lead it towards its object, provided that object is not unalterably hostile – to let it find rest where—"

He stopped abruptly, and the eyes of the two men met in a single glance of comprehension.

"Joan?" Maloney exclaimed, under his breath.

"Joan!" replied John Silence.

* * *

We all went to bed early. The day had been unusually warm, and after sunset a curious hush descended on the island. Nothing was audible but that faint, ghostly singing which is inseparable from a pinewood even on the stillest day – a low, searching sound, as though the wind had hair and trailed it o'er the world.

With the sudden cooling of the atmosphere a sea fog began to form. It appeared in isolated patches over the water, and then these patches slid together and a white wall advanced upon us. Not a breath of air stirred; the firs stood like flat metal outlines; the sea became as oil. The whole scene lay as though held motionless by some huge weight in the air; and the flames from our fire – the largest we had ever made – rose upwards, straight as a church steeple.

As I followed the rest of our party tent-wards, having kicked the embers of the fire into safety, the advance guard of the fog was creeping slowly among the trees, like white arms feeling their way. Mingled with the smoke was the odour of moss and soil and bark, and the peculiar flavour of the Baltic, half salt, half brackish, like the smell of an estuary at low water.

It is difficult to say why it seemed to me that this deep stillness masked an intense activity; perhaps in every mood lies the suggestion of its opposite, so that I became aware of the contrast of furious energy, for it was like moving through the deep pause before a thunderstorm, and I trod gently lest by breaking a twig or moving a stone I might set the whole scene into some sort of tumultuous movement. Actually, no doubt, it was nothing more than a result of overstrung nerves.

There was no more question of undressing and going to bed than there was of undressing and going to bathe. Some sense in me was alert and expectant. I sat in my tent and waited. And at the end of half an hour or so my waiting was justified, for the canvas suddenly shivered, and someone tripped over the ropes that held it to the earth. John Silence came in.

The effect of his quiet entry was singular and prophetic: it was just as though the energy lying behind all this stillness had pressed forward to the edge of action. This, no doubt, was merely the quickening of my own mind, and had no other justification; for the presence of John Silence always suggested the near possibility of vigorous action, and as a matter of fact, he came in with nothing more than a nod and a significant gesture.

He sat down on a corner of my ground-sheet, and I pushed the blanket over so that he could cover his legs. He drew the flap of the tent after him and settled down, but hardly had he done so when the canvas shook a second time, and in blundered Maloney.

"Sitting in the dark?" he said self-consciously, pushing his head inside, and hanging up his lantern on the ridge-pole nail. "I just looked in for a smoke. I suppose—"

He glanced round, caught the eye of Dr. Silence, and stopped. He put his pipe back into his pocket and began to hum softly – that underbreath humming of a nondescript melody I knew so well and had come to hate.

Dr. Silence leaned forward, opened the lantern and blew the light out. "Speak low," he said, "and don't strike matches. Listen for sounds and movements about the Camp, and be ready to follow me at a moment's notice." There was light enough to distinguish our faces easily, and I saw Maloney glance again hurriedly at both of us.

"Is the Camp asleep?" the doctor asked presently, whispering.

"Sangree is," replied the clergyman, in a voice equally low. "I can't answer for the women; I think they're sitting up."

"That's for the best." And then he added: "I wish the fog would thin a bit and let the moon through; later – we may want it."

"It is lifting now, I think," Maloney whispered back. "It's over the tops of the trees already."

I cannot say what it was in this commonplace exchange of remarks that thrilled. Probably Maloney's swift acquiescence in the doctor's mood had something to do with it; for his quick obedience certainly impressed me a good deal. But, even without that slight evidence, it was clear that each recognised the gravity of the occasion, and understood that sleep was impossible and sentry duty was the order of the night.

"Report to me," repeated John Silence once again, "the least sound, and do nothing precipitately."

He shifted across to the mouth of the tent and raised the flap, fastening it against the pole so that he could see out. Maloney stopped humming and began to force the breath through his teeth with a kind of faint hissing, treating us to a medley of church hymns and popular songs of the day.

Then the tent trembled as though someone had touched it.

"That's the wind rising," whispered the clergyman, and pulled the flap open as far as it would go. A waft of cold damp air entered and made us shiver, and with it came a sound of the sea as the first wave washed its way softly along the shores.

"It's got round to the north," he added, and following his voice came a long-drawn whisper that rose from the whole island as the trees sent forth a sighing response. "The fog'll move a bit now. I can make out a lane across the sea already."

"Hush!" said Dr. Silence, for Maloney's voice had risen above a whisper, and we settled down again to another long period of watching and waiting, broken only by the occasional rubbing of shoulders against the canvas as we shifted our positions, and the increasing noise of waves on the outer coast-line of the island. And over all whirred the murmur of wind sweeping the tops of the trees like a great harp, and the faint tapping on the tent as drops fell from the branches with a sharp pinging sound.

We had sat for something over an hour in this way, and Maloney and I were finding it increasingly hard to keep awake, when suddenly Dr. Silence rose to his feet and peered out. The next minute he was gone.

Relieved of the dominating presence, the clergyman thrust his face close into mine. "I don't much care for this waiting game," he whispered, "but Silence wouldn't hear of my sitting up with the others; he said it would prevent anything happening if I did."

"He knows," I answered shortly.

"No doubt in the world about that," he whispered back; "it's this 'Double' business, as he calls it, or else it's obsession as the Bible describes it. But it's bad, whichever it is, and I've got my Winchester outside ready cocked, and I brought this too." He shoved a pocket Bible under my nose. At one time in his life it had been his inseparable companion.

"One's useless and the other's dangerous," I replied under my breath, conscious of a keen desire to laugh, and leaving him to choose. "Safety lies in following our leader—"

"I'm not thinking of myself," he interrupted sharply; "only, if anything happens to Joan tonight I'm going to shoot first – and pray afterwards!"

Maloney put the book back into his hip-pocket, and peered out of the doorway. "What is he up to now, in the devil's name, I wonder!" he added; "going round Sangree's tent and making gestures. How weird he looks disappearing in and out of the fog."

"Just trust him and wait," I said quickly, for the doctor was already on his way back. "Remember, he has the knowledge, and knows what he's about. I've been with him through worse cases than this."

Maloney moved back as Dr. Silence darkened the doorway and stooped to enter.

"His sleep is very deep," he whispered, seating himself by the door again. "He's in a cataleptic condition, and the Double may be released any minute now. But I've taken steps to imprison it in the tent, and it can't get out till I permit it. Be on the watch for signs of movement." Then he looked hard at Maloney. "But no violence, or shooting, remember, Mr. Maloney, unless you want a murder on your hands. Anything done to the Double acts by repercussion upon the physical body. You had better take out the cartridges at once."

His voice was stern. The clergyman went out, and I heard him emptying the magazine of his rifle. When he returned he sat nearer the door than before, and from that moment until we left the tent he never once took his eyes from the figure of Dr. Silence, silhouetted there against sky and canvas.

And, meanwhile, the wind came steadily over the sea and opened the mist into lanes and clearings, driving it about like a living thing.

It must have been well after midnight when a low booming sound drew my attention; but at first the sense of hearing was so strained that it was impossible exactly to locate it, and I imagined it was the thunder of big guns far out at sea carried to us by the rising wind. Then Maloney, catching hold of my arm and leaning forward, somehow brought the true relation, and I realised the next second that it was only a few feet away.

"Sangree's tent," he exclaimed in a loud and startled whisper.

I craned my head round the corner, but at first the effect of the fog was so confusing that every patch of white driving about before the wind looked like a moving tent and it was some seconds before I discovered the one patch that held steady. Then I saw that it was shaking all over, and the sides, flapping as much as the tightness of the ropes allowed, were the cause of the booming sound we had heard. Something alive was tearing frantically about inside, banging against the stretched canvas in a way that made me think of a great moth dashing against the walls and ceiling of a room. The tent bulged and rocked.

"It's trying to get out, by Jupiter!" muttered the clergyman, rising to his feet and turning to the side where the unloaded rifle lay. I sprang up too, hardly knowing what purpose was in my mind, but anxious to be prepared for anything. John Silence, however, was before us both, and his figure slipped past and blocked the doorway of the tent. And there was some quality in his voice next minute when he began to speak that brought our minds instantly to a state of calm obedience.

"First – the women's tent," he said low, looking sharply at Maloney, "and if I need your help, I'll call."

The clergyman needed no second bidding. He dived past me and was out in a moment. He was labouring evidently under intense excitement. I watched him picking his way silently over the slippery ground, giving the moving tent a wide berth, and presently disappearing among the floating shapes of fog.

Dr. Silence turned to me. "You heard those footsteps about half an hour ago?" he asked significantly.

"I heard nothing."

"They were extraordinarily soft – almost the soundless tread of a wild creature. But now, follow me closely," he added, "for we must waste no time if I am to save this poor man from his affliction and lead his werewolf Double to its rest. And, unless I am much mistaken" – he peered at me through the darkness, whispering with the utmost distinctness – "Joan and Sangree are absolutely made for one another. And I think she knows it too – just as well as he does."

My head swam a little as I listened, but at the same time something cleared in my brain and I saw that he was right. Yet it was all so weird and incredible, so remote from the commonplace facts of life as commonplace people know them; and more than once it flashed upon me that the whole scene – people, words, tents, and all the rest of it – were delusions created by the intense excitement of my own mind somehow, and that suddenly the sea-fog would clear off and the world become normal again.

The cold air from the sea stung our cheeks sharply as we left the close atmosphere of the little crowded tent. The sighing of the trees, the waves breaking below on the rocks, and the lines and patches of mist driving about us seemed to create the momentary illusion that the whole island had broken loose and was floating out to sea like a mighty raft.

The doctor moved just ahead of me, quickly and silently; he was making straight for the Canadian's tent where the sides still boomed and shook as the creature of sinister life raced and tore about impatiently within. A little distance from the door he paused and held up a hand to stop me. We were, perhaps, a dozen feet away.

"Before I release it, you shall see for yourself," he said, "that the reality of the werewolf is beyond all question. The matter of which it is composed is, of course, exceedingly attenuated, but you are partially clairvoyant – and even if it is not dense enough for normal sight you will see something."

He added a little more I could not catch. The fact was that the curiously strong vibrating atmosphere surrounding his person somewhat confused my senses. It was the result, of course, of his intense concentration of mind and forces, and pervaded the entire Camp and all the persons in it. And as I watched the canvas shake and heard it boom and flap I heartily welcomed it. For it was also protective.

At the back of Sangree's tent stood a thin group of pine trees, but in front and at the sides the ground was comparatively clear. The flap was wide open and any ordinary animal would have been out and away without the least trouble. Dr. Silence led me up to within a few feet, evidently careful not to advance beyond a certain limit, and then stooped down and signalled to me to do the same. And looking over his shoulder I saw the interior lit faintly by the spectral light reflected from the fog, and the dim blot upon the balsam boughs and blankets signifying Sangree; while over him, and round him, and up and down him, flew the dark mass of 'something' on four legs, with pointed muzzle and sharp ears plainly visible against the tent sides, and the occasional gleam of fiery eyes and white fangs.

I held my breath and kept utterly still, inwardly and outwardly, for fear, I suppose, that the creature would become conscious of my presence; but the distress I felt went far deeper than the mere sense of personal safety, or the fact of watching something so incredibly active and real. I became keenly aware of the dreadful psychic calamity it involved. The realisation that Sangree lay confined in that narrow space with this species of monstrous projection of himself – that he was wrapped there in the cataleptic sleep, all unconscious that this thing was masquerading with his own life and energies – added a distressing touch of horror to the scene. In all the cases of John Silence – and they were many and often terrible – no other psychic affliction has ever, before or since, impressed me so convincingly with the pathetic impermanence of the human personality, with its fluid nature, and with the alarming possibilities of its transformations.

"Come," he whispered, after we had watched for some minutes the frantic efforts to escape from the circle of thought and will that held it prisoner, "come a little farther away while I release it."

We moved back a dozen yards or so. It was like a scene in some impossible play, or in some ghastly and oppressive nightmare from which I should presently awake to find the blankets all heaped up upon my chest.

By some method undoubtedly mental, but which, in my confusion and excitement, I failed to understand, the doctor accomplished his purpose, and the next minute I heard him say sharply under his breath, "It's out! Now watch!"

At this very moment a sudden gust from the sea blew aside the mist, so that a lane opened to the sky, and the moon, ghastly and unnatural as the effect of stage limelight, dropped down in a momentary gleam upon the door of Sangree's tent, and I perceived that something had moved forward from the interior darkness and stood clearly defined upon the threshold. And, at the same moment, the tent ceased its shuddering and held still.

There, in the doorway, stood an animal, with neck and muzzle thrust forward, its head poking into the night, its whole body poised in that attitude of intense rigidity that precedes the spring into freedom, the running leap of attack. It seemed to be about the size of a calf, leaner than a mastiff, yet more squat than a wolf, and I can swear that I saw the fur ridged sharply upon its back. Then its upper lip slowly lifted, and I saw the whiteness of its teeth.

Surely no human being ever stared as hard as I did in those next few minutes. Yet, the harder I stared the clearer appeared the amazing and monstrous apparition. For, after all, it was Sangree – and yet it was not Sangree. It was the head and face of an animal, and yet it was the face of Sangree: the face of a wild dog, a wolf, and yet his face. The eyes were sharper, narrower, more fiery, yet they were his eyes – his eyes run wild; the teeth were longer, whiter, more pointed – yet they were his teeth, his teeth grown cruel; the expression was flaming, terrible, exultant – yet it was his expression carried to the border of savagery – his expression as I had already surprised it more than once, only dominant now, fully released from human constraint, with the mad yearning of a hungry and importunate soul. It was the soul of Sangree, the long suppressed, deeply loving Sangree, expressed in its single and intense desire – pure utterly and utterly wonderful.

Yet, at the same time, came the feeling that it was all an illusion. I suddenly remembered the extraordinary changes the human face can undergo in circular insanity, when it changes from melancholia to elation; and I recalled the effect of hascheesh, which shows the human countenance in the form of the bird or animal to which in character it most approximates; and for a moment I attributed this mingling of Sangree's face with a wolf to some kind of similar delusion of the senses. I was mad, deluded, dreaming! The excitement of the day, and this dim light of stars and bewildering mist combined to trick me. I had been amazingly imposed upon by some false wizardry of the senses. It was all absurd and fantastic; it would pass.

And then, sounding across this sea of mental confusion like a bell through a fog, came the voice of John Silence bringing me back to a consciousness of the reality of it all –

"Sangree – in his Double!"

And when I looked again more calmly, I plainly saw that it was indeed the face of the Canadian, but his face turned animal, yet mingled with the brute expression a curiously pathetic look like the soul seen sometimes in the yearning eyes of a dog – the face of an animal shot with vivid streaks of the human.

The doctor called to him softly under his breath –

"Sangree! Sangree, you poor afflicted creature! Do you know me? Can you understand what it is you're doing in your 'Body of Desire'?"

For the first time since its appearance the creature moved. Its ears twitched and it shifted the weight of its body on to the hind legs. Then, lifting its head and muzzle to the sky, it opened its long jaws and gave vent to a dismal and prolonged howling.

But, when I heard that howling rise to heaven, the breath caught and strangled in my throat and it seemed that my heart missed a beat; for, though the sound was entirely animal, it was at the same time entirely human. But, more than that, it was the cry I had so often heard in the Western States of America where the Indians still fight and hunt and struggle – it was the cry of the Redskin!

"The Indian blood!" whispered John Silence, when I caught his arm for support; "the ancestral cry."

And that poignant, beseeching cry, that broken human voice, mingling with the savage howl of the brute beast, pierced straight to my very heart and touched there something that no music, no voice, passionate or tender, of man, woman or child has ever stirred before or since for one second into life. It echoed away among the fog and the trees and lost itself somewhere out over the hidden sea. And some part of myself – something that was far more than the mere act of intense listening – went out with it, and for several minutes I lost consciousness of my surroundings and felt utterly absorbed in the pain of another stricken fellow-creature.

Again the voice of John Silence recalled me to myself.

"Hark!" he said aloud. "Hark!"

His tone galvanised me afresh. We stood listening side by side.

Far across the island, faintly sounding through the trees and brushwood, came a similar, answering cry. Shrill, yet wonderfully musical, shaking the heart with a singular wild sweetness that defies description, we heard it rise and fall upon the night air.

"It's across the lagoon," Dr. Silence cried, but this time in full tones that paid no tribute to caution. "It's Joan! She's answering him!"

Again the wonderful cry rose and fell, and that same instant the animal lowered its head, and, muzzle to earth, set off on a swift easy canter that took it off into the mist and out of our sight like a thing of wind and vision.

The doctor made a quick dash to the door of Sangree's tent, and, following close at his heels, I peered in and caught a momentary glimpse of the small, shrunken body lying upon the branches but half covered by the blankets – the cage from which most of the life, and not a little of the actual corporeal substance, had escaped into that other form of life and energy, the body of passion and desire.

By another of those swift, incalculable processes which at this stage of my apprenticeship I failed often to grasp, Dr. Silence reclosed the circle about the tent and body.

"Now it cannot return till I permit it," he said, and the next second was off at full speed into the woods, with myself close behind him. I had already had some experience of my companion's ability to run swiftly through a dense wood, and I now had the further proof of his power almost to see in the dark. For, once we left the open space about the tents, the trees seemed to absorb all the remaining vestiges of light, and I understood that special sensibility that is said to develop in the blind – the sense of obstacles.

And twice as we ran we heard the sound of that dismal howling drawing nearer and nearer to the answering faint cry from the point of the island whither we were going.

Then, suddenly, the trees fell away, and we emerged, hot and breathless, upon the rocky point where the granite slabs ran bare into the sea. It was like passing into the clearness of open day. And there, sharply defined against sea and sky, stood the figure of a human being. It was Joan.

I at once saw that there was something about her appearance that was singular and unusual, but it was only when we had moved quite close that I recognised what caused it. For while the lips wore a smile that lit the whole face with a happiness I had never seen there before, the eyes themselves were fixed in a steady, sightless stare as though they were lifeless and made of glass.

I made an impulsive forward movement, but Dr. Silence instantly dragged me back.

"No," he cried, "don't wake her!"

"What do you mean?" I replied aloud, struggling in his grasp.

"She's asleep. It's somnambulistic. The shock might injure her permanently."

I turned and peered closely into his face. He was absolutely calm. I began to understand a little more, catching, I suppose, something of his strong thinking.

"Walking in her sleep, you mean?"

He nodded. "She's on her way to meet him. From the very beginning he must have drawn her – irresistibly."

"But the torn tent and the wounded flesh?"

"When she did not sleep deep enough to enter the somnambulistic trance he missed her – he went instinctively and in all innocence to seek her out – with the result, of course, that she woke and was terrified—"

"Then in their heart of hearts they love?" I asked finally.

John Silence smiled his inscrutable smile. "Profoundly," he answered, "and as simply as only primitive souls can love. If only they both come to realise it in their normal waking states his Double will cease these nocturnal excursions. He will be cured, and at rest."

The words had hardly left his lips when there was a sound of rustling branches on our left, and the very next instant the dense brushwood parted where it was darkest and out rushed the swift form of an animal at full gallop. The noise of feet was scarcely audible, but in that utter stillness I heard the heavy panting breath and caught the swish of the low bushes against its sides. It went straight towards Joan – and as it went the girl lifted her head and turned to meet it. And the same instant a canoe that had been creeping silently and unobserved round the inner shore of the lagoon, emerged from the shadows and defined itself upon the water with a figure at the middle thwart. It was Maloney.

It was only afterwards I realised that we were invisible to him where we stood against the dark background of trees; the figures of Joan and the animal he saw plainly, but not Dr. Silence and myself standing just beyond them. He stood up in the canoe and pointed with his right arm. I saw something gleam in his hand.

"Stand aside, Joan girl, or you'll get hit," he shouted, his voice ringing horribly through the deep stillness, and the same instant a pistol-shot cracked out with a burst of flame and smoke, and the figure of the animal, with one tremendous leap into the air, fell back in the shadows and disappeared like a shape of night and fog. Instantly, then, Joan opened her eyes, looked in a dazed fashion about her, and pressing both hands against her heart, fell with a sharp cry into my arms that were just in time to catch her.

And an answering cry sounded across the lagoon – thin, wailing, piteous. It came from Sangree's tent.

"Fool!" cried Dr. Silence, "you've wounded him!" and before we could move or realise quite what it meant, he was in the canoe and half-way across the lagoon.

Some kind of similar abuse came in a torrent from my lips, too – though I cannot remember the actual words – as I cursed the man for his disobedience and tried to make the girl comfortable on the ground. But the clergyman was more practical. He was spreading his coat over her and dashing water on her face.

"It's not Joan I've killed at any rate," I heard him mutter as she turned and opened her eyes and smiled faintly up in his face. "I swear the bullet went straight."

Joan stared at him; she was still dazed and bewildered, and still imagined herself with the companion of her trance. The strange lucidity of the somnambulist still hung over her brain and mind, though outwardly she appeared troubled and confused.

"Where has he gone to? He disappeared so suddenly, crying that he was hurt," she asked, looking at her father as though she did not recognise him. "And if they've done anything to him – they have done it to me too – for he is more to me than—"

Her words grew vaguer and vaguer as she returned slowly to her normal waking state, and now she stopped altogether, as though suddenly aware that she had been surprised into telling secrets. But all the way back, as we carried her carefully through the trees, the girl smiled and murmured Sangree's name and asked if he was injured, until it finally became clear to me that the wild soul of the one had called to the wild soul of the other and in the secret depths of their beings the call had been heard and understood. John Silence was right. In the abyss of her heart, too deep at first for recognition, the girl loved him, and had loved him from the very beginning. Once her normal waking consciousness recognised the fact they would leap together like twin flames, and his affliction would be at an end; his intense desire would be satisfied; he would be cured.

And in Sangree's tent Dr. Silence and I sat up for the remainder of the night – this wonderful and haunted night that had shown us such strange glimpses of a new heaven and a new hell – for the Canadian tossed upon his balsam boughs with high fever in his blood, and upon each cheek a dark and curious contusion showed, throbbing with severe pain although the skin was not broken and there was no outward and visible sign of blood.

"Maloney shot straight, you see," whispered Dr. Silence to me after the clergyman had gone to his tent, and had put Joan to sleep beside her mother, who, by the way, had never once awakened. "The bullet must have passed clean through the face, for both cheeks are stained. He'll wear these marks all his life – smaller, but always there. They're the most curious scars in the world, these scars transferred by repercussion from an injured Double. They'll remain visible until just before his death, and then with the withdrawal of the subtle body they will disappear finally."

His words mingled in my dazed mind with the sighs of the troubled sleeper and the crying of the wind about the tent. Nothing seemed to paralyse my powers of realisation so much as these twin stains of mysterious significance upon the face before me.

It was odd, too, how speedily and easily the Camp resigned itself again to sleep and quietness, as though a stage curtain had suddenly dropped down upon the action and concealed it; and nothing contributed so vividly to the feeling that I had been a spectator of some kind of visionary drama as the dramatic nature of the change in the girl's attitude.

Yet, as a matter of fact, the change had not been so sudden and revolutionary as appeared. Underneath, in those remoter regions of consciousness where the emotions, unknown to their owners, do secretly mature, and owe thence their abrupt revelation to some abrupt psychological climax, there can be no doubt that Joan's love for the Canadian had been growing steadily and irresistibly all the time. It had now rushed to the surface so that she recognised it; that was all.

And it has always seemed to me that the presence of John Silence, so potent, so quietly efficacious, produced an effect, if one may say so, of a psychic forcing-house, and hastened incalculably the bringing together of these two 'wild' lovers. In that sudden awakening had occurred the very psychological climax required to reveal the passionate emotion accumulated below. The deeper knowledge had leaped across and transferred itself to her ordinary consciousness, and in that shock the collision of the personalities had shaken them to the depths and shown her the truth beyond all possibility of doubt.

"He's sleeping quietly now," the doctor said, interrupting my reflections. "If you will watch alone for a bit I'll go to Maloney's tent and help him to arrange his thoughts." He smiled in anticipation of that 'arrangement'. "He'll never quite understand how a wound on the Double can transfer itself to the physical body, but at least I can persuade him that the less he talks and 'explains' tomorrow, the sooner the forces will run their natural course now to peace and quietness."

He went away softly, and with the removal of his presence Sangree, sleeping heavily, turned over and groaned with the pain of his broken head.

And it was in the still hour just before the dawn, when all the islands were hushed, the wind and sea still dreaming, and the stars visible through clearing mists, that a figure crept silently over the ridge and reached the door of the tent where I dozed beside the sufferer, before I was aware of its presence. The flap was cautiously lifted a few inches and in looked – Joan.

That same instant Sangree woke and sat up on his bed of branches. He recognised her before I could say a word, and uttered a low cry. It was pain and joy mingled, and this time all human. And the girl too was no longer walking in her sleep, but fully aware of what she was doing. I was only just able to prevent him springing from his blankets.

"Joan, Joan!" he cried, and in a flash she answered him, "I'm here – I'm with you always now," and had pushed past me into the tent and flung herself upon his breast.

"I knew you would come to me in the end," I heard him whisper.

"It was all too big for me to understand at first," she murmured, "and for a long time I was frightened—"

"But not now!" he cried louder; "you don't feel afraid now of – of anything that's in me—"

"I fear nothing," she cried, "nothing, nothing!"

I led her outside again. She looked steadily into my face with eyes shining and her whole being transformed. In some intuitive way, surviving probably from the somnambulism, she knew or guessed as much as I knew.

"You must talk tomorrow with John Silence," I said gently, leading her towards her own tent. "He understands everything."

I left her at the door, and as I went back softly to take up my place of sentry again with the Canadian, I saw the first streaks of dawn lighting up the far rim of the sea behind the distant islands.

And, as though to emphasise the eternal closeness of comedy to tragedy, two small details rose out of the scene and impressed me so vividly that I remember them to this very day. For in the tent where I had just left Joan, all aquiver with her new happiness, there rose plainly to my ears the grotesque sounds of the Bo'sun's Mate heavily snoring, oblivious of all things in heaven or hell; and from Maloney's tent, so still was the night, where I looked across and saw the lantern's glow, there came to me, through the trees, the monotonous rising and falling of a human voice that was beyond question the sound of a man praying to his God.

Moonskin

Charlotte Bond

Yorkshire, 1534

THERE WAS A LEGEND that those who spied on a werewolf's transformation would be turned to stone, but Thomas discovered that this couldn't be true when he saw his intended wife slip, in wolf form, into a river, slough off her skin then turn into a human. A human of unsurpassed beauty and the most remarkable grey hair – not the grey of withered age but the silver of fur in moonlight.

He hadn't intended to spy that night. He'd been out checking his rabbit snares and was just returning to his village along the riverbank when a great howl rose around him. Dropping his catch, he sprinted towards and then up a nearby tree, where he hid himself among the branches. If it hadn't been summer, if it had been bare branches instead of leafy boughs, he might well have been spotted, and this story would have been much shorter. As it was, he was well-concealed and thankfully downwind when a pack of wolves came snapping and prancing into the clearing below. These weren't wolves on the hunt, fierce and intent on finding prey; these were wolves enjoying the warmth of a summer's night, creatures more intent on games than game.

Despite his fear, Thomas peered curiously through the branches. He'd only seen a few wolf carcasses in his life, but that had been enough for him to know that these wolves were shaped differently. Their bodies were longer, their ribcages more pronounced like a greyhound's. Their legs were longer too, but in a spindly way.

The pack snapped and snarled, yipped and barked, playing a game of chase or tag by the look of it. Then one of them plunged into the water and started swimming. Thomas watched in amazement as the skin started to detach itself from the body until it was entirely separate and at risk of floating away. Beneath the skin was a naked man, and he seized his wolf skin before it could escape.

"The water is fine and cool!" he called out. "Join me!"

The wolves on the bank all charged into the water, and within moments, there were no longer eight wolves but five men and three women, all laughing and splashing each other after hanging their skins on nearby tree branches to dry out.

One woman caught Thomas' eye in particular: the one with the silvery hair. He found himself aching with lust for her as he watched her naked body twist and slide through the water. In their human form, he recognised them as a group of travelling bards and musicians that were touring the villages and towns hereabouts. A perfect guise for werewolves, he reflected.

Time lost all meaning, and as he continued to watch without being seen, Thomas felt his fear receding – always a dangerous thing to happen when wolves are around.

Eventually, the werewolves got out of the river, and one of them proposed a race to some tree or other. So they ran – five naked men and three naked women – and Thomas suspected that anyone meeting them in the forest that night would be no less shocked than if the werewolves had been charging about in their hairy form.

Filled with boldness now, he slipped down the tree and ran over to the skins, seizing the one belonging to the beautiful woman. His grandmother had been Scottish and had filled his head with tales of kelpies and selkies, so he knew if you stole a shapechanger's skin, you had power over them, and he desperately wanted power over that silver-haired woman.

However, it had been an impulsive decision to turn thief and, as he ran, Thomas began to see the foolishness of it. Once the theft was noticed, the others would merely transform into wolves and run him down. But putting the skin back would be even more dangerous, and he wasn't far from his home, so the best course seemed to be to keep going.

Just as his little cottage on the outskirts of the village came into sight, terrible howls raced through the darkness, giving him an extra burst of speed. He didn't dare look behind him as he threw himself at the door, and he didn't even dare to look out of the window once he was safely inside. Instead, clutching the skin tightly, he seized a fish-gutting knife and sank to the floor, panting, trying to purge himself of the terror that had set his limbs trembling.

* * *

The naked woman stood before the door of the cottage and knocked. Not far away, her pack circled. They'd told her that the smell of her moonskin led to this door then stopped, so inside her skin must be.

A man opened the door, clutching a knife. She recognised him from the play they'd put on in the village just yesterday; he'd been in the crowd, staring at her.

"Hello," he said. "I suppose you've come for your skin."

"Indeed," she replied.

"You know the laws governing your kind," the man continued. She noticed, with satisfaction, how his gaze was caught by her pack mates slinking through the darkness. His house was some way from the other houses of the village, and no one would get here in time to save him if her fellow werewolves struck. "I have your skin and you have to stay with me until I give it back."

What he said was true, and growls rumbled through the darkness.

"Three days," he said quickly. "Stay three days and I will give it back."

The woman glanced at the other werewolves; none offered advice. She was intrigued by this trembling human who was willing to brave the wrath of her pack just to have her in his house for a short time.

"Three days, then," she agreed. He stood aside to let her in.

* * *

After three days, he convinced her to stay until the next full moon. "You won't need your skin until then anyway," he said.

This wasn't true because the moonskin could be used whenever the wearer was in moonlight. But she felt it wiser not to tell him that; the secrets of her kind were not to be given up so easily.

Besides, she was enjoying herself. Life with the pack was all she had known, and she had lived the same life for a long time so she found this change a welcome curiosity. Beds, she concluded, were far superior to the ground. A stewpot that could bubble on the fire for days gave a richer, heartier meal than a pot that had to be used, then cleaned, then stowed in a cart within the space of a few hours. She could cut flowers from the fields and bring them inside to marvel at their beauty whenever she desired. And Thomas, for all that he had come to her as a thief, was a gentle lover and a considerate host.

She agreed to his proposal, and when she'd spent a week in his company, she answered the door to find her pack there. "We're leaving," said one of her brothers. "Have you your moonskin?"

"No. He will return it at the next full moon."

There were some uneasy glances at that since, just as humans have cautionary tales of werewolves, so werewolves have stories about humans. But her brother spoke again. "Very well. We shall return then. Take care, little sister."

When Thomas heard that the travelling entertainers had moved on, he rushed home from his job at the water mill, certain he'd find an empty home. But his very own werewolf was there, welcoming him with a smile, so he swept her up and made passionate love to her.

After, as she lay sleepy in his arms, he murmured, "I must know your name, beloved, so that I can take you into the village and show off your beauty."

"Werewolves don't have names," she replied.

"Then I shall choose one for you. You shall be Constance, because our love and desire for each other will be constant."

She thought on this a while and decided she liked it well enough, so Constance she became. She didn't see the name for what it was: a chain tying her to this new life.

* * *

Constance found a mixed reception among the villagers. Without exception, all the men desired her. The women, however, treated her with either scorn, derision, or outright hatred, sensing how their husbands and brothers were drawn to her. But a few women were kind and welcoming, and Constance found that if she stayed with these women, she could easily ignore the others who bore her ill-will.

Fortuitously, as she spent time with these kind, quiet women and completely ignored the menfolk, the jealous wives began to soften towards her. It was clear that she had no interest in anyone other than Thomas, and she couldn't be blamed if the other men were ruled by their breeches over their brains.

* * *

The day before the next full moon, Constance said to Thomas, "Don't forget to give me my moonskin tomorrow."

"Of course not. Or…" He pulled out a small brass ring from the pouch at his waist. "Would you plight your troth to me and become my wife?"

Constance was intrigued. A wife? Devoted to one man, with one man devoted to her? In the pack, monogamy did not exist, and while she had always enjoyed varying her partners, the idea of singular devotion was curiously appealing.

"What does it involve?" she asked.

"We must stand before God and promise ourselves to each other, and then we must consummate the marriage."

Werewolves have only a little concept of God and no concept at all of promises, so she readily agreed, knowing it could be easily undone if necessary.

* * *

Thomas had thought that being married to a beautiful woman who was bound to him utterly would be wonderful. At first, it was. While she considered him a gentle lover, he found her wild and greedy in her lovemaking, so that in those first few months he was constantly excited to see her. Her face would light up whenever he walked in, and she would rise from her chair by the fire to embrace him. Her cooking was adequate but quickly got better as she got used to the regular supply of flour, eggs, vegetables, and honey – all of which had been scarce during her life on the move.

"We mostly ate meat," she told him, and indeed, when he was fortunate enough to afford meat, she could make amazing dishes out of it.

When her old wolf pack came to call at the next full moon, his heart thrilled at how she politely told them to go away before she came back to his arms. Their howls outside were joyous to listen to as he snuggled by the hearth with his new wife.

But while Thomas craved the unusual and beautiful, he soon found that what he really wanted was sensible and normal. He had hoped to take on something ethereal and bend it to his will, make it mundane. Yet no matter how long she lived with him or how he tried to encourage her to be like other women, Constance's wildness kept showing through.

As the winter months drew in, everyone started to put on their furs, but Constance walked through the village in a summer dress, her skin warm and her lips a pale pink rather than the frigid blue they should be when the frost had a tight grip on the ground.

While the jealous stares of the other men had made Thomas puff as proud as a peacock at first, as the months wore on, he grew irritated then enraged by their attention. What was worse was that Constance didn't even seem to notice their stares.

"They are just being friendly," she said, "and I want to fit in. Their wives don't mind – why should you?"

He'd hit her then, like he would strike any stubborn and stupid creature, and she recoiled.

"Constance, beloved, I'm sorry..." he began, but she stood up, went to the bedroom and barred the door against him. He slept by the fire that night, and the next as well, but then she took him to bed and made love to him, and all settled between them, if a little uneasily.

That was another thing that was beginning to grate on him: their lovemaking. When he brought her to the height of pleasure, she would arch her back and howl. He'd found it a wild, wonderful sound to begin with, but as the trees became bare and the ground hardened, when the wind bit and the rain stung, what a man did not want was to hear the cry of a wolf in the night. So he began to be quicker in his lovemaking, ensuring that he was spent before she was. While that solved one problem, it did lead to a certain coldness between them, and he often found himself falling asleep, hoping he'd dream of a pliant wife who lay soft and quiet beneath him, a woman like so many in the village that he hadn't married and wished now that he had.

* * *

Constance was desperate to leave, and while promises and rings and consummation wouldn't stop her, the lack of a moonskin did. If she left without it, she would be forever human-shaped – but, crucially, never a human. She'd merely be a werewolf who could not change, and such a state brought only misery.

So she started to look for the skin. She searched the cottage, the rafters, the vegetable patch, the outhouse, the mill, and even the roadsides that Thomas passed along every day, but nothing. When her pack passed back through, she asked them to use their noses to sniff out its hiding place, but they couldn't locate it either.

"We shall wait until he comes home," one of her sisters said, "and then we shall rip him apart for such wickedness."

"But if you do that," Constance said bitterly, "I shall never get my skin back."

Miserable, tired, and constantly plagued with a stomach complaint, she began to descend into despair. Until, that is, she found her stomach complaint was not an illness but the sign of a babe growing inside her.

* * *

Thomas was thrilled to learn he would become a father. He felt sure a werewolf would give him strong sons and beautiful daughters. He became kinder to Constance, more attentive. While she was pregnant and after the baby was born (a strapping, healthy son as he'd hoped), things went well between them. But they quickly soured when he saw that motherhood didn't soften her peculiarities but enhanced them.

If the baby started to crawl somewhere it shouldn't, she snarled at him; if he misbehaved, she snapped her perfect white teeth. As well as teaching him to talk, she encouraged him to howl. Her lullabies were interspersed with gentle growls that the child seemed to find soothing. While other mothers carried their children in slings, Constance let their son crawl on all fours behind her, slowing her pace so he could keep up.

"It's unnatural," Thomas heard people whisper.

"Is she a woman or a beast?"

"That child will grow up feral."

"Poor Thomas. How ashamed he must be."

Again and again he berated her, beat her even, but she would not change her ways. "I act only as I feel a mother should," was her repeated response.

"Look at the other mothers in the village," he snapped. "They don't behave like you."

"But they are not me," she said, and never had he had such a strong urge to strangle a willful creature.

More and more, Thomas was thinking that there was only one way to solve the problem of his beastly wife.

* * *

The baby was a source of great joy to Constance. Her kind struggled to procreate, so any offspring was to be celebrated. At first, she had been disappointed that her son showed no signs of wolfishness. But when she noticed Thomas watching the child carefully and yelling at her for encouraging the boy to snarl or walk on all fours, she felt somewhat relieved that any traits he might have were well-hidden.

However, she doubted that he was a werewolf at all. Her afterbirth had not contained a moonskin, which might make him fully human. She'd searched for it frantically while the midwife cleaned and swaddled the baby. Thomas, looking mortified, had scooped the sac up and thrown it on the fire, and that had been the final proof: burning or cutting the moonskin would inflict similar physical injuries on the werewolf's body. Since their baby boy did not cry out at the agony of flames, there must have been no moonskin in there.

Only when she saw Thomas with his son, Henry ("Named for our great and gracious king"), did Constance realise just how little affection he showed her these days. Love and kindness emanated from him every time he spoke to or held his son, while there was only a kind of genial accord between mother and father, as if they were mere acquaintances. He no longer made love to her, claiming the smell of her milk made him queasy – and while she did, indeed, have a dairy aroma to her, she sensed this was nothing but a convenient excuse. In the darkness of the marriage bed, while her son snuffled between them, she mourned the loss of intimacy and the shattering of her illusions about the man she had been bound to.

The search for her skin intensified; she didn't want to be Constance, the shackled wife, anymore. She wanted to be unnamed and wild and free, running with her pack, her little son scampering at her side. Even though he'd been born without a moonskin, she had an idea of how that might be fixed. But her plan would only succeed if she worked quickly, before he grew too big. Each morning, when she woke still a wife, the dread and urgency inside her increased.

* * *

Any love built on the back of lust and possession is a love that rests on unstable foundations. Yet as much as Constance had grown to displease Thomas, he still experienced moments when his desire for her was a powerful wave that crashed against the wall of his growing dislike. One evening, he came home from work, tired and hot, to find the house empty, the evening meal uncooked. Incensed by this lack of wifely consideration, he stormed into their sleeping quarters. But on the threshold he froze, struck to the heart by what he saw. Surely, if an angel and a cherub had descended from heaven to rest in his house, they could not have looked more beautiful than his wife and son lying asleep on the pallet, her long silver hair draped over both of them like a blanket.

If only she could be like this all the time, he thought with deep regret.

At that moment, a plan that had been lurking in his brain for several months came forward. *If I destroy her skin, she'll be less of a wolf and more of a woman. Then she'll be perfect.*

Fetching his skinning knife from his poacher's bag, Thomas went out behind the house and heaved a huge stone out of its place on a patch of earth at the end of the vegetable patch. Beneath it was a metal box, something his grandfather had put there years before for storing meat in the summer. The earth kept it cool and the box kept the insects out. Inside, scrunched into the tiny space, was Constance's moonskin.

Reverently, he took it out, running his hand down the fur, marvelling at how soft it was, even after all this time. Within the house (although he did not hear it), Constance sighed and shifted, as if a lover had run his hand down her back.

Laying the skin on the ground, Thomas took his knife and started to cut the skin, intending to slice it into two pieces then cut those into smaller chunks. He'd expected the knife to glide through, given the soft suppleness of it, but the pelt resisted as if it was old, hardened leather.

With great effort, he sawed a gash in the skin, at which point a terrible scream rent the air. It came from inside the house, and he leaped up and dashed inside to find Constance on the bed, clutching her side, blood flowing through her fingertips.

"What happened?" he asked, aghast.

"I don't know," she moaned.

But Thomas suddenly understood, and he raced out to stuff the skin back in the box. Just as he was about to close the lid, pain erupted at the back of his head and everything went black.

* * *

When Constance had barricaded the doors and windows as best she could, she took her skin back into the bedroom. Last she'd seen through the shutters, Thomas had still been lying motionless where she'd hit him with a stone. It had taken a few minutes after she woke to pain and blood to realise what was going on, but a gash in the side was a small price to pay to have her skin returned.

Her son was in the other room, wrapped in a blanket and crying for her, but that couldn't be helped – not yet. Taking Thomas's skinning knife, she placed a block of wood between her teeth and began to cut the skin at the front left shoulder. Things became much harder as blood coursed down her left arm, and she gradually lost the use of it as it slowly detached itself from her shoulder.

When the deed was done, she was dizzy with the pain and had to lie down for a minute while the blood in her stump clotted and congealed. Had she been human, she would have bled to death, but a werewolf's body is a strange thing and more resilient than most. Eventually, she sat up; once she'd sewn the loose ends of her arm stump together, she took the scrap of cut skin through to her son. Awkwardly, she lay it over his naked body and then unfastened one of the shutters and held him up to the moonlight. He changed before her eyes, and it was a marvellous thing. Her heart sang as he gave a tiny little howl, and as quiet as it was, there came an answering howl from the distant wood.

* * *

Thomas awoke to pain, his mind groggy. He sat up, and it took a few minutes to remember where he was and what he had been doing. The box was empty. The door and shutters of his home were closed. What was his beastly wife doing in there?

Unsteadily, he got to his feet and started shuffling towards the house, but halfway he stopped. Something was moving in the gloom to his left. And his right too. A growl came from behind him. There were glowing eyes in the gloaming and then, with howls of vengeance, the pack descended.

* * *

The night had been full of howls and screams, so all the villagers had stayed steadfastly indoors.

One man, who'd been late coming back from market, told of a feeling that something was keeping pace with him in the trees along the lonely path home.

"And then," he told horrified friends the next morning, "I swear a wolf ran across my path. It had only three legs – a front one was missing. And it was carrying something in its mouth." Everybody shook their heads and crossed themselves, thanking God that this man had avoided such a close call.

When it was noted that Thomas was not at the mill, a collection of villagers (because none would go alone) made their way to his cottage. There, they found his mauled and ragged corpse in the garden. And on the blood-soaked sheets of his sleeping pallet, they discovered a woman's slender arm, severed at the shoulder.

The Claws Come Out

B.A. Boober

BEFORE AISLING RAE could switch between gas and brake, a sickeningly thick thump heralded the spray of fur from the Jeep Scrambler's rusted-out passenger floor. The rear wheels rocked with a wet crunch that echoed the front collision. The Jeep burnt long skidmarks on the asphalt, catching the loose gravel on the road's edge. The world somersaulted. Corn stalks whipped past her open cab, slapping and scratching Aisling's face and arms. Everything became weightless, only to crash down with the earth above and her horn screaming into the night.

Gravel bit into Aisling's palms as she pushed herself up. Training kicked in – cervical spine stable, no numbness or tingling. Her arms worked. Legs too. The metallic taste in her mouth was from biting her cheek, not internal bleeding. The nurse in her cataloged injuries with clinical detachment while adrenaline screamed through her system.

A deer, Aisling pleaded. *Please be a deer.*

Aisling fumbled for her phone light. The Jeep was a broken-backed beast bleeding radiator fluid. Steam curled from the engine like dragon's breath. Droplets led into the cornfield – too much blood for a deer. Was someone bleeding out in there?

"Hello? Anyone there?" she called out. "I'm a nurse. Do you need help?" Something deep within her whispered: *Run.*

Movement between the stalks made Aisling's pulse quicken. She caught sight of amber eyes, too large for a human, floating at chest height – studying her, calculating. A knot of fear tightened in her stomach as its labored breathing filled the space between them. The mingled scents of copper and wet fur with fertilizer and hot antifreeze made her feel dizzy. The eyes narrowed, and a chill ran down her spine. Another grunt, softer now, only heightened her anxiety. As the creature shifted and the eyes retreated, its breathing faded until only the tick of her cooling engine broke the night's silence. She exhaled slowly, unaware she'd been holding her breath, her hands still shaking on the steering wheel.

***

The cornfields parted on either side of Aisling's rental, their stalks having turned gold since the last time she had ventured out this way. From the pet carrier in the passenger seat came a disgruntled 'mrrp'. Aisling glanced over at Morph, her gray Scottish Fold whose squashed face perfectly matched his perpetually judgmental expression. "Almost there." She'd been clear at the agency that Morph was non-negotiable. If they wanted Aisling as a live-in, Morph came too.

Black vines crawled up the Victorian ironwork beside the security keypad that blinked at her from its stone housing. Aisling punched in the code she'd been given, and the gates swung open, the corn canyons giving way to a sylvan landscape. Old-growth maples and oaks formed a natural scarlet and gold archway over the private drive, dappling sunlight across her windshield. Lake Grinmore's steel-blue waters peeked through breaks in the trees. The Hundt house was a mansion of steel and glass rising from local limestone as if grown from the hillside itself. The floor-to-ceiling windows and expansive decks blurred the edge of the interior with the exterior. The greenhouse dominated the house's eastern wing, a glass cathedral that trapped the late afternoon light and glowed like a copper lantern.

She parked. A cool breeze carried the scent of water and wood smoke, making her shiver despite her sweater. A wind chime rang somewhere above, its hollow song emphasizing the profound quiet. Aisling sat, her hands still on the wheel. She grabbed her nursing bag beside Morph's carrier and tried to summon the professional confidence that usually came so easily. She reminded herself it was just another home healthcare assignment, and bedpans were bedpans.

"Ms. Rae?" A shadow fell across Aisling's window. She jumped, barely stifling a yelp.

"You must be Mr. Wurmig."

"Emil, please. I apologize for startling you." His close-cropped silver hair caught the late afternoon light as he offered a formal bow that seemed to belong to another century. "Allow me to help with your bags."

Once the bags were balanced in their arms, Emil said, "I must brief you quickly. My flight leaves in three hours, and the training cannot be postponed."

Aisling bit back a smile. "Important butler conference?"

Emil's spine, if possible, stiffened further. "The nature of my training is confidential, Ms. Rae."

The foyer opened into a great room where steel beams met limestone walls, everything precisely angled to draw the eye toward the lake view. Emil led her through with practiced efficiency, pointing out essential locations. "Kitchen through there. Your efficiency apartment is on the ground floor, east wing. Mrs. Hundt occupies the master suite and adjacent rooms on the west wing's second floor. She is not to attempt stairs unassisted."

They arrived at her apartment – a modern studio with a kitchenette and lake view. "I trust your… companion will remain within these quarters?" His tone suggested this was less a question than a requirement.

"Yep," Aisling assured him, though Morph's indignant meow from his carrier seemed less convinced.

They paused at a heavy wooden door. "The greenhouse," Emil said, producing an iron key. "This is crucial. Mrs. Hundt requires a special tea blend each evening at sunset. The ingredients must be fresh-picked daily." He unlocked the door, and humid air wrapped around them, rich with earth and green things.

"The plants are clearly labeled," Emil said as he harvested small amounts of each plant and placed them in separate pouches. "Monkshood in the blue pots. Garlic and thyme in the terra cotta. Mistletoe hanging in the north corner. Belladonna – handle with gloves – in the black containers. Mountain ash berries over there."

In the kitchen, Emil retrieved an ancient-looking stone mortar with strange symbols carved around its rim. The matching pestle gleamed with a silver tip that caught the light. He demonstrated the precise measurements and grinding technique, his movements almost ritualistic. "The proportions are written in the leather journal by the preparation station, but I must emphasize: this blend is for Mrs. Hundt alone. Under no circumstances should you prepare a cup for yourself or sample it. Some of these herbs can be… quite potent."

"The tea must be served precisely at sunset," he continued, his voice grave. "Mrs. Hundt is quite particular about timing."

Back in the house proper, Emil's pace quickened. "Mrs. Hundt follows a strict carnivore diet. No vegetables, no seasonings except salt. The butcher delivers twice weekly. Everything is labeled in the industrial refrigerator."

"I strongly recommend staying in your quarters after dark unless Mrs. Hundt requires assistance. The house can be… disorienting at night. Between the old wings settling and the sounds that drift in from the forest, it's best not to wander. Additionally, Mrs. Hundt has exacting standards for the house's cleanliness. Best not to leave a trail. And everyone leaves a trail. So, the fewer areas accessed, the fewer opportunities for… disturbance."

Aisling glanced around the immaculate hallway. "I don't see any signs of your trail, Mr. Wurmig."

His expression could have frozen the lake. "Don't be absurd." He checked his watch. "Mrs. Hundt will be waking from her afternoon rest soon. She'll want to meet you before I leave for the airport."

He hesitated at the door. "One final thing, Ms. Rae. If you hear anything unusual at night – creaking, scratching, even voices – remember that old houses near forests harbor many sounds. Best to stay in your room with the door locked." He managed a thin smile. "Shall we meet Mrs. Hundt?"

"Lead the way, Jeeves," Aisling muttered under her breath.

Emil's shoulders tightened fractionally, but he said nothing as he turned toward the west wing.

The master suite doors were solid oak, ancient and dark with oil. Emil's knock seemed to wake something in the wood – a deep, resonant sound that made Aisling's bones ache. He pressed his palm flat against the grain, and the doors swung inward on silent hinges. "Wait here," he murmured, stepping inside. Aisling caught fragments of low conversation, the words unclear but the tone unmistakable – supplication.

When Emil returned, his usual precision had hardened into something more brittle. "Mrs. Hundt will see you now." He ushered Aisling in, then closed the doors behind them with a soft click that felt inexplicably final. The master suite was a temple to shadow and light. Copper-hued sunlight poured through wall-to-wall windows, catching dust motes that danced like embers in the still air. The space smelled of something Aisling couldn't quite place – green things and earth and beneath that, a metallic note that triggered memories of trauma-bay shifts. Blood, but not quite.

"Come forward, child." The voice emerged from the shadows where the sun couldn't reach. Low, resonant, with an accent that spoke of old money and older secrets. "Let me look at you properly."

Aisling's shoes whispered against hardwood as she approached the hospital bed that had been arranged like a throne. The woman who reclined there bore little resemblance to typical hip fracture patients. Otsana Hundt's silver-streaked hair cascaded over silk pillows like spilled ink, and her amber eyes caught the dying sun in a way that made them glow. Even bedridden, she made Aisling want to check her posture.

"So," Otsana's voice deep, husky, commanding, "you're the one they've sent to cage-sit."

"Mrs. Hundt—"

"Oh, don't fuss, Emil. We both know that's what this is." Her gaze never left Aisling. "Come closer, dear. My eyes aren't what they used to be."

Aisling approached, professional mask firmly in place. The chart had said broken hip from a fall, but the extensive bruising visible at Otsana's collar suggested massive trauma. The particular pattern of healing – yellowish at the edges, deep purple-black at the centers – told a story of a trauma that should have filled a body bag, not a hospital bed.

"See anything interesting?" Otsana asked.

"Your chart mentioned a fall," Aisling said carefully, "but these injuries suggest—"

"Do they?" Otsana's smile showed too many teeth. "I must tell you a funny story. You brought the cat, yes? When the agency said Morphine was non-negotiable, we were perplexed and about to pass on you until we realized it was your cat's name. We had a bit of a chuckle at your gallows humor, didn't we, Emil?"

"Yes, madam."

"The tea service is quite specific," Otsana continued as if discussing the weather. "Each herb must be measured precisely. Ground with intention." Her fingers traced patterns on the silk sheets. "The proportions matter greatly, like the difference between medicine and poison. One must be so careful with doses. Some of these herbs can be volatile, like me when I'm… unsettled."

Emil cleared his throat softly. "I've explained the protocol—"

"Quiet." The word rumbled, and Otsana's eyes never left her face. "Do you feel the sun setting? The way the light changes. The way the shadows… stretch."

She was right. The copper light had deepened to blood-red.

Otsana's sonorous voice dropped to a growl. "Time to make the tea."

* * *

A week into the job, Aisling had settled into the rhythm of the house like a heartbeat. Wake before dawn. Prep medications. Check vitals. Assist with morning hygiene. Prepare raw breakfast (trying not to think too hard about the deep red meat). Change dressings on injuries that seemed to heal a little too quickly. Afternoon rest. Evening tea ritual as the sun bled across the lake. She'd learned to time her movements to Otsana's schedule, like prey adapting to a predator's patterns. When to fade into the background. When to approach. When to speak and when silence was safer.

One night, with tomorrow's full moon hanging fat and yellow through the windows, Morph slipped past her legs as she returned from the evening tea service.

"No, no, no—" She lunged for his tail, but he was already streaking down the hallway, a gray ghost in the shadows. Aisling cursed under her breath, weighing options. Otsana would be deep in her post-tea drowse, but Emil's warnings about nighttime wandering echoed in her mind.

The alternative was explaining to Otsana why a cat was loose in her pristine house.

Morph's bell jingled faintly from somewhere below. Aisling followed, her nurse's shoes silent on the hardwood. The basement door stood slightly ajar – odd since she distinctly remembered it being locked earlier. The darkness beyond seemed to breathe.

"Morph," she whispered, fishing out her phone for light. "Come here, you little shit."

The stairs creaked under her weight despite her careful steps. The beam of her phone caught glimpses of wine racks and storage shelves before something glinted in the darkness – Morph's reflective eyes disappearing around a corner.

A sound from above – the distinct click of claws on wood, steady and deliberate.

Aisling's heart hammered as she pressed herself into a shadowed alcove. The clicking descended the stairs, each step measured, hunting. She held her breath as it reached the bottom, waiting for it to move away before she dared peek around the corner.

The temperature dropped with each step deeper into the basement. Her phone light revealed a corridor she hadn't been shown during orientation, its walls lined with rough stone that looked much older than the house above. The clicking echoed somewhere behind her, driving her forward.

A heavy wooden door offered escape. Aisling slipped inside, finding herself in a circular chamber. Elaborate tapestries covered the walls, depicting scenes that made her eyes hurt to focus on. Carved wooden panels filled the spaces between, etched with symbols that seemed to writhe in her peripheral vision. The air felt thick with incense and something metallic that triggered her trauma ward instincts.

In the center stood a stone altar, its surface stained dark and deeply grooved. Around it, arranged in a perfect circle, were thirteen chairs carved from some black wood she couldn't identify. Each bore a silver plaque. The nearest read *Hunter*.

Morph sat in the thirteenth chair, slightly larger than the others, grooming himself without a care.

The clicking grew closer. Aisling snatched Morph and ducked behind a tapestry, discovering a door hidden in the paneling. She slipped through just as the creature entered the ritual room.

She found herself in what had to be Heinrich's study, illuminated by moonlight streaming through high windows. Ancient Persian texts on wolf cults lay scattered among modern psychiatric journals, meticulous notes bridging millennia. Post-it notes in precise German connected behavioral conditioning techniques to ritual ceremonies penciled in the margins of crumbling manuscripts.

The clicking moved into the ritual room. Aisling eased toward a cabinet left ajar, seeking better cover. Inside, her fingers found an ornate silver collar, heavy and inscribed with intricate patterns that hurt her eyes. In the center, words were etched in elegant script: "To my fierce huntress – may you always return to my hand."

Letters spilled from a hidden drawer – correspondence with wealthy European and Asian elite. They addressed her as 'Sacred Hunter' and 'Living Deity'. Meeting minutes labeled 'The Pack' listed attendees: judges, CEOs, old money families.

A growl from the ritual room sent her scrambling behind the desk. Her hand brushed something slick, a tablet, its screen dark. Her finger trembled as she pressed the home button.

The video gallery opened automatically: Heinrich moved with calculated grace in the footage, directing Otsana through complex patterns with subtle hand gestures. She followed with inhuman fluidity, her amber eyes never leaving his fingers. She dropped to all fours in one clip at a single finger snap. He'd documented everything, treating the footage like research data, complete with timestamps and notes.

The clicking returned to the doorway. Aisling spotted another hidden door behind a bookcase, already slightly open. She slipped through with Morph just as something large entered the study.

The greenhouse's tea ritual haunted her as she found Heinrich's translations of ancient Persian texts describing identical preparations – the specific herbs, the silver-tipped pestle, the timing at sunset. All designed to enable transformation while maintaining control of the beast within.

Aisling's blood ran cold when she found the hunting records in the next room. Heinrich documented everything with scientific precision. 'Prey acquisition methods.' 'Hunt duration.' 'Disposal protocols.' Missing person reports from local papers matched his dates exactly. She counted them with horror – twelve disappearances per year, one for each full moon.

The freezer behind the wine cellar held the final proof. Trophy cases lined the walls, each containing 'hunting memorabilia' – watches, rings, wallets. Personal effects cataloged by date. A leather-bound volume nearby contained photographs of the 'hunts' – Otsana in her other form pursuing terrified figures through torch-lit woods while cultists in robes chanted from the periphery.

The clicking resumed, urgent now, too close. Aisling clutched Morph and fled upstairs, pieces falling into place with each step. The bruising pattern on Otsana's body wasn't from a fall. The injuries had been reported the day after Aisling had hit – something – and totaled her Scrambler at the end of last month. Those amber eyes in the cornfield. The way it had looked at her with calculation, with rage... Aisling was sure it was Otsana.

But who would believe her? A werewolf? A cult of wealthy killers? They'd dismiss her as mad, if they found enough of her to question. Tonight was the full moon, time for a hunt.

Back in her room, Aisling's hands trembled as she stroked Morph's fur. She was pretty sure she was the next hunt's red fox. If anyone was going to deal with this, it had to be her. Her mind raced to the evening herbs, to Heinrich's journal, to the strictly controlled diet. A plan began to form. She'd poison the beast with Heinrich's own methods.

She did her best to appear calm as she got the mortar and pestle from the kitchen and proceeded to the greenhouse. Her heart raced as she measured the evening herbs. The tea had to fool Otsana. Emil had said the ingredients could be volatile; Aisling aimed to find out.

"Something smells... interesting." Otsana's voice carried from the doorway, making Aisling's spine stiffen.

"Mrs. Hundt, I—"

"The tea. You've changed it." Otsana crossed the greenhouse in three fluid steps, her nostrils flaring. "Don't lie to me, girl. I can smell the deception. The extra warfarin." Her hand shot out, knocking the mortar to the floor. The precious tea mixture scattered across the stone. "Did you think I wouldn't notice? That my senses aren't heightened as the moon rises? That I wouldn't be able to follow your trail?"

Aisling backed away, shoving her hand into her pocket and buying time. "Not sensitive enough to avoid my Scrambler. That was you I hit the other night, wasn't it? She was cherry, you know," she lied. "Now she's totaled, and you've barely a limp."

"Clever girl," Otsana said. "Though you cracked three ribs and shattered my hip. Do you know how hard it is to shift forms with broken bones? Emil wanted to take you that night. But I had trouble enough running down that Haitian gentleman. After your pristine driving, that is." Otsana licked her lips. "That man could run. Those glutes..." She glared down at Aisling and snarled. "But I said some prey deserve to die properly, to satiate revenge's hunger. Imagine my surprise when I found out your profession. Does not the moon provide?"

Aisling gripped the syringe in her pocket. "Your husband's tea mix wasn't for any kind of delusions. It's about managing your blood chemistry during transformation."

Otsana's laugh was all growl now. "Heinrich understood the beast's needs. The sacred hunt requires perfect balance."

"Perfect coagulation," Aisling corrected. "Warfarin from the mountain ash berries. Precisely counterbalanced with vitamin K from the thyme. The garlic and belladonna to manage blood pressure. Without it, the transformation would trigger massive internal hemorrhage."

"You think knowledge will save you?" Bones cracked as Otsana's flesh rippled unnaturally.

Aisling faced those predatory eyes. "You're a murderer. All those people in the trophy room—"

"Sacred sacrifices." Otsana sniffed. "Heinrich understood that. Made me a goddess among our circle." Blood dripped as her skin ripped and tore, only for the wounds to melt closed beneath her silk robes. "The others worship the beast. Feed it. Guide it. The hunts are our communion."

Aisling thought of the photos in Heinrich's study. The ones of Otsana kneeling, collared, performing for her husband's camera. Not submission – satisfaction. A predator indulging her handler's illusion of control while she fed her true nature. No point running – a predator would only chase. "They'll look for me. The agency—"

"Will receive your resignation letter. Poor thing, moved back home. Emil is very good at paperwork." Otsana's face elongated, bones reshaping. "Your heart is racing. Good. Fear makes the meat sweeter."

Aisling lunged forward, driving the syringe deep into Otsana's exposed shoulder. The transformation stuttered, caught between forms as Otsana stumbled back.

"What... what did you...?"

"There's more than one way to dose a bitch," Aisling said, backing toward the door. "You've got about thirty seconds before your blood gets too thin to shift."

Otsana's roar of rage turned to a wet cough. Blood trickled from her nose, her ears, the corners of her eyes. The hemorrhaging had begun. "You can't…"

"Should I call an ambulance?" Aisling said, phone already in hand. "Tell them exactly what I see – a wealthy woman with a severe coagulation crisis? They'll pump you full of vitamin K and fresh plasma. You'll live. But you'll never shift again without hemorrhaging. The beast dies tonight."

Otsana tried to lunge but collapsed, her hybrid form shuddering. "They'll never… believe…"

"That you're a werewolf? No. But internal bleeding in a patient with documented clotting issues? That they'll understand. Of course, you'll need to help them understand your trophy room. Or turn into that wolf, and I'll call animal control, but you'll have a headstart, right? I'm not sure who I'd call if you want to maintain the wolf-woman look, but I'm sure some lab would love you."

Aisling checked her watch. "Fifteen seconds. What will it be: kennel, lab hell, or padded cell?"

Otsana's eyes locked onto Aisling with predatory focus. "We'll see." Her voice was thick and wet. "The moon calls. **Best** you run."

Aisling ran. Her shoes slapped against hardwood, then gravel, each footfall echoing with Otsana's wet, gurgling growls growing fainter behind her. The moon hung low and swollen over Lake Grinmore, painting everything in cruel silver light. She snatched Morph from his windowsill perch, ignoring his startled yowl as she clutched him to her chest.

Her rental's engine roared to life just as something crashed through the greenhouse glass. The sound of splintering wood and shattering panes sent ice through her veins. Morph dug his claws into the passenger seat as Aisling threw the car into drive, tires spraying gravel. In her rearview mirror, a dark shape loped across the manicured lawn.

Aisling punched in the gate code, watching shadows dance at the edge of her headlights. Once the gap was wide enough, she stomped on the gas. In her mirror, the gates stood open, a maw of pooling darkness. Something might have moved in that darkness – a shadow, a wolf, or just her imagination painting monsters in the spaces her headlights couldn't reach.

Whatever ran in the shadows, be it hallucination or not, Aisling aimed for the moon and didn't stop until morning.

The White Wolf of Kostopchin

Gilbert Edward Campbell

A WIDE SANDY expanse of country, flat and uninteresting in appearance, with a great staring whitewashed house standing in the midst of wide fields of cultivated land; whilst far away were the low sand hills and pine forests to be met with in the district of Lithuania, in Russian Poland. Not far from the great white house was the village in which the serfs dwelt, with the large bakehouse and the public bath which are invariably to be found in all Russian villages, however humble. The fields were negligently cultivated, the hedges broken down and the fences in bad repair, shattered agricultural implements had been carelessly flung aside in remote corners, and the whole estate showed the want of the superintending eye of an energetic master. The great white house was no better looked after, the garden was an utter wilderness, great patches of plaster had fallen from the walls, and many of the Venetian shutters were almost off the hinges. Over all was the dark lowering sky of a Russian autumn, and there were no signs of life to be seen, save a few peasants lounging idly towards the vodki ship, and a gaunt halt-starved cat creeping stealthily abroad in quest of a meal.

The estate, which was known by the name of Kostopchin, was the property of Paul Sergevitch, a gentleman of means, and the most discontented man in Russian Poland. Like most wealthy Muscovites, he had traveled much, and had spent the gold which had been amassed by serf labor, like water, in all the dissolute revelries of the capitals of Europe. Paul's figure was as well known in the boudoirs of the demi *mondaines* as his face was familiar at the public gaming tables. He appeared to have no thought for the future, but only to live in the excitement of the mad career of dissipation which he was pursuing. His means, enormous as they were, were all forestalled, and he was continually sending to his intendant for fresh supplies of money. His fortune would not have long held out against the constant inroads that were being made upon it, when an unexpected circumstance took place which stopped his career like a flash of lightning. This was a fatal duel, in which a young man of great promise, the son of the prime minister of the country in which he then resided, fell by his hand. Representatives were made to the Tsar, and Paul Sergevitch was recalled, and, after receiving a severe reprimand was ordered to return to his estates in Lithuania. Horribly discontented, yet not daring to disobey the Imperial mandate, Paul buried himself at Kostopchin, a place he had not visited since his boyhood. At first he endeavored to interest himself in the workings of the vast estate; but agriculture had no charm for him, and the only result was that he quarreled with and dismissed his German intendant, replacing him by an old serf, Michal Vassilitch, who had been his father's valet. Then he took to wandering about the country, gun in hand, and upon his return home would sit moodily drinking brandy and smoking innumerable cigarettes, as he cursed his lord and master, the emperor, for consigning him to such a course of dullness and ennui. For a couple of years he led this aimless life, and at last, hardly knowing the reason for so doing, he married the daughter of a neighboring landed proprietor. The marriage was a most unhappy one; the girl had really never cared for Paul, but had married him in obedience to her father's mandates, and the man, whose temper was always brutal and violent, treated her, after a brief interval of contemptuous indifference, with savage cruelty. After three years the unhappy woman expired, leaving behind her two children – a boy, Alexis, and a girl, Katrina. Paul treated his wife's death with the most perfect indifference; but he did not put any one in her place. He was very fond of the little Katrina, but did not take much notice of the boy, and resumed his lonely wanderings about the country with dog and gun. Five years had passed since the death of his wife. Alexis was a fine, healthy boy of seven, whilst Katrina was some eighteen months younger. Paul was lighting one of his eternal cigarettes at the door of his house, when the little girl came running up to him.

"You bad, wicked papa," said she. "How is it that you have never brought me the pretty gray squirrels that you promised I should have the next time you went to the forest?"

"Because I have never yet been able to find any, my treasure," returned her father, taking up his child in his arms and half smothering her with kisses. "Because I have not found them yet, my golden queen; but I am bound to find Ivanovitch, the poacher, smoking about the woods, and if he can't show me where they are, no one can."

"Ah, little father," broke in old Michal, using the term of address with which a Russian of humble position usually accosts his superior; "Ah, little father, take care; you will go to those woods once too often."

"Do you think I am afraid of Ivanovitch?" returned his master, with a coarse laugh. "Why, he and I are the best of friends; at any rate, if he robs me, he does so openly, and keeps other poachers away from my woods."

"It is not of Ivanovitch that I am thinking," answered the old man. "But oh! Gospodin, do not go into these dark solitudes; there are terrible tales told about them, of witches that dance in the moonlight, of strange, shadowy forms that are seen amongst the trunks of the tall pines, and of whispered voices that tempt the listeners to eternal perdition."

Again the rude laugh of the lord of the manor rang out, as Paul observed, "If you go on addling your brain, old man, with these nearly half-forgotten legends, I shall have to look out for a new intendant."

"But I was not thinking of these fearful creatures only," returned Michal, crossing himself piously. "It was against the wolves that I meant to warn you."

"Oh, father, dear, I am frightened now," whimpered little Katrina, hiding her head on her father's shoulder. "Wolves are such cruel, wicked things."

"See there, graybearded dotard," cried Paul, furiously, "you have terrified this sweet angel by your farrago of lies; besides, who ever heard of wolves so early as this? You are dreaming, Michal Vassilitch, or have taken your morning dram of *vodki* too strong."

"As I hope for future happiness," answered the old man, solemnly, "as I came through the marsh last night from Kosma the herdsman's cottage – you know, my lord, that he has been bitten by a viper, and is seriously ill – as I came through the marsh, I repeat, I saw something like sparks of fire in the clump of alders on the right-hand side. I was anxious to know what they could be, and cautiously moved a little nearer, recommending my soul to the protection of Saint Vladamir. I had not gone a couple of paces when a wild howl came that chilled the very marrow of my bones, and a pack of some ten or a dozen wolves, gaunt and famished as you see them, my lord, in the winter, rushed out. At their head was a white she-wolf, as big as any of the male ones, with gleaming tusks and a pair of yellow eyes that blazed with lurid fire. I had round my neck a crucifix that had been given me by the priest of Streletza, and the savage beasts knew this and broke away across the marsh, sending up the mud and water in showers in the air; but the white she-wolf, little father, circled round me three times, as though endeavoring to find some place from which to attack me. Three times she did this, and then, with a snap of her teeth and a howl of impotent malice, she galloped away some fifty yards and sat down, watching my every movement with her fiery eyes. I did not delay any longer in so dangerous a spot, as you may well imagine, Gospodin, but walked hurriedly home, crossing myself at every step; but, as I am a living man, that white devil followed me the whole distance, keeping fifty paces in the rear, and every now and then licking her lips with a sound that made my flesh creep. When I got to the last fence before you come to the house I raised up my voice and shouted for the dogs, and soon I heard the deep bay of Troska and Bransköe as they came bounding towards me. The white devil heard it, too, and, giving a high bound into the air, she uttered a loud howl of disappointment, and trotted back leisurely towards the marsh."

"But why did you not set the dogs after her?" asked Paul, interested, in spite of himself, at the old man's narrative. "In the open Troska and Bransköe would run down any wolf that ever set foot to the ground in Lithuania."

"I tried to do so, little father," answered the old man, solemnly; "but directly they got up to the spot where the beast had executed her last devilish gambol, they put their tails between their legs and ran back to the house as fast as their legs could carry them."

"Strange," muttered Paul, thoughtfully, "that is, if it is truth and not *vodki* that is speaking."

"My lord," returned the old man, reproachfully, "man and boy, I have served you and my lord your father for fifty years, and no one can say that they ever saw Michal Vassilitch the worse for liquor."

"No one doubts that you are a sly old thief, Michal," returned his master, with his coarse, jarring laugh; "but for all that, your long stories of having been followed by white wolves won't prevent me from going to the forest today. A couple of good buckshot cartridges will break any spell, though I don't think that the she-wolf, if she existed anywhere than in your own imagination, has anything to do with magic. Don't be frightened, Katrina, my pet; you shall have a fine white wolf skin to put your feet on, if what this old fool says is right."

"Michal is not a fool," pouted the child, "and it is very wicked of you to call him so. I don't want any nasty wolf skins, I want the gray squirrels."

"And you shall have them, my precious," returned her father, setting her down upon the ground. "Be a good girl, and I will not be long away."

"Father," said the little Alexis, suddenly, "let me go with you. I should like to see you kill a wolf, and then I should know how to do so, when I grow older and taller."

"Pshaw," returned his father, irritably. "Boys are always in the way. Take the lad away, Michal; don't you see that he is worrying his sweet little sister?"

"No, no, he does not worry me at all," answered the impetuous little lady, as she flew to her brother and covered him with kisses. "Michal, you shan't take him away, do you hear?"

"There, there, leave the children together," returned Paul, as he shouldered his gun, and kissing the tips of his fingers to Katrina, stepped away rapidly in the direction of the dark pine woods. Paul walked on, humming the fragment of an air that he had heard in a very different place many years ago. A strange feeling of elation crept over him, very different to the false excitement which his solitary drinking bouts were wont to produce. A change seemed to have come over his whole life, the skies looked brighter, the *spiculæ* of the pine trees of a more vivid green, and the landscape seemed to have lost that dull cloud of depression which had for years appeared to hang over it. And beneath all this exaltation of the mind, beneath all this unlooked-for promise of a more happy future, lurked a heavy, inexplicable feeling of a power to come, a something without form or shape, and yet the more terrible because it was shrouded by that thick veil which conceals from the eyes of the soul the strange fantastic designs of the dwellers beyond the line of earthly influences.

There were no signs of the poacher, and wearied with searching for him, Paul made the woods echo with his name. The great dog, Troska, which had followed his master, looked up wistfully into his face, and at a second repetition of the name "Ivanovitch," uttered a long plaintive howl, and then, looking round at Paul as though entreating him to follow, moved slowly ahead towards a denser portion of the forest. A little mystified at the hound's unusual proceedings, Paul followed, keeping his gun ready to fire at the least sign of danger. He thought that he knew the forest well, but the dog led the way to a portion which he never remembered to have visited before. He had got away from the pine trees now, and had entered a dense thicket formed of stunted oaks and hollies. The great dog kept only a yard or so ahead; his lips were drawn back, showing the strong white fangs, the hair upon his neck and back was bristling, and his tail firmly pressed between his hind legs. Evidently the animal was in a state of the most extreme terror, and yet it proceeded bravely forward. Struggling through the dense thicket, Paul suddenly found himself in an open space of some ten or twenty yards in diameter. At one end of it was a slimy pool, into the waters of which several strange-looking reptiles glided as the man and dog made their appearance. Almost in the center of the opening was a shattered stone cross, and at its base lay a dark heap, close to which Troska stopped, and again raising his head, uttered a long melancholy howl. For an instant or two, Paul gazed hesitatingly at the shapeless heap that lay beneath the cross, and then, mustering up all his courage, he stepped forwards and bent anxiously over it. Once glance was enough, for he recognized the body of Ivanovitch the poacher, hideously mangled. With a cry of surprise, he turned over the body and shuddered as he gazed upon the terrible injuries that had been inflicted. The unfortunate man had evidently been attacked by some savage beast, for there were marks of teeth upon the throat, and the jugular vein had been almost torn out. The breast of the corpse had been torn open, evidently by long sharp claws, and there was a gaping orifice upon the left side, round which the blood had formed in a thick coagulated patch. The only animals to be found in the forests of Russia capable of inflicting such wounds are the bear or the wolf, and the question as to the class of the assailant was easily settled by a glance at the dank ground, which showed the prints of a wolf so entirely different from the plantegrade traces of the bear.

"Savage brutes," muttered Paul. "So, after all, there may have been some truth in Michal's story, and the old idiot may for once in his life have spoken the truth. Well, it is no concern of mine, and if a fellow chooses to wander about the woods at night to kill my game, instead of remaining in his own hovel, he must take his chance. The strange thing is that the brutes have not eaten him, though they have mauled him so terribly."

He turned away as he spoke, intending to return home and send out some of the serfs to bring in the body of the unhappy man, when his eye was caught by a small white object, hanging from a bramble bush near the pond. He made towards the spot, and taking up the object, examined it curiously. It was a tuft of coarse white hair, evidently belonging to some animal.

"A wolf's hair, or I am much mistaken," muttered Paul, pressing the hair between his fingers, and then applying it to his nose. "And from its color, I should think that it belonged to the white lady who so terribly alarmed old Michal on the occasion of his night walk through the marsh."

Paul found it no easy task to retrace his steps towards those parts of the forest with which he was acquainted, and Troska seemed unable to render him the slightest assistance, but followed moodily behind. Many times Paul found his way blocked by impenetrable thicket or dangerous quagmire, and during his many wanderings he had the ever-present sensation that there was a something close to him, an invisible something, a noiseless something, but for all that a presence which moved as he advanced, and halted as he stopped in vain to listen. The certainty that an impalpable thing of some shape or other was close at hand grew so strong, that as the short autumn day began to close, and darker shadows to fall between the trunks of the lofty trees, it made him hurry on at his utmost speed. At length, when he had grown almost mad with terror, he suddenly came upon a path he knew, and with a feeling of intense relief, he stepped briskly forward in the direction of Kostopchin. As he left the forest and came into the open country, a faint wail seemed to ring through the darkness; but Paul's nerves had been so much shaken that he did not know whether this was an actual fact or only the offspring of his own excited fancy.

As he crossed the neglected lawn that lay in front of the house, old Michal came rushing out of the house with terror convulsing every feature.

"Oh, my lord, my lord!" gasped he, "is not this too terrible?"

"Nothing has happened to my Katrina?" cried the father, a sudden sickly feeling of terror passing through his heart.

"No, no, the little lady is quite safe, thanks to the Blessed Virgin and Saint Alexander of Nevskoi," returned Michal; "but oh, my lord, poor Marta, the herd's daughter—"

"Well, what of the slut?" demanded Paul, for now that his momentary fear for the safety of his daughter had passed away, he had but little sympathy to spare for so insignificant a creature as a serf girl.

"I told you that Kosma was dying," answered Michal. "Well, Marta went across the marsh this afternoon to fetch the priest, but alas! she never came back."

"What detained her, then?" asked his master.

"One of the neighbors, going in to see how Kosma was getting on, found the poor old man dead; his face was terribly contorted, and he was half in the bed, and half out, as though he had striven to reach the door. The man ran to the village to give the alarm, and as the men returned to the herdsman's hut, they found the body of Marta in a thicket by the clump of alders on the marsh."

"Her body – she was dead then?" asked Paul.

"Dead, my lord, killed by wolves," answered the old man. "And oh, my lord, it is too horrible, her breast was horribly lacerated, and her heart had been taken out and eaten, for it was nowhere to be found."

Paul started, for the horrible mutilation of the body of Ivanovitch the poacher occurred to his recollection.

"And, my lord," continued the old man, "this is not all; on a bush close by was this tuft of hair," and, as he spoke, he took it from a piece of paper in which it was wrapped and handed it to his master.

Paul took it and recognized a similar tuft of hair to that which he had seen upon the bramble bush beside the shattered cross.

"Surely, my lord," continued Michal, not heeding his master's look of surprise, "you will have out men and dogs to hunt down this terrible creature, or, better still, send for the priest and holy water, for I have my doubts whether the creature belongs to this earth."

Paul shuddered, and, after a short pause, he told Michal of the ghastly end of Ivanovitch the poacher.

The old man listened with the utmost excitement, crossing himself repeatedly, and muttering invocations to the Blessed Virgin and the saints every instant; but his master would no longer listen to him, and, ordering him to place brandy on the table, sat drinking moodily until daylight.

The next day a fresh horror awaited the inhabitants of Kostopchin. An old man, a confirmed drunkard, had staggered out of the *vodki* shop with the intention of returning home; three hours later he was found at a turn of the road, horribly scratched and mutilated, with the same gaping orifice in the left side of the breast, from which the heart had been forcibly torn out.

Three several times in the course of the week the same ghastly tragedy occurred – a little child, an able-bodied laborer, and an old woman, were all found with the same terrible marks of mutilation upon them, and in every case the same tuft of white hair was found in the immediate vicinity of the bodies. A frightful panic ensued, and an excited crowd of serfs surrounded the house at Kostopchin, calling upon their master, Paul Sergevitch, to save them from the fiend that had been let loose upon them, and shouting out various remedies, which they insisted upon being carried into effect at once.

Paul felt a strange disinclination to adopt any active measures. A certain feeling which he could not account for urged him to remain quiescent; but the Russian serf when suffering under an access of superstitious terror is a dangerous person to deal with, and, with extreme reluctance, Paul Sergevitch issued instructions for a thorough search through the estate, and a general battue of the pine woods.

The army of beaters convened by Michal was ready with the first dawn of sunrise, and formed a strange and almost grotesque-looking assemblage, armed with rusty old firelocks, heavy bludgeons, and scythes fastened on to the end of long poles. Paul, with his double-barreled gun thrown across his shoulder and a keen hunting knife thrust into his belt, marched at the head of the serfs, accompanied by the two great hounds, Troska and Bransköe. Every nook and corner of the hedgerows were examined, and the little outlying clumps were thoroughly searched, but without success; and at last a circle was formed round the larger portion of the forest, and with loud shouts, blowing of horns, and beating of copper cooking utensils, the crowd of eager serfs pushed their way through the brushwood. Frightened birds flew up, whirring through the pine branches; hares and rabbits darted from their hiding places behind tufts and hummocks of grass, and scurried away in the utmost terror. Occasionally a roe deer rushed through the thicket, or a wild boar burst through the thin lines of beaters, but no signs of wolves were to be seen. The circle grew narrower and yet more narrow, when all at once a wild shriek and a confused murmur of voices echoed through the pine trees. All rushed to the spot, and a young lad was discovered weltering in his blood and terribly mutilated, though life still lingered in the mangled frame. A few drops of *vodki* were poured down the throat, and he managed to gasp out that the white wolf had sprung upon him suddenly, and, throwing him to the ground, had commenced tearing at the flesh over his heart. He would inevitably have been killed, had not the animal quitted him, alarmed by the approach of the other beaters.

"The beast ran into that thicket," gasped the boy, and then once more relapsed into a state of insensibility.

But the words of the wounded boy had been eagerly passed round, and a hundred different propositions were made.

"Set fire to the thicket," exclaimed one.

"Fire a volley into it," suggested another.

"A bold dash in, and trample the beast's life out," shouted a third.

The first proposal was agreed to, and a hundred eager hands collected dried sticks and leaves, and then a light was kindled. Just as the fire was about to be applied, a soft, sweet voice issued from the center of the thicket.

"Do not set fire to the forest, my dear friends; give me time to come out. Is it not enough for me to have been frightened to death by that awful creature?"

All started back in amazement, and Paul felt a strange, sudden thrill pass through his heart as those soft musical accents fell upon his ear.

There was a light rustling in the brushwood, and then a vision suddenly appeared, which filled the souls of the beholders with surprise. As the bushes divided, a fair woman, wrapped in a mantle of soft white fur, with a fantastically shaped traveling cap of green velvet upon her head, stood before them. She was exquisitely fair, and her long Titian red hair hung in disheveled masses over her shoulders.

"My good man," began she, with a certain tinge of aristocratic hauteur in her voice, "is your master here?"

As moved by a spring, Paul stepped forward and mechanically raised his cap.

"I am Paul Sergevitch," said he, "and these woods are on my estate of Kostopchin. A fearful wolf has been committing a series of terrible devastations upon my people, and we have been endeavoring to hunt it down. A boy whom he has just wounded says that he ran into the thicket from which you have just emerged, to the surprise of us all."

"I know," answered the lady, fixing her clear, steel-blue eyes keenly upon Paul's face. "The terrible beast rushed past me, and dived into a large cavity in the earth in the very center of the thicket. It was a huge white wolf, and I greatly feared that it would devour me."

"Ho, my men," cried Paul, "take spade and mattock, and dig out the monster, for she has come to the end of her tether at last. Madam, I do not know what chance has conducted you to this wild solitude, but the hospitality of Kostopchin is at your disposal, and I will, with your permission, conduct you there as soon as this scourge of the countryside has been dispatched."

He offered his hand with some remains of his former courtesy, but started back with an expression of horror on his face.

"Blood," cried he; "why, madam, your hand and fingers are stained with blood."

A faint color rose to the lady's cheek, but it died away in an instant as she answered, with a faint smile:

"The dreadful creature was all covered with blood, and I suppose I must have stained my hands against the bushes through which it had passed, when I parted them in order to escape from the fiery death with which you threatened me."

There was a ring of suppressed irony in her voice, and Paul felt his eyes drop before the glance of those cold steel-blue eyes. Meanwhile, urged to the utmost exertion by their fears, the serfs plied spade and mattock with the utmost vigor. The cavity was speedily enlarged, but, when a depth of eight feet had been attained, it was found to terminate in a little burrow not large enough to admit a rabbit, much less a creature of the white wolf's size. There were none of the tufts of white hair which had hitherto been always found beside the bodies of the victims, nor did that peculiar rank odor which always indicates the presence of wild animals hang about the spot.

The superstitious Muscovites crossed themselves, and scrambled out of the hole with grotesque alacrity. The mysterious disappearance of the monster which had committed such frightful ravages had cast a chill over the hearts of the ignorant peasants, and, unheeding the shouts of their master, they left the forest, which seemed to be overcast with the gloom of some impending calamity.

"Forgive the ignorance of these boors, madam," said Paul, when he found himself alone with the strange lady, "and permit me to escort you to my poor house, for you must have need of rest and refreshment, and—"

Here Paul checked himself abruptly, and a dark flush of embarrassment passed over his face.

"And," said the lady, with the same faint smile, "and you are dying with curiosity to know how I suddenly made my appearance from a thicket in your forest. You say that you are the lord of Kostopchin; then you are Paul Sergevitch, and should surely know how the ruler of Holy Russia takes upon himself to interfere with the doings of his children?"

"You know me, then?" exclaimed Paul, in some surprise.

"Yes, I have lived in foreign lands, as you have, and have heard your name often. Did you not break the bank at Blankburg? Did you not carry off Isola Menuti, the dancer, from a host of competitors; and, as a last instance of my knowledge, shall I recall to your memory a certain morning, on a sandy shore, with two men facing each other pistol in hand, the one young, fair, and boyish-looking, hardly twenty-two years of age, the other—"

"Hush!" exclaimed Paul, hoarsely; "you evidently know me, but who in the fiend's name are you?"

"Simply a woman who once moved in society and read the papers, and who is now a hunted fugitive."

"A fugitive!" returned Paul, hotly; 'who dare to persecute you?"

The lady moved a little closer to him, and then whispered in his ear:

"The police!"

"The police!" repeated Paul, stepping back a pace or two. "The police!"

"Yes, Paul Sergevitch, the police," returned the lady, "that body at the mention of which it is said the very Emperor trembles as he sits in his gilded chambers in the Winter Palace. Yes, I have had the imprudence to speak my mind too freely, and – well, you know what women have to dread who fall into the hands of the police in Holy Russia. To avoid such infamous degradations I fled, accompanied by a faithful domestic. I fled in hopes of gaining the frontier, but a few versts from here a body of mounted police rode up. My poor old servant had the imprudence to resist, and was shot dead. Half wild with terror I fled into the forest, and wandered about until I heard the noise your serfs made in the beating of the woods. I thought it was the police, who had organized a search for me, and I crept into the thicket for the purpose of concealment. The rest you know. And now, Paul Sergevitch, tell me whether you dare give shelter to a proscribed fugitive such as I am."

"Madam," returned Paul, gazing into the clear-cut features before him, glowing with the animation of the recital, "Kostopchin is ever open to misfortune – and beauty," added he, with a bow.

"Ah!" cried the lady, with a laugh in which there was something sinister; "I expect that misfortune would knock at your door for a long time, if it was unaccompanied by beauty. However, I thank you, and will accept your hospitality; but if evil come upon you, remember that I am not to be blamed."

"You will be safe enough at Kostopchin," returned Paul. "The police won't trouble their heads about me; they know that since the Emperor drove me to lead this hideous existence, politics have no charm for me, and that the brandy bottle is the only charm of my life."

"Dear me," answered the lady, eyeing him uneasily, "a morbid drunkard, are you? Well, as I am half perished with cold, suppose you take me to Kostopchin; you will be conferring a favor on me, and will get back all the sooner to your favorite brandy."

She placed her hand upon Paul's arm as she spoke, and mechanically he led the way to the great solitary white house. The few servants betrayed no astonishment at the appearance of the lady, for some of the serfs on their way back to the village had spread the report of the sudden appearance of the mysterious stranger; besides, they were not accustomed to question the acts of their somewhat arbitrary master.

Alexis and Katrina had gone to bed, and Paul and his guest sat down to a hastily improvised meal.

"I am no great eater," remarked the lady, as she played with the food before her; and Paul noticed with surprise that scarcely a morsel passed her lips, though she more than once filled and emptied a goblet of the champagne which had been opened in honor of her arrival.

"So it seems," remarked he; "and I do not wonder, for the food in this benighted hole is not what either you or I have been accustomed to."

"Oh, it does well enough," returned the lady, carelessly. "And now, if you have such a thing as a woman in the establishment, you can let her show me to my room, for I am nearly dead for want of sleep."

Paul struck a hand bell that stood on the table beside him, and the stranger rose from her seat, and with a brief "Good night," was moving towards the door, when the old man Michal suddenly made his appearance on the threshold. The aged intendant started backwards as though to avoid a heavy blow, and his fingers at once sought for the crucifix which he wore suspended round his neck, and on whose protection he relied to shield him from the powers of darkness.

"Blessed Virgin!" he exclaimed. "Holy Saint Radislas protect me, where have I seen her before?"

The lady took no notice of the old man's evident terror, but passed away down the echoing corridor.

The old man now timidly approached his master, who, after swallowing a glass of brandy, had drawn his chair up to the stove, and was gazing moodily at its polished surface.

"My lord," said Michal, venturing to touch his master's shoulder, "is that the lady that you found in the forest?"

"Yes," returned Paul, a smile breaking out over his face; "she is very beautiful, is she not?"

"Beautiful!" repeated Michal, crossing himself, "she may have beauty, but it is that of a demon. Where have I seen her before? –Where have I seen those shining teeth and those cold eyes? She is not like any one here, and I have never been ten versts from Kostopchin in my life. I am utterly bewildered. Ah, I have it, the dying herdsman – save the mark! Gospodin, have a care. I tell you that the strange lady is the image of the white wolf."

"You old fool," returned his master, savagely, "let me ever hear you repeat such nonsense again, and I will have you skinned alive. The lady is highborn, and of good family; beware how you insult her. Nay, I give you further commands: see that during her sojourn here she is treated with the utmost respect. And communicate this to all the servants. Mind, no more tales about the vision that your addled brain conjured up of wolves in the marsh, and above all do not let me hear that you have been alarming little Katrina with your senseless babble."

The old man bowed humbly, and, after a short pause, remarked:

"The lad that was injured at the hunt today is dead, my lord."

"Oh, dead is he, poor wretch!" returned Paul, to whom the death of a serf lad was not a matter of overweening importance. "But look here, Michal, remember that if any inquiries are made about the lady, that no one knows anything about her; that, in fact, no one has seen her at all."

"Your lordship shall be obeyed," answered the old man; and then, seeing that his master had relapsed into his former moody reverie, he left the room, crossing himself at every step he took.

Late into the night Paul sat up thinking over the occurrences of the day. He had told Michal that his guest was of noble family, but in reality he knew nothing more of her than she had condescended to tell him."

"Why, I don't even know her name," muttered he; "and yet somehow or other it seems as if a new feature of my life was opening before me. However, I have made one step in advance by getting her here, and if she talks about leaving, why, all that I have to do is threaten her with the police."

After his usual custom he smoked cigarette after cigarette, and poured out copious tumblers of brandy. The attendant serf replenished the stove from a small den which opened into the corridor, and after a time Paul slumbered heavily in his armchair. He was aroused by a light touch upon the shoulder, and, starting up, saw the stranger of the forest standing by his side.

"This is indeed kind of you," said she, with her usual mocking smile. "You felt that I should be strange here, and you got up early to see to the horses, or can it really be, those ends of cigarettes, that empty bottle of brandy? Paul Sergevitch, you have not been to bed at all."

Paul muttered a few indistinct words in reply, and then, ringing the bell furiously, ordered the servant to clear away the *débris* of last night's orgy, and lay the table for breakfast; then, with a hasty apology, he left the room to make a fresh toilet, and in about half an hour returned with his appearance sensibly improved by his ablutions and change of dress.

"I dare say," remarked the lady, as they were seated at the morning meal, for which she manifested the same indifference that she had for the dinner of the previous evening, "that you would like to know my name and who I am. Well, I don't mind telling you my name. It is Ravina, but as to my family and who I am, it will perhaps be best for you to remain in ignorance. A matter of policy, my dear Paul Sergevitch, a mere matter of policy, you see. I leave you to judge from my manners and appearance whether I am of sufficiently good form to be invited to the honor of your table—"

"None more worthy," broke in Paul, whose bemuddled brain was fast succumbing to the charms of his guest; "and surely that is a question upon which I may be deemed a competent judge."

"I do not know about that," returned Ravina, "for from all accounts the company that you used to keep was not of the most select character."

"No, but hear me," began Paul, seizing her hand and endeavoring to carry it to his lips. But as he did so an unpleasant chill passed over him, for those slender fingers were icy cold.

"Do not be foolish," said Ravina, drawing away her hand, after she had permitted it to rest for an instant in Paul's grasp, "do you not hear someone coming?"

As she spoke the sound of tiny pattering feet was heard in the corridor, then the door was flung violently open, and with a shrill cry of delight, Katrina rushed into the room, followed more slowly by her brother Alexis.

"And are these your children?" asked Ravina, as Paul took up the little girl and placed her fondly upon his knee, whilst the boy stood a few paces from the door gazing with eyes of wonder upon the strange woman, for whose appearance he was utterly unable to account. "Come here, my little man," continued she; "I suppose you are the heir of Kostopchin, though you do not resemble your father much."

"He takes after his mother, I think," returned Paul carelessly; "and how has my darling Katrina been?" he added, addressing his daughter.

"Quite well, papa dear," answered the child; "but where is the fine white wolf skin that you promised me?"

"Your father did not find her," answered Ravina, with a little laugh; "the white wolf was not so easy to catch as he fancied."

Alexis had moved a few steps nearer to the lady, and was listening with grave attention to every word she uttered.

"Are white wolves so difficult to kill, then?" asked he.

"It seems so, my little man," returned the lady, "since your father and all the serfs of Kostopchin were unable to do so."

"I have got a pistol, that good old Michal has taught me to fire, and I am sure I could kill her if ever I got sight of her," observed Alexis, boldly.

"There is a brave boy," returned Ravina, with one of her shrill laughs; "and now, won't you come and sit on my knee, for I am very fond of little boy?"

"No, I don't like you," answered Alexis, after a moment's consideration, "for Michal says—"

"Go to your room, you insolent young brat," broke in the father, in a voice of thunder. "You spend so much of your time with Michal and the serfs that you have learned all their boorish habits."

Two tiny tears rolled down the boy's cheeks as in obedience to his father's orders he turned about and quitted the room, whilst Ravina darted a strange look of dislike after him. As soon, however, as the door had closed, the fair woman addressed Katrina.

"Well, perhaps you will not be so unkind to me as your brother," said she. "Come to me," and as she spoke she held out her arms.

The little girl came to her without hesitation, and began to smooth the silken tresses which were coiled and wreathed around Ravina's head.

"Pretty, pretty," she murmured, "beautiful lady."

"You see, Paul Sergevitch, that your little daughter has taken to me at once," remarked Ravina.

"She takes after her father, who was always noted for his good taste," returned Paul, with a bow; "but take care, madam, or the little puss will have your necklace off."

The child had indeed succeeded in unclasping the glittering ornament, and was now inspecting it in high glee.

"That is a curious ornament," said Paul, stepping up to the child and taking the circlet from her hand.

It was indeed a quaintly fashioned ornament, consisting as it did of a number of what were apparently curved pieces of sharp-pointed horn set in gold, and depending from a snake of the same precious metal.

"Why, these are claws," continued he, as he looked at them more carefully.

"Yes, wolves' claws," answered Ravina, taking the necklet from the child and reclasping it round her neck. "It is a family relic which I have always worn."

Katrina at first seemed inclined to cry at her new plaything being taken from her, but by caresses and endearments Ravina soon contrived to lull her once more into a good temper.

"My daughter has certainly taken to you in a most wonderful manner," remarked Paul, with a pleased smile. "You have quite obtained possession of her heart."

"Not yet, whatever I may do later on," answered the woman, with her strange cold smile, as she pressed the child closer towards her and shot a glance at Paul which made him quiver with an emotion that he had never felt before. Presently, however, the child grew tired of her new acquaintance, and sliding down from her knee, crept from the room in search of her brother Alexis.

Paul and Ravina remained silent for a few instants, and then the woman broke the silence.

"All that remains for me now, Paul Sergevitch, is to trespass on your hospitality, and to ask you to lend me some disguise, and assist me to gain the nearest post town, which, I think, is Vitroski."

"And why should you wish to leave this at all," demanded Paul, a deep flush rising to his cheek. "You are perfectly safe in my house, and if you attempt to pursue your journey there is every chance of your being recognized and captured."

"Why do I wish to leave this house?" answered Ravina, rising to her feet and casting a look of surprise upon her interrogator. "Can you ask me such a question? How is it possible for me to remain here?"

"It is perfectly impossible for you to leave; of that I am quite certain," answered the man, doggedly. "All I know is, that if you leave Kostopchin, you will inevitably fall into the hands of the police."

"And Paul Sergevitch will tell them where they can find me?" questioned Ravina, with an ironical inflection in the tone of her voice.

"I never said so," returned Paul.

"Perhaps not," answered the woman, quickly, "but I am not slow in reading thoughts; they are sometimes plainer to read than words. You are saying to yourself, 'Kostopchin is but a dull hole after all; chance has thrown into my hands a woman whose beauty pleases me; she is utterly friendless, and is in fear of the pursuit of the police; why should I not bend her to my will?' That is what you have been thinking – is it not so, Paul Sergevitch?"

"I never thought, that is—" stammered the man.

"No, you never thought that I could read you so plainly," pursued the woman, pitilessly; "but it is the truth that I have told you, and sooner than remain an inmate of your house, I would leave it, even if all the police of Russia stood ready to arrest me on its very threshold."

"Stay, Ravina," exclaimed Paul, as the woman made a step towards the door. "I do not say whether your reading of my thoughts is right or wrong, but before you leave, listen to me. I do not speak to you in the usual strain of a pleading lover – you, who know my past, would laugh at me should I do so; but I tell you plainly that from the first moment that I set eyes upon you, a strange new feeling has risen up in my heart, not the cold thing that society calls love, but a burning resistless flood which flows down like molten lava from the volcano's crater. Stay, Ravina, stay, I implore you, for if you go from here you will take my heart with you."

"You may be speaking more truthfully than you think," returned the fair woman, as, turning back, she came close up to Paul, and placing both her hands upon his shoulders, shot a glance of lurid fire from her eyes. "Still, you have but given me a selfish reason for my staying, only your own self-gratification. Give me one that more nearly affects myself."

Ravina's touch sent a tremor through Paul's whole frame which caused every nerve and sinew to vibrate. Gaze as boldly as he might into those steel-blue eyes, he could not sustain their intensity.

"Be my wife, Ravina," faltered he. "Be my wife. You are safe enough from all pursuit here, and if that does not suit you I can easily convert my estate into a large sum of money, and we can fly to other lands, where you can have nothing to fear from the Russian police."

"And does Paul Sergevitch actually mean to offer his hand to a woman whose name he does not even know, and of whose feelings towards him he is entirely ignorant?" asked the woman, with her customary mocking laugh.

"What do I care for name or birth," returned he, hotly, "I have enough for both, and as for love, my passion would soon kindle some sparks of it in your breast, cold and frozen as it may now be."

"Let me think a little," said Ravina; and throwing herself into an armchair she buried her face in her hands and seemed plunged in deep reflection, whilst Paul paced impatiently up and down the room like a prisoner awaiting the verdict that would restore him to life or doom him to a shameful death.

At length Ravina removed her hands from her face and spoke.

"Listen," said she. "I have thought over your proposal seriously, and upon certain conditions, I will consent to become your wife."

"They are granted in advance," broke in Paul, eagerly.

"Make no bargains blindfold," answered she, "but listen. At the present moment I have no inclination for you, but on the other hand I feel no repugnance for you. I will remain here for a month, and during that time I shall remain in a suite of apartments which you will have prepared for me. Every evening I will visit you here, and upon your making yourself agreeable my ultimate decision will depend."

"And suppose that decision should be an unfavorable one?" asked Paul.

"Then," answered Ravina, with a ringing laugh, "I shall, as you say, leave this and take your heart with me."

"These are hard conditions," remarked Paul. "Why not shorten the time of probation?"

"My conditions are unalterable," answered Ravina, with a little stamp of the foot. "Do you agree to them or not?"

"I have no alternative," answered he, sullenly; "but remember that I am to see you every evening."

"For two hours," said the woman, "so you must try and make yourself as agreeable as you can in that time; and now, if you will give orders regarding my rooms, I will settle myself in them with as little delay as possible."

Paul obeyed her, and in a couple of hours three handsome chambers were got ready for their fair occupant in a distant part of the great rambling house.

The Awakening of the Wolf

THE DAYS SLIPPED slowly and wearily away, but Ravina showed no signs of relenting. Every evening, according to her bond, she spent two hours with Paul and made herself most agreeable, listening to his far-fetched compliments and asseverations of love and tenderness either with a cold smile or with one of her mocking laughs. She refused to allow Paul to visit her in her own apartments, and the only intruder she permitted there, save the servants, was little Katrina, who had taken a strange fancy to the fair woman. Alexis, on the contrary, avoided her as much as he possibly could, and the pair hardly ever met. Paul, to while away the time, wandered about the farm and the village, the inhabitants of which had recovered from their panic as the white wolf appeared to have entirely desisted from her murderous attacks upon belated peasants. The shades of evening had closed in as Paul was one day returning from his customary round, rejoiced with the idea that the hour for Ravina's visit was drawing near, when he was startled by a gentle touch upon the shoulder, and turning round, saw the old man Michal standing just behind him. The intendant's face was perfectly livid, his eyes gleamed with the luster of terror, and his fingers kept convulsively clasping and unclasping.

"My lord," exclaimed he, in faltering accents; "oh, my lord, listen to me, for I have terrible news to narrate to you."

"What is the matter?" asked Paul, more impressed than he would have liked to confess by the old man's evident terror.

"The wolf, the white wolf! I have seen it again," whispered Michal.

"You are dreaming," retorted his master, angrily. "You have got the creature on the brain, and have mistaken a white calf or one of the dogs for it."

"I am not mistaken," answered the old man, firmly. "And oh, my lord, do not go into the house, for she is there."

"She – who – what do you mean?" cried Paul.

"The white wolf, my lord. I saw her go in. You know the strange lady's apartments are on the ground floor on the west side of the house. I saw the monster cantering across the lawn, and, as if it knew its way perfectly well, make for the center window of the reception room; it yielded to a touch of the fore paw, and the beast sprang through. Oh, my lord, do not go in; I tell you that it will never harm the strange woman. Ah! let me—"

But Paul cast off the detaining arm with a force that made the old man reel and fall, and then, catching up an ax, dashed into the house, calling upon the servants to follow him to the strange lady's rooms. He tried the handle, but the door was securely fastened, and then, in all the frenzy of terror, he attacked the panels with heavy blows of his ax. For a few seconds no sound was heard save the ring of metal and the shivering of panels, but then the clear tones of Ravina were heard asking the reason for this outrageous disturbance.

"The wolf, the white wolf," shouted half a dozen voices.

"Stand back and I will open the door," answered the fair woman. "You must be mad, for there is no wolf here."

The door flew open and the crowd rushed tumultuously in; every nook and corner were searched, but no signs of the intruder could be discovered, and with many shamefaced glances Paul and his servants were about to return, when the voice of Ravina arrested their steps.

"Paul Sergevitch," said she, coldly, "explain the meaning of this daring intrusion on my privacy."

She looked very beautiful as she stood before them; her right arm extended and her bosom heaved violently, but this was doubtless caused by her anger at the unlooked-for invasion.

Paul briefly repeated what he had heard from the old serf, and Ravina's scorn was intense.

"And so," cried she, fiercely, "it is to the crotchets of this old dotard that I am indebted for this. Paul, if you ever hope to succeed in winning me, forbid that man ever to enter the house again."

Paul would have sacrificed all his serfs for a whim of the haughty beauty, and Michal was deprived of the office of intendant and exiled to a cabin in the village, with orders never to show his face again near the house. The separation from the children almost broke the old man's heart, but he ventured on no remonstrance and meekly obeyed the mandate which drove him away from all he loved and cherished.

Meanwhile, curious rumors began to be circulated regarding the strange proceedings of the lady who occupied the suite of apartments which had formerly belonged to the wife of the owner of Kostopchin. The servants declared that the food sent up, though hacked about and cut up, was never tasted, but that the raw meat in the larder was frequently missing. Strange sounds were often heard to issue from the rooms as the panic-stricken serfs hurried past the corridor upon which the doors opened, and dwellers in the house were frequently disturbed by the howlings of wolves, the footprints of which were distinctly visible the next morning, and, curiously enough, invariably in the gardens facing the west side of the house in which the lady dwelt. Little Alexis, who found no encouragement to sit with his father, was naturally thrown a great deal amongst the serfs, and heard the subject discussed with many exaggerations. Weird old tales of folklore were often narrated as the servants discussed their evening meal, and the boy's hair would bristle as he listened to the wild and fanciful narratives of wolves, witches, and white ladies with which the superstitious serfs filled his ears. One of his most treasured possessions was an old brass-mounted cavalry pistol, a present from Michal; this he has learned to load, and by using both hands to the cumbrous weapon could contrive to fire it off, as many an ill-starred sparrow could attest. With his mind constantly dwelling upon the terrible tales he had so greedily listened to, this pistol became his daily companion, whether he was wandering about the long echoing corridors of the house or wandering through the neglected shrubberies of the garden. For a fortnight matters went on in this manner, Paul becoming more and more infatuated by the charms of his strange guest, and she every now and then letting drop occasional crumbs of hope which led the unhappy man further and further upon the dangerous course that he was pursuing. A mad, soul-absorbing passion for the fair woman and the deep draughts of brandy with which he consoled himself during her hours of absence were telling upon the brain of the master of Kostopchin, and except during the brief space of Ravina's visit, he would relapse into moods of silent sullenness from which he would occasionally break out into furious bursts of passion for no assignable cause. A shadow seemed to be closing over the house of Kostopchin; it became the abode of grim whispers and undeveloped fears; the men and maid servants went about their work glancing nervously over their shoulders, as though they were apprehensive that some hideous thing was following at their heels.

After three days of exile, poor old Michal could endure the state of suspense regarding the safety of Alexis and Katrina no longer; and, casting aside his superstitious fears, he took to wandering by night about the exterior of the great white house, and peering curiously into such windows as had been left unshuttered. At first he was in continual dread of meeting the terrible white wolf; but his love for the children and his confidence in the crucifix he wore prevailed, and he continued his nocturnal wanderings about Kostopchin and its environs. He kept near the western front of the house, urged on to do so from some vague feeling which he could in no wise account for. One evening as he was making his accustomed tour of inspection, the wail of a child struck upon his ear. He bent down his head and eagerly listened, again he heard the same faint sounds, and in them he fancied he recognized the accents of his dear little Katrina. Hurrying up to one of the ground-floor windows, from which a dim light streamed, he pressed his face against the pane, and looked steadily in. A horrible sight presented itself to his gaze. By the faint light of a shaded lamp, he saw Katrina stretched upon the ground; but her wailing had now ceased, for a shawl had been tied across her little mouth. Over her was bending a hideous shape, which seemed to be clothed in some white and shaggy covering. Katrina lay perfectly motionless, and the hands of the figure were engaged in hastily removing the garments from the child's breast. The task was soon effected; then there was a bright gleam of steel, and the head of the thing bent closely down to the child's bosom.

With a yell of apprehension, the old man dashed in the window frame, and, drawing the cross from his breast, sprang boldly into the room. The creature sprang to its feet, and the white fur cloak falling from its head and shoulders disclosed the pallid features of Ravina, a short, broad knife in her hand, and her lips discolored with blood.

"Vile sorceress!" cried Michal, dashing forward and raising Katrina in his arms. "What hellish work are you about?"

Ravina's eyes gleamed fiercely upon the old man, who had interfered between her and her prey. She raised her dagger, and was about to spring in upon him, when she caught sight of the cross in his extended hand. With a low cry, she dropped the knife, and, staggering back a few paces, wailed out: "I could not help it; I liked the child well enough, but I was so hungry."

Michal paid but little heed to her words, for he was busily engaged in examining the fainting child, whose head was resting helplessly on his shoulder. There was a wound over the left breast, from which the blood was flowing; but the injury appeared slight, and not likely to prove fatal. As soon as he had satisfied himself on this point, he turned to the woman, who was crouching before the cross as a wild beast shrinks before the whip of the tamer.

"I am going to remove the child," said he, slowly. "Dare you to mention a word of what I have done or whither she has gone, and I will arouse the village. Do you know what will happen then? Why, every peasant in the place will hurry here with a lighted brand in his hand to consume this accursed house and the unnatural dwellers in it. Keep silence, and I leave you to your unhallowed work. I will no longer seek to preserve Paul Sergevitch, who has given himself over to the powers of darkness by taking a demon to his bosom."

Ravina listened to him as if she scarcely comprehended him; but, as the old man retreated to the window with his helpless burden, she followed him step by step; and as he turned to cast one last glance at the shattered window, he saw the woman's pale face and bloodstained lips glued against an unbroken pane, with a wild look of unsatiated appetite in her eyes.

Next morning the house of Kostopchin was filled with terror and surprise, for Katrina, the idol of her father's heart, had disappeared, and no signs of her could be discovered. Every effort was made, the woods and fields in the neighborhood were thoroughly searched; but it was at last concluded that robbers had carried off the child for the sake of the ransom that they might be able to extract from the father. This seemed the more likely as one of the windows in the fair stranger's room bore marks of violence, and she declared that, being alarmed by the sound of crashing glass, she had risen and confronted a man who was endeavoring to enter her apartment, but who, on perceiving her, turned and fled away with the utmost precipitation.

Paul Sergevitch did not display as much anxiety as might have been expected from him, considering the devotion which he had ever evinced for the lost Katrina, for his whole soul was wrapped up in one mad, absorbing passion for the fair woman who had so strangely crossed his life. He certainly directed the search, and gave all the necessary orders; but he did so in a listless and half-hearted manner, and hastened back to Kostopchin as speedily as he could as though fearing to be absent for any length of time from the casket in which his new treasure was enshrined. Not so Alexis; he was almost frantic at the loss of his sister, and accompanied the searchers daily until his little legs grew weary, and he had to be carried on the shoulders of a sturdy *moujik*. His treasured brass-mounted pistol was now more than ever his constant companion; and when he met the fair woman who had cast a spell upon his father, his face would flush, and he would grind his teeth in impotent rage.

The day upon which all search had ceased, Ravina glided into the room where she knew that she would find Paul awaiting her. She was fully an hour before her usual time, and the lord of Kostopchin started to his feet in surprise.

"You are surprised to see me," said she; 'but I have only come to pay you a visit for a few minutes. I am convinced that you love me, and could I but relieve a few of the objections that my heart continues to raise, I might be yours."

"Tell me what these scruples are," cried Paul, springing towards her, and seizing her hands in his; "and be sure that I will find means to overcome them."

Even in the midst of all the glow and fervor of anticipated triumph, he could not avoid noticing how icily cold were the fingers that rested in his palm, and how utterly passionless was the pressure with which she slightly returned his enraptured clasp.

"Listen," said she, as she withdrew her hand; "I will take two more hours for consideration. By that time the whole of the house of Kostopchin will be cradled in slumber; then meet me at the old sundial near the yew tree at the bottom of the garden, and I will give you my reply. Nay, not a word," she added, as he seemed about to remonstrate, "for I tell you that I think it will be a favorable one."

"But why not come back here?" urged he; "there is a hard frost tonight, and—"

"Are you so cold a lover," broke in Ravina, with her accustomed laugh, "to dread the changes of the weather? But not another word; I have spoken."

She glided from the room, but uttered a low cry of rage. She had almost fallen over Alexis in the corridor.

"Why is that brat not in his bed?" cried she, angrily; "he gave me quite a turn."

"Go to your room, boy," exclaimed his father, harshly; and with a malignant glance at his enemy, the child slunk away.

Paul Sergevitch paced up and down the room for the two hours that he had to pass before the hour of meeting. His heart was very heavy, and a vague feeling of disquietude began to creep over him. Twenty times he made up his mind not to keep his appointment, and as often the fascination of the fair woman compelled him to rescind his resolution. He remembered that he had from childhood disliked that spot by the yew tree, and had always looked upon it as a dreary, uncanny place; and he even now disliked the idea of finding himself here after dark, even with such fair companionship as he had been promised. Counting the minutes, he paced backwards and forwards, as though moved by some concealed machinery. Now and again he glanced at the clock, and at last its deep metallic sound, as it struck the quarter, warned him that he had but little time to lose, if he intended to keep his appointment. Throwing on a heavily furred coat and pulling a traveling cap down over his ears, he opened a side door and sallied out into the grounds. The moon was at its full, and shone coldly down upon the leafless trees, which looked white and ghostlike in its beams. The paths and unkept lawns were now covered with hoar frost, and a keen wind every now and then swept by, which, in spite of his wraps, chilled Paul's blood in his veins. The dark shape of the yew tree soon rose up before him, and in another moment he stood beside its dusky boughs. The old gray sundial stood only a few paces off, and by its side was standing a slender figure, wrapped in a white, fleecy-looking cloak. It was perfectly motionless, and again a terror of undefined dread passed through every nerve and muscle of Paul Sergevitch's body.

"Ravina!" said he, in faltering accents. "Ravina!"

"Did you take me for a ghost?" answered the fair woman, with her shrill laugh; "no, no, I have not come to that yet. Well, Paul Sergevitch, I have come to give you my answer; are you anxious about it?"

"How can you ask me such a question?" returned he; "do you not know that my whole soul has been aglow with anticipations of what your reply might be? Do not keep me any longer in suspense. Is it yes, or no?"

"Paul Sergevitch," answered the young woman, coming up to him and laying her hands upon his shoulders, and fixing her eyes upon his with that strange weird expression before which he always quailed; "do you really love me, Paul Sergevitch?" asked she.

"Love you!" repeated the lord of Kostopchin; "have I not told you a thousand times how much my whole soul flows out towards you, how I only live and breathe in your presence, and how death at your feet would be more welcome than life without you?"

"People often talk of death, and yet little know how near it is to them," answered the fair lady, a grim smile appearing upon her face; "but say, do you give me your whole heart?"

"All I have is yours, Ravina," returned Paul, "name, wealth, and the devoted love of a lifetime."

"But your heart," persisted she; "it is your heart that I want; tell me, Paul, that it is mine and mine only."

"Yes, my heart is yours, dearest Ravina," answered Paul, endeavoring to embrace the fair form in his impassioned grasp; but she glided from him, and then with a quick bound sprang upon him and glared in his face with a look that was absolutely appalling. Her eyes gleamed with a lurid fire, her lips were drawn back, showing her sharp, white teeth, whilst her breath came in sharp, quick gasps.

"I am hungry," she murmured, "oh, so hungry; but now, Paul Sergevitch, your heart is mine."

Her movement was so sudden and unexpected that he stumbled and fell heavily to the ground, the fair woman clinging to him and falling upon his breast. It was then that the full horror of his position came upon Paul Sergevitch, and he saw his fate clearly before him; but a terrible numbness prevented him from using his hands to free himself from the hideous embrace which was paralyzing all his muscles. The face that was glaring into his seemed to be undergoing some fearful change, and the features to be losing their semblance of humanity. With a sudden, quick movement, she tore open his garments, and in another moment she had perforated his left breast with a ghastly wound, and, plunging in her delicate hands, tore out his heart and bit at it ravenously. Intent upon her hideous banquet she heeded not the convulsive struggles which agitated the dying form of the lord of Kostopchin. She was too much occupied to notice a diminutive form approaching, sheltering itself behind every tree and bush until it had arrived within ten paces of the scene of the terrible tragedy. Then the moonbeams glistened upon the long shining barrel of a pistol, which a boy was leveling with both hands at the murderess. Then quick and sharp rang out the report, and with a wild shriek, in which there was something beastlike, Ravina leaped from the body of the dead man and staggered away to a thick clump of bushes some ten paces distant. The boy Alexis had heard the appointment that had been made, and dogged his father's footsteps to the trysting place. After firing the fatal shot his courage deserted him, and he fled backwards to the house, uttering loud shrieks for help. The startled servants were soon in the presence of their slaughtered master, but aid was of no avail, for the lord of Kostopchin had passed away. With fear and trembling the superstitious peasants searched the clump of bushes, and started back in horror as they perceived a huge white wolf, lying stark and dead, with a half-devoured human heart clasped between its forepaws.

* * *

No signs of the fair lady who had occupied the apartments in the western side of the house were ever again seen. She had passed away from Kostopchin like an ugly dream, and as the *moujiks* of the village sat around their stoves at night they whispered strange stories regarding the fair woman of the forest and the white wolf of Kostopchin. By order of the Tsar a surtee was placed in charge of the estate of Kostopchin, and Alexis was ordered to be sent to a military school until he should be old enough to join the army. The meeting between the boy and his sister, whom the faithful Michal, when all danger was at an end, had produced from his hiding place, was most affecting; but it was not until Katrina had been for some time resident at the house of a distant relative at Vitepak, that she ceased to wake at night and cry out in terror as she again dreamed that she was in the clutches of the white wolf.

The Change

Ramsey Campbell

AS SOON AS HE REACHED the flat Don started writing. Walking home, he'd shaped the chapter in his mind. *What transformations does the werewolf undergo?* he wrote. The new streetlamp by the bus-stop snapped alight as the October evening dimmed. *Does he literally change into another creature, or is it simply a regression?*

"How's it coming?" Margaret asked when she came in.

"Pretty well." It was, though she'd distracted him. He stared out at the bluish lamp and searched for the end of his sentence.

After dinner, during which his mind had been constructing paragraphs, he hurried back to his desk. The bluish light washed out the lines of ink; the rest of the page looked arctically indifferent, far too wide to fill. His prepared paragraphs grew feeble. When he closed the curtains and wrote a little, his sentences seemed dull. Tomorrow was Saturday. He'd begin early.

He had forgotten the queues at the bus-stop. He went unshaven to his desk, but already shoppers were chattering about the crowds they would avoid. They were less than three yards from him, and the glass seemed very thin. He was sure the noise grew worse each week. Still, he could ignore it, use the silences.

Aren't we all still primitive? he wrote. *Hasn't civilisation* Children whined, tugging at their mothers. *Hasn't civilisation* Now the women were shaking the children, cuffing them, shouting. *Hasn't bloody civilisation* A bus bore the queue away, but as many people missed the bus and began complaining loudly, repetitively.

"Yes, it's going all right," he told Margaret, and pretended to turn back to check a reference. He wasn't lying. Just a temporary block.

Hasn't civilisation simply trapped and repressed our primitive instincts? he managed to stutter at last. *But the more strongly* Scarved crowds were massing outside, chanting football slogans. There's tribal behaviour for you. *But the more strongly* Youths stared in at him, shouting inanities. If only there was room in the bedroom for his desk, if only they had erected the bus-stop just a few houses away – He forced himself to keep his head down. *But the more strongly primitive instincts are repressed the more savage their occasional outburst will be, whether in mass murder or actual lycanthropy.* God, that was enough. Sunday would be better.

Sunday was full of children, playing itinerant games. He abandoned writing, and researched in library books while Margaret wrote her case reports. He was glad he'd taken time off to read the books. Now he had new insights, which would mean a stronger chapter.

Monday was hectic. The most complicated tax assessments were being calculated, now that all the information had arrived. Taxpayers phoned, demanding why they were waiting; the office rang incessantly. "Inland Revenue," Don and his colleagues kept saying. "Inland Revenue." Still, he managed to calculate three labyrinthine assessments.

He felt more confident on the way home. He was already on the third chapter, and his publisher had said that this book should be more commercial than his first. Perhaps it would pay for a house, then Margaret could give up social work and have her baby; perhaps he could even write full time. He strode home, determined to improve the book. Dissolving bars of gold floated in the deep blue sky, beyond the tower blocks.

He was surprised how well the opening chapters read. He substituted phrases here and there. The words grew pale as bluish light invaded his desk-lamp's. When the text gave out, his mind went on. His nib scratched faintly. At the end of the second paragraph he gazed out, frowning.

The street had the unnatural stillness of a snowscape. Street and houses stretched away in both directions, gleaming faintly blue. The cross-street on his right was lit similarly; the corner house had no shadow. The pavement seemed oppressively close with no garden intervening. Everything looked unreal, glary with lightning.

He was so aware of the silence now that it distracted him. He must get an idea moving before the silence gave way, before someone came to stare. Write, for God's sake write. Repression, regression, lycanthropy. It sounded like a ditty in his mind.

Animal traits of primitive man. Distrust of the unfamiliar produces a savage response. He scribbled, but there seemed to be no continuity; his thoughts were flowing faster than his ink. Someone crossed at the intersection, walking oddly. He glared at the shadowless corner, but it was deserted. At the edge of his vision the figure had looked as odd as the light. He scribbled, crossing out and muttering to deafen himself to the silence. As he wrote the end of a paragraph, a face peered at him, inches from his. Margaret had tiptoed up to smile. He crumpled the book as he slammed it shut, but managed to smile as she came in.

Later he thought an idea was stirring, a paragraph assembling. Margaret began to tell him about her latest case. "Right, yes, all right," he muttered and sat at the window, his back to her. The blank page blotted thought from his mind. The bluish light tainted the page and the desk, like a sour indefinable taste.

The light bothered him. It changed his view of the quiet street he'd used to enjoy while working. This new staged street was unpleasantly compelling. Passers-by looked discoloured, almost artificial. If he drew the curtains, footsteps conjured up caricatures that strolled across his mind. If he sat at the dining-table he could still hear any footsteps, and was nearer Margaret, the rustling of her case reports, her laughter as she read a book.

His head was beginning to feel like the approach of a storm; he wasn't sure how long it had felt that way. The first sign of violence was almost a relief. It was Thursday night, and he was straining at a constipated paragraph. When someone arrived at the bus-stop, Don forced himself not to look. He gazed at the blot that had gathered at the end of his last word, where he'd rested his pen. The blot had started to look like an obstacle he would never be able to pass. The bluish light appeared to be making it grow, and there was another blot on the edge of his vision – another man at the bus-stop. If he looked he would never be able to write, he knew. At last he glanced up, to get it over with, and then he stared. Something was wrong.

They looked almost like two strangers at a bus-stop, their backs to each other. One shrugged his shoulders loosely, as though he was feeling the cold; the other stretched, baring huge calloused hands. Their faces were neutral as masks. All at once Don saw that was just a pretence. Each man was waiting for the other to make a move. They were wary as animals in a cage.

Now he could see how whenever one shifted the other turned towards him, almost imperceptibly. The light had changed their faces into plastic, bluish plastic masks that might at any moment slip awry. Suddenly Don's mouth tasted sour, for he'd realised that the men were turning their backs on the roadway; before they came face to face, they would see him. He was protected by the window, and anyway he could retreat to Margaret. But the sound of her rustling pages seemed very far away. Now the masks were almost facing him, and a roar was growing – the sound of a bus. He managed to gulp back a sigh of relief before Margaret could notice that anything was wrong. How could he explain to her when he didn't understand it himself?

When the men had boarded the bus, making way stiffly for each other, he closed the curtains hastily. His fingers were trembling, and he had to go into the kitchen to splash cold water on his face. Trying to appear nonchalant as he passed Margaret, he felt as false as the masks in the street.

A face came towards the window, grinning. It was discoloured, shiny, plastic; its eyes shone, unnaturally blue. As it reached the window it cracked like an egg from forehead to chin, and its contents leapt at him, smashing the glass and his dream. Beside him Margaret was sound asleep. He lay in his own dark and wondered what was true about the dream.

The next night he pretended to write, and watched. His suspicion was absurd, but fascinating. As he gazed unblinking at the people by the bus-stop they looked increasingly deformed; their heads were out of proportion, or their faces lopsided; their dangling hands looked swollen and clumsy. Christ, nobody was perfect; the clinical light simply emphasised imperfections, or his eyes were tired. Yet the people looked self-conscious, pretending to be normal. That light would make anyone feel awkward. He would be glad of Saturday and daylight.

He'd forgotten the crowds again. Once they would have set him scribbling his impressions in his notebook; now their mannerisms looked studied and ugly, their behaviour uncivilised. The women were mannequins, in hideous taste: hives of artificially senile hair squatted on their heads, their eyes looked enlarged with blue paint. The men were louder and more brutal, hardly bothering to pretend at all.

Margaret returned, laden with shopping. "I saw your book in the supermarket. I improved their display."

"Good, fine," he snarled, and tried to reconstruct the sentence she had ruined. He was gripping his pen so hard it almost cracked.

On Sunday afternoon he managed a page, as late sunlight turned the street amber. In one case, he wrote, a man interested in transmogrification took LSD and "became" a tiger, even to seeing a tiger in the mirror. *Doesn't this show how fragile human personality is?* Too many bloody rhetorical questions in this book. *Very little pressure is needed to break the shell of civilisation, of all that we call human* – five minutes more of that bloody radio upstairs was about all it would take. There was no silence anywhere, except the strained unnerving quiet of the street at night.

Next week Margaret was on call. After being surrounded by the office phones all day, he was even more on edge for the shrilling of the phone. Yet when she was called out he was surprised to find that he felt relieved. The flat was genuinely silent, for the people overhead were out too. Though he was tired from persuading irate callers that they owed tax, he uncapped his pen and sat at the window.

Why is the full moon important to lycanthropy? Does moonlight relate to a racial memory, a primitive fear? Its connotations might stir up the primitive elements of the personality, most violently where they were most repressed, or possibly where they were closest to the surface. Come to think, it must be rather like the light outside his window.

There was his suspicion again, and yet he had no evidence. He'd seen how the light caricatured people, and perhaps its spotlighting made them uneasy. But how could a streetlight make anyone more savage – for example, the gang of youths he could hear approaching loudly? It was absurd. Nevertheless his palms were growing slick with apprehension, and he could hardly keep hold of his pen.

When they came abreast of the window they halted and began to jeer at him, at his pose behind the desk. Teeth gleamed metallically in the discoloured faces, their eyes glittered like glass. For a moment he was helpless with panic, then he realised that the glass protected him. He held that thought steady, though his head was thumping. Let them try to break through, he'd rip their throats out on the glass, drag their faces over the splinters. He sat grinning at the plastic puppets while they jeered and gestured jerkily. At last they dawdled away, shouting threats.

He sat coated with the light, and felt rather sick. He seemed unable to clear his mind of a jumble of images: glass, flesh, blood, screams. He got up to find a book, any distraction at all, and then he saw his bluish shadow. Its long hands dangled, its distorted head poked forward. As he stooped to peer closer he felt as if it was dragging him down, stretching his hands down to meet its own. All at once he darted to the light-switch. He clawed the curtains shut and left the light burning, then he went into the bedroom and sat for a long time on the bed. He held his face as though it was a mask that was slipping.

On Thursday the bus home was delayed by a car crash. While the other passengers stared at blood and deformed metal, Don was uneasily watching the night seep across the sky. When he reached home the house looked worse than he'd feared: thin, cardboardy, bricks blackened by the light – not much of a refuge at all.

He was overworked, that was why he felt nervous. He must find time to relax. He'd be all right once he was inside with the curtains drawn, away from the dead light that seemed to have soaked into everything, even his fingers as they fumbled with the key. He glanced up to see who was watching him from the upstairs flat, then he looked away hastily. Maybe someone up there was really as deformed as that; he never met the tenants, they had a separate entrance. No, surely the figure must have looked like that because of a flaw in the glass.

In his flat he listened to the footsteps overhead, and couldn't tell if anything was wrong with them. Eventually he cooked the dinner Margaret had left him when she was called away. He tried to write, but the fragility of the silence made him too nervous. When he held his breath, he could hear the jungle of sound beyond the curtains: snarls of cars, the low thunder of planes, shouts, things falling, shrieks of metal, cries. The bluish flat stood emptily behind him.

The last singers were spilling out of pubs. Surely Margaret would be home soon. Wasn't that Margaret now? No, the hurrying footsteps were too uneven and too numerous: a man and a woman. He could hear the man shouting incoherently, almost wordlessly. Now the woman was running, and the man was stumbling heavily after her. When he caught her outside the window she began to scream.

Don squirmed in his chair. She was screaming abuse, not with fear. He could stand it, surely it wouldn't last long, her screeching voice that seemed to be in the room with him, scraping his nerves. All at once a body thumped the window; the frame shook. They were fighting, snarling. Christ! He struggled to his feet and forced himself to reach towards the curtains.

Then he saw the shadows, and barely managed not to cry out himself. Though the curtains blurred them, they were all too clear to him. As they clawed at each other, he was sure their arms were lengthening. Surely their heads were swelling like balloons and changing shape; perhaps that was why they sounded as though they never could have formed words. The window juddered and he flinched back, terrified they might sense him beyond the glass. For a moment he saw their mouths lunging at each other's faces, tearing.

All at once there was silence. Footsteps stumbled away, he couldn't tell whose. It took him a long time to part the curtains, and much longer to open the front door. But the street was deserted, and he might have doubted everything he'd seen but for a smear of blood on the window. He ran for tissues and wiped it away, shuddering. The lamp stood behind him, bright and ruthless; its dead eye gazed from the pane. He was surrounded. He could only take refuge in bed and try to keep his eyes closed.

The next day he rang the Engineering Department (Mechanical & Lighting) from the office, and told them where he lived. "What exactly have you put in those lights?"

The girl was probably just a clerk. "No, they're not mercury vapour," he said. "You might think they were, but not if you had to live with them, I can tell you. Will you connect me with someone who knows?"

Perhaps she felt insulted, or perhaps his tone disturbed her. "Never mind why I want to know. You don't want me to know, do you? Well, I know there's something else in them, let me tell you, and I'll be in touch with someone who can do something about it."

As he slammed the receiver down, he saw that his colleagues were staring at him. What was wrong with them? Had the politeness the job demanded possessed them completely? Were they scared of a bit of honest rage?

On the way home he wandered until he found a derelict area, though the start of winter time had made him more nervous. Already the sky was black, an hour earlier than yesterday, and he was dismayed to find he dreaded going home. Outside his flat the lamp stood waiting, in a street that looked alien as the moon. Nobody was in sight. He unlocked the front door, then he lifted the brick he was carrying and hurled it at the lamp. As the bulb shattered, he closed the door quickly. He spent the evening pretending to write, and stared out at the dark.

Saturday brought back the crowds. Their faces were pink putty, all too malleable. He cursed himself for wasting last night's dark. If he went to the library for quiet he would have walked two miles for nothing: there would be crowds there too. If only he could afford to move! But it was only the cheap rent here that was allowing him and Margaret to save.

She emerged from the mass of putty faces and dumped shopping on the table. "Isn't it going well?"

"What do you mean, isn't it going well? It won't go better for questions like that, will it? Yes, of course it's going well." There was no point in telling her the truth; he had enough to bear without her anxiety. That evening he wrote a few paragraphs, but they were cumbersome and clumsy.

On Sunday he tried to relax, but whenever Margaret spoke he felt there was an idea at the edge of his mind, waiting to be glimpsed and written. "Yes, later, later," he muttered, trying vainly to recapture the idea. That night she turned restlessly in bed for hours. He lay beside her and wondered uneasily what had gone wrong with the dark.

His lack of sleep nagged him on Monday. His skull felt tight and fragile. Whenever he tried to add up a column of figures a telephone rang, his colleagues laughed inanely, a fragment of conversation came into focus. People wandered from desk to desk. His surroundings were constantly restless, distracting.

One of his taxpayers called and refused to believe he owed four hundred pounds. Don sensed how the man's hands were clenching, seeking a victim, reaching for him. There was no need to panic, not with the length of the telephone cable between them. He couldn't be bothered to conceal his feelings. "You owe the money. There's nothing I can do."

"You bastards," the man was screaming, "you f—" as Don put down the receiver.

Some of his colleagues were staring at him. Maybe they could have done better, except that they probably wouldn't even have realised they were threatened. Did they honestly believe that words and printed forms were answers to the violence? Couldn't they see how false it all was? Only his triumph over the streetlamp helped him through the day.

He walked most of the way home, enjoying the darkness where lamps were smashed. As he neared his street the bluish light closed in. It didn't matter, it couldn't reach his home now. When he began to run, anxious to take refuge, his footsteps sounded flat and false as the light. He turned the corner into his street. Outside his flat the lamp was lit.

It craned its bony concrete neck, a tall thin ghost, its face blazing. It had defeated him. However many times he destroyed it, it would return. He locked himself in and grabbed blindly for the light-switch.

After dinner he sat at his desk and read his chapters, in case Margaret suspected he had failed. The words on the bluish pages seemed meaningless; even his handwriting looked unfamiliar. His hot eyes felt unfamiliar too.

And now it was Margaret's noises. They sounded forced, unnervingly artificial, sound effects. When he frowned at her she muted them, which only made them more infuriating. Her eyes were red, but he couldn't help it if she was distressed while he felt as he did, besieged deep in himself. "I'm going to bed," she said eventually, like a rebuke. When he couldn't bear sitting alone any longer, she was still awake. He lay with his back to her in order to discourage conversation, which would distract him. Something was certainly wrong with the dark.

In the morning, when she'd gone to work, he saw what he must do. Since he had no chance of writing at weekends or in the evenings, he must give up his daytime job, which was false anyway. His book was more important, it would say things that needed saying – they would be clear when the time came to write them. In the shaving mirror his grin looked weaker than he felt.

He grinned more widely as he phoned to report himself sick. That falseness was enjoyable. He sat grinning at his desk, waiting for words. But he couldn't reach back to the self who had written the chapters; however deep in his mind he groped, there was nothing but a dialogue. Isn't it going well? No, it isn't going well. No, it isn't, no, it isn't, no, it isn't going well. Repression, regression, lycanthropy. Putty faces bobbed past the window. Now here was the bluish light, moulding them into caricatures or worse. Repression, regression, lycanthropy.

"You're home early," Margaret said. He stared at her, probing for the implication, until she looked away.

After dinner she watched television in the bedroom, with the sound turned to a whisper. He followed her, to place more distance between himself and the tinged curtains. As soon as he switched off the light, the living-room was a dead bluish box. When he clawed at the switch, the bluish tinge seemed to have invaded the light of the room.

"You've left the light on."

"Leave it on!" He couldn't tell her why. He was trapped in himself, and his shell felt brittle. In a way it was a relief to be cut off from her that way; at least he needn't struggle to explain. She stared at the screen, she swallowed aspirin, she glanced at him and flinched from his indifferent gaze. Shrunken figures jerked about as though they were trying to escape the box of the television, and they felt as real as he did. After a while Margaret slipped into bed and hid her face. He supposed she was crying.

He lay beside her. Voices crowded his mind, shouting. Repression, regression, lycanthropy. Margaret's hand crept around his waist, but he couldn't bear to be touched; he shook her off. Perhaps she was asleep. Around him the room was faintly luminous. He gazed at it suspiciously until his eyelids drooped.

When he woke, he seemed hardly to have slept. Perhaps the revelation had woken him, for he knew at last what was wrong with the dark. It had developed a faint bluish tinge. How could the light penetrate the closed door? Was it reaching beneath the door for him? Or had the colour settled on his eyeballs, seeped into them?

It hadn't trapped him yet. He sneaked into his clothes. Margaret was a vague draped huddle, dimly bluish. He tiptoed to the front door and let himself out, then he began to run.

At the tower blocks he slowed. Concrete, honeycombed with curtained rectangles, massed above him. Orange sodium mushrooms glared along the paths, blackening the grass. The light outside his flat was worse than that; it was worse than moonlight, because it infected everyone, not just the few. That was why he'd felt so strange lately. It had been transforming him.

He must go back for Margaret. They must leave now, this minute. Tomorrow they'd find somewhere else to live, draw on their savings; they could come back in daylight for their possessions. He must go back, he'd left her alone with the light. He ran, closing his eyes against the light as far as he could.

As he reached the street he heard someone padding towards him – padding like an animal. He dodged into an alley almost opposite the flat, but the padding turned aside somewhere. He grinned at the dark; he could outwit the light now that he knew its secret. But as soon as he emerged into the street he sensed that he was being watched.

He saw the face almost at once. It was staring at him between curtains, beside a reflection of the lamp. The face was a luminous dead mask, full of the light. He could see the animal staring out through the eyes. The mask was inside his flat, staring out at him.

He made himself go forward, or perhaps the light was forcing him. Certainty it had won. His head felt cold and hollow, cut off from his trudging. The eyes widened in the mask; the creature was ready to fly at him. The mask writhed, changing.

Suddenly he caught sight of his shadow. The light was urging it towards the window. Its claws were dangling, its head swelled forward eagerly, and this time there was nothing familiar to hold him back, no light he could switch on to change the dead street and the shadow. There was only the enemy in his home. He was the shadow, one hand dangling near the gutter. He snatched up the brick and smashing the window, struggled in through the splintering frame.

The creature backed away, into a corner. For a moment it seemed to be beaten. But when he leapt, hurling the curtains aside, it fought him with its claws. He struggled with it, breaking it, biting, tearing. At last it was still. He staggered blindly into the bedroom, mopping blood from his eyes with the rags of his sleeve.

He switched on the light, but couldn't tell what colour it was. He felt like a hollow shell. When at last he noticed that the bed was empty, it took him a very long time to force himself to look in the living-room. As he looked, he became less and less sure of what he was seeing. As to who was seeing it, he had no idea at all.

The Thing in the Forest

Bernard Capes

INTO THE SNOW-LOCKED FORESTS of Upper Hungary steal wolves in winter; but there is a footfall worse than theirs to knock upon the heart of the lonely traveller.

One December evening Elspet, the young, newly wedded wife of the woodman Stefan, came hurrying over the lower slopes of the White Mountains from the town where she had been all day marketing. She carried a basket with provisions on her arm; her plump cheeks were like a couple of cold apples; her breath spoke short, but more from nervousness than exhaustion. It was nearing dusk, and she was glad to see the little lonely church in the hollow below, the hub, as it were, of many radiating paths through the trees, one of which was the road to her own warm cottage yet a half-mile away.

She paused a moment at the foot of the slope, undecided about entering the little chill, silent building and making her plea for protection to the great battered stone image of Our Lady of Succour which stood within by the confessional box; but the stillness and the growing darkness decided her, and she went on. A spark of fire glowing through the presbytery window seemed to repel rather than attract her, and she was glad when the convolutions of the path hid it from her sight. Being new to the district, she had seen very little of Father Ruhl as yet, and somehow the penetrating knowledge and burning eyes of the pastor made her feel uncomfortable.

The soft drift, the lane of tall, motionless pines, stretched on in a quiet like death. Somewhere the sun, like a dead fire, had fallen into opalescent embers faintly luminous: they were enough only to touch the shadows with a ghastlier pallor. It was so still that the light crunch in the snow of the girl's own footfalls trod on her heart like a desecration.

Suddenly there was something near her that had not been before. It had come like a shadow, without more sound or warning. It was here – there – behind her. She turned, in mortal panic, and saw a wolf. With a strangled cry and trembling limbs she strove to hurry on her way; and always she knew, though there was no whisper of pursuit, that the gliding shadow followed in her wake. Desperate in her terror, she stopped once more and faced it.

A wolf! – Was it a wolf? O who could doubt it! Yet the wild expression in those famished eyes, so lost, so pitiful, so mingled of insatiable hunger and human need! Condemned, for its unspeakable sins, to take this form with sunset, and so howl and snuffle about the doors of men until the blessed day released it. A werewolf – not a wolf.

That terrific realization of the truth smote the girl as with a knife out of darkness: for an instant she came near fainting. And then a low moan broke into her heart and flooded it with pity. So lost, so infinitely hopeless. And so pitiful – yes, in spite of all, so pitiful. It had sinned, beyond any sinning that her innocence knew or her experience could gauge; but she was a woman, very blest, very happy, in her store of comforts and her surety of love. She knew that it was forbidden to succour these damned and nameless outcasts, to help or sympathize with them in any way.

But –

There was good store of meat in her basket, and who need ever know or tell? With shaking hands she found and threw a sop to the desolate brute – then, turning, sped upon her way. But at home her secret sin stood up before her, and, interposing between her husband and herself, threw its shadow upon both their faces. What had she dared – what done? By her own act forfeited her birthright of innocence; by her own act placed herself in the power of the evil to which she had ministered. All that night she lay in shame and horror, and all the next day, until Stefan had come about his dinner and gone again, she moved in a dumb agony. Then, driven unendurably by the memory of his troubled, bewildered face, as twilight threatened she put on her cloak and went down to the little church in the hollow to confess her sin.

"Mother, forgive, and save me," she whispered, as she passed the statue.

After ringing the bell for the confessor, she had not knelt long at the confessional box in the dim chapel, cold and empty as a waiting vault, when the chancel rail clicked, and the footsteps of Father Ruhl were heard rustling over the stones. He came, he took his seat behind the grating; and, with many sighs and falterings, Elspet avowed her guilt. And as, with bowed head, she ended, a strange sound answered her – it was like a little laugh, and yet not so much like a laugh as a snarl. With a shock as of death she raised her face. It was Father Ruhl who sat there – and yet it was not Father Ruhl. In that time of twilight his face was already changing, narrowing, becoming wolfish – the eyes rounded and the jaw slavered. She gasped, and shrunk back; and at that, barking and snapping at the grating, with a wicked look he dropped – and she heard him coming. Sheer horror lent her wings. With a scream she sprang to her feet and fled. Her cloak caught in something – there was a wrench and crash and, like a flood, oblivion overswept her.

It was the old deaf and near senile sacristan who found them lying there, the woman unhurt but insensible, the priest crushed out of life by the fall of the ancient statue, long tottering to its collapse. She recovered, for her part: for his, no one knows where he lies buried. But there were dark stories of a baying pack that night, and of an empty, bloodstained pavement when they came to seek for the body.

Dance, Mephisto

Catherine Cavendish

I WAS THERE the day Hitler's troops marched into Vienna. March 12th, 1938. It was called the Anschluss – union – but it really meant the total surrender of Austria and absorption into the Nazi state.

I was in Heldenplatz – Heroes Square – alone among a cast of thousands of cheering men, women and children, while that absurd peacock postured, gesticulated, and bathed in adulation.

But here is not where my story begins. Of my early life you need know only this: I was born Liesel Kessler, in a small village nestling in the foothills of the Oetscher Mountains of Lower Austria. My mother died shortly after giving birth to me and my father was killed a month later. I was raised by Oma – my maternal grandmother – in a two-roomed wooden shack, isolated from its neighbors by fields and forests. With no siblings or other children to play with, my best friends were wild animals who seemed to sense a kindred spirit in me and posed no danger. I always felt safe in the forest even when I spent entire nights out in the open, nestled under a tall, aromatic pine tree, allowing the sounds of the night creatures to lull me to sleep.

On one such balmy summer night on my sixteenth birthday, the full moon cast silvery beams, illuminating the forest floor. Overhead, an owl hooted, the tone of its cry issuing a warning that set my hackles rising. I listened intently. A twig snapped nearby. Leaves rustled, their movement catching my eye. A few feet away something moved. I felt its eyes on me. My heart beat faster. My mouth ran dry.

The bushes parted and I saw him – a sleek, beautiful wolf with gleaming black fur, a long snout and eyes of the brightest azure. He advanced toward me, seemingly concerned not to frighten me, closer and closer until the tips of my fingers touched his fur. I wanted to sink my fingers into its luxurious depths. I smelled the animal warmth of him, and stroked his velvety ears. From his throat emanated a low-pitched rumble of pleasure so soporific, my eyes closed as the desire to sleep overwhelmed me.

Then I was waking up, in bed, the early morning sun pouring into my room. That was the last time I would awaken in my beloved Oetscher for, mere hours later, we were packed and my grandmother told me she was taking me to Vienna, miles to the east.

"It is time, Liesel. There is someone you must meet. A man. He is your cousin, Johannes."

Although I always trusted and never questioned Oma, this time fear struck me. I had so little experience of anyone. Not other children and certainly not men. Now Oma was suggesting that I should move to the city? I had read about Vienna in books and old magazines that Oma used when teaching me my letters and words. I knew it was our country's capital and our Emperor lived there but nothing else. I didn't want to go, but Oma said I must.

I could smell the city long before we reached it. Unfamiliar and unpleasant aromas wafted toward us on the breeze. Smoke from the many chimneys and, as we came closer, other noisome fumes entered the mix, the detritus of many thousands of people and horses living in close proximity. I had never seen so many houses and magnificent buildings built of stone when everywhere around me had been constructed of timber. And the roads… Oma told me the Emperor had ordered the old center of Vienna to be swept away and a wide circular road called the Ringstrasse to be built. All around this stylish thoroughfare, were magnificent buildings, and palatial residences for the many aristocratic families of our sprawling Empire.

We turned into a narrow street and there before me rose the baroque elegance of the Palais Dachstein.

"This is your new home," Oma announced, and I stared up at it. Dumbstruck.

Oma kissed me. Something she never did. She had tears in her eyes, and she never wept. "I must leave you, child. Here is where you belong, among your own kind. Your cousin is your guardian now. Goodbye, Liesel."

And she was gone. I never saw her again. But I had little time to mourn. The next days and weeks were a blur while they taught me how to be a young lady. My first teacher was my maid, Gerda, who dressed me, styled my hair, showed me how to eat and use the correct cutlery and introduced me to my ancestors.

Their portraits adorned the Long Gallery on the first floor and Gerda steered me along, stopping at each one. A general here, a financier there, various patrons of the arts. Elegant men with portraits of their wives next to them. And we were nobility. My rightful name was Kessler von Dachstein, and Johannes was the current Count.

The portrait of the cousin I had yet to meet enthralled me. Like all his male forebears, he possessed vivid blue eyes – the same eyes I saw every time I looked in a mirror. His shiny black hair was slicked back over his head, and the hand that held his sword hilt was ungloved, displaying long, slender fingers. His lips showed the merest hint of a smile and despite my fears and trepidations, I couldn't wait to meet him. I was told he was on a lengthy tour of Asia but would return in the autumn. And, one day, he did.

A poor reader, I had barely set foot in the library but, as the footman opened the door, I felt drawn in by a warm aroma of leather, beeswax and rich tobacco.

He stood by the fire, a cigar in one hand and a crystal glass containing a drink I later learned to be schnapps, in the other. At my entrance, he diverted his attention from the darting flames to me, and straightened to his full height revealing himself to be the tallest man I had ever laid eyes on. At well over six feet, he was a good six inches taller than any of the male servants. Being at least eighteen inches shorter, I had never felt so small. In that second my already miniscule self-confidence waned, only to disappear altogether by what happened next.

From nowhere, a creature resembling a small, slender, long-limbed black monkey leaped, screeching, onto the shoulder of my cousin who dissolved into gales of hearty laughter while I backed away and slammed into the closed door behind me. My left hand scrabbled in vain for the handle, as Johannes took a few strides closer, while the monkey screamed warnings at me to keep away. Clearly the animal believed his master to be his sole possession and no one was allowed near. My cousin laid his glass and cigar down before deftly maneuvering the creature off his shoulder and onto the floor amid much caterwauling. I was frozen to the spot, afraid any movement would send the monkey racing to scratch my eyes out.

"Now, Mephisto. That is no way to behave. This is my cousin, Liesel. She has come to live here and you must be nice to her. Come, say hello." But all this served to anger the animal still further until it seemed to have hysterics.

"I know what we'll do." Johannes strode over to a concert piano in the corner of the book-lined room and sat down to play. I didn't know it then but it was one of Mozart's dances. As soon as Johannes hit the first note, Mephisto quietened his racket and began to dance, swaying, leaping, performing moves I would now say Nijinsky himself could not have bettered.

"Yes!" Johannes exclaimed. "Dance, Mephisto. Dance!"

When Johannes finished his final note, the monkey sank to a graceful bow and I found myself applauding. Mephisto raised his black eyes and blinked at me and in them I read a curious mix of high intelligence and curiosity, along with an emerging empathy. Tentatively he approached me.

"He likes you," Johannes said. "Stay still and let him come to you. Don't make any sudden moves. Let him smell you and see you are his friend."

Johannes's baritone voice was softly modulated and almost hypnotic. I did as he advised and Mephisto came up to me, sniffed my feet, and then, apparently satisfied, reached up his arms.

"He wants you to pick him up. This is a great honor. I am the only person he allows to do that."

"Is it permitted for me to do this?"

"Of course. If Mephisto wants you to, then so it must be. I deny him nothing. He is my friend, my confidante and even on occasion, has been known to save my life. Maybe one day he will do the same for you."

Mephisto was surprisingly light and lay comfortably in my arms. He sniffed my face and planted a soft kiss on my lips which was surprisingly pleasant, before nestling his warm, furry head in my neck. His aroma wasn't unpleasant. Animal-like, but clean and warm. He linked his long, wiry arms around my shoulders and made a snuffling noise I took to be contentment, not unlike a cat's purr.

"You see, Mephisto is like us. He is a breed apart, and so are we." Johannes seemed to be studying me as I was studying him. I wondered if he was drawn to me in the same way. For the first time in my life, I experienced feelings I couldn't explain, warm, sensual awakenings and stirrings. His fingers stroked the crystal glass and I wanted to feel his hands caressing my face. His eyes drew me into their depths, making me want to go to him and, as his lips savored the drink, I yearned to know how it would taste if my lips were pressed to his, partaking in that drink with him, sharing a kiss that perhaps first cousins should not permit themselves. Yet weren't our Emperor and Empress also cousins?

* * *

In the weeks and months that followed, I never once questioned my place at Palais Dachstein. It seems incredible now that I had been there fully two years before I learned the full story of who I was and why I was there. I suppose it was because for the first time in my life I was experiencing true happiness and never wanted it to end. My life was with Johannes, by his side at all times while he taught me everything a young aristocratic lady should know.

Johannes threw lavish parties and an invitation was much coveted in Viennese society. Ah, those long-ago golden days at the end of the nineteenth century; the last years of our great Empire, although we didn't know it then.

Mephisto had the run of the house. Occasionally he would make an impromptu appearance at a party and cause general mayhem. He took great delight in leaping down from chandeliers and scaring ladies who ran screaming away. This set him off on one of his hysterical rages and Johannes would leap to the piano and play Mozart.

"Dance, Mephisto!" he would yell and the monkey would stun everyone into silence by his prowess, earning himself a standing ovation.

The day of my eighteenth birthday is one I will never forget. How could I? It was the day I learned what I have been ever since.

It was the day Johannes revealed his true nature to me.

After dinner, he took me into the library and poured me my first schnapps. We toasted each other and I raised the glass to my lips. I was aware of movement and, in the flickering firelight, glimpsed Mephisto slinking across the room to sit at the feet of his beloved master.

I took my first sip and the liquid burned my tongue. I screwed up my eyes and swallowed hard. The sharpness of it made me cough.

"Now another sip," Johannes said.

I hesitated.

"No, I insist. You will see. This time it will warm you and you will taste the flavor of the pears."

Reluctantly I did what I was told and he was right. Instead of burning, the liquid warmed and soothed. "It tastes of summer," I said, and Johannes laughed.

"Now you're ready, my Liesel."

I loved it when he called me 'his' Liesel. It always made me tingle inside and the combination of that, and the unaccustomed strong alcohol, sent my head spinning.

Johannes came toward me. His warm, familiar, natural scent seemed especially intoxicating tonight. He took the glass from my hand and set it down on the table next to my chair before taking my hand and raising me to my feet.

"Come, my Liesel," he murmured and I followed him.

He led me to a corner of the library where he indicated a shelf of books on medieval history. He touched three volumes in order and made me watch closely. "You must remember this. Only in this sequence will it work. One day you may need this. It could save your life."

I forced myself to concentrate and commit what I saw to my memory where it has resided ever since. An audible click followed by a slight movement of the entire case of books revealed a hidden door. Johannes opened it and removed a candelabra from a shelf inside. He took a matchbox from his pocket and lit each candle, then led me inside, swiftly followed by Mephisto who scampered ahead, making barely a sound, as did my soft-soled shoes. Only Johannes's dress shoes tapped against the stone floor as we proceeded along the fusty corridor within the walls of Palais Dachstein until we reached a closed door. Johannes showed me a loose stone in the wall – something else I would need to remember for behind it lay the key that would unlock the intricate mechanism that had protected what lay beyond for centuries. The candles flickered wildly as a rush of air greeted the opening of the heavy door. Shadows danced off the walls and the flames lit up a stone staircase leading down into a black abyss. The effect of the alcohol had abated and fear propelled a cold hand to clutch my heart.

Johannes must have sensed this. "You have nothing to fear," he said. "Come with me. I will show you."

We reached the bottom and I touched the wall. My hand felt heat. The chimney must be on the other side. That explained the relative warmth in this cellar. I felt a light breeze and looked for its source. Sure enough, ahead was a grating. I knew it was a full moon tonight and the sky was clear. Silvery light filtered through into the dark cellar.

Johannes touched my hand. "You must listen to me, Liesel. I haven't long and you mustn't question anything I say. In a short while you will watch me change from the person you see before you, and become something you haven't seen since the day of your sixteenth birthday. Do you remember?"

I nodded. As he spoke, his voice grew deeper, rougher, and there was something about the smell he was giving off. It had become more feral…yet familiar.

"What I will tell you now will seem the stuff of folklore. But most folk tales have an element of truth in them and so it is with us. You and I are different, Liesel. There are few of us left but we come from a long line of shapeshifters that trace their ancestry back to the dawn of time. You will see me transform and you'll come with me. You will watch me hunt tonight and see me kill to eat as I am bound to do. Next month we will hunt together. Have no fear, my Liesel, for no harm shall come to you from me. Not tonight and not ever. Do you understand?"

I didn't, of course, but strangely I wasn't afraid, and stranger still, it was as if a door had opened in my mind and everything about myself became clear. Fascinated, I watched as, in the flickering candlelight, his features changed, almost imperceptibly at first. While still in human form, he removed his clothes and stood before me, a naked man, but within seconds, he was on all fours and silky black fur spread across his skin as if some invisible hand had laid a blanket over him.

You don't need me to explain the strange and awful sounds of cracking bones that accompanied the transformation from man to wolf, but when it was done and the exquisite beast stood there, his gleaming azure eyes upon me, I couldn't resist the urge to put my arms around him and bury my face in his warm fur. The heady aroma of it intoxicated me. But there was work to do and Mephisto took charge. I realized how valuable the monkey's dexterous fingers were to a creature with wolf's paws. Mephisto manipulated the catch on the grating, which, as a wolf, would have been beyond his master's capabilities. Mephisto let himself out and held the grating open for Johannes to slip through. I followed, shutting it behind me.

The moon illuminated our way. Mephisto darted this way and that, watchful for his master's safety. I followed his lead, moving from doorway to doorway, learning to be alert to every sound that might signal a human abroad late in the silent city streets.

Then, an almost indistinguishable noise. Mephisto grabbed my hand and tugged me inside a courtyard where I could see a man, alone, staggering from the effects of too much alcohol. A sudden flash of black, the slightest of protesting cries and he was brought down. Dead.

Johannes feasted that night.

* * *

We never spoke of it. There seemed no need. We were what we were and I knew what I would need to do.

My first metamorphosis felt strange. The bone-cracking didn't hurt, much to my surprise. It was merely an odd sensation and a compulsion to get down on all fours before the inevitable happened and I had no choice. I saw my paws for the first time – as black as Johannes's. I must look just like him. That night we ran together and I made my first kill.

It wasn't as clean as Johannes. That took around six moons to perfect, but I learned. I would like to say we only took the old, sick and infirm, but we didn't. We usually took those who would provide us with the greatest sustenance. Young, tender, on the plump side. I loved how my senses were heightened. I could smell my prey before I saw them, and my eyesight was so keen I could see them long before my human senses would have even been aware of anyone.

The years progressed but I never aged physically from that day to this. Johannes, too, remained young and strong. Our love deepened, strengthened. Never physically consummated, although we came close many times especially in our wolf state, but Johannes made it clear, the risk was too great. We must not bring more of our kind into the world. It was preordained. Our course was run. It was time to be truly designated to the stuff of myth and fantasy. I learned that was why my father had been killed. He refused to accept this and had escaped from his family in order to start one of his own. Yes, my beloved Johannes killed my father and, to be sure he could not regenerate, consumed his body. I forgave him. I loved him too much not to and my father had, after all, done wrong in procreating me.

Johannes taught me the only ways shapeshifters like us can die. One that may surprise you is that we can end our own lives. If all seems completely hopeless, we can starve our bodies, lock ourselves away with no means of escape during a full moon, lay down and, in the absence of lunar light, use our mental strength of mind to shut ourselves down, allowing the ageing process to catch up in a matter of hours so we die quickly. Painlessly.

* * *

The First World War ended in defeat for Austria, the break-up of the Empire and the end of monarchy. It also meant the end of the nobility. Johannes and I became Herr and Fräulein Kessler-Dachstein. We still lived in the palace but only on the ground floor with no servants, Johannes's finances having been much depleted during Austria's terrible interwar financial crises.

After the Anschluss, life grew harsher for many in Austria. First the Jews were persecuted, rounded up and transported off to concentration camps, then more of us began to fear the dreaded knock at the door. Only our most trusted servants had known our secret. But the SS had methods of extracting information few could resist. With Mephisto our constant and sole companion, Johannes and I spent every night in the cellar. One morning we emerged to find our home had been ransacked. The Nazis had taken everything of any value. All the paintings, silverware, crystal.

The day they took Johannes, I was late rising from my bed. Johannes and Mephisto had gone up before me to try to find food for the day. I was climbing the steps when the sounds of shouting followed by a couple of shots sent fear coursing through me. I forced myself to pause at the entrance to the library. The noise died away to nothing. I opened the door, saw blood and knew it was Johannes's. No sign of Mephisto, although he would have been there. He never left his master.

I crept to the front door which stood half off its hinges. Outside, chaos. Rubble and shattered glass greeted me. People milled around. A scarf concealing my face, I managed to blend in with the crowd and that's when I saw him.

He lay, beaten and battered, on the ground. Blood poured from a wound in his shoulder and my heart cried out to him. I wanted to run to him but his voice in my head told me to stay back.

I struggled to the front and our eyes locked one last time. I felt our mutual love pouring out, finding each other. Mingling. Somewhere across that wrecked, bloodied street our spirits met for one brief moment before the soldier raised his bayonet and drove it through my beloved's heart.

That was two years ago.

Now they say the war is over. The Americans, British, French and Russians are all claiming victory and have taken over the city they have done their best to destroy with their bombs. The magnificent cathedral lies in ruins, its spire somehow managing to still point upward to a heaven I no longer believe exists. The Opera House is unrecognizable. The grand buildings on the Ringstrasse are collapsed mountains of twisted metal, broken concrete, shattered glass. There is no food, the water is impure, and disease and starvation stalk the streets. Of Mephisto there has been no sign since that awful day they murdered my beloved Johannes.

I have decided to end my life. I'm now a very old woman although to the world I still look eighteen. I've closed the grating I had wedged open. Without Mephisto I couldn't open it in my wolf-state. Now I won't need to.

I have made myself comfortable here. I even found a gramophone and some records upstairs in what remains of our home. I play it now and again. Mozart of course. In case he can hear it…

* * *

It is time.

The sun has set and I feel my body wanting to change but I'm ready. I've blocked up the grating with heavy dark material so not one drop of moonlight can seep in. A solitary candle illuminates my surroundings as I place the record on the gramophone and lay down, ready to drift away.

I snatch a quick look at the cracked carriage clock. Midnight. My body is protesting. It wants to change but I won't allow it. Soon, my spirit will beg for release.

I fancy I hear Mephisto. Yes, I smell his fur. He's here. He has returned. He nuzzles my cheek… kisses my lips… The music plays on.

"Dance, Mephisto!" I cry. "Dance for me. One more time."

The Lay of the Were-Wolf

French Medieval Romance by Marie de France

AMONGST THE TALES I tell you once again, I would not forget the Lay of the Were-Wolf. Such beasts as he are known in every land. Bisclavaret he is named in Brittany; whilst the Norman calls him Garwal.

It is a certain thing, and within the knowledge of all, that many a christened man has suffered this change, and ran wild in woods, as a Were-Wolf. The Were-Wolf is a fearsome beast. He lurks within the thick forest, mad and horrible to see. All the evil that he may, he does. He goeth to and fro, about the solitary place, seeking man, in order to devour him. Hearken, now, to the adventure of the Were-Wolf, that I have to tell.

In Brittany there dwelt a baron who was marvellously esteemed of all his fellows. He was a stout knight, and a comely, and a man of office and repute. Right private was he to the mind of his lord, and dear to the counsel of his neighbours. This baron was wedded to a very worthy dame, right fair to see, and sweet of semblance. All his love was set on her, and all her love was given again to him. One only grief had this lady. For three whole days in every week her lord was absent from her side. She knew not where he went, nor on what errand. Neither did any of his house know the business which called him forth.

On a day when this lord was come again to his house, altogether joyous and content, the lady took him to task, right sweetly, in this fashion, "Husband," said she, "and fair, sweet friend, I have a certain thing to pray of you. Right willingly would I receive this gift, but I fear to anger you in the asking. It is better for me to have an empty hand, than to gain hard words."

When the lord heard this matter, he took the lady in his arms, very tenderly, and kissed her.

"Wife," he answered, "ask what you will. What would you have, for it is yours already?"

"By my faith," said the lady, "soon shall I be whole. Husband, right long and wearisome are the days that you spend away from your home. I rise from my bed in the morning, sick at heart, I know not why. So fearful am I, lest you do aught to your loss, that I may not find any comfort. Very quickly shall I die for reason of my dread. Tell me now, where you go, and on what business! How may the knowledge of one who loves so closely, bring you to harm?"

"Wife," made answer the lord, "nothing but evil can come if I tell you this secret. For the mercy of God do not require it of me. If you but knew, you would withdraw yourself from my love, and I should be lost indeed."

When the lady heard this, she was persuaded that her baron sought to put her by with jesting words. Therefore she prayed and required him the more urgently, with tender looks and speech, till he was overborne, and told her all the story, hiding naught.

"Wife, I become Bisclavaret. I enter in the forest, and live on prey and roots, within the thickest of the wood."

After she had learned his secret, she prayed and entreated the more as to whether he ran in his raiment, or went spoiled of vesture.

"Wife," said he, "I go naked as a beast."

"Tell me, for hope of grace, what you do with your clothing?"

"Fair wife, that will I never. If I should lose my raiment, or even be marked as I quit my vesture, then a Were-Wolf I must go for all the days of my life. Never again should I become man, save in that hour my clothing were given back to me. For this reason never will I show my lair."

"Husband," replied the lady to him, "I love you better than all the world. The less cause have you for doubting my faith, or hiding any tittle from me. What savour is here of friendship? How have I made forfeit of your love; for what sin do you mistrust my honour? Open now your heart, and tell what is good to be known."

So at the end, outwearied and overborne by her importunity, he could no longer refrain, but told her all.

"Wife," said he, "within this wood, a little from the path, there is a hidden way, and at the end thereof an ancient chapel, where oftentimes I have bewailed my lot. Near by is a great hollow stone, concealed by a bush, and there is the secret place where I hide my raiment, till I would return to my own home."

On hearing this marvel the lady became sanguine of visage, because of her exceeding fear. She dared no longer to lie at his side, and turned over in her mind, this way and that, how best she could get her from him. Now there was a certain knight of those parts, who, for a great while, had sought and required this lady for her love. This knight had spent long years in her service, but little enough had he got thereby, not even fair words, or a promise. To him the dame wrote a letter, and meeting, made her purpose plain.

"Fair friend," said she, "be happy. That which you have coveted so long a time, I will grant without delay. Never again will I deny your suit. My heart, and all I have to give, are yours, so take me now as love and dame."

Right sweetly the knight thanked her for her grace, and pledged her faith and fealty. When she had confirmed him by an oath, then she told him all this business of her lord – why he went, and what he became, and of his ravening within the wood. So she showed him of the chapel, and of the hollow stone, and of how to spoil the Were-Wolf of his vesture. Thus, by the kiss of his wife, was Bisclavaret betrayed. Often enough had he ravished his prey in desolate places, but from this journey he never returned. His kinsfolk and acquaintance came together to ask of his tidings, when this absence was noised abroad. Many a man, on many a day, searched the woodland, but none might find him, nor learn where Bisclavaret was gone.

The lady was wedded to the knight who had cherished her for so long a space. More than a year had passed since Bisclavaret disappeared. Then it chanced that the King would hunt in that self-same wood where the Were-Wolf lurked. When the hounds were unleashed they ran this way and that, and swiftly came upon his scent. At the view the huntsman winded on his horn, and the whole pack were at his heels. They followed him from morn to eve, till he was torn and bleeding, and was all adread lest they should pull him down. Now the King was very close to the quarry, and when Bisclavaret looked upon his master, he ran to him for pity and for grace. He took the stirrup within his paws, and fawned upon the prince's foot. The King was very fearful at this sight, but presently he called his courtiers to his aid.

"Lords," cried he, "hasten hither, and see this marvellous thing. Here is a beast who has the sense of man. He abases himself before his foe, and cries for mercy, although he cannot speak. Beat off the hounds, and let no man do him harm. We will hunt no more today, but return to our own place, with the wonderful quarry we have taken."

The King turned him about, and rode to his hall, Bisclavaret following at his side. Very near to his master the Were-Wolf went, like any dog, and had no care to seek again the wood. When the King had brought him safely to his own castle, he rejoiced greatly, for the beast was fair and strong, no mightier had any man seen. Much pride had the King in his marvellous beast. He held him so dear, that he bade all those who wished for his love, to cross the Wolf in naught, neither to strike him with a rod, but ever to see that he was richly fed and kennelled warm. This commandment the Court observed willingly. So all the day the Wolf sported with the lords, and at night he lay within the chamber of the King. There was not a man who did not make much of the beast, so frank was he and debonair. None had reason to do him wrong, for ever was he about his master, and for his part did evil to none. Every day were these two companions together, and all perceived that the King loved him as his friend.

Hearken now to that which chanced.

The King held a high Court, and bade his great vassals and barons, and all the lords of his venery to the feast. Never was there a goodlier feast, nor one set forth with sweeter show and pomp. Amongst those who were bidden, came that same knight who had the wife of Bisclavaret for dame. He came to the castle, richly gowned, with a fair company, but little he deemed whom he would find so near. Bisclavaret marked his foe the moment he stood within the hall. He ran towards him, and seized him with his fangs, in the King's very presence, and to the view of all. Doubtless he would have done him much mischief, had not the King called and chidden him, and threatened him with a rod. Once, and twice, again, the Wolf set upon the knight in the very light of day. All men marvelled at his malice, for sweet and serviceable was the beast, and to that hour had shown hatred of none. With one consent the household deemed that this deed was done with full reason, and that the Wolf had suffered at the knight's hand some bitter wrong. Right wary of his foe was the knight until the feast had ended, and all the barons had taken farewell of their lord, and departed, each to his own house. With these, amongst the very first, went that lord whom Bisclavaret so fiercely had assailed. Small was the wonder that he was glad to go.

No long while after this adventure it came to pass that the courteous King would hunt in that forest where Bisclavaret was found. With the prince came his wolf, and a fair company. Now at nightfall the King abode within a certain lodge of that country, and this was known of that dame who before was the wife of Bisclavaret. In the morning the lady clothed her in her most dainty apparel, and hastened to the lodge, since she desired to speak with the King, and to offer him a rich present. When the lady entered in the chamber, neither man nor leash might restrain the fury of the Wolf. He became as a mad dog in his hatred and malice. Breaking from his bonds he sprang at the lady's face, and bit the nose from her visage. From every side men ran to the succour of the dame. They beat off the wolf from his prey, and for a little would have cut him in pieces with their swords. But a certain wise counsellor said to the King,

"Sire, hearken now to me. This beast is always with you, and there is not one of us all who has not known him for long. He goes in and out amongst us, nor has molested any man, neither done wrong or felony to any, save only to this dame, one only time as we have seen. He has done evil to this lady, and to that knight, who is now the husband of the dame. Sire, she was once the wife of that lord who was so close and private to your heart, but who went, and none might find where he had gone. Now, therefore, put the dame in a sure place, and question her straitly, so that she may tell – if perchance she knows thereof – for what reason this Beast holds her in such mortal hate. For many a strange deed has chanced, as well we know, in this marvellous land of Brittany."

The King listened to these words, and deemed the counsel good. He laid hands upon the knight, and put the dame in surety in another place. He caused them to be questioned right straitly, so that their torment was very grievous. At the end, partly because of her distress, and partly by reason of her exceeding fear, the lady's lips were loosed, and she told her tale. She showed them of the betrayal of her lord, and how his raiment was stolen from the hollow stone.

Since then she knew not where he went, nor what had befallen him, for he had never come again to his own land. Only, in her heart, well she deemed and was persuaded, that Bisclavaret was he.

Straightway the King demanded the vesture of his baron, whether this were to the wish of the lady, or whether it were against her wish. When the raiment was brought him, he caused it to be spread before Bisclavaret, but the Wolf made as though he had not seen. Then that cunning and crafty counsellor took the King apart, that he might give him a fresh rede.

"Sire," said he, "you do not wisely, nor well, to set this raiment before Bisclavaret, in the sight of all. In shame and much tribulation must he lay aside the beast, and again become man. Carry your wolf within your most secret chamber, and put his vestment therein. Then close the door upon him, and leave him alone for a space. So we shall see presently whether the ravening beast may indeed return to human shape."

The King carried the Wolf to his chamber, and shut the doors upon him fast. He delayed for a brief while, and taking two lords of his fellowship with him, came again to the room. Entering therein, all three, softly together, they found the knight sleeping in the King's bed, like a little child. The King ran swiftly to the bed and taking his friend in his arms, embraced and kissed him fondly, above a hundred times. When man's speech returned once more, he told him of his adventure. Then the King restored to his friend the fief that was stolen from him, and gave such rich gifts, moreover, as I cannot tell. As for the wife who had betrayed Bisclavaret, he bade her avoid his country, and chased her from the realm. So she went forth, she and her second lord together, to seek a more abiding city, and were no more seen.

The adventure that you have heard is no vain fable. Verily and indeed it chanced as I have said. The Lay of the Were-Wolf, truly, was written that it should ever be borne in mind.

Rougarou Moon

E.C. Dorgan

Sarah

I'M ONLY PRETENDING to play bingo. The game's in my blood, but I'm rusty. I spent days in these bingo halls as a child, sitting beside my grandma. It's my first time back in thirteen years. Now I have a degree and a research question. A university expense account. Training in field methods. A plan to find myself.

The first few games are a write-off; I'm missing half the caller's numbers. I'm not here to play, but it still irks me. By the second hour, I can almost keep up. I feel muscle memory awakening. Between games, my ears prick.

"I was berry-picking…something in the bush…"

I scan the hall for the speaker, and then I see her – an old lady eating cheese twists at the back. She takes her time, choosing her words with care. I reach for my pen. Her companions roll their eyes. The old lady trails off.

I see her at the break at the snacks table. Come up beside her while she's pouring coffee. This time, I'm prepared. She puts down her styrofoam, and I'm there with the creamer. Our eyes meet, and I ask about the rougarou.

Elzéar

I'm looking out at the city from the skyscraper, trying to get through my client meetings, but the hunger's too much, rising from my haunches in waves. I take five for an Americano with an extra shot. Drink it fast and torch my tongue. My appetite's hotter.

Back in my office, I'm killing it. It's a cut-throat industry – my salary's based on sales. Me and my co-workers are bad-ass – when we're not selling up clients, we're one-upping each other's extreme workouts and competing to see who can drink the most high-end whiskey at the bar.

But this new boss – she's not normal. She's hardcore on sales, then makes us sit in a circle and share. We're supposed to keep "reflection journals." I don't reflect. I have my own way of coping: I go home and put my headphone volume to the max. Get naked and howl at the shower head. Curl in a ball on stained carpet and bite my thumbs until they bleed.

When the new boss convenes us, I press my pen into my blank pad and smash the nib. My co-workers complain about their lives and responsibilities. I would kill to be owned by the man, the job, the mortgage. I have the moon in my bones.

Sarah

Four days of spinning my wheels on Saskatchewan roads, getting weird looks in bingo halls, and I have only two pages to show for it. My notes aren't even good – more observations than actual research. I should be farther ahead by now. I'm from here, I'm Métis. The university approved my topic: *Otipemisiwak (The People Who Own Themselves) and the Rougarou*. They're paying for my rental car. I came all the way here from Ontario.

I know this place. Spent time here when I was little, berry picking and playing bingo with my grandma, swimming in prairie lakes with my cousins. I thought I'd get more from that old lady at the bingo hall. But she clocked me right away as an outsider. Was it my clothes? And to think, she was a berry-picker.

Berry-picking – that's something special. I can't come out and say it in my research plan, but it's couched there in my field methods, the one thing that didn't come from a book. I learned about berry-picking from my grandma.

You're more likely to meet a rougarou on a deserted road at night. They'll come after you if you're alone, or if you've been gambling or playing cards. Berry-picking, on the other hand – you have to be sharp. Don't want to run into a bear, or an angry moose. You have to keep your wits. Sometimes, you find more than berries. My grandma thought berry-picking was the world.

Elzéar

I start a damn journal. But it's a man's journal: black alligator leather, with brushed metal edges. We sit in our circle, and I write about gouging clients and beating my record on pull-ups. I break three pens.

The moon swells. I lie in bed without sleeping. The bones in my hands and feet arch skyward, and my teeth pine for things to crunch. Spine itches, hungry to make ribs. There's vomit on my pillow in the morning. I can read the moon by it. Macaroni and undercooked steak when it's waxing. Eyeglasses, clothes tags, and acrylic nails when it wanes. The full moon is in three days – tomorrow will be worse.

It must be moon madness that makes me open that alligator leather over breakfast. I know I shouldn't, but once I start writing, I can't stop. I'm not writing about workouts anymore. Now, what I write makes me break prongs off my forks, and crack the kitchen table with my grip. Things like her name...

I arrive to work late, still wearing my headphones, serviette tucked in collar. My co-workers' eyes widen when they see me. I show them teeth and ramp up the volume. I take my journal, and lock myself in my office. Look out the window and write.

Sarah

Three days later, I've exhausted the bingo halls, and I can't take any more country markets with all their crocheted things and jams. I have to be back at the university on Monday. They're expecting a field study. I thought it would be easier, that people would still know me. All these years in the east, cut off from family... I don't want to be a failure.

My grandma knew the old stories about rougarou, but I never asked her. I was too busy trying to leave, hungry to become someone else. I was seventeen when I moved east. I learned Métis folklore from books.

My grandma grew up around here. I remember the name of the community, but when I put it in my phone, I can't find it. I plug what I remember into my methodology: an old settlement based on river lots, links to the Resistance, those old Métis families. It meets all the indicators for my study.

I don't have a better idea, so I try it. Five minutes off the paved highway, my rental car GPS becomes a revolving circle. I know the general direction, maybe I can find it. My grandma didn't use maps. She navigated by land and bush, and especially by berries. She knew all the places for berries in this landscape.

The road is over-gravelled, so I have to drive slow. I pass sloughs and willows, and dust clouds rise from my wheels. The air is thick with dragonflies. There are no other cars. I have no idea where I am on the map, but I know I'm in saskatoon and chokecherry country – land for berry-picking, land for rougarou.

Elzéar

Tonight's the full moon. Client meetings are intolerable. I've set my headphones to the max, while I babble to some fool on a screen. Don't know what I'm saying. No idea who I'm meeting. I'm looking out the window at the city below. It's like any prairie city: there's a perfect line where the city stops, and the land opens up to sky.

I've had this view for years, but only now it hits me – it faces east. That's where my home is. My wife. That's where the moon took me.

When we gather for the reflection session, that journal's burning up in my hands. It's cursed, what it's doing to me, stirring up memories, feeding this crazy July moon. They say the Wolf Moon's in winter, but I know it's these long days and short nights that fuel the moon's rage.

I seethe in my suit while my co-workers reflect. I can't bear another moment in this skyscraper, this city. Another morning, waking to a nightmare on my pillow. I'm tired of shitting eyeglasses.

When my boss asks me to share, I put down my work phone and laptop. I rip off my lanyard and tell her, "I'm done."

I hold that journal so tight, it scalds my knuckles. I take the elevator all 32 floors down, and step eastward into sun.

Sarah

The sky looms and looms. It's hard to see, with all the dragonflies splattered on the windshield. The only sound for miles is crickets. The gravel thins. Now the road is mostly potholes. A coyote crosses in front of my car. I'm going to need gas soon.

My indicator light's flashing red, and I'm almost on empty, when I come to a town. It's not my grandma's but it's close. There's a gas station with an old-fashioned pump. I have to ask the attendant how to use it. Something about her face nags at me.

I follow her to the cash and take my time rummaging for my wallet.

"Have you seen the rougarou?" The gravel's parched my throat. I stumble on the syllables.

Her lip twitches, but her slouch stills.

I change tack, and ask if she knows my grandma's town.

Her face changes. "Who's your grandma?"

I should have known – we're related. It's a risk in these parts – all these big Métis families. She declares us third cousins.

"You should meet my Uncle Joe."

She tells me he knows old stories. He's not on the map either, so she sends me off with directions. His dogs find me before I reach his house. I follow tire tracks through long grass, to what might have been a farm. Rocks and twigs crunch under the chassis, and I hope the rental company won't ding me.

When I park the car, the dogs mob me, leaving slobber on my jeans, then they run back to the road, after a distant car. An old man in a walker shuffles to the screen door. I have no idea what time it is.

"Florence's granddaughter?"

My third cousin told him about me. We sit in his kitchen, and I make him tea.

"A big one, I saw." He points to the road. "That rougarou, it almost got me."

I pull out my notebook. He says it's from grandma's community. She even met it, once. He touches his suspenders when he speaks. My grandpa wore suspenders.

I want to ask more, but Uncle Joe changes the subject. He asks about my relatives. I shake my head. We were closer before I moved.

"Florence, she loved picking berries."

I shouldn't digress, but I put down my pen to listen.

"She picked berries all around here. She knew the best patches. Them saskatoons, chokecherries."

I can taste them. We'd be driving on the highway, and my grandma would say, "Here." My grandpa would park his hatchback and put down his seat for a nap, while I'd follow my grandma into bush.

Uncle Joe asks about my cousins. I have nothing to say. I search in my notebook for the question to bring us back.

He invites me to stay for dinner – my third cousin and some other relatives are coming. I almost consider it. What it would be, to see them. But how would I explain myself, after so long away? I make an excuse. He tells me I'm always welcome. The dogs chase me out.

Elzéar

I'm in a daze till I hit the refineries on the eastern edge of the city. There's a new scratch on the windshield. Could be the music; it's loud enough. But I'm wearing headphones, so it must be the moon.

Past the refineries, my ethmoid starts to rattle. There's a bump on the road, and the bone elongates. It twists without warning, and I come up fast behind a hatchback. Barely brake to avoid rear-ending it. I flash my lights, and open my window. I throw a pop can at the car, but miss.

I drive on. My mind is half dog. I might not have my wallet. No idea what happened to my phone. That journal burns on the passenger seat. Memories roar when I look at it. Sweat is dripping off the steering wheel. My curling fingers can't start the AC.

By the time the sun sets, I'm in Saskatchewan, long off paved highway. This is the landscape I know, where open prairie turns to willow bushes and poplar bluffs, and farther north, spruce. I can smell the South Saskatchewan winding nearby. There's good hunting in this bush. I had traplines in these trees. This wasn't Saskatchewan when I lived here.

My headphones are deafening, but the crickets are louder. I left the road some time ago. Grass and bush tangle under my car. I taste the night with the roof of my mouth. There's river, bush, and something older. Close my eyes, and I feel it coming up through the gas and steering wheel. I'm not far now.

Sarah

I eat dinner in my room – cold pizza from the nearby gas station. It leaves a layer of grease on my teeth. I'd eat better at Uncle Joe's. But the thought of the questions… Would my relatives still know me? They don't even know I'm back.

Growing up, we were close. I can't think of a childhood memory without them. Even when I moved away, they were always calling, asking after me, inviting me home to visit. I was too busy with my studies, and my new life in the east. After a while, they stopped calling. All those years in Ontario – I worked, I studied, but I never belonged. I don't know what happened to me. Sometimes, I think my research is less about Métis folklore and more about finding my way home.

Elzéar

I leave the car by the river. It's faster on these feet. They know this land, they curve to the shape of it. Sometimes, I'm on road, sometimes, I'm walking through bush, or staggering through sloughs. I'm leaning on willows, and breathing in night. The moon is getting brighter.

There's a clap that's not thunder, and the world cracks in two. Something in my skull bursts, and my vision turns grey. The curve of my spine snaps straight, and my new ribs reach for the sky. My whole body shudders, then my head whips back, and the moon pulls me up like a hook. I'm a moment suspended. Then my knees change their bend, and I fall.

I lift my head and howl into the night. My jaws open and open, and I eat the alligator-skin journal in a single bite. I open my mouth wider, this time for the moon – but it's too big to eat.

The bush is thick with things to stalk, and I'm moon-hungry, famished. But even now, something else pulls at me: that damn journal, burning a hole in my gut. This is where I made a home, this is where I had a family.

I went out only once, under that angry July moon. They said not to go alone – I should have listened. This is where I was damned. I still remember, our horse, lying gutless in the morning. Pitou, that yapper, missing. I never did find the cow… My gut was so heavy I couldn't dress. And the pain – I passed horse teeth and a terrier jaw that evening.

Sarah

My phone buzzes. It's an invitation from the university to present my findings on Monday morning. I stare at the date. Can't understand how this week has sped by. I thought it would be easier, that this land would take me back. I feel like a stranger. I'll never be a real scholar. Would my family take me back? Or have they disowned me, too? I don't even own myself anymore.

I stare at the pizza box. The motel room's thick with the stench of congealed grease. It's suddenly unbearable. I need air.

When I step outside, the moon takes my breath. All these years in the closed-in city – it's like I'm seeing it for the first time. Didn't even realize it was the full moon. And I should know, I've read the literature.

I get a thought. I scroll to maps, and my grandma's town is showing again. This time, it's closer. GPS is a crapshoot around here, I'd have just as much luck on foot. Could try navigating by berry and bush. Maybe I can salvage something, get some notes out of it.

It feels good to be outside, after all these days in the car. The sky's even bigger at night. And that moon… Each time I look, it gets me. There are fewer mosquitoes on the road. Dust and gravel wedge in my toes and make my flip-flops slide.

The night helps me think. It gives me perspective. It's not the end of the world if I don't complete this field study. I can revert to the literature. Spend a week at the library. I'll survive.

By the time I stop for my bearings, I've lost track of time. The gas station is somewhere behind me. The motel is farther back, I barely see it. Can't believe I've come this far. I should go back.

The sky's so bright, it could be day. I still hear crickets. I scan the landscape. My grandma would say this is berry country. I breathe it in. So many memories in the bush with her. I shouldn't have left.

I blink and I see it. A big dog, no – a rougarou. All this time studying, and still, I'm not ready for it. I blink again, and it's still there, in the middle of the road, straightening – no, turning toward me. My breath catches. I lose a flip-flop. I never believed the stories, but now… I don't like what my heart is doing.

The beast shifts. Something rises from my stomach. I've read too many sources. I search for my shoe. My heart is wild. I try to summon the literature, but nothing comes. It sniffs the air. My knees falter – I catch myself. It turns its head. Please don't let it see me.

Elzéar

My baby boy loved that terrier. Everything that dog did made him laugh. My boy was my world. I can still see him, gurgling and clapping. I smell the air – it's baby skin. Those crickets – they're my wife's laugh. They're all around me. I look up at the moon, it's nothing next to my wife. My baby boy laughs, he makes the moon small. We were family.

The landscape bows to them. Sticks on the road are my wife's comb. A dead rabbit for the fur-lined boots she made our boy. He grew out of them fast, so I trapped another rabbit, and she made another pair. He didn't grow out of those.

Now, the memories won't stop. These are different memories, these are unspeakable memories. They're tiny fingers and tiny feet, the tiny toys and tiny boots.

I howl, but my voice cracks. I bite my thumb, but it doesn't bleed. The moon ignores me. Shame is bigger than everything.

Sarah

I blink again. It doesn't look so much like a dog now. More like a man, prostrate on the road. My heart hasn't slowed. Legs still shaking.

The man, or animal, lifts his head. It doesn't move, but now I'm certain it sees me. It sniffs the air. The literature can't help me now. The gas station must be five hundred metres away. The rougarou's closer.

I head for the gas station, and it follows, steady, behind me. I try to go faster, but my flip-flops slip from my feet. I am getting blisters. I should have asked Uncle Joe how he got away. I reach for my notebook, but must have dropped it. I look back and shudder – the monster's closer. I can barely keep my pace, and I'm getting out of breath. I look to the land. Panic rises. I try to distract myself.

I picked berries with my grandma in places like this. We'd bring back our pails, tired and happy, and climb back into my grandpa's hatchback. He'd adjust his hat, and we'd go bringing berries to relatives. Sometimes, on the way, we'd stop for bingo. My grandma owned herself.

Something in the moonlight catches my eye. I stop. It might be saskatoons. Or chokecherries. I can't see from the road, but somehow I feel it, must be muscle memory. The gas station isn't so far now. The monster's not slowing, but if I walk fast, I might reach it. I look back at those berries and think of my grandma.

Elzéar

Something rustles in the bush. I stop and sniff. It might be prey. I hesitate, then step off the gravel. I've always been a good tracker. My footsteps are soft on the long grass. I smell fear. I let the scent lead me.

She surprises me when she steps out from the bush. That woman from the road. She's wearing flip-flops, impractical. Does she not know the dangers? There are monsters that roam under that angry July moon, monsters like me…

She doesn't move, but something glistens in her hand. I sniff. Her smell is different. I step forward. She opens her palm – it's the moon.

I blink, and she eats it. She reaches into the bush and takes another. The Wolf Moon is nothing compared to it. Our eyes meet. She doesn't look like prey.

I turn away. A memory awakens. Her face reminds me. Another time, this same bush. Those same eyes. I tracked the woman all the way from the hatchback. Thought she was easy prey. But when she opened her hands – the whole world was in there. I still cower when I think of it.

The light of the gas station shines back at me. Somewhere beyond, I've abandoned my car. I could drive to the city, or build a den in it. Tomorrow, I'll shit paper and black alligator leather, but in this moment, I own myself. The thought's too much. I try to howl, but can only whine.

A Pastoral Horror

Arthur Conan Doyle

FAR ABOVE THE level of the Lake of Constance, nestling in a little corner of the Tyrolese Alps, lies the quiet town of Feldkirch. It is remarkable for nothing save for the presence of a large and well-conducted Jesuit school and for the extreme beauty of its situation. There is no more lovely spot in the whole of the Vorarlberg. From the hills which rise behind the town, the great lake glimmers some fifteen miles off, like a broad sea of quicksilver. Down below in the plains the Rhine and the Danube prattle along, flowing swiftly and merrily, with none of the dignity which they assume as they grow from brooks into rivers. Five great countries or principalities – Switzerland, Austria, Baden, Wurtemburg, and Bavaria – are visible from the plateau of Feldkirch.

Feldkirch is the centre of a large tract of hilly and pastoral country. The main road runs through the centre of the town, and then on as far as Anspach, where it divides into two branches, one of which is larger than the other. This more important one runs through the valleys across Austrian Tyrol into Tyrol proper, going as far, I believe, as the capital of Innsbruck. The lesser road runs for eight or ten miles amid wild and rugged glens to the village of Laden, where it breaks up into a network of sheep-tracks. In this quiet spot, I, John Hudson, spent nearly two years of my life, from the June of '65 to the March of '67, and it was during that time that those events occurred which for some weeks brought the retired hamlet into an unholy prominence, and caused its name for the first, and probably for the last time, to be a familiar word to the European press. The short account of these incidents which appeared in the English papers was, however, inaccurate and misleading, besides which, the rapid advance of the Prussians, culminating in the battle of Sadowa, attracted public attention away from what might have moved it deeply in less troublous times. It seems to me that the facts may be detailed now, and be new to the great majority of readers, especially as I was myself intimately connected with the drama, and am in a position to give many particulars which have never before been made public.

And first a few words as to my own presence in this out of the way spot. When the great city firm of Sprynge, Wilkinson, and Spragge failed, and paid their creditors rather less than eighteen-pence in the pound, a number of humble individuals were ruined, including myself. There was, however, some legal objection which held out a chance of my being made an exception to the other creditors, and being paid in full. While the case was being brought out I was left with a very small sum for my subsistance.

I determined, therefore, to take up my residence abroad in the interim, since I could live more economically there, and be spared the mortification of meeting those who had known me in my more prosperous days. A friend of mine had described Laden to me some years before as being the most isolated place which he had ever come across in all his experience, and as isolation and cheap living are usually synonymous, I bethought use of his words. Besides, I was in a cynical humour with my fellow-man, and desired to see as little of him as possible for some time to come. Obeying, then, the guidances of poverty and of misanthropy, I made my way to Laden, where my arrival created the utmost excitement among the simple inhabitants. The manners and customs of the red-bearded Englander, his long walks, his check suit, and the reasons which had led him to abandon his fatherland, were all fruitful sources of gossip to the topers who frequented the Gruner Mann and the Schwartzer Bar – the two alehouses of the village.

I found myself very happy at Laden. The surroundings were magnificent, and twenty years of Brixton had sharpened my admiration for nature as an olive improves the flavour of wine. In my youth I had been a fair German scholar, and I found myself able, before I had been many months abroad, to converse even on scientific and abstruse subjects with the new curé of the parish.

This priest was a great godsend to me, for he was a most learned man and a brilliant conversationalist. Father Verhagen – for that was his name – though little more than forty years of age, had made his reputation as an author by a brilliant monograph upon the early Popes – a work which eminent critics have compared favourably with Von Ranke's. I shrewdly suspect that it was owing to some rather unorthodox views advanced in this book that Verhagen was relegated to the obscurity of Laden. His opinions upon every subject were ultra-Liberal, and in his fiery youth he had been ready to vindicate them, as was proved by a deep scar across his chin, received from a dragoon's sabre in the abortive insurrection at Berlin. Altogether the man was an interesting one, and though he was by nature somewhat cold and reserved, we soon established an acquaintanceship.

The atmosphere of morality in Laden was a very rarefied one. The position of Intendant Wurms and his satellites had for many years been a sinecure. Non-attendance at church upon a Sunday or feast-day was about the deepest and darkest crime which the most advanced of the villagers had attained to. Occasionally some hulking Fritz or Andreas would come lurching home at ten o'clock at night, slightly under the influence of Bavarian beer, and might even abuse the wife of his bosom if she ventured to remonstrate, but such cases were rare, and when they occurred the Ladeners looked at the culprit for some time in a half admiring, half horrified manner, as one who had committed a gaudy sin and so asserted his individuality.

It was in this peaceful village that a series of crimes suddenly broke out which astonished all Europe, and for atrocity and for the mystery which surrounded them surpassed anything of which I have ever heard or read. I shall endeavour to give a succinct account of these events in the order of their sequence, in which I am much helped by the fact that it has been my custom all my life to keep a journal – to the pages of which I now refer.

It was, then, I find upon the 19th of May in the spring of 1866, that my old landlady, Frau Zimmer, rushed wildly into the room as I was sipping my morning cup of chocolate and informed me that a murder had been committed in the village. At first I could hardly believe the news, but as she persisted in her statement, and was evidently terribly frightened, I put on my hat and went out to find the truth. When I came into the main street of the village I saw several men hurrying along in front of me, and following them I came upon an excited group in front of the little stadthaus or town hall – a barn-like edifice which was used for all manner of public gatherings. They were collected round the body of one Maul, who had formerly been a steward upon one of the steamers running between Lindau and Fredericshaven, on the Lake of Constance. He was a harmless, inoffensive little man, generally popular in the village, and, as far as was known, without an enemy in the world. Maul lay upon his face, with his fingers dug into the earth, no doubt in his last convulsive struggles, and his hair all matted together with blood, which had streamed down over the collar of his coat. The body had been discovered nearly two hours, but no one appeared to know what to do or whither to convey it. My arrival, however, together with that of the curé, who came almost simultaneously, infused some vigour into the crowd. Under our direction the corpse was carried up the steps, and laid on the floor of the town hall, where, having made sure that life was extinct, we proceeded to examine the injuries, in conjunction with Lieutenant Wurms, of the police. Maul's face was perfectly placid, showing that he had had no thought of danger until the fatal blow was struck. His watch and purse had not been taken. Upon washing the clotted blood from the back of his head a singular triangular wound was found, which had smashed the bone and penetrated deeply into the brain. It had evidently been inflicted by a heavy blow from a sharp-pointed pyramidal instrument. I believe that it was Father Verhagen, the curé, who suggested the probability of the weapon in question having been a short mattock or small pickaxe, such as are to be found in every Alpine cottage. The Intendant, with praiseworthy promptness, at once obtained one and striking a turnip, produced just such a curious gap as was to be seen in poor Maul's head. We felt that we had come upon the first link of a chain which might guide us to the assassin. It was not long before we seemed to grasp the whole clue.

A sort of inquest was held upon the body that same afternoon, at which Pfiffor, the maire, presided, the curé, the Intendant, Freckler, of the post office, and myself forming ourselves into a sort of committee of investigation. Any villager who could throw a light upon the case or give an account of the movements of the murdered man upon the previous evening was invited to attend. There was a fair muster of witnesses, and we soon gathered a connected series of facts. At half-past eight o'clock Maul had entered the Gruner Mann public-house, and had called for a flagon of beer. At that time there were sitting in the tap-room Waghorn, the butcher of the village, and an Italian pedlar named Cellini, who used to come three times a year to Laden with cheap jewellery and other wares. Immediately after his entrance the landlord had seated himself with his customers, and the four had spent the evening together, the common villagers not being admitted beyond the bar. It seemed from the evidence of the landlord and of Waghorn, both of whom were most respectable and trustworthy men, that shortly after nine o'clock a dispute arose between the deceased and the pedlar. Hot words had been exchanged, and the Italian had eventually left the room, saying that he would not stay any longer to hear his country decried. Maul remained for nearly an hour, and being somewhat elated at having caused his adversary's retreat, he drank rather more than was usual with him. One witness had met him walking towards his home, about ten o'clock, and deposed to his having been slightly the worse for drink. Another had met him just a minute or so before he reached the spot in front of the stadthaus where the deed was done. This man's evidence was most important. He swore confidently that while passing the town hall, and before meeting Maul, he had seen a figure standing in the shadow of the building, adding that the person appeared to him, as far as he could make him out, to be not unlike the Italian.

Up to this point we had then established two facts – that the Italian had left the Gruner Mann before Maul, with words of anger on his lips; the second, that some unknown individual had been seen lying in wait on the road which the ex-steward would have to traverse. A third, and most important, was reached when the woman with whom the Italian lodged deposed that he had not returned the night before until half-past ten, an unusually late hour for Laden. How had he employed the time, then, from shortly after nine, when he left the public-house, until half-past ten, when he returned to his rooms? Things were beginning to look very black, indeed, against the pedlar.

It could not be denied, however, that there were points in the man's favour, and that the case against him consisted entirely of circumstantial evidence. In the first place, there was no sign of a mattock or any other instrument which could have been used for such a purpose among the Italian's goods; nor was it easy to understand how he could come by any such a weapon, since he did not go home between the time of the quarrel and his final return. Again, as the curé pointed out, since Cellini was a comparative stranger in the village, it was very unlikely that he would know which road Maul would take in order to reach his home. This objection was weakened, however, by the evidence of the dead man's servant, who deposed that the pedlar had been hawking his wares in front of their house the day before, and might very possibly have seen the owner at one of the windows. As to the prisoner himself, his attitude at first had been one of defiance, and even of amusement; but when he began to realise the weight of evidence against him, his manner became cringing, and he wrung his hands hideously, loudly proclaiming his innocence. His defence was that after leaving the inn, he had taken a long walk down the Anspach-road in order to cool down his excitement, and that this was the cause of his late return. As to the murder of Maul, he knew no more about it than the babe unborn.

I have dwelt at some length upon the circumstances of this case, because there are events in connection with it which makes it peculiarly interesting. I intend now to fall back upon my diary, which was very fully kept during this period, and indeed during my whole residence abroad. It will save me trouble to quote from it, and it will be a teacher for the accuracy of facts.

May 20th. – Nothing thought of and nothing talked of but the recent tragedy. A hunt has been made among the woods and along the brook in the hope of finding the weapon of the assassin. The more I think of it, the more convinced I am that Cellini is the man. The fact of the money being untouched proves that the crime was committed from motives of revenge, and who would bear more spite towards poor innocent Maul except the vindictive hot-blooded Italian whom he had just offended. I dined with Pfiffor in the evening, and he entirely agreed with me in my view of the case.

May 21st. – Still no word as far as I can hear which throws any light upon the murder. Poor Maul was buried at twelve o'clock in the neat little village churchyard. The curé led the service with great feeling, and his audience, consisting of the whole population of the village, were much moved, interrupting him frequently by sobs and ejaculations of grief. After the painful ceremony was over I had a short walk with our good priest. His naturally excitable nature has been considerably stirred by recent events. His hand trembles and his face is pale.

"My friend," said he, taking me by the hand as we walked together, "you know something of medicine." (I had been two years at Guy's). "I have been far from well of late."

"It is this sad affair which has upset you," I said.

"No," he answered, "I have felt it coming on for some time, but it has been worse of late. I have a pain which shoots from here to there," he put his hand to his temples. "If I were struck by lightning, the sudden shock it causes me could not be more great. At times when I close my eyes flashes of light dart before them, and my ears are for ever ringing. Often I know not what I do. My fear is lest I faint some time when performing the holy offices."

"You are overworking yourself," I said, "you must have rest and strengthening tonics. Are you writing just now? And how much do you do each day?"

"Eight hours," he answered. "Sometimes ten, sometimes even twelve, when the pains in my head do not interrupt me."

"You must reduce it to four," I said authoritatively. "You must also take regular exercise. I shall send you some quinine which I have in my trunk, and you can take as much as would cover a gulden in a glass of milk every morning and night."

He departed, vowing that he would follow my directions.

I hear from the maire that four policemen are to be sent from Anspach to remove Cellini to a safer gaol.

May 22nd. – To say that I was startled would give but a faint idea of my mental state. I am confounded, amazed, horrified beyond all expression. Another and a more dreadful crime has been committed during the night. Freckler has been found dead in his house – the very Freckler who had sat with me on the committee of investigation the day before. I write these notes after a long and anxious day's work, during which I have been endeavouring to assist the officers of the law. The villagers are so paralysed with fear at this fresh evidence of an assassin in their midst that there would be a general panic but for our exertions. It appears that Freckler, who was a man of peculiar habits, lived alone in an isolated dwelling. Some curiosity was aroused this morning by the fact that he had not gone to his work, and that there was no sign of movement about the house. A crowd assembled, and the doors were eventually forced open. The unfortunate Freckler was found in the bed-room upstairs, lying with his head in the fireplace. He had met his death by an exactly similar wound to that which had proved fatal to Maul, save that in this instance the injury was in front. His hands were clenched, and there was an indescribable look of horror, and, as it seemed to me, of surprise upon his features. There were marks of muddy footsteps upon the stairs, which must have been caused by the murderer in his ascent, as his victim had put on his slippers before retiring to his bed-room. These prints, however, were too much blurred to enable us to get a trustworthy outline of the foot. They were only to be found upon every third step, showing with what fiendish swiftness this human tiger had rushed upstairs in search of his victim. There was a considerable sum of money in the house, but not one farthing had been touched, nor had any of the drawers in the bed-room been opened.

As the dismal news became known the whole population of the village assembled in a great crowd in front of the house – rather, I think, from the gregariousness of terror than from mere curiosity. Every man looked with suspicion upon his neighbour. Most were silent, and when they spoke it was in whispers, as if they feared to raise their voices. None of these people were allowed to enter the house, and we, the more enlightened members of the community, made a strict examination of the premises. There was absolutely nothing, however, to give the slightest clue as to the assassin. Beyond the fact that he must be an active man, judging from the manner in which he ascended the stairs, we have gained nothing from this second tragedy. Intendant Wurms pointed out, indeed, that the dead man's rigid right arm was stretched out as if in greeting, and that, therefore, it was probable that this late visitor was someone with whom Freckler was well acquainted. This, however, was, to a large extent, conjecture. If anything could have added to the horror created by the dreadful occurrence, it was the fact that the crime must have been committed at the early hour of half-past eight in the evening – that being the time registered by a small cuckoo clock, which had been carried away by Freckler in his fall.

No one, apparently, heard any suspicious sounds or saw any one enter or leave the house. It was done rapidly, quietly, and completely, though many people must have been about at the time. Poor Pfiffor and our good curé are terribly cut up by the awful occurrence, and, indeed, I feel very much depressed myself now that all the excitement is over and the reaction set in. There are very few of the villagers about this evening, but from every side is heard the sound of hammering – the peasants fitting bolts and bars upon the doors and windows of their houses. Very many of them have been entirely unprovided with anything of the sort, nor were they ever required until now. Frau Zimmer has manufactured a huge fastening which would be ludicrous if we were in a humour for laughter.

I hear tonight that Cellini has been released, as, of course, there is no possible pretext for detaining him now; also that word has been sent to all the villages near for any police that can be spared.

My nerves have been so shaken that I remained awake the greater part of the night, reading Gordon's translation of Tacitus by candlelight. I have got out my navy revolver and cleaned it, so as to be ready for all eventualities.

May 23rd. – The police force has been recruited by three more men from Anspach and two from Thalstadt at the other side of the hills. Intendant Wurms has established an efficient system of patrols, so that we may consider ourselves reasonably safe. Today has cast no light upon the murders. The general opinion in the village seems to be that they have been done by some stranger who lies concealed among the woods. They argue that they have all known each other since childhood, and that there is no one of their number who would be capable of such actions. Some of the more daring of them have made a hunt among the pine forests today, but without success.

May 24th. – Events crowd on apace. We seem hardly to have recovered from one horror when something else occurs to excite the popular imagination. Fortunately, this time it is not a fresh tragedy, although the news is serious enough.

The murderer has been seen, and that upon the public road, which proves that his thirst for blood has not been quenched yet, and also that our reinforcements of police are not enough to guarantee security. I have just come back from hearing Andreas Murch narrate his experience, though he is still in such a state of trepidation that his story is somewhat incoherent. He was belated among the hills, it seems, owing to mist. It was nearly eleven o'clock before he struck the main road about a couple of miles from the village. He confesses that he felt by no means comfortable at finding himself out so late after the recent occurrences. However, as the fog had cleared away and the moon was shining brightly, he trudged sturdily along. Just about a quarter of a mile from the village the road takes a very sharp bend. Andreas had got as far as this when he suddenly heard in the still night the sound of footsteps approaching rapidly round this curve. Overcome with fear, he threw himself into the ditch which skirts the road, and lay there motionless in the shadow, peering over the side. The steps came nearer and nearer, and then a tall dark figure came round the corner at a swinging pace, and passing the spot where the moon glimmered upon the white face of the frightened peasant, halted in the road about twenty yards further on, and began probing about among the reeds on the roadside with an instrument which Andreas Murch recognised with horror as being a long mattock. After searching about in this way for a minute or so, as if he suspected that someone was concealed there, for he must have heard the sound of the footsteps, he stood still leaning upon his weapon. Murch describes him as a tall, thin man, dressed in clothes of a darkish colour. The lower part of his face was swathed in a wrapper of some sort, and the little which was visible appeared to be of a ghastly pallor. Murch could not see enough of his features to identify him, but thinks that it was no one whom he had ever seen in his life before. After standing for some little time, the man with the mattock had walked swiftly away into the darkness, in the direction in which he imagined the fugitive had gone. Andreas, as may be supposed, lost little time in getting safely into the village, where he alarmed the police. Three of them, armed with carbines, started down the road, but saw no signs of the miscreant. There is, of course, a possibility that Murch's story is exaggerated and that his imagination has been sharpened by fear. Still, the whole incident cannot be trumped up, and this awful demon who haunts us is evidently still active.

There is an ill-conditioned fellow named Hiedler, who lives in a hut on the side of the Spiegelberg, and supports himself by chamois hunting and by acting as guide to the few tourists who find their way here. Popular suspicion has fastened on this man, for no better reason than that he is tall, thin, and known to be rough and brutal. His chalet has been searched today, but nothing of importance found. He has, however, been arrested and confined in the same room which Cellini used to occupy.

At this point there is a gap of a week in my diary, during which time there was an entire cessation of the constant alarms which have harassed us lately. Some explained it by supposing that the terrible unknown had moved on to some fresh and less guarded scene of operations. Others imagine that we have secured the right man in the shape of the vagabond Hiedler. Be the cause what it may, peace and contentment reign once more in the village, and a short seven days have sufficed to clear away the cloud of care from men's brows, though the police are still on the alert. The season for rifle shooting is beginning, and as Laden has, like every other Tyrolese village, butts of its own, there is a continual pop, pop, all day. These peasants are dead shots up to about four hundred yards. No troops in the world could subdue them among their native mountains.

My friend Verhagen, the curé, and Pfiffor, the maire, used to go down in the afternoon to see the shooting with me. The former says that the quinine has done him much good and that his appetite is improved. We all agree that it is good policy to encourage the amusements of the people so that they may forget all about this wretched business. Vaghorn, the butcher, won the prize offered by the maire. He made five bulls, and what we should call a magpie out of six shots at 100 yards. This is English prize-medal form.

June 2nd. – Who could have imagined that a day which opened so fairly could have so dark an ending? The early carrier brought me a letter by which I learned that Spragge and Co. have agreed to pay my claim in full, although it may be some months before the money is forthcoming. This will make a difference of nearly £400 a year to me – a matter of moment when a man is in his seven-and-fortieth year.

And now for the grand events of the hour. My interview with the vampire who haunts us, and his attempt upon Frau Bischoff, the landlady of the Gruner Mann – to say nothing of the narrow escape of our good cure. There seems to be something almost supernatural in the malignity of this unknown fiend, and the impunity with which he continues his murderous course. The real reason of it lies in the badly lit state of the place – or rather the entire absence of light – and also in the fact that thick woods stretch right down to the houses on every side, so that escape is made easy. In spite of this, however, he had two very narrow escapes tonight – one from my pistol, and one from the officers of the law. I shall not sleep much, so I may spend half an hour in jotting down these strange doings in my dairy. I am no coward, but life in Laden is becoming too much for my nerves. I believe the matter will end in the emigration of the whole population.

To come to my story, then. I felt lonely and depressed this evening, in spite of the good news of the morning. About nine o'clock, just as night began to fall, I determined to stroll over and call upon the curé, thinking that a little intellectual chat might cheer me up. I slipped my revolver into my pocket, therefore – a precaution which I never neglected – and went out, very much against the advice of good Frau Zimmer. I think I mentioned some months ago in my diary that the curé's house is some little way out of the village upon the brow of a small hill. When I arrived there I found that he had gone out – which, indeed, I might have anticipated, for he had complained lately of restlessness at night, and I had recommended him to take a little exercise in the evening. His housekeeper made me very welcome, however, and having lit the lamp, left me in the study with some books to amuse me until her master's return.

I suppose I must have sat for nearly half an hour glancing over an odd volume of Klopstock's poems, when some sudden instinct caused me to raise my head and look up. I have been in some strange situations in my life, but never have I felt anything to be compared to the thrill which shot through me at that moment. The recollection of it now, hours after the event, makes me shudder. There, framed in one of the panes of the window, was a human face glaring in, from the darkness, into the lighted room – the face of a man so concealed by a cravat and slouch hat that the only impression I retain of it was a pair of wild-beast eyes and a nose which was whitened by being pressed against the glass. It did not need Andreas Murch's description to tell me that at last I was face to face with the man with the mattock. There was murder in those wild eyes. For a second I was so unstrung as to be powerless; the next I cocked my revolver and fired straight at the sinister face. I was a moment too late. As I pressed the trigger I saw it vanish, but the pane through which it had looked was shattered to pieces. I rushed to the window, and then out through the front door, but everything was silent. There was no trace of my visitor. His intention, no doubt, was to attack the curé, for there was nothing to prevent his coming through the folding window had he not found an armed man inside.

As I stood in the cool night air with the curé's frightened housekeeper beside me, I suddenly heard a great hubbub down in the village. By this time, alas! such sounds were so common in

Laden that there was no doubting what it forboded. Some fresh misfortune had occurred there. Tonight seemed destined to be a night of horror. My presence might be of use in the village, so I set off there, taking with me the trembling woman, who positively refused to remain behind. There was a crowd round the Gruner Mann public-house, and a dozen excited voices were explaining the circumstances to the curé, who had arrived just before us. It was as I had thought, though happily without the result which I had feared. Frau Bischoff, the wife of the proprietor of the inn, had, it seems, gone some twenty minutes before a few yards from her door to draw some water, and had been at once attacked by a tall disguised man, who had cut at her with some weapon. Fortunately he had slipped, so that she was able to seize him by the wrist and prevent his repeating his attempt, while she screamed for help. There were several people about at the time, who came running towards them, on which the stranger wrested himself free, and dashed off into the woods, with two of our police after him. There is little hope of their overtaking or tracing him, however, in such a dark labyrinth. Frau Bischoff had made a bold attempt to hold the assassin, and declares that her nails made deep furrows in his right wrist. This, however, must be mere conjecture, as there was very little light at the time. She knows no more of the man's features than I do. Fortunately she is entirely unhurt. The curé was horrified when I informed him of the incident at his own house. He was returning from his walk, it appears, when hearing cries in the village, he had hurried down to it. I have not told anyone else of my own adventure, for the people are quite excited enough already.

As I said before, unless this mysterious and bloodthirsty villain is captured, the place will become deserted. Flesh and blood cannot stand such a strain. He is either some murderous misanthrope who has declared a vendetta against the whole human race, or else he is an escaped maniac. Clearly after the unsuccessful attempt upon Frau Bischoff he had made at once for the cures house, bent upon slaking his thirst for blood, and thinking that its lonely situation gave hope of success. I wish I had fired at him through the pocket of my coat. The moment he saw the glitter of the weapon he was off.

June 3rd. – Everybody in the village this morning has learned about the attempt upon the curé last night. There was quite a crowd at his house to congratulate him on his escape, and when I appeared they raised a cheer and hailed me as the "tapferer Englander". It seems that his narrow shave must have given the ruffian a great start, for a thick woollen muffler was found lying on the pathway leading down to the village, and later in the day the fatal mattock was discovered close to the same place. The scoundrel evidently threw those things down and then took to his heels. It is possible that he may prove to have been frightened away from the neighbourhood altogether. Let us trust so!

June 4th. – A quiet day, which is as remarkable a thing in our annals as an exciting one elsewhere. Wurms has made strict inquiry, but cannot trace the muffler and mattock to any inhabitant. A description of them has been printed, and copies sent to Anspach and neighbouring villages for circulation among the peasants, who may be able to throw some light upon the matter. A thanksgiving service is to be held in the church on Sunday for the double escape of the pastor and of Martha Bischoff. Pfiffer tells me that Herr von Weissendorff, one of the most energetic detectives in Vienna, is on his way to Laden. I see, too, by the English papers sent me, that people at home are interested in the tragedies here, although the accounts which have reached them are garbled and untrustworthy.

How well I can recall the Sunday morning following upon the events which I have described, such a morning as it is hard to find outside the Tyrol! The sky was blue and cloudless, the gentle breeze wafted the balsamic odour of the pine woods through the open windows, and away up on the hills the distant tinkling of the cow bells fell pleasantly upon the ear, until the musical rise and fall which summoned the villagers to prayer drowned their feebler melody. It was hard to believe, looking down that peaceful little street with its quaint topheavy wooden houses and old-fashioned church, that a cloud of crime hung over it which had horrified Europe. I sat at my window watching the peasants passing with their picturesquely dressed wives and daughters on their way to church. With the kindly reverence of Catholic countries, I saw them cross themselves as they went by the house of Freckler and the spot where Maul had met his fate. When the bell had ceased to toll and the whole population had assembled in the church, I walked up there also, for it has always been my custom to join in the religious exercises of any people among whom I may find myself.

When I arrived at the church I found that the service had already begun. I took my place in the gallery which contained the village organ, from which I had a good view of the congregation. In the front seat of all was stationed Frau Bischoff, whose miraculous escape the service was intended to celebrate, and beside her on one side was her worthy spouse, while the maire occupied the other. There was a hush through the church as the curé turned from the altar and ascended the pulpit. I have seldom heard a more magnificent sermon. Father Verhagen was always an eloquent preacher, but on that occasion he surpassed himself. He chose for his text: – "In the midst of life we are in death," and impressed so vividly upon our minds the thin veil which divides us from eternity, and how unexpectedly it may be rent, that he held his audience spell-bound and horrified. He spoke next with tender pathos of the friends who had been snatched so suddenly and so dreadfully from among us, until his words were almost drowned by the sobs of the women, and, suddenly turning he compared their peaceful existence in a happier land to the dark fate of the gloomy-minded criminal, steeped in blood and with nothing to hope for either in this world or the next – a man solitary among his fellows, with no woman to love him, no child to prattle at his knee, and an endless torture in his own thoughts. So skilfully and so powerfully did he speak that as he finished I am sure that pity for this merciless demon was the prevailing emotion in every heart.

The service was over, and the priest, with his two acolytes before him, was leaving the altar, when he turned, as was his custom, to give his blessing to the congregation. I shall never forget his appearance. The summer sunshine shining slantwise through the single small stained glass window which adorned the little church threw a yellow lustre upon his sharp intellectual features with their dark haggard lines, while a vivid crimson spot reflected from a ruby-coloured mantle in the window quivered over his uplifted right hand. There was a hush as the villagers bent their heads to receive their pastor's blessing – a hush broken by a wild exclamation of surprise from a woman who staggered to her feet in the front pew and gesticulated frantically as she pointed at Father Verhagen's uplifted arm. No need for Frau Bischoff to explain the cause of that sudden cry, for there – there in full sight of his parishioners, were lines of livid scars upon the cure's white wrist – scars which could be left by nothing on earth but a desperate woman's nails. And what woman save her who had clung so fiercely to the murderer two days before!

That in all this terrible business poor Verhagen was the man most to be pitied I have no manner of doubt. In a town in which there was good medical advice to be had, the approach of the homicidal mania, which had undoubtedly proceeded from overwork and brain worry, and which assumed such a terrible form, would have been detected in time and he would have been spared the awful compunction with which he must have been seized in the lucid intervals between his fits – if, indeed, he had any lucid intervals. How could I diagnose with my smattering of science the existence of such a terrible and insidious form of insanity, especially from the vague symptoms of which he informed me. It is easy now, looking back, to think of many little circumstances which might have put us on the right scent; but what a simple thing is retrospective wisdom! I should be sad indeed if I thought that I had anything with which to reproach myself.

We were never able to discover where he had obtained the weapon with which he had committed his crimes, nor how he managed to secrete it in the interval. My experience proved that it had been his custom to go and come through his study window without disturbing his housekeeper. On the occasion of the attempt on Frau Bischoff he had made a dash for home, and then, finding to his astonishment that his room was occupied, his only resource was to fling away his weapon and muffler, and to mix with the crowd in the village. Being both a strong and an active man, with a good knowledge of the footpaths through the woods, he had never found any difficulty in escaping all observation.

Immediately after his apprehension, Verhagen's disease took an acute form, and he was carried off to the lunatic asylum at Feldkirch. I have heard that some months afterwards he made a determined attempt upon the life of one of his keepers, and afterwards committed suicide. I cannot be positive of this, however, for I heard it quite accidentally during a conversation in a railway carriage.

As for myself, I left Laden within a few months, having received a pleasing intimation from my solicitors that my claim had been paid in full. In spite of my tragic experience there, I had many a pleasing recollection of the little Tyrolese village, and in two subsequent visits I renewed my acquaintance with the maire, the Intendant, and all my old friends, on which occasion, over long pipes and flagons of beer, we have taken a grim pleasure in talking with bated breath of that terrible month in the quiet Vorarlberg hamlet.

The Werewolf

Eugene Field

IN THE REIGN of Egbert the Saxon there dwelt in Britain a maiden named Yseult, who was beloved of all, both for her goodness and for her beauty. But, though many a youth came wooing her, she loved Harold only, and to him she plighted her troth.

Among the other youth of whom Yseult was beloved was Alfred, and he was sore angered that Yseult showed favor to Harold, so that one day Alfred said to Harold: "Is it right that old Siegfried should come from his grave and have Yseult to wife?" Then added he, "Prithee, good sir, why do you turn so white when I speak your grandsire's name?"

Then Harold asked, "What know you of Siegfried that you taunt me? What memory of him should vex me now?"

"We know and we know," retorted Alfred. "There are some tales told us by our grandmas we have not forgot."

So ever after that Alfred's words and Alfred's bitter smile haunted Harold by day and night.

Harold's grandsire, Siegfried the Teuton, had been a man of cruel violence. The legend said that a curse rested upon him, and that at certain times he was possessed of an evil spirit that wreaked its fury on mankind. But Siegfried had been dead full many years, and there was naught to mind the world of him save the legend and a cunning-wrought spear which he had from Brunehilde, the witch. This spear was such a weapon that it never lost its brightness, nor had its point been blunted. It hung in Harold's chamber, and it was the marvel among weapons of that time.

Yseult knew that Alfred loved her, but she did not know of the bitter words which Alfred had spoken to Harold. Her love for Harold was perfect in its trust and gentleness. But Alfred had hit the truth: the curse of old Siegfried was upon Harold – slumbering a century, it had awakened in the blood of the grandson, and Harold knew the curse that was upon him, and it was this that seemed to stand between him and Yseult. But love is stronger than all else, and Harold loved.

Harold did not tell Yseult of the curse that was upon him, for he feared that she would not love him if she knew. Whensoever he felt the fire of the curse burning in his veins he would say to her, "Tomorrow I hunt the wild boar in the uttermost forest," or, "Next week I go stag-stalking among the distant northern hills." Even so it was that he ever made good excuse for his absence, and Yseult thought no evil things, for she was trustful; ay though he went many times away and was long gone, Yseult suspected no wrong. So none beheld Harold when the curse was upon him in its violence.

Alfred alone bethought himself of evil things. "'Tis passing strange," quoth he, "that ever and anon this gallant lover should quit our company and betake himself whither none knoweth. In sooth 't will be well to have an eye on old Siegfried's grandson."

Harold knew that Alfred watched him zealously and he was tormented by a constant fear that Alfred would discover the curse that was on him; but what gave him greater anguish was the fear that mayhap at some moment when he was in Yseult's presence, the curse would seize upon him and cause him to do great evil unto her, whereby she would be destroyed or her love for him would be undone forever. So Harold lived in terror, feeling that his love was hopeless, yet knowing not how to combat it.

Now, it befell in those times that the country round about was ravaged of a werewolf, a creature that was feared by all men howe'er so valorous. This werewolf was by day a man, but by night a wolf given to ravage and to slaughter, and having a charmed life against which no human agency availed aught. Wheresoever he went he attacked and devoured mankind, spreading terror and desolation round about, and the dream-readers said that the earth would not be freed from the werewolf until some man offered himself a voluntary sacrifice to the monster's rage.

Now, although Harold was known far and wide as a mighty huntsman, he had never set forth to hunt the werewolf, and, strange enow, the werewolf never ravaged the domain while Harold was therein. Whereat Alfred marvelled much, and oftentimes he said: "Our Harold is a wondrous huntsman. Who is like unto him in stalking the timid doe and in crippling the fleeing boar? But how passing well doth he time his absence from the haunts of the werewolf. Such valor beseemeth our young Siegfried."

Which being brought to Harold his heart flamed with anger, but he made no answer, lest he betray the truth he feared.

It happened so about that time that Yseult said to Harold, "Wilt thou go with me tomorrow even to the feast in the sacred grove?"

"That can I not do," answered Harold. "I am privily summoned hence to Normandy upon a mission of which I shall some time tell thee. And I pray thee, on thy love for me, go not to the feast in the sacred grove without me."

"What say'st thou?" cried Yseult. "Shall I not go to the feast of Ste. Aelfreda? My father would be sore displeased were I not there with the other maidens. 'T were greatest pity that I should despite his love thus."

"But do not, I beseech thee," Harold implored. "Go not to the feast of Ste. Aelfreda in the sacred grove! And thou would thus love me, go not – see, thou my life, on my two knees I ask it!"

"How pale thou art," said Yseult, "and trembling."

"Go not to the sacred grove upon the morrow night," he begged.

Yseult marvelled at his acts and at his speech. Then, for the first time, she thought him to be jealous – whereat she secretly rejoiced (being a woman).

"Ah," quoth she, "thou dost doubt my love," but when she saw a look of pain come on his face she added – as if she repented of the words she had spoken – "or dost thou fear the werewolf?"

Then Harold answered, fixing his eyes on hers, "Thou hast said it; it is the werewolf that I fear."

"Why dost thou look at me so strangely, Harold?" cried Yseult. "By the cruel light in thine eyes one might almost take three to be the werewolf!"

"Come hither, sit beside me," said Harold tremblingly "and I will tell thee why I fear to have thee go to the feast of Ste. Aelfreda tomorrow evening. Hear what I dreamed last night. I dreamed I was the werewolf – do not shudder, dear love, for 't was only a dream."

"A grizzled old man stood at my bedside and strove to pluck my soul from my bosom.

"'What would'st thou?' I cried.

"'Thy soul is mine,' he said, 'thou shalt live out my curse. Give me thy soul – hold back thy hands – give me thy soul, I say.'

"'Thy curse shall not be upon me,' I cried. 'What have I done that thy curse should rest upon me? Thou shalt not have my soul.'

"'For my offence shalt thou suffer, and in my curse thou shalt endure hell – it is so decreed.'

"So spake the old man, and he strove with me, and he prevailed against me, and he plucked my soul from my bosom, and he said, 'Go, search and kill' – and – and lo, I was a wolf upon the moor.

"The dry grass crackled beneath my tread. The darkness of the night was heavy and it oppressed me. Strange horrors tortured my soul, and it groaned and groaned gaoled in that wolfish body. The wind whispered to me; with its myriad voices it spake to me and said, 'Go, search and kill.' And above these voices sounded the hideous laughter of an old man. I fled the moor – whither I knew not, nor knew I what motive lashed me on.

"I came to a river and I plunged in. A burning thirst consumed me, and I lapped the waters of the river – they were waves of flame, and they flashed around me and hissed, and what they said was, 'Go, search and kill,' and I heard the old man's laughter again.

"A forest lay before me with its gloomy thickets and its sombre shadows – with its ravens, its vampires, its serpents, its reptiles, and all its hideous brood of night. I darted among its thorns and crouched amid the leaves, the nettles, and the brambles. The owls hooted at me and the thorns pierced my flesh. 'Go, search and kill,' said everything. The hares sprang from my pathway; the other beasts ran bellowing away; every form of life shrieked in my ears – the curse was on me – I was the werewolf.

"On, on I went with the fleetness of the wind, and my soul groaned in its wolfish prison, and the winds and the waters and the trees bade me, 'Go, search and kill, thou accursed brute; go, search and kill.'

"Nowhere was there pity for the wolf; what mercy, thus, should I, the werewolf, show? The curse was on me and it filled me with hunger and a thirst for blood. Skulking on my way within myself I cried, 'Let me have blood, oh, let me have human blood, that this wrath may be appeased, that this curse may be removed.'

"At last I came to the sacred grove. Sombre loomed the poplars, the oaks frowned upon me. Before me stood an old man – 'twas he, grizzled and taunting, whose curse I bore. He feared me not. All other living things fled before me, but the old man feared me not. A maiden stood beside him. She did not see me, for she was blind.

"'Kill, kill,' cried the old man, and he pointed at the girl beside him.

"Hell raged within me – the curse impelled me – I sprang at her throat. I heard the old man's laughter once more, and then – then I awoke, trembling, cold, horrified."

Scarce was this dream told when Alfred strode the way.

"Now, by'r Lady," quoth he, "I bethink me never to have seen a sorrier twain."

Then Yseult told him of Harold's going away and how that Harold had besought her not to venture to the feast of Ste. Aelfreda in the sacred grove.

"These fears are childish," cried Alfred boastfully. "And thou sufferest me, sweet lady, I will bear thee company to the feast, and a score of my lusty yeoman with their good yew-bows and honest spears, they shall attend me. There be no werewolf, I trow, will chance about with us."

Whereat Yseult laughed merrily, and Harold said: "'T is well; thou shalt go to the sacred grove, and may my love and Heaven's grace forefend all evil."

Then Harold went to his abode, and he fetched old Siegfried's spear back unto Yseult, and he gave it into her two hands, saying, "Take this spear with thee to the feast tomorrow night. It is old Siegfried's spear, possessing mighty virtue and marvellous."

And Harold took Yseult to his heart and blessed her, and he kissed her upon her brow and upon her lips, saying, "Farewell, oh, my beloved. How wilt thou love me when thou know'st my sacrifice. Farewell, farewell, forever, oh, alder-liefest mine."

So Harold went his way, and Yseult was lost in wonderment.

On the morrow night came Yseult to the sacred grove wherein the feast was spread, and she bore old Siegfried's spear with her in her girdle.

Alfred attended her, and a score of lusty yeomen were with him. In the grove there was great merriment, and with singing and dancing and games withal did the honest folk celebrate the feast of the fair Ste. Aelfreda.

But suddenly a mighty tumult arose, and there were cries of "The werewolf!" "The werewolf!" Terror seized upon all – stout hearts were frozen with fear. Out from the further forest rushed the werewolf, wood wroth, bellowing hoarsely, gnashing his fangs and tossing hither and thither the yellow foam from his snapping jaws. He sought Yseult straight, as if an evil power drew him to the spot where she stood. But Yseult was not afeared; like a marble statue she stood and saw the werewolf's coming. The yeomen, dropping their torches and casting aside their bows, had fled; Alfred alone abided there to do the monster battle.

At the approaching wolf he hurled his heavy lance, but as it struck the werewolf's bristling back the weapon was all to-shivered.

Then the werewolf, fixing his eyes upon Yseult, skulked for a moment in the shadow of the yews and thinking then of Harold's words, Yseult plucked old Siegfried's spear from her girdle, raised it on high, and with the strength of despair sent it hurtling through the air.

The werewolf saw the shining weapon, and a cry burst from his gaping throat – a cry of human agony. And Yseult saw in the werewolf's eyes the eyes of someone she had seen and known, but 't was for an instant only, and then the eyes were no longer human, but wolfish in their ferocity.

A supernatural force seemed to speed the spear in its flight. With fearful precision the weapon smote home and buried itself by half its length in the werewolf's shaggy breast just above the heart, and then, with a monstrous sigh – as if he yielded up his life without regret – the werewolf fell dead in the shadow of the yews.

Then, ah, then in very truth there was great joy, and loud were the acclaims, while, beautiful in her trembling pallor, Yseult was led unto her home, where the people set about to give great feast to do her homage, for the werewolf was dead, and she it was that had slain him.

But Yseult cried out: "Go, search for Harold – go, bring him to me. Nor eat, nor sleep till he be found."

"Good my lady," quoth Alfred, "how can that be, since he hath betaken himself to Normandy?"

"I care not where he be," she cried. "My heart stands still until I look into his eyes again."

"Surely he hath not gone to Normandy?" outspake Hubert. "This very eventide I saw him enter his abode."

They hastened thither – a vast company. His chamber door was barred.

"Harold, Harold, come forth!" they cried, as they beat upon the door, but no answer came to their calls and knockings. Afeared, they battered down the door, and when it fell they saw that Harold lay upon his bed.

"He sleeps," said one. "See, he holds a portrait in his hand – and it is her portrait. How fair he is and how tranquilly he sleeps."

But no, Harold was not asleep. His face was calm and beautiful, as if he dreamed of his beloved, but his raiment was red with the blood that streamed from a wound in his breast – a gaping, ghastly spear wound just above his heart.

We Are Not the Wolf

Roy Graham

"**EAMES HAS ESCAPED** the facility," Levi told us. "But the important thing to remember is, there's no reason to panic. Remember: Panic is the strung-out uncle of Concern."

He'd cut himself shaving that morning and hadn't put a bandage over it. Levi was always shaving, two or three times a day. In all the excitement the scab had broken open and now he sported a little dot of red on his chin. I tried not to stare. Directed my eyes anywhere else: his cat-covered tie, his starchy white shirt, the linoleum floor. The other residents.

"I'm sure this is a stressful time for everybody. I'm sure emotions are running high. And that's why I'd like to do a few rounds of our mantra, just to center everyone. Can we do that?"

I took a deep breath. Collectively, the other teenage residents of the Tranquility Center took one with me.

"We are not the wolf. His teeth are not our teeth. His horrible claws are not our horrible claws. We possess the fearsome natural weapons of kindness, restraint, and respect for others. We are not the wolf."

Early that morning, residents of the Tranquility Center had woken to chanting. We did plenty of chanting ourselves, but this was no mantra of Levi's: "Munsen! Ain't! For monsters! Munsen! Ain't! For monsters!"

There they were, assembled on the lawn of the Tranquility Center–farmers, ditch diggers, men who made their living through some combination of selling bootleg alcohol and shoveling driveways in the colder months. Red faces, withered sports jerseys. They all looked like they had survived something vague and horrible. A few of the protestors were holding signs; on one, illustrated in two-tone marker, a woodsman chopped the big bad wolf into little disks of meat. On another, the words HUMANS ONLY were painted in big red letters. They were all belting their little slogan, over and over. "Munsen! Ain't! For monsters!"

Munsen County. So poor and remote, someone like Levi could actually buy land. The Tranquility Center was his baby, as I understood, and despite all the corny meditation junk and weird fixation with keeping his cheeks marble-smooth, I actually thought he was all right. The residents of Munsen County apparently disagreed. Now, on top of that, Eames was out.

When my parents told me I was going upstate, I didn't understand what they meant. I thought we already lived upstate. But there were six solid hours between the suburb where we lived and the Tranquility Center. My father volunteered to drive the whole way.

"Look, Justin! Goats! I didn't know they had those in this corner of the country."

"So much green up here. Can't you already taste the difference in the air?"

"Wow, that man's on a tractor!"

On and on and on. We drove into what I thought of as the country, the real backwoods, and then we kept going; deeper and deeper, until it looked like we were driving through some minor apocalypse. Barns with the paint stripped by wind and rain, creeper vines spilling out the window like an infection. He'd bought donuts on our way out of town, and then came the talking. It didn't seem to matter to him that I wasn't talking back.

I would have preferred, I think, the icy silence of my mother. She wouldn't have stopped for donuts or said "Gee!" or tried to make this seem like some kind of vacation. When my father was scared he babbled, but her fear was muffling and silent. It would have suited the occasion, I think. I had eaten the neighbor's poodle and that wasn't even the worst of it.

Most of the people at the Center wanted to be there. Not Eames. His first change, Eames had killed another kid at his high school. His lawyer had gotten it down to a manslaughter charge, on account of the unusual circumstances of the crime, and because Eames was white and a minor and came from money, he managed to avoid jail time. The judge settled instead for community service and a mandatory enrollment in the Tranquility Center.

I knew all this because Eames told us. He bragged about how he'd gotten away with eating a classmate. "What do you think people taste like?" he'd said to me once in the cafeteria. "A lot of people say pork. Because of the movies, you know? Long pig? But I'd say it's closer to venison. Gamey." When Levi wasn't around he liked to chomp on contraband Slim Jims, just to remind everyone where he stood.

So, that was Eames. And now he was out there, somewhere.

* * *

By the afternoon the protest had petered out. Hay to bale, buckets to kick, or something. I called my parents. Levi advised against making many calls during our first month at the Center – "We have to look inward before we can look outward" – but the day Eames escaped, I needed to hear a normal voice.

"Dad?"

"Hey, Champ! How's it going? Your mother and I were just thinking of you."

"It's all right, I guess."

"How's that fresh air and good food? The brochures talked a lot about the food. You've got real chefs out there cooking for you."

"Yeah, it's all right." It really was, for being all-vegetarian.

"Your, uh, your first full moon is coming up. Isn't that right?"

"Yeah. We've been practicing for it. Deep breaths and all that."

"Good, good. Breathing is good."

"How's Peter?"

A beat of silence. "Peter's still in the hospital," said my father. "But the doctors say he's doing much better."

* * *

The night of the full moon, they strapped me down to the bed. I hadn't noticed the metal rings on the bed frame, or maybe I just hadn't connected them to their intended purpose. They used steel cables, like the kind on crab-fishing boats. I heard a rumor there was silver woven into them but it didn't seem necessary. When they were pulled taut, even the strongest kid couldn't have moved a muscle.

One cable went around my shoulders and chest, one around my arms and midriff – tight, so I wouldn't be able to slip my hands out. The last cable was right above my knees. The whole time, the nurse strapping me down was talking about breakfast the next day.

"Everyone's always so tired the night after a full moon," she said. "And hungry too! That's why we have plenty of waffles, eggs, oatmeal, whatever you want. Oh, and coffee, of course!"

From the tinny speakers in the hallway, I heard the kind of jazz a catalog might describe as "soothing" or "gentle." Levi's choice, surely. When I was secured to the bed, the nurse paused, setting her hand on my knee.

"You boys," she said. "You're not as bad as they say. You're going to turn out okay."

When she left, I heard someone flip a larger lock into place outside the door.

* * *

At first I thought it was a piñata. Very bright red, swaying gently in the morning breeze. Hanging from that great oak that framed the Center's driveway. I could see it from my window as I got dressed, though not clearly – too many branches in the way. I had to kind of press my face into the side of the glass, around the bars. Maybe it was someone's birthday. High school wasn't that far from piñata-age.

At breakfast someone outside started screaming. That was an uncomfortable moment for the residents. I heard spoons and forks clatter to a halt all down my table, and then some very deliberate breathing. One-two-three pause, one-two-three. Everyone just trying to get a handle on their shit. Screaming was tough for us.

Levi didn't miss a beat. He was up and power-walking to the front of the building, bony elbows pumping, pizza-tie flapping wildly.

Ray Baines. The name made the rounds. He owned fifty acres of apple tree land barely two miles from the Center. I'd seen him before and I hadn't even realized. Apparently he'd been part of the protest, though how anyone could identify that visually was beyond me, because he'd also been skinned. *Inexpertly skinned*. Which seemed decidedly worse.

When the situation was more or less under control, Levi called us into the cafeteria for a general-body. "Everyone, I'm sorry for that unpleasantness this morning, but I need you to know that we've gotten the situation *completely* under control. And – unrelatedly – there will be some men coming to help us with repairs around the facility, so you might see a few unfamiliar faces. We want everyone to feel welcome here, so make sure you give 'em a hearty hello," he said, with a little wave of his hand.

I called home twice before anyone picked up. I wanted to say, *Okay, time for me to come home! Skinned bodies are now showing up at this rehabilitation center and it is time to go!*

"Carver's residence," said my mother. My mind emptied.

"Hi, Mom."

"Justin?"

"Yes, that's me. That's my name."

"Well," she said. Her voice like a pick. "I didn't know they let you make calls from the facility."

There was some noise in the background, two distorted voices talking to one another with some urgency. Then motion.

"Hoo boy, son," said my father into the receiver, a little too flustered. "You catch that big game?!"

I tried to return to the image of that man, bloody, obscured by broad oak leaves. I couldn't muster the same horror I'd felt a moment ago. All I could hear was my mother's voice on the other end of the phone. A little faint, like she couldn't bear to hold it up against her ear.

* * *

All week, a steady trickle of men in trucks arrived at the facility. Their uniforms were gray and nondescript. They had mysterious equipment – once, I saw them lifting huge black boxes made of hard plastic from the bed of their truck. Like the stage manager of a school play, Levi brought them here and there, shepherding them into unoccupied rooms, hosting clandestine meetings during meal times.

In group sessions, Bart broke down. He'd gotten into a pet store on his first change and was still haunted by the memory. Whenever it was my turn I always found a way to talk around Peter, around what had happened. "School was so stressful. All those tests," I'd say, while picturing Peter lying in his hospital bed, Peter with his leg all torn to meat.

Eames was a constant presence, even if no one said his name. Levi's slogans started to have the air of political debate. "When you worry that you might lose control, remember that you always have a choice. Don't forget to HOWL: Hold up, Own your feelings, Weigh your options, and Let go of your animal urges."

Once, after dark, I saw beams of white light sweeping through the hills outside through the bars of my window. Swinging back and forth in the night. The distant buzz of radios.

* * *

Most nights at the Center, I dreamed animal dreams. The pads of my feet on dewey grass, the quickness of thought unfiltered by human interpretation. A rabbit, darting from the entrance to its warren, sprinting into night and panic; in a few strides I had caught him. It wasn't anger or viciousness I felt when I bit down, punching my teeth through the rabbit's baby-soft skull. Nothing so human. When I killed the rabbit in my dream, I felt a great and abiding tranquility.

The first change, because of its unpredictability, was often the worst. Levi told us that early on in our time at the center. Showed us slide after horrible Powerpoint slide: apartments torn to shreds, lawns drenched in human blood. One particularly ghoulish anecdote about a car at Makeout Point discovered the next morning, the windows papered in viscera, a naked boy shivering in the backseat amidst the remains of his date.

When I think about that night it's like it's happening all over again. A car alarm singing somewhere in the distance. The world open and raw, unfiltered by my sluggish daylight brain. No more nerves or second-guessing, no words or symbols cluttering my wolf-thoughts. I remember Pom-Pom, Mrs. Bergstram's poodle, barking at me through the white boards of her fence. I cleared those boards effortlessly, and then I was in her yard, with Pom-Pom, who tried to run but not nearly fast enough.

I didn't feel out of control when I opened Pom-Pom's neck with a swipe of my claws, or when I bit into her soft underbelly. They were all choices, and I was happy to have made them. I was ripping into one of Pom-Pom's back legs when our front porch light turned on.

Peter, my little brother, stood there under the warm yellow light. Pajamas on. Squinting into the dark.

And the whole time, it's me. That's the worst part. Me crunching down on the skull of that poodle. Me seeing my younger brother in the doorway. Me wondering what that beating heart, what that hot blood I can hear running through his veins will taste like.

I don't know how you can come back from that. I don't know how Levi lives an ordinary life. Goes into town. Has a bank account, pays his taxes. Eames is an asshole, but I get it. It would be so much easier to lean in.

* * *

Around midnight there was a lot of shouting. I could hear Levi's voice among the racket, shrill and pronounced, and under all of it was a noise like a broken machine; grinding, low, constant with fluctuations in pitch and volume. I listened for some time before I realized it was the sound of a man dying. Or the sound of his body, telling everyone around him that he was dying. With my ear pressed to the door I only caught a few words: "Monster," "Treeline," "Contract." Nobody sounded happy.

The next day, the handy-men were gone. They took everything with them: their black equipment cases, their trucks, their aura, which was in character something between "There's a rattlesnake under the house, so nobody go outside" and "The principal has suspended the school bully, ushering in an uneasy period of peace." I was astounded at the speed with which they'd erased any trace of their presence here, but I guess they were professionals.

Breakfast was piles of cereal and jugs of milk from the fridge. I didn't see any of the kitchen staff or nurses.

When we filed into our Awareness and Guidance meeting that morning, Levi was already waiting for us. He had a book in his lap; on the glossy cover was a photo of snow-swept pines beneath the words *Ogden's Guide to the North American Wolf: Gray to Timber*. Blue, green and purple post-its were sticking out to mark a few particular pages.

"Eames paid us a visit last night. As some of you may have heard," said Levi. He scratched at his chin. There was, I noticed, stubble carpeting his narrow jaw. It was the first time I'd seen any trace of hair on him that wasn't eyebrow. "I thought maybe we'd take a different approach today. Unless anyone really wants to meditate, of course."

I exchanged side-eyes with a few other residents. Without really waiting, he opened the book to the first post-it. "Originally, the gray wolf occupied all of North America above a certain latitude. As an apex predator, almost no other animal threatened their presence on the continent before the arrival of European colonists."

He turned to another note, farther into the book. "Fear of wolves among American settlers resulted in predator control programs that virtually eliminated the animal from the Western United States. The most common method was poisoning, but the National Park Service had a shoot-to-kill policy for almost ten years. The myth of the wolf declared it an unkillable monster, a child-eating beast. They did, every now and then, attack children. But the unkillable part was very much myth."

"Despite the popular image of the "lone wolf," there is no subspecies that operates as solitary creatures. Wolves are social animals. They depend on one another for survival."

"Wolves kill, but unlike tigers and humans, they never do so for sport."

"Wolves kill deer, but no wolf has ever *been* a deer. It is unknown if wolves would continue to kill deer if they had a good understanding of the inner lives of said deer. Of their hopes for the future, or their love for other deer. For example."

"Scientists disagree on whether or not wolves would, in that case, have a moral obligation to not kill deer. Or to try and coexist with deer. But if the deer were the ones poisoning and shooting the wolves, because of their fear, one would think an attempt to build bridges would be a wise move as far as survival of the species is concerned."

Finally, he closed the book. We all sat there, together. I thought maybe he was going to cry, but instead he said, "There's a better life than the one they want for us. I know things haven't been going so well around the Center but I'm asking for your trust. The full moon is tonight. Just stay in your rooms until morning, and I will make pancakes tomorrow. With fruit in them."

I called my parents six times after that. Over and over I got the voicemail machine. *You've reached the Carvers' residence*, said Peter's disembodied voice. *Please leave a message after the tone.*

* * *

That night, no one came to strap me down. I finally got around to wondering what happened to the nurse that had been so kind to me before. Maybe one of the hard men in jumpsuits had swept her off her feet, took her far from Munsen county to live as a glamorous mercenary wife. Without any steel cables, I couldn't even make an effort at restraining myself, so I just sat in bed and tried not to think of Eames. What new horrors he might visit onto the men and women of this place. Last full moon he had skinned someone, hung them like a Christmas ornament. If it was this hard to be good it must be so much easier to slide into bad, and now he was a full month worse than he had been last time.

The change is never as dramatic as the movies make it out to be. In truth I hardly noticed it was happening. Just looked down and my hands were big and hairy and tipped with these little black talons, harder than stone.

Then I could smell the grass. Like grass times a thousand. And all the signals that normal people can't see, the billion signs and symbols of the yard: the territorial bluster of the chipmunk mob, the invader dandelion on the wind, the wild cat that still smelled like house, the birdly terror at his arrival. The sudden emptiness in my belly.

And clear as a hunting call, my wolf-nose scented men.

I couldn't see them from my window. They were coming quickly from the other side of the Center, down the road, towards the front doors. I couldn't hear the rum-tum-tum of their hearts but soon, when they were here, when they got to the front door, when they came inside I would NO.

I wouldn't. Not again.

I tried to remember one of Levi's slogans, any one of them. "Remember, it has never been more true that you *are* what you *eat*!"

I could smell them and then I could hear them and then I could *really* smell them: pollen, dirt, fear, vodka. They jiggled the front doors frantically against the lock. "Let us in!" one of them shouted. "Please! There's something out here!"

Eames. Finally I understood, and knew just as quickly what I had to do. I stood up from my bed and looked at the simple door knob, then down at my claws. It took me a few tries, but with both hands I managed to twist it open, and I was out of my room. Werewolf on the loose. A ghostly oboe from the speaker system warbled from the speakers.

It was harder to navigate the tiled hallway than I expected. My long digitigrade feet couldn't get much traction so I kept falling, catching myself on the walls, accidentally putting my claws right through the plaster. I followed the frenzied banging. Everything was so different. At night, as a wolf, I had never walked the halls like this before.

Finally, the front doors. There was a little latch holding them shut – that was easy enough, even with the men outside nearly shaking them off the hinges. I flipped the latch and the Munsenites spilled inside.

I knew I couldn't speak like this, couldn't tell them it would all be okay, that I wasn't going to hurt them. Not with my flopping tongue, my black lips, my many teeth. Instead I tried to smile. Ludicrously, I gave them one clawed thumbs-up. Trying, in some Levi-like fashion, to communicate the essentials: that they were safe from Eames. That it was going to be all right. That we were in this together. Then one of them shot me.

At first I was surprised. Surprised at the little revolver in his hand, at the deafening noise it had made. Then the room tilted and I fell over and the other men closed the double doors while the pain approached like an oncoming train.

The bullet in my chest was a piece of burning coal and I twisted around it, writhing on the ground. I don't know if it was silver or if being shot just hurt worse than anything else a sixteen-year-old might encounter in the world. All the while the man with the gun – a little portly, wearing a hockey shirt and glasses – circumnavigated me slowly, keeping the pistol fixed in my direction while he peeked around the corner.

"I thought they were all supposed to be locked up."

"I don't know about this anymore."

"Where are the fucking *people*?"

"Doesn't matter. Let's do what we came here to do."

One of them opened a backpack and pulled out a bottle of vodka with a rag poking from the neck. "Who's got the lighter?"

I whimpered. I couldn't help it – the pain in my chest was too much.

"Will you fucking kill that thing already?" someone said. Which is when Levi came around the corner.

Not the Levi that I had known – the bald, obsessive little man in the goofy ties and loafers – but Levi all the same. Shaggy and huge, a salt-and-pepper hue to his coarse fur, leaving deep gouges in the tiled floor with each loping stride. The man with the pistol managed to fire two shots into the wall and ceiling before Levi hit him and they tumbled together into the others. Deep inside, the Justin part of me said to close my eyes.

Darkness, and then the iron stench of blood filling my nostrils. Bone snapping, a nightmare snarl, then hooting and moaning and yapping as the men died, involuntary noises, body sounds. Glass breaking – the reek of liquor. Some ripping, like fabric overstretched, and then silence. Someone touched my head.

When I opened my eyes, it was Levi. Naked, fur falling off in clumps, absolutely covered in blood. His hands were still claws and with one he stroked my canine ears while the other delicately searched my chest for the breach. I felt him brush very lightly against the edge of the wound. The wave of pain was so great I nearly passed out.

"Shh," he said. The last thing I remember from that night: no more slogans, just comforting animal sounds. "Shh, shhh. It's going to be okay."

Margaery the Wolf

Maria Haskins

IT WAS THE KIND OF VILLAGE where some were born wolves, and others were born human.

This all happened long ago, of course, and I am old now, but I remember it as it was when I grew up, across the road from Margaery's house.

Everyone lived together, as it had always been. Wolves and humans married and had children, and it mattered little what your parents were. Some wolves gave birth to humans, some humans gave birth to wolves. Cubs and children played together, went to the village school together, ate their midday meals together beneath the trees on sunny days: cracked beef bones and marrow for some, bread and soup for others.

It happened when the cubs grew that sharp teeth would sometimes rip a dress or pant leg, would draw blood, maybe give a deeper cut, teeth marks set in flesh. "Just wash and bind it, Ellinore," my mother would say, like all the adults said. And the children did, nursing old wounds and scars beneath sleeves and petticoats.

As they grew bigger still, sometimes a child would go missing, and a cub – or two or three – would return home from the woods with washed-clean muzzles and no story to tell, their still-hot tongues licking red dribbles from the corners of their mouths.

"Children get lost in the woods," the parents would say, "it happens. The trails are narrow and winding, and some children stray too far, too deep, too dark. We should have taught them better, to keep steady on the trails, not to step in between the roots and shadows. Not to walk off untended."

Maybe some thought that cubs, too, should be kept on trails more straight and narrow, but if they did, they kept those words tucked deep inside.

The day Margaery got bitten by a cub, she came home, arm torn from elbow to wrist, bone showing through. I heard her wailing as she ran from the woods, blood soaked through her dress and stockings, dripping dark from dirty fingers.

"Just wash and bind it," said her mother, shaking somewhat as she helped her.

Once Margaery stopped crying, she said, "I am a cub, too." After that, she ran on all-fours through the village, brandishing teeth and nails instead of playing hide and seek, cuffing cubs around the head, knocking children over as she ran. She was fourteen, just like me. Too old for playing cub in fields and streets, as younger children sometimes did, and Margaery's parents watched perturbed. Some neighbours laughed. Until Margaery bit a cub, and a child.

She did it in the schoolyard, where everyone could see: teeth bared, leaping at them, the way she did when they'd called her something foul. She kept that wounded arm of hers aside while she bit and tore, ripping into a cheek and a leg.

The teacher sent her home, and I watched her go scampering down the street. By the time I got home, Margaery's father had already been at her with his belt, and she lay stretched out on the porch, face turned so I couldn't see.

"You cannot go around biting others," said her mother, changing the soiled bandage on Margaery's arm, wrapping clean linen around the weeping wound, dabbing resin-ointment at the fresh belt-streaks across her back.

Margaery growled. "Cubs do it. I am a cub. They can wash and bind it, same as I."

She was not allowed to go to school for a week. When she returned, everyone knew her father had whipped her for what she'd done.

"Cubs don't mind whippings," Margaery said, and kept going about on all-fours: at school, at home, and in the fields and forest, too. I saw her sometimes, sneaking between the trees at the edges of the fields – dress soiled, face grubby, hair unbraided.

"Come with me, Ellinore," she called out once when she caught me looking, but all I did was turn and run.

* * *

The children didn't want to play with her, and neither did the cubs. For a while she was all alone.

Then Rebecca, who'd been bitten by some cubs the year before, and Alistair, whose brother had wandered too far and deep in the company of cubs that past winter, and not been seen since, started walking on all-fours with her. They'd go off into the woods together, like cubs did, chasing through the deep glades and dark hollows, eating rabbits and squirrels raw, rolling in the muck, washing hands and lips in the creek, licking red dribbles from the corners of their mouths.

By the time first one cub and then another disappeared and didn't come home for supper or breakfast, the village was in uproar. Margaery and her friends had wiped their chins clean, washed their hands, and had no tales to tell. But others had stories, and Margaery denied nothing.

"Why do you care?" she said when two elders came to speak to her. "Two children disappeared last winter. You didn't even look for them. Maybe these cubs strayed too far, too deep, too dark, just like those children did. Maybe they lost their way. Maybe someone found them, and searched out that warm spot in their gut, all the cubs know it and so do I, that soft part of the belly where the skin is thinnest."

She licked her lips.

The elders left, saying they'd be back next morning. Margaery's father took her to the shed, saying he'd strip the hide off her backside this time. I heard the snap of that leather belt, the thump of that buckle, but afterwards, he was the one tending a bleeding hand, his flesh gouged out in strips. Margaery wiped her eyes and mouth, shook herself, wolf-like, and said her hide wasn't his to strip anymore.

It made me shiver, the way she said it. The way her words burned beneath my skin, the way her voice tore at me, even though I did nought but listen.

At the village council that night, wolves and humans alike were raging, with the parents of the missing cubs shouting and crying, some thinking that Margaery should be put to death right then and there. Burning was the way to do it, most agreed.

Next morning, Margaery was brought before the council, chained. They made her stand on two-legs when she spoke, though she snapped her jaws and tried to scratch as best she could, even then.

"What makes the others cubs and not me?" asked Margaery. "You call them wolves, and so you let them bite and claw and kill. Those are things wolves do. You've all seen the bones in the forest glades, the skulls emptied, the knuckles gnawed clean. You know the deeds. Yet you act now as though these things had never happened before. As if the forest were safe before I stalked there."

She looked around at the faces in the village hall, bared her teeth at some, mouth wide and leering. I looked at her and thought of Margaery before she'd had her arm torn: wearing dresses, neat shoes, and ribboned pigtails, loath to speak up in class, just like me.

"I am a cub, as much as any other. I bite and claw and kill. That makes me wolf. Would you call me human now? Can a human bite and claw and kill as well as a wolf? Is that what you tell me?"

The people looked at each other, then back at Margaery, and it seemed to many of them that perhaps Margaery had always been wolf, and that they just hadn't noticed until now. She was led away on all-fours, shaggy-haired and snarling. "Much like a cub," some whispered in the crowd, uneasy.

"The midwives know best how to tell cub from child," a man piped up. "They know it from when they're born. We should ask them what Margaery is for certain."

The midwives had their house near the village well, and they were always fair busy, drying herbs and roots, making ointments and potions, seeing to the pregnant wolves and humans.

"You can tell when they're born, of course," the oldest midwife said, impatient with the askers. "You see them squeezed out into the world, and there you are: some are born wolves, some human. You know which one's what soon as you see them."

"Sometimes it takes a bit of looking," said the other midwife. "But you can always tell."

"You just know," said the third and youngest midwife. "You see it in them. And later of course the wolves walk on all-fours and do all sorts of things that only wolves do."

But what to do, then, about a child who had walked on twos, and now went about on all-fours?

The midwives thought on it, whispering amongst themselves about Margaery and Rebecca and Alistair. Then they shook their heads. No, they said, each of those had been a child at birth, and surely was a child still.

"I see what they are, and they are what I see," said the oldest midwife with her hackles raised, a growl prickling beneath her words, and then she'd say no more.

Meanwhile, Margaery was howling in her cell, Rebecca and Alistair in their cages joining their howls to hers. Margaery ripped and scratched the guards, bit and chewed her chains.

Not even her mother was allowed to see her, though she was stood across the way, listening all day, saying nothing if you spoke to her.

Thinking this matter harder to unravel than first thought, the elders went reluctantly to Henrick, the oldest of the villagers and therefore named lore-keeper. He was half-blind and hobbling, living mostly off rope-work and handouts, housed in a hut on the outskirts: dirt-floor, sod-roof, three goats roaming free outside.

He chuckled when they asked him if he'd ever heard of a child turned wolf before, sipping at his sweet-root tea. How old he was he did not know himself, but no one in the village could remember him as anything but ancient and hairless. Whatever family he'd had were all done and gone, bones beneath the grass and oak at forest's edge.

"I don't right recall," Henrick answered, savouring the words as if they were burned-sugar candies, melting slowly on his tongue. "My life's too long for me to remember all that's happened and been done to me, and to this village. Once we were all alike, so the oldest stories say. But if so, were we wolves or humans, then, and why did some turn while others didn't? I'm not sure of that, if that is what you're asking."

I listened as he spoke those words, hiding behind Father in the crowd, and when he saw me there, trembling, he winked and twitched his ears. Father would have slapped me if I laughed, so I only blushed and turned to go with the others.

* * *

Deep into the night the village spoke and argued, wolves and humans gathered in the church; us children and cubs playing in the hall while the adults talked, or sleeping in the back pew.

There were village laws, rules spoken and unspoken, and all agreed Margaery had broken them. It was not right for a child to kill a cub. One woman grumbled that her daughter had disappeared that past fall, and wondered why no fuss had been made about the cubs seen with her before she got lost. Both wolves and humans shook their heads and looked away.

"Your daughter wandered too far and deep. You should have told her it weren't safe."

"Wiser mothers teach their children not to stray."

"Just teach your cub the same," the woman said, a sting in her voice.

"You wolves are all of one kind," another man's voice, rising. Alistair's father it might have been. "All killing and a-slaughtering."

"I've never," cried one wolf. Others joining in, saying they had not been anywhere near the woods or trails or darker hollows, at least since they were cubs themselves.

"What kind of wolf are you, then?" the man asked. "If not for the snarling and the biting? Seems to me, you're nothing but a human, except walking 'round on all-fours."

The wolves raised their voices, howling that being wolf was more than snarls and teeth; that they were villagers of worth and import and should be treated such. In that moment, there was a sudden heat like spark and kindling in the room, a flicker of a feral glow. All could feel it: words and voices likely to catch fire, to set each house ablaze before long.

Flasks and tea were passed around to douse the flames, some were sent home to sleep their rage off, others told to get out of doors to cool their heads.

"Might it be that everyone, wolf and human both, should be treated the same and follow the same rules?" one wolf wondered, glancing about anxiously when most were settled in the pews again. Heads shook. No. Wolves were not like humans, and humans not like wolves.

Wolves had sharper senses, smell and hearing for a start. That was known.

"Say a wolf smells blood," one wolf put in, "even a smidgen of it, a drop. Their jaws will start a-snapping before they even know they're doing it."

All wolves nodded in agreement. Most humans nodded, too. "That's right, so it is," they said. "We don't care over-much for the smell of blood." Neither did they have the taste for raw meat or howling or stalking between the trees. Those were wolf cravings, surely. And if some humans thought that they might have felt a twinge or two when they smelled blood or flesh, a stirring in the heart and the saliva running freely, they did not speak up that night.

When the lots were cast at dawn, the verdict was decided: not death, but banishment.

That rustled through the village right-quick. It had been years uncounted since such a ruling had been handed down.

Margaery's mother stood quiet while the lots were counted, while the sentence was read aloud to all the villagers in the square. There were fresh cuts and scrapes on her face and paws, same as I'd seen on Margaery more than once when she'd disobeyed her father.

Margaery saw it, too, from her place on the steps where she had been brought out in chains.

I looked away, but I felt Margaery's eyes on me, and didn't dare raise my head: afraid of what I'd see in her face, afraid of what she'd see in mine.

Next full moon, Margaery and her pack, as they called Rebecca and Alistair by then, were taken deep into the woods. Deeper than the hunters went, deeper than the berry pickers and herbalists would go. So far they almost crossed the edge of the world into the realms of other beings and their habitations. There the three were let go, bonds cut, and the wagon drove off, horses whipped into a froth as the driver headed back.

* * *

Not even cubs roamed the woods for a good while after that, and neither wolves nor humans would go by themselves into the farther fields. Everyone closed and barred their doors and stayed inside when darkness fell. All except Henrick, who sat out on his porch among the goats most nights it seemed, braiding rope or drinking sweet-root tea, rheumy eyes fixed on the woods as if he were waiting.

"She couldn't make it in the woods," I said to him when I went there one evening to pass along some fresh-baked bread from grandmother. I kept looking half with dread, half with hope at the edge of the forest where Henrick's eyes were roaming. "Could she? Might she?"

Henrick only chuckled and dunked a crust of bread into his mug, those hairy knuckles of his almost turning into paws in the dusk-light.

"Who knows what such a one as Margaery might do," he said, rubbing the smallest of the goats between the horns until the creature bucked and skipped off the porch. He winked at me and smiled. "I've seen you wondering, Ellinore, seen you wondering about the way the world is made around you. It's not easy to live like this, with wolves and humans side by side, so alike that we need the midwives to tell us who is who, and yet told we are so different that the same rules can't apply." He peeked at me sideways. "What do you see, when you look at me? Wolf or human?"

I shifted where I sat, unsettled, looking at his face in the dusk-light, the gleam of those grey-clouded eyes.

"I see human, since that is what you are. You're like me."

He nodded.

"Yes. Of course. And some days I see it too. But do you see it because it is what I am, or because that's what you've been told to see?" I didn't know how to answer that, and Henrick turned towards the woods again. "No matter. Maybe you're too young, yet, to know the difference between becoming what others see, and seeing what you are without their gaze.

"And besides, if I've gained any wisdom in my old age it's only this: that it's safer to wait and be told what I am, rather than make up my own mind. The world shapes itself to what we believe. That's the way it's always been."

He drank from his cup, licked his lips clean after.

"As for that Margaery," he said, "when she comes again, she'll bring a fire with her. I've dreamed it so. Or maybe what I've seen is memory or story. Sometimes it seems to me that all this has happened before, once or many times, but always been forgotten. Either way, you'd best be ready, Ellinore, whether you think yourself cub or child."

I sat with him as the sun went down, even though I knew Mother wanted me back sharpish, sat and thought of woods and trails, thought of cubs and children lost or found within the dark.

* * *

Margaery's mother put away her daughter's dresses, her ribbons, and her shoes.

She folded them and placed them in a chest. "Have another child," my mother told her, "if you've still got a patch as where to plant the seeds." But everyone knew by then she wouldn't let her human husband touch her since Margaery had gone.

Some nights I saw her, sitting next to Henrick, holding a mug of sweet-root tea between her paws, staring at the woods like he did, like I did all those times I couldn't sleep.

* * *

It was a quiet year, mostly. Summer and harvest slipping past to winter, cubs and children almost playing together again by next spring, even those of us still nursing deeper wounds, washed and bound and festering.

Margaery's pack waited for the first new moon in early summer: night all dark, clouds pulled over stars, no light to glimpse their faces by. Then they came: fierce and silent, fang and claw unsheathed, tearing through the village like a hunter's blade slits a carcass open from ribs to tail, spilling guts and entrails.

Wolves and humans alike were dragged from their beds into the square past midnight, made to stand before the bonfire where the jail had been: Margaery on all-fours in the glow, blood and gore trickling from her chin and tongue. Three elders and some others were missing, my mother among them, charred limbs and skulls showing in the fire, the sight of it enough to make us all try to turn away, though no turning made the smell of roasted flesh easier to abide.

Rebecca stood beside Margaery, and so did Alistair, as well as at least two-dozen wolves none of us had seen before. They were other cubs Margaery had found in the woods, hurt or lost or wandering, some still thinking they were children until they'd heard Margaery calling them with her howl.

"By morning, there will be no humans in this village," Margaery said, and when she fell silent, not a word or sound was heard besides the crackle of the flames. Then we were all let go.

Only Henrick smiled that night, nodding as though he'd seen it all before.

* * *

When we gathered in the square at sun-up, there was not one human to be found.

Elders, midwives, teachers, parents, children, everyone was all-fours in the dirt. And if some had tender soles and palms from walking the ground, they said nought that day.

Margaery stood on all-fours high atop a roof next to the smoldering pile of wood and bones that had been her prison once. That long and ragged scar where the cubs had bitten her was white against her skin, scruffy hair tangled down her back, sharp claws digging deep into the wooden tiles. I saw then how much she'd grown: strong and tall, muscles taut, voice that made you listen. Grand and mighty had she become, like some creature out of history and legend. At her feet, slung across the ridge of the roof, lay her father, bound and bleeding. I'd seen him walk out of his house on two-legs that morning, looking Margaery in the eye and telling her she couldn't make him into other than he was.

"Neither could you make me other than I am," she'd said. "Not even with the whip and belt, not even with the iron-plated handle of a shovel."

She glanced first at the three midwives, gathered in a huddle below.

"There will be no more children born here, only cubs. You will see them born, and you will call them what they are."

They nodded, heads bent, crouching in the dust and ashes.

"All are wolves, now," she said as her pack howled and yipped below. "Same rules and laws for every wolf, for every one of us. Pack and village, one. All are the same. All wolves.

"All fierce. All teeth. All claws. None more or less than any other. Be wolves, together."

I felt the stirring of those words, can feel it still, sitting here so many years past thinking on it. Then she rolled her father off the roof into the dirt. He hit the ground, heavy, like a rain-wet sack of grain. We smelled the blood – all fierce, all teeth, all claws, all wolves – and all went forward, Margaery's mother at the forefront, all our jaws a-snapping, none could keep away.

And oh, the smell of it, the taste of it, that feeling when you're wolf with other wolves, of knowing I was wolf, that we were all the same; knowing I was strong with my jaws a-snapping, my paws a-tearing. I scarce recalled whether I'd been wolf or human before that day, and besides, it didn't matter none: we were all wolf from that day forward.

"I remember now," Henrick crowed next to me when it was all done, his ears twitching in the dawn-light, blood-spattered paws scratching at the dirt. "First time I saw this village burn I was just a cub, but I turned human as the sun rose, standing up on two-legs next to mother. And now the world has turned and turned again as it does after every fire, and here I am. Same as I was, anew."

Then he cried a little there on all-fours, and so did I. Crying for the smoke lingering in our eyes from the pyre. For love of our new-won claws and fangs. For love of being wolf.

For love of Margaery.

The Were-Wolf

Clemence Housman

THE GREAT FARM HALL was ablaze with the fire-light, and noisy with laughter and talk and many-sounding work. None could be idle but the very young and the very old: little Rol, who was hugging a puppy, and old Trella, whose palsied hand fumbled over her knitting. The early evening had closed in, and the farm-servants, come from their outdoor work, had assembled in the ample hall, which gave space for a score or more of workers. Several of the men were engaged in carving, and to these were yielded the best place and light; others made or repaired fishing-tackle and harness, and a great seine net occupied three pairs of hands. Of the women most were sorting and mixing eider feather and chopping straw to add to it. Looms were there, though not in present use, but three wheels whirred emulously, and the finest and swiftest thread of the three ran between the fingers of the house-mistress. Near her were some children, busy too, plaiting wicks for candles and lamps. Each group of workers had a lamp in its centre, and those farthest from the fire had live heat from two braziers filled with glowing wood embers, replenished now and again from the generous hearth. But the flicker of the great fire was manifest to remotest corners, and prevailed beyond the limits of the weaker lights.

Little Rol grew tired of his puppy, dropped it incontinently, and made an onslaught on Tyr, the old wolf-hound, who basked dozing, whimpering and twitching in his hunting dreams. Prone went Rol beside Tyr, his young arms round the shaggy neck, his curls against the black jowl. Tyr gave a perfunctory lick, and stretched with a sleepy sigh. Rol growled and rolled and shoved invitingly, but could only gain from the old dog placid toleration and a half-observant blink. "Take that then!" said Rol, indignant at this ignoring of his advances, and sent the puppy sprawling against the dignity that disdained him as playmate. The dog took no notice, and the child wandered off to find amusement elsewhere.

The baskets of white eider feathers caught his eye far off in a distant corner. He slipped under the table, and crept along on all-fours, the ordinary common-place custom of walking down a room upright not being to his fancy. When close to the women he lay still for a moment watching, with his elbows on the floor and his chin in his palms. One of the women seeing him nodded and smiled, and presently he crept out behind her skirts and passed, hardly noticed, from one to another, till he found opportunity to possess himself of a large handful of feathers. With these he traversed the length of the room, under the table again, and emerged near the spinners. At the feet of the youngest he curled himself round, sheltered by her knees from the observation of the others, and disarmed her of interference by secretly displaying his handful with a confiding smile. A dubious nod satisfied him, and presently he started on the play he had devised. He took a tuft of the white down, and gently shook it free of his fingers close to the whirl of the wheel. The wind of the swift motion took it, spun it round and round in widening circles, till it floated above like a slow white moth. Little Rol's eyes danced, and the row of his small teeth shone in a silent laugh of delight. Another and another of the white tufts was sent whirling round like a winged thing in a spider's web, and floating clear at last. Presently the handful failed.

Rol sprawled forward to survey the room, and contemplate another journey under the table. His shoulder, thrusting forward, checked the wheel for an instant; he shifted hastily. The wheel flew on with a jerk, and the thread snapped. "Naughty Rol!" said the girl. The swiftest wheel stopped also, and the house-mistress, Rol's aunt, leaned forward, and sighting the low curly head, gave a warning against mischief, and sent him off to old Trella's corner.

Rol obeyed, and after a discreet period of obedience, sidled out again down the length of the room farthest from his aunt's eye. As he slipped in among the men, they looked up to see that their tools might be, as far as possible, out of reach of Rol's hands, and close to their own. Nevertheless, before long he managed to secure a fine chisel and take off its point on the leg of the table. The carver's strong objections to this disconcerted Rol, who for five minutes thereafter effaced himself under the table.

During this seclusion he contemplated the many pairs of legs that surrounded him, and almost shut out the light of the fire. How very odd some of the legs were: some were curved where they should be straight, some were straight where they should be curved, and, as Rol said to himself, "they all seemed screwed on differently." Some were tucked away modestly under the benches, others were thrust far out under the table, encroaching on Rol's own particular domain. He stretched out his own short legs and regarded them critically, and, after comparison, favourably. Why were not all legs made like his, or like *his*?

These legs approved by Rol were a little apart from the rest. He crawled opposite and again made comparison. His face grew quite solemn as he thought of the innumerable days to come before his legs could be as long and strong. He hoped they would be just like those, his models, as straight as to bone, as curved as to muscle.

A few moments later Sweyn of the long legs felt a small hand caressing his foot, and looking down, met the upturned eyes of his little cousin Rol. Lying on his back, still softly patting and stroking the young man's foot, the child was quiet and happy for a good while. He watched the movement of the strong deft hands, and the shifting of the bright tools. Now and then, minute chips of wood, puffed off by Sweyn, fell down upon his face. At last he raised himself, very gently, lest a jog should wake impatience in the carver, and crossing his own legs round Sweyn's ankle, clasping with his arms too, laid his head against the knee. Such act is evidence of a child's most wonderful hero-worship. Quite content was Rol, and more than content when Sweyn paused a minute to joke, and pat his head and pull his curls. Quiet he remained, as long as quiescence is possible to limbs young as his. Sweyn forgot he was near, hardly noticed when his leg was gently released, and never saw the stealthy abstraction of one of his tools.

Ten minutes thereafter was a lamentable wail from low on the floor, rising to the full pitch of Rol's healthy lungs; for his hand was gashed across, and the copious bleeding terrified him. Then was there soothing and comforting, washing and binding, and a modicum of scolding, till the loud outcry sank into occasional sobs, and the child, tear-stained and subdued, was returned to the chimney-corner settle, where Trella nodded.

In the reaction after pain and fright, Rol found that the quiet of that fire-lit corner was to his mind. Tyr, too, disdained him no longer, but, roused by his sobs, showed all the concern and sympathy that a dog can by licking and wistful watching. A little shame weighed also upon his spirits. He wished he had not cried quite so much. He remembered how once Sweyn had come home with his arm torn down from the shoulder, and a dead bear; and how he had never winced nor said a word, though his lips turned white with pain. Poor little Rol gave another sighing sob over his own faint-hearted shortcomings.

The light and motion of the great fire began to tell strange stories to the child, and the wind in the chimney roared a corroborative note now and then. The great black mouth of the chimney, impending high over the hearth, received as into a mysterious gulf murky coils of smoke and brightness of aspiring sparks; and beyond, in the high darkness, were muttering and wailing and strange doings, so that sometimes the smoke rushed back in panic, and curled out and up to the roof, and condensed itself to invisibility among the rafters. And then the wind would rage after its lost prey, and rush round the house, rattling and shrieking at window and door.

In a lull, after one such loud gust, Rol lifted his head in surprise and listened. A lull had also come on the babel of talk, and thus could be heard with strange distinctness a sound outside the door – the sound of a child's voice, a child's hands. "Open, open; let me in!" piped the little voice from low down, lower than the handle, and the latch rattled as though a tiptoe child reached up to it, and soft small knocks were struck. One near the door sprang up and opened it. "No one is here," he said. Tyr lifted his head and gave utterance to a howl, loud, prolonged, most dismal.

Sweyn, not able to believe that his ears had deceived him, got up and went to the door. It was a dark night; the clouds were heavy with snow, that had fallen fitfully when the wind lulled. Untrodden snow lay up to the porch; there was no sight nor sound of any human being. Sweyn strained his eyes far and near, only to see dark sky, pure snow, and a line of black fir trees on a hill brow, bowing down before the wind. "It must have been the wind," he said, and closed the door.

Many faces looked scared. The sound of a child's voice had been so distinct – and the words "Open, open; let me in!" The wind might creak the wood, or rattle the latch, but could not speak with a child's voice, nor knock with the soft plain blows that a plump fist gives. And the strange unusual howl of the wolf-hound was an omen to be feared, be the rest what it might. Strange things were said by one and another, till the rebuke of the house-mistress quelled them into far-off whispers. For a time after there was uneasiness, constraint, and silence; then the chill fear thawed by degrees, and the babble of talk flowed on again.

Yet half-an-hour later a very slight noise outside the door sufficed to arrest every hand, every tongue. Every head was raised, every eye fixed in one direction. "It is Christian; he is late," said Sweyn.

No, no; this is a feeble shuffle, not a young man's tread. With the sound of uncertain feet came the hard tap-tap of a stick against the door, and the high-pitched voice of eld, "Open, open; let me in!" Again Tyr flung up his head in a long doleful howl.

Before the echo of the tapping stick and the high voice had fairly died away, Sweyn had sprung across to the door and flung it wide. "No one again," he said in a steady voice, though his eyes looked startled as he stared out. He saw the lonely expanse of snow, the clouds swagging low, and between the two the line of dark fir-trees bowing in the wind. He closed the door without a word of comment, and re-crossed the room.

A score of blanched faces were turned to him as though he must be solver of the enigma. He could not be unconscious of this mute eye-questioning, and it disturbed his resolute air of composure. He hesitated, glanced towards his mother, the house-mistress, then back at the frightened folk, and gravely, before them all, made the sign of the cross. There was a flutter of hands as the sign was repeated by all, and the dead silence was stirred as by a huge sigh, for the held breath of many was freed as though the sign gave magic relief.

Even the house-mistress was perturbed. She left her wheel and crossed the room to her son, and spoke with him for a moment in a low tone that none could overhear. But a moment later her voice was high-pitched and loud, so that all might benefit by her rebuke of the "heathen chatter" of one of the girls. Perhaps she essayed to silence thus her own misgivings and forebodings.

No other voice dared speak now with its natural fulness. Low tones made intermittent murmurs, and now and then silence drifted over the whole room. The handling of tools was as noiseless as might be, and suspended on the instant if the door rattled in a gust of wind. After a time Sweyn left his work, joined the group nearest the door, and loitered there on the pretence of giving advice and help to the unskilful.

A man's tread was heard outside in the porch. "Christian!" said Sweyn and his mother simultaneously, he confidently, she authoritatively, to set the checked wheels going again. But Tyr flung up his head with an appalling howl.

"Open, open; let me in!"

It was a man's voice, and the door shook and rattled as a man's strength beat against it. Sweyn could feel the planks quivering, as on the instant his hand was upon the door, flinging it open, to face the blank porch, and beyond only snow and sky, and firs aslant in the wind.

He stood for a long minute with the open door in his hand. The bitter wind swept in with its icy chill, but a deadlier chill of fear came swifter, and seemed to freeze the beating of hearts. Sweyn stepped back to snatch up a great bearskin cloak.

"Sweyn, where are you going?"

"No farther than the porch, mother," and he stepped out and closed the door.

He wrapped himself in the heavy fur, and leaning against the most sheltered wall of the porch, steeled his nerves to face the devil and all his works. No sound of voices came from within; the most distinct sound was the crackle and roar of the fire.

It was bitterly cold. His feet grew numb, but he forbore stamping them into warmth lest the sound should strike panic within; nor would he leave the porch, nor print a foot-mark on the untrodden white that declared so absolutely how no human voices and hands could have approached the door since snow fell two hours or more ago. "When the wind drops there will be more snow," thought Sweyn.

For the best part of an hour he kept his watch, and saw no living thing – heard no unwonted sound. "I will freeze here no longer," he muttered, and re-entered.

One woman gave a half-suppressed scream as his hand was laid on the latch, and then a gasp of relief as he came in. No one questioned him, only his mother said, in a tone of forced unconcern, "Could you not see Christian coming?" as though she were made anxious only by the absence of her younger son. Hardly had Sweyn stamped near to the fire than clear knocking was heard at the door. Tyr leapt from the hearth, his eyes red as the fire, his fangs showing white in the black jowl, his neck ridged and bristling; and overleaping Rol, ramped at the door, barking furiously.

Outside the door a clear mellow voice was calling. Tyr's bark made the words undistinguishable. No one offered to stir towards the door before Sweyn.

He stalked down the room resolutely, lifted the latch, and swung back the door.

A white-robed woman glided in.

No wraith! Living – beautiful – young.

Tyr leapt upon her.

Lithely she baulked the sharp fangs with folds of her long fur robe, and snatching from her girdle a small two-edged axe, whirled it up for a blow of defence.

Sweyn caught the dog by the collar, and dragged him off yelling and struggling.

The stranger stood in the doorway motionless, one foot set forward, one arm flung up, till the house-mistress hurried down the room; and Sweyn, relinquishing to others the furious Tyr, turned again to close the door, and offer excuse for so fierce a greeting. Then she lowered her arm, slung the axe in its place at her waist, loosened the furs about her face, and shook over her shoulders the long white robe – all as it were with the sway of one movement.

She was a maiden, tall and very fair. The fashion of her dress was strange, half masculine, yet not unwomanly. A fine fur tunic, reaching but little below the knee, was all the skirt she wore;

below were the cross-bound shoes and leggings that a hunter wears. A white fur cap was set low upon the brows, and from its edge strips of fur fell lappet-wise about her shoulders; two of these at her entrance had been drawn forward and crossed about her throat, but now, loosened and thrust back, left unhidden long plaits of fair hair that lay forward on shoulder and breast, down to the ivory-studded girdle where the axe gleamed.

Sweyn and his mother led the stranger to the hearth without question or sign of curiosity, till she voluntarily told her tale of a long journey to distant kindred, a promised guide unmet, and signals and landmarks mistaken.

"Alone!" exclaimed Sweyn in astonishment. "Have you journeyed thus far, a hundred leagues, alone?"

She answered "Yes" with a little smile.

"Over the hills and the wastes! Why, the folk there are savage and wild as beasts."

She dropped her hand upon her axe with a laugh of some scorn.

"I fear neither man nor beast; some few fear me." And then she told strange tales of fierce attack and defence, and of the bold free huntress life she had led.

Her words came a little slowly and deliberately, as though she spoke in a scarce familiar tongue; now and then she hesitated, and stopped in a phrase, as though for lack of some word.

She became the centre of a group of listeners. The interest she excited dissipated, in some degree, the dread inspired by the mysterious voices. There was nothing ominous about this young, bright, fair reality, though her aspect was strange.

Little Rol crept near, staring at the stranger with all his might. Unnoticed, he softly stroked and patted a corner of her soft white robe that reached to the floor in ample folds. He laid his cheek against it caressingly, and then edged up close to her knees.

"What is your name?" he asked.

The stranger's smile and ready answer, as she looked down, saved Rol from the rebuke merited by his unmannerly question.

"My real name," she said, "would be uncouth to your ears and tongue. The folk of this country have given me another name, and from this" (she laid her hand on the fur robe) "they call me 'White Fell.'"

Little Rol repeated it to himself, stroking and patting as before. "White Fell, White Fell."

The fair face, and soft, beautiful dress pleased Rol. He knelt up, with his eyes on her face and an air of uncertain determination, like a robin's on a doorstep, and plumped his elbows into her lap with a little gasp at his own audacity.

"Rol!" exclaimed his aunt; but, "Oh, let him!" said White Fell, smiling and stroking his head; and Rol stayed.

He advanced farther, and panting at his own adventurousness in the face of his aunt's authority, climbed up on to her knees. Her welcoming arms hindered any protest. He nestled happily, fingering the axe head, the ivory studs in her girdle, the ivory clasp at her throat, the plaits of fair hair; rubbing his head against the softness of her fur-clad shoulder, with a child's full confidence in the kindness of beauty.

White Fell had not uncovered her head, only knotted the pendant fur loosely behind her neck. Rol reached up his hand towards it, whispering her name to himself, "White Fell, White Fell," then slid his arms round her neck, and kissed her – once – twice. She laughed delightedly, and kissed him again.

"The child plagues you?" said Sweyn.

"No, indeed," she answered, with an earnestness so intense as to seem disproportionate to the occasion.

Rol settled himself again on her lap, and began to unwind the bandage bound round his hand. He paused a little when he saw where the blood had soaked through; then went on till his hand was bare and the cut displayed, gaping and long, though only skin deep. He held it up towards White Fell, desirous of her pity and sympathy.

At sight of it, and the blood-stained linen, she drew in her breath suddenly, clasped Rol to her – hard, hard – till he began to struggle. Her face was hidden behind the boy, so that none could see its expression. It had lighted up with a most awful glee.

Afar, beyond the fir-grove, beyond the low hill behind, the absent Christian was hastening his return. From daybreak he had been afoot, carrying notice of a bear hunt to all the best hunters of the farms and hamlets that lay within a radius of twelve miles. Nevertheless, having been detained till a late hour, he now broke into a run, going with a long smooth stride of apparent ease that fast made the miles diminish.

He entered the midnight blackness of the fir-grove with scarcely slackened pace, though the path was invisible; and passing through into the open again, sighted the farm lying a furlong off down the slope. Then he sprang out freely, and almost on the instant gave one great sideways leap, and stood still. There in the snow was the track of a great wolf.

His hand went to his knife, his only weapon. He stooped, knelt down, to bring his eyes to the level of a beast, and peered about; his teeth set, his heart beat a little harder than the pace of his running insisted on. A solitary wolf, nearly always savage and of large size, is a formidable beast that will not hesitate to attack a single man. This wolf-track was the largest Christian had ever seen, and, so far as he could judge, recently made. It led from under the fir-trees down the slope. Well for him, he thought, was the delay that had so vexed him before: well for him that he had not passed through the dark fir-grove when that danger of jaws lurked there. Going warily, he followed the track.

It led down the slope, across a broad ice-bound stream, along the level beyond, making towards the farm. A less precise knowledge had doubted, and guessed that here might have come straying big Tyr or his like; but Christian was sure, knowing better than to mistake between footmark of dog and wolf.

Straight on – straight on towards the farm.

Surprised and anxious grew Christian, that a prowling wolf should dare so near. He drew his knife and pressed on, more hastily, more keen-eyed. Oh that Tyr were with him!

Straight on, straight on, even to the very door, where the snow failed. His heart seemed to give a great leap and then stop. There the track *ended*.

Nothing lurked in the porch, and there was no sign of return. The firs stood straight against the sky, the clouds lay low; for the wind had fallen and a few snowflakes came drifting down. In a horror of surprise, Christian stood dazed a moment: then he lifted the latch and went in. His glance took in all the old familiar forms and faces, and with them that of the stranger, fur-clad and beautiful. The awful truth flashed upon him: he knew what she was.

Only a few were startled by the rattle of the latch as he entered. The room was filled with bustle and movement, for it was the supper hour, when all tools were laid aside, and trestles and tables shifted. Christian had no knowledge of what he said and did; he moved and spoke mechanically, half thinking that soon he must wake from this horrible dream. Sweyn and his mother supposed him to be cold and dead-tired, and spared all unnecessary questions. And he found himself seated beside the hearth, opposite that dreadful Thing that looked like a beautiful girl; watching her every movement, curdling with horror to see her fondle the child Rol.

Sweyn stood near them both, intent upon White Fell also; but how differently! She seemed unconscious of the gaze of both – neither aware of the chill dread in the eyes of Christian, nor of Sweyn's warm admiration.

These two brothers, who were twins, contrasted greatly, despite their striking likeness. They were alike in regular profile, fair brown hair, and deep blue eyes; but Sweyn's features were perfect as a young god's, while Christian's showed faulty details. Thus, the line of his mouth was set too straight, the eyes shelved too deeply back, and the contour of the face flowed in less generous curves than Sweyn's. Their height was the same, but Christian was too slender for perfect proportion, while Sweyn's well-knit frame, broad shoulders, and muscular arms, made him pre-eminent for manly beauty as well as for strength. As a hunter Sweyn was without rival; as a fisher without rival. All the countryside acknowledged him to be the best wrestler, rider, dancer, singer. Only in speed could he be surpassed, and in that only by his younger brother. All others Sweyn could distance fairly; but Christian could outrun him easily. Ay, he could keep pace with Sweyn's most breathless burst, and laugh and talk the while. Christian took little pride in his fleetness of foot, counting a man's legs to be the least worthy of his members. He had no envy of his brother's athletic superiority, though to several feats he had made a moderate second. He loved as only a twin can love – proud of all that Sweyn did, content with all that Sweyn was; humbly content also that his own great love should not be so exceedingly returned, since he knew himself to be so far less love-worthy.

Christian dared not, in the midst of women and children, launch the horror that he knew into words. He waited to consult his brother; but Sweyn did not, or would not, notice the signal he made, and kept his face always turned towards White Fell. Christian drew away from the hearth, unable to remain passive with that dread upon him.

"Where is Tyr?" he said suddenly. Then, catching sight of the dog in a distant corner, "Why is he chained there?"

"He flew at the stranger," one answered.

Christian's eyes glowed. "Yes?" he said, interrogatively.

"He was within an ace of having his brain knocked out."

"Tyr?"

"Yes; she was nimbly up with that little axe she has at her waist. It was well for old Tyr that his master throttled him off."

Christian went without a word to the corner where Tyr was chained. The dog rose up to meet him, as piteous and indignant as a dumb beast can be. He stroked the black head. "Good Tyr! brave dog!"

They knew, they only; and the man and the dumb dog had comfort of each other.

Christian's eyes turned again towards White Fell: Tyr's also, and he strained against the length of the chain. Christian's hand lay on the dog's neck, and he felt it ridge and bristle with the quivering of impotent fury. Then he began to quiver in like manner, with a fury born of reason, not instinct; as impotent morally as was Tyr physically. Oh! the woman's form that he dare not touch! Anything but that, and he with Tyr would be free to kill or be killed.

Then he returned to ask fresh questions.

"How long has the stranger been here?"

"She came about half-an-hour before you."

"Who opened the door to her?"

"Sweyn: no one else dared."

The tone of the answer was mysterious.

"Why?" queried Christian. "Has anything strange happened? Tell me."

For answer he was told in a low undertone of the summons at the door thrice repeated without human agency; and of Tyr's ominous howls; and of Sweyn's fruitless watch outside.

Christian turned towards his brother in a torment of impatience for a word apart. The board was spread, and Sweyn was leading White Fell to the guest's place. This was more awful: she would break bread with them under the roof-tree!

He started forward, and touching Sweyn's arm, whispered an urgent entreaty. Sweyn stared, and shook his head in angry impatience.

Thereupon Christian would take no morsel of food.

His opportunity came at last. White Fell questioned of the landmarks of the country, and of one Cairn Hill, which was an appointed meeting-place at which she was due that night. The house-mistress and Sweyn both exclaimed.

"It is three long miles away," said Sweyn; "with no place for shelter but a wretched hut. Stay with us this night, and I will show you the way tomorrow."

White Fell seemed to hesitate. "Three miles," she said; "then I should be able to see or hear a signal."

"I will look out," said Sweyn; "then, if there be no signal, you must not leave us."

He went to the door. Christian rose silently, and followed him out.

"Sweyn, do you know what she is?"

Sweyn, surprised at the vehement grasp, and low hoarse voice, made answer:

"She? Who? White Fell?"

"Yes."

"She is the most beautiful girl I have ever seen."

"She is a Were-Wolf."

Sweyn burst out laughing. "Are you mad?" he asked.

"No; here, see for yourself."

Christian drew him out of the porch, pointing to the snow where the footmarks had been. Had been, for now they were not. Snow was falling fast, and every dint was blotted out.

"Well?" asked Sweyn.

"Had you come when I signed to you, you would have seen for yourself."

"Seen what?"

"The footprints of a wolf leading up to the door; none leading away."

It was impossible not to be startled by the tone alone, though it was hardly above a whisper. Sweyn eyed his brother anxiously, but in the darkness could make nothing of his face. Then he laid his hands kindly and re-assuringly on Christian's shoulders and felt how he was quivering with excitement and horror.

"One sees strange things," he said, "when the cold has got into the brain behind the eyes; you came in cold and worn out."

"No," interrupted Christian. "I saw the track first on the brow of the slope, and followed it down right here to the door. This is no delusion."

Sweyn in his heart felt positive that it was. Christian was given to day-dreams and strange fancies, though never had he been possessed with so mad a notion before.

"Don't you believe me?" said Christian desperately. "You must. I swear it is sane truth. Are you blind? Why, even Tyr knows."

"You will be clearer headed tomorrow after a night's rest. Then come too, if you will, with White Fell, to the Hill Cairn; and if you have doubts still, watch and follow, and see what footprints she leaves."

Galled by Sweyn's evident contempt Christian turned abruptly to the door. Sweyn caught him back.

"What now, Christian? What are you going to do?"

"You do not believe me; my mother shall."

Sweyn's grasp tightened. "You shall not tell her," he said authoritatively.

Customarily Christian was so docile to his brother's mastery that it was now a surprising thing when he wrenched himself free vigorously, and said as determinedly as Sweyn, "She shall know!" but Sweyn was nearer the door and would not let him pass.

"There has been scare enough for one night already. If this notion of yours will keep, broach it tomorrow." Christian would not yield.

"Women are so easily scared," pursued Sweyn, "and are ready to believe any folly without shadow of proof. Be a man, Christian, and fight this notion of a Were-Wolf by yourself."

"If you would believe me," began Christian.

"I believe you to be a fool," said Sweyn, losing patience. "Another, who was not your brother, might believe you to be a knave, and guess that you had transformed White Fell into a Were-Wolf because she smiled more readily on me than on you."

The jest was not without foundation, for the grace of White Fell's bright looks had been bestowed on him, on Christian never a whit. Sweyn's coxcombery was always frank, and most forgiveable, and not without fair colour.

"If you want an ally," continued Sweyn, "confide in old Trella. Out of her stores of wisdom, if her memory holds good, she can instruct you in the orthodox manner of tackling a Were-Wolf. If I remember aright, you should watch the suspected person till midnight, when the beast's form must be resumed, and retained ever after if a human eye sees the change; or, better still, sprinkle hands and feet with holy water, which is certain death. Oh! never fear, but old Trella will be equal to the occasion."

Sweyn's contempt was no longer good-humoured; some touch of irritation or resentment rose at this monstrous doubt of White Fell. But Christian was too deeply distressed to take offence.

"You speak of them as old wives' tales; but if you had seen the proof I have seen, you would be ready at least to wish them true, if not also to put them to the test."

"Well," said Sweyn, with a laugh that had a little sneer in it, "put them to the test! I will not object to that, if you will only keep your notions to yourself. Now, Christian, give me your word for silence, and we will freeze here no longer."

Christian remained silent.

Sweyn put his hands on his shoulders again and vainly tried to see his face in the darkness.

"We have never quarrelled yet, Christian?"

"I have never quarrelled," returned the other, aware for the first time that his dictatorial brother had sometimes offered occasion for quarrel, had he been ready to take it.

"Well," said Sweyn emphatically, "if you speak against White Fell to any other, as tonight you have spoken to me – we shall."

He delivered the words like an ultimatum, turned sharp round, and re-entered the house. Christian, more fearful and wretched than before, followed.

"Snow is falling fast: not a single light is to be seen."

White Fell's eyes passed over Christian without apparent notice, and turned bright and shining upon Sweyn.

"Nor any signal to be heard?" she queried. "Did you not hear the sound of a sea-horn?"

"I saw nothing, and heard nothing; and signal or no signal, the heavy snow would keep you here perforce."

She smiled her thanks beautifully. And Christian's heart sank like lead with a deadly foreboding, as he noted what a light was kindled in Sweyn's eyes by her smile.

That night, when all others slept, Christian, the weariest of all, watched outside the guest-chamber till midnight was past. No sound, not the faintest, could be heard. Could the old tale be true of the midnight change? What was on the other side of the door, a woman or a beast? he would have given his right hand to know. Instinctively he laid his hand on the latch, and drew it softly, though believing that bolts fastened the inner side. The door yielded to his hand; he stood on the threshold; a keen gust of air cut at him; the window stood open; the room was empty.

So Christian could sleep with a somewhat lightened heart.

In the morning there was surprise and conjecture when White Fell's absence was discovered. Christian held his peace. Not even to his brother did he say how he knew that she had fled before midnight; and Sweyn, though evidently greatly chagrined, seemed to disdain reference to the subject of Christian's fears.

The elder brother alone joined the bear hunt; Christian found pretext to stay behind. Sweyn, being out of humour, manifested his contempt by uttering not a single expostulation.

All that day, and for many a day after, Christian would never go out of sight of his home. Sweyn alone noticed how he manœuvred for this, and was clearly annoyed by it. White Fell's name was never mentioned between them, though not seldom was it heard in general talk. Hardly a day passed but little Rol asked when White Fell would come again: pretty White Fell, who kissed like a snowflake. And if Sweyn answered, Christian would be quite sure that the light in his eyes, kindled by White Fell's smile, had not yet died out.

Little Rol! Naughty, merry, fairhaired little Rol. A day came when his feet raced over the threshold never to return; when his chatter and laugh were heard no more; when tears of anguish were wept by eyes that never would see his bright head again: never again, living or dead.

He was seen at dusk for the last time, escaping from the house with his puppy, in freakish rebellion against old Trella. Later, when his absence had begun to cause anxiety, his puppy crept back to the farm, cowed, whimpering and yelping, a pitiful, dumb lump of terror, without intelligence or courage to guide the frightened search.

Rol was never found, nor any trace of him. Where he had perished was never known; how he had perished was known only by an awful guess – a wild beast had devoured him.

Christian heard the conjecture "a wolf"; and a horrible certainty flashed upon him that he knew what wolf it was. He tried to declare what he knew, but Sweyn saw him start at the words with white face and struggling lips; and, guessing his purpose, pulled him back, and kept him silent, hardly, by his imperious grip and wrathful eyes, and one low whisper.

That Christian should retain his most irrational suspicion against beautiful White Fell was, to Sweyn, evidence of a weak obstinacy of mind that would but thrive upon expostulation and argument. But this evident intention to direct the passions of grief and anguish to a hatred and fear of the fair stranger, such as his own, was intolerable, and Sweyn set his will against it. Again Christian yielded to his brother's stronger words and will, and against his own judgment consented to silence.

Repentance came before the new moon, the first of the year, was old. White Fell came again, smiling as she entered, as though assured of a glad and kindly welcome; and, in truth, there was only one who saw again her fair face and strange white garb without pleasure. Sweyn's face glowed with delight, while Christian's grew pale and rigid as death. He had given his word to keep silence; but he had not thought that she would dare to come again. Silence was impossible, face to face with that Thing, impossible. Irrepressibly he cried out:

"Where is Rol?"

Not a quiver disturbed White Fell's face. She heard, yet remained bright and tranquil. Sweyn's eyes flashed round at his brother dangerously. Among the women some tears fell at the poor child's name; but none caught alarm from its sudden utterance, for the thought of Rol rose naturally. Where was little Rol, who had nestled in the stranger's arms, kissing her; and watched for her since; and prattled of her daily?

Christian went out silently. One only thing there was that he could do, and he must not delay. His horror overmastered any curiosity to hear White Fell's smooth excuses and smiling apologies for her strange and uncourteous departure; or her easy tale of the circumstances of her return; or to watch her bearing as she heard the sad tale of little Rol.

The swiftest runner of the country-side had started on his hardest race: little less than three leagues and back, which he reckoned to accomplish in two hours, though the night was moonless and the way rugged. He rushed against the still cold air till it felt like a wind upon his face. The dim homestead sank below the ridges at his back, and fresh ridges of snowlands rose out of the obscure horizon-level to drive past him as the stirless air drove, and sink away behind into obscure level again. He took no conscious heed of landmarks, not even when all sign of a path was gone under depths of snow. His will was set to reach his goal with unexampled speed; and thither by instinct his physical forces bore him, without one definite thought to guide.

And the idle brain lay passive, inert, receiving into its vacancy restless siftings of past sights and sounds: Rol, weeping, laughing, playing, coiled in the arms of that dreadful Thing: Tyr – O Tyr! – white fangs in the black jowl: the women who wept on The foolish puppy, precious for the child's last touch: footprints from pine wood to door: the smiling face among furs, of such womanly beauty – smiling – smiling: and Sweyn's face.

"Sweyn, Sweyn, O Sweyn, my brother!"

Sweyn's angry laugh possessed his ear within the sound of the wind of his speed; Sweyn's scorn assailed more quick and keen than the biting cold at his throat. And yet he was unimpressed by any thought of how Sweyn's anger and scorn would rise, if this errand were known.

Sweyn was a sceptic. His utter disbelief in Christian's testimony regarding the footprints was based upon positive scepticism. His reason refused to bend in accepting the possibility of the supernatural materialised. That a living beast could ever be other than palpably bestial – pawed, toothed, shagged, and eared as such, was to him incredible; far more that a human presence could be transformed from its god-like aspect, upright, free-handed, with brows, and speech, and laughter. The wild and fearful legends that he had known from childhood and then believed, he regarded now as built upon facts distorted, overlaid by imagination, and quickened by superstition. Even the strange summons at the threshold, that he himself had vainly answered, was, after the first shock of surprise, rationally explained by him as malicious foolery on the part of some clever trickster, who withheld the key to the enigma.

To the younger brother all life was a spiritual mystery, veiled from his clear knowledge by the density of flesh. Since he knew his own body to be linked to the complex and antagonistic forces that constitute one soul, it seemed to him not impossibly strange that one spiritual force should possess divers forms for widely various manifestation. Nor, to him, was it great effort to believe that as pure water washes away all natural foulness, so water, holy by consecration, must needs cleanse God's world from that supernatural evil Thing. Therefore, faster than ever man's foot had covered those leagues, he sped under the dark, still night, over the waste, trackless snow-ridges to the far-away church, where salvation lay in the holy-water stoup at the door. His faith was as firm as any that wrought miracles in days past, simple as a child's wish, strong as a man's will.

He was hardly missed during these hours, every second of which was by him fulfilled to its utmost extent by extremest effort that sinews and nerves could attain. Within the homestead the while, the easy moments went bright with words and looks of unwonted animation, for the kindly, hospitable instincts of the inmates were roused into cordial expression of welcome and interest by the grace and beauty of the returned stranger.

But Sweyn was eager and earnest, with more than a host's courteous warmth. The impression that at her first coming had charmed him, that had lived since through memory, deepened now in her actual presence. Sweyn, the matchless among men, acknowledged in this fair White Fell a spirit high and bold as his own, and a frame so firm and capable that only bulk was lacking for equal strength. Yet the white skin was moulded most smoothly, without such muscular swelling as made his might evident. Such love as his frank self-love could concede was called forth by an ardent admiration for this supreme stranger. More admiration than love was in his passion, and therefore he was free from a lover's hesitancy and delicate reserve and doubts. Frankly and boldly he courted her favour by looks and tones, and an address that came of natural ease, needless of skill by practice.

Nor was she a woman to be wooed otherwise. Tender whispers and sighs would never gain her ear; but her eyes would brighten and shine if she heard of a brave feat, and her prompt hand in sympathy fall swiftly on the axe-haft and clasp it hard. That movement ever fired Sweyn's admiration anew; he watched for it, strove to elicit it, and glowed when it came. Wonderful and beautiful was that wrist, slender and steel-strong; also the smooth shapely hand, that curved so fast and firm, ready to deal instant death.

Desiring to feel the pressure of these hands, this bold lover schemed with palpable directness, proposing that she should hear how their hunting songs were sung, with a chorus that signalled hands to be clasped. So his splendid voice gave the verses, and, as the chorus was taken up, he claimed her hands, and, even through the easy grip, felt, as he desired, the strength that was latent, and the vigour that quickened the very fingertips, as the song fired her, and her voice was caught out of her by the rhythmic swell, and rang clear on the top of the closing surge.

Afterwards she sang alone. For contrast, or in the pride of swaying moods by her voice, she chose a mournful song that drifted along in a minor chant, sad as a wind that dirges:

> *"Oh, let me go!*
> *Around spin wreaths of snow;*
> *The dark earth sleeps below.*
> *Far up the plain*
> *Moans on a voice of pain:*
> *'Where shall my babe be lain?'*
> *In my white breast*
> *Lay the sweet life to rest!*
> *Lay, where it can lie best!*
> *'Hush! hush' its cries!*
> *Dense night is on the skies:*
> *Two stars are in thine eyes.*
> *Come, babe, away!*
> *But lie thou till dawn be grey,*
> *Who must be dead by day.*
> *This cannot last;*
> *But, ere the sickening blast,*
> *All sorrow shall be past;*
> *And kings shall be*
> *Low bending at thy knee,*
> *Worshipping life from thee.*
> *For men long sore*
> *To hope of what's before, –*
> *To leave the things of yore.*

> *Mine, and not thine,*
> *How deep their jewels shine!*
> *Peace laps thy head, not mine."*

Old Trella came tottering from her corner, shaken to additional palsy by an aroused memory. She strained her dim eyes towards the singer, and then bent her head, that the one ear yet sensible to sound might avail of every note. At the close, groping forward, she murmured with the high-pitched quaver of old age:

"So she sang, my Thora; my last and brightest. What is she like, she whose voice is like my dead Thora's? Are her eyes blue?"

"Blue as the sky."

"So were my Thora's! Is her hair fair, and in plaits to the waist?" "Even so," answered White Fell herself, and met the advancing hands with her own, and guided them to corroborate her words by touch.

"Like my dead Thora's," repeated the old woman; and then her trembling hands rested on the fur-clad shoulders, and she bent forward and kissed the smooth fair face that White Fell upturned, nothing loth, to receive and return the caress.

So Christian saw them as he entered.

He stood a moment. After the starless darkness and the icy night air, and the fierce silent two hours' race, his senses reeled on sudden entrance into warmth, and light, and the cheery hum of voices. A sudden unforeseen anguish assailed him, as now first he entertained the possibility of being overmatched by her wiles and her daring, if at the approach of pure death she should start up at bay transformed to a terrible beast, and achieve a savage glut at the last. He looked with horror and pity on the harmless, helpless folk, so unwitting of outrage to their comfort and security. The dreadful Thing in their midst, that was veiled from their knowledge by womanly beauty, was a centre of pleasant interest. There, before him, signally impressive, was poor old Trella, weakest and feeblest of all, in fond nearness. And a moment might bring about the revelation of a monstrous horror – a ghastly, deadly danger, set loose and at bay, in a circle of girls and women and careless defenceless men: so hideous and terrible a thing as might crack the brain, or curdle the heart stone dead.

And he alone of the throng prepared!

For one breathing space he faltered, no longer than that, while over him swept the agony of compunction that yet could not make him surrender his purpose.

He alone? Nay, but Tyr also; and he crossed to the dumb sole sharer of his knowledge.

So timeless is thought that a few seconds only lay between his lifting of the latch and his loosening of Tyr's collar; but in those few seconds succeeding his first glance, as lightning-swift had been the impulses of others, their motion as quick and sure. Sweyn's vigilant eye had darted upon him, and instantly his every fibre was alert with hostile instinct; and, half divining, half incredulous, of Christian's object in stooping to Tyr, he came hastily, wary, wrathful, resolute to oppose the malice of his wild-eyed brother.

But beyond Sweyn rose White Fell, blanching white as her furs, and with eyes grown fierce and wild. She leapt down the room to the door, whirling her long robe closely to her. "Hark!" she panted. "The signal horn! Hark, I must go!" as she snatched at the latch to be out and away.

For one precious moment Christian had hesitated on the half-loosened collar; for, except the womanly form were exchanged for the bestial, Tyr's jaws would gnash to rags his honour of manhood. Then he heard her voice, and turned – too late.

As she tugged at the door, he sprang across grasping his flask, but Sweyn dashed between, and caught him back irresistibly, so that a most frantic effort only availed to wrench one arm free. With that, on the impulse of sheer despair, he cast at her with all his force. The door swung behind her, and the flask flew into fragments against it. Then, as Sweyn's grasp slackened, and he met the questioning astonishment of surrounding faces, with a hoarse inarticulate cry: "God help us all!" he said. "She is a Were-Wolf."

Sweyn turned upon him, "Liar, coward!" and his hands gripped his brother's throat with deadly force, as though the spoken word could be killed so; and as Christian struggled, lifted him clear off his feet and flung him crashing backward. So furious was he, that, as his brother lay motionless, he stirred him roughly with his foot, till their mother came between, crying shame; and yet then he stood by, his teeth set, his brows knit, his hands clenched, ready to enforce silence again violently, as Christian rose staggering and bewildered.

But utter silence and submission were more than he expected, and turned his anger into contempt for one so easily cowed and held in subjection by mere force. "He is mad!" he said, turning on his heel as he spoke, so that he lost his mother's look of pained reproach at this sudden free utterance of what was a lurking dread within her.

Christian was too spent for the effort of speech. His hard-drawn breath laboured in great sobs; his limbs were powerless and unstrung in utter relax after hard service. Failure in his endeavour induced a stupor of misery and despair. In addition was the wretched humiliation of open violence and strife with his brother, and the distress of hearing misjudging contempt expressed without reserve; for he was aware that Sweyn had turned to allay the scared excitement half by imperious mastery, half by explanation and argument, that showed painful disregard of brotherly consideration. All this unkindness of his twin he charged upon the fell Thing who had wrought this their first dissension, and, ah! most terrible thought, interposed between them so effectually, that Sweyn was wilfully blind and deaf on her account, resentful of interference, arbitrary beyond reason.

Dread and perplexity unfathomable darkened upon him; unshared, the burden was overwhelming: a foreboding of unspeakable calamity, based upon his ghastly discovery, bore down upon him, crushing out hope of power to withstand impending fate.

Sweyn the while was observant of his brother, despite the continual check of finding, turn and glance when he would, Christian's eyes always upon him, with a strange look of helpless distress, discomposing enough to the angry aggressor. "Like a beaten dog!" he said to himself, rallying contempt to withstand compunction. Observation set him wondering on Christian's exhausted condition. The heavy labouring breath and the slack inert fall of the limbs told surely of unusual and prolonged exertion. And then why had close upon two hours' absence been followed by open hostility against White Fell?

Suddenly, the fragments of the flask giving a clue, he guessed all, and faced about to stare at his brother in amaze. He forgot that the motive scheme was against White Fell, demanding derision and resentment from him; that was swept out of remembrance by astonishment and admiration for the feat of speed and endurance. In eagerness to question he inclined to attempt a generous part and frankly offer to heal the breach; but Christian's depression and sad following gaze provoked him to self-justification by recalling the offence of that outrageous utterance against White Fell; and the impulse passed. Then other considerations counselled silence; and afterwards a humour possessed him to wait and see how Christian would find opportunity to proclaim his performance and establish the fact, without exciting ridicule on account of the absurdity of the errand.

This expectation remained unfulfilled. Christian never attempted the proud avowal that would have placed his feat on record to be told to the next generation.

That night Sweyn and his mother talked long and late together, shaping into certainty the suspicion that Christian's mind had lost its balance, and discussing the evident cause. For Sweyn, declaring his own love for White Fell, suggested that his unfortunate brother, with a like passion, they being twins in loves as in birth, had through jealousy and despair turned from love to hate, until reason failed at the strain, and a craze developed, which the malice and treachery of madness made a serious and dangerous force.

So Sweyn theorised, convincing himself as he spoke; convincing afterwards others who advanced doubts against White Fell; fettering his judgment by his advocacy, and by his staunch defence of her hurried flight silencing his own inner consciousness of the unaccountability of her action.

But a little time and Sweyn lost his vantage in the shock of a fresh horror at the homestead. Trella was no more, and her end a mystery. The poor old woman crawled out in a bright gleam to visit a bed-ridden gossip living beyond the fir-grove. Under the trees she was last seen, halting for her companion, sent back for a forgotten present. Quick alarm sprang, calling every man to the search. Her stick was found among the brushwood only a few paces from the path, but no track or stain, for a gusty wind was sifting the snow from the branches, and hid all sign of how she came by her death.

So panic-stricken were the farm folk that none dared go singly on the search. Known danger could be braced, but not this stealthy Death that walked by day invisible, that cut off alike the child in his play and the aged woman so near to her quiet grave.

"Rol she kissed; Trella she kissed!" So rang Christian's frantic cry again and again, till Sweyn dragged him away and strove to keep him apart, albeit in his agony of grief and remorse he accused himself wildly as answerable for the tragedy, and gave clear proof that the charge of madness was well founded, if strange looks and desperate, incoherent words were evidence enough.

But thenceforward all Sweyn's reasoning and mastery could not uphold White Fell above suspicion. He was not called upon to defend her from accusation when Christian had been brought to silence again; but he well knew the significance of this fact, that her name, formerly uttered freely and often, he never heard now: it was huddled away into whispers that he could not catch.

The passing of time did not sweep away the superstitious fears that Sweyn despised. He was angry and anxious; eager that White Fell should return, and, merely by her bright gracious presence, reinstate herself in favour; but doubtful if all his authority and example could keep from her notice an altered aspect of welcome; and he foresaw clearly that Christian would prove unmanageable, and might be capable of some dangerous outbreak.

For a time the twins' variance was marked, on Sweyn's part by an air of rigid indifference, on Christian's by heavy downcast silence, and a nervous apprehensive observation of his brother. Superadded to his remorse and foreboding, Sweyn's displeasure weighed upon him intolerably, and the remembrance of their violent rupture was a ceaseless misery. The elder brother, self-sufficient and insensitive, could little know how deeply his unkindness stabbed. A depth and force of affection such as Christian's was unknown to him. The loyal subservience that he could not appreciate had encouraged him to domineer; this strenuous opposition to his reason and will was accounted as furious malice, if not sheer insanity.

Christian's surveillance galled him incessantly, and embarrassment and danger he foresaw as the outcome. Therefore, that suspicion might be lulled, he judged it wise to make overtures for peace. Most easily done. A little kindliness, a few evidences of consideration, a slight return of the old brotherly imperiousness, and Christian replied by a gratefulness and relief that might have touched him had he understood all, but instead, increased his secret contempt.

So successful was this finesse, that when, late on a day, a message summoning Christian to a distance was transmitted by Sweyn, no doubt of its genuineness occurred. When, his errand proved useless, he set out to return, mistake or misapprehension was all that he surmised. Not till he sighted the homestead, lying low between the night-grey snow ridges, did vivid recollection of the time when he had tracked that horror to the door rouse an intense dread, and with it a hardly-defined suspicion.

His grasp tightened on the bear-spear that he carried as a staff; every sense was alert, every muscle strung; excitement urged him on, caution checked him, and the two governed his long stride, swiftly, noiselessly, to the climax he felt was at hand.

As he drew near to the outer gates, a light shadow stirred and went, as though the grey of the snow had taken detached motion. A darker shadow stayed and faced Christian, striking his life-blood chill with utmost despair.

Sweyn stood before him, and surely, the shadow that went was White Fell.

They had been together – close. Had she not been in his arms, near enough for lips to meet?

There was no moon, but the stars gave light enough to show that Sweyn's face was flushed and elate. The flush remained, though the expression changed quickly at sight of his brother. How, if Christian had seen all, should one of his frenzied outbursts be met and managed: by resolution? by indifference? He halted between the two, and as a result, he swaggered.

"White Fell?" questioned Christian, hoarse and breathless.

"Yes?"

Sweyn's answer was a query, with an intonation that implied he was clearing the ground for action.

From Christian came: "Have you kissed her?" like a bolt direct, staggering Sweyn by its sheer prompt temerity.

He flushed yet darker, and yet half-smiled over this earnest of success he had won. Had there been really between himself and Christian the rivalry that he imagined, his face had enough of the insolence of triumph to exasperate jealous rage.

"You dare ask this!"

"Sweyn, O Sweyn, I must know! You have!"

The ring of despair and anguish in his tone angered Sweyn, misconstruing it. Jealousy urging to such presumption was intolerable.

"Mad fool!" he said, constraining himself no longer. "Win for yourself a woman to kiss. Leave mine without question. Such an one as I should desire to kiss is such an one as shall never allow a kiss to you."

Then Christian fully understood his supposition.

"I – I!" he cried. "White Fell – that deadly Thing! Sweyn, are you blind, mad? I would save you from her: a Were-Wolf!"

Sweyn maddened again at the accusation – a dastardly way of revenge, as he conceived; and instantly, for the second time, the brothers were at strife violently.

But Christian was now too desperate to be scrupulous; for a dim glimpse had shot a possibility into his mind, and to be free to follow it the striking of his brother was a necessity. Thank God! he was armed, and so Sweyn's equal.

Facing his assailant with the bear-spear, he struck up his arms, and with the butt end hit hard so that he fell. The matchless runner leapt away on the instant, to follow a forlorn hope. Sweyn, on regaining his feet, was as amazed as angry at this unaccountable flight. He knew in his heart that his brother was no coward, and that it was unlike him to shrink from an encounter because defeat was certain, and cruel humiliation from a vindictive victor probable. Of the uselessness of pursuit he was well aware: he must abide his chagrin, content to know that his time for advantage would come. Since White Fell had parted to the right, Christian to the left, the event of a sequent encounter did not occur to him. And now Christian, acting on the dim glimpse he had had, just as Sweyn turned upon him, of something that moved against the sky along the ridge behind the homestead, was staking his only hope on a chance, and his own superlative speed. If what he saw was really White Fell, he guessed she was bending her steps towards the open wastes; and there was just a possibility that, by a straight dash, and a desperate perilous leap over a sheer bluff, he might yet meet her or head her. And then: he had no further thought.

It was past, the quick, fierce race, and the chance of death at the leap; and he halted in a hollow to fetch his breath and to look: did she come? Had she gone?

She came.

She came with a smooth, gliding, noiseless speed, that was neither walking nor running; her arms were folded in her furs that were drawn tight about her body; the white lappets from her head were wrapped and knotted closely beneath her face; her eyes were set on a far distance. So she went till the even sway of her going was startled to a pause by Christian.

"Fell!"

She drew a quick, sharp breath at the sound of her name thus mutilated, and faced Sweyn's brother. Her eyes glittered; her upper lip was lifted, and shewed the teeth. The half of her name, impressed with an ominous sense as uttered by him, warned her of the aspect of a deadly foe. Yet she cast loose her robes till they trailed ample, and spoke as a mild woman.

"What would you?"

Then Christian answered with his solemn dreadful accusation:

"You kissed Rol – and Rol is dead! You kissed Trella: she is dead! You have kissed Sweyn, my brother; but he shall not die!"

He added: "You may live till midnight."

The edge of the teeth and the glitter of the eyes stayed a moment, and her right hand also slid down to the axe haft. Then, without a word, she swerved from him, and sprang out and away swiftly over the snow.

And Christian sprang out and away, and followed her swiftly over the snow, keeping behind, but half-a-stride's length from her side.

So they went running together, silent, towards the vast wastes of snow, where no living thing but they two moved under the stars of night.

Never before had Christian so rejoiced in his powers. The gift of speed, and the training of use and endurance were priceless to him now. Though midnight was hours away, he was confident that, go where that Fell Thing would, hasten as she would, she could not outstrip him nor escape from him. Then, when came the time for transformation, when the woman's form made no longer a shield against a man's hand, he could slay or be slain to save Sweyn. He had struck his dear brother in dire extremity, but he could not, though reason urged, strike a woman.

For one mile, for two miles they ran: White Fell ever foremost, Christian ever at equal distance from her side, so near that, now and again, her out-flying furs touched him. She spoke no word; nor he. She never turned her head to look at him, nor swerved to evade him; but, with set face looking forward, sped straight on, over rough, over smooth, aware of his nearness by the regular beat of his feet, and the sound of his breath behind.

In a while she quickened her pace. From the first, Christian had judged of her speed as admirable, yet with exulting security in his own excelling and enduring whatever her efforts. But, when the pace increased, he found himself put to the test as never had he been before in any race. Her feet, indeed, flew faster than his; it was only by his length of stride that he kept his place at her side. But his heart was high and resolute, and he did not fear failure yet.

So the desperate race flew on. Their feet struck up the powdery snow, their breath smoked into the sharp clear air, and they were gone before the air was cleared of snow and vapour. Now and then Christian glanced up to judge, by the rising of the stars, of the coming of midnight. So long – so long!

White Fell held on without slack. She, it was evident, with confidence in her speed proving matchless, as resolute to outrun her pursuer as he to endure till midnight and fulfil his purpose. And

Christian held on, still self-assured. He could not fail; he would not fail. To avenge Rol and Trella was motive enough for him to do what man could do; but for Sweyn more. She had kissed Sweyn, but he should not die too: with Sweyn to save he could not fail.

Never before was such a race as this; no, not when in old Greece man and maid raced together with two fates at stake; for the hard running was sustained unabated, while star after star rose and went wheeling up towards midnight, for one hour, for two hours.

Then Christian saw and heard what shot him through with fear. Where a fringe of trees hung round a slope he saw something dark moving, and heard a yelp, followed by a full horrid cry, and the dark spread out upon the snow, a pack of wolves in pursuit.

Of the beasts alone he had little cause for fear; at the pace he held he could distance them, four-footed though they were. But of White Fell's wiles he had infinite apprehension, for how might she not avail herself of the savage jaws of these wolves, akin as they were to half her nature. She vouchsafed to them nor look nor sign; but Christian, on an impulse to assure himself that she should not escape him, caught and held the back-flung edge of her furs, running still.

She turned like a flash with a beastly snarl, teeth and eyes gleaming again. Her axe shone, on the upstroke, on the downstroke, as she hacked at his hand. She had lopped it off at the wrist, but that he parried with the bear-spear. Even then, she shore through the shaft and shattered the bones of the hand at the same blow, so that he loosed perforce.

Then again they raced on as before, Christian not losing a pace, though his left hand swung useless, bleeding and broken.

The snarl, indubitable, though modified from a woman's organs, the vicious fury revealed in teeth and eyes, the sharp arrogant pain of her maiming blow, caught away Christian's heed of the beasts behind, by striking into him close vivid realisation of the infinitely greater danger that ran before him in that deadly Thing.

When he bethought him to look behind, lo! the pack had but reached their tracks, and instantly slunk aside, cowed; the yell of pursuit changing to yelps and whines. So abhorrent was that fell creature to beast as to man.

She had drawn her furs more closely to her, disposing them so that, instead of flying loose to her heels, no drapery hung lower than her knees, and this without a check to her wonderful speed, nor embarrassment by the cumbering of the folds. She held her head as before; her lips were firmly set, only the tense nostrils gave her breath; not a sign of distress witnessed to the long sustaining of that terrible speed.

But on Christian by now the strain was telling palpably. His head weighed heavy, and his breath came labouring in great sobs; the bear spear would have been a burden now. His heart was beating like a hammer, but such a dullness oppressed his brain, that it was only by degrees he could realise his helpless state; wounded and weaponless, chasing that terrible Thing, that was a fierce, desperate, axe-armed woman, except she should assume the beast with fangs yet more formidable.

And still the far slow stars went lingering nearly an hour from midnight.

So far was his brain astray that an impression took him that she was fleeing from the midnight stars, whose gain was by such slow degrees that a time equalling days and days had gone in the race round the northern circle of the world, and days and days as long might last before the end – except she slackened, or except he failed.

But he would not fail yet.

How long had he been praying so? He had started with a self-confidence and reliance that had felt no need for that aid; and now it seemed the only means by which to restrain his heart from swelling beyond the compass of his body, by which to cherish his brain from dwindling and shrivelling quite away. Some sharp-toothed creature kept tearing and dragging on his maimed left hand; he never could see it, he could not shake it off; but he prayed it off at times.

The clear stars before him took to shuddering, and he knew why: they shuddered at sight of what was behind him. He had never divined before that strange things hid themselves from men under pretence of being snow-clad mounds or swaying trees; but now they came slipping out from their harmless covers to follow him, and mock at his impotence to make a kindred Thing resolve to truer form. He knew the air behind him was thronged; he heard the hum of innumerable murmurings together; but his eyes could never catch them, they were too swift and nimble. Yet he knew they were there, because, on a backward glance, he saw the snow mounds surge as they grovelled flatlings out of sight; he saw the trees reel as they screwed themselves rigid past recognition among the boughs.

And after such glance the stars for awhile returned to steadfastness, and an infinite stretch of silence froze upon the chill grey world, only deranged by the swift even beat of the flying feet, and his own – slower from the longer stride, and the sound of his breath. And for some clear moments he knew that his only concern was, to sustain his speed regardless of pain and distress, to deny with every nerve he had her power to outstrip him or to widen the space between them, till the stars crept up to midnight. Then out again would come that crowd invisible, humming and hustling behind, dense and dark enough, he knew, to blot out the stars at his back, yet ever skipping and jerking from his sight.

A hideous check came to the race. White Fell swirled about and leapt to the right, and Christian, unprepared for so prompt a lurch, found close at his feet a deep pit yawning, and his own impetus past control. But he snatched at her as he bore past, clasping her right arm with his one whole hand, and the two swung together upon the brink.

And her straining away in self preservation was vigorous enough to counter-balance his headlong impulse, and brought them reeling together to safety.

Then, before he was verily sure that they were not to perish so, crashing down, he saw her gnashing in wild pale fury as she wrenched to be free; and since her right hand was in his grasp, used her axe left-handed, striking back at him.

The blow was effectual enough even so; his right arm dropped powerless, gashed, and with the lesser bone broken, that jarred with horrid pain when he let it swing as he leaped out again, and ran to recover the few feet she had gained from his pause at the shock.

The near escape and this new quick pain made again every faculty alive and intense. He knew that what he followed was most surely Death animate: wounded and helpless, he was utterly at her mercy if so she should realise and take action. Hopeless to avenge, hopeless to save, his very despair for Sweyn swept him on to follow, and follow, and precede the kiss doomed to death. Could he yet fail to hunt that Thing past midnight, out of the womanly form alluring and treacherous, into lasting restraint of the bestial, which was the last shred of hope left from the confident purpose of the outset?

"Sweyn, Sweyn, O Sweyn!" He thought he was praying, though his heart wrung out nothing but this: "Sweyn, Sweyn, O Sweyn!"

The last hour from midnight had lost half its quarters, and the stars went lifting up the great minutes; and again his greatening heart, and his shrinking brain, and the sickening agony that swung at either side, conspired to appal the will that had only seeming empire over his feet.

Now White Fell's body was so closely enveloped that not a lap nor an edge flew free. She stretched forward strangely aslant, leaning from the upright poise of a runner. She cleared the ground at times by long bounds, gaining an increase of speed that Christian agonised to equal.

Because the stars pointed that the end was nearing, the black brood came behind again, and followed, noising. Ah! If they could but be kept quiet and still, nor slip their usual harmless masks to encourage with their interest the last speed of their most deadly congener. What shape had they? Should he ever know? If it were not that he was bound to compel the fell Thing that ran before him into her truer form, he might face about and follow them. No – no – not so; if he might do anything but what he did – race, race, and racing bear this agony, he would just stand still and die, to be quit of the pain of breathing.

He grew bewildered, uncertain of his own identity, doubting of his own true form. He could not be really a man, no more than that running Thing was really a woman; his real form was only hidden under embodiment of a man, but what it was he did not know. And Sweyn's real form he did not know. Sweyn lay fallen at his feet, where he had struck him down – his own brother – he: he stumbled over him, and had to overleap him and race harder because she who had kissed Sweyn leapt so fast. "Sweyn, Sweyn, O Sweyn!"

Why did the stars stop to shudder? Midnight else had surely come!

The leaning, leaping Thing looked back at him with a wild, fierce look, and laughed in savage scorn and triumph. He saw in a flash why, for within a time measurable by seconds she would have escaped him utterly. As the land lay, a slope of ice sunk on the one hand; on the other hand a steep rose, shouldering forwards; between the two was space for a foot to be planted, but none for a body to stand; yet a juniper bough, thrusting out, gave a handhold secure enough for one with a resolute grasp to swing past the perilous place, and pass on safe.

Though the first seconds of the last moment were going, she dared to flash back a wicked look, and laugh at the pursuer who was impotent to grasp.

The crisis struck convulsive life into his last supreme effort; his will surged up indomitable, his speed proved matchless yet. He leapt with a rush, passed her before her laugh had time to go out, and turned short, barring the way, and braced to withstand her.

She came hurling desperate, with a feint to the right hand, and then launched herself upon him with a spring like a wild beast when it leaps to kill. And he, with one strong arm and a hand that could not hold, with one strong hand and an arm that could not guide and sustain, he caught and held her even so. And they fell together. And because he felt his whole arm slipping, and his whole hand loosing, to slack the dreadful agony of the wrenched bone above, he caught and held with his teeth the tunic at her knee, as she struggled up and wrung off his hands to overleap him victorious.

Like lightning she snatched her axe, and struck him on the neck, deep – once, twice – his life-blood gushed out, staining her feet.

The stars touched midnight.

The death scream he heard was not his, for his set teeth had hardly yet relaxed when it rang out; and the dreadful cry began with a woman's shriek, and changed and ended as the yell of a beast. And before the final blank overtook his dying eyes, he saw that She gave place to It; he saw more, that Life gave place to Death – causelessly, incomprehensibly.

For he did not presume that no holy water could be more holy, more potent to destroy an evil thing than the life-blood of a pure heart poured out for another in free willing devotion.

His own true hidden reality that he had desired to know grew palpable, recognisable. It seemed to him just this: a great glad abounding hope that he had saved his brother; too expansive to be contained by the limited form of a sole man, it yearned for a new embodiment infinite as the stars.

What did it matter to that true reality that the man's brain shrank, shrank, till it was nothing; that the man's body could not retain the huge pain of his heart, and heaved it out through the red exit riven at the neck; that the black noise came again hurtling from behind, reinforced by that dissolved shape, and blotted out for ever the man's sight, hearing, sense.

* * *

In the early grey of day Sweyn chanced upon the footprints of a man – of a runner, as he saw by the shifted snow; and the direction they had taken aroused curiosity, since a little farther their line must be crossed by the edge of a sheer height. He turned to trace them. And so doing, the length of the stride struck his attention – a stride long as his own if he ran. He knew he was following Christian.

In his anger he had hardened himself to be indifferent to the night-long absence of his brother; but now, seeing where the footsteps went, he was seized with compunction and dread. He had failed to give thought and care to his poor frantic twin, who might – was it possible? – have rushed to a frantic death.

His heart stood still when he came to the place where the leap had been taken. A piled edge of snow had fallen too, and nothing but snow lay below when he peered. Along the upper edge he ran for a furlong, till he came to a dip where he could slip and climb down, and then back again on the lower level to the pile of fallen snow. There he saw that the vigorous running had started afresh.

He stood pondering; vexed that any man should have taken that leap where he had not ventured to follow; vexed that he had been beguiled to such painful emotions; guessing vainly at Christian's object in this mad freak. He began sauntering along, half unconsciously following his brother's track; and so in a while he came to the place where the footprints were doubled.

Small prints were these others, small as a woman's, though the pace from one to another was longer than that which the skirts of women allow.

Did not White Fell tread so?

A dreadful guess appalled him, so dreadful that he recoiled from belief. Yet his face grew ashy white, and he gasped to fetch back motion to his checked heart. Unbelievable? Closer attention showed how the smaller footfall had altered for greater speed, striking into the snow with a deeper onset and a lighter pressure on the heels. Unbelievable? Could any woman but White Fell run so? Could any man but Christian run so? The guess became a certainty. He was following where alone in the dark night White Fell had fled from Christian pursuing.

Such villainy set heart and brain on fire with rage and indignation: such villainy in his own brother, till lately love-worthy, praiseworthy, though a fool for meekness. He would kill Christian; had he lives many as the footprints he had trodden, vengeance should demand them all. In a tempest of murderous hate he followed on in haste, for the track was plain enough, starting with such a burst of speed as could not be maintained, but brought him back soon to a plod for the spent, sobbing breath to be regulated. He cursed Christian aloud and called White Fell's name on high in a frenzied expense of passion. His grief itself was a rage, being such an intolerable anguish of pity and shame at the thought of his love, White Fell, who had parted from his kiss free and radiant, to be hounded straightway by his brother mad with jealousy, fleeing for more than life while her lover was housed at his ease. If he had but known, he raved, in impotent rebellion at the cruelty of events, if he had but known that his strength and love might have availed in her defence; now the only service to her that he could render was to kill Christian.

As a woman he knew she was matchless in speed, matchless in strength; but Christian was matchless in speed among men, nor easily to be matched in strength. Brave and swift and strong though she were, what chance had she against a man of his strength and inches, frantic, too, and intent on horrid revenge against his brother, his successful rival?

Mile after mile he followed with a bursting heart; more piteous, more tragic, seemed the case at this evidence of White Fell's splendid supremacy, holding her own so long against Christian's famous speed. So long, so long that his love and admiration grew more and more boundless, and his grief and indignation therewith also. Whenever the track lay clear he ran, with such reckless prodigality of strength, that it soon was spent, and he dragged on heavily, till, sometimes on the ice of a mere, sometimes on a wind-swept place, all signs were lost; but, so undeviating had been their line that a course straight on, and then short questing to either hand, recovered them again.

Hour after hour had gone by through more than half that winter day, before ever he came to the place where the trampled snow showed that a scurry of feet had come – and gone! Wolves' feet – and gone most amazingly! Only a little beyond he came to the lopped point of Christian's bear-spear; farther on he would see where the remnant of the useless shaft had been dropped. The snow here was dashed with blood, and the footsteps of the two had fallen closer together. Some hoarse sound of exultation came from him that might have been a laugh had breath sufficed. "O White Fell, my poor, brave love! Well struck!" he groaned, torn by his pity and great admiration, as he guessed surely how she had turned and dealt a blow.

The sight of the blood inflamed him as it might a beast that ravens. He grew mad with a desire to have Christian by the throat once again, not to loose this time till he had crushed out his life, or beat out his life, or stabbed out his life; or all these, and torn him piecemeal likewise: and ah! then, not till then, bleed his heart with weeping, like a child, like a girl, over the piteous fate of his poor lost love.

On – on – on – through the aching time, toiling and straining in the track of those two superb runners, aware of the marvel of their endurance, but unaware of the marvel of their speed, that, in the three hours before midnight had overpassed all that vast distance that he could only traverse from twilight to twilight. For clear daylight was passing when he came to the edge of an old marl-pit, and saw how the two who had gone before had stamped and trampled together in desperate peril on the verge. And here fresh blood stains spoke to him of a valiant defence against his infamous brother; and he followed where the blood had dripped till the cold had staunched its flow, taking a savage gratification from this evidence that Christian had been gashed deeply, maddening afresh with desire to do likewise more excellently, and so slake his murderous hate. And he began to know that through all his despair he had entertained a germ of hope, that grew apace, rained upon by his brother's blood.

He strove on as best he might, wrung now by an access of hope, now of despair, in agony to reach the end, however terrible, sick with the aching of the toiled miles that deferred it.

And the light went lingering out of the sky, giving place to uncertain stars.

He came to the finish.

Two bodies lay in a narrow place. Christian's was one, but the other beyond not White Fell's. There where the footsteps ended lay a great white wolf.

At the sight Sweyn's strength was blasted; body and soul he was struck down grovelling.

The stars had grown sure and intense before he stirred from where he had dropped prone. Very feebly he crawled to his dead brother, and laid his hands upon him, and crouched so, afraid to look or stir farther.

Cold, stiff, hours dead. Yet the dead body was his only shelter and stay in that most dreadful hour. His soul, stripped bare of all sceptic comfort, cowered, shivering, naked, abject; and the living clung to the dead out of piteous need for grace from the soul that had passed away.

He rose to his knees, lifting the body. Christian had fallen face forward in the snow, with his arms flung up and wide, and so had the frost made him rigid: strange, ghastly, unyielding to Sweyn's lifting, so that he laid him down again and crouched above, with his arms fast round him, and a low heart-wrung groan.

When at last he found force to raise his brother's body and gather it in his arms, tight clasped to his breast, he tried to face the Thing that lay beyond. The sight set his limbs in a palsy with horror and dread. His senses had failed and fainted in utter cowardice, but for the strength that came from holding dead Christian in his arms, enabling him to compel his eyes to endure the sight, and take into the brain the complete aspect of the Thing. No wound, only blood stains on the feet. The great grim jaws had a savage grin, though dead-stiff. And his kiss: he could bear it no longer, and turned away, nor ever looked again.

And the dead man in his arms, knowing the full horror, had followed and faced it for his sake; had suffered agony and death for his sake; in the neck was the deep death gash, one arm and both hands were dark with frozen blood, for his sake! Dead he knew him, as in life he had not known him, to give the right meed of love and worship. Because the outward man lacked perfection and strength equal to his, he had taken the love and worship of that great pure heart as his due; he, so unworthy in the inner reality, so mean, so despicable, callous, and contemptuous towards the brother who had laid down his life to save him. He longed for utter annihilation, that so he might lose the agony of knowing himself so unworthy such perfect love. The frozen calm of death on the face appalled him. He dared not touch it with lips that had cursed so lately, with lips fouled by kiss of the horror that had been death.

He struggled to his feet, still clasping Christian. The dead man stood upright within his arm, frozen rigid. The eyes were not quite closed; the head had stiffened, bowed slightly to one side; the arms stayed straight and wide. It was the figure of one crucified, the blood-stained hands also conforming.

So living and dead went back along the track that one had passed in the deepest passion of love, and one in the deepest passion of hate. All that night Sweyn toiled through the snow, bearing the weight of dead Christian, treading back along the steps he before had trodden, when he was wronging with vilest thoughts, and cursing with murderous hatred, the brother who all the while lay dead for his sake.

Cold, silence, darkness encompassed the strong man bowed with the dolorous burden; and yet he knew surely that that night he entered hell, and trod hell-fire along the homeward road, and endured through it only because Christian was with him. And he knew surely that to him Christian had been as Christ, and had suffered and died to save him from his sins.

In the Forest of Villefère

Robert E. Howard

THE SUN HAD SET. The great shadows came striding over the forest. In the weird twilight of a late summer day, I saw the path ahead glide on among the mighty trees and disappear. And I shuddered and glanced fearfully over my shoulder. Miles behind lay the nearest village – miles ahead the next.

I looked to left and to right as I strode on, and anon I looked behind me. And anon I stopped short, grasping my rapier, as a breaking twig betokened the going of some small beast. Or was it a beast?

But the path led on and I followed, because, forsooth, I had naught else to do.

As I went I bethought me, "My own thoughts will rout me, if I be not aware. What is there in this forest, except perhaps the creatures that roam it, deer and the like? Tush, the foolish legends of those villagers!"

And so I went and the twilight faded into dusk. Stars began to blink and the leaves of the trees murmured in the faint breeze. And then I stopped short, my sword leaping to my hand, for just ahead, around a curve of the path, someone was singing. The words I could not distinguish, but the accent was strange, almost barbaric.

I stepped behind a great tree, and the cold sweat beaded my forehead. Then the singer came in sight, a tall, thin man, vague in the twilight. I shrugged my shoulders. A *man* I did not fear. I sprang out, my point raised.

"Stand!"

He showed no surprise. "I prithee, handle thy blade with care, friend," he said.

Somewhat ashamed, I lowered my sword.

"I am new to this forest," I quoth, apologetically. "I heard talk of bandits. I crave pardon. Where lies the road to Villefère?"

"*Corbleu*, you've missed it," he answered. "You should have branched off to the right some distance back. I am going there myself. If you may abide my company, I will direct you."

I hesitated. Yet why should I hesitate?

"Why, certainly. My name is de Montour, of Normandy."

"And I am Carolus le Loup."

"No!" I started back.

He looked at me in astonishment.

"Pardon," said I; "the name is strange. Does not *loup* mean wolf?"

"My family were always great hunters," he answered. He did not offer his hand.

"You will pardon my staring," said I as we walked down the path, "but I can hardly see your face in the dusk."

I sensed that he was laughing, though he made no sound.

"It is little to look upon," he answered.

I stepped closer and then leaped away, my hair bristling.

"A mask!" I exclaimed. "Why do you wear a mask, *m'sieu*?"

"It is a vow," he exclaimed. "In fleeing a pack of hounds I vowed that if I escaped I would wear a mask for a certain time."

"Hounds, *m'sieu?*"

"Wolves," he answered quickly; "I said wolves."

We walked in silence for awhile and then my companion said, "I am surprised that you walk these woods by night. Few people come these ways even in the day."

"I am in haste to reach the border," I answered. "A treaty has been signed with the English, and the Duke of Burgundy should know of it. The people at the village sought to dissuade me. They spoke of – a wolf that was purported to roam these woods."

"Here the path branches to Villefère," said he, and I saw a narrow, crooked path that I had not seen when I passed it before. It led in amid the darkness of the trees. I shuddered.

"You wish to return to the village?"

"No!" I exclaimed. "No, no! Lead on."

So narrow was the path that we walked single file, he leading. I looked well at him. He was taller, much taller than I, and thin, wiry. He was dressed in a costume that smacked of Spain. A long rapier swung at his hip. He walked with long easy strides, noiselessly.

Then he began to talk of travel and adventure. He spoke of many lands and seas he had seen and many strange things. So we talked and went farther and farther into the forest.

I presumed that he was French, and yet he had a very strange accent, that was neither French nor Spanish nor English, not like any language I had ever heard. Some words he slurred strangely and some he could not pronounce at all.

"This path is often used, is it?" I asked.

"Not by many," he answered and laughed silently. I shuddered. It was very dark and the leaves whispered together among the branches.

"A fiend haunts this forest," I said.

"So the peasants say," he answered, "but I have roamed it oft and have never seen his face."

Then he began to speak of strange creatures of darkness, and the moon rose and shadows glided among the trees. He looked up at the moon.

"Haste!" said he. "We must reach our destination before the moon reaches her zenith."

We hurried along the trail.

"They say," said I, "that a werewolf haunts these woodlands."

"It might be," said he, and we argued much upon the subject.

"The old women say," said he, "that if a werewolf is slain while a wolf, then he is slain, but if he is slain as a man, then his half-soul will haunt his slayer forever. But haste thee, the moon nears her zenith."

We came into a small moonlit glade and the stranger stopped.

"Let us pause a while," said he.

"Nay, let us be gone," I urged; "I like not this place."

He laughed without sound. "Why," said he, "This is a fair glade. As good as a banquet hall it is, and many times have I feasted here. Ha, ha, ha! Look ye, I will show you a dance." And he began bounding here and there, anon flinging back his head and laughing silently. Thought I, the man is mad.

As he danced his weird dance I looked about me. *The trail went not on but stopped in the glade.*

"Come," said I "we must on. Do you not smell the rank, hairy scent that hovers about the glade? Wolves den here. Perhaps they are about us and are gliding upon us even now."

He dropped upon all fours, bounded higher than my head, and came toward me with a strange slinking motion.

"That dance is called the Dance of the Wolf," said he, and my hair bristled.

"Keep off!" I stepped back, and with a screech that set the echoes shuddering he leaped for me, and though a sword hung at his belt he did not draw it. My rapier was half out when he grasped my arm and flung me headlong. I dragged him with me and we struck the ground together. Wrenching a hand free I jerked off the mask. A shriek of horror broke from my lips. Beast eyes glittered beneath that mask, white fangs flashed in the moonlight. *The face was that of a wolf.*

In an instant those fangs were at my throat. Taloned hands tore the sword from my grasp. I beat at that horrible face with my clenched fists, but his jaws were fastened on my shoulders, his talons tore at my throat. Then I was on my back. The world was fading. Blindly I struck out. My hand dropped, then closed automatically about the hilt of my dagger, which I had been unable to get at. I drew and stabbed. A terrible, half-bestial bellowing screech. Then I reeled to my feet, free. At my feet lay the werewolf.

I stooped, raised the dagger, then paused, looked up. The moon hovered close to her zenith. *If I slew the thing as a man its frightful spirit would haunt me forever.* I sat down waiting. The *thing* watched me with flaming wolf eyes. The long wiry limbs seemed to shrink, to crook; hair seemed to grow upon them. Fearing madness, I snatched up the *thing's* own sword and hacked it to pieces. Then I flung the sword away and fled.

Morraha

Celtic Fairy Tale

MORRAHA ROSE IN the morning and washed his hands and face, and said his prayers, and ate his food; and he asked God to prosper the day for him. So he went down to the brink of the sea, and he saw a currach, short and green, coming towards him; and in it there was but one youthful champion, and he was playing hurly from prow to stern of the currach. He had a hurl of gold and a ball of silver; and he stopped not till the currach was in on the shore; and he drew her up on the green grass, and put fastenings on her for a year and a day, whether he should be there all that time or should only be on land for an hour by the clock. And Morraha saluted the young man courteously; and the other saluted him in the same fashion, and asked him would he play a game of cards with him; and Morraha said that he had not the wherewithal; and the other answered that he was never without a candle or the making of it; and he put his hand in his pocket and drew out a table and two chairs and a pack of cards, and they sat down on the chairs and went to card-playing. The first game Morraha won, and the Slender Red Champion bade him make his claim; and he asked that the land above him should be filled with stock of sheep in the morning. It was well; and he played no second game, but home he went.

The next day Morraha went to the brink of the sea, and the young man came in the currach and asked him would he play cards; they played, and Morraha won. The young man bade him make his claim; and he asked that the land above should be filled with cattle in the morning. It was well; and he played no other game, but went home.

On the third morning Morraha went to the brink of the sea, and he saw the young man coming. He drew up his boat on the shore and asked him would he play cards. They played, and Morraha won the game; and the young man bade him give his claim. And he said he would have a castle and a wife, the finest and fairest in the world; and they were his. It was well; and the Red Champion went away.

On the fourth day his wife asked him how he had found her. And he told her. "And I am going out," said he, "to play again today."

"I forbid you to go again to him. If you have won so much, you will lose more; have no more to do with him."

But he went against her will, and he saw the currach coming; and the Red Champion was driving his balls from end to end of the currach; he had balls of silver and a hurl of gold, and he stopped not till he drew his boat on the shore, and made her fast for a year and a day. Morraha and he saluted each other; and he asked Morraha if he would play a game of cards, and they played, and he won. Morraha said to him, "Give your claim now."

Said he, "You will hear it too soon. I lay on you bonds of the art of the Druid, not to sleep two nights in one house, nor finish a second meal at the one table, till you bring me the sword of light and news of the death of Anshgayliacht."

He went home to his wife and sat down in a chair, and gave a groan, and the chair broke in pieces.

"That is the groan of the son of a king under spells," said his wife; "and you had better have taken my counsel than that the spells should be on you."

He told her he had to bring news of the death of Anshgayliacht and the sword of light to the Slender Red Champion.

"Go out," said she, "in the morning of the morrow, and take the bridle in the window, and shake it; and whatever beast, handsome or ugly, puts its head in it, take that one with you. Do not speak a word to her till she speaks to you; and take with you three pint bottles of ale and three sixpenny loaves, and do the thing she tells you; and when she runs to my father's land, on a height above the castle, she will shake herself, and the bells will ring, and my father will say, 'Brown Allree is in the land. And if the son of a king or queen is there, bring him to me on your shoulders; but if it is the son of a poor man, let him come no further.'"

He rose in the morning, and took the bridle that was in the window, and went out and shook it; and Brown Allree came and put her head in it. He took the three loaves and three bottles of ale, and went riding; and when he was riding she bent her head down to take hold of her feet with her mouth, in hopes he would speak in ignorance; but he spoke not a word during the time, and the mare at last spoke to him, and told him to dismount and give her her dinner. He gave her the sixpenny loaf toasted, and a bottle of ale to drink.

"Sit up now riding, and take good heed of yourself: there are three miles of fire I have to clear at a leap."

She cleared the three miles of fire at a leap, and asked if he were still riding, and he said he was. Then they went on, and she told him to dismount and give her a meal; and he did so, and gave her a sixpenny loaf and a bottle; she consumed them and said to him there were before them three miles of hill covered with steel thistles, and that she must clear it. She cleared the hill with a leap, and she asked him if he were still riding, and he said he was. They went on, and she went not far before she told him to give her a meal, and he gave her the bread and the bottleful. She went over three miles of sea with a leap, and she came then to the land of the King of France; she went up on a height above the castle, and she shook herself and neighed, and the bells rang; and the king said that it was Brown Allree was in the land.

"Go out," said he; "and if it is the son of a king or queen, carry him in on your shoulders; if it is not, leave him there."

They went out; and the stars of the son of a king were on his breast; they lifted him high on their shoulders and bore him in to the king. They passed the night cheerfully, playing and drinking, with sport and with diversion, till the whiteness of the day came upon the morrow morning.

Then the young king told the cause of his journey, and he asked the queen to give him counsel and good luck, and she told him everything he was to do.

"Go now," said she, "and take with you the best mare in the stable, and go to the door of Rough Niall of the Speckled Rock, and knock, and call on him to give you news of the death of Anshgayliacht and the sword of light: and let the horse's back be to the door, and apply the spurs, and away with you."

In the morning he did so, and he took the best horse from the stable and rode to the door of Niall, and turned the horse's back to the door, and demanded news of the death of Anshgayliacht and the sword of light; then he applied the spurs, and away with him. Niall followed him hard, and, as he was passing the gate, cut the horse in two. His wife was there with a dish of puddings and flesh, and she threw it in his eyes and blinded him, and said, "Fool! whatever kind of man it is that's mocking you, isn't that a fine condition you have got your father's horse into?"

On the morning of the next day Morraha rose, and took another horse from the stable, and went again to the door of Niall, and knocked and demanded news of the death of Anshgayliacht and the sword of light, and applied the spurs to the horse and away with him. Niall followed, and as Morraha was passing, the gate cut the horse in two and took half the saddle with him; but his wife met him and threw flesh in his eyes and blinded him.

On the third day, Morraha went again to the door of Niall; and Niall followed him, and as he was passing the gate, cut away the saddle from under him and the clothes from his back. Then his wife said to Niall:

"The fool that's mocking you, is out yonder in the little currach, going home; and take good heed to yourself, and don't sleep one wink for three days."

For three days the little currach kept in sight, but then Niall's wife came to him and said:

"Sleep as much as you want now. He is gone."

He went to sleep, and there was heavy sleep on him, and Morraha went in and took hold of the sword that was on the bed at his head. And the sword thought to draw itself out of the hand of Morraha; but it failed. Then it gave a cry, and it wakened Niall, and Niall said it was a rude and rough thing to come into his house like that; and said Morraha to him:

"Leave your much talking, or I will cut the head off you. Tell me the news of the death of Anshgayliacht."

"Oh, you can have my head."

"But your head is no good to me; tell me the story."

"Oh," said Niall's wife, "you must get the story."

"Well," said Niall, "let us sit down together till I tell the story. I thought no one would ever get it; but now it will be heard by all."

The Story

WHEN I WAS GROWING UP, my mother taught me the language of the birds; and when I got married, I used to be listening to their conversation; and I would be laughing; and my wife would be asking me what was the reason of my laughing, but I did not like to tell her, as women are always asking questions. We went out walking one fine morning, and the birds were arguing with one another. One of them said to another:

"Why should you be comparing yourself with me, when there is not a king nor knight that does not come to look at my tree?"

"What advantage has your tree over mine, on which there are three rods of magic mastery growing?"

When I heard them arguing, and knew that the rods were there, I began to laugh.

"Oh," asked my wife, "why are you always laughing? I believe it is at myself you are jesting, and I'll walk with you no more."

"Oh, it is not about you I am laughing. It is because I understand the language of the birds."

Then I had to tell her what the birds were saying to one another; and she was greatly delighted, and she asked me to go home, and she gave orders to the cook to have breakfast ready at six o'clock in the morning. I did not know why she was going out early, and breakfast was ready in the morning at the hour she appointed. She asked me to go out walking. I went with her. She went to the tree, and asked me to cut a rod for her.

"Oh, I will not cut it. Are we not better without it?"

"I will not leave this until I get the rod, to see if there is any good in it."

I cut the rod and gave it to her. She turned from me and struck a blow on a stone, and changed it; and she struck a second blow on me, and made of me a black raven, and she went home and left me after her. I thought she would come back; she did not come, and I had to go into a tree till morning. In the morning, at six o'clock, there was a bellman out, proclaiming that everyone who killed a raven would get a fourpenny-bit. At last you could not find man or boy without a gun, nor, if you were to walk three miles, a raven that was not killed. I had to make a nest in the top of the parlour chimney, and hide myself all day till night came, and go out to pick up a bit to support me, till I spent a month. Here she is herself to say if it is a lie I am telling.

"It is not," said she.

Then I saw her out walking. I went up to her, and I thought she would turn me back to my own shape, and she struck me with the rod and made of me an old white horse, and she ordered me to be put to a cart with a man, to draw stones from morning till night. I was worse off then. She spread abroad a report that I had died suddenly in my bed, and prepared a coffin, and waked and buried me. Then she had no trouble. But when I got tired I began to kill everyone who came near me, and I used to go into the haggard every night and destroy the stacks of corn; and when a man came near me in the morning I would follow him till I broke his bones. Everyone got afraid of me. When she saw I was doing mischief she came to meet me, and I thought she would change me. And she did change me, and made a fox of me. When I saw she was doing me every sort of damage I went away from her. I knew there was a badger's hole in the garden, and I went there till night came, and I made great slaughter among the geese and ducks. There she is herself to say if I am telling a lie.

"Oh! you are telling nothing but the truth, only less than the truth."

When she had enough of my killing the fowl she came out into the garden, for she knew I was in the badger's hole. She came to me and made me a wolf. I had to be off, and go to an island, where no one at all would see me, and now and then I used to be killing sheep, for there were not many of them, and I was afraid of being seen and hunted; and so I passed a year, till a shepherd saw me among the sheep and a pursuit was made after me. And when the dogs came near me there was no place for me to escape to from them; but I recognised the sign of the king among the men, and I made for him, and the king cried out to stop the hounds. I took a leap upon the front of the king's saddle, and the woman behind cried out, "My king and my lord, kill him, or he will kill you!"

"Oh! he will not kill me. He knew me; he must be pardoned."

The king took me home with him, and gave orders I should be well cared for. I was so wise, when I got food, I would not eat one morsel until I got a knife and fork. The man told the king, and the king came to see if it was true, and I got a knife and fork, and I took the knife in one paw and the fork in the other, and I bowed to the king. The king gave orders to bring him drink, and it came; and the king filled a glass of wine and gave it to me.

I took hold of it in my paw and drank it, and thanked the king.

"On my honour," said he, "it is some king or other has lost him, when he came on the island; and I will keep him, as he is trained; and perhaps he will serve us yet."

And this is the sort of king he was – a king who had not a child living. Eight sons were born to him and three daughters, and they were stolen the same night they were born. No matter what guard was placed over them, the child would be gone in the morning. A twelfth child now came to the queen, and the king took me with him to watch the baby. The women were not satisfied with me.

"Oh," said the king, "what was all your watching ever good for? One that was born to me I have not; I will leave this one in the dog's care, and he will not let it go."

A coupling was put between me and the cradle, and when everyone went to sleep I was watching till the person woke who attended in the daytime; but I was there only two nights; when it was near the day, I saw a hand coming down through the chimney, and the hand was so big that it took round the child altogether, and thought to take him away. I caught hold of the hand above the wrist, and as I was fastened to the cradle, I did not let go my hold till I cut the hand from the wrist, and there was a howl from the person without. I laid the hand in the cradle with the child, and as I was tired I fell asleep; and when I awoke, I had neither child nor hand; and I began to howl, and the king heard me, and he cried out that something was wrong with me, and he sent servants to see what was the matter with me, and when the messenger came he saw me covered with blood, and he could not see the child; and he went to the king and told him the child was not to be got. The king came and saw the cradle coloured with the blood, and he cried out "Where was the child gone?" and everyone said it was the dog had eaten it.

The king said: "It is not: loose him, and he will get the pursuit himself."

When I was loosed, I found the scent of the blood till I came to a door of the room in which the child was. I went back to the king and took hold of him, and went back again and began to tear at the door. The king followed me and asked for the key. The servant said it was in the room of the stranger woman. The king caused search to be made for her, and she was not to be found. "I will break the door," said the king, "as I can't get the key." The king broke the door, and I went in, and went to the trunk, and the king asked for a key to unlock it. He got no key, and he broke the lock. When he opened the trunk, the child and the hand were stretched side by side, and the child was asleep. The king took the hand and ordered a woman to come for the child, and he showed the hand to everyone in the house. But the stranger woman was gone, and she did not see the king; – and here she is herself to say if I am telling lies of her.

"Oh, it's nothing but the truth you have!"

The king did not allow me to be tied any more. He said there was nothing so much to wonder at as that I cut the hand off, as I was tied.

The child was growing till he was a year old. He was beginning to walk, and no one cared for him more than I did. He was growing till he was three, and he was running out every minute; so the king ordered a silver chain to be put between me and the child, that he might not go away from me. I was out with him in the garden every day, and the king was as proud as the world of the child. He would be watching him everywhere we went, till the child grew so wise that he would loose the chain and get off. But one day that he loosed it I failed to find him; and I ran into the house and searched the house, but there was no getting him for me. The king cried to go out and find the child, that had got loose from the dog. They went searching for him, but could not find him. When they failed altogether to find him, there remained no more favour with the king towards me, and everyone disliked me, and I grew weak, for I did not get a morsel to eat half the time. When summer came, I said I would try and go home to my own country. I went away one fine morning, and I went swimming, and God helped me till I came home. I went into the garden, for I knew there was a place in the garden where I could hide myself, for fear my wife should see me. In the morning I saw her out walking, and the child with her, held by the hand. I pushed out to see the child, and as he was looking about him everywhere, he saw me and called out, "I see my shaggy papa. Oh!" said he; "oh, my heart's love, my shaggy papa, come here till I see you!"

I was afraid the woman would see me, as she was asking the child where he saw me, and he said I was up in a tree; and the more the child called me, the more I hid myself. The woman took the child home with her, but I knew he would be up early in the morning.

I went to the parlour-window, and the child was within, and he playing. When he saw me he cried out, "Oh! my heart's love, come here till I see you, shaggy papa." I broke the window and went in, and he began to kiss me. I saw the rod in front of the chimney, and I jumped up at the rod and knocked it down. "Oh! my heart's love, no one would give me the pretty rod," said he. I hoped he would strike me with the rod, but he did not. When I saw the time was short I raised my paw, and I gave him a scratch below the knee. "Oh! you naughty, dirty, shaggy papa, you have hurt me so much, I'll give you a blow of the rod." He struck me a light blow, and so I came back to my own shape again. When he saw a man standing before him he gave a cry, and I took him up in my arms. The servants heard the child. A maid came in to see what was the matter with him. When she saw me she gave a cry out of her, and she said, "Oh, if the master isn't come to life again!"

Another came in, and said it was he really. When the mistress heard of it, she came to see with her own eyes, for she would not believe I was there; and when she saw me she said she'd drown herself. But I said to her, "If you yourself will keep the secret, no living man will ever get the story from me until I lose my head." Here she is herself to say if I am telling the truth. "Oh, it's nothing but truth you are telling."

When I saw I was in a man's shape, I said I would take the child back to his father and mother, as I knew the grief they were in after him. I got a ship, and took the child with me; and as I journeyed I came to land on an island, and I saw not a living soul on it, only a castle dark and gloomy. I went in to see was there any one in it. There was no one but an old hag, tall and frightful, and she asked me, "What sort of person are you?" I heard someone groaning in another room, and I said I was a doctor, and I asked her what ailed the person who was groaning.

"Oh," said she, "it is my son, whose hand has been bitten from his wrist by a dog."

I knew then that it was he who had taken the child from me, and I said I would cure him if I got a good reward.

"I have nothing; but there are eight young lads and three young women, as handsome as any one ever laid eyes on, and if you cure him I will give you them."

"Tell me first in what place his hand was cut from him?"

"Oh, it was out in another country, twelve years ago."

"Show me the way, that I may see him."

She brought me into a room, so that I saw him, and his arm was swelled up to the shoulder. He asked me if I would cure him; and I said I would cure him if he would give me the reward his mother promised.

"Oh, I will give it; but cure me."

"Well, bring them out to me."

The hag brought them out of the room. I said I should burn the flesh that was on his arm. When I looked on him he was howling with pain. I said that I would not leave him in pain long. The wretch had only one eye in his forehead. I took a bar of iron, and put it in the fire till it was red, and I said to the hag, "He will be howling at first, but will fall asleep presently, and do not wake him till he has slept as much as he wants. I will close the door when I am going out." I took the bar with me, and I stood over him, and I turned it across through his eye as far as I could. He began to bellow, and tried to catch me, but I was out and away, having closed the door. The hag asked me, "Why is he bellowing?"

"Oh, he will be quiet presently, and will sleep for a good while, and I'll come again to have a look at him; but bring me out the young men and the young women."

I took them with me, and I said to her, "Tell me where you got them."

"My son brought them with him, and they are all the children of one king."

I was well satisfied, and I had no wish for delay to get myself free from the hag, so I took them on board the ship, and the child I had myself. I thought the king might leave me the child I nursed myself; but when I came to land, and all those young people with me, the king and queen were out walking. The king was very aged, and the queen aged likewise. When I came to converse with them, and the twelve with me, the king and queen began to cry. I asked, "Why are you crying?"

"It is for good cause I am crying. As many children as these I should have, and now I am withered, grey, at the end of my life, and I have not one at all."

I told him all I went through, and I gave him the child in his hand, and "These are your other children who were stolen from you, whom I am giving to you safe. They are gently reared."

When the king heard who they were he smothered them with kisses and drowned them with tears, and dried them with fine cloths silken and the hair of his own head, and so also did their mother, and great was his welcome for me, as it was I who found them all. The king said to me, "I will give you the last child, as it is you who have earned him best; but you must come to my court every year, and the child with you, and I will share with you my possessions."

"I have enough of my own, and after my death I will leave it to the child."

I spent a time, till my visit was over, and I told the king all the troubles I went through, only I said nothing about my wife. And now you have the story.

* * *

And now when you go home, and the Slender Red Champion asks you for news of the death of Anshgayliacht and for the sword of light, tell him the way in which his brother was killed, and say you have the sword; and he will ask the sword from you. Say you to him, "If I promised to bring it to you, I did not promise to bring it for you"; and then throw the sword into the air and it will come back to me.

* * *

He went home, and he told the story of the death of Anshgayliacht to the Slender Red Champion, "And here," said he, "is the sword." The Slender Red Champion asked for the sword; but he said: "If I promised to bring it to you, I did not promise to bring it for you"; and he threw it into the air and it returned to Blue Niall.

When It Happens

Rebecca Jones-Howe

KATE CRINGED as the emergency-room doctor pulled a needle through Michael's wound. His skin swelled against the stitches. Blood and pus oozed through the broken flesh. The doctor dressed the wound in gauze and then turned for the vaccine.

"It was just a *wolf*," Michael protested.

The doctor pressed the syringe into the bottle. "It's a precaution, Mr. Freeman. Our records show that you haven't been—"

"Werewolves don't exist," Michael said.

Kate reached for her husband but Michael swatted her away.

The doctor straightened. "Were you not aware of the reported sighting in the area?"

"I knew," Kate said.

Signs had littered every post along the hiking trail, but Michael always knew better. He'd insisted they go hiking after dinner under the full moon. It was their wedding anniversary, after all. What Kate failed to mention was that her period had just started, and she was sure that the smell of the blood was what drew the wolf near.

Michael straightened as the doctor approached with the syringe. "The moon isn't real," he said. "Werewolves can't exist if the moon isn't real."

"Mr. Freeman, you have to understand—"

"Michael, please don't do this here." Kate met her husband's gaze but his expression only hardened. The vein pulsed in his neck.

"There's proof," he said. "There are videos on the Internet that clearly explain that the moon is a hologram."

The doctor sighed. "For the benefit of those around you, for your *wife*, Mr. Freeman, I urge you—"

Michael laughed, the maniacal sound vibrating through the emergency room.

A menstrual cramp worked against Kate's gut. She pursed her lips, gripping at the straps of her backpack, tension swelling against the bind of her wedding ring.

"Mr. Freeman, I can't legally force you to take the vaccine, but I *will* have to log you down as a carrier if you refuse."

"So I end up on some government watch-list, or you inject me with your mind-control drugs?"

Kate caught his elbow. "Let it go, Michael. You're causing a scene."

"*Everyone* should be causing a scene! This entire program is a globalist scheme to control us!"

Heads turned. Voices whispered. Patients in the other beds raised their phones and hit record.

"This is fascism!" Michael roared. "It's blatant fascism and you people are willingly letting it happen!"

Kate gripped at her stomach as the doctor paged for security. She still hadn't gotten herself a tampon and she could feel a gush of blood working its way out of her.

* * *

Kate wasn't going to tell Michael about her period.

He had already gotten his hopes up about her being pregnant. They'd been trying for two years, and the only thing that kept Michael from talking about the vaccine was the prospect of them becoming parents.

At home, Kate rushed to the bathroom and popped an extra-strength Tylenol before sliding a tampon in. She washed her hands and returned to the kitchen, where Michael eased his bandaged arm out of his jacket. Kate pulled out the informational pamphlet on Lycanthropy from her backpack. Listed were the symptoms to watch out for:

Hallucinations.

Hunger.

Stiff limbs.

Cravings for raw meat.

Michael winced, cracking open a beer. The red stain on the bandage looked like an eye on his arm, an outside gaze observing their marriage and the problems it contained.

"Don't let this government-created bullshit ruin your critical thinking skills, babe," he said, nodding at the pamphlet.

"I don't want you to turn into a werewolf," Kate said. "Immunization is the best prevention."

The pamphlet said so, but Michael snatched it out of Kate's hold.

"You're paranoid, babe. The vaccine makes you paranoid. I read on InfoCrusaders that it makes you infertile, too."

"It doesn't do that, Michael."

"Maybe you're proof that it does."

Kate bit over her lip. "Don't make this about something it's not."

Tendons twitched in his arm. He made a fist, sucking air through his teeth. Aggression worked through his gaze, though he looked at her long enough for his anger to ease. His throat bobbed. Wobbled. "Fine," he said. "I'm sorry." He wiped sweat off his brow, his hand shaking. "I just, I can't take that fucking vaccine, babe. You know that."

"I wish you would," Kate said.

He braced himself, picking up the beer he'd opened. He took a swig and laughed. "I'll make a believer out of you yet, babe."

* * *

Michael snored, which kept Kate awake, which kept her staring out at the full moon, its glow slipping over the sheets. She rolled over and touched the edge of her silver wedding band to Michael's arm.

Nothing.

Another snore reverberated against the walls.

Kate took her pillow into the office, the place where Michael did most of his research after losing his pipeline surveying job two years before.

InfoCrusaders claimed that Lycanthropy was a myth. Satellites all over the world projected the moon into the sky. Michael swore that the video feed often lapsed. Sometimes lines would blink and flicker. Sometimes the orientation of the satellites would fall out of sync and the moon would appear bigger, smaller, or brighter. It was all a scheme, devised by the global elite to control the masses.

Kate lifted the blinds. She squinted at the full moon, seeing nothing but reality.

* * *

Part of Kate's job as a public health nurse was to make house calls on new mothers. She knocked on the door of a newly built townhouse. The mother answered. Kate slipped on a pair of disposable slippers over her shoes and followed the mother's lead up the stairs.

The stairwell wall featured a selection of snapshots of a happy couple in love. Already, there was a printed photo of the newborn baby in a blue cap.

The woman's husband was home, seated in the rocking chair, holding the sleeping baby that Kate weighed and assessed. Kate then pulled out the questionnaire she was to ask of all new mothers. Most of the questions were to assess the general health and well-being of mother and baby, but there was one lingering question at the end that she hated asking.

"Do you feel safe?"

The mother hesitated. "Safe in what way?"

Kate glanced at a living room full of happy smiling photos. A canvas sign hung over the kitchen table: *Love lives here.*

"This question is really about security." Kate shifted against the menstrual cramp plaguing her. "How do you feel about your home and work balance? How do you feel about your ability to provide for your child?"

The husband and wife looked at each other.

"Really good!" the mother said. "We're excited. Things are great!"

Kate believed them.

* * *

The man from the InfoCrusaders website was screaming again: *"People think I'm crazy when I tell them the truth!"*

Kate winced before letting herself into the apartment. She tread down the hallway, glancing at the single wedding picture featured on the beige wall. She and Michael stood posed in front of the waterfall at the end of the Peterson Creek trail, both smiling in their hiking gear, she with a veil and he with a top hat. A budget wedding, but a happy one.

Now five years old, the photo sat crooked in its frame.

"The moon isn't a physical object in the sky, people! It's a mirror they're using to reflect all of their lies about society back to us, and the longer you look, the longer you'll be corrupted. Make sure you arm yourself! Protect your family because I'm telling you now that nobody else will!"

The office door stood open. Michael sat at his desk, reaching into a bag of beef jerky.

"They're pulling this trick to try to divert us!"

"Hey babe." He smiled, sinking his teeth into the meat. His nostrils flared and Kate shifted in the threshold, wondering if he could smell her blood. He paused the video. "How was work?"

"It was fine. How are you feeling?"

He reached into the bag of jerky again, leaning back in his seat. "Do I look like a monster yet?"

She pressed her thighs together. "No."

"Well, I feel fine," he said. "So you don't need to worry, okay?"

Kate nodded with no choice but to believe, the blood leaking out of her. The second day of her period was always the worst. She found solace in the bathroom, washing her stained panties under the cold tap. It'd get better from here, she thought, but nothing could overpower the sound of the man screaming on the computer screen.

"We should be ready! We need to identify our enemy! That's the fight! That's the key! That's everything!"

* * *

Kate woke to the smell of bacon cooking. Michael stood over the stove in his red Visions Electronics shirt. Grease was smeared over the MANAGER title embroidered on the breast pocket. He held a slice of bacon to her mouth. "Take a bite, babe."

The salty cured meat looked as sick and sweaty as he did.

At least it was cooked, she reasoned.

"Did you pack a lunch?" she asked.

Michael laughed. "I'll grab something from the store, babe." He ate another piece of bacon before pulling his jacket on, leaving a greasy kiss on her forehead before he said goodbye.

* * *

Another house. Another mother.

Kate counted the children in the photos. Four kids plus the newborn. Kate weighed and measured the baby. She helped the mother get the baby to latch properly. While the baby nursed, Kate pulled out her questionnaire.

The father wasn't in the home, though photos of him were featured prominently.

"Do you feel safe?" Kate asked.

The mother nodded. "What do you do if the woman says no?"

"Well, we offer them a card with emergency numbers and counselling options."

"What if you *know* the woman's not okay but she insists she is?"

Kate stared at a picture of the happy father reading *Goodnight Moon* to the kids in bed, knowing Michael would never be able to do the same.

"There's only so far we can intervene," Kate said. "It's tough."

"I can only imagine," the mother said. "How awful that must be." She glanced down at the baby, bringing it close so she could kiss its little forehead.

* * *

The moon loomed over the city, waning.

Kate sat on the deck with a mug of tea. Chamomile. She hoped it would calm her. Gone were the cramps that accommodated the first days of her period. She'd made herself a salad for dinner, enjoyed a night to herself while Michael worked late.

Her nerves flared when the sliding door creaked open behind her. Michael placed his hand over her shoulder. Kate took a heavy sip from her mug. She imagined claws forming, hair growing.

"Are you trying to see what I see, babe?" His expression was hopeful. Human.

She put her tea down. "I'll never see what you see."

Michael's hand fell from her shoulder. He moved in front of her. The glow touched his back, his hands, his neck. Nothing changed.

"Werewolves only change under the full moon, Michael."

"Said like a true member of the flock."

Kate brought her hands to her face. She groaned, pressing fingers to her eyelids until her vision went painful and spotty. For a moment, Michael was a blur, a mess, but it didn't take long for Kate's vision to clear. He still looked like the man she married, still smiled like the man she married.

"What did you have for lunch today?" she asked.

"A vegan burger," he said, "saturated with chemicals."

"Michael, please, just stop. I can't talk to you."

He gripped at the deck railing. The moon made shadows out of his expression. "You're scared of me, aren't you? Is that it? You're scared of me now?"

She couldn't answer.

"You think I'm going to hurt you, babe?" He leaned over her and snarled. He bared teeth.

"Stop it."

"*You* got the vaccine," he said, grabbing her shoulders. "It's in your brain, babe! It's making you paranoid."

Kate twisted in her seat. "Michael, stop. I don't want to talk about this."

He grabbed her hand, only to flinch when he touched the ring on her finger. "Fuck!" His groan echoed in the night. He made a fist and held it at his side. "This is why you won't have a fucking baby with me, isn't it?"

Kate wrestled herself out of the chair. She turned for the patio door.

Michael followed. "Tell me, Kate. Fucking *tell* me! It's been two fucking years, Kate!"

Kate slammed the door over his hand.

* * *

In the living room, Kate knelt down in front of him, pressing a bag of frozen peas over the swelling.

"I wasn't trying to scare you," Michael said. "We used to joke. We used to pretend."

Kate nodded with a sigh, remembering when she'd leave the lights off in the apartment when when she was ovulating. Michael would call her, would find her. She liked the danger, the flight or fight. The dread in her stomach always rose up into a lustful rush when he wrestled her down onto the bed or the couch or the floor.

Trying. They had fun trying.

Then the government halted the nearby pipeline expansion and Michael was left with nothing to survey. Every month he'd fade a little. Stubble lined his jaw. Lines settled over his brow, only to remain there as his skepticism grew.

Secretly, Kate made an appointment to get an IUD.

They tried. They kept trying.

Michael kept tackling Kate down in the dark, recreating the past only to later wonder why a baby never resulted from their effort.

Kate started leaving the curtains open, leaving the lights on.

No more trying. No more thrill.

She was a sheep, after all. Paranoid. Brainwashed.

Michael cradled his hand beneath the bag of frozen peas. He tried to make a fist, his breath catching, his voice breaking. "I wasn't trying to scare you, babe."

Kate believed it.

She leaned forward and undid the buttons beneath the collar of his Visions Electronics shirt, her fingertips grazing against the warmth of human skin.

"Let's go to bed, okay?"

* * *

"I've got a headache," he groaned, gripping at her thighs. He rolled away when he finished, passing out immediately, his mouth slacked, filling the room with snores.

In the night, he rolled in close again. He brought his arm around her and clutched his injured hand over her belly.

Kate pressed her elbow against his side in return.

Michael snarled against her ear. "You don't smell like Kate."

She turned to face him. His eyes were wide open, pupils dilated but unfocused.

Kate wrestled herself out of his hold, scrambling off the bed as Michael thrashed, his limbs spasming, body tangled in the sheets.

"Kate!"

She wedged a chair beneath the doorknob and raced into the office again. Michael's hallucinated calls penetrated through the wall.

"Kate, where'd you go? What happened to you, Kate?"

A thud sounded, followed by a series of grunts. Kate imagined him on all fours, desperate for the smell of her. He clawed at the wall that separated the rooms.

"We'll fix this, Kate! We'll get it right! Our kids will know the truth! We'll tell them the truth!"

Kate dug through the closet and found one of her old hiking poles, which she clutched tight, poised and ready. Michael scratched the wall, his groans turning into sobs, his cries withering into exhaustion as the moon gave way to dawn.

* * *

The next house Kate visited was a worn-down post-war home with a rusty chain-link fence. Stacks of undelivered newspapers turned into pulp on the rain-soaked grass. Kate tread up the front steps and knocked on the door.

A dog barked on the other side. A woman yelled.

Kate waited, glancing back at her car as the dog scratched. The woman inside yelled again. She opened the door and held the dog back by its collar. It jumped at her, sniffed at her.

"Sorry," the woman said. "He's just defending the baby."

Kate dodged the dog's swipes as she struggled to pull her disposable slippers over her shoes. Treading across the toy-littered living room, she followed the woman into the baby's nursery. The dog barked behind the nursery door as Kate weighed and measured the baby. She touched the baby's yellowed skin.

"She's got a bit of jaundice," Kate said.

"All my kids had jaundice," the mom said, taking the baby into her arms. "It'll be fine."

"Jaundice goes away in most cases, yes, but it's worth knowing when to be concerned."

The mother grimaced. Then Kate pulled out the questionnaire.

"You're going to ask about vaccines, aren't you?"

"It is one of the questions, yes."

"I've done my own research, alright? I get that you're a nurse, but *I'm* the parent, here."

"I have to give you the package with the information. You're free to throw it in the recycling bin just like my husband does."

The mother raised her brow. "Did you vaccinate your kids?"

"I don't have kids yet."

The mother stood, popped the baby on her hip. "But your husband's against vaccines? How would you deal with that?"

"It's something we haven't discussed."

The mother laughed. "That's why my husband left me, honestly."

"Was it amicable?"

"Oh, fuck no. He filed for custody. He wants them shot full of mind control."

Kate clenched her toes in her disposable slippers, hospital pastel blue, the same colour as the emergency-room curtains.

"You'd love my husband," Kate said.

He's turning into a werewolf, she wanted to say.

He'll eat your children, she wanted to say.

Instead, she finished her questionnaire and carefully slipped a vaccination pamphlet between the cushions of the rocking chair. She peeled off the slippers at the door and dropped another pamphlet by the shoe rack. She dropped a stack of pamphlets on top of the decaying newspapers, the dog barking behind her, angry with her, wanting her gone.

* * *

She ended up at the grocery store, where she loaded up her cart with a salad kit and some saltine crackers and a bottle of white wine. She went down the canned food aisle, where she found Michael with his back turned. He tossed a can of SPAM into his basket.

Kate paused, unsure whether or not to move, but he could sense her now, smell her now. The moon was in its waxing phase now. She gripped the bar of the shopping cart, turning around only to knock over a display of coffee.

"Dammit." She tried to right the display but the bags scattered over the floor.

"What are you doing here, babe?" Michael leaned down to help. His knuckles flexed around the vacuum-sealed packages. He did his best to file them back onto the cardboard shelf of the display, but his fingers seized and the coffee slipped out of his grasp.

"Shit."

Michael struggled to stand. Kate offered help but he swatted her back with his curled fingers.

"I'm fine," he said, using the cart to pull himself up. His leg spasmed as he stood.

"Michael—"

"I'm *fine*, babe."

Another couple entered the aisle. They were young, early twenties, hands still clasped with inexperience. The woman rubbed her free hand over her swollen belly, where a baby was fully grown, ready to meet reality.

Michael commandeered the cart and placed his basket inside. Beneath the canned meat was a fresh steak. The slab of red pressed against the plastic wrap. Juices settled in the base of the Styrofoam container, sloshing around white sinews of fat.

A tightness built in Kate's throat. A sickness worked its way up. She squeezed her eyes shut and swallowed.

"Oh please," Michael said, leaning in, his nostrils flared. "I can smell the blood, babe. You didn't even tell me you were ovulating two weeks ago."

Kate parted her lips.

Michael fidgeted with the cart. He pushed it against Kate's stomach.

"Michael, stop." The alarm in her voice caught the attention of the pregnant woman. Kate put her hand out but Michael shoved her with the cart again. He smiled, tried to make the action playful even though the aggression lingered in his tendons.

"Let's go, babe."

The pregnant woman stared, her eyes narrowed, seeing nothing but reality.

* * *

Michael scratched again at the walls, vigorous, desperate, his voice breaking with need.

Kate moved her base to the living room. It gave her more distance from Michael and allowed for a quick exit if she needed to run. She dug through the dining room hutch for the silver knife they used to cut their wedding cake. She kept it tucked between the couch cushions.

Inside, her uterus cramped.

She felt the sickness in her throat.

The moon was nearly full again.

* * *

She woke to the smell of ground beef in mid-fry.

Michael stood at the stove in his red shirt with his back turned. He scratched at the wound on his arm. The bandage was missing now, his wound healed to scar tissue. The bruise on his hand was missing too.

Like it never happened.

Like everything was normal, even though the beef he loaded onto his plate was streaked with pink and the InfoCrusaders man still yelled from the video playing on Michael's phone: *"If they start quarantining the truth-tellers, then all hell will break loose! This is about individual liberty! Do not let them imprison you for knowing the truth!"*

He picked a fork out of the utensil drawer and shovelled the half-cooked meat into his mouth.

"Michael?"

The fork slipped out of his hand. He leaned over the plate so he could lick at the juices before returning to the stove for another serving.

"Michael!" Kate stood, the cake knife gripped behind her back.

He fisted the next batch of meat into his mouth. As Kate stepped closer, she noticed the hair growing in the scar tissue, thick follicles pushing through his flesh.

Finally, he turned, licking his fingers clean. "Oh, I thought I smelled you, babe."

Clutching the knife behind her back, Kate reached for a sheet of paper towel, wiping the grease away from his face.

"I love you," he said, smiling.

* * *

Do you feel safe?

She got a McDonald's salad for dinner. She ate in the restaurant, watching a breaking story on the local news. A werewolf victim had been found on the Peterson Creek trail.

"I'm terrified," one of the locals said.

"This is horrible," another person said. "The government really needs to step things up. I don't understand why they won't quarantine these people!"

A mother cried. "Everyone out there *needs* to get vaccinated."

Kate ate, savouring the acidic taste of her balsamic vinaigrette.

* * *

At home, the Styrofoam container sat in the sink. The kitchen reeked of raw meat. The smell twisted in her stomach. Her hormones reacted. Her uterus cramped, reminding Kate that her body's ticking clock was ready to spill again. Kate retched into the trash, her eyes closed tight. She imagined Michael's hand on her shoulder, imagined him shoving her into the bed.

He'd find out about the IUD eventually.

In the office, the InfoCrusaders man was yelling again: *"This is the New World Order, people! This is about mass surveillance! This is about social engineering! They're making us impotent and they're taking our liberty away!"*

"Is that you, Kate?" Michael appeared in the office doorway, steak juices dripping off his chin.

Kate wiped the bile off her lips.

"Why don't we eat together anymore?" he asked. Black circled his eyes. "We used to go out every Friday night. Remember that? Remember?"

She could leave, call the police, let them know. They'd take him for a while. They'd put him into a cell without a window. He wouldn't turn without the moon. They couldn't quarantine him if he didn't turn.

"Please," she begged. "Please just get the vaccine."

Michael's gaze hardened. His shoulders broadened. He turned and locked the office door behind him, the crusader screams bleeding out.

* * *

Kate walked up the front steps of another home. She knocked, the colour draining from her face when the once-pregnant woman from the grocery store answered, her swollen belly replaced with a swaddled infant that she clutched against her chest.

Kate put on the flimsy blue slippers and tread over the white shag carpet in the living room. Her fingers shook when she pulled out the scale.

"I was worried," the mother said. "When he hit you with the cart, I—"

It's fine.

I'm okay.

Kate smiled and read off her questionnaire. "Do you feel safe?"

"Do *you* feel safe?" the mother asked.

Kate thought of the steak, pressed up against the plastic wrap.

"Michael wouldn't hurt me," Kate said. "He seems bad, but he's confused. He's scared."

"Scared of what?"

Kate shook her head. "He's scared of losing me."

"Oh, he'll be fine," the mother scoffed. "He'll live."

It wasn't exactly the best answer, but it filled Kate with dread.

* * *

Kate returned to an empty apartment.

The garbage had been taken out.

Outside, the moon beamed in its full form. The cramps worsened. He could already smell the blood she'd soon be spilling. Kate sat down on the couch. She made her makeshift bed and turned on the news. She kept the lights on, the blinds open. On the evening's news, another breaking story flashed, showing images of emergency vehicles surrounding the Visions Electronics parking lot.

A key turned in the door.

Michael entered in his red Visions Electronics shirt. The red was deeper now. Saturated. The fabric was torn. Michael stumbled out of his shoes, leaving a bloody handprint on a door frame, a bloody handprint on the wall. Blood stained his face, his hands, his chest.

Kate swallowed, watching as he approached her. He fell to his knees in the moonlight.

He buried his face over her lap and sobbed over her thighs. "I'm sorry," he said. "I did something bad, babe."

Kate shook her head, reaching beneath the cushions. "I'm sorry, too."

He gathered a shaking breath. "What are you sorry for?"

She swallowed.

Michael raised his head, hurt in his expression. "Babe?"

"I don't want to have a baby with you," she said, raising the knife.

Boy-Beautiful, the Golden Apples, and the Were-Wolf

Romanian Fairy Tale

ONCE UPON A TIME, a long while ago, when the very flies wrote upon the walls more beautifully than the mind can picture, there lived an Emperor and an Empress who had three sons, and a very beautiful garden alongside their palace. At the bottom of this garden there grew an apple-tree, entirely of gold from the top to the bottom. The Emperor was wild with joy at the thought that he had in his garden an apple-tree, the like of which was not to be found in the wide world. He used to stand in front of it, and poke his nose into every part of it, and look at it again and again, till his eyes nearly started out of his head. One day he saw this tree bud, blossom, and form its fruit, which began to ripen before him. The Emperor twisted his moustache, and his mouth watered at the thought that the next day he would have a golden apple or two on his table, an unheard-of thing up to that moment since the world began.

Day had scarcely begun to dawn next morning, when the Emperor was already in the garden to feast his eyes to the full on the golden apples; but he almost went out of his mind when, instead of the ripened golden apples, he saw that the tree was budding anew, but of apples there was no sign. While he stood there he saw the tree blossom, the blossoms fall off, and the young fruit again appear.

At this sight his heart came back to him again, and he joyfully awaited the morrow, but on the morrow also the apples had gone – goodness knows where! The Emperor was very wroth. He commanded that the tree should be strictly guarded, and the thief seized; but, alas! where were they to find him?

The tree blossomed every day, put forth flowers, formed its fruit, and towards evening the fruit began to ripen. But in the middle of the night somebody always came and took away the fruit, without the Emperor's watchers being aware of it. It was just as if it were done on purpose. Every night, sure enough, somebody came and took the apples, as if to mock at the Emperor and all his guards! So though this Emperor had the golden apple-tree in his garden, he not only never could have a golden apple on his table, but never even saw it ripen. At last the poor Emperor took it so to heart that he said he would give up his throne to whosoever would catch and bind the thief.

Then the sons of the Emperor came to him, and asked him to let them watch also. Great was the joy of the Emperor when he heard from the mouth of his eldest son the vow he made to lay hands upon the thief. So the Emperor gave him leave, and he set to work. The eldest son watched the first night, but he suffered the same disgrace that the other watchers had suffered before him.

On the second night the second son watched, but he was no cleverer than his brother, and returned to his father with his nose to the earth.

Both the brothers said that up to midnight they had watched well enough, but after that they could not keep their feet for weariness, but fell down in a deep sleep, and recollected nothing else.

The youngest son listened to all this in silence, but when his big brothers had told their story, he begged his father to let *him* watch too. Now, sad as his father was at being unable to find a valiant warrior to catch the thief, yet he burst out laughing when he heard the request of his youngest son.

Nevertheless, he yielded at last, though only after much pressing, and now the youngest son set about guarding the tree.

When the evening had come, he took his bow, and his quiver full of arrows, and his sword, and went down into the garden. Here he chose out a lonely place, quite away from wall and tree, or any other place that he might have been able to lean against, and stood on the trunk of a felled tree, so that if he chanced to doze off, it might slip from under him and awake him. This he did, and when he had fallen two or three times, sleep forsook him, and weariness ceased to torment him.

Just as it was drawing nigh to dawn, at the hour when sleep is sweetest, he heard a fluttering in the air, as if a swarm of birds was approaching. He pricked up his ears, and heard something or other pecking away at the golden apples. He pulled an arrow from his quiver, placed it on his bow, and drew it with all his might – but nothing stirred. He drew his bow again – still there was nothing. When he had drawn it once more, he heard again the fluttering of wings, and was conscious that a flock of birds was flying away. He drew near to the golden apples, and perceived that the thief had not had time to take all of them. He had taken one here, and one there, but most of them still remained. As now he stood there he fancied he saw something shining on the ground. He stooped down and picked up the shining thing, and, lo and behold! It was two feathers entirely of gold.

When it was day he plucked the apples, placed them on a golden salver, and with the golden feathers in his hat, went to find his father. The Emperor, when he saw the apples, very nearly went out of his mind for joy; but he controlled himself, and proclaimed throughout the city that his youngest son had succeeded in saving the apples, and that the thief was discovered to be a flock of birds.

Boy-Beautiful now asked his father to let him go and search out the thief; but his father would hear of nothing but the long-desired apples, which he was never tired of feasting his eyes upon.

But the youngest son of the Emperor was not to be put off, and importuned his father till at last the Emperor, in order to get rid of him, gave him leave to go and seek the thief. So he got ready, and when he was about to depart, he took the golden feathers out of his cap, and gave them to his mother, the Empress, to keep for him till he returned. He took raiment and money for his journey, fastened his quiverful of arrows to his back, and his sword on his right hip, and with his bow in one hand and the reins in the other, and accompanied by a faithful servant, set off on his way. He went on and on, along roads more and more remote, till at last he came to a desert. Here he dismounted, and taking counsel with his faithful servant, hit upon a road that led to the east. They went on a good bit further, till they came to a vast and dense wood. Through this tangle of a wood they had to grope their way (and it was as much as they could do to do that), and presently they saw, a long way off, a great and terrible wolf, with a head of steel. They immediately prepared to defend themselves, and when they were within bow-shot of the wolf, Boy-Beautiful put his bow to his eye.

The wolf seeing this, cried: "Stay thy hand, Boy-Beautiful, and slay me not, and it will be well for thee one day!" Boy-Beautiful listened to him, and let his bow fall, and the wolf drawing nigh, asked them where they were going, and what they were doing in that wood, untrodden by the foot of man. Then Boy-Beautiful told him the whole story of the golden apples in his father's garden, and said they were seeking after the thief.

The wolf told him that the thief was the Emperor of the Birds, who, whenever he set out to steal apples, took with him in his train all the birds of swiftest flight, that so they might strip the orchards more rapidly, and that these birds were to be found in the city on the confines of this wood. He also told them that the whole household of the Emperor of the Birds lived by the robbing of gardens and orchards; and he showed them the nearest and easiest way to the city.

Then giving them a little apple most lovely to look upon, he said to them: "Accept this apple, Boy-Beautiful! Whenever thou shouldst have need of me, look at it and think of me, and immediately I'll be with thee!"

Boy-Beautiful took the apple, and concealed it in his bosom, and bidding the wolf good-day, struggled onwards with his faithful servant through the thickets of the forest, till he came to the city where the robber-bird dwelt. All through the city he went, asking where it was, and they told him that the Emperor of that realm had it in a gold cage in his garden.

That was all he wanted to know. He took a turn round the court of the Emperor, and noted in his mind all the ramparts which surrounded the court. When it was evening, he came thither with his faithful servant, and hid himself in a corner, waiting till all the dwellers in the palace had gone to rest. Then the faithful servant gave him a leg-up, and Boy-Beautiful, mounting on his back, scaled the wall, and leaped down into the garden. But the moment he put his hand on the cage, the Emperor of the Birds chirped, and before you could say boo! he was surrounded by a flock of birds, from the smallest to the greatest, all chirping in their own tongues. They made such a noise that they awoke all the servants of the Emperor. They rushed into the garden, and there they found Boy-Beautiful, with the cage in his hand, and all the birds darting at him, and he defending himself as best he could. The servants laid their hands upon him, and led him to the Emperor, who had also got up to see what was the matter.

"I am sorry to see thee thus, Boy-Beautiful," cried the Emperor, for he knew him. "If thou hadst come to me with good words, or with entreaties, and asked me for the bird, I might, perhaps, have been persuaded to give it to thee of my own good-will and pleasure; but as thou hast been taken hand-in-sack, as they say, the reward of thy deed according to our laws is death, and thy name will be covered with dishonour."

"Illustrious Emperor," replied Boy-Beautiful, "these same birds have stolen the golden apples from the apple-tree of my father's garden, and therefore have I come all this way to lay hands on the thief."

"What thou dost say may be true, Boy-Beautiful, but I have no power to alter the laws of this land. Only a signal service rendered to our empire can save thee from a shameful death."

"Say what that service is, and I will venture it."

"Listen then! If thou dost succeed in bringing me the saddle-horse in the court of the Emperor my neighbour, thou wilt depart with thy face unblackened, and thou shalt take the bird in its cage along with thee."

Boy-Beautiful agreed to these conditions, and that same day he departed with his faithful servant.

On reaching the court of the neighbouring Emperor he took note of the horse and of all the environs of the court. Then as evening drew near, he hid with his faithful servant in a corner of the court which seemed to him to be a safe ambuscade. He saw the horse walked out between two servants, and he marvelled at its beauty. It was white, its bridle was of gold set with gems inestimable, and it shone like the sun.

In the middle of the night, when sleep is most sweet, Boy-Beautiful bade his faithful servant stoop down, leaped on to his back, and from thence on to the wall, and leaped down into the Emperor's courtyard. He groped his way along on the tips of his toes till he came to the stable, and opening the door, put his hand on the bridle and drew the horse after him. When the horse got to the door of the stable and sniffed the keen air, it sneezed once with a mighty sneeze that awoke the whole court. In an instant they all rushed out, laid hands on Boy-Beautiful, and led him before the Emperor, who had also been aroused, and who when he saw Boy-Beautiful knew him at once. He reproached him for the cowardly deed he had nearly accomplished, and told him that the laws of the land decreed death to all thieves, and that he had no power against those laws. Then Boy-Beautiful told him of the theft of the golden apples by the birds, and of what the neighbouring Emperor had told him to do. Then said the Emperor: "If, Boy-Beautiful, thou canst bring me the divine Craiessa, thou mayest perhaps escape death, and thy name shall remain untarnished." Boy-Beautiful risked the adventure, and accompanied by his faithful servant set off on his quest. While he was on the road, the thought of the little apple occurred to him. He took it from his bosom, looked at it, and thought of the wolf, and before he could wipe his eyes the wolf was there.

"What dost thou desire, Boy-Beautiful?" said he.

"What do I desire, indeed! – Look here, look here, look here, what has happened to me! Whatever am I to do to get out of this mess with a good conscience?"

"Rely upon me, for I see I must finish this business for thee." So they all three went on together to seek the divine Craiessa.

When they drew nigh to the land of the divine Craiessa they halted in the midst of a vast forest, where they could see the Craiessa's dazzling palace, and it was agreed that Boy-Beautiful and his servant should await the return of the wolf by the trunk of a large tree. The proud palace of the divine Craiessa was so grand and beautiful, and the style and arrangement thereof so goodly, that the wolf could scarce take his eyes therefrom. But when he came up to the palace he did what he could, and crept furtively into the garden.

And what do you think he saw there? Not a single fruit-tree was any longer green. The stems, branches, and twigs stood there as if someone had stripped them naked. The fallen leaves had turned the ground into a crackling carpet. Only a single rose-bush was still covered with leaves and full of buds, some wide open and some half closed. To reach this rose-bush the wolf had to tread very gingerly on the tips of his toes, so as not to make the carpet of dry leaves crackle beneath him; and so he hid himself behind this leafy bush. As now he stood there on the watch, the door of the dazzling palace was opened, and forth came the divine Craiessa, attended by four-and-twenty of her slaves, to take a walk in the garden.

When the wolf beheld her he was very near forgetting what he came for and coming out of his lair, though he restrained himself; for she was so lovely that the like of her never had been and never will be seen on the face of the whole earth. Her hair was of nothing less than pure gold, and reached from top to toe. Her long and silken eyelashes seemed almost to put out her eyes. When she looked at you with those large sloe-black eyes of hers, you felt sick with love. She had those beautifully-arched eyebrows which look as if they had been traced with compasses, and her skin was whiter than the froth of milk fresh from the udder.

After taking two or three turns round the garden with her slaves behind her, she came to the rose-bush and plucked one or two flowers, whereupon the wolf who was concealed in the bush darted out, took her in his front paws, and sped down the road. Her servants scattered like a bevy of young partridges, and in an instant the wolf was there, and put her, all senseless as she was, in the arms of Boy-Beautiful. When he saw her he changed colour, but the wolf reminded him that he was a warrior and he came to himself again. Many Emperors had tried to steal her, but they had all been repulsed.

Boy-Beautiful had compassion upon her, and he now made up his mind that nobody else should have her.

When the divine Craiessa awoke from her swoon and found herself in the arms of Boy-Beautiful, she said: "If thou art the wolf that hath stolen me away, I'll be thine." Boy-Beautiful replied: "Mine thou shalt be till death do us part."

So they made a compact of it, and they told each other their stories.

When the wolf saw the tenderness that had grown up between them he said: "Leave everything to me, and your desires shall be fulfilled!" Then they set out to return from whence they had just come, and, while they were on the road, the wolf turned three somersaults and made himself exactly like the divine Craiessa, for you must know that this wolf was a magician.

Then they arranged among themselves that the faithful servant of Boy-Beautiful should stand by the trunk of a great tree in the forest till Boy-Beautiful returned with the steed. So on reaching the court of the Emperor who had the steed, Boy-Beautiful gave him the made-up divine Craiessa, and when the Emperor saw her his heart died away within him, and he felt a love for her which told in words would be foolishness.

"Thy merits, Boy-Beautiful," said the Emperor, "have saved thee this time also from a shameful death, and now I'll pay thee for this by giving thee the steed." Then Boy-Beautiful put his hand on the steed and leaped into the jewelled saddle, and, reaching the tree, placed the divine Craiessa in front of him and galloped across the boundaries of that empire.

And now the Emperor called together all his counsellors and went to the cathedral to be married to the divine Craiessa. When they got to the door of the cathedral, the pretended Craiessa turned a somersault three times and became a wolf again, which, gnashing its teeth, rushed straight at the Emperor's retinue, who were stupefied with terror when they saw it. On coming to themselves a little, they gave chase with hue-and-cry: but the wolf, take my word for it! took such long strides that not one of them could come near him, and joining Boy-Beautiful and his friends went along with them. When they drew nigh to the court of the Emperor with the bird, they played him the same trick they had played on the Emperor with the horse. The wolf changed himself into the horse, and was given to the Emperor, who could not contain himself for joy at the sight of it.

After entertaining Boy-Beautiful with great honour, the Emperor said to him: "Boy-Beautiful, thou hast escaped a shameful death. I will keep my imperial word and my blessing shall always follow thee." Then he commanded them to give him the bird in the golden cage, and Boy-Beautiful took it, wished him good-day, and departed. Arriving in the wood where he had left the divine Craiessa, his horse, and his faithful servant, he set off with them for the court of his father.

But the Emperor who had received the horse commanded that his whole host and all the grandees of his empire should assemble in the plain to see him mount his richly-caparisoned goodly steed. And when the soldiers saw him they all cried: "Long live the Emperor who hath won such a goodly steed, and long live the steed that doth the Emperor so much honour!"

And, indeed, there was the Emperor mounting on the back of the horse, but no sooner did it put its foot to the ground than it flew right away. They all set off in pursuit, but there was never the slightest chance of any of them catching it, for it left them far behind from the first. When it had got a good way ahead the pretended horse threw the Emperor to the ground, turned head over heels three times and became a wolf, and set off again in full flight, and ran and ran till it overtook Boy-Beautiful. Then said the wolf to him: "I have now fulfilled all thy demands. Look to thyself better in future, and strive not after things beyond thy power, or it will not go well with thee." Then their roads parted, and each of them went his own way.

When he arrived at the empire of his father the old Emperor came out to meet his youngest son with small and great as he had agreed. Great was the public joy when they saw him with a consort the like of whom is no longer to be found on the face of the earth, and with a steed the excellence whereof lives only in the tales of the aged. When he got home Boy-Beautiful ordered a splendid stable to be made for his good steed, and put the bird-cage in the terrace of the garden. Then his father prepared for the wedding, and after not many days Boy-Beautiful and the divine Craiessa were married; the tables were spread for good and bad, and they made merry for three days and three nights. After that they lived in perfect happiness, for Boy-Beautiful had now nothing more to desire. And they are living to this day, if they have not died in the meantime.

And now I'll mount my steed again and say an "Our Father" before I go.

How William of Palermo Was Carried off by the Werwolf

Medieval Romance

MANY HUNDREDS of years ago there lived in the beautiful city of Palermo a little prince who was thought, not only by his parents but by everyone who saw him, to be the handsomest child in the whole world. When he was four years old, his mother, the queen, made up her mind that it was time to take him away from his nurses, so she chose out two ladies of the court who had been friends of her own youth, and to them she entrusted her little son. He was to be taught to read and write, and to talk Greek, the language of his mother's country, and Latin, which all princes ought to know, while the Great Chamberlain would see that he learned to ride and shoot, and, when he grew bigger, how to wield a sword.

For a while everything went on as well as the king and queen could wish. Prince William was quick, and, besides, he could not bear to be beaten in anything he tried to do, whether it was making out the sense of a roll of parchment written in strange black letters, which was his reading-book, or mastering a pony which wanted to kick him off. And the people of Palermo looked on, and whispered to each other:

"Ah! what a king he will make!"

But soon a terrible end came to all these hopes!

William's father, king Embrons, had a brother who would have been the heir to the throne but for the little prince. He was a wicked man, and hated his nephew, but when the boy was born he was away at the wars, and did not return till five years later. Then he lost no time in making friends with the two ladies who took care of William, and slowly managed to gain their confidence. By-and-by he worked upon them with his promises and gifts, till they became as wicked as he was, and even agreed to kill not only the child, but the king his father.

Now adjoining the palace at Palermo was a large park, planted with flowering trees and filled with wild beasts. The royal family loved to roam about the park, and often held jousts and sports on the green grass, while William played with his dogs or picked flowers.

One day – it was a festival – the whole court went into the park at noon, after they had finished dining, and the queen and her ladies busied themselves with embroidering a quilt for the royal bed, while the king and his courtiers shot at a mark. Suddenly there leapt from a bush a huge grey wolf with his mouth open and his tongue hanging out. Before anyone had time to recover from his surprise, the great beast had caught up the child, and was bounding with him through the park, and over the wall into the plain by the sea. When the courtiers had regained their senses, both the wolf and boy were out of sight.

Oh! What weeping and wailing burst forth from the king and queen when they understood that their little son was gone from them for ever, only, as they supposed, to die a cruel death! For of course they did not know that one far worse had awaited him at home.

After the first shock, William did not very much mind what was happening to him. The wolf jerked him on to his back, and told him to hold fast by his ears, and the boy sat comfortably among the thick hair, and did not even get his feet wet as they swam across the Straits of Messina. On the other side, not far from Rome, was a forest of tall trees, and as by this time it was getting dark, the wolf placed William on a bed of soft fern, and broke off a branch of delicious fruits, which he gave him for supper. Then he scooped out a deep pit with his paws, and lined it with moss and feathery grasses, and there they both lay down and slept till morning; in spite of missing his mother, in all his life William had never been so happy.

For eight days they stayed in the forest, and it seemed to the boy as if he had never dwelt anywhere else. There was so much to see and to do, and when he was tired of playing the wolf told him stories.

But one morning, before he was properly awake, he felt himself gently shaken by a paw, and he sat up, and looked about him. "Listen to me," said the wolf. "I have to go right over to the other side of the wood, on some business of a friend's, and I shall not be back till sunset. Be careful not to stray out of sight of this pit, for you may easily lose yourself. You will find plenty of fruit and nuts piled up under that cherry tree."

So the wolf went away, and the child curled himself up for another sleep, and when the sun was high and its beams awakened him, he got up and had his breakfast. While he was eating, birds with blue and green feathers came and hopped on his shoulder and pecked at the fruit he was putting into his mouth, and William made friends with them all, and they suffered him to stroke their heads.

* * *

Now there dwelt in the forest an old cowherd, who happened that morning to have work to do not far from the pit where William lived with the wolf. He took with him a big dog, which helped him to collect the cows when they wandered, and to keep off any strange beasts that threatened to attack them. On this particular morning there were no cows, so the dog ran hither and thither as he would, enjoying himself mightily, when suddenly he set up a loud barking, as if he had found a prey, and the noise caused the old man to hasten his steps.

When he reached the spot from which the noise came, the dog was standing at the edge of a pit, out of which came a frightened cry. The old man looked in, and there he saw a child clad in garments that shone like gold, shrinking timidly into the farthest corner.

"Fear nothing, my boy," said the cowherd; "he will never hurt you, and even if he wished I would not let him;" and as he spoke he held out his hand. At this William took courage. He was not really a coward, but he felt lonely and it seemed a long time since the wolf had gone away. Would he really ever come back? This old man looked kind, and there could be no harm in speaking to him. So he took the outstretched hand and scrambled out of the pit, and the cowherd gathered apples for him, and other fruits that grew on the tops of trees too high for the wolf to reach. And all the day they wandered on and on, till they came to the cowherd's cottage, before which an old woman was standing.

"I have brought you a little boy," he said, "whom I found in the forest."

"Ah, a lucky star was shining when you got up today," answered she. "And what is your name, my little man? And will you stay and live with me?"

"My name is William, and you look kind like my grandmother, and I will stay with you," said the boy; and the old people were very glad, and they milked a cow, and gave him warm milk for his supper.

When the wolf returned – he was not a wolf at all, but the son of the king of Spain, who had been enchanted by his stepmother – he was very unhappy at finding the pit empty. Indeed, his first thought was that a lion must have carried off the boy and eaten him, or that an eagle must have pounced on him from the sky, and borne him away to his young ones for supper. But after he had cried till he could cry no more, it occurred to him that before he gave up the boy for dead it would be well to make a search, as perchance there might be some sign of his whereabouts. So he dried his eyes with his tail and jumped up quite cheerfully.

He began by looking to see if the bushes round about were broken and torn as if some great beast had crashed through them. But they were all just as he had left them in the morning, with the creepers still knotting tree to tree. No, it was clear that no lion had been near the spot. Then he examined the ground carefully for a bird's feather or a shred of a child's dress; he did not find these either, but the marks of a man's foot were quite plain, and these he followed.

The track turned and twisted for about two miles, and then stopped at a little cottage with roses climbing up the walls. The wolf did not want to show himself, so he crept quietly round to the back, where there was a hole in the door just big enough for the cats to come in and out of. The wolf peeped through this hole and saw William eating his supper, and chattering away to the old woman as if he had known her all his life, for he was a friendly little boy, and purred like a pussy-cat when he was pleased. And when the wolf saw that all was well with the child, he was glad and went his way.

"William will be safer with them than with me," he said to himself.

Many years went by, and William had grown a big boy, and was very useful to the cowherd and his wife. He could shoot now with his bow and arrow in a manner which would have pleased his first teacher, and he and his playfellows – the sons of charcoal-burners and woodmen – were wont to keep the pots supplied at home with the game they found in the forest. Besides this, he filled the pails full of water from the stream, and chopped wood for the fire, and, sometimes, was even trusted to cook the dinner. And when this happened William was a very proud boy indeed.

One day the emperor planned a great hunt to take place in the forest, and, while following a wild boar, he outstripped all his courtiers and lost his way. Turning first down one path and then the other, he came upon a boy gathering fruit, and so beautiful was he that the emperor thought that he must be of a fairy race.

"What is your name, my child?" asked the emperor; "and where do you live?"

The boy looked round at the sound of his voice, and, taking off his cap, bowed low.

"I am called William, noble sir," he answered, "and I live with a cowherd, my father, in a cottage near by. Other kindred have I none that ever I heard of;" for the gardens of Palermo and the life of the palace had now faded into dreams in the memory of the child.

"Bid your father come hither and speak to me," said the emperor, but William did not move.

"I fear lest harm should befall him through me," he answered, "and that shall never be." But the emperor smiled as he heard him.

"Not harm, but good," he said; and William took courage and hastened down the path to the cottage.

"I am the emperor," said the stranger, when the boy and the cowherd returned together. "Tell me truly, is this your son?"

Then the cowherd, trembling all over, told the whole story, and when he had finished the emperor said quietly:

"You have done well, but from today the boy shall be mine, and shall grow up with my daughter."

The heart of the cowherd sank as he thought how sorely he and his wife would miss William, but he kept silence. Not so William, who broke into sobs and wails.

"I should have fared ill if this good man and his wife had not taken me and nourished me. I know not whence I came or whither I shall go! None can be so kind as they have been."

"Cease weeping, fair child," said the emperor, "some day you shall be able to reward the good that they have done you," and then the cowherd spoke and gave him wise counsel how to behave himself at court.

"Be no teller of tales, and let your words be few. Be true to your lord, and fair of speech to all men; and seek to help the poor when you may."

"Set him on my horse," said the emperor, and, though William wept still as he bade farewell to the cowherd, and sent a sorrowful greeting to his wife and to his playfellows Hugonet, and Abelot, and Akarin, yet he was pleased to be riding in such royal fashion, and soon dried his tears.

They reached the palace at last, and the emperor led William into the hall, and sent a messenger for Melior, his daughter.

"I have brought home a present for you," he cried, as she entered; "and be sure to treat him as you would your brother, for he has come of goodly kindred, though now he does not know where he was born, or who was his father." And with that he told her the tale of how he had found the boy in the wood.

"I shall care for him willingly," answered Melior, and she took him away, and saw that supper was set before him, and clothes provided for him, and made him ready for his duties as page to the emperor.

So the boy and girl grew up together, and everyone loved William, who was gentle and pleasant to all, and was skilled in what a gentleman should know. Wise he was too, beyond his years, and the emperor kept him ever at his side, and took counsel with him on many subjects touching his honour and the welfare of his people.

And if the people loved him, how much more Melior, who saw him about the court all day long, and knew the store her father set on him? Yet she remembered with sadness certain whispers she had heard of a match between herself and a foreign prince, and if her father had promised her hand nought would make him break his word.

So she sighed and bewailed herself in secret, till her cousin Alexandrine marked that something was amiss.

"Tell me all your sickness," said Alexandrine one day, "and what grieves you so sorely. You know that you can trust me, for I have served you truly, and perhaps I may be able to help you in this strait!"

Then Melior told her, and Alexandrine listened in amaze. From his childhood William and the two girls had played together, and well Alexandrine knew that the emperor had cast his eyes upon another son-in-law. Still, she loved her cousin, and she loved William too, so she said.

"Mourn no longer, madam; I am skilled in magic, and can heal you. So weep no more." And Melior took heart and was comforted.

That night Alexandrine caused William to dream a dream in which the whole world vanished away, and only he and Melior were left. In a moment he felt that as long as she was there the rest might go, and that she was the princess that was waiting for every prince. But who was he that he should dare to ask for the emperor's daughter? and what chance had he amongst the noble suitors who now began to throng the palace? These thoughts made him very sad, and he went about his duties with a face as long as Melior's was now.

Alexandrine paid no heed to his gloomy looks. She was very wise, and for some days left her magic to work. At last one morning she thought the time had come to heal the wounds she had caused, and planned a meeting between them. After this they had no more need of her, neither did Melior weep any longer.

For a while they were content, and asked nothing more than to see each other every day, as they had always done. But soon a fresh source of grief came. A war broke out, in which William, now a knight, had to follow the emperor, and more than once saved the life of his master. On their return, when the enemy was put to flight, the expected ambassadors from Greece arrived at court, to seek the hand of Melior, which was readily granted by her father. This news made William sick almost unto death, and Melior, who was resolved not to marry the stranger, hastened to Alexandrine in order to implore her help.

But Alexandrine only shook her head.

"It is true," said she, "that, unless you manage to escape, you will be forced to wed the prince; but how are you to get away when there are guards before every door of the palace, except by the little gate, and to reach that you will have first to pass by the sentries, who know you?"

"O dear Alexandrine," cried Melior, clasping her hands in despair. "Do try to think of some way to save us! I am sure you can; you are always clever, and there is nobody else."

And Alexandrine did think of a way, but what it was must be told in the next chapter.

The Disenchantment of the Werwolf
(William of Palermo)

EVERYBODY WILL REMEMBER that William and Melior trusted to Alexandrine to help them to escape from the palace, before Melior was forced into marriage by her father with the prince of Greece. At first Alexandrine declared that it was quite impossible to get them away unseen, but at length she thought of something which might succeed, though, if it failed, all three would pay a heavy penalty.

And this was her plan, and a very good one too.

She would borrow some boy's clothes, and put them on, hiding her hair under one of those tight caps that kitchen varlets wore covering all their heads; she would then go down into the big kitchens underneath the palace, where the wild beasts shot by the emperor were skinned and made into coats for the winter. Here she would have a chance of slipping out unnoticed with the skins of two white bears, and in these she would sew up William and Melior, and would let them through the little back gate, from which they could easily escape into the forest.

"Oh, I knew you would find a way!" said Melior, throwing her arms joyfully round her cousin's neck. "I am quite sure it will all go right, only let us make haste, for my father may find us out, or perhaps I may lose my courage."

"I will set about it at once," said Alexandrine, "and you and William must be ready tonight."

So she got her boy's clothes, which her maid stole for her out of the room of one of the scullions, and dressed herself in them, smearing her face and hands with walnut-juice, that their whiteness might not betray her. She slipped down by some dark stairs into the kitchen, and joined a company of men who were hard at work on a pile of dead animals. The sun had set, and in the corner of the great hall where the flaying was going on, there was very little light, but Alexandrine marked that close to an open door was a heap of bearskins, and she took up her position as near them as she could. But the girl was careful not to stand too long in one place; she moved about from one group of men to another, lending a hand here and there and passing a merry jest, and as she did so she gave the topmost skins a little shove with her foot, getting them each time closer to the open door, and always watching her chance to pick them up and run off with them.

It came at last. The torch which lighted that end of the hall flared up and went out, leaving the men in darkness. One of them rose to fetch another, and, quick as thought, Alexandrine caught up the bearskins and was outside in the garden. From that it was easy to make her way upstairs unseen.

"See how I have sped!" she said, throwing the skins on the floor. "But night is coming on apace, and we have no time to lose; I must sew you up in them at once."

The skins were both so large that Melior and William wore all their own clothes beneath, and did not feel at all hot, as they expected to do.

"Am I not a bold beast?" asked Melior in glee, as she caught sight of herself in a polished shield on the wall. "Methinks no handsomer bear was ever seen!"

"Yes, verily, madam," answered her maiden, "you are indeed a grisly ghost, and no man will dare to come near you. But now stand aside, for it is William's turn."

"How do you like me, sweetheart?" asked he, when the last stitches had been put in.

"You have so fierce an air, and are so hideous a sight, that I fear to look on you!" said she. And William laughed and begged Alexandrine to guide them through the garden, as they were not yet used to going on all fours, and might stumble.

As they passed through the bushes, galloping madly – for in spite of the danger they felt as though they were children again – a Greek who was walking up to the palace saw them afar, and, seized with dread, took shelter in the nearest hut, where he told his tale. The men who heard it paid but little heed at the time, though they remembered it after; but bears were common in that country, and often came out of the forest at night.

Not knowing what a narrow escape they had had, the two runaways travelled till sunrise, when they hid themselves in a cave on the side of a hill. They had nothing to eat, but were too tired to think of that till they had had a good sleep, though when they woke up they began to wonder how they should get any food.

"Oh, it will be all right!" said Melior; "there are blackberries in plenty and acorns and hazelnuts, and there is a stream just below the cave – do you not hear it? It will all be much nicer than anything in the palace."

But William did not seem to agree with her, and wished to seek out some man who would give him something he liked better than nuts and acorns. This, however, Melior would not hear of; they would certainly be followed and betrayed, she said, and, to please her, William ate the fruit and stayed in the cave, wondering what would happen on the morrow.

Luckily for themselves, they did not have to wait so long before they got a good supper. Their friend the werwolf had spied them from afar, and was ready to come to their rescue. During that day he had hidden himself under a clump of bushes close to the highway, and by-and-by he saw a man approaching, carrying a very fat wallet over his shoulder. The wolf bounded out of his cover, growling fiercely, which so frightened the man that he dropped the wallet and ran into the wood. Then the wolf picked up the wallet, which contained a loaf of bread and some meat ready cooked, and galloped away with it to William.

They felt quite strong and hearty again when they had finished their supper, and quite ready to continue their journey. As it was night, and the country was very lonely, they walked on two feet, but when morning came, or they saw signs that men were about, they speedily dropped on all fours. And all the way the werwolf followed them, and saw that they never lacked for food.

Meanwhile the preparations for Melior's marriage to the prince of Greece were going on blithely in the palace, and none thought of asking for the bride. At last, when everything was finished, the emperor bade the high chamberlain fetch the princess.

"She is not in her room, your Majesty," said the chamberlain, when he re-entered the hall; but the emperor only thought that his daughter was timid, and answered that he would go and bring her himself.

Like the chamberlain, he found the outer room empty and passed on to the door of the inner one, which was locked. He shook and thumped and yelled with anger, till Alexandrine heard him from her distant turret, and, terrified though she was, hastened to find out what was the matter.

"My daughter! Where is my daughter?" he cried, stammering with rage.

"Asleep, sire," answered Alexandrine.

"Asleep still!" said the emperor; "then wake her instantly, for the bridegroom is ready and I am waiting to lead her to him."

"Alas! sire, Melior has heard that in Greece royal brides pass their lives shut in a tower, and she has sworn that she will never wed one of that race. But, indeed, for my part, I think that is not her true reason, and that she has pledged her faith to another, whom you also know and love."

"And who may that be?" asked the emperor.

"The man who saved your life in battle, William himself," answered Alexandrine boldly, though her limbs shook with fear.

At this news the emperor was half beside himself with grief and rage.

"Where is she?" he cried; "speak, girl, or I will shut you up in the tower."

"Where is William?" asked Alexandrine. "If Melior is not here, and William is not here, then of a surety they have gone away together."

The emperor looked at her in silence for a moment.

"The Greeks will make war on me for this insult," he said; "and, as for William, a body of soldiers shall go in search of him this moment, and when he is found I will have his head cut off, and stuck on my palace gate as a warning to traitors."

But the soldiers could not find him. Perhaps they did not look very carefully, for, like everyone else, they loved William. Party after party was sent out by the emperor, but they all returned without finding a trace of the runaways. Then at last the Greek who had seen the two white bears galloping through the garden came to the high chamberlain and told his tale.

"Send to the kitchen at once and ask if any bearskins are missing," ordered the chamberlain; and the page returned with the tidings that the skins of two white bears could not be found.

Now the werwolf had been lurking round the palace seeking for news, and as soon as he heard that the emperor had ordered out his dogs to hunt the white bears, he made a plan in his head to save William and Melior. He hid in some bushes that lay in the path of the hounds, and let them get quite near him. As soon as they were close, he sprang out in front of their noses and they gave chase at once. And a fine dance he led them! Over mountains and through swamps, under ferns that were thickly matted together, and past wide lakes. And every step they took brought them further away from the bears, who were lying snugly in their den.

* * *

At last even the patience of the emperor was exhausted. He gave up the hunt, and bade his men call off the dogs and go home.

"They have escaped me this time," said he, "but I will have them by-and-by. Let a reward be offered, and posted up on the gate of every city. After all, that is the surest way of capturing them."

And the emperor was right: the shepherds and goatherds were told that if they could bring the two white bears to the gates of the palace they would not need to work for the rest of their lives, and they kept a sharp look-out as they followed their flocks. Once a man actually saw them, and gave notice to one of the royal officials, who brought a company of spearmen and surrounded the cave. Another moment, and they would have been seized, had not the wolf again come to their rescue. He leapt out from behind a rock, and snatched up the officer's son, who had followed his father. The poor man shrieked in horror, and cried out to save the boy, so they all turned and went after the wolf as before.

"We are safer now in our own clothes," said William; and they hastily stripped off the bearskins, and stole away, but they would not leave the skins behind, for they had learnt to love them.

For a long while they wandered through the forest, the werwolf ever watching over them, and bringing them food. At length the news spread abroad, no one knew how, that William and Melior were running about as bears no more, but in the garments they always wore. So men began to look out for them, and once they were very nearly caught by some charcoal-burners. Then the wolf killed a hart and a hind, and sewed them in their skins and guided them across the Straits of Messina into the kingdom of Sicily.

Very dimly, and one by one, little things that had happened in his childhood began to come back to William; but he wondered greatly how he seemed to know this land, where he had never been before. The king his father had been long dead, but the queen (his mother) and his sister were besieged in the city of Palermo by the king of Spain, who was full of wrath because the princess had refused to marry his son. The queen was in great straits, when one night she dreamed that a wolf and two harts had come to help her, and one bore the face of her son, while both had crowns on their heads.

She could sleep no more that night, so she rose and looked out of the window on the park which lay below, and there, under the trees, were the hart and the hind! Panting for joy, the queen summoned a priest, and told him her dream, and, as she told it, behold the skins cracked, and shining clothes appeared beneath.

"Your dream has been fulfilled," said the priest. "The hind is the daughter of the emperor of Rome, who fled away with yonder knight dressed in a hart skin!"

Joyfully the queen made herself ready, and she soon joined the animals, who had wandered off to a part of the park that was full of rocks and caves. She greeted them with fair words, and begged William to take service under her, which he did gladly.

"Sweet sir, what token will you wear on your shield?" asked she; and William answered, "Good madam, I will have a werwolf on a shield of gold, and let him be made hideous and huge."

"That shall be done," said she.

When the shield was painted, William prayed her to give him a horse, and she led him into the stable, and bade him choose one for himself. And he chose one that had been ridden by the late king his father. And the horse knew him, though his mother did not, and it neighed from pure delight. After that William called to the soldiers to rally round him, and there was fought a great battle, and the Spaniards were put to flight, and throughout Palermo the people rejoiced mightily.

When the enemy had retreated far away, and William returned to the palace, where the queen and Melior were awaiting him; suddenly, from the window, they beheld the werwolf go by, and as he passed he held up his foot as if he craved mercy.

"What does he mean by that?" asked the queen.

"It betokens great good to us," answered William.

"That is well," said the queen; "but the sight of that beast causes me much sorrow. For my fair son was stolen away from me by such a one, when he was four years old, and never more have I heard of him." But in her heart she felt, though she said nothing, that she had found him again.

By-and-by the king of Spain came back with another army, and there was more fighting. In the end the Spanish king was forced to yield up his sword to William, who carried him captor to his mother Felice. The queen received him with great courtesy, and placed him next her at dinner, and the peers who had likewise been taken prisoners sat down to feast.

The next day a council was held in the hall of the palace to consider the terms of peace. The king of Spain and his son were present also, and everyone said in turn what penalty the enemy should pay for having besieged their city and laid waste their cornfields. In the midst of this grave discussion a werwolf entered through the open door, and, trotting up to the Spanish king, he kissed his feet. Then he bowed to the queen and to William, and went away as he came.

The sight of his tail disappearing through the door restored to the guards their courage, which had vanished in the presence of anything so unexpected. They sprang up to pursue him, but like a flash of lightning William flung himself in their path, crying, "If any man dare to hurt that beast, I will do him to death with my own hands;" and, as they all knew that William meant what he said, they slunk back to their places.

"Tell me, gracious king," asked William when they were all seated afresh round the council table, "why did the wolf bow to you more than to other men?"

Then the king made answer that long ago his first wife had died, leaving him with a son, and that in a little while he had married again, and that his second wife had had a son also. One day when he came back from the wars she told him that his eldest son had been drowned, but he found out afterwards that she had changed him into a werwolf, so that her own child might succeed to the crown.

"And I think," he added, "that this werwolf may be indeed the son I lost."

"It may right well be thus," cried William, "for he has the mind of a man, and of a wise man too. Often has he succoured me in my great need, and if your wife had skill to turn him into a werwolf her charms can make him a man again. Therefore, sire, neither you nor your people shall go hence out of prison till he has left his beast's shape behind him. So bid your queen come hither, and if she says you nay I will fetch her myself!"

Then the king called one of his great lords, and he bade him haste to Spain and tell the queen what had befallen him, and to bring her with all speed to Palermo. Little as she liked the summons, the Spanish queen dared not refuse, and on her arrival she was led at once into the great hall, which was filled with a vast company, both of Spaniards and Sicilians. When all were assembled William fetched the werwolf from his chamber, where he had lain for nights and days, waiting till his stepmother should come.

Together they entered the hall, but at the sight of the wicked woman who had done him such ill the wolf's bristles stood up on his back, and with a snarl that chilled the blood of all that heard it he sprang towards the dais. But, luckily, William was on the watch, and, flinging his arms round the wolf's neck, he held him back, saying in a whisper:

"My dear, sweet beast, trust to me as truly as to your own brother. I sent for her for your sake, and if she does not undo her evil spells I will have her body burned to coals, and her ashes scattered to the winds."

The wicked queen knew well what doom awaited her, and that she could resist no longer. Sinking on her knees before the wolf, she confessed the ill she had wrought, and added:

"Sweet Alfonso, soon shall the people see your seemly face, and your body as it would have been but for me!" At that she led the wolf into a private chamber, and, drawing from her wallet a thread of red silk, she bound it round a ring she wore, which no witchcraft could prevail against. This ring she hung round the wolf's neck, and afterwards read him some rhymes out of a book. Then the werwolf looked at his body, and, behold, he was a man again!

There were great rejoicings at the court of Palermo when prince Alfonso came among them once more. He forgave the queen for her wickedness, and rebuked his father for having stirred up such a wanton and bloody war.

"Plague and famine would have preyed upon this land," he said, "had not this knight, whose real name is unknown to you, come to your aid. He is the rightful lord of this country, for he is the son of king Embrons and queen Felice, and I am the werwolf who carried him away, to save him from a cruel death that was planned for him by his own uncle!"

So the tale ends and everyone was made happy. The werwolf, now prince Alfonso, married William's sister, and in due time ruled the kingdom of Spain, and William and Melior lived at Palermo till the emperor her father died, when the Romans offered him the crown in his stead.

And if you want to know any more about them, you must read the story for yourselves.

The White Wolf

Andrew Lang

ONCE UPON A TIME there was a king who had three daughters; they were all beautiful, but the youngest was the fairest of the three. Now it happened that one day their father had to set out for a tour in a distant part of his kingdom. Before he left, his youngest daughter made him promise to bring her back a wreath of wild flowers. When the king was ready to return to his palace, he bethought himself that he would like to take home presents to each of his three daughters; so he went into a jeweller's shop and bought a beautiful necklace for the eldest princess; then he went to a rich merchant's and bought a dress embroidered in gold and silver thread for the second princess, but in none of the flower shops nor in the market could he find the wreath of wild flowers that his youngest daughter had set her heart on. So he had to set out on his homeward way without it. Now his journey led him through a thick forest. While he was still about four miles distant from his palace, he noticed a white wolf squatting on the roadside, and, behold! on the head of the wolf, there was a wreath of wild flowers.

Then the king called to the coachman, and ordered him to get down from his seat and fetch him the wreath from the wolf's head. But the wolf heard the order and said: "My lord and king, I will let you have the wreath, but I must have something in return."

"What do you want?" answered the king. "I will gladly give you rich treasure in exchange for it."

"I do not want rich treasure," replied the wolf. "Only promise to give me the first thing that meets you on your way to your castle. In three days I shall come and fetch it."

And the king thought to himself: *I am still a good long way from home, I am sure to meet a wild animal or a bird on the road, it will be quite safe to promise.* So he consented, and carried the wreath away with him. But all along the road he met no living creature till he turned into the palace gates, where his youngest daughter was waiting to welcome him home.

That evening the king was very sad, remembering his promise; and when he told the queen what had happened, she too shed bitter tears. And the youngest princess asked them why they both looked so sad, and why they wept. Then her father told her what a price he would have to pay for the wreath of wild flowers he had brought home to her, for in three days a white wolf would come and claim her and carry her away, and they would never see her again. But the queen thought and thought, and at last she hit upon a plan.

There was in the palace a servant maid the same age and the same height as the princess, and the queen dressed her up in a beautiful dress belonging to her daughter, and determined to give her to the white wolf, who would never know the difference.

On the third day the wolf strode into the palace yard and up the great stairs, to the room where the king and queen were seated.

"I have come to claim your promise," he said. "Give me your youngest daughter."

Then they led the servant maid up to him, and he said to her: "You must mount on my back, and I will take you to my castle." And with these words he swung her on to his back and left the palace.

When they reached the place where he had met the king and given him the wreath of wild flowers, he stopped, and told her to dismount that they might rest a little.

So they sat down by the roadside.

"I wonder," said the wolf, "what your father would do if this forest belonged to him?"

And the girl answered: "My father is a poor man, so he would cut down the trees, and saw them into planks, and he would sell the planks, and we should never be poor again; but would always have enough to eat."

Then the wolf knew that he had not got the real princess, and he swung the servant-maid on to his back and carried her to the castle. And he strode angrily into the king's chamber, and spoke.

"Give me the real princess at once. If you deceive me again I will cause such a storm to burst over your palace that the walls will fall in, and you will all be buried in the ruins."

Then the king and the queen wept, but they saw there was no escape. So they sent for their youngest daughter, and the king said to her: "Dearest child, you must go with the white wolf, for I promised you to him, and I must keep my word."

So the princess got ready to leave her home; but first she went to her room to fetch her wreath of wild flowers, which she took with her. Then the white wolf swung her on his back and bore her away. But when they came to the place where he had rested with the servant-maid, he told her to dismount that they might rest for a little at the roadside. Then he turned to her and said: "I wonder what your father would do if this forest belonged to him?"

And the princess answered: "My father would cut down the trees and turn it into a beautiful park and gardens, and he and his courtiers would come and wander among the glades in the summer time."

This is the real princess, said the wolf to himself. But aloud he said: "Mount once more on my back, and I will bear you to my castle."

And when she was seated on his back he set out through the woods, and he ran, and ran, and ran, till at last he stopped in front of a stately courtyard, with massive gates.

"This is a beautiful castle," said the princess, as the gates swung back and she stepped inside. "If only I were not so far away from my father and my mother!"

But the wolf answered: "At the end of a year we will pay a visit to your father and mother."

And at these words the white furry skin slipped from his back, and the princess saw that he was not a wolf at all, but a beautiful youth, tall and stately; and he gave her his hand, and led her up the castle stairs.

One day, at the end of half a year, he came into her room and said: "My dear one, you must get ready for a wedding. Your eldest sister is going to be married, and I will take you to your father's palace. When the wedding is over, I shall come and fetch you home. I will whistle outside the gate, and when you hear me, pay no heed to what your father or mother say, leave your dancing and feasting, and come to me at once; for if I have to leave without you, you will never find your way back alone through the forests."

When the princess was ready to start, she found that he had put on his white fur skin, and was changed back into the wolf; and he swung her on to his back, and set out with her to her father's palace, where he left her, while he himself returned home alone. But, in the evening, he went back to fetch her, and, standing outside the palace gate, he gave a long, loud whistle. In the midst of her dancing the princess heard the sound, and at once she went to him, and he swung her on his back and bore her away to his castle.

Again, at the end of half a year, the prince came into her room, as the white wolf, and said: "Dear heart, you must prepare for the wedding of your second sister. I will take you to your father's palace today, and we will remain there together till tomorrow morning."

So they went together to the wedding. In the evening, when the two were alone together, he dropped his fur skin, and, ceasing to be a wolf, became a prince again. Now they did not know that the princess's mother was hidden in the room. When she saw the white skin lying on the floor, she crept out of the room, and sent a servant to fetch the skin and to burn it in the kitchen fire. The moment the flames touched the skin there was a fearful clap of thunder heard, and the prince disappeared out of the palace gate in a whirlwind, and returned to his palace alone.

But the princess was heart-broken, and spent the night weeping bitterly. Next morning she set out to find her way back to the castle, but she wandered through the woods and forests, and she could find no path or track to guide her. For fourteen days she roamed in the forest, sleeping under the trees, and living upon wild berries and roots, and at last she reached a little house. She opened the door and went in, and found the wind seated in the room all by himself, and she spoke to the wind and said: "Wind, have you seen the white wolf?"

And the wind answered: "All day and all night I have been blowing round the world, and I have only just come home; but I have not seen him."

But he gave her a pair of shoes, in which, he told her, she would be able to walk a hundred miles with every step. Then she walked through the air till she reached a star, and she said: "Tell me, star, have you seen the white wolf?"

And the star answered: "I have been shining all night, and I have not seen him."

But the star gave her a pair of shoes, and told her that if she put them on she would be able to walk two hundred miles at a stride. So she drew them on, and she walked to the moon, and she said: "Dear moon, have you not seen the white wolf?"

But the moon answered, "All night long I have been sailing through the heavens, and I have only just come home; but I did not see him."

But he gave her a pair of shoes, in which she would be able to cover four hundred miles with every stride. So she went to the sun, and said: "Dear sun, have you seen the white wolf?"

And the sun answered, "Yes, I have seen him, and he has chosen another bride, for he thought you had left him, and would never return, and he is preparing for the wedding. But I will help you. Here are a pair of shoes. If you put these on you will be able to walk on glass or ice, and to climb the steepest places. And here is a spinning-wheel, with which you will be able to spin moss into silk. When you leave me you will reach a glass mountain. Put on the shoes that I have given you and with them you will be able to climb it quite easily. At the summit you will find the palace of the white wolf."

Then the princess set out, and before long she reached the glass mountain, and at the summit she found the white wolf's palace, as the sun had said.

But no one recognised her, as she had disguised herself as an old woman, and had wound a shawl round her head. Great preparations were going on in the palace for the wedding, which was to take place next day. Then the princess, still disguised as an old woman, took out her spinning-wheel, and began to spin moss into silk. And as she spun the new bride passed by, and seeing the moss turn into silk, she said to the old woman: "Little mother, I wish you would give me that spinning-wheel."

And the princess answered, "I will give it to you if you will allow me to sleep tonight on the mat outside the prince's door."

And the bride replied, "Yes, you may sleep on the mat outside the door."

So the princess gave her the spinning-wheel. And that night, winding the shawl all round her, so that no one could recognise her, she lay down on the mat outside the white wolf's door. And when everyone in the palace was asleep she began to tell the whole of her story. She told how she had been one of three sisters, and that she had been the youngest and the fairest of the three, and that her father had betrothed her to a white wolf. And she told how she had gone first to the wedding of one sister, and then with her husband to the wedding of the other sister, and how her mother had ordered the servant to throw the white fur skin into the kitchen fire. And then she told of her wanderings through the forest; and of how she had sought the white wolf weeping; and how the wind and star and moon and sun had befriended her, and had helped her to reach his palace. And when the white wolf heard all the story, he knew that it was his first wife, who had sought him, and had found him, after such great dangers and difficulties.

But he said nothing, for he waited till the next day, when many guests – kings and princes from far countries – were coming to his wedding. Then, when all the guests were assembled in the banqueting hall, he spoke to them and said: "Hearken to me, ye kings and princes, for I have something to tell you. I had lost the key of my treasure casket, so I ordered a new one to be made; but I have since found the old one. Now, which of these keys is the better?"

Then all the kings and royal guests answered: "Certainly the old key is better than the new one."

"Then," said the wolf, "if that is so, my former bride is better than my new one."

And he sent for the new bride, and he gave her in marriage to one of the princes who was present, and then he turned to his guests, and said: "And here is my former bride" – and the beautiful princess was led into the room and seated beside him on his throne. "I thought she had forgotten me, and that she would never return. But she has sought me everywhere, and now we are together once more we shall never part again."

The Son of the Wolf Chief

From Tlingit Mythology

ONCE UPON A TIME a town near the North Pacific Ocean suffered greatly from famine and many of the Indians who lived there died of hunger. It was terrible to see them sitting before their doors, too weak and listless to move, and waiting silently and hopelessly for death to come. But there was one boy who behaved quite differently from the rest of the tribe. For some reason or other he seemed quite strong on his legs, and all day long he would go into the fields or the woods, with his bow and arrows slung to his back, hoping to bring back a supper for himself and his mother.

One morning when he was out as usual, he found a little animal that looked like a dog. It was such a round, funny little thing that he could not bear to kill it, so he put it under his warm blanket, and carried it home, and as it was very dirty from rolling about in the mud and snow, his mother washed it for him. When it was quite clean, the boy fetched some red paint which his uncle who had died of famine had used for smearing over their faces, and put it on the dog's head and legs so that he might always be able to trace it when they were hunting together.

The boy got up early next morning and took his dog into the woods and the hills. The little beast was very quick and sharp, and it was not long before the two got quite a number of grouse and birds of all sorts; and as soon as they had enough for that day and the next, they returned to the wigwam and invited their neighbours to supper with them.

A short time after, the boy was out on the hills wondering where the dog had gone, for, in spite of the red paint, he was to be seen nowhere. At length he stood still and put his ear to the ground and listened with all his might, and that means a great deal, for Indian ears are much cleverer at hearing than European ones. Then he heard a whine which sounded as if it came from a long way off, so he jumped up at once and walked and walked till he reached a small hollow, where he found that the dog had killed one of the mountain sheep.

"Can it really *be* a dog?" said the boy to himself. "I don't know; I wish I did. But at any rate, it deserves to be treated like one," and when the sheep was cooked, the dog – if it was a dog – was given all the fat part.

After this, never a day passed without the boy and the dog bringing home meat, and thanks to them the people began to grow fat again. But if the dog killed many sheep at once, the boy was always careful to give it first the best for itself.

* * *

Some weeks later the husband of the boy's sister came to him and said:

"Lend me your dog, it will help me greatly." So the boy went and brought the dog from the little house he had made for it, and painted its head and its feet, and carried it to his brother-in-law.

"Give it the first thing that is killed as I always do," observed the boy, but the man answered nothing, only put the dog in his blanket.

Now the brother-in-law was greedy and selfish and wanted to keep everything for himself; so after the dog had killed a whole flock of sheep in the fields, the man threw it a bit of the inside which nobody else would touch, exclaiming rudely:

"Here, take that! It is quite good enough for you."

But the dog would not touch it either, and ran away to the mountains, yelping loudly.

The man had to bring back all the sheep himself, and it was evening before he reached the village. The first person he saw was the boy who was waiting about for him.

"Where is the dog?" asked he, and the man answered:

"It ran away from me."

On hearing this the boy put no more questions, but he called his sister and said to her:

"Tell me the truth. What did your husband do to the dog? I did not want to let it go, because I guessed what would happen."

And the wife answered:

"He threw the inside of a sheep to it, and that is why it ran off."

When the boy heard this, he felt very sad, and turned to go into the mountains in search of the dog. After walking some time he found the marks of its paws, and smears of red paint on the grass. But all this time the boy never knew that the dog was really the son of the Wolf Chief and had been sent by his father to help him, and he did not guess that from the day that he painted red paint round its face and on its feet a wolf can be told far off by the red on its paws and round its mouth.

The marks led a long, long way, and at length they brought him to a lake, with a town on the opposite side of it, where people seemed to be playing some game, as the noise that they made reached all the way across.

"I must try if I can get over there," he said, and as he spoke, he noticed a column of smoke coming right up from the ground under his feet, and a door flew open.

"Enter!" cried a voice, so he entered, and discovered that the voice belonged to an old woman, who was called 'Woman-always-wondering'.

"Grandchild, why are you here?" she asked, and he answered:

"I found a young dog who helped me to get food for the people, but it is lost and I am seeking it."

"Its people live right across there," replied the woman. "It is the Wolf Chief's son, and that is his father's town where the noise comes from."

'How can I get over the lake?' he said to himself, but the old woman guessed what he was thinking and replied:

"My little canoe is just below here."

'It might turn over with me,' he thought, and again she answered him:

"Take it down to the shore and shake it before you get in, and it will soon become large. Then stretch yourself in the bottom, and, instead of paddling, wish with all your might to reach the town."

The boy did as he was told, and by and by he arrived on the other side of the lake. He shook the canoe a second time, and it shrunk into a mere toy-boat which he put in his pocket, and after that he went and watched some boys who were playing with a thing that was like a rainbow.

"Where is the chief's house?" he asked when he was tired of looking at their game.

"At the other end of the village," they said, and he walked on till he reached a place where a large fire was burning, with people sitting round it. The chief was there too, and the boy saw his little wolf playing about near his father.

"There is a man here," exclaimed the Wolf Chief. "Vanish all of you!" And the wolf-people vanished instantly, all but the little wolf, who ran up to the boy and smelt him and knew him at once. As soon as the Wolf Chief beheld that, he said:

"I am your friend; fear nothing. I sent my son to help you because you were starving, and I am glad you have come in quest of him." But after a pause, he added:

"Still, I do not think I will let him go back with you; but I will aid you in some other way," and the boy did not guess that the reason the chief was so pleased to see him was because he had painted the little wolf. Yet, as he glanced at the little beast again, he observed with surprise that it did not look like a wolf any longer, but like a human being.

"Take out the fish-hawk's quill that is hanging on the wall, and if you should meet a bear point the quill straight at it, and it will fly out of your hand. I will also give you this," and he opened a box and lifted out a second quill stuck in a blanket. "If you lay this side on a sick person, it will cure him; and if you lay the other side on your enemy, it will kill him. Thus you can grow rich by healing sick people."

So the boy and the Wolf Chief made friends, and they talked together a long time, and the boy put many questions about things he had seen in the town, which puzzled him.

"What was the toy the children were playing with?" he asked at last.

"That toy belongs to me," answered the chief. "If it appears to you in the evening it means bad weather, and if it appears in the morning it means fine weather. Then we know that we can go out on the lake. It is a good toy."

"But," continued he, "you must depart now, and, before you leave eat this, for you have a long journey to make and you will need strength for it," and he dropped something into the boy's mouth.

And the boy did not guess that he had been absent for two years, and thought it was only two nights.

* * *

Then he journeyed back to his own town, not a boy any more, but a man. Near the first house he met a bear and he held the quill straight towards it. Away it flew and hit the bear right in the heart; so there was good meat for hungry people. Further on, he passed a flock of sheep, and the quill slew them all and he drew it out from the heart of the last one. He cooked part of a sheep for himself and hid the rest where he knew he could find them. After that he entered the town.

It seemed strangely quiet. What had become of all his friends and of the children whom he had left behind him when he left to seek for his dog? He opened the door of a hut and peeped in: three or four bodies were stretched on the floor, their bones showing through their skin, dead of starvation; for after the boy had gone to the mountains there was no one to bring them food. He opened another door, and another and another; everywhere it was the same story. Then he remembered the gift of the Wolf Chief, and he drew the quill out of his blanket and laid one side of it against their bodies, so that they all came to life again, and once more the town was full of noise and gaiety.

"Now come and hunt with me," he said; but he did not show them his quill lest he should lose it as he had lost the dog. And when they beheld a flock of mountain sheep grazing, he let fly the quill so quickly that nobody saw it go, neither did they see him pull out the quill and hide it in his blanket. After that they made a fire and all sat down to dine, and those who were not his friends gave him payment for the meat.

For the rest of his life the man journeyed from place to place, curing the sick and receiving payment from their kinsfolk. But those who had been dead for many years took a long while to get well, and their eyes were always set deep back in their heads, and had a look as if they had seen something.

The Feelings of Sheep

Andrew Lyall

OLENA'S ATTENDANTS helped her out of the large copper tub and led her, one at each arm, through the steam to a plush dressing room. They lowered her in front of a dressing table and gilded mirror and began towelling and combing her dark hair while she sagged and slumped in her chair. In this moment of calm, she let herself fancy that she was a princess and these handmaidens were preparing her for some magnificent ball. It was a nice fantasy and she wanted to wallow in it like the hot bath she'd been pulled from.

She'd been drugged, of course. It would not do to have her screaming and thrashing when the gentlemen came calling throughout the night. That would be unseemly in such a grand old country mansion house. However, the sedative they'd given her wasn't quite strong enough to dull the edge of the cramps which were coming more frequently now.

One of the young women at her side whispered some words of comfort as she patted her arms and shoulders with a fluffy towel. Olena couldn't concentrate on the words but could tell that this woman was from her home country. She might be her sister or cousin. Undoubtedly her story was the same: she'd answered an ad for a job vacancy in England; she'd simply wanted a better life. Olena wondered dreamily if this woman had fallen afoul of the same man who'd arranged her own travel documents and work visa. The one with a chipped front tooth who had spun her tales of an English family who needed a nanny for their two children – a well-to-do family who would provide board and lodging as well as an ample salary, which she could send home to her own family.

How long had she been in England now? Months only, she thought, but long enough for her home to seem like a poorly remembered dream. Time had become slippery. Ever since they'd abducted her, she'd found it hard to keep things straight in her head. No, that wasn't quite right, it wasn't ever since they'd abducted her, it was ever since they'd taken her to see Old Mother. Had that even happened? That seemed like a dream as well.

Sitting in this opulent room now, her reflection in the mirror coming in and out of focus, she could only remember scattered shards of that wintry night somewhere in Europe. The crunch of snow as they led her out to a barn; the darkness inside, save for beams of pearl moonlight cutting through gaps in the boards; the heavy, musty smell which filled the place; the large cage in the middle of the barn, strewn with hay, and that pathetic, wheezing mound of grey fur inside, like a mouldering old rug; a large man forcing her left arm through the bars.

The memory went all swimmy.

It must have been a fever dream because it was around that time she'd fallen ill and delirious. That was when her memories began to unpick. She could remember a rocking boat and the smell of the sea. She remembered rough hands and the stench of cheap aftershave and sweat. Some of the other things she remembered were too strange to be real. Her next clear memory was waking as if from a nightmare in her anonymous room somewhere in England, except the nightmare never really ended.

Olena's left hand ached and she lifted it to her face. The chunky chain of the handcuffs which were attached to the arm of her chair snapped taut. She gazed woozily at the ragged scar which ran in a crescent over the back of her hand. It looked red and angry. Her whole hand looked strange, as if it belonged to someone else.

More cramps shot through her like venom, bending her double. It felt as if there were hooks deep inside her which were being slowly pulled out from between her legs. The women around her fussed. One of them ran out of the room and returned with a plate which they dropped onto the dressing table in front of her. It smelt good. Olena swallowed as her mouth filled with saliva. Three raw steaks sat on the plate. They would be drugged too, but she needed them. The handcuffs around both wrists clinked as she grabbed the topmost steak and pressed it to her face. The flat, metallic taste of meat and blood bloomed inside her mouth and the claws raking at her insides were blunted almost instantly. She turned the pink steaks to mash in her mouth and sucked on them, unaware that she was rocking in her chair and moaning deep in the back of her throat as she ate. After she had licked the plate clean of its blood she fell into a stupor and her ladies in waiting approached again to clean her hands and face.

As they fluttered around her, Olena daydreamed. She imagined that she was the owner of this grand estate which she'd been brought to. Her ladies loved her. At night she would roam the grounds and soak up the heady fragrance from the night-blooming jessamine, and a large shape would move among the trees, eyes like sodium lamps – Old Mother keeping her distance but always watching.

She began to shake and the seizure took hold quickly. Her ladies in waiting flapped and squawked like birds, and suddenly there were men at her side with tight grips and stubbly chins, lifting her up and through to the bedroom. They dragged her to the four-poster bed and secured her there, legs and arms, face down and bent over a velvet roll cushion so that her backside was in the air.

Downstairs, Henry Norris kept track of proceedings through his earpiece. The slight twitch at the corner of his otherwise flat mouth was the only indication of his disquiet. From the adjoining room the ting of silver cutlery on bone china was diminishing. The roasted game birds had either been consumed or discarded, and Norris could hear the squeaky pop of bottles being uncorked. Cordial conversation bubbled, punctuated by the occasional braying laugh, and doubtless many of their number would be taking their little blue pills in anticipation of the night's entertainment.

Norris had never been overly burdened by qualms, but there was something about tonight's event which did not sit well with him. He could tell himself that it was the concentration of VIPs in the room beyond – a member of the Royal Family was here tonight, along with cabinet ministers, business leaders, and, of course, newspaper owners – but that would be untrue. It was the girl upstairs that bothered him. It was what was going to happen.

He was an aide-de-camp of sorts for these people. Some of them called him their "fixer" but he thought of himself as a Groom of the Stool, those courtiers of yore who used to clean the King's shit. And as then, so now – with such intimate acquaintance came confidence and information. He knew all their peccadilloes and facilitated most of them. He knew who in that room liked their heroin; he knew who liked to hurt their conquests; he knew the ones who liked children and whether they preferred girls or boys. The morality of such behaviour was of no concern or consequence to him. This was the way of things; these people owned and ran the world and everything in it was theirs to do with as they pleased. So it was, and so it would ever be.

The young woman upstairs, though. She was a different proposition altogether. Young girls were easy to obtain; even procuring one from overseas and getting them into the country was not bothersome. This one came from Poland or Ukraine or some such, he believed. But finding someone who could take on board the infection – someone who could survive the bite – and then managing her while the infection took hold, month on month, until she was ready, that had stretched him. Nothing could be left to chance. He'd personally overseen her progress once she'd arrived on these shores. He'd watched her twist and transform so he could guarantee he was delivering what had been asked of him. He'd observed the monster to ensure the right precautions were in place to subdue and contain her, and eventually to put her down when the night was over and they were done with her.

Seeing her like that had shaken his long-held notions of the natural order of things. Perhaps it also challenged his clients' certainties of their station above the herd, which might explain their desire to dominate and degrade it. Or perhaps a lifelong gratification of every whim and desire had so blunted their sense of pleasure that more extreme depravity was required to regain any feeling of satisfaction. His was not to reason why, his one job was to supply.

A voice in his earpiece told him that she was secure and ready. He checked his tie and cuffs, moved through the now vacated dining room, and followed the sounds of bonhomie into the wood-panelled drawing room opposite. The air was already a fug of cigar smoke and some were helping themselves to the lines of cocaine which had been prepared while others quaffed port or champagne.

Beyond the drawing room was a private chamber, guarded by one of the Personal Protection Officers who were present tonight. Norris knocked efficiently and waited for the door to be opened. Inside, the prince had already undressed and was standing in the middle of the room in a silken, oriental robe which hung open. A young blonde girl was on her knees in front of him, fluffing him in preparation for the amusement to come. Norris cleared his throat politely, but before he could speak an ungodly noise tore through the house from the floor above; a long, tortured howl which abruptly stopped the chatter and activity in the drawing room and sent all eyes towards the ceiling. When the howl eventually dwindled and died, Norris had to clear his throat again because it was suddenly tight.

"Everything is prepared, Your Royal Highness," he said.

Upstairs, Olena writhed and screamed against her bonds. She was shredding the bedclothes and mattress with her flexing fingers but was held fast and laid out taut. She felt as if she were burning, but the intense pain was receding a little, and she became aware of the heartbeats of the people in the room with her, even if she could not twist her neck enough to see them. She could smell their sweat and adrenaline; one of them was pregnant but did not know it. She could hear the conversation and laughter of a gathering on a lower floor, and she heard it stop dead when she screamed.

Her head was still foggy but she heard Old Mother more clearly now. Not a dream, then, nor a fevered delusion. Her left hand throbbed where Old Mother had bitten her, and her hands and arms looked very strange stretched out in front of her, coarse and sinewy. From thousands of miles away, Old Mother soothed her. She spoke calming words from her cage across the sea, except she didn't really speak in words; Old Mother spoke in feelings and images – the delight of running through the forest at night in packs; the music of the moon; the lust of the hunt – but her meaning was clear.

Old Mother was perhaps the last of her kind. They had hunted her, caged and beaten her, and now she was old, riddled with pain, and dying. But still she spent what little energy she had reaching out to Olena, cooing to her as one does a distressed child, rocking her with promises of the cold ground beneath the pads of her feet, of running free and wild.

Two men entered the room. Olena tensed and sounded a warning note which rolled low and long in the back of her throat. The women left, filing out quickly, and one of these men approached her tentatively. She saw his round, white belly protruding from the robe which hung about him, and below that a thin prick at attention. This man circled behind her as if he were inspecting the flanks of a potential brood mare for his stables. He spoke and the second man left the room, leaving them alone, although she knew he waited just outside the door. Downstairs the chatter had begun again, more raucous than before.

He was talking to her now, this pasty, priapic man. She could feel the heat coming off him but she couldn't understand his words. She shouted and shook in rage when he laid a hand on the shaggy back of her thigh, but Old Mother shushed her and bade her to lie still and quiet.

This man wants to mount you, Old Mother said, *as do all the men below.*

He laid a second, trembling hand on her other leg and slid it up to her buttocks.

They want to subjugate and domineer, Old Mother said.

He was right up against her now.

They believe they own everything, Old Mother chuckled. *But they are fools.*

She felt his flabby weight pressing down on her, but she didn't really feel it when he entered her.

Fools, Old Mother continued, *because they believe they can control everything; because they believe they can control you. Yet each month you grow stronger; each month you burn more quickly through the narcotics they give you to keep you docile.*

The prince made a small, personal noise which quickly turned into a shriek when she suddenly tensed inside and he could not withdraw.

Be free, my child! Free and wild!

At the sound of the prince's screech, the officer waiting in the hall burst back in. His gun was drawn, but with his royal charge flopping naked across Olena's back, desperately trying to disengage himself, there was no clear shot. Instead, he gaped as she flexed her limbs and snapped the chains around her wrists and ankles. She leapt off the bed towards him, her arms outstretched and greedy for his body, dragging the prince with her, his screams reaching a new pitch. The guard's face was within reach and she squeezed his cheeks as if he were a chubby toddler. Her hands were huge now, and that face crumpled beneath them. The guard dropped to the floor, twitching, and gurgled from the red hole which had been his mouth. She crouched low over him, sniffing the blood bubbles which popped from his ruined face. In amongst those hot, short bursts of breath she detected the stale molecules of disease and pulled back in disgust.

No matter. There were more downstairs.

She lunged for the door and dropped onto all fours in the thick-carpeted hallway, dragging the whimpering prince behind her as she prowled towards the stairs. Let him enjoy his fuck while he could.

Norris heard the muffled sounds of commotion above and tried to reach the officer upstairs on the radio. No reply. The gathering downstairs was getting rowdy and loud, as it always did, and he moved discreetly to another part of the house. He called for the three other armed officers on site to come to his position. Their clipped, professional responses reassured him until he reached the foot of the grand staircase and saw what was coming down.

The thing looked like a nightmare, much larger than when he had previously seen it. It was descending on all fours and he could see the muscles in its forearms and shoulders standing proud like ropes beneath dark fur. Its clawed hands were huge and splayed across each step as it advanced, slowly but steadily. And its smile as it watched him looked almost too wide for its head; it seemed to have more teeth than could fit in its mouth. It was only then that he noticed the moaning prince being dragged behind it like a ragdoll, but he had no time to react because the thing launched itself upon him. Its weight toppled him instantly, knocking the wind from him, and its claws were in his shoulders like steak knives before that awful mouth opened and enveloped most of his head. He couldn't even scream. The last thing he saw was its quivering gullet as the teeth clamped down and scraped across the bone of his skull. The last thing he felt was a blast of hot breath on his face and an unbearable pressure inside his head as those jaws worked on him like a vice. The last thing he heard was the cracking of his own skull, and then it was all over for Henry Norris.

Olena knew this one, she recognised his scent; he'd been there for her other changes. After the eggshell crunch of his head, she felt the warm jelly of his brain on her tongue, but she had no time to enjoy it before more men arrived, guns drawn. Two of them stood aghast, but the third began to fire, which prompted the others into action. Olena roared as she was struck by stinging bullets. She reached behind her and grabbed her bruised and terrified rapist by the first flailing limb which came into her grasp. Rising onto her hind legs she whipped him round, breaking his arm in the process, and hurled him at her attackers, sending two of them crashing to the ground in a mess of limbs. She jumped at the third as he took aim and caught his outstretched arms in the wide arc of her swinging hand. Her claws flensed his muscles from the bone and he staggered back, soundless, staring at the ribbons of meat which now dangled below his elbows.

Now she stalked towards her downed attackers who were scrambling beneath the lolling, naked weight of their royal charge. Remarkably, one of them still had a hold of his gun, and as she approached, all teeth and fury, he pressed it to his throat and pulled the trigger. His head snapped back and hit the polished wooden floor with the sound of a baseball bat. There was a small, scorched hole just below his chin and blood began to pour thickly from his nostrils.

The third guard was screaming, desperate to be free from the body pinning him to the ground, struggling like a hare in a snare. Olena placed a foot on his chest to stop his wriggling and curled her lips at the tang of piss and shit which suddenly filled his trousers. She took a moment to assess her injuries. Those bullets had teeth, but the wounds to her bicep, shoulders and chest were only oozing, already healing.

The guard beneath her raised his hands, palms out, placating and pleading. She grabbed his wrists with a snort of contempt, yanked both arms out of their sockets, and tossed them aside like chicken legs.

Far off to the east, Old Mother was singing and it made Olena's heart soar.

The prince at her feet was still breathing, so she took his shin in her mouth and dragged him through the mansion house towards the sound of gathered heartbeats and the smell of rising alarm.

Inside the drawing room the air of good cheer and anticipation of wild delights had soured with the dull pop of gunfire and shrill screams. When Olena entered, the puce-faced and sweaty revellers looked like nothing more than turkeys in a coop, staring at the fox. She let go of the prince's mangled leg and rose onto her hind legs again. She lifted his broken, naked body by the neck and held him in front of her. There were murmurs of fear and noises of sickened recognition, and some even marked that His Royal Highness was still alive when she cupped his flaccid genitals in her other hand and twisted them from his body. Now they squawked like fowl, and their screams filled the room like puffs of aphrodisiac, driving her wild.

"Darlings!" she said, although her vocal cords were rough and knotted, so the word came out as a strained bark which sounded like broken crockery in a sack.

The room exploded in panic and her frenzy began. She hooked her fingers around the jawbone of one and ripped it from his face, then they embraced and she swallowed his tongue as it flapped from the hole in his throat. Another tried to run past her and she unzipped him with a slash of her foot. His insides spilled out like a burst bin bag and he thudded to the ground, trying to scoop them back up. His last thought was, *Nanny will be so cross if she sees this mess.* She grabbed another by the neck and bit into the flabby flesh of his back to reach his kidneys. Her desire was so vibrant that when she swallowed those morsels, she squeezed his throat until his eyes ruptured.

Some of her sisters were also in the room, women like her who had been kidnapped or coerced, but her desire wasn't so great that she could not distinguish one from the other. Some of these women froze in abject fear and she passed them by, others scrambled for the door and she let them pass.

One man wrangled a sword from a suit of armour which stood in the corner of the room. He blubbered incoherently as he tried to raise its tip off the floor but the ancient weapon was too heavy. Olena snatched it from him contemptuously. She bent him over an armchair roughly and ceased his squealing by pushing the wide blade up inside him until the hilt met his buttocks.

The air had become misty with blood and the floor was slick with innards. Some men scrabbled on their hands and knees trying to hide, sliding in gore, and she plucked them off the ground one at a time and opened them up with her hands and teeth. She buried her face in their chests and ate their beating hearts. She tore at their throats and showered in the arterial spray. Of course, some slipped past her in the heat of the moment, or jumped from windows out into the chill night, but this country estate was isolated and there were acres of grounds to hunt them through before daybreak.

After she had finished playing inside, she stepped out into the gardens and waded in the glorious moonlight. She breathed deeply and caught the scent of those near and far who had enslaved and abused her. With time she would be able to find them all, even the chip-toothed man. She would track them back to their hiding places and sniff out their accomplices wherever they went to ground, and she would free all her captive sisters.

Old Mother was still singing and Olena joined that song, howling high and long at the fat moon. *Show them*, Old Mother sang, *show them all what a true wolf thinks of the feelings of sheep.*

When Sleeping Wolves Lie

Mark Patrick Lynch

THE OVERNIGHT TRAIN arrived as the first sunlight of the day caught the city.

Disembarking, bag in hand, Jonathan left the station and found a cab to take him to the rendezvous. Floating on the glass of the taxi's rear windows, the architecture of old London passed by as weary ghosts haunting the new. It offered nothing in the way of consolation. A bad business was a bad business, and he was about its work today.

He sighed. He was back in the metropolis and as far from the full moon as possible, and with that all too human.

* * *

At journey's end, he mounted the steps to the library. In the expansive lobby, Wilson was dawdling by the grand staircase as people passed by. Seeing Jonathan, he stepped forward, offering a handshake. He wore an unsure smile as out-of-keeping with the man as the lake of cologne he must have bathed in that morning. Jonathan could scent that at least.

"Dear boy, how good to see you," Wilson said. "I know it's not a day we'd either of us choose to be out on the… ah, out on the prowl. I do appreciate this."

"Could have done without the trip. Getting to London's quite the haul these days."

"I rather fear there's no other way, but we'll talk of it later."

From there, in their version of spy-craft, they crisscrossed the city to shake any tails, using black cabs and public transport. After some time in a park they spent an hour in a coffee house, then took in a string recital (not Jonathan's choice) in a dinky hall close to a tube station.

By the time they arrived at Wilson's den it was raining, a thin slanted rain that contained the first chill of autumn.

Inside, with day waning to night, the subject of the moon and how far away it was came to their lips, as it was always going to. Because of who they were, because of *what* they were.

"Dulls the senses, don't you find, when it's so distant? You lose your strength, your senses. It's a terrible come-down, being human again."

Wilson spoke, drink in hand, plate before him. He'd played the chef earlier, busy in the kitchen, and now they were dining. Wilson: one of Jonathan's kind, and if you believed him, was so out of choice. A risky cut after midnight, decades ago, when the moon was in full light and a beast the other side of a parade of iron bars. A month later he'd experienced his first transformation, along with his first blooding.

His face spoiled as he sipped his wine. "Even this barely has a flavour to it. I swear, Jonathan, it's bloody inconvenient, being human, it really is. More so for me at my age. Whippersnapper like you, you'll probably not notice."

Whippersnapper? Well, hardly. They lived long lives, did their kind. Longer than a natural human span at any rate.

"You're not that old," Jonathan said. "For one of us."

Wilson, his leanness noticeably visible this far from the moon, laughed. "Aren't I?"

Jonathan studied him, asking himself the question. Wilson was smooth-skinned, with a high forehead that lacked for worry-lines. Usually his eyes were bright, often containing a mocking twinkle, though tonight they looked tired. The business ahead troubling him, worries showing?

"I'm feeling a few things myself," Jonathan settled for saying.

"Well that little scratch you so readily complain about has seen to it that you're in perfect health for most of the month. Thousands would beg for a life like yours."

"Maybe, but it comes at a price. And it wasn't a little scratch."

The evidence of his *Becoming* was still with him, ragged scar tissue across his flank. The claws had nearly loosed his innards on the world. He winced at the memory of the pain.

Wilson was unimpressed.

"Why can't you just take what fortune has delivered you and enjoy it? You're so tiresome, Jonathan. I have tried with you, I really have."

"I don't like eating people."

"But you're not one of them any longer. Haven't been for years. Both of us are different. Better."

"Yet here we are," Jonathan said. "Human. Today. Just like them."

"A painful reminder is what it is. So we remember how lucky we are when the wolf is in full pomp."

Jonathan held his companion's gaze. "It's always in us."

"But sleeping now. Not stalking around our blood waiting to emerge. Which is why, alas, we are as we are today. Feeble and pathetic."

"Perhaps." As Jonathan ate he couldn't really deny the truth of what Wilson was saying. They were perilously human. Inside them, the wolf slept. But its nose would start to twitch tomorrow, an eye slink open the next day, and so on. Until transformation. Full moon, full wolf.

"So what's the deal with this woman you were telling me about? Not the reporter. Your bit of stuff," Jonathan asked, patting his lips with a linen napkin. The candles Wilson had lighted were scented, but not unpleasantly so. "Not your style at all."

"Yes, she's hardly a delight. But I can endure her. Convenience, I suppose. Saves the effort of seeking fresh game. She'll be there for me when it's time."

"Does she think she's laying a trap? On the lookout for someone with a few pounds to their name?"

Wilson's self-satisfaction returned. "Any trap is mine. Baited and caught. She's ready to accompany me on a little trip to the country come the fortnight."

"And in the meantime, you'll keep her entertained?"

Wilson tsk-tsked, stirring the last of his rare beef through rich gravy. "Oh, you know me. I'm ever so chaste, Jonathan. A gentleman. And when the time comes... Well, she doesn't have much in the way of friends and family. I've done my due diligence, and been, as you would expect, most circumspect about being seen with her."

"And what about the boy? No doubt there is one, somewhere."

"Yes, well, there is indeed. But you know, I'm growing rather fond of this latest one. He is very talented, quite the artist. I might keep him around a while longer. Even the wolf's enjoying the pleasure of his company, and you know how particular the wolf can be."

"I suppose it's a life-hack everyone should stick to – don't eat what you fuck."

"Please, Jonathan. Less of the crudity. You know I can't bear it. Especially at dinner."

"Sorry. My mistake. Should we get back to the cannibalism?"

Wilson stilled his knife and fork. They were stainless steel rather than silver, not that it mattered to them today, and caught the candlelight. "We are not cannibals."

"Aren't we?"

"We are wolves, Jonathan. And everyone else is prey."

Except it wasn't quite true and they both knew it. Other wolves were not their prey; that was one of their few rules. But there were others out there, frustrated men – usually men, though women were not unheard of – who fancied themselves hunters and sought the most elusive game. They were hardly prey. And of course, when Jonathan and Wilson were as human as they ever got, it really was best to be out of their way, when a single bullet could do the trick of ending them.

"You're sure we're doing the right thing?" Jonathan asked, knife and fork laid on his plate. The beef had settled his stomach, but he didn't like what was still to come of their night. "We have to do it?"

"Yes."

"No question about it?"

"None."

"Your information's correct? She knows?"

A tired sigh of defeat. "Yes."

"You're certain?"

"I can't be certain of everything, Jonathan. Not a hundred per cent. I'm as sure as I can be, let's leave it at that."

"Then there's a possibility she doesn't know, that we'll be doing it for the wrong reasons."

"Oh, do relax, will you? You're spoiling things."

"Well, I wouldn't want to do that. Obviously. I mean, it's not as if it's a matter of life and death we're discussing here."

"We'll tend to her."

It felt like a confession when Jonathan said, "I don't know if I can. It's not the same. Not when we're like this."

"Well, we could hardly involve anyone else in this. We'll just have to remember what it's like to be a wolf."

"Without claws? With dull human teeth? It'll take some doing. I don't like it."

"And you think I do?" Wilson looked away. "I'll sort some coffee out for us. We've time. She's not due for a while."

"If she knows, why the hell is she coming here anyway?"

"Because knowing isn't necessarily believing, dear child."

"But she still picked this date?"

"Wouldn't be moved on the matter."

"Then she does know. With no moon she thinks she's safe."

"Well, she isn't."

They fell into silence. Wilson's phone rang.

* * *

"Change of plan," Wilson said when he'd ended the call. "We're going to hers."

"Jesus, Wilson. She was coming *here*. That was the arrangement. We should call it off."

"And do what? She has our names. She knows us. We can't run. She'll follow."

"What she's thinking are impossible things."

"*We* are impossible things, Jonathan."

"Not today, we're not. You didn't even argue with her."

"Because the arrangements are in place. All this calls for is a small change of plan, a little improvisation on our part."

Jonathan shook his head. "No one will believe her. She prints any of her suspicions and people will laugh."

"Some will. Others won't."

Wilson didn't have to spell it out. The hunt, looking for a wolf's head, frozen for eternity, to snarl from a lodge wall.

He'd wanted to avoid this, he really had. Jonathan closed his eyes, knowing all the while what had to be done.

* * *

"Jaguar. Quite the car," Jonathan said.

"Big enough to cope with the motorways and nimble enough for the country lanes," Wilson explained, pulling on a pair of deerskin gloves to handle the steering wheel. "You have to give your guests a bit of luxury. Their blood thickens, tastes all the sweeter when there's terror in it after such treats."

He triggered the engine. Jonathan glanced at his wristwatch.

"Easy, my boy," Wilson said. "We'll be there in time. We'll get this done."

Jonathan fidgeted. He hadn't been worried about the time till their assignation, not exactly; he was thinking of how soon it would be until the wolf started making itself known in him again, how quickly his enhanced senses would return. Both their senses, his and Wilson's. Enough to suss out the truth from the girl they were going to meet, to root out her bluffs and lies? "You know where you're going?"

"Looked it up on my phone while you were getting changed."

"Right." Jonathan was in black now, dark jeans and a hoodie. Wilson was dressed as if for walking his dog in the country. "You've not got a scent for her?"

"That is the one thing worrying me about all of this, I have to confess," Wilson said. "The only occasions we've met, she's timed it for days like today, when I've only had my wits to take her measure, no help from the wolf. Three months, two meetings, and all of it culminating tonight."

"This is a mistake."

"She might think it's a trap, else it's extreme caution on her part. But really it's my trap, Jonathan."

"Then why are we following her directions?"

"Now now. We had this argument in the flat. Steady ahead, eh?"

He drove. Jonathan sighed. He felt like an actor uncertain of his lines. Better to say nothing, then, let Wilson be the lead. Jonathan just had to make sure he himself saw out the script, ready for the applause after the curtain fell, or to be first through the theatre door and into the night before the catcalls of the critics landed home.

* * *

They left the major roads for the dowdy end of wherever they'd been led to, a rougher district of the city. Houses were gone, replaced by motor mechanics, tyre warehouses, timber yards, and welders' units, all shut for the night. The railway was close. Trains, both lighted and dim, clattered past behind shadowy buildings.

"I think we're there," Wilson said, playing his part. "Up ahead. I believe that's us."

"Not her house, then."

At the end of the road Wilson slowed the car before open flat-board gates stencilled with a company name that gave no real clue to its business. The headlights showed nothing but darkness beyond them.

"Be vigilant, dear boy, and we'll come through this all right." By the dashboard's illumination, Wilson's face had an amber hue to it. Jonathan thought it looked sickly.

They rolled forward, cautious, watchful, passing the gates. The yard appeared to be empty. There were no lights but the Jaguar's, not even a security LED raised on a pole.

A world-weary portacabin stood on slabs and breezeblocks, catching what little ambient light bounced back from the underside of the clouds. There was nothing to indicate anyone was inside, though of course there might be, someone secreted away with camera or rifle. The windows were dark, the door padlocked on the outside.

Still, Jonathan knew Wilson wouldn't want him to dismiss it… The lock might be stage-dressing, easily opened with a heavy push from inside. All the same…

"I don't see anything."

"No."

Wilson stopped the car and let the engine idle for a minute and then shut it down. The dashboard illuminations died, as did the headlights. Then it was just the pair of them, he and Wilson in the dark.

"What now?" Jonathan asked on a breath.

"Revelations, I suppose. Let's be about it." Wilson opened his door, stepping out before Jonathan could protest.

Taking a breath to fortify himself, Jonathan did the same. The air struck him first of all, how cold it was compared to the interior of the car. Then the smell of vegetables, more pungent than the diesel of the train passing by with a loud shriek just now, suggesting it was a processing centre for something; cabbages and lettuces, perhaps, and by their odour many of them gone to rot. The train went by, taking the sound of its passage with it.

In the new silence, Jonathan's and Wilson's gazes met across the roof of the car. A breeze, gentle as a child's first flirtation with sin, licked their hair, wetting the nape of their necks.

"I don't like this," Jonathan said.

"You're not meant to."

It wasn't Wilson who'd spoken. Both men turned around, seeking the owner of the voice. It had come from behind them. She stepped out from the side of the portacabin, leaving the deepest shadows there to themselves.

"Gregory Wilson and Jonathan Vickers," she said, wearing a reporter's mac over a trouser suit. Her hair was loose, her hands empty. "Werewolves."

* * *

The nomenclature hung in the air, absurd as the notion that the brightness of the moon could exact a transformation on a man, turn him inside out, breaking everything within and tear what was without, re-knit his bones, strengthen his muscles, extend his nose into a snout and fill the insides of his mouth with teeth as grim as a hundred vicious tusks, all of them the better to eat you with, my dear, all of them the better to dismember and devour you with.

Jonathan found that he couldn't even raise a disparaging laugh to try to ward off the truth. To hear it from her, so blatant, stole something from him. Here they stood, with nothing by way of the moon to strengthen them. He inhaled, but his useless nose caught no scent from her, not even any perfume she might be wearing. He glanced at Wilson, and saw his senses were equally as dull. *Just a man,* Jonathan thought. *And tonight prey as well.*

"Sally Boone," Wilson said, his composure admirable given his intentions. "How sweet of you to invite us here tonight. Not quite a cosy little place for drinks and a chat, though. If you're living in that cabin, I hope you have a kerosene heater to keep off the chill."

"You don't need to worry about me," Sally Boone said.

"Brought a silver pentagram with you, have you? In one of your pockets, is it? Presumably the one that doesn't contain your phone, which is no doubt recording this conversation." Wilson didn't seem perturbed at the thought. "I do hope you're not – what's the term – streaming it live. Still, if it makes you feel better to have such a thing."

She didn't reply. Wilson glanced around the yard, as did Jonathan. If anyone was hanging back in the shadows, behind the containers, he couldn't see them. Actually, the more he thought about why Sally Boone had picked this place to meet, the more he understood. The scent of spoiled vegetables might disguise her own scent, or that of anyone with her, for a while.

Wilson, still in his own cloud of cologne, said, "Well, obviously we deny everything. Because werewolves don't exist. Cut us and we bleed."

"Oh, I'm sure you do, Mister Wilson. Especially when there isn't a moon to help you."

Wilson laughed softly. "Yes, yes. Here's where you are with things. You see, you half-believe but aren't entirely convinced by your findings. After all, what you're suggesting is incredible. Perhaps a part of you thinks we merely believe we're wolves, and, driven mad by the moon, go out on killing sprees for the joy of it. A terrible but prosaic explanation."

"It's something to consider."

"A more likely explanation."

"Except it doesn't fit, not when it comes down to it. There are witnesses."

"People who've glimpsed a big dog near a murder scene, heard what they thought was a wolf howling at the full moon? Slim pickings for evidence, Sally Boone. Slim, slim pickings. What do you say, Jonathan?"

"I say I don't get any of this. This is a conversation the two of you could have had anywhere, any time. Why now, why here?"

Wilson's head dipped. When he lifted it, he looked to Sally Boone. "He does have a point. This is all a bit theatrical, isn't it? Perhaps it's time to come clean."

He turned to Jonathan.

"Bit of bad news. I've brought you here under false pretences, Jonathan."

Jonathan kept his voice steady. "What do you mean?"

"Well, to be blunt about it – rather afraid I've sold you out. Sorry. I truly am."

The car was still between them. Wilson meant to keep it that way. He looked wary, as if Jonathan might leap at him. But Jonathan didn't move. Wilson rubbed his chin.

"Told you, I'm old, dear boy. Failing. Slowing down. I wouldn't make much sport for them. I've to drag old women into the country to hunt these days. It's embarrassing. Anything younger, they elude me. Elude the wolf. He's tiring too, coming to his end. It wouldn't take someone with a gun or silver-tipped arrow long to bring me down, an ailing wolf, fur all grey. Where's the fun in that?"

Jonathan read his face, finding little in the way of remorse. "You'd do this to me?"

"Have done. The arrangements are in place." He lifted his hands, still wearing the driving gloves. "You go with them and I get a free pass. A few more months and I'll be done with anyway. Cancer's in me. Doesn't shift, not even after a transformation. That's one of the reasons it had to be today, you see, all of this. You're not just weaker, you can't smell it on me either. The rot. It's appalling. There all the time."

Jonathan understood. When the wolf was awake he could smell human sickness a mile away. It was one of the reasons he stayed away from cities. He took his prey on lonely moorlands, went through forests noting wild campers in the days before he became the wolf.

The rot explained Wilson's reason for covering himself in all those colognes. When cancer advances enough, even someone plainly human could smell death in a person.

Wilson nodded. "Sally's one of them. Game-hunter, not a reporter."

"That's why you didn't give me her name. So I wouldn't check on her."

"In case you didn't trust me to do my due diligence."

She walked to Wilson, the car between her and Jonathan, the charade almost done.

"That reporter's coat's a bit central casting," Jonathan told her. "I'm surprised you don't have one of those big flashbulb cameras around your neck."

"It's only stage-dressing. Mister Wilson didn't want to alert you to things. If it's any comfort, he didn't want you to notice the capture, or realise he'd betrayed you. You'd have been taken to the hunt and they'd have... Well, a chase and a killing come the full moon."

Wilson looked down at this. When he did lift his eyes, he said softly, "I thought it was a kindness. For you not to know."

"Someone from behind?" Jonathan said. "With what? A tranquilizer dart or needle? I come to elsewhere, chained up and caged, thinking you're going through the same thing elsewhere. What a gentleman you are."

"No. Not a gentleman. A wolf. I have been for a long, long time, Jonathan. And this is what comes of it." He turned to the woman beside him. "Miss Boone, could you call them out please, and have them take my friend with some gentleness?"

"Actually," she said. "I'm afraid I can't."

Wilson raised his objection quickly enough. "They don't have to hurt him. We're unarmed. Say you'll go quietly, Jonathan. Tell her. It's for the best."

"Gregory," Jonathan said. "Gregory."

Wilson shot a look at him, hearing something in Jonathan's tone.

"There aren't any others, Gregory. It's just us. You, me, and Sally. There are no hunters. We're the only ones here."

"I don't...?"

"Oh, but I think you do."

Wilson turned to the woman beside him, seeing her with new eyes. Maybe the wolf, for all its age, was stirring in him a little, now danger was in the air.

She said, "As I understand it, it needn't be silver today. But I thought you'd appreciate it if it was."

A stiletto blade, catching the ambient light from the undersides of the clouds. It had been inside the coat. She flourished it expertly, no stranger to its ways.

"I can carry it without burning myself today, too," she told him.

Understanding took Wilson by the scruff of the neck, and Jonathan could see it shaking him. "You're...?"

"Yes."

"And you two... You're together?"

"Have been for a while. Sorry I couldn't introduce you properly earlier," Jonathan said. "I had to be sure you wouldn't change your mind."

Wilson tried to recover, to extract himself from the situation. He put a hand through his hair, as if a great worry had dissipated. "But this is tremendous news. There's three of us, then. Imagine the fun we could get up to. Yes, yes, I know I'm ailing, done for. But there's a few moons left in me yet. We could go to my place in the country. Before, you know, the end finds me. And of course the property's yours, as will be all my assets. Some small business with the paperwork to attend to as yet, but it'll be done. No worries on that score."

His laughter almost sounded genuine.

Jonathan shook his head. "You thought she was from the hunt."

"But she isn't. That was your joke, wasn't it?"

Jonathan shook his head. "We know. Sally had been tracking the first one who contacted you. We'd been wary of this particular individual for a while, and then, when you spoke with them… and you were so quick to give me away… All I can say is that I was genuinely disappointed, Gregory. It hurts when trust is broken. That first one met my wolf in the moonlight. Sally took up their role afterwards, to see how far you'd really go with giving me up."

"Hence this?" Wilson said, any pretence at charm fallen away. "An end here. In some grisly yard in the dark?"

"You think you deserve better?"

"Poor, Jonathan. It's poor."

Wilson couldn't back away. Sally Boone had the stiletto pressed to the small of his back. It would pass through his jacket in a moment and he knew it.

Jonathan produced his own blade. He'd brought it with him from Scotland. And in all that time journeying, he'd been hoping Wilson would not go through with his plan.

"You're not a wolf, Jonathan. Not today. You said so yourself."

"No, no, I'm not. Wolves don't kill wolves. That's the rule. But today I'm human, just a man. And men kill each other all the time."

Wilson raised a cry, calling for help. But it was lost in the roar of another train clattering over the rails behind the yard, and Jonathan did his work. Did it in the darkness, without the moon, without, for this one day and night, the help of the wolf. Brought forth blood, and with it the ending of two lives: a man's and a wolf's.

The Gray Wolf

George MacDonald

ONE EVENING-TWILIGHT in spring, a young English student, who had wandered northwards as far as the outlying fragments of Scotland called the Orkney and Shetland Islands, found himself on a small island of the latter group, caught in a storm of wind and hail, which had come on suddenly. It was in vain to look about for any shelter; for not only did the storm entirely obscure the landscape, but there was nothing around him save a desert moss.

At length, however, as he walked on for mere walking's sake, he found himself on the verge of a cliff, and saw, over the brow of it, a few feet below him, a ledge of rock, where he might find some shelter from the blast, which blew from behind. Letting himself down by his hands, he alighted upon something that crunched beneath his tread, and found the bones of many small animals scattered about in front of a little cave in the rock, offering the refuge he sought. He went in, and sat upon a stone. The storm increased in violence, and as the darkness grew he became uneasy, for he did not relish the thought of spending the night in the cave. He had parted from his companions on the opposite side of the island, and it added to his uneasiness that they must be full of apprehension about him. At last there came a lull in the storm, and the same instant he heard a footfall, stealthy and light as that of a wild beast, upon the bones at the mouth of the cave. He started up in some fear, though the least thought might have satisfied him that there could be no very dangerous animals upon the island. Before he had time to think, however, the face of a woman appeared in the opening. Eagerly the wanderer spoke. She started at the sound of his voice. He could not see her well, because she was turned towards the darkness of the cave.

"Will you tell me how to find my way across the moor to Shielness?" he asked.

"You cannot find it tonight," she answered, in a sweet tone, and with a smile that bewitched him, revealing the whitest of teeth.

"What am I to do, then?"

"My mother will give you shelter, but that is all she has to offer."

"And that is far more than I expected a minute ago," he replied. "I shall be most grateful."

She turned in silence and left the cave. The youth followed.

She was barefooted, and her pretty brown feet went catlike over the sharp stones, as she led the way down a rocky path to the shore. Her garments were scanty and torn, and her hair blew tangled in the wind. She seemed about five and twenty, lithe and small. Her long fingers kept clutching and pulling nervously at her skirts as she went. Her face was very gray in complexion, and very worn, but delicately formed, and smooth-skinned. Her thin nostrils were tremulous as eyelids, and her lips, whose curves were faultless, had no colour to give sign of indwelling blood. What her eyes were like he could not see, for she had never lifted the delicate films of her eyelids.

At the foot of the cliff, they came upon a little hut leaning against it, and having for its inner apartment a natural hollow within. Smoke was spreading over the face of the rock, and the grateful odour of food gave hope to the hungry student. His guide opened the door of the cottage; he followed her in, and saw a woman bending over a fire in the middle of the floor. On the fire lay a large fish broiling. The daughter spoke a few words, and the mother turned and welcomed the stranger.

She had an old and very wrinkled, but honest face, and looked troubled. She dusted the only chair in the cottage, and placed it for him by the side of the fire, opposite the one window, whence he saw a little patch of yellow sand over which the spent waves spread themselves out listlessly. Under this window there was a bench, upon which the daughter threw herself in an unusual posture, resting her chin upon her hand. A moment after, the youth caught the first glimpse of her blue eyes. They were fixed upon him with a strange look of greed, amounting to craving, but, as if aware that they belied or betrayed her, she dropped them instantly. The moment she veiled them, her face, notwithstanding its colourless complexion, was almost beautiful.

When the fish was ready, the old woman wiped the deal table, steadied it upon the uneven floor, and covered it with a piece of fine table-linen. She then laid the fish on a wooden platter, and invited the guest to help himself. Seeing no other provision, he pulled from his pocket a hunting knife, and divided a portion from the fish, offering it to the mother first.

"Come, my lamb," said the old woman; and the daughter approached the table. But her nostrils and mouth quivered with disgust.

The next moment she turned and hurried from the hut.

"She doesn't like fish," said the old woman, "and I haven't anything else to give her."

"She does not seem in good health," he rejoined.

The woman answered only with a sigh, and they ate their fish with the help of a little rye bread. As they finished their supper, the youth heard the sound as of the pattering of a dog's feet upon the sand close to the door; but ere he had time to look out of the window, the door opened, and the young woman entered. She looked better, perhaps from having just washed her face. She drew a stool to the corner of the fire opposite him. But as she sat down, to his bewilderment, and even horror, the student spied a single drop of blood on her white skin within her torn dress. The woman brought out a jar of whisky, put a rusty old kettle on the fire, and took her place in front of it. As soon as the water boiled, she proceeded to make some toddy in a wooden bowl.

Meantime the youth could not take his eyes off the young woman, so that at length he found himself fascinated, or rather bewitched. She kept her eyes for the most part veiled with the loveliest eyelids fringed with darkest lashes, and he gazed entranced; for the red glow of the little oil-lamp covered all the strangeness of her complexion. But as soon as he met a stolen glance out of those eyes unveiled, his soul shuddered within him. Lovely face and craving eyes alternated fascination and repulsion.

The mother placed the bowl in his hands. He drank sparingly, and passed it to the girl. She lifted it to her lips, and as she tasted – only tasted it – looked at him. He thought the drink must have been drugged and have affected his brain. Her hair smoothed itself back, and drew her forehead backwards with it; while the lower part of her face projected towards the bowl, revealing, ere she sipped, her dazzling teeth in strange prominence. But the same moment the vision vanished; she returned the vessel to her mother, and rising, hurried out of the cottage.

Then the old woman pointed to a bed of heather in one corner with a murmured apology; and the student, wearied both with the fatigues of the day and the strangeness of the night, threw himself upon it, wrapped in his cloak. The moment he lay down, the storm began afresh, and the wind blew so keenly through the crannies of the hut, that it was only by drawing his cloak over his head that he could protect himself from its currents. Unable to sleep, he lay listening to the uproar which grew in violence, till the spray was dashing against the window. At length the door opened, and the young woman came in, made up the fire, drew the bench before it, and lay down in the same strange posture, with her chin propped on her hand and elbow, and her face turned towards the youth. He moved a little; she dropped her head, and lay on her face, with her arms crossed beneath her forehead. The mother had disappeared.

Drowsiness crept over him. A movement of the bench roused him, and he fancied he saw some four-footed creature as tall as a large dog trot quietly out of the door. He was sure he felt a rush of cold wind. Gazing fixedly through the darkness, he thought he saw the eyes of the damsel encountering his, but a glow from the falling together of the remnants of the fire revealed clearly enough that the bench was vacant. Wondering what could have made her go out in such a storm, he fell fast asleep.

In the middle of the night he felt a pain in his shoulder, came broad awake, and saw the gleaming eyes and grinning teeth of some animal close to his face. Its claws were in his shoulder, and its mouth in the act of seeking his throat. Before it had fixed its fangs, however, he had its throat in one hand, and sought his knife with the other. A terrible struggle followed; but regardless of the tearing claws, he found and opened his knife. He had made one futile stab, and was drawing it for a surer, when, with a spring of the whole body, and one wildly contorted effort, the creature twisted its neck from his hold, and with something betwixt a scream and a howl, darted from him. Again he heard the door open; again the wind blew in upon him, and it continued blowing; a sheet of spray dashed across the floor, and over his face. He sprung from his couch and bounded to the door.

It was a wild night – dark, but for the flash of whiteness from the waves as they broke within a few yards of the cottage; the wind was raving, and the rain pouring down the air. A gruesome sound as of mingled weeping and howling came from somewhere in the dark. He turned again into the hut and closed the door, but could find no way of securing it.

The lamp was nearly out, and he could not be certain whether the form of the young woman was upon the bench or not. Overcoming a strong repugnance, he approached it, and put out his hands – there was nothing there. He sat down and waited for the daylight: he dared not sleep any more.

When the day dawned at length, he went out yet again, and looked around. The morning was dim and gusty and gray. The wind had fallen, but the waves were tossing wildly. He wandered up and down the little strand, longing for more light.

At length he heard a movement in the cottage. By and by the voice of the old woman called to him from the door.

"You're up early, sir. I doubt you didn't sleep well."

"Not very well," he answered. "But where is your daughter?"

"She's not awake yet," said the mother. "I'm afraid I have but a poor breakfast for you. But you'll take a dram and a bit of fish. It's all I've got."

Unwilling to hurt her, though hardly in good appetite, he sat down at the table. While they were eating, the daughter came in, but turned her face away and went to the farther end of the hut. When she came forward after a minute or two, the youth saw that her hair was drenched, and her face whiter than before. She looked ill and faint, and when she raised her eyes, all their fierceness had vanished, and sadness had taken its place. Her neck was now covered with a cotton handkerchief. She was modestly attentive to him, and no longer shunned his gaze. He was gradually yielding to the temptation of braving another night in the hut, and seeing what would follow, when the old woman spoke.

"The weather will be broken all day, sir," she said. "You had better be going, or your friends will leave without you."

Ere he could answer, he saw such a beseeching glance on the face of the girl, that he hesitated, confused. Glancing at the mother, he saw the flash of wrath in her face. She rose and approached her daughter, with her hand lifted to strike her. The young woman stooped her head with a cry. He darted round the table to interpose between them. But the mother had caught hold of her; the handkerchief had fallen from her neck; and the youth saw five blue bruises on her lovely throat – the marks of the four fingers and the thumb of a left hand. With a cry of horror he darted from the house, but as he reached the door he turned. His hostess was lying motionless on the floor, and a huge gray wolf came bounding after him.

There was no weapon at hand; and if there had been, his inborn chivalry would never have allowed him to harm a woman even under the guise of a wolf. Instinctively, he set himself firm, leaning a little forward, with half outstretched arms, and hands curved ready to clutch again at the throat upon which he had left those pitiful marks. But the creature as she sprung eluded his grasp, and just as he expected to feel her fangs, he found a woman weeping on his bosom, with her arms around his neck. The next instant, the gray wolf broke from him, and bounded howling up the cliff. Recovering himself as he best might, the youth followed, for it was the only way to the moor above, across which he must now make his way to find his companions.

All at once he heard the sound of a crunching of bones – not as if a creature was eating them, but as if they were ground by the teeth of rage and disappointment; looking up, he saw close above him the mouth of the little cavern in which he had taken refuge the day before. Summoning all his resolution, he passed it slowly and softly. From within came the sounds of a mingled moaning and growling.

Having reached the top, he ran at full speed for some distance across the moor before venturing to look behind him. When at length he did so, he saw, against the sky, the girl standing on the edge of the cliff, wringing her hands. One solitary wail crossed the space between. She made no attempt to follow him, and he reached the opposite shore in safety.

Skin Traders

Clara MacGauffin

RORY DIDN'T KNOW what he was, not exactly. He only knew that something darker than hunger lived inside him, that a pulse deep in his marrow throbbed in sync with the moon. And now, after that last full moon, after the torn limbs and the blood on his clothes, he knew he couldn't keep this life. Couldn't keep his *skin*.

He'd found the ad late one night. *"Got a bit of you you'd like gone? New skin, new life, guaranteed."* It was his last hope, and so, at 2 a.m., he waited in the alley behind the butcher shop, thick envelopes of cash stuffed in his pocket.

The figure that met him stepped out of the shadows without a sound, her pale green coat a sickly glow under the streetlight. Her face looked almost right, but stretched, as if it had been painted onto the wrong skull.

"Are you Rory?" she asked, though her gaze seemed to drift over him, almost *through* him.

"Yeah," he managed, and her eyes lingered on him for a moment, almost... sniffing him out.

She unfurled an old-fashioned beach umbrella, stabbing it into the pavement and twisting. Colors swirled around her, as though they were slipping between worlds. When the colors settled, they'd formed a doorway in the brick wall, yawning open like a black mouth.

"Shall we?" she said with a nod.

Rory followed, his pulse racing. The darkness in him stirred, restless, *hungry*, but he swallowed it down, reminding himself why he was here.

The room they stepped into was cold and filled with mirrors, though each reflection felt a little... off. He couldn't help but notice that each one showed him with different eyes: golden, green, slit-pupiled. Eyes that didn't look quite human.

At the far end of the room, a man in a mustard-yellow suit stood at a workbench covered in pale, fleshy slabs of... skin. As Rory approached, the man turned, revealing a face dotted with small, spinning cogs beneath a thin veil of skin. He eyed Rory for a moment, nostrils flaring.

"This one smells different," he said, his voice scraping out like rusted gears. "Strange... Thick."

The woman beside Rory smiled. Her teeth were slightly translucent, like old porcelain. "Yes, he has something *unique* about him."

Rory shifted uncomfortably, but steeled himself. "I want a new start. A new life. Just like you said."

The man in yellow didn't look convinced, but he gestured to the workbench. "Very well. Let's begin. Remove your shirt."

Rory stripped down, leaving his skin bare to the cold air, though the thing inside him shifted, snarling. He clenched his fists, biting down the urge to let it out. Soon, he reminded himself. Soon, he'd be someone else. Free.

The man approached with a thin, glimmering knife. "Now, this will be... uncomfortable. We'll need to *peel* what's there before we can apply the new one."

Rory's breath hitched. *Peel.* His skin prickled, but he nodded, telling himself it would be worth it.

The knife sank in, a quick, burning slice across his arm. The man in yellow grinned, pulling the flap of skin back, revealing dark, coarse hair beneath. Rory stifled a gasp, the pain hitting him hard, but the man just murmured, "Fascinating... So *that's* what you're hiding."

The woman leaned closer, her nostrils flaring. "A werewolf," she hissed, almost reverent.

A shock ran through Rory. *They know.*

"Let me go," he growled, but the knife had already cut deeper, dragging along his shoulder, revealing sinewy, furred muscle beneath. The wolf inside him roared, straining against the bonds of human form, but the woman held him fast, her grip iron-strong.

"We don't let go, dear," she whispered, her voice like silk on glass. "We *trade*."

Rory bucked, his growl slipping into a snarl, but the man kept cutting, peeling away layer after layer of human skin, exposing the beast beneath. Pain mingled with a rising, feral rage, but the woman only tightened her hold, eyes gleaming.

The man in yellow let out a long, low chuckle. "We've never done this to a werewolf," he said, voice tinged with an almost childlike glee. "Imagine – layer after layer of soul-rich skin, each carrying a bit of the beast."

The walls seemed to close in as he worked, and Rory felt the strange sensations of the wolf slipping from him, the skin peeled and flayed, his human and animal forms unraveling into separate, vulnerable pieces.

When the knife reached his neck, Rory's vision blurred, the wolf fighting him, thrashing for freedom, but he felt his body weakening. He opened his mouth to scream, to let out the beast, but all that came was a faint whimper.

The man leaned back, admiring the thin, empty shell of human skin in his hands, holding it up to the dim light. "A magnificent piece... You'll be *useful*, Rory. Not as one, but as many."

Rory tried to focus, to keep hold of himself, but as the darkness closed in, he felt them peeling him apart – *one layer for the man, one for the beast* – until nothing remained but empty fragments of his stolen life.

The last thing he heard was the woman's whisper. "The wolf's fury makes such a fine skin to sell. Welcome to the collection."

* * *

The skin sat on the workbench, folded and waiting like an empty suit. The next customer arrived a week later, desperate and sunken-eyed, who muttered about escaping his past, starting over. He didn't know what he was truly buying, didn't understand the *weight* of it. He only knew the Skin Traders offered new lives, and he was desperate enough to pay any price.

The woman in the pale green coat handed him the skin, her smile thin and satisfied. "This," she said, her fingers brushing over it like silk, "is a very rare piece. Fresh, potent. It will give you everything you're looking for, Evan."

Evan took the skin, slightly bewildered but captivated by the way it seemed to shimmer in the low light. It looked *alive* somehow, though he brushed the thought aside. With her instruction, he slipped it over his own body, inch by inch, feeling it mold to him with an unnatural warmth. The skin clung to him tightly, sinking into his flesh, merging until it felt as though he'd never had any other skin at all. He looked down at his hands, marveling at how powerful he felt, how his senses seemed sharper, clearer.

But as he left, that warm feeling turned prickly, like an itch he couldn't scratch. A faint growling began somewhere in his mind, a voice that wasn't his, something dark and feral curling up from inside him.

In the days that followed, the changes started slowly. His sense of smell grew unnaturally strong. The sounds of the city – traffic, voices, distant music – became oppressive, their edges harsh and grating. His temper frayed, snapping at the smallest things, an irrational fury simmering under his skin that he couldn't control.

Then the memories started.

Flashes of dark forests under the moonlight, the taste of iron-rich blood, the scent of wet fur. Faces he didn't recognize, some screaming, others torn and limp in his hands. He'd catch glimpses in mirrors of something *else* in his eyes – golden, bestial, a creature pacing just beneath the surface, waiting to break through.

One night, unable to shake the restless energy coursing through him, he found himself at the edge of a park, staring up at the full moon. His hands shook as that foreign, furious voice returned, louder, clawing at the edges of his mind, demanding release. He doubled over, a low growl slipping from his lips, his skin crawling as though it didn't quite fit. Then, in a flash of violent agony, his bones cracked, his muscles tore, and he felt himself shift into something monstrous, something *hungry*.

As he tore through the darkened park, his mind fractured into shards of memories he didn't own, a life he didn't understand. The memories belonged to Rory, and they were bleeding into him with every howl, every clawed swipe through the night.

And the worst part? Somewhere, deep inside him, he felt Rory's presence. The original owner of the skin was there, his spirit melded to the flesh, his fury spreading like a contagion. Rory's thoughts and memories pressed against Evan's, a mind driven by the same bloodthirsty instinct that now consumed him. Trapped in a skin that didn't belong to him, Evan realized the truth: *the skin came with a soul attached.*

Every transformation brought him closer to Rory, to the monster lurking just beneath the surface. And there was nothing he could do to stop it – no way to peel away the horror stitched to him like a second soul.

On the next full moon, when the wolf took over completely, Evan felt his mind slip away, disappearing beneath the tide of Rory's wrath. The wolf ran wild, tearing through the city streets, each snarl and bite an act of vengeance, a punishment for whoever wore this stolen skin.

As the Skin Traders had promised, Rory's skin had granted a new life… only it was Rory's, relentless and cursed, reborn again and again in an endless night.

* * *

The woman in the pale green coat ran her fingers across the bristling pelt as her assistant, a jittery young man, watched her work with a mix of awe and unease.

"So, uh… what exactly are you doing with that?" he asked, eyeing the fur as though it might bite.

"Ah, Callum," she replied, her voice soft, almost reverent. "This isn't just any fur. This is *alive*. Feel it." She lifted the edge of the thick pelt toward him, her fingers guiding his hand onto the surface.

He winced as his hand brushed against the coarse hair, recoiling when he felt the faint, almost inaudible *rumble* beneath his fingers, as if it held a heartbeat. "It's like… it's like it's angry."

"It is," she said, a smile twitching at the corners of her mouth. "This fur remembers. It remembers the freedom of the forest, the thrill of the hunt." She lifted the pelt delicately, examining it in the low light. "The fury of its owner lives within every hair."

He glanced around the room nervously. "But… what's the point? No one's going to wear… well, *that*."

"Oh, they will." She chuckled, unfurling the fur with a graceful twist, laying it flat on the workbench. "Collectors, thrill-seekers… those who crave power, even just a taste of it. They'll wear it, Callum. And they'll *pay*." She picked up a pair of shears, slicing through the fur with careful precision.

Callum watched as she began stitching the pieces into grotesque shapes. "So… gloves? Boots? You're turning that—" he nodded to the fur "—into… accessories?"

The woman arched an eyebrow, her fingers working steadily, threading the dark sinewy thread through each piece. "Not accessories, Callum. *Instruments*. These claws, these fangs – when worn, they give a taste of the hunt, a glimpse of the darkness." She held up a pair of clawed gloves, the fingertips long and sharp, dark as night. "And those foolish enough to put these on will understand what it means to *be hunted*."

He shifted, uncomfortable. "Is that… is that safe? I mean, for the customers?"

She laughed, the sound rich and indulgent. "Oh, safe? Hardly. This isn't for the safe and the sane. Those who wear it will feel Rory's memories press against their minds – the thrill, the fury, the bloodlust." She paused, examining the gloves in her hands. "And maybe… just a touch of his madness."

"So… they'll want a refund?" he asked with a nervous grin, only half-joking.

"They usually do." She smiled back, but there was a knowing look in her eyes. "They come back, clutching the fur with trembling hands, pale and rattled. They beg for their money, desperate to rid themselves of the thing." She set down the gloves, tying a ribbon around the grotesque pieces and tucking them into a sleek black box. "But by then, the fur has already taken what it wanted."

Callum blinked. "Taken what?"

"Ah," she said softly, gazing at the fur with something close to fondness. "It feeds on them, bit by bit. They leave their humanity in every clawed grip, every step in those boots. Rory's rage grows stronger each time."

He swallowed, glancing down at the fur in the box. "So… why do you take it back?"

"Because the fur always returns, Callum," she said simply, fastening the box with care. "It's *hungry*. It remembers him, piece by piece." She glanced at the gloves with a satisfied gleam in her eye. "Someday, it might even be whole again."

The assistant took a step back, watching as she placed the box neatly on the shelf. "What if… what if someone keeps it?" he asked, voice trembling.

"Oh, dear," she murmured, a hint of a smile dancing on her lips. "Then they're Rory's for good."

* * *

The first customer who wore a glove crafted from Rory's fur didn't know what was inside it, of course. But the moment the glove touched his skin, Rory's rage seeped into the customer's veins. A twisted echo of Rory's memories flooded their mind: nights spent racing through shadowed forests, the coppery taste of blood, the intoxicating power of the hunt. And always, that same savage fury that had burned inside him – now amplified by the tortures he had endured.

The glove was returned, along with the boots and the hood, every customer fleeing from the darkness that seemed to crawl up from the fur itself. The Skin Traders would reclaim each piece, watching with a bemused smile as their creation grew stronger with each attempt to wear it. But Rory's spirit, his fragmented soul, wasn't just growing stronger – it was learning, adapting.

Piece by piece, each item stored on the shelves of the Skin Traders' back room began to pulse with something like life. The fur held his wrath, his bitterness; it felt the humiliation and pain of betrayal and longing for the wild. And somewhere in the depths of that fragmented consciousness,

Rory remembered who he was. He remembered each moonlit hunt, each breath of the wild night air.

So, each piece of fur lay in wait, biding its time, knowing that one day, another unwitting customer would place it on, and Rory would seize the opportunity. But he wouldn't settle for mere glimpses into his past, nor for the borrowed moments he snatched through the minds of others.

Rory, scattered across gloves, boots, and hood, waited for his soul to pull itself back together, stitch by stitch. And when it did, he would return – not as the man they had taken, nor as the werewolf he once was.

But as something far, far darker.

It began in the dark, slowly, on the shelf where Rory's pieces lay, each fragment of his stolen pelt folded and packed away in black silk. The gloves, the boots, the hood – all stored neatly among the trinkets and cursed wares in the back of the Skin Traders' shop. But this night, as the air grew thick and the moon rose high, a tremor pulsed through the fur. It began as a faint hum, a vibration that made the shelves shake, rippling through each piece as though something inside them had woken up.

The gloves twitched, fingers curling of their own accord. The boots shifted, heels clicking softly against the wood. And in the hood, a pair of hollow eyes seemed to blink open, two pinpricks of a deep, bestial gold glinting in the empty sockets. Threads of sinew began to unravel, reaching out, creeping toward one another, finding their way like roots in the soil. The leather bindings snapped, and each piece drifted toward the others, defying gravity, drawn together by some dark, unbreakable force.

With a shuddering pull, the pieces fused, the fur re-knitting, each thread finding its place, binding tighter than before. The pelt became whole again, a monstrous patchwork, the fur alive with all the memories, rage, and stolen fears of those who had dared to wear it. The coarse, bristling hairs rose as if stirred by a phantom wind, and the thing that was Rory took its first ragged breath.

A low, guttural growl echoed in the silence, filling the shop with the smell of blood and earth and damp fur. His muscles stretched under his reformed skin, a body born anew from every piece that had been sold, worn, and returned. Rory's memories, once fractured and scattered, surged back to him – each stolen moment, each dark thrill, each scream he had tasted.

The pelt stretched, filling out with sinew and flesh, a twisted, snarling wolf-man shape that shifted between human and beast, something forged from both but belonging to neither. And as he rose from the shelf, Rory flexed his claws, feeling the strength that had been torn from him now reforged, reborn.

Rory's golden eyes, slit-pupiled and sharp as broken glass, scanned the room, landing on the narrow door that led out into the shop. He sniffed the air, catching the faint scent of the woman in the green coat – her, the one who had ordered his skin stripped and scattered.

"Time to finish what you started," he snarled, his voice a guttural rasp, half-human, half-beast. With a low, menacing growl, he stalked forward, leaving nothing but darkness in his wake.

* * *

When he found the woman in the green coat in the front of the shop, she was leaning over the counter, cataloging her new wares with her usual, detached elegance. She didn't hear him at first, but Callum did, looking up just in time to see the hulking shadow filling the doorway.

"Wh—what is that?" Callum stammered, backing away, his eyes widening in horror as Rory's massive, furred shape emerged from the darkness.

The woman in the green coat turned, her face paling. "It can't be…" she whispered, her voice barely audible.

Rory's lip curled, revealing rows of sharp, glistening teeth. "Oh, but it is."

Before she could respond, Callum bolted for the door, but Rory's clawed hand shot out, gripping him by the throat. He lifted the boy off the ground with an ease that sent a thrill through his reformed body. Callum's terrified eyes met Rory's, his lips moving in a silent plea, but Rory tightened his grip, savoring the look of pure, helpless fear.

"That's right," he growled, his voice rumbling through the room. "Fear. That's what you gave me, isn't it? What you all gave me." And with a flick of his wrist, he threw Callum to the ground, leaving him motionless, his eyes wide and empty.

The woman stumbled back, her expression now twisted in horror, her lips trembling as she searched for words. But Rory only stalked forward, the faint scent of blood filling his senses as he closed the gap between them.

She tried to back away, tried to speak, but his voice cut through the air, low and venomous.

"You thought I'd stay broken, didn't you?" he snarled, crouching down so his face was inches from hers. "Thought you'd strip me of everything, tear me into parts, sell me like some… product. But every time someone slipped on a piece of me, I took something back. A little fear, a little pain, a little anger. You thought you'd turned me into scraps. But you only made me stronger."

She opened her mouth to scream, but his claws were on her throat, silencing her, forcing her to meet his blazing, golden gaze.

"You wore a piece of me yourself, didn't you?" he murmured, his voice almost gentle. "Just once… to show it off, to make a sale. And in that moment, I felt you – your emptiness, your greed, your hunger." He bared his teeth in a twisted smile. "You took me apart, bit by bit. Now I wear you."

He loosened his grip just enough for her to gasp, to take a shuddering breath, her eyes wide with the dawning realization of what he'd become.

"Fear…" he said, voice low, almost like a chant, "when it festers, becomes armor. Pain becomes strength. And anger – oh, anger becomes purpose."

Her face went slack, her eyes glistening with the terror he'd craved.

"You thought you'd sell me off, thought I'd disappear into the lives of those foolish enough to try me on." He leaned closer, his breath hot against her cheek. "But now, I wear *you*, every last one of you who thought they could own me. You thought you'd stay safe, untouched. You thought wrong."

And as she choked, her final breath slipping from her, he watched her with satisfaction, each piece of himself reveling in her terror. The light faded from her eyes, leaving her lifeless and broken, and Rory rose, his form a shadowed giant of fur, flesh, and rage.

He looked down at her still body, a cold satisfaction settling over him.

"Remember this," he whispered to the silence, his voice carrying a twisted sense of triumph. "I'm not just what you made me. I'm everything you'll never escape."

And with that, he turned and slipped into the shadows, leaving nothing behind but the faint, metallic scent of blood and the memory of the creature they had tried – and failed – to destroy.

Madame Bisclavret

Natasha Marshall

MADAME BISCLAVRET was going to steal her husband's skin.

She did not know what possessed her to do it. She knew that when she followed him into the woods, he would appear before her not as a man, but as a wolf-man: a *werewolf*, he'd called himself, when he'd revealed to her his deepest truth. When she looked upon him, that was exactly what she saw. In place of the man she had loved so much, there stood a wolf with a human physicality, switching between running on all fours and standing on his hind legs. He was much larger than any hunting dog she'd ever seen. And his eyes were a wolf's amber, but there was humanity in them – she could tell he was looking straight at her, almost *through* her, into her soul.

She had expected to be afraid of him in this form. She had not expected what was actually happening inside of her – the primal, deep twisting in her gut that drove her towards the betrayal she was about to commit.

Her dear Bisclavret trusted her, and perhaps that had been his mistake. But why would he not? She was a good wife. She was beautiful, kind, and devoted. She cooked and cleaned and tended to all matters of the house. She did all of the things a good wife and companion would do, and he cared for her deeply.

And yet, she hesitated not for a moment as she crept up to the bush in which he hid his human clothes. She grabbed his tunic and his pants, both a deep brown color, and tucked them into her arms. Instinctively, she brought the fabric up to her nose and breathed deep. They smelled like warm skin and dirt, which made her feel a strange sadness.

A branch broke behind her, and she whipped her head around to look. Two amber eyes, halfway between man and wolf, stared at her. Even with such an animalistic face, she could see the pain she'd wrought on her poor Bisclavret. And yet still, she turned away from him, and, clutching his clothes as tightly as possible, she ran. His last words to her rang in her ears the whole way home.

"My dearest wife, I must share with you my secret. Each month, I go into the wild and become a werewolf. I am ashamed of this, and wish for no one to know. But in my love for you, I will bring you to the woods with me so that you may see I speak the truth. I only ask that you do not touch my clothes, for without them, I may not return to my human form."

When she reached the house, she threw open the door and leapt inside. She locked it tight behind her and peered out the window. She found nothing. Bisclavret had not followed her home.

She leaned against the door and slid onto the floor, clutching Bisclavret's clothes up to her face. As she cried, her tears seeped into the fabric. The scent of the salt mixed with the scent of Bisclavret, and she knew she would never forget the smell for as long as she lived.

Madame Bisclavret fell asleep there on the floor, cuddling up close to the clothes, Bisclavret's human skin that she'd stolen away. In her dreams she saw the world through amber eyes, running wild with the body of a wolf. It was the most at peace she'd ever felt.

* * *

Madame Bisclavret married another. She was no fool, and she knew there was no good life for her as a widow. Her new husband adored her deeply, and she told herself that she was happy. She had freed herself of the terror of the werewolf who had shared her last bed. She was safe now, and all was well.

"You are the most beautiful woman in all the world," her new husband told her often. "It is a shame that you were once widowed, but I feel so fortunate to share your heart now."

Fortunate was a strange word, she thought. Her husband felt fortunate, and she certainly should have as well. Not all women got the opportunity to remarry, much less to a man who loved them so wholeheartedly. But she felt, often, that the most fortunate person she'd ever met was Bisclavret, though she knew he suffered.

Her dreams haunted her. Sometimes, she had night terrors where Bisclavret caught her on her run away from the woods, ripping her body apart with his sharp canine teeth. Other times, she dreamt that she killed him, tearing into his wolf-body with a knife before tossing his clothes away into a fire to be destroyed forever. But the dream that returned most often was the one she'd had on that fateful night. Over and over again, in her sleep, she watched the world through the amber eyes of a wolf. She howled and ran free in the woods, her body free of clothing, the wind on her back. When she awoke from this dream, she shed more tears than she did for any of the night terrors.

Her husband was often away at court, and for this she was grateful. She appreciated his company and the life he provided her. But when he was around, she had to hide away the part of herself that she'd discovered through her betrayal of Bisclavret.

The very first day after she'd stolen Bisclavret's clothes, she tucked them away under his side of the bed. She spent the whole day feeling ill, as if her body was yearning for some sort of remedy she could not find. The air seemed thinner than usual, and she often found herself doubling over and gasping for breath. She could not help but constantly kneel on the floor next to the bed, running her fingers over the fabric of Bisclavret's clothes over and over again.

That night, she decided to try something. She pulled Bisclavret's clothes back out and donned them herself. When the moon was high, she stepped out into the cool night air. The breeze brushed past her face but she shivered, not from the chill, but from anticipation. Would she, too, be able to transform, to run wild and free as a wolf in the wood?

Her body did not change. Desperate for a kind of freedom she could not taste, she instead walked forward into the high grass. She dropped to her knees and realized that in these clothes, she could feel the air and the earth so much more freely than in any of her tunics or dresses. She dug her fingers into the ground and brought a chunk of wet soil up to her nose. Her hands smelled like her last memory of Bisclavret – dirt and skin.

She fell back into the grass and laughed and laughed, until the sounds grew so loud they became a howl.

Madame Bisclavret had the sense to keep this behavior from her new husband, though each day she went without feeling the pure earth on her body, she felt like she was suffocating. When her husband left to attend the king's court, she would kiss him goodbye and put on a solemn air, telling him to hurry home to be back with her. But she was always glad, for when she was alone, she was free to spend her nights donning the stolen clothes. She would walk out into the woods with them, lay in the grass with them, sleep in them. Sometimes, she would even go out to the market with a dress on, but don the clothes underneath her own. Any time that fabric was touching her skin, she found it infinitely easier to breathe.

Many months passed like this, with Madame Bisclavret counting down the days until her husband would leave for court. But the most recent time he returned home, her husband greeted her with a great excitement in his eyes.

"My dearest wife, I have the most incredible story to tell you. The king has found himself the strangest companion."

Madame Bisclavret smiled. As much as she preferred her solitude, she did enjoy hearing her husband's tales of court drama.

"Tell me more!" she said.

"He has a wolf by his side! But it is not a normal wolf. This one has a human-like intelligence about him, as if he understands everything the king says to him. He has an odd physicality as well. His shoulders hunch forward and he seems more comfortable sitting back on his haunches, imitating the way the king himself sits."

Madame Bisclavret's smile faltered. She looked down at her hands. There was dirt under her fingernails.

"Pray, dear husband, tell me – what do his eyes look like?"

"They are the amber eyes of a wolf. But of course, when he looks at you, you really feel as though he is looking *through* you."

Madame Bisclavret's heart quickened. Her husband grabbed her shoulders.

"Are you well? You look pale, dear."

"It is just… a very interesting story. If I may, I would love to accompany you to court the next time you go, so I may meet this wolf you speak of."

Her husband considered this for a moment, but then nodded.

"Very well. I plan to return to court next week. Prepare your finest outfit, and I will prepare for us to make the journey together."

Madame Bisclavret had never been so thankful for her husband. She spent the next few days mentally preparing for what would await her at court. And though she still had her night terrors and amber-eyed dreams, she slept more soundly these nights than she had in a long, long time.

* * *

When Madame Bisclavret arrived at court, she was greeted kindly by the various knights and noblemen who had previously fraternized with her husband. They called her beautiful, comely, kind. She smiled back at them, but their compliments barely penetrated past the surface of her skin.

She scanned the crowd, searching for her husband. But he had faded into the sea of people, all wearing the same courtly clothing, standing in the same practiced posture. She walked closer to the dais instead, preparing to be as close to the king and his companions as she possibly could.

Suddenly, everyone turned toward the grand doors at the entrance of the throne room. The king, flanked by guards, walked down the aisle. Along with the others, Madame Bisclavret bowed, but her attention was not really on the king at all. She was focused instead on the wolf that trotted behind him.

The wolf was larger than any dog she'd ever seen, walking with a strangely human gait. He looked as if he wanted to step onto his hind legs but knew he should not. And when he finally reached the throne, settling himself on the ground beside it, she looked into his eyes. Those amber, all-knowing eyes.

It was Bisclavret.

As soon as he met her eyes, he launched off the dais and ran straight for Madame Bisclavret, knocking her to the ground. He leaned down and snarled right in her face, his amber eyes narrowing.

A guard sprinted over and grabbed him by the scruff, pulling him back. He went to strike Bisclavret, but the king leapt to his feet.

"Halt! This wolf has never shown violence towards anyone except this woman. I believe she must have wronged my dear companion."

Madame Bisclavret sat up, and saw the king was looking at her with severe distrust. Bisclavret stalked back over to the king and sat at his feet. The king pet him gently on the head, and Bisclavret nuzzled into his hand.

"Take her to the dungeons and question her. If she has harmed this wolf, she will be punished."

She did not fight when the guards came and grabbed her arms, dragging her away. She heard her husband cry out for her, but she did not turn back to look at him. To go into the dungeons, to have her time alone with Bisclavret, was something she knew she needed to do.

* * *

Her cell was cold and smelled like damp rocks. They locked her up and left her alone for hours, giving her endless time to regret how easily she'd complied with the king's order. She tucked herself away in the corner, hugging her knees as close to her body as she could get them. Perhaps if she made herself small enough, she would disappear, and all of this would end as fast as it had begun.

She heard the footsteps of a guard approaching, followed by the clicking of four clawed paws behind him. The guard came and knocked on the bars of the cell. Bisclavret stayed close behind him, his teeth bared.

"I invite you to speak the truth on how you have wronged the king's wolf companion. If you refuse to speak, I will let him into this cage to have his way with you."

She was about to open her mouth, but she paused. She had more to gain by letting Bisclavret in. She tucked herself even closer to the wall, staying silent.

"Speak, woman!" the guard yelled, banging his hand again on the bars of the cell. But again, Madame Bisclavret said nothing.

"Fine. You have made your choice. The beast will have his turn with you now."

True to his word, the guard unlocked the cell door just wide enough for Bisclavret to slip through. Madame Bisclavret turned to look at his wolfish form. Bisclavret stalked up to her, his teeth bared. His earlier urgency had been replaced with a slow, simmering anger.

"Bisclavret," she whispered. He actually *whined* in response. It had been over a year since she had betrayed him – a year since anyone would have called him by his name.

"I don't expect forgiveness," she continued, "but I need you to know how sorry I am."

Bisclavret growled at her. But she went on.

"I understand now how painful it is to be locked into a body that does not answer to your wishes. Since I saw you in this form, all I have wished for was to follow behind you and to run free and wild. But I took your freedom and yourself away from you. And I will carry the regret and sorrow as long as I breathe."

She crawled forward on her knees, sliding her dress off her shoulders as she moved. Underneath, she was wearing Bisclavret's clothes.

"I am here to right that wrong," she said. "Take these, and be free."

He leaned forward and sniffed the fabric on her torso. He bowed his head down, whimpering. She knew he was crying in the only way he could.

She put her hand under his furry chin and raised his head so that his eyes met her own.

"I do not deserve it, but if you would, I would beg you to help me be free, too."

His eyes softened, and she knew that he understood. He had woken the spirit of the wolf hidden inside of her, and he was the only one who could give her this gift.

Bisclavret lunged forward and tackled her. He was still for a brief moment, scanning her face. And then he let out a howl and dove down, his teeth ripping apart the flesh of her nose, leaving bite marks and bruises and blood in their wake. When he pulled back, she did not even register the pain. She only laughed. He had done it. She could feel the change instantly.

She sat up and disrobed, unbuttoning his clothes and laying them on the ground before him. He took them in his lupine mouth and made for the cage door, pawing at the bars to get the guard's attention. When the guard let him out, he snuck off into a dark corner.

The guard walked into the cell and pulled Madame Bisclavret up, leading her out. But as quickly as he took her arm, he dropped it when he beheld the man who now stood before him in the place of the wolf he'd known minutes before.

"The wrong has been righted, and all is well between us. Now that I have taken back my original form, if I may, I would stay by the king to serve as his companion."

The guard said nothing. He only led the two of them out of the dungeons, back in front of the king. Madame Bisclavret's husband ran to her instantly, and threw his arms around her. But then he took a good look at her face and jumped away. He could tell, too, that she had changed irrevocably.

The king was overjoyed to see Bisclavret in the form of a man. He stood up and pulled the other man into his arms, and kissed his cheek. Bisclavret glanced over his shoulder and smiled at his once-wife, and she felt a settling in her heart. Bisclavret was himself now, completely.

The king allowed Madame Bisclavret and her husband to return home, and so they did. She knew that the deep love her husband had once had for her was fading and would only fade more as she grew into herself. The cuts on her nose would heal, but the memory of the marks would not go away. Her husband would never be able to unsee this version of her, and he could not love her the same. But she found that this thought did not make her sad.

That first night back home, when her husband was fast asleep, she crept outside to breathe in the chilly air with her scarred nose. Something stirred deep inside of her. She shed her clothes and ran out into the woods, laughing all the way.

And finally, her body transformed. She leapt from two feet onto four, running even faster than she knew her body could take her. She howled at the moon, she dug her hairy paws into the dirt, she rolled around and felt the earth all over her body, this body that felt so much more *real* than the one she'd had before. She saw the world through amber eyes.

At last, Madame Bisclavret was free.

Hugues, the Wer-Wolf

Sutherland Menzies

ON THE CONFINES of that extensive forest-tract formerly spreading over so large a portion of the county of Kent, a remnant of which, to this day, is known as the weald of Kent, and where it stretched its almost impervious covert midway between Ashford and Canterbury during the prolonged reign of our second Henry, a family of Norman extraction by name Hugues (or Wulfric, as they were commonly called by the Saxon inhabitants of that district) had, under protection of the ancient forest laws, furtively erected for themselves alone and miserable habitation. And amidst those sylvan fastnesses, ostensibly following the occupation of woodcutters, the wretched outcasts, for such, from some cause or other, they evidently were, had for many years maintained a secluded and precarious existence. Whether from the rooted antipathy still actively cherished against all of that usurping nation from which they derived their origin, or from recorded malpractice by their superstitious Anglo-Saxon neighbours, they had long been looked upon as belonging to the accursed race of wer-wolves, and as such churlishly refused work on the domains of the surrounding franklins or proprietors, so thoroughly was accredited the descent of the original lycanthropic stain transmitted from father to son through several generations. That the Hugues Wulfric reckoned not a single friend among the adjacent homesteads of serf or freedman was not to be wondered at, possessing as they did so unenviable a reputation; for to them was invariably attributed even the misfortunes which chance alone might seem to have given birth. Did midnight fire consume the grange; – did the time-decayed barn, over-stored with an abundant harvest, tumble into ruins; – were the shocks of wheat lain prostrate over the fields by a tempest; – did the smut destroy the grain; – or the cattle perish, decimated by a murrain; – a child sink under some wasting malady; – or a woman give premature birth to her offspring, it was ever the Hugues Wulfric who were openly accused, eyed askance with mingled fear and detestation, the finger of young and old pointing them out with bitter execrations – in fine, they were almost as nearly classed feroe natura as their fabled prototype, and dealt with accordingly.

That woody district, at the period to which our tale belongs, was an immense forest, desolate of inhabitants, and only occupied by wild swine and deer; and though it is now filled with towns and villages and well peopled, the woods that remain sufficiently indicate its former extent.

King Edgar is said to have been the first who attempted to rid England of these animals; criminals even being pardoned by producing a stated number of these creatures' tongues. Some centuries after they increased to such a degree as to become again the object of royal attention; and Edward I appointed persons to extirpate this obnoxious race. It is one of the principal bearings in armoury. Hugh, surnamed Lupus, the first Earl of Kent, bore for his crest a wolf's head.

Terrible, indeed, were the tales told of them round the glowing hearth at eventide, whilst spinning the flax, or plucking the geese; equally affirmed too, in broad daylight, whilst driving the cows to pasturage, and most circumstantially discussed on Sundays between mass and vespers, by the gossip groups collected within Ashford parvyse, with most seasonable admixture of anathema and devout crossings. Witchcraft, larceny, murther, and sacrilege, formed prominent features in the bloody and mysterious scenes of which the Hugues Wulfric were the alleged actors: sometimes they were ascribed to the father, at others to the mother, and even the sister escaped not her share of vilification; fair would they have attributed an atrocious disposition to the unweaned babe, so great, so universal was the horror in which they held that race of Cain! The churchyard at Ashford, and the stone cross, from whence diverged the several roads to London, Canterbury, and Ashford, situated midway between the two latter places, served, so tradition avouched, as nocturnal theatres for the unhallowed deeds of the Wulfrics, who thither prowled by moonlight, it was said, to batten on the freshly-buried dead, or drain the blood of any living wight who might be rash enough to venture among those solitary spots. True it was that the wolves had, during some of the severe winters, emerged from their forest lairs, and, entering the cemetery by a breach in its walls, goaded by famine, had actually disinterred the dead; true was it, also, that the Wolf's Cross, as the hinds commonly designated it, had been stained with gore on one occasion through the fall of a drunken mendicant, who chanced to fracture his skull against a pointed angle of its basement. But these accidents, as well as a multitude of others, were attributed to the guilty intervention of the Wulfrics, under their fiendish guise of wer-wolves.

These poor people, moreover, took no pains to justify themselves from a prejudice so monstrous: full well apprised of what calumny they were the victims, but alike conscious of their impotence to contradict it, they tacitly suffered its infliction, and fled all contact with those to whom they knew themselves repulsive. Shunning the highways, and never venturing to pass through the town of Ashford in open day, they pursued such labour as might occupy them within doors, or in unfrequented places. They appeared not at Canterbury market, never numbered themselves amongst the pilgrims at Becket's far-famed shrine, or assisted at any sport, merry-making, hay-cutting, or harvest home: the priest had interdicted them from all communion with the church – the ale-bibbers from the hostelry.

The primitive cabin which they inhabited was built of chalk and clay, with a thatch of straw, in which the high winds had made huge rents and closed up by a rotten door, exhibiting wide gaps, through which the gusts had free ingress. As this wretched abode was situated at considerable distance from any other, if, perchance, any of the neighbouring serfs strayed within its precincts towards nightfall, their credulous fears made them shun near approach so soon as the vapours of the marsh were seen to blend their ghastly wreaths with the twilight; and as that darkling time drew on which explains the diabolical sense of the old saying, "tween dog and wolf," "twixt hawk and buzzard", at that hour the will-o'-wisps began to glimmer around the dwelling of the Wulfrics, who patriarchally supped – whenever they had a supper – and forthwith betook themselves to their rest.

Sorrow, misery, and the putrid exhalations of the steeped hemp, from which they manufactured a rude and scanty attire, combined eventually to bring sickness and death into the bosom of this wretched family, who, in their utmost extremity, could neither hope for pity or succour. The father was first attacked, and his corpse was scarce cold ere the mother rendered up her breath. Thus passed that fated couple to their account, unsolaced by the consolation of the confessor, or the medicaments of the leech. Hugues Wulfric, their eldest son, himself dug their grave, laid their bodies within it swathed with hempen shreds for grave cloths, and raised a few clods of earth to mark their last resting-place. A hind, who chanced to see him fulfilling this pious duty in the dusk of evening, crossed himself, and fled as fast as his legs would carry him, fully believing that he had assisted at some hellish incantation. When the real event transpired, the neighbouring gossips congratulated one another upon the double mortality, which they looked upon as the tardy chastisement of heaven: they spoke of ringing the bells, and singing masses of thanks for such an action of grace.

It was All Souls' eve, and the wind howled along the bleak hillside, whistling drearily through the naked branches of the forest trees, whose last leaves it had long since stripped; the sun had disappeared; a dense and chilling fog spread through the air like the mourning veil of the widowed, whose day of love hath early fled. No star shone in the still and murky sky. In that lonely hut, through which death had so lately passed, the orphan survivors held their lonely vigil by the fitful blaze emitted by the reeking logs upon their hearth. Several days had elapsed since their lips had been imprinted for the last time upon the cold hands of their parents; several dreary nights had passed since the sad hour in which their eternal farewell had left them desolate on earth.

Poor lone ones! Both, too, in the flower of their youth – how sad, yet how serene did they appear amid their grief! But what sudden and mysterious terror is it that seems to overcome them? It is not, alas! The first time since they were left alone upon earth that they have found themselves at this hour of the night by their deserted hearth, enlivened of old by the cheerful tales of their mother. Full often had they wept together over her memory, but never yet had their solitude proved so appalling; and, pallid as very spectres, they tremblingly gazed upon one another as the flickering ray from the wood-fire played over their features.

"Brother! Heard you not that loud shriek which every echo of the forest repeated? It sounds to me as if the ground were ringing with the tread of some gigantic phantom, and whose breath seems to have shaken the door of our hut. The breath of the dead they say is icy cold. A mortal shivering has come over me."

"And I, too, sister, thought I heard voices as it were at a distance, murmuring strange words. Tremble not thus – am I not beside you?"

"Oh, brother! Let us pray the Holy Virgin, to the end that she may restrain the departed from haunting our dwelling."

"But, perhaps, our mother is amongst them: she comes, unshrived and unshrouded, to visit her forlorn offspring – her well-beloved! For, knowest thou not, sister, 'tis the eve on which the dead forsake their tombs. Let us open the door, that our mother may enter and resume her wonted place by hearthstone."

"Oh, brother, how gloomy is all without doors, how damp and cold the gust sweeps by. Hearest thou, what groans the dead are uttering round our hut? Oh, close the door, in heaven's name!"

"Take courage, sister, I have thrown upon the fire that holy branch, plucked as it flowered on last palm Sunday, which thou knowest will drive away all evil spirits, and now our mother can enter alone."

"But how will she look, brother? They say the dead are horrible to gaze upon; that their hair has fallen away; their eyes become hollow; and that, in walking, their bones rattle hideously. Will our mother, then, be thus?"

"No; she will appear with the features we loved to behold; with the affectionate smile that welcomes us home from our perilous labours; with the voice which, in early youth, sought us when, belated, the closing night surprised its far from our dwelling."

The poor girl busied herself awhile in arranging a few platters of scanty fare upon the tottering board which served them for a table; and this last pious offering of filial love, as she deemed it, appeared accomplished only by the greatest and last effort, so enfeebled had her frame become.

"Let our dearly-beloved mother enter then," she exclaimed, sinking exhausted upon the settle. "I have prepared her evening meal, that she may not be angry with me, and all is arranged as she was wont to have it. But what ails thee, my brother, for now thou tremblest as I did awhile agone?"

"See'st thou not, sister, those pale lights which are rising at a distance across the marsh? They are the dead coming to seat themselves before the repast prepared for then. Hark! list to the funeral tones of the Allhallowtide bells, as they come upon the gale, blended with their hollow voices. – Listen, listen!"

On this eve formally the Catholic church performed a most solemn office for the repose of the dead.

"Brother, this horror grows insupportable. This, I feel, of a verity, will be my last night upon earth! And is there no word of hope to cheer me, mingling with those fearful sounds? Oh, mother! Mother!"

"Hush, sister, hush I see'st thou now the ghastly lights which herald the dead, gleaming athwart the horizon? Hearest thou the prolonged tolling of the bell? They come! They come!"

"Eternal repose to their ashes!" exclaimed the bereaved ones, sinking upon their knees, and bowing down their heads in the extremity of terror and lamentation; and as they uttered the words, the door was at the same moment closed with violence, as though it had been slammed to by a vigorous hand. Hugues started to his feet, for the cracking of the timber which supported the roof seemed to announce the fall of the frail tenement; the fire was suddenly extinguished, and a plaintive groan mingled itself with the blast that whistled through the crevices of the door. On raising his sister, Hugues found that she too was no longer to be numbered among the living.

Hugues, on becoming the head of his family, composed of two sisters younger than himself, saw them likewise descend into the grave in the short space of a fortnight; and when he had laid the last within her parent earth, he hesitated whether he should not extend himself beside them, and share their peaceful slumber. It was not by tears and sobs that grief so profound as his manifested itself, but in a mute and sullen contemplation over the supulture of his kindred and his own future happiness. During three consecutive nights he wandered, pale and haggard, from his solitary hut, to prostrate himself and kneel by turns upon the funeral turf. For three days food had not passed his lips.

Winter had interrupted the labours of the woods and fields, and Hugues had presented himself in vain among the neighbouring domains to obtain a few days' employment to thresh grain, cut wood, or drive the plough; no one would employ him from fear of drawing upon himself the fallity attached to all bearing the name of Wulfric. He met with brutal denials at all hands, and not only were these accompanied by taunts and menace, but dogs were let loose upon him to rend his limbs; they deprived him even of the alms accorded to beggars by profession; in short, he found himself overwhelmed with injuries and scorn.

Was he, then, to expire of inanition or deliver himself from the tortures of hunger by suicide? He would have embraced that means, as a last and only consolation, had he not been retained earthward to struggle with his dark fate by a feeling of love. Yes, that abject being, forced in very desperation, against his better self, to abhor the human species in the abstract, and to feel a savage joy in waging war against it; that paria who scarce longer felt confidence in that heaven which seemed an apathetic witness of his woes; that man so isolated from those social relations which alone compensate us for the toils and troubles of life, without other stay than that afforded by his conscience, with no other fortune in prospect than the bitter existence and miserable death of his departed kin: worn to the bone by privation and sorrow, swelling with rage and resentment, he yet consented to live – to cling to life; for, strange – he loved! But for that heaven-sent ray gleaming across his thorny path, a pilgrimage so lone and wearisome would he have gladly exchanged for the peaceful slumber of the grave.

Hugues Wulfric would have been the finest youth in all that part of Kent, were it not that the outrages with which he had so unceasingly to contend, and the privations he was forced to undergo, had effaced the colour from his cheeks, and sunk his eyes deep in their orbits: his brows were habitually contracted, and his glance oblique and fierce. Yet, despite that recklessness and anguish which clouded his features, one, incredulous of his atrocities, could not have failed to admire the savage beauty of his head, cast in nature's noblest mould, crowned with a profusion of waving hair, and set upon shoulders whose robust and harmonious proportions were discoverable through the tattered attire investing them. His carriage was firm and majestic; his motions were not without a species of rustic grace, and the tone of his naturally soft voice accorded admirably with the purity in which he spoke his ancestral language – the Norman-French: in short, he differed so widely from people of his imputed condition that one is constrained to believe that jealousy or prejudice must originally have been no stranger to the malicious persecution of which he was the object. The women alone ventured first to pity his forlorn condition, and endeavoured to think of him in a more favourable light.

Branda, niece of Willieblud, the flesher of Ashford, had, among other, of the town maidens, noticed Hugues with a not unfavouring eye, as she chanced to pass one day on horseback, through a coppice near the outskirts of the town, into which the latter had been led by the eager chase of a wild hog, and which animal, from the nature of the country was, single-handed, exceedingly difficult of capture. The malignant falsehoods of the ancient crones, continually buzzed in her ears, in nowise diminished the advantageous opinion she had conceived of this ill-treated and good-looking wer-wolf. She sometimes, indeed, went so far as to turn considerably out of her way, in order to meet and exchange his cordial greeting: for Hugues, recognizing the attention of which he had now become the object, had, in his turn, at last summoned up courage to survey more leisurely the pretty Branda; and the result was that he found her as buxom and pretty a lass as, in his hitherto restricted rambles out of the forest, his timorous gaze had ever encountered. His gratitude increased proportionally; and at the moment when his domestic losses came one after another to overwhelm him, he was actually on the eve of making Branda, on the first opportunity presenting itself, an avowal of the love he bore her.

It was chill winter – Christmas-tide – the distant roll of the curfew had long ceased, and all the inhabitants of Ashford were safe housed in their tenements for the night. Hugues, solitary, motionless, silent, his forehead grasped between his hands, his gaze dully faced upon the decaying brands that feebly glimmered upon his hearth: he heeded not the cutting north wind, whose sweeping gusts shook the crazy roof, and whistled through the chinks of the door; he started not at the harsh cries of the herons fighting for prey in the marsh, nor at the dismal croaking of the ravens perched over his smoke-vent. He thought of his departed kindred, and imagined that his hour to join them would soon be at hand; for the intense cold congealed the marrow of his bones, and fell hunger gnawed and twisted his entrails. Yet, at intervals, would a recollection of nascent love, of Branda, suddenly appease his else intolerable anguish, and cause a faint smile to gleam across his wan features.

"Oh, blessed Virgin! Grant that my sufferings may speedily cease!" murmured he, despairingly. "Oh, would I might be a wer-wolf, as they call me! I could then requite them for all the foul wrong done me. True, I could not nourish myself with their flesh; I would not shed their blood; but I would be able to terrify and torment those who have wrought my parents' and sisters' death – who have persecuted our family even to extermination! Why have I not the power to change my nature into that of a wolf, if, of a verity, my ancestors possessed it, as they avouch? I should at least find carrion to devour, and not die thus horribly. Branda is the sole being in this world who cares for me; and that conviction alone reconciles me to life!"

Horseflesh was an article of food among our Saxon forefathers in England.

Hugues gave free current to these gloomy reflections. The smouldering embers now emitted but a feeble and vacillating light, faintly struggling with the surrounding gloom, and Hugues felt the horror of darkness coming strong upon him; frozen with the ague-fit one instant, and troubled the next by the hurried pulsation of his veins, he arose, at last, to seek some fuel, and threw upon the fire a heap of faggot-chips, heath and straw, which soon raised a clear and crackling flame. His stock of wood had become exhausted, and, seeking wherewith to replenish his dying hearth-light, whilst foraging under the rude oven amongst a pile of rubbish placed there by his mother wherewith to bake bread – handles of tools, fractured joint-stools, and cracked platters, he discovered a chest rudely covered with a dressed hide, and which he had never seen before; and seizing upon it as though he had discovered a treasure, broke open the lid, strongly secured by a string.

This chest, which had evidently remained long unopened, contained the complete disguise of a wer-wolf: a dyed sheepskin, with gloves in the form of paws, a tail, a mask with an elongated muzzle, and furnished with formidable rows of yellow horse-teeth.

Hugues started backwards, terrified at his discovery – so opportune, that it seemed to him the work of sorcery; then, on recovering from his surprise, he drew forth one by one the several pieces of this strange envelope, which had evidently seen some service, and from long neglect had become somewhat damaged. Then rushed confusedly upon his mind the marvellous recitals made him by his grandfather, as he nursed him upon his knees during earliest childhood; tales, during the narration of which his mother wept silently, as he laughed heartily. In his mind there was a mingled strife of feelings and purposes alike undefinable. He continued his silent examination of this criminal heritage, and by degrees his imagination grew bewildered with vague and extravagant projects.

Hunger and despair conjointly hurried him away: he saw objects no longer save through a bloody prism: he felt his very teeth on edge with an avidity for biting; he experienced an inconceivable desire to run: he set himself to howl as though he had practised wer-wolfery all his life, and began thoroughly to invest himself with the guise and attributes of his novel vocation. A more startling change could scarcely have been wrought in him, had that so horribly grotesque metamorphosis really been the effect of enchantment; aided, too, as it was, by the, fever which generated a temporary insanity in his frenzied brain.

Scarcely did he thus find himself travestied into a wer-wolf through the influence of his vestment, ere he darted forth from the hut, through the forest and into the open country, white with hoar frost, and across which the bitter north wind swept, howling in a frightful manner and traversing the meadows, fallows, plains, and marshes, like a shadow. But, at that hour, and during such a season, not a single belated wayfarer was there to encounter Hugues, whom the sharpness of the air, and the excitation of his course, had worked up to the highest pitch of extravagance and audacity: he howled the louder proportionally as his hunger increased.

Suddenly the heavy rumbling of an approaching vehicle arrested his attention; at first with indecision, then with a stupid fixity, he struggled with two suggestions, counselling him at one and the same time to fly and to advance. The carriage, or whatever it might be, continued, rolling towards him; the night was not so obscure but that he was enabled to distinguish the tower of Ashford church at a short distance off, and hard by which stood a pile of unhewn stone, destined either for the execution of some repair, or addition to the saintly edifice, in the shade of which he ran to crouch himself down, and so await the arrival of his prey.

It proved to be the covered cart of Willieblud, the Ashford flesher, who was wont twice a week to carry meat to Canterbury, and travelled by night in order that he might be among the first at market-opening. Of this Hugues was fully aware, and the departure of the flesher naturally suggested to him the inference that his niece must be keeping house by herself, for our lusty flesher had been long a widower. For an instant he hesitated whether he should introduce himself there, so favourable an opportunity thus presenting itself, or whether he should attack the uncle and seize upon his viands. Hunger got the better of love this once, and the monotonous whistle with which the driver was accustomed to urge forward his sorry jade warning him to be in readiness, he howled in a plaintive tone, and, rushing forward, seized the horse by the bit.

"Willieblud, flesher," said he, disguising his voice, and speaking to him in the lingua Franca of that period, "I hunger; throw me two pounds of meat if thou would'st have me live."

"St. Willifred have mercy on me!" cried the terrified flesher, "is it thou, Hugues Wulfric, of Wealdmarsh, the born wer-wolf?"

"Thou say'st sooth – it is I," replied Hugues, who had sufficient address to avail himself of the credulous superstition of Willieblud; "I would rather have raw meat than eat of thy flesh, plump as thou art. Throw me, therefore, what I crave, and forget not to be ready with the like portion each time thou settest out for Canterbury market; or, failing thereof, I tear thee limb from limb."

Hugues, to display his attributes of a wer-wolf before the gaze of the confounded flesher, had mounted himself upon the spokes of the wheel, and placed his forepaw upon the edge of the cart, which he made semblance of snuffing at with his snout. Willieblud, who believed in wer-wolves as devoutly as he did in his patron saint, had no sooner perceived this monstrous paw, than, uttering a fervent invocation to the latter, he seized upon his daintiest joint of meat, let it fall to the ground, and whilst Hugues sprung eagerly down to pick it up, the butcher at the same instant having bestowed a sudden and violent blow upon the flank of his beast, the latter set off at a round gallop without waiting for any reiterated invitation from the lash.

Hugues was so satisfied with a repast which had cost him far less trouble to procure than any he had long remembered, readily promised himself the renewal of an expedient, the execution of which was at once easy and diverting; for though smitten with the charms of the fair-haired Branda, he not the less found a malicious pleasure in augmenting the terror of her uncle Willieblud. The latter, for a long while, revealed not to a living being the tale of his terrible encounter and strange compact, which had varied according to circumstances, and he submitted unmurmuringly to the imposts levied each time the wer-wolf presented himself before him, without being very nice about either the weight or quality of the meat; he no longer even waited to be asked for it, anything to avoid the sight of that fiend-like form clinging to the side of his cart, or being brought into such immediate contact with that hideous misshapen paw stretched forth, as it were to strangle him, that paw too, which had once been a human hand. He had become dull and thoughtful of late; he set out to market unwillingly, and seemed to dread the hour of departure as it approached, and no longer beguiled the tedium of his nocturnal journey by whistling to his horse, or trolling snatches of ballads, as was his wont formerly; he now invariably returned in a melancholy and restless mood.

Branda, at loss to conceive what had given birth to this new and permanent depression which had taken possession of her uncle's mind, after in vain exhausting conjecture, proceeded to interrogate, importune, and supplicate him by turns, until the unhappy flesher, no longer proof against such continued appeals, at last disburthened himself of the load which he had at heart, by recounting the history of his adventure with the wer-wolf.

Branda listened to the whole of the recital without offering interruption or comment; but, at its close –

"Hugues is no more a wer-wolf than thou or I," exclaimed she, offended that such unjust suspicion should be cherished against one for whom she had long felt more than an interest; "'tis an idle tale, or some juggling device; I fear me thou must needs dream these sorceries, uncle Willieblud, for Hugues of the Wealmarsh, or Wulfric, as the silly fools call him, is worth far more, I trow, than his reputation."

"Girl, it boots not saying me nay, in this matter," replied Willieblud, pertinaciously urging the truth of his story; "the family of Hugues, as everybody knows, were wer-wolves born, and, since they are all of late, by the blessing of heaven, defunct, save one, Hugues now inherits the wolf's paw."

"I tell thee, and will avouch it openly, uncle, that Hugues is of too gentle and seemly a nature to serve Satan, and turn himself into a wild beast, and that will I never believe until I have seen the like."

"Mass, and that thou shalt right speedily, if thou wilt but along with me. In very troth 'tis he, besides, he made confession of his name, and did I not recognize his voice, and am I not ever bethinking me of his knavish paw, which he places me on the shaft while he stays the horse. Girl, he is in league with the foul fiend:

Branda had, to a certain degree, imbibed the superstition in the abstract, equally with her uncle, and, excepting so far as it touched the hitherto, as she believed, traduced being on whom her affections, as if in feminine perversity, had so strangely lighted. Her woman's curiosity, in this instance, less determined her resolution to accompany the flesher on his next journey, than the desire to exculpate her lover, fully believing the strange tale of her kinsman's encounter with, and spoliation by the latter, to be the effect of some illusion, and of which to find him guilty, was the sole fear she experienced on mounting the rude vehicle laden with its ensanguined viands.

It was just midnight when they started from Ashford, the hour alike dear to wer-wolves as to spectres of every denomination. Hugues was punctual at the appointed spot; his howlings, as they drew nigh, though horrible enough, had still something human in them, and disconcerted not a little the doubts of Branda. Willieblud, however, trembled even more than she did, and sought for the wolf's portion; the latter raised himself upon his hind legs, and extended one of his forepaws to receive his pittance as soon as the cart stopped at the heap of stones.

"Uncle, I shall swoon with affright," exclaimed Branda, clinging closely to the flesher, and tremblingly pulling the coverchief over her eyes: "loose rein and smite thy beast, or evil will surely betide us."

"Thou are not alone, gossip," cried Hugues, fearful of a snare; "if thou essay'st to play me false, thou art at once undone."

"Harm us not friend Hugues, thou know'st I weigh not my pounds of meat with thee; I shall take care to keep my troth. It is Branda, my niece, who goes with me tonight to buy wares at Canterbury."

"Branda with thee? By the mass 'tis she indeed, more buxom and rosy too, than ever; come pretty one, descend and tarry awhile, that I may have speech with thee."

"I conjure thee, good Hugues, terrify not so cruelly my poor wench, who is wellnigh dead already with fear; suffer us to; hold our way, for we have far to go, and the morrow is early, market-day."

"Go thy ways then alone, uncle Willieblud, 'tis thy niece I would have speech with, in all courtesy and honour; the which, if thou permittest not readily, and of a good grace, I will rend thee both to death."

All in vain was it that Willieblud exhausted himself in prayers and lamentations in hopes of softening the bloodthirsty wer-wolf, as he believed him to be, refusing as the latter did, every sort of compromise in avoidance of his demand, and at last replying only by horrible threats, which froze the hearts of both. Branda, although especially interested in the debate, neither stirred foot, or opened her mouth, so greatly had terror and surprise overwhelmed her; she kept her eyes fixed upon the wolf, who peered at her likewise through his mask, and felt incapable of offering resistance when she found herself forcibly dragged out of the vehicle, and deposited by an invisible power, as it seemed to her, beside the piles of stones; she swooned without uttering a single scream.

The flesher was no less dumbfounded at the turn which the adventure had taken, and he, too, fell back among his meat as though stricken by a blinding blow; he fancied that the wolf had swept his bushy tail violently across his eyes, and on recovering the use of his senses found himself alone in the cart, which rolled joltingly at a swift pace towards Canterbury. At first he listened, but in vain, for the wind bringing him either the shrieks of his niece, or the howlings of the wolf; but stop his beast he could not, which, panic-stricken, kept trotting as though bewitched, or felt the spur of some fiend pricking her flanks.

Willieblud, however, reached his journey's end in safety, sold his meat, and returned to Ashford, reckoning full sure upon having to say a De Profundis for his niece, whose fate he had not ceased to bemoan during the whole night. But how great was his astonishment to find her safe at home, a little pale, from recent fright and want of sleep, but without a scratch; still more was he astonished to hear that the wolf had done her no injury whatsoever, contenting himself, after she had recovered from her swoon, with conducting her back to their dwelling, and acting in every respect like a loyal suitor, rather than a sanguinary wer-wolf. Willieblud knew not what to think of it.

This nocturnal gallantry towards his niece had additionally irritated the burly Saxon against the wer-wolf, and although the fear of reprisals kept him from making a direct and public attack upon Hugues, he ruminated not the less upon taking some sure and secret revenge; but previous to putting his design into execution, it struck him that he could not do better than relate his misadventures to the ancient sacristan and parish grave-digger of St. Michael's, a worthy of profound sagacity in those sort of matters, endowed with a clerk-like erudition, and consulted as an oracle by all the old crones and lovelorn maidens throughout the township of Ashford and its vicinity.

"Slay a wer-wolf thou canst not," was the repeated rejoinder of the wiseacre to the earnest queries of the tormented flesher; "for his hide is proof against spear or arrow, though vulnerable to the edge of a cutting weapon of steel. I counsel thee to deal him a slight flesh wound, or cut him over the paw, in order to know of a surety whether it really be Hugues or no; thou'lt run no danger, save thou strikest him a blow from which blood flows not therefrom, for, so soon as his skin is severed he taketh flight."

Resolving implicitly to follow the advice of the sacristan, Willieblud that same evening determined to know with what wer-wolf it was with whom he had to do, and with that view hid his cleaver, newly sharpened for the occasion, under the load in his cart, and resolutely prepared to make use of it as a preparatory step towards proving the identity of Hugues with the audacious spoiler of his meat, and eke his peace. The wolf presented himself as usual, and anxiously inquired after Branda, which stimulated the flesher the more firmly to follow out his design.

"Here, Wolf," said Willieblud, stooping down as if to choose a piece of meat; "I give thee double portion tonight; up with thy paw, take toll, and be mindful of my frank alms."

"Sooth, I will remember me, gossip," rejoined our wer-wolf; "but when shall the marriage be solemnized for certain, betwixt the fair Branda and myself?"

Hugues believing he had nothing to fear from the flesher, whose meats he so readily appropriated to himself, and of whose fair niece he hoped shortly no less to make lawful possession; both that he really loved, and viewed his union with her as the surest means of placing him within the pale of that sociality from which he had been so unjustly exiled, could he but succeed in making intercession with the holy fathers of the church to remove their interdict. Hugues placed his extended paw upon the edge of the cart; but instead of handing him his joint of beef, or mutton, Willieblud raised his cleaver, and at a single blow lopped off the paw laid there as fittingly for the purpose as though upon a block. The flesher flung down his weapon, and belaboured his beast, the wer-wolf roared aloud with agony, and disappeared amid the dark shades of the forest, in which, aided by the wind, his howling was soon lost.

The next day, on his return, the flesher, chuckling and laughing, deposited a gory cloth upon the table, among the trenchers with which his niece was busied in preparing his noonday meal, and which, on being opened, displayed to her horrified gaze a freshly severed human hand enveloped in wolf-skin. Branda, comprehending what had occurred, shrieked aloud, shed a flood of tears, and then hurriedly throwing her mantle round her, whilst her uncle amused himself by turning and twitching the hand about with a ferocious delight, exclaiming, whilst he staunched the blood which still flowed:

"The sacristan said sooth; the wer-wolf has his need I trow, at last, and now I wot of his nature, I fear no more his witchcraft."

Although the day was far advanced, Hugues lay writhing in torture upon his couch, his coverings drenched with blood, as well also the floor of his habitation; his countenance of a ghastly pallor, expressed as much moral, as physical pain; tears gushed from beneath his reddened eyelids, and he listened to every noise without, with an increased inquietude, painfully visible upon his distorted features. Footsteps were heard rapidly approaching, the door was hurriedly flung open, and a female threw herself beside his couch, and with mingled sobs and imprecations sought tenderly for his mutilated arm, which, rudely bound round with hempen wrappings, no longer dissembled the absence of its wrist, and from which a crimson stream still trickled. At this piteous spectacle she grew loud in her denunciations against the sanguinary flesher, and sympathetically mingled her lamentations with those of his victim.

These effusions of love and dolour, however, were doomed to sudden interruption; someone knocked at the door. Branda ran to the window that she might recognize who the visitor was that had dared to penetrate the lair of a wer-wolf, and on perceiving who it was, she raised her eyes and hands on high, in token of her extremity of despair, whilst the knocking momentarily grew louder.

"'Tis my uncle," faltered she. "Ah! Woe's me, how shall I escape hence without his seeing me? Whither hide? Oh, here, here, nigh to thee, Hugues, and we will die together," and she crouched herself into an obscure recess behind his couch. "If Willieblud should raise his cleaver to slay thee, he shall first strike through his kinswoman's body."

Branda hastily concealed herself amidst a pile of hemp, whispering Hugues to summon all his courage, who, however, scarce found strength sufficient to raise himself to a sitting posture, whilst his eyes vainly sought around for some weapon of defence.

"A good morrow to thee, Wulfric!" exclaimed Willieblud, as he entered, holding in his hand a napkin tied in a knot, which he proceeded to place upon the coffer beside the sufferer. "I come to offer thee some work, to bind and stack me a faggot-pile, knowing that thou art no laggard at bill-hook and wattle. Wilt do it?"

"I am sick," replied Hugues, repressing the wrath which, despite of pain, sparkled in his wild glance; "I am not in fitting state to work."

"Sick, gossip, sick, art thou indeed? Or is it but a sloth fit? Come, what ails thee? Where lieth the evil? Your hand, that I may feel thy pulse."

Hugues reddened, and for an instant hesitated whether he should resist a solicitation, the bent of which he too readily comprehended; but in order to avoid exposing Branda to discovery, he thrust forth his left hand from beneath the coverlid, all imbrued in dried gore.

"Not that hand, Hugues, but the other, the right one. Alack, and well-a-day, hast thou lost thy hand, and I must find it for thee?"

Hugues, whose purpling flush of rage changed quickly to a death-like hue, replied not to this taunt, nor testified by the slightest gesture or movement that he was preparing to satisfy a request as cruel in its preconception as the object of it was slenderly cloaked. Willieblud laughed, and ground his teeth in savage glee, maliciously revelling in the tortures he had inflicted upon the sufferer. He seemed already disposed to use violence, rather than allow himself to be baffled in the attainment of the decisive proof he aimed at. Already had he commenced untying the napkin, giving vent all the while to his implacable taunts; one hand alone displaying itself upon the coverlid, and which Hugues, wellnigh senseless with anguish, thought not of withdrawing.

"Why tender me that hand?" continued his unrelenting persecutor, as he imagined himself on the eve of arriving at the conviction he so ardently desired – "That I should lop it off? Quick, quick, Master Wulfric, and do my bidding; I demanded to see your right hand."

"Behold it then!" ejaculated a suppressed voice, which belonged to no supernatural being, however it might seem appertaining to such; and Willieblud to his utter confusion and dismay saw a second hand, sound and unmutilated, extend itself towards him as though in silent accusation. He started back; he stammered out a cry for mercy, bent his knees for an instant, and raising himself, palsied with terror, fled from the hut, which he firmly believed under the possession of the foul fiend.

He carried not with him the severed hand, which henceforward became a perpetual vision ever present before his eyes, and which all the potent exorcisms of the sacristan, at whose hands he continually sought council and consolation, signally failed to dispel.

"Oh, that hand! To whom then, belongs that accursed hand?" groaned he, continually. "Is it really the fiend's, or that of some wer-wolf? Certain 'tis, that Hugues is innocent, for have I not seen both his hands? But wherefore was one bloody? There's sorcery at bottom of it."

The next morning, early, the first object that struck his sight on entering his stall, was the severed hand that he had left the preceding night upon the coffer in the forest hut; it was stripped of its wolf's-skin covering, and lay among the viands. He dared no longer touch that hand, which now, he verily believed to be enchanted; but in hopes of getting rid of it for ever, he had it flung down a well, and it was with no small increase of despair that he found it shortly afterwards again lying upon his block. He buried it in his garden, but still without being able to rid himself of it; it returned livid and loathsome to infect his shop, and augment the remorse which was unceasingly revived by the reproaches of his niece.

At last, flattering himself to escape all further persecution from that fatal hand, it struck him that he would have it carried to the cemetery at Canterbury, and try whether exorcism, and supulture in holy ground would effectually bar its return to the light of day. This was also done; but lo! on the following morning he perceived it nailed to his shutter. Disheartened by these dumb, yet awful reproaches, which wholly robbed him of his peace, and impatient to annihilate all trace of an action with which heaven itself seemed to upbraid him, he quitted Ashford one morning without bidding adieu to his niece, and some days after was found drowned in the river Stour. They drew out his swollen and discoloured body, which was discovered floating on the surface among the sedge, and it was only by piecemeal that they succeeded in tearing away from his death-contracted clutch, the phantom hand, which, in his suicidal convulsions he had retained firmly grasped.

A year after this event, Hugues, although minus a hand, and consequently a confirmed wer-wolf, married Branda, sole heiress to the stock and chattels of the late unhappy flesher of Ashford.

Arthur and Gorlagon

From Arthurian Legend

Here Begins About the Wolf

THERE WAS A KING well known to me, noble, accomplished, rich, and far-famed for justice and for truth. He had provided for himself a delightful garden which had no equal, and in it he had caused to be sown and planted all kinds of trees and fruits, and spices of different sorts: and among the other shrubs which grew in the garden there was a beautiful slender sapling of exactly the same height as the King himself, which broke forth from the ground and began to grow on the same night and at the same hour as the King was born. Now concerning this sapling, it had been decreed by fate that whoever should cut it down, and striking his head with the slenderer part of it, should say, "Be a wolf and have the understanding of a wolf," he would at once become a wolf, and have the understanding of a wolf. And for this reason the King watched the sapling with great care and with great diligence, for he had no doubt that his safety depended upon it. So he surrounded the garden with a strong and steep wall, and allowed no one but the guardian, who was a trusted friend of his own, to be admitted into it; and it was his custom to visit that sapling three or four times a day, and to partake of no food until he had visited it, even though he should fast until the evening. So it was that he alone understood this matter thoroughly.

Now this king had a very beautiful wife, but though fair to look upon she did not prove chaste, and her beauty was the cause of her undoing. For she loved a youth, the son of a certain pagan king; and preferring his love to that of her lord, she had taken great pains to involve her husband in some danger so that the youth might be able lawfully to enjoy the embraces for which he longed. And observing that the King entered the garden so many times a day, and desiring to know the reason, she often purposed to question him on the subject, but never dared to do so. But at last one day, when the King had returned from hunting later than usual, and according to his wont had entered the plantation alone, the Queen, in her thirst for information, and unable to endure that the thing should be concealed from her any longer (as it is customary for a woman to wish to know everything), when her husband had returned and was seated at table, asked him with a treacherous smile why he went to the garden so many times a day, and had been there even then late in the evening before taking food. The King answered that that was a matter which did not concern her, and that he was under no obligation to divulge it to her; whereupon she became furious, and improperly suspecting that he was in the habit of consorting with an adulteress in the garden, cried out, "I call all the gods of heaven to witness that I will never eat with you henceforth until you tell me the reason." And rising suddenly from the table she went to her bedchamber, cunningly feigning sickness, and lay in bed for three days without taking any food.

On the third day, the King, perceiving her obstinacy and fearing that her life might be endangered in consequence, began to beg and exhort her with gentle words to rise and eat, telling her that the thing she wished to know was a secret which he would never dare to tell anyone. To which she replied, "You ought to have no secrets from your wife, and you must know for certain that I would rather die than live, so long as I feel that I am so little loved by you," and he could not by any means persuade her to take refreshment. Then the King, in too changeable and irresolute a mood and too devoted in his affection for his wife, explained to her how the matter stood, having first exacted an oath from her that she would never betray the secret to anyone, and would keep the sapling as sacred as her own life.

The Queen, however, having got from him that which she had so dearly wished and prayed for, began to promise him greater devotion and love, although she had already conceived in her mind a device by which she might bring about the crime she had been so long deliberating. So on the following day, when the King had gone to the woods to hunt, she seized an axe, and secretly entering the garden, cut down the sapling to the ground, and carried it away with her. When, however, she found that the King was returning, she concealed the sapling under her sleeve, which hung down long and loose, and went to the threshold of the door to meet him, and throwing her arms around him she embraced him as though she would have kissed him, and then suddenly thrust the sapling out from her sleeve and struck him on the head with it once and again, crying, "Be a wolf, be a wolf," meaning to add "and have the understanding of a wolf," but she added instead the words "have the understanding of a man." Nor was there any delay, but it came about as she had said; and he fled quickly to the woods with the hounds she set on him in pursuit, but his human understanding remained unimpaired. Arthur, see, you have now learned in part the heart, the nature, and the ways of woman. Dismount now and eat, and afterwards I will relate at greater length what remains. For yours is a weighty question, and there are few who know how to answer it, and when I have told you all you will be but little the wiser.

Arthur. The matter goes very well and pleases me much. Follow up, follow up what you have begun.

Gorlagon. You are pleased then to hear what follows. Be attentive and I will proceed. Then the Queen, having put to flight her lawful husband, at once summoned the young man of whom I have spoken, and having handed over to him the reins of government became his wife. But the wolf, after roaming for a space of two years in the recesses of the woods to which he had fled, allied himself with a wild she-wolf, and begot two cubs by her. And remembering the wrong done him by his wife (as he was still possessed of his human understanding), he anxiously considered if he could in any way take his revenge upon her. Now near that wood there was a fortress at which the Queen was very often wont to sojourn with the King. And so this human wolf, looking out for his opportunity, took his shewolf with her cubs one evening, and rushed unexpectedly into the town, and finding the two little boys of whom the aforesaid youth had become the father by his wife, playing by chance under the tower without anyone to guard them, he attacked and slew them, tearing them cruelly limb from limb. When the bystanders saw too late what had happened they pursued the wolves with shouts. The wolves, when what they had done was made known, fled swiftly away and escaped in safety. The Queen, however, overwhelmed with sorrow at the calamity, gave orders to her retainers to keep a careful watch for the return of the wolves. No long time had elapsed when the wolf, thinking that he was not yet satisfied, again visited the town with his companions, and meeting with two noble counts, brothers of the Queen, playing at the very gates of the palace, he attacked them, and tearing out their bowels gave them over to a frightful death. Hearing the noise, the servants assembled, and shutting the doors caught the cubs and hanged them. But the wolf, more cunning than the rest, slipped out of the hands of those who were holding him and escaped unhurt.

Arthur, dismount and eat, for yours is a weighty question and there are few who know how to answer it. And when I have told you all, you will be but little the wiser.

Gorlagon. The wolf, overwhelmed with very great grief for the loss of his cubs and maddened by the greatness of his sorrow, made nightly forays against the flocks and herds of that province, and attacked them with such great slaughter that all the inhabitants, placing in ambush a large pack of hounds, met together to hunt and catch him; and the wolf, unable to endure these daily vexations, made for a neighbouring country and there began to carry on his usual ravages. However, he was at once chased from thence by the inhabitants, and compelled to go to a third country: and now he began to vent his rage with implacable fury, not only against the beasts but also against human beings. Now it chanced that a king was reigning over that country, young in years, of a mild disposition, and far-famed for his wisdom and industry: and when the countless destruction both of men and beasts wrought by the wolf was reported to him, he appointed a day on which he would set about to track and hunt the brute with a strong force of huntsmen and hounds. For so greatly was the wolf held in dread that no one dared to go to rest anywhere around, but everyone kept watch the whole night long against his inroads.

So one night when the wolf had gone to a neighbouring village, greedy for bloodshed, and was standing under the eaves of a certain house listening intently to a conversation that was going on within, it happened that he heard the man nearest him tell how the King had proposed to seek and track him down on the following day, much being added as to the clemency and kindness of the King. When the wolf heard this he returned trembling to the recesses of the woods, deliberating what would be the best course for him to pursue. In the morning the huntsmen and the King's retinue with an immense pack of hounds entered the woods, making the welkin ring with the blast of horns and with shouting; and the King, accompanied by two of his intimate friends, followed at a more moderate pace. The wolf concealed himself near the road where the King was to pass, and when all had gone by and he saw the King approaching (for he judged from his countenance that it was the King) he dropped his head and ran close after him, and encircling the King's right foot with his paws he would have licked him affectionately like a suppliant asking for pardon, with such groanings as he was capable of. Then two noblemen who were guarding the King's person, seeing this enormous wolf (for they had never seen any of so vast a size), cried out, "Master, see here is the wolf we seek! See, here is the wolf we seek! Strike him, slay him, do not let the hateful beast attack us!" The wolf, utterly fearless of their cries, followed close after the King, and kept licking him gently. The King was wonderfully moved, and after looking at the wolf for some time and perceiving that there was no fierceness in him, but that he was rather like one who craved for pardon, was much astonished, and commanded that none of his men should dare to inflict any harm on him, declaring that he had detected some signs of human understanding in him; so putting down his right hand to caress the wolf he gently stroked his head and scratched his ears. Then the King seized the wolf and endeavoured to lift him up to him. But the wolf, perceiving that the King was desirous of lifting him up, leapt up, and joyfully sat upon the neck of the charger in front of the King.

The King recalled his followers, and returned home. He had not gone far when lo! a stag of vast size met him in the forest pasture with antlers erect. Then the King said "I will try if there is any worth or strength in my wolf, and whether he can accustom himself to obey my commands." And crying out he set the wolf upon the stag and thrust him from him with his hand. The wolf, well knowing how to capture this kind of prey, sprang up and pursued the stag, and getting in front of it attacked it, and catching it by the throat laid it dead in sight of the King. Then the King called him back and said, "Of a truth you must be kept alive and not killed, seeing that you know how to show such service to us." And taking the wolf with him he returned home.

Arthur, dismount and eat. For yours is a weighty question, and there are few who know how to answer it; and when I have told you all my tale you will be but little the wiser.

Arthur. If all the gods were to cry from heaven "Arthur, dismount and eat," I would neither dismount nor eat until I had learnt the rest.

Gorlagon. So the wolf remained with the King, and was held in very great affection by him. Whatever the King commanded him he performed, and he never showed any fierceness towards or inflicted any hurt upon any one. He daily stood at table before the King at dinner time with his forepaws erect, eating of his bread and drinking from the same cup. Wherever the King went he accompanied him, so that even at night he would not go to rest anywhere save beside his master's couch.

Now it happened that the King had to go on a long journey outside his kingdom to confer with another king, and to go at once, as it would be impossible for him to return in less than ten days. So he called his Queen, and said, "As I must go on this journey at once, I commend this wolf to your protection, and I command you to keep him in my stead, if he will stay, and to minister to his wants." But the Queen already hated the wolf because of the great sagacity which she had detected in him (and as it so often happens that the wife hates whom the husband loves), and she said, "My lord, I am afraid that when you are gone he will attack me in the night if he lies in his accustomed place and will leave me mangled." The King replied, "Have no fear of that, for I have detected no such symptom in him all the long time he has been with me. However, if you have any doubt of it, I will have a chain made and will have him fastened up to my bed-ladder." So the King gave orders that a chain of gold should be made, and when the wolf had been fastened up by it to the steps, he hastened away to the business he had on hand.

Arthur, dismount and eat. For yours is a weighty question, there are few who know how to answer it; and when I have told you all my tale you will be but little the wiser.

Arthur. I have no wish to eat; and I beg you not to invite me to eat any more.

Gorlagon. So the King set out, and the wolf remained with the Queen. But she did not show the care for him which she ought to have done. For he always lay chained up though the King had commanded that he should be chained up at night only. Now the Queen loved the King's sewer with an unlawful love, and went to visit him whenever the King was absent. So on the eighth day after the King had started, they met in the bedchamber at midday and mounted the bed together, little heeding the presence of the wolf. And when the wolf saw them rushing into each other's impious embraces he blazed forth with fury, his eyes reddening, and the hair on his neck standing up, and he began to make as though he would attack them, but was held back by the chain by which he was fastened. And when he saw they had no intention of desisting from the iniquity on which they had embarked, he gnashed his teeth, and dug up the ground with his paws, and venting his rage over all his body, with awful howls he stretched the chain with such violence that it snapped in two. When loose he rushed with fury upon the sewer and threw him from the bed, and tore him so savagely that he left him half-dead. But to the Queen he did no harm at all, but only gazed upon her with venom in his eye. Hearing the mournful groans of the sewer, the servants tore the door from its hinges and rushed in. When asked the cause of all the tumult, that cunning Queen concocted a lying story, and told the servants that the wolf had devoured her son, and had torn the sewer as they saw while he was attempting to rescue the little one from death, and that he would have treated her in the same way had they not arrived in time to succour her. So the sewer was brought half dead to the guest-chamber. But the Queen fearing that the King might somehow discover the truth of the matter, and considering how she might take her revenge on the wolf, shut up the child, whom she had represented as having been devoured by the wolf, along with his nurse in an underground room far removed from any access; everyone being under the impression that he had in fact been devoured.

Arthur, dismount and eat. For yours is a weighty question, and few there are who know how to answer it: and when I have told my tale you will be but little the wiser.

Arthur. I pray you, order the table to be removed, as the service of so many dishes interrupts our conversation.

Gorlagon. After these events news was brought to the Queen that the King was returning sooner than had been expected. So the deceitful woman, full of cunning, went forth to meet him with her hair cut close, and cheeks torn, and garments splashed with blood, and when she met him cried,

"Alas! Alas! Alas! My lord, wretched that I am, what a loss have I sustained during your absence!" At this the King was dumbfounded, and asked what was the matter, and she replied, "That wretched beast of yours, of yours I say, which I have but too truly suspected all this time, has devoured your son in my lap; and when your sewer was struggling to come to the rescue the beast mangled and almost killed him, and would have treated me in the same way had not the servants broken in; see here the blood of the little one splashed upon my garments is witness of the thing." Hardly had she finished speaking, when lo! the wolf hearing the King approach, sprang forth from the bedchamber, and rushed into the King's embraces as though he well deserved them, jumping about joyfully, and gambolling with greater delight than he had ever done before. At this the King, distracted by contending emotions, was in doubt what he should do, on the one hand reflecting that his wife would not tell him an untruth, on the other that if the wolf had been guilty of so great a crime against him he would undoubtedly not have dared to meet him with such joyful bounds.

So while his mind was driven hither and thither on these matters and he refused food, the wolf sitting close by him touched his foot gently with his paw, and took the border of his cloak into his mouth, and by a movement of the head invited him to follow him. The King, who understood the wolf's customary signals, got up and followed him through the different bedchambers to the underground room where the boy was hidden away. And finding the door bolted the wolf knocked three or four times with his paw, as much as to ask that it might be opened to him. But as there was some delay in searching for the key – for the Queen had hidden it away – the wolf, unable to endure the delay, drew back a little, and spreading out the claws of his four paws he rushed headlong at the door, and driving it in, threw it down upon the middle of the floor broken and shattered. Then running forward he took the infant from its cradle in his shaggy arms, and gently held it up to the King's face for a kiss. The King marvelled and said, "There is something beyond this which is not clear to my comprehension." Then he went out after the wolf, who led the way, and was conducted by him to the dying sewer; and when the wolf saw the sewer, the King could scarcely restrain him from rushing upon him. Then the King sitting down in front of the sewer's couch, questioned him as to the cause of his sickness, and as to the accident which had occasioned his wounds. The only confession, however, he would make was that in rescuing the boy from the wolf, the wolf had attacked him; and he called the Queen to witness to the truth of what he said. The King in answer said, "You are evidently lying: my son lives: he was not dead at all, and now that I have found him and have convicted both you and the Queen of treachery to me, and of forging lying tales, I am afraid that something else may be false also. I know the reason why the wolf, unable to bear his master's disgrace, attacked you so savagely, contrary to his wont. Therefore confess to me at once the truth of the matter, else I swear by the Majesty of highest Heaven that I will deliver thee to the flames to burn." Then the wolf making an attack upon him pressed him close, and would have mangled him again had he not been held back by the bystanders.

What need of many words? When the King insisted, sometimes with threats, sometimes with coaxing, the sewer confessed the crime of which he had been guilty, and humbly prayed to be forgiven. But the King, blazing out in an excess of fury, delivered the sewer up to be kept in prison, and immediately summoned the chief men from the whole of his kingdom to meet, and through them he held an investigation into the circumstances of this great crime, Sentence was given. The sewer was flayed alive and hanged. The Queen was torn limb from limb by horses and thrown into balls of flame.

Arthur, dismount and eat. For yours is a mighty question, and there are few who know how to answer it: and when I have told my tale you will be but little the wiser.

Arthur. If you are not tired of eating, you need not mind my fasting a little longer.

Gorlagon. After these events the King pondered over the extraordinary sagacity and industry of the wolf with close attention and great persistence, and afterwards discussed the subject more fully with his wise men, asserting that a being who was clearly endued with such great intelligence must have the understanding of a man, "For no beast," he argued, "was ever found to possess such great wisdom, or to show such great devotion to any one as this wolf has shown to me. For he understands perfectly whatever we say to him: he does what he is ordered: he always stands by me, wherever I may be: he rejoices when I rejoice, and when I am in sorrow, he sorrows too. And you must know that one who has avenged with such severity the wrong which has been done me must undoubtedly have been a man of great sagacity and ability, and must have assumed the form of a wolf under some spell or incantation." At these words the wolf, who was standing by the King, showed great joy, and licking his hands and feet and pressing close to his knees, showed by the expression of his countenance and the gesture of his whole body that the King had spoken the truth.

Then the King said, "See with what gladness he agrees with what I say, and shows by unmistakable signs that I have spoken the truth. There can now be no further doubt about the matter, and would that power might be granted me to discover whether by some act or device I might be able to restore him to his former state, even at the cost of my worldly substance; nay, even at the risk of my life." So, after long deliberation, the King at length determined that the wolf should be sent off to go before him, and to take whatever direction he pleased whether by land or by sea. "For perhaps," said he, "if we could reach his country we might get to know what has happened and find some remedy for him."

So the wolf was allowed to go where he would, and they all followed after him. And he at once made for the sea, and impetuously dashed into the waves as though he wished to cross. Now his own country adjoined that region, being, however, separated from it on one side by the sea, though in another direction it was accessible by land, but by a longer route. The King, seeing that he wished to cross over, at once gave orders that the fleet should be launched and that the army should assemble.

Arthur, dismount and eat. For yours is a weighty question: and few there are who know how to answer it: and when I have told my tale you will be but little the wiser.

Arthur. The wolf being desirous of crossing the sea, is standing on the beach. I am afraid that if he is left alone he will be drowned in his anxiety to get over.

Gorlagon. So the King, having ordered his ship, and duly equipped his army, approached the sea with a great force of soldiers, and on the third day he landed safely at the wolf's country; and when they reached the shore the wolf was the first to leap from the ship, and clearly signified to them by his customary nod and gesture that this was his country. Then the King, taking some of his men with him, hastened secretly to a certain neighbouring city, commanding his army to remain on shipboard until he had looked into the affair and returned to them. However, he had scarcely entered the city when the whole course of events became clear to him. For all the men of that province, both of high and low degree, were groaning under the intolerable tyranny of the king who had succeeded to the wolf, and were with one voice lamenting their master, who by the craft and subtilty of his wife had been changed into a wolf, remembering what a kind and gentle master he was.

So having discovered what he wanted to know, and having ascertained where the king of that province was then living, the King returned with all speed to his ships, marched out his troops, and attacking his adversary suddenly and unexpectedly, slew or put to flight all his defenders, and captured both him and his Queen and made them subject to his dominion.

Arthur, dismount and eat. For yours is a mighty question: and there are few who know how to answer it: and when I have finished my tale you will be but little the wiser for it.

Arthur. You are like a harper who almost before he has finished playing the music of a song, keeps on repeatedly interposing the concluding passages without anyone singing to his accompaniment.

Gorlagon. So the King, relying on his victory, assembled a council of the chief men of the kingdom, and setting the Queen in the sight of them all, said, "O most perfidious and wicked of women, what madness induced you to plot such great treachery against your lord! But I will not any longer bandy words with one who has been judged unworthy of intercourse with anyone; so answer the question I put to you at once, for I will certainly cause you to die of hunger and thirst and exquisite tortures, unless you show me where the sapling lies hidden with which you transformed your husband into a wolf. Perhaps the human shape which he has lost may thereby be recovered." Whereupon she swore that she did not know where the sapling was, saying that it was well known that it had been broken up and burnt in the fire. However, as she would not confess, the King handed her over to the tormentors, to be daily tortured and daily exhausted with punishments, and allowed her neither food nor drink. So at last, compelled by the severity of her punishment, she produced the sapling and handed it to the King. And the King took it from her, and with glad heart brought the wolf forward into the midst, and striking his head with the thicker part of the sapling, added these words, "Be a man and have the understanding of a man." And no sooner were the words spoken than the effect followed. The wolf became a man as he had been before, though far more beautiful and comely, being now possessed of such grace that one could at once detect that he was a man of great nobility. The King seeing a man of such great beauty metamorphosed from a wolf standing before him, and pitying the wrongs the man had suffered, ran forward with great joy and embraced him, kissing and lamenting him and shedding tears. And as they embraced each other they drew such long protracted sighs and shed so many tears that all the multitude standing around were constrained to weep. The one returned thanks for all the many kindnesses which had been shown him: the other lamented that he had behaved with less consideration than he ought. What more? Extraordinary joy is shown by all, and the King, having received the submission of the principal men, according to ancient custom, retook possession of his sovereignty. Then the adulterer and adulteress were brought into his presence, and he was consulted as to what he judged ought to be done with them. And he condemned the pagan king to death. The Queen he only divorced, but of his inborn clemency spared her life, though she well deserved to lose it. The other King, having been honoured and enriched with costly presents, as was befitting, returned to his own kingdom.

Now, Arthur, you have learned what the heart, the nature, and the ways of women are. Have a care for yourself and see if you are any the wiser for it. Dismount now and eat, for we have both well deserved our meal, I for the tale I have told, and you for listening to it.

Arthur. I will by no means dismount until you have answered the question I am about to ask you.

Gorlagon. What is that?

Arthur. Who is that woman sitting opposite you of a sad countenance, and holding before her in a dish a human head bespattered with blood, who has wept whenever you have smiled, and who has kissed the bloodstained head whenever you have kissed your wife during the telling of your tale?

Gorlagon. If this thing were known to me alone, Arthur (he replied), I would by no means tell it you; but as it is well known to all who are sitting at table with me, I am not ashamed that you also should be made acquainted with it. That woman who is sitting opposite me, she it was who, as I have just told you, wrought so great a crime against her lord, that is to say against myself. In me you may recognise that wolf who, as you have heard, was transformed first from a man into a wolf, and then from a wolf into a man again. When I became a wolf it is evident that the kingdom to which I first went was that of my middle brother, King Gorleil. And the King who took such great pains to care for me you can have no doubt was my youngest brother, King Gargol, to whom you came in the first instance. And the bloodstained head which that woman sitting opposite me embraces in the dish she has in front of her is the head of that youth for love of whom she wrought so great a crime against me. For when I returned to my proper shape again, in sparing her life, I subjected her to this penalty only, namely, that she should always have the head of her paramour before her, and that when I kissed the wife I had married in her stead she should imprint kisses on him for whose sake she had committed that crime. And I had the head embalmed to keep it free from putrefaction. For I knew that no punishment could be more grievous to her than a perpetual exhibition of her great wickedness in the sight of all the world. Arthur, dismount now, if you so desire, for now that I have invited you, you will, so far as I am concerned, from henceforth remain where you are.

So Arthur dismounted and ate, and on the following day returned home a nine days' journey, marvelling greatly at what he had heard.

Sigmund, Sinfjotli and the Wolf Pelts
from The Story of the Volsungs
translated by William Morris & Eiríkur Magnússon

THE TALE TELLS that Sigmund thought Sinfjotli over young to help him to his revenge, and will first of all harden him with manly deeds; so in summer-tide they fare wide through the woods and slay men for their wealth; Sigmund deems him to take much after the kin of the Volsungs, though he thinks that he is Siggeir's son, and deems him to have the evil heart of his father, with the might and daring of the Volsungs; withal he must needs think him in no wise a kinsome man, for full oft would he bring Sigmund's wrongs to his memory, and prick him on to slay King Siggeir.

Now on a time as they fare abroad in the wood for the getting of wealth, they find a certain house, and two men with great gold rings asleep therein: now these twain were spell-bound skin-changers, and wolf-skins were hanging up over them in the house; and every tenth day might they come out of those skins; and they were kings' sons: so Sigmund and Sinfjotli do the wolf-skins on them, and then might they nowise come out of them, though forsooth the same nature went with them as heretofore; they howled as wolves howl, but both knew the meaning of that howling; they lay out in the wild-wood, and each went his way; and a word they made betwixt them, that they should risk the onset of seven men, but no more, and that he who was first to be set on should howl in wolfish wise: "Let us not depart from this," says Sigmund, "for thou art young and over-bold, and men will deem the quarry good, when they take thee."

Now each goes his way, and when they were parted, Sigmund meets certain men, and gives forth a wolf's howl; and when Sinfjotli heard it, he went straightway thereto, and slew them all, and once more they parted. But ere Sinfjotli has fared long through the woods, eleven men meet him, and he wrought in such wise that he slew them all, and was awearied therewith, and crawls under an oak, and there takes his rest. Then came Sigmund thither, and said –

"Why didst thou not call on me?"

Sinfjotli said, "I was loth to call for thy help for the slaying of eleven men."

Then Sigmund rushed at him so hard that he staggered and fell, and Sigmund bit him in the throat. Now that day they might not come out of their wolf-skins: but Sigmund lays the other on his back, and bears him home to the house, and cursed the wolf-gears and gave them to the trolls. Now on a day he saw where two weasels went, and how that one bit the other in the throat, and then ran straightway into the thicket, and took up a leaf and laid it on the wound, and thereon his fellow sprang up quite and clean whole; so Sigmund went out and saw a raven flying with a blade of that same herb to him; so he took it and drew it over Sinfjotli's hurt, and he straightway sprang up as whole as though he had never been hurt. Thereafter they went home to their earth-house, and abode there till the time came for them to put off the wolf-shapes; then they burnt them up with fire, and prayed that no more hurt might come to any one from them; but in that uncouth guise they wrought many famous deeds in the kingdom and lordship of King Siggeir.

The Cage in the Forest

Jim Moss

HANNAH AND TREVOR sat inside the cage with their backs against the tree. It had taken Trevor two weeks to weld the cage around the old oak, and another three days to wire and insulate it. He eyed each fused joint, admiring his work. The grid of bars was uneven in places, but sturdy, with no more than eight inches between each, which would suit his purpose. Hannah stared through the gaps into the forest. To the east, an amber slice of moon peeked over the tree line. Hannah pulled her legs in against her body, and shivered.

"Cold?" Trevor glanced at her.

"Nerves."

"Relax, the most they can reach in is two and a half feet." Trevor stretched out his legs.

"You couldn't have set another trap?"

"They're not mindless beasts, you know that."

"That's what worries me." Hannah glanced at the braced door that held them inside.

"Be ready, and we'll be fine." Trevor plucked a twig off the ground. "Wanna test it again?"

Hannah looked down at the battery box attached to the base of the tree, and placed her finger on the switch.

"Go ahead," said Trevor.

"Won't it drain the battery?"

"Nah, there's enough power for a week."

Hannah flipped the switch. A low hum buzzed. Trevor rose and took two steps towards the bars. He flung the twig at a joint. It struck the wired bar, sparked with a crackle, then fell to the ground.

"Fifteen thousand volts. Enough to hurt 'em good, maybe even knock 'em out."

"What happens if you get knocked out?" Hannah flipped the switch to the off position.

"If that happens, cut the power, and drag me away from the bars so I'm not touching them. Then flip it back on if you need to." Trevor stepped back to the base of the tree and plopped down next to Hannah. "Just remember, don't turn it on until after I get bit."

"What if they slash you?"

"I can slash back." Trevor unsnapped the sheath on his belt. He slid his bowie knife out and held it before his face. "And if I draw some blood, that might be good enough." Trevor angled the knife so that moonlight glinted along the sharp edge. "If they reach through the bars... get zapped, get knocked out... I could pull an arm or limb inside. That'd be ideal." He turned to look at Hannah. "So have your finger ready on that switch, and when you hear me—"

A howl echoed through the trees. Trevor and Hannah froze. Their eyes darted left to right. Trevor slid his knife back into the sheath, but left it unbuckled. He rose to his feet and stared at the full moon, now halfway over the tree tops. A second howl sounded from the west. Trevor cupped his hands around his mouth and released a deep howl. One... two... three... Trevor counted seconds in his head. On the eighth, a return howl from the west, followed by another from the north.

"Good... They heard." Trevor looked down at Hannah. "Stand up, and howl with me."

"Do I have to?"

"Yeah. C'mon," Trevor urged. He cupped his hands again, and howled into the night, modulating the tone higher and ending it with staccato ouu-ouus.

Hannah stood and brushed the dirt from her jeans. She took a deep breath, cupped her hands, and let out a high-pitched howl.

"Doesn't that feel good?" Trevor whispered to her. "When it comes from your soul? When it vibrates through your whole body? Makes your hair stand on end?"

A few seconds later three return howls sounded, louder, closer. Hannah shrunk back against the tree and slumped to the ground. She pulled her backpack onto her lap and unzipped a side pouch.

"What are you doing?" Trevor stared at her.

"I just..." Hannah pulled out her cell-phone.

"You can't get a signal here."

"Thought I'd check anyway. At least the time." Hands shaking, Hannah tapped at the phone, stared at it a moment, then stuffed it back in the pouch.

"We'll be okay."

"You sure you want to go through with this?"

* * *

Six sets of howls later, they heard rustling nearby. Hannah moved a shaky finger over the switch. Trevor stared through the bars at the underbrush. The full moon hung in the sky like an old urine-yellow ball frozen in mid-toss. The snout of a wolf poked through the tall grass. A tip of white fang flashed in the moonlight. The hairy silhouette rose on two legs and lurched towards the cage. Trevor caught his breath. The creature stopped six feet from the bars, lifted its head and sniffed the air. It stood about six feet tall. Patches of brown and gray fur filled its upper torso; torn jeans covered its bottom half. Trevor stared at its face. Would there be, beyond those flaring nostrils, something to reveal who this person was as a human? The werewolf turned its head. Its amber eyes locked onto Trevor's baby blues.

It growled.

"Get rea-dy," Trevor whispered in sing-song to Hannah.

The werewolf languidly paced around the cage, never taking its eyes off Trevor, or getting closer than five feet.

C'mon... Trevor mouthed to himself.

The creature broke eye contact, turned left, and uttered a short howl. Then it folded its arms across its chest, stared at Trevor, and sneered. It looked like it was waiting for something to happen. Trevor pulled up the right cuff of his cargo pants. He yanked off his right hiking boot and sock. Staring at the werewolf, with a serene expression, Trevor lifted his bare foot towards an opening in the bars.

"Yummy foot," Trevor smiled. "Come bite the yummy foot."

The werewolf looked from Trevor, to his foot, to Hannah, then back at Trevor and sneered even more.

"Yummy foot-foot," Trevor trilled in a high-pitched voice as if he were talking to a pet dog. "With yummy-yum-yum toesies." Trevor wiggled his toes.

The werewolf growled: "Yer feet stink!"

Trevor stumbled backwards in surprise.

"Omigod – they talk!" Hannah's hand shot up to her neck.

"Yeah, I talk. I'm still part human," said the werewolf.

"This is great!" Trevor exclaimed as he staggered to balance his bare foot on a tree root. He turned to Hannah. "Haven't I been saying that you don't lose your mind when you transform?"

Trevor turned back to the werewolf. "Hey, can I get a bite? Just deep enough to infect me with lycanthropy?"

"I'm not gonna fucking bite you."

"Why not?" Trevor demanded.

"Trust me, pal," the werewolf shook his head. "You won't like being a werewolf."

"Yes, I will! I've been dreaming of being a werewolf since I was a kid!"

"Dream all you want, but the reality sucks." The werewolf spat a wad of saliva to the side. "I lost my wife. I lost my job. I can't *hold* a job. My family is pissed because I miss weddings, funerals, vacations, you name it, because of this curse."

"I can handle it." Trevor strode towards the bars.

"You're an idiot."

"I've already worked my schedule out. I'm a pagan, I take off all nights with full moons as religious holidays."

"It ain't just that," the werewolf snarled. "The transformation is painful and leaves you ravenous for raw meat. You don't sleep well, you gotta avoid hunters, you get ticks, you shed everywhere—"

Two howls echoed from the forest. The werewolf cocked his head and listened.

"What are they saying?" Trevor turned his head to hear.

"Listen…" the werewolf sighed. "My pack doesn't need, or want, any more werewolves. We each gotta eat a good ten pounds of fresh meat every full moon. That's about a lamb each. It ain't cheap, and sometimes we gotta hunt deer, or take down a—"

A low-pitched howl rumbled out of the forest.

"Can I talk to your other packmates about this?" Trevor insisted.

"I gotta go." The werewolf turned away from the cage and began shambling towards the forest.

"Hey. Hey! You come back here!" Trevor scrambled over to the cage door. He quickly unlocked and lifted the two bracing bars.

"Trevor!" Hannah yelled in alarm.

"I'm not planning on being part of your pack!" Trevor shouted at the werewolf. "I live ninety miles away!" Trevor stumbled out of the cage and marched after the retreating creature.

"Trevor, come back!" Hannah jumped up and reached for the cage door. "Don't leave me here alone!" Hannah grabbed the middle door bar. She hesitated a second before pulling the door shut. There were other werewolves out there that may not be as… *could she call this one, friendly?* She pulled down only one brace in case she needed to quickly let Trevor back in. She rushed over to the other side of the cage to look through the bars at Trevor, who stomped after the werewolf in one hiking boot, and one bare foot.

"Look, I'll pay you…" said Trevor.

"Get away from me," the werewolf snarled.

"Trevor, please…" Hannah said as she watched Trevor follow the werewolf. Both were silhouetted in the moonlight. She saw Trevor place his hand on the shoulder of the hairy figure in front of him.

"How much you want for biting me?"

The werewolf whipped its body around and barked at Trevor. "Leave me alone!"

"It's gotta be worth somethin' to ya!" Trevor thrust his arms out. "C'mon, man!"

"I'm not a man, anymore!" the werewolf roared as he pulled back one arm and flung a paw with splayed claws at Trevor's neck.

From her barred vantage, Hannah gasped. She saw tiny black flecks fly into the air. The figure of Trevor staggered, and just as his body leaned over, the werewolf swung his other arm up and caught Trevor's chin. Trevor's head snapped back and his knees folded. His body crumpled to the ground. Hannah screamed. The werewolf turned and stared at her, and, with surprising speed, ran towards the cage. Hannah stumbled backwards, she tripped, and her left knee came down hard on a tree root. She heard werewolf paws thrashing through underbrush growing closer. On hands and knees, she scrambled for the switch. She slammed her palm on it. She strived to hear the hum beneath her panting breath. She felt a vibration from where her legs and arms pressed on the ground, but she wasn't sure if it was from the electric field, or her own trembling. She gasped a couple of deep breaths, then slowly turned back to look through the bars. The werewolf stood three feet on the other side, panting, ears twitching, staring at her. Its arms hung by its sides, clawed hands stained with dirt and blood.

"He shoulda left me alone," it growled.

Hannah stared at the werewolf's face, into its eyes, searching, hoping for some hint of humanity. Its ears tilted to the left. Hannah heard rustling, shifted her gaze left, and saw a second stooped figure creep towards the section of grass where Trevor had fallen. The figure stopped, raised its muzzle to the moon and howled. Then it spun around to face the cage.

"Hey Dex, ya sharin'?" it called out to the werewolf that stood before Hannah.

Dex turned away from Hannah and called back, "Take all ya want, Al."

Hannah's muscles tightened. It felt like some black hole had opened in her gut and was trying to suck the life out of her. She heard rips; clothes were being torn.

"Thanks. Never ate a man before," cried Al.

Hannah dared one glance at the werewolf kneeling in the grass. She saw it open its mouth and lean in for a chomp. She shut her eyes tight and concentrated her listening on Dex's retreating paw patter, to cover what could be the sound of flesh being ripped and chewed.

Could be...

Hannah opened her eyes and stared at the spot where the two werewolves crouched. One was shaking its head to tear apart a chunk of meat it held in one paw. The other chewed and licked at its claws.

"Tastes more like pork than chicken."

"Yeah."

"And there's somethin' kinda astringent..."

"Probably Axe bodywash."

"Yuck."

"Hey, you want a foot? This guy thought his foot would taste good."

"Nah – looks boney."

Hannah's cold sweat began to dissipate.

This was a prank! It had to be! Talking werewolves? This couldn't be real. Though that Dex guy had to be wearing the most realistic werewolf costume ever. Why else would Trevor run out and fall into the grass some forty feet away where she couldn't see everything? The bastard was probably laughing his ass off at the stupid banter of his friends.

Hannah, left knee throbbing and still shaking from what she saw, rose to her feet. She took two steps closer to the bars.

"OK Trev – you had your laugh!" Hannah called out, a sarcastic edge to her tone. "Ha-ha. I know this is a prank!"

No response.

"You can come back now!" Hannah yelled louder to cover the nerves that threw little tremors into her voice. "I'd like to take a good look at those costumes."

Silence.

Except for the chewing.

"Trevor, I don't wanna stay out here all night!" Hannah yelled even louder. "Game's over, Trevor! Do you hear me, Trevor!? You hear me? I wanna go home!"

Hannah watched the one called Al yank at something that had to be a tree branch. It arched one arm back and hurled it at the cage. Hannah tottered back two steps and fell against the tree as the object crashed into the bars and sparked.

Smooth, peach-colored, streaked with red – this was no branch. Angling her head to look where it fell, she could make out the fingers, the ring, the thin blonde hair that lined the side of the arm. Wisps of blonde hair that Trevor always told her he wished would grow longer and thicker and cover his body, so that he could really be a werewolf. Blonde arm hair flattened in places under smears of blood, sticking up in others as if frozen in fright. More blood pooled out of one side where an elbow should have been. This was no prop; this *was* Trevor's arm.

Hannah screamed. Outside, the werewolves howled. A night breeze blew into the cage, bringing the scent of roadkill. Throat sore from yelling, Hannah gulped down the last of the bitter saliva left in her mouth. She wiped cold sweat and tears from her face. She blinked her eyes, and dared glances through the bars. Two more werewolves had joined the two feasting kneelers. They stood looking down at the lifeless lump. Senses heightened from adrenaline, Hannah strained to hear them while she panted.

"Did you have to, Dex?" One of the newly arrived werewolves growled in a high pitch.

"Sorry," said Dex. "He got aggressive, and I… just lost it."

"Trevor McGinty," said another new, lower-pitched voice.

"You know him, Kurt?"

"Know of him," said Kurt. "He hangs out in forums we track. A pesky wanna-wolf. But he must have found out something."

"…Government?"

"Nah. He would've been tagged by our sources earlier."

"What about the gal?"

Hannah could make out the silhouettes of the two standing werewolves turning to look at the cage. One mumbled something she couldn't make out.

"…cage is electrified…" she heard Dex tell them.

The standing werewolves began to lumber towards her. She whipped her head around to look at the door. It was barred from the inside. Would one bar be enough? Wired on the outside, they'd get shocked if they tried to touch it, but what if they could work out some way of disabling the electricity? She grabbed her backpack and moved it to hide the switch. She stood and backed herself up against the tree. As the pair drew closer, she noticed one was shorter than the other, with a curvy feminine shape. A female werewolf? The pair ceased their advance four feet from the bars. They glanced at her, but didn't stare. They raised their muzzles and sniffed the air. They began circling the cage, the male, with long black fur and beady green eyes, in the lead. The female wore a cropped brown halter top and torn jeans. She had yellowish fur. A blonde werewolf, *like Trevor would have been if…* Hannah banished that thought from her mind. She had to focus on what they looked like in case she escaped so she could—

The male shuffled closer to the cage. He stooped and reached down. Hannah tilted her head, to keep what she knew he picked off the ground out of her sight. After standing back up, the male again circled the cage with the female beside him. They moved to the backside of the tree, and this was more frightening; she couldn't see them to get a handle on what they might be doing. Her heart beat faster. She listened to their paws crunching leaves. They stopped for a moment, and Hannah braced herself against the tree, expecting something awful to happen. After what could have been seconds, or minutes, their steps resumed, and it sounded like they were moving around to the right side of the cage. She caught their eyes as they reappeared. The male stared at her a moment, then turned and walked away. The female followed. They stopped about eight feet away and began whispering to each other. The male gestured with both hands; he was no longer carrying what he had picked up. Hannah's pulse beat so hard in her ears she didn't bother to try to decipher their mutters. *I can survive this. I will survive...* she repeated to herself like a mantra.

The two werewolves walked back to stand just a foot away from the bars. The female looked at the ground; the male stared at Hannah. Hannah shot him one glance, then turned her head to avoid his stare. She did not want those green eyes bearing down on the windows to her soul.

"On behalf of my pack..." Kurt intoned, "I want to apologize for what happened tonight... This is not how we normally handle non-violent intruders."

Hannah said nothing. She took a breath, then another. *I can survive this. I will survive...*

"Your name is Hannah Cruz, right?" The female's voice was soft.

Hannah remained silent and told herself not to nod, not to indicate in any way who she was. The less information they had on her, the better.

"We recognize you from your Facebook posts on Lair of the Lycans," said Kurt.

"You're a member of about three or four other werewolf groups on Instagram, and Discord too," the female added.

Hannah closed her eyes, muttered her new mantra, and added: *please let morning come soon.*

"We mean you no harm," said Kurt. "But this cage is on our property and must be dismantled. We'll do that tomorrow afternoon. We ask that you leave at dawn."

Hannah released a breath in a quiver. This sounded too easy. She had to be careful.

Kurt turned and walked away. Suddenly, he broke into a run. The swash of underbrush told her he was moving fast and far into the forest. The female sat down on the ground to Hannah's right, and moved closer to the bars.

"Hey," she whispered to Hannah. "You'll be alright... My name's Tara. Sorry for not introducing myself sooner."

Hannah looked away, but kept Tara in her periphery.

"I'm also sorry for what happened," said Tara softly.

Minutes passed as Hannah listened to the hum of electric fence, the one thing preventing these monsters from reaching her.

"I guess you don't want to talk," said Tara.

Hannah glanced to where Trevor had fallen. The two werewolves who had been feasting on him were gone. So too was the lump of Trevor's body. How had they all moved away without her noticing? Had she been concentrating so hard on ignoring Tara that she failed to hear them leave? The throbbing pain in her right knee grew worse, and her hip pressing into the tree began to ache. Hannah slowly lowered herself to sit on the ground.

Tara looked at Hannah, then at the ground, and flicked at a blade of grass with her index claw. "Was Trevor your boyfriend?"

"He was..." Hannah heard herself say, and wondered why she was saying anything, but now that she'd started, she felt the need to clarify. "Just a friend."

"I think I saw your profile and that you were single," said Tara. "Sorry if I know stuff about you, and I'm sure this is weird. For our own protection we must keep track of people who..." Tara sighed. "Try to seek us out for whatever reason. The government knows about us, and we've had to make deals with them." Tara turned her amber eyes on Hannah's. "They don't want too many more of us than there already are. There are... quotas. That's why we keep to ourselves, and why Dex wasn't..." Tara looked away. "There's a lot of guys that want to be werewolves. Too many." Tara slowly stood up and stretched. "The appeal can be intoxicating." Tara took an expansive breath, her halter tightened against her chest. She raised her arms to the sky and leisurely pirouetted. "The power, the strength, the stealth, the *wildness!*" Tara smiled, baring her fangs. She stared at Hannah, a glow lighting her amber eyes. "Isn't that why you are fascinated by them?"

"I don't know." Hannah began sobbing.

"Haven't you wanted a werewolf boyfriend? Wanted to be one?"

"Not anymore," Hannah whispered. She felt like vomiting.

"Well, maybe you'll change your mind back," Tara smirked. "I sure hope so."

Hannah heard a rustle from her left side. She began to turn her head, but was a split second too late. With a whoosh, something struck her left shoulder. Hannah yelped in pain and clutched her arm. A dart stuck out of it. She looked up to see Kurt lowering a blow gun. Hannah yanked the dart out of her arm and hurled it at the ground.

"What!? Why!?" Hannah cried.

"The 'what' is a shot of our saliva. The 'why' is to give you lycanthropy," said Kurt.

"Too many males, and not enough females in our pack," Tara added. "We've got quotas to take advantage of."

"No! No!" Hannah shook, tears sprouting from her eyes. "I don't wanna be a werewolf!" She kicked the dart with her foot. "I don't wanna be *with* werewolves!"

"Not true – I've read some of that werewolf porn you posted," said Tara. "Talk about smut!"

"Please, please!" Hannah looked back and forth at the furry faces of Tara and her mate.

"You got four weeks till your first change," said Kurt. "We'll send you an email and a guide to the newly bitten."

"Don't cry, sweetheart." Tara crouched down, tilted her head, and stared through the bars at Hannah with puppy-dog eyes. Her ferocious smile broadened, baring two rows of jagged teeth. "You're going to *love* it!"

Fangs Fur Love

James Musgrave

THEY SAY you can't choose your family, but believe me, if I could, I'd trade mine for a pack of rabid bats. Being the only son of the illustrious Von Gorgon vampyr clan comes with definite perks: eternal life, inimitable fashion sense, and an unquenchable thirst for O-positive. Of course, there's the minor inconvenience of turning into a furry nightmare every full moon, thanks to that werewolf cub who decided I looked like a chew toy when I was two.

Strutting through the shadowy halls of Gorgon Castle, I felt every bit the heir to a vampyr dynasty. My reflection in the polished obsidian columns showed a tall, lean figure draped in a midnight-blue cloak that contrasted with my pale skin. Dark hair fell in controlled waves around my face, framing eyes that held a hint of mischief. Sharp cheekbones and an even sharper wit – that's me, Andrei Von Gorgon.

As I turned a corner, I spotted Carinthia Basecourt lounging in the lap of a gargoyle statue as if it were a throne. She exuded an effortless allure that could rival any vampyr noble. Her silver hair cascaded over one shoulder, and her eyes – cold and sharp like chipped ice – matched the silver locket she twirled between her fingers. Dressed in a form-fitting black dress adorned with intricate lace, she looked every bit the enigma she was rumored to be.

"Well, if it isn't Andrei Von Gorgon," she purred, her voice smoother than aged bloodwine.

"Carinthia," I replied, attempting nonchalance but probably sounding like I'd swallowed a fur ball. "Fancy seeing you haunting these halls."

She slid off the gargoyle with feline grace, her boots making no sound on the stone floor. "I heard rumors that you're not just any vampyr."

"Rumors are like howling – mostly harmless," I quipped, eyeing the silver locket that matched the glint in her eyes.

She let out a throaty laugh that made my fangs tingle. "Oh, I do love a good secret."

"Who doesn't?" I returned with a sly smile, though my heart – or what's left of it – was doing somersaults.

Before I knew it, we were strolling under the moonlit arches of the castle gardens. The air was thick with the scent of night-blooming flowers, their petals glowing softly. We debated everything from the latest in nocturnal fashion to the political nuances of vampyr–werewolf relations.

She tilted her head, allowing the moonlight to accentuate the sharp angles of her face. "Imagine if our clans could find common ground," she mused.

"Peace between vampyrs and werewolves?" I chuckled, brushing a stray leaf off my cloak. "That's like expecting a garlic clove to win 'Vegetable of the Year' at a vampyr convention."

"Perhaps with the right encouragement," she said, her eyes meeting mine with an intensity that was both alluring and unsettling.

I should have sensed the hidden agenda lurking behind those silver eyes, but I was too busy being sixteen and feeling invincible. After all, who wouldn't trust a girl who could probably bench-press a carriage in her wolf form?

"Count me in," I declared. "What's the worst that could happen?"

Famous last words.

* * *

If there's one thing I dislike more than sunrises, it's melodramatic shapeshifters. The next evening, Carinthia suggested we attend the annual Night Market – a dubious assembly of magical misfits selling everything from hexed trinkets to potions promising eternal youth, not that I needed it.

"Trust me," she said, linking her arm with mine as we walked through the towering iron gates. Her touch was warm, a stark contrast to my naturally cold skin.

"Is it your tailor? Because I have questions about that cloak," I teased, glancing at her attire – a dark ensemble accentuated with silver chains and amulets.

She rolled her eyes, a small smile playing on her lips. "Very funny. No, he's a magician who claims he can help us with our peace plan."

"Nothing says 'trustworthy' like a self-proclaimed magician at a black market," I muttered, eyeing the stalls filled with glowing artifacts and bottled curses.

We weaved through the bustling crowd until a flamboyantly dressed figure in purple robes caught our attention. His stall was adorned with flashing lights and swirling smoke.

"Step right up! Witness the wonders of Alaric the Astonishing!" he proclaimed, his eyes gleaming under thick eyebrows.

"More like Alaric the Appalling," I whispered to Carinthia, who stifled a giggle.

"Ah, young love!" Alaric exclaimed, zeroing in on us. His grin revealed more gold teeth than seemed practical. "Looking to spice things up? Perhaps a love potion?"

"Actually, we're here for a peace potion," Carinthia corrected.

"Peace, love – two sides of the same coin!" Alaric declared, producing a vial filled with swirling, iridescent liquid. "This, my friends, is the ultimate solution."

I scrutinized the concoction, noticing faint wisps of smoke forming questionable shapes. "And what's in it? Essence of gullibility?"

"Only the finest ingredients," he assured, placing a hand over his heart. "A sip, and all animosities will vanish!"

"Sounds legitimate," I said, my tone dripping with sarcasm.

Before I could protest further, Carinthia purchased the potion. "This could be the key," she insisted, her eyes reflecting the swirling liquid.

"To what? Our untimely demise?"

As we turned to leave, a commotion erupted behind us. A group of shapeshifters, shifting erratically between forms, were causing chaos.

"Unsatisfied customers?" I remarked.

One of them, mid-transformation between a man and a fox, bumped into Carinthia, causing her to drop the vial.

"Watch it!" I snapped, baring my fangs.

"Apologies!" the shapeshifter replied before morphing into a raven and flying off with what looked suspiciously like my coin pouch.

"Great, now we're broke and potion-less," I sighed.

A shimmering trail of the spilled potion led away from us. "Looks like it didn't all go to waste," Carinthia observed.

"We can follow it," I agreed, though with little enthusiasm.

What followed was a ludicrous chase through the winding paths around the castle. The shapeshifters transformed into various creatures – a cat darting under stalls, a toad leaping into a pond – each escape more frustrating than the last.

At one point, I confronted a particularly disgruntled goat chewing on a piece of parchment. "You wouldn't happen to be a shapeshifter, would you?"

The goat stared blankly before bleating and trotting away.

"Figures," I muttered.

Meanwhile, other creatures had come into contact with the spilled potion. Squirrels gazed adoringly at stone gargoyles, and a garden gnome recited poetry to a bewildered hedgehog.

"This is absurd," I declared.

Finally, we cornered Alaric near the stables. "Give us the real potion!" Carinthia demanded, her eyes flashing with a dangerous glint.

"Ah, but that was the real potion!" he insisted, backing away slowly. "Perhaps it was a tad miscalibrated."

"A tad?" I echoed. "You've got rodents proposing to inanimate objects!"

"Love works in mysterious ways," he shrugged, attempting a disarming smile.

By the night's end, we retrieved the potion – now a muddy paste – and more questions than answers. As we trudged back to the castle, Carinthia huffed, "Well, that didn't go as planned."

"On the contrary," I smirked. "It went exactly as I expected."

She shot me a playful glare. "Always the pessimist."

"Realist, darling. Realist."

Little did I know, the real chaos was just beginning.

* * *

After the Night Market fiasco, doubts crept in like fog over a graveyard. Carinthia's undeniable charm was matched only by her willingness to involve shady magicians and dubious potions. I decided to test her honesty.

"Meet me at the East Tower tonight," I told her the next day. "There's something I want to show you."

"Another one of your surprises?" she inquired, arching an elegant eyebrow.

"You'll see."

I enlisted the help of my cousin Vlad, a master of illusion spells and someone who owed me a favor after that incident with the disappearing mirror. As dusk settled, I waited atop the East Tower, the wind tousling my dark hair. The panoramic view of the castle grounds below was both majestic and foreboding.

Carinthia arrived, her silver hair glowing under the moonlight. "So, what's this grand reveal?" she asked, her gaze curious yet cautious.

"First, a question: Do you trust me?"

She tilted her head thoughtfully. "Trust is earned, but yes, I think I do."

"Good," I nodded. "Because I've arranged a little demonstration."

At that moment, Vlad's illusion materialized – a towering figure resembling Lord Mortimer, a vampyr known for his disdain of werewolves. His crimson cloak billowed as if caught in an invisible breeze, and his eyes glowed with a sinister light.

"Andrei Von Gorgon!" the illusion thundered. "What is the meaning of this fraternization with the enemy?"

Carinthia stiffened beside me. "Is that Lord Mortimer?"

"Apparently so," I feigned surprise. "He must have followed us."

"You will bring shame upon your clan!" the illusion continued. "This alliance is forbidden!"

Carinthia's eyes darted between me and the apparition. "We need to explain—"

"No time!" I interrupted. "Tell him we're working undercover!"

"Undercover? That's your plan?" she whispered incredulously.

"Do you have a better one?"

Before she could respond, the illusion declared, "Silence! The werewolf must be eliminated!"

Her expression hardened. Without warning, she stepped between me and the illusion, her posture defensive. "You'll have to go through me first," she growled, a hint of her wolf form edging into her features.

"Stand down!" the illusion commanded.

"Never!" she shot back, her nails elongating into claws.

Seeing her willingness to protect me, guilt gnawed at me. I signaled to Vlad to end the charade. The illusion flickered before dissipating into wisps of smoke.

"What just happened?" Carinthia demanded, turning to face me.

I sighed, rubbing the back of my neck. "Alright, you caught me. It was a test."

"A test?" Her eyes flashed with anger. "You orchestrated that entire scene?"

"I needed to know where your loyalties lie," I admitted.

She laughed bitterly. "You're questioning my loyalty? You're the one setting up fake ambushes!"

"Technically, Vlad did the heavy lifting," I mumbled.

"You know, for someone aiming to build trust between our clans, you have a peculiar way of showing it."

"Can you blame me?" I countered. "You're mysterious, cunning, and perhaps a bit too charming for your own good."

She softened slightly, the tension easing from her shoulders. "Flattery won't get you out of this."

"Not even a little?" I asked, offering a sheepish grin.

She sighed. "Maybe a little. But promise me – no more tricks."

"Agreed," I said, though a part of me remained skeptical. "Honesty from now on."

"Good," she nodded. "Because I have a surprise for you tomorrow."

"Should I be concerned?"

"Only if you don't trust me," she replied with a cryptic smile.

As she descended the tower stairs, I couldn't shake the feeling that I might have underestimated her.

* * *

The next evening, anticipation and a hint of dread coursed through me as I waited in the grand hall. Carinthia had arranged a 'special event', and given recent events, I wasn't sure what to expect.

"Ready for our adventure?" Carinthia's voice echoed as she entered, her attire a blend of elegance and mystery. She wore a deep green cloak that accentuated her eyes, and a subtle pendant hung around her neck – a wolf's head crafted from silver.

"As ready as I'll ever be," I replied. "So, what's the plan? A nocturnal picnic? A séance?"

"You'll find out soon enough." She handed me a similar pendant. "Wear this. It will help you embrace your true nature."

I eyed the pendant warily. "Matching jewelry already? We must be getting serious."

She chuckled. "Just put it on."

We ventured into the dense forest surrounding the castle, the canopy above filtering moonlight into scattered beams. The sounds of nocturnal creatures filled the air – owls hooting, leaves rustling.

"Where exactly are we headed?" I inquired.

"Patience," she said, stepping over a fallen log with ease.

"Trust, right?" I muttered, fastening the pendant around my neck.

After navigating through tangled underbrush, we arrived at a secluded clearing. A circle of ancient stones surrounded a roaring bonfire, casting flickering shadows on the surrounding trees.

"Welcome to the Gathering of the Clans," Carinthia announced.

Before I could respond, figures emerged from the darkness – werewolves in human form, their eyes reflecting the firelight. Their presence was imposing; muscles taut, postures confident.

"Carinthia, what's going on?" I whispered.

She faced me, her expression earnest. "It's time for you to embrace your werewolf side."

"Funny, I was just getting comfortable with my vampyr half."

An elder stepped forward, his eyes a piercing amber. Scars etched his weathered face, telling tales of battles long past. "So, this is the hybrid we've heard about."

"Hybrid?" I forced a smile. "I prefer 'uniquely versatile.'"

Carinthia placed a reassuring hand on my arm. "Tonight, you'll undergo a ritual to awaken your inner wolf."

"Awaken? It's already pretty awake, thank you."

She gestured toward a stone altar where a wooden chalice rested. "Drink this elixir. It will help you connect with your true nature."

I approached the altar, eyeing the concoction that shimmered with a silvery hue. "Of course. Another mysterious potion."

"Do you trust me?" Carinthia asked softly.

I met her gaze, seeing sincerity in her eyes. "I suppose I do."

Taking a deep breath, I lifted the chalice and drank. A warmth spread through my body, followed by a tingling sensation that intensified with each heartbeat.

"See? Not so bad," Carinthia smiled.

Suddenly, a sharp pain coursed through me. My senses heightened – the scent of the forest became overwhelming, the sound of crackling fire deafening.

"What's happening?" I gasped.

"You're transforming," she explained, a hint of concern in her voice.

"But it's not the full moon!"

"The pendant accelerates the process," she admitted.

"Fantastic," I groaned as my bones shifted and muscles contorted. Fur sprouted along my arms, and my hands morphed into clawed paws.

Panic surged. "I didn't sign up for this!"

"Embrace it!" Carinthia urged. "Don't fight it."

Overwhelmed, I stumbled away from the circle, crashing through the underbrush. The forest seemed alive, branches clawing at me as I ran.

"Andrei, wait!" her voice called after me.

"Stay back!" I snarled, my voice a guttural growl.

I collapsed beside a stream, gazing into the water. The reflection that stared back was neither fully vampyr nor werewolf – a distorted amalgamation that sent a shiver down my spine.

"Great, I look like I lost a fight with a lawnmower," I muttered.

Carinthia approached cautiously, her own features partially transformed. "Now you understand what it's like."

"Uncontrollable transformations and identity crises? Delightful."

"It's who you are," she insisted.

"Or who you want me to be?"

She sighed. "I just wanted to help you see both sides."

As the transformation subsided, exhaustion weighed me down. "I need time to process this."

"Take all the time you need," she replied gently.

We walked back in silence, the distance between us palpable. I realized that before I could help bridge our worlds, I needed to understand my own.

* * *

The following morning, a scroll was slipped under my chamber door.

Meet me at dusk by the old oak. – Carinthia.

Determined to get answers, I prepared for whatever she had planned, ensuring I had a few tricks up my sleeve.

As the sun dipped below the horizon, I arrived at the ancient oak, its twisted branches silhouetted against the darkening sky.

"You're punctual," Carinthia observed, stepping from behind the tree. She wore a simple dress, devoid of her usual adornments.

"And you're cryptic," I retorted. "What's this about?"

"I wanted to apologize for last night."

"Which part? The forced transformation or the identity crisis?"

"All of it," she admitted. "I realize I may have pushed you too far."

I crossed my arms. "Go on."

She produced a small vial containing a translucent liquid. "This is a truth serum. If we both take it, we can clear the air."

"A truth serum? Sounds risky."

"Only if you're hiding something," she challenged.

I hesitated before accepting the vial. "Fine."

We each took a sip, the liquid leaving a bitter taste.

She spoke first. "Why do you really want peace between our clans?"

The serum compelled honesty. "At first, it was about proving myself. Being a hero. But now, I see the potential for real change."

She nodded thoughtfully. "Your turn."

"Are you using me to gain favor with your clan?"

Her gaze dropped. "Yes."

I felt a sting of betrayal. "So, it was all a game?"

"It started that way," she confessed. "But things changed."

"Convenient timing," I remarked.

Before she could respond, figures emerged from the shadows – members of both our clans, their expressions grim.

"What's going on?" I demanded.

Carinthia stepped back, her face unreadable. "I'm sorry, Andrei. This was the only way."

"The only way for what?"

The werewolf elder stepped forward. "To expose you as the threat you are."

Lord Mortimer appeared beside him. "Your existence jeopardizes the balance."

"Fantastic," I sighed. "An intervention."

"Your time is up," the elder declared.

As they closed in, a surge of defiance welled up. Drawing upon both sides of my lineage, I prepared to defend myself.

"Wait!" Carinthia shouted. "There must be another way."

"You've done your part," the elder snapped. "Stand aside."

She looked at me, regret evident in her eyes. "I never wanted this."

"Could've fooled me," I replied.

Just as tensions reached a breaking point, a commanding voice echoed through the clearing. "Enough!"

* * *

My father, Count Vladislav Von Gorgon, emerged from the shadows, his crimson cloak billowing behind him. His eyes, a deep shade of burgundy, surveyed the scene with a mix of anger and disappointment. "This conflict ends now," he declared.

Behind him stood a contingent of vampyrs, their pale faces stern, fangs glinting under the moonlight. Opposite them, werewolves began to shift, muscles rippling as fur sprouted along their bodies. Their eyes glowed amber, low growls emanating from deep within.

The werewolf elder snarled, "Stay out of this, Vladislav. The hybrid must be eliminated."

"I will not allow senseless violence to taint our lands," my father retorted, his voice steady.

Lord Mortimer stepped forward, his features sharp and unforgiving. "The abomination threatens our very existence. It is our duty to cleanse this impurity."

"Abomination?" I scoffed. "That's rich coming from someone who sleeps in a coffin."

"I also sleep in a coffin, when the mood strikes me." Carinthia confessed. "I am a hybrid as well."

Tensions snapped. With a howl, a massive werewolf lunged forward. His form was towering – easily eight feet tall – with matted gray fur and claws like daggers. His jaws snapped, revealing rows of razor-sharp teeth designed to rend flesh from bone.

A vampyr met his charge, leaping with supernatural agility. Clad in dark armor, she wielded a blade forged from silver, its edge glowing faintly. They clashed mid-air, the impact sending a shockwave that rustled the surrounding trees.

Chaos erupted. Werewolves transformed en masse, their human forms giving way to beasts of legend. Some were hulking brutes with muscles bulging under thick fur; others were lean and agile, moving with predatory grace. Their howls filled the night, a haunting chorus that echoed across the landscape.

The vampyrs retaliated with equal ferocity. They moved like shadows, disappearing and reappearing in blurs of motion. Eyes glowing red, they struck with precision, utilizing centuries of combat experience. Some wielded swords and spears, while others relied on their claws and fangs.

I stood at the center of the maelstrom, unsure where to turn. Carinthia transformed beside me, her werewolf form sleek and powerful. Silver fur covered her lithe frame, and her eyes retained their icy clarity.

"Andrei, we have to stop this!" she shouted over the din, her voice a mix of human and beast.

"Agreed, but how?" I responded, feeling the pull of my own transformation.

A werewolf charged toward us, eyes wild. He swung a massive paw, aiming for my head. Instinct took over. I ducked and countered with a swift kick to his midsection, sending him sprawling.

"Nice move," Carinthia noted, fending off a vampyr who attempted to stake her with a sharpened piece of wood.

"Thanks," I replied. "But we can't keep fighting our own."

The battlefield was a whirlwind of snarls, clashes, and flashes of steel. Vampyrs and werewolves were locked in combat, each side refusing to yield. The ground became slick with mud and traces of dark, unnatural blood.

Amidst the chaos, I spotted my father dueling with the werewolf elder. Vladislav moved with calculated elegance, his blade weaving intricate patterns as he parried and struck. The elder, in his wolf form, was a formidable opponent – muscles coiled like springs, jaws snapping inches from my father's face.

"Father!" I called out, but he was too engrossed in the fight to hear.

Carinthia grabbed my arm. "We have to do something drastic."

An idea sparked. "The bell tower!"

She nodded in understanding. Together, we sprinted toward the towering structure at the edge of the courtyard. Dodging skirmishes, we made our way inside and began ascending the spiral staircase.

Reaching the top, we found the massive iron bell suspended above us. Its surface was etched with ancient runes, designed to amplify its sound.

"Think this will work?" she asked, her features shifting back to human form.

"It has to," I replied, grasping the thick rope attached to the bell's clapper.

We pulled with all our might. The bell swung, emitting a deep, resonant toll that cut through the cacophony below. The sound reverberated across the castle grounds, causing everyone to pause.

The fighters hesitated, glancing around in confusion.

Seizing the moment, I projected my voice with all the authority I could muster. "Enough! Look at what we're doing!"

All eyes turned toward the bell tower.

"This battle serves no purpose," Carinthia shouted. "We are destroying ourselves over fear and mistrust."

My father lowered his weapon, breathing heavily. The werewolf elder did the same, his chest heaving.

"Listen to them," Vladislav urged. "Our children see a future beyond this endless conflict."

Lord Mortimer scowled but remained silent.

I continued, "We stand here as proof that our kinds can coexist. That we can find strength in our differences."

Murmurs spread through the crowd. Weapons were lowered, and the tension began to dissipate.

The werewolf elder transformed back into his human form – a grizzled man with tired eyes. "Perhaps we've let old wounds fester for too long."

Vladislav approached him. "Agreed. It's time we forge a new path."

* * *

Preparations for the wedding were swift. The castle transformed, adorned with a blend of vampyr elegance and werewolf rusticity. Flowers and dark draperies intertwined, symbolizing the merging of our worlds.

As I stood at the altar, a sense of hope filled me. Carinthia approached, radiant in a gown that seemed to shimmer with every color of the moon. Her eyes met mine, and we shared a moment of understanding.

"Ready?" she whispered.

"Absolutely," I replied.

The ceremony proceeded without incident until the moon reached its zenith. A cloud moved aside, revealing its full brilliance.

I felt the familiar tingling of transformation. "Not again," I murmured.

Carinthia's eyes widened. "The full moon…"

Our changes were swift. In moments, we stood before the gathered guests in our hybrid forms – a vampyr-werewolf and a werewolf with vampyr heritage. Gasps echoed through the hall.

"Behold," I announced. "We are the embodiment of unity."

Silence hung heavy until a young vampyr stepped forward. "They're beautiful," she said softly.

A werewolf joined her. "Perhaps there's more to us than we thought."

Applause broke out, hesitant at first but growing in enthusiasm. The elders smiled, and a sense of genuine acceptance filled the room.

As we exchanged vows, I knew that while challenges lay ahead, we had taken the first crucial step toward a shared future.

Later, during the feast, Carinthia and I stood on a balcony overlooking the mingling clans.

"So," she began, a playful glint in her eye, "about our future children."

I chuckled. "Wondering if they'll inherit the best – or worst – of both worlds?"

"Perhaps they'll be hybrids like us," she mused. "Or maybe something entirely new."

"Either way, they'll have quite the lineage," I remarked. "Vampyr elegance and werewolf strength."

She smiled. "And hopefully your sarcasm."

"Perish the thought," I grinned.

She leaned into me. "Do you think the clans will accept them?"

I wrapped an arm around her. "They'll have to. Our union is the bridge between worlds."

"True," she agreed. "But it's up to us to ensure that bridge remains strong."

"With you by my side, I'm ready for whatever comes next."

She looked up, eyes reflecting the stars. "Always."

Under the watchful gaze of the full moon, we embraced our future – not just for ourselves, but for the generations that would follow. The night was filled with possibilities, and for the first time, I felt at peace with who I was.

"Ready to face eternity together?" I asked.

She nodded. "As long as we have each other."

"Then let's get started," I said, taking her hand as we joined our clans below.

Bran, the Wolf Dog

Jane Pentzer Myers

ON A HIGH CLIFF overlooking the ocean, on the western coast of Ireland, stand the ruins of an old castle. The short grass grows on the floor of the great hall, and the wind sighs and howls through its broken walls, with a sound half human, half animal.

The peasants for generations have named it 'The Wolf's Castle'. Even long years ago, when it was tenanted by kindly folk and was running over with life and happiness, it had already earned its grim name.

Max had been out hunting. He had spent the day in the woods and fields, and now as night fell, dark and lowering, he hastened his steps. The first scattering drops of rain struck his face, and the wind was rising. It moaned and howled like the distant cry of a wolf; it made Max feel strangely nervous and frightened. "Frightened!" – he laughed at the thought. "A boy of twelve frightened by the wind!"

And yet, listen! The patter of the rain (coming faster now) sounds on the leaves like the stealthy tread of some animal.

"If it is a wolf, it is the ghost of one; for there are no wolves in this country now," thought Max. "How like a sigh from human lips the wind sounds!"

"Home at last, I am thankful to say," and Max ran swiftly round to the back door. As he closed it, the wind gave a long-drawn wail, and he almost fancied a hand strove to draw him back into the darkness.

"I think I need my supper," thought he. "Fasting makes a fellow light-headed."

Entering the kitchen with exultant heart but studied indifference, he threw his game down on the table before the admiring cook, and then hastened to change his dress. Soon, over a good supper, he had forgotten the uncanny night outside, though the wind still howled and the rain beat against the window.

After supper Max went into the library. How cosy and comfortable it was, with a fire in the grate, an easy-chair drawn in front of it, and the shadows dancing over books and pictures!

"I'll sit here in front of the fire and rest," thought he. He sat there mentally reviewing the day's sport. "I need a good dog," he said. "I must have one. Why, what is that?" For there, lying in front of the fire, basking in the heat, was an immense dog, with shaggy coat and pointed ears. Max called to him:

"Here, old fellow; here, Bran – why, he knows his name. How did I come to know it, I wonder!" For at the first call, the dog had raised his head and beat his great tail upon the floor. At the mention of his name he sprang to his feet, and came crouching and trembling with joy to lick the hands and shoes of the lad.

"What is it then, good dog? Tell me your story, for I'm sure you have one to tell," coaxed Max.

Did he tell it, or did Max dream? For as the dog rested his head on the boy's knee and looked with liquid, loving eyes into his face, Max glanced round the room and saw a strange transformation: the walls widened, the ceiling rose to a greater height, and was crossed by great black beams. On the walls hung shields, spears, great swords, and numerous other articles of war and of the chase.

The polished grate had grown into an immense fireplace, and the floor was covered with what Max supposed were rushes. But the people in the room interested him most of all. On the opposite side of the fireplace, in a great carven chair, sat a lady, young and very lovely – her dress some rich dark green material clasped at the throat and waist by heavy golden clasps, her bare arms heavy with gold armlets, her long black hair falling in shining waves around her, and her eyes – the sea was in them – gray or dark blue, and in moments of anger flashing greenish yellow like the eyes of some animal.

She sat with her elbow on the arm of her chair, her head resting on her hand, looking into the fire and listening to the music of an ancient harper, who sat in the background, softly striking the chords of his harp.

The firelight, dancing over the room, caused strange shadows; and Max fancied himself one of the shadows, for his chair was filled by a boy of his own age, sitting just as he had been sitting, with the great dog's head on his knee; and notwithstanding his strange dress, Max started with a feeling almost of terror, for the boy was his double; it was like seeing himself in the glass.

A storm was raging around the castle, and above the soft music of the harp could be heard the rush of the wind, and the roar of the ocean dashing at the foot of the cliff.

The lady shivered and glanced round the room. "I wish your father were home, Patrick. How glad I shall be when peace comes again."

"I wish I were old enough to lead the clan to battle, then father could remain with you."

"What? become a dotard? Out upon you!" Her eyes flashed at the boy, and the dog, raising his head, gave a low growl. "Why do you not have that beast speared? You know I hate him," said the lady.

"He was given to me (as you know) by the good fathers at the monastery. They told me always to cherish Bran, for he would save me from demons, as well as wolves. See the silver crosses on his collar. Nothing can harm us while Bran is here."

The lady cast a look of fear and hatred at the boy and the dog. "Be not too sure," she said. Springing to her feet, she walked back and forth through the room. Her step was smooth and graceful; she made no sound on the rushes as she walked.

Presently there came a lull in the storm, and from somewhere back in the hills came the howl of a wolf. The lady paused and listened, then turning to the boy she said in a hurried manner, while her eyes sought the floor: "I feel ill; I am going to my room. Let no one disturb me tomorrow; if I need help I will call." And as she turned to leave the room, suddenly she paused. "Get you to bed, Patrick, chain up that dog, and – you are the hope and pride of your father – I lay my commands on you – do not hunt tomorrow."

Then the lady was gone; but Bran was trembling and growling. "He heard the wolves howl," said Patrick to the harper. The old man looked into the fire and was silent.

Presently Patrick arose, and bidding the harper good-night, went to his room, closely followed at the heels by the great dog. To his surprise, awaiting him in his room was the housekeeper, an ancient woman, who had been his father's nurse. She rose when Patrick entered, and came toward him.

"My mind is troubled, child," she said; "I must tell you my story."

"What is it, nurse?"

"It is about my lady Eileen, your stepmother. May I speak?"

"Tell on," said Patrick. "But remember, I will hear nothing against my lady," for he well knew that the nurse bore the young stepmother no good will.

"Well, listen, child. You were not here when your father married my lady. You had not left the monastery where your father placed you for safety while he was beyond seas. I must tell you first how she came here."

"Fingal, the huntsman, told me that one day, when your father was hunting alone, he was followed all day by a wolf. It would lurk from one hillock to another, but when he turned to pursue it, it would disappear. Finally, at noon, when he sat down to rest, it came creeping and fawning to his feet. He was tempted to spear it, but did not, out of surprise. Presently it disappeared; but in the gloaming it returned, and followed him clear to the gate of the castle. This my lord told to Fingal, and greatly did he marvel. That same night," whispered the nurse, mysteriously, "came a call for help, and when the gate was opened, there stood a beautiful woman (my lady Eileen) who told how she had lost her way and her company as she journeyed to St. Hilda's shrine. Your father bade her enter, and she has abode here ever since; for soon he married her, and she became our lady."

"Well, well, nurse, I knew of her coming, and I know also that she was no waif, but of a noble house and high lineage, as her coat of arms bears witness – a wolf couchant. But why explain all this to you? Right glad am I that she came to gladden my father's heart and brighten our home."

"Yes, child, but listen; this only brings me to my story. My lady has strange spells of illness, and always after a wolf howls." The boy started impatiently, but the old dame, laying her hand on his arm, compelled him to listen. "The last time it was moonlight. I was up in the turret opposite her window; her lamp was lit, and I saw a strange sight. My lady was springing with long leaps backward and forward over the floor, and wringing her hands. Presently she went to her closet, took from it a wolf's skin, slipped it over her dress, and I do not know how she got outside the walls, but I saw her presently speeding away with long leaps toward the hills."

"Nurse, nurse, are you crazy? It is my lady of whom you speak. Never let me hear you breathe that story again. Think of my father's wrath, should this come to his ears."

Still the old woman shook her head and mumbled in wrath, and speedily betook herself away; while Patrick, laughing heartily at her foolish story, went to bed. But all night above the roar of the storm could be heard the howling of wolves.

The morning broke wild and gloomy; the castle seemed lonely and dreary without the cheery presence of Lady Eileen. Patrick went once to her door and knocked, but received no answer. Presently Fingal, the huntsman, came in, armed for the chase. Bran followed close at his heels. "Will my lord hunt today? The wolves were among the flocks last night, the shepherds tell me."

Patrick hesitated, remembering his lady's commands, but he decided finally to go. Soon he was ready, and issuing from the gates, he and Fingal and the dog were lost in the mists that enveloped the hills.

Long did the household wait their return. Night was brooding over the castle when Fingal's horn was heard at the gate. In answer to the warder's call his voice came sternly through the night: "Bring help, and come quickly; my lady is dead." To the grievous outcries and questions that arose he would return no answer.

Soon an excited group were hurrying toward the hills, and presently the torches revealed a sad sight. The first to come into view was their young lord, crouching on the ground, with the dog's head clasped in his arms; Bran's throat had been torn and mangled, and he had been thrust through with a spear. Patrick was wounded and torn in many places; blood was flowing down his face and throat, and his tears were falling on the dog's head. Not far away lay Lady Eileen, quite dead. Very beautiful and placid she looked, as if sleeping; but on her throat were marks of great teeth.

"Take up my lady and bear her to the castle," said Patrick; "as for Bran, you must bury him here."

"Nay, child, he is only a dead dog," said the old nurse, fussily. But she was met by a stern command to be quiet.

"Do as I bid you," he said to the servants, and then added, "The good dog went mad, and attacked my lady. I could not save her. Let my father know this, should I die," and then the boy fell backward, fainting.

To the father it was a sad home-coming when, a few days later, he returned from war – his beautiful young wife lying cold and dead in the chapel; his son very ill, calling always for Bran to save him from some deadly peril.

Greatly the household marvelled how their lady came to be out in the mist and the storm, alone on the hills; but Fingal, the huntsman, sought his two gossips, the nurse and the harper, and told this tale of the day's hunt.

"We had followed the wolves all day, and several had been killed. But there was one gray wolf, who seemed the leader of the pack. This one my lord singled out, and followed from valley to valley. Bran would not pursue it, but slunk and cowered after his master, whining pitifully. All day we followed it, until, late in the gloaming, it had headed toward the castle; and we pressed it hard. It finally turned at bay, and, springing at my lord's throat, it brought him to the ground. Bran was lagging behind, and I was urging him forward. When he heard my lord's cries, the dog flew at the wolf. The beast then turned on the dog, and as I ran to help to spear it, I saw—" here the huntsman's voice sank into a whisper – "I saw no wolf, but my lady, tearing and rending the dog, while Bran's teeth were buried in her throat.

"'Separate them! Save them!' cried my lord; and I, not knowing what else to do, watched my chance and thrust the dog through the body. He sank without a groan, relaxing his grasp on my lady's throat. My lord gave a cry of despair, and my lady, hearing it, crept over to him and whispering, 'Forgive; I could not help it,' sank dead at his feet. But Lord Patrick passed her by, and threw himself down by the dog; while I, half distraught, came home for help."

Then said the nurse, "See that you hold your tongue, man, for if this story come to the ears of my lord, your body will want a head."

But from that time forth the Lady Eileen was spoken of as 'The Wolf Lady', and in time, the grim name of the 'Wolf's Castle' clung to her old home.

In the years that came and passed, Patrick became chief in his father's place; and then a cairn was raised over the body of the faithful dog.

Max awoke to find the fire out; shivered, and sprang to his feet. "What a strange dream!" he said.

Happy Dancing Rejects

Plangdi Neple

ONCE, THERE WAS half a man, hidden away in the mountains and bushes around his village. And then there was a woman with a body made in a stolen mortar and rats' blood.

This is how they met, and what happened because of it.

* * *

One night, while her farmer husband slept, the woman ventured behind the mountains, to the place of her yearly remaking.

As she stepped on drying leaves and sticks and stones, she made sure the sound of her footsteps matched the sound of the forest beyond the mountains. She slammed the bag of rats in her hand on her back to silence their squealing.

Usually, she would keep a careful eye out for beasts, hyenas, rogue goats, snakes and the occasional antelope. And, of course, the magical rejects.

But that night, her mind was elsewhere, and so her eyes did not see the leopard slinking from oak tree to mango tree to shrub, silently dogging her steps.

She couldn't stop thinking of her afternoon with Kyenpia. She had just finished cleaning and blowing acha under the guava tree behind her hut when her best friend came to see her. She groaned as she saw the woman bent over the raffia weaved sieve, adjusting the wrapper tied under her armpit.

"Muplang again? You said you'd be free this afternoon."

Maybe it was the sun, and its assault on Muplang all afternoon, but she was irritated.

"Eh toh. I still have things to do," she spat. "Not everyone can be as free and adventurous as you and your husband."

Kyenpia simply hummed as her long fingers inspected the fruit on the guava tree, but the tightening of her lips immediately made Muplang feel guilty for her sharp tone, and she rose and dropped the sieve on the stool.

"I'm sorry, but I've told you before, I'd rather we go in the night."

Kyenpia hissed and shook her head. "Is it because of that your husband or what? I told you you shouldn't have married him. If you can't even be honest with him about something like this, how can you stay married to him?"

How long did it take for a dissenting voice to plant itself in your head, and then become yours? Even five years after their wedding, Kyenpia didn't like to be around Muplang's husband, and had apparently grown tired of hiding it. And after five years of sneaking off to the forest at night, Muplang was starting to tire too. But of what, she could never tell Kyenpia. So, she simply promised her best friend that she would go alone that night and perform the ritual.

* * *

There were many reasons she should not be in the forest at night.

It was at night that cursed beasts came out, rejects of children who tried to use magic to turn their pets or parents' animals into something else. The first time Muplang had seen a cat with a pig's snout and tail, her father had to seal her mouth with his palm.

"Don't scream. It'll feel bad if you do."

At seven years old, her father's comment made no sense to her, nor did his saddened eyes whenever he saw the spliced animals. All she knew was fear that the strange things would chase her down, and she would never eat groundnut or cow leg peppersoup again. Yet, her heart yearned to see them again. So, the next day, she'd pulled her father from his dinner and into the bushes near their house, so they could see pig-cats and chicken-lizards again.

It was at fifteen that she started to see the creatures in a different way, and wanted to know exactly the spells and incantations and potions that had turned them into what they were. But she never told anyone, because then, she would have to explain how she had started to be envious of her mother and sisters, how everyone called them "women", but called Muplang "man". She would have to tell them how when she followed her father to the forest on his nightly fortnightly trips, she would linger at moonlit puddles, imagining her reflection with the breasts and long hair that she knew people would demand before they called her woman.

Can one miss a part of themselves if they have never seen it?

Kyenpia was the first person she told, because she was her friend… and a prostitute's daughter. Who would she be to judge, Muplang had thought. The two girls had been returning from school when Muplang broke the news. Kyenpia barely glanced at her, eyes fixed on the groundnuts she was popping and throwing into her mouth.

"Okay," she said. "I can help you."

The widening of Muplang's eyes and confused stuttering made Kyenpia laugh. What regular child just had a transformation spell lying around?

"You have magic?" Muplang asked. Kyenpia's lips flattened and she nodded, beaded plaits bouncing.

"I want to change my face," she said, her hand circling her rodent-like visage.

Muplang understood the plaintive yearning on Kyenpia's face; she would bet anything that anytime the other girl looked into a mirror, she wished to see something, *someone*, else. But where Muplang wanted to look more like herself, the woman she knew she was, Kyenpia wanted to look like someone else, someone who would not draw mocking fingers and taunts and 'look, that's that whore's child, do you think she'll start sleeping around too?' Both girls had cried and laughed and danced on the evening they'd performed the ritual, and had been inseparable since then. It only made sense that they ran away from Shendam together.

Now, as she weaved between gnarled tree trunks and stooped under low-hanging branches, she couldn't help but wonder. Where had she gone, the girl who had been so excited that night, grinding lizard bones in the mortar she stole from her mother, slitting the throats of four rats, and sprinkling the mixture of blood and bones with firewood ash, then painting her whole body with it? As it was, she didn't even look forward to the dance she would have to do after the mixing. Not when it meant she would have to sneak out of her house and do it all over again, or risk returning to *that* body.

Her chest ached. She was tired. So tired.

* * *

In over ten years, the leopard had not interacted with another human being at night, seen his skin under the moonlight.

So, really, who could blame him as he watched the strange woman from the treetops. Having followed her from the moment she entered the forest, he'd borne witness to her relentless lip-chewing and sighs. He was surprised she hadn't chewed it off completely. That obvious worry and pensiveness, different from the other times he'd seen her in the forest, had made him follow.

She stopped by a pond, and dropped the bag she carried. From it, she withdrew materials that made the leopard's heart stutter. A short knife, bones, and one brown, squirming rat.

Skin tingling, he leaped from the tree straight into the pond. Water sprayed everywhere and the woman screamed and fell back onto her buttocks. Though he'd gotten the desired result, he wondered. She had never screamed at the cursed animals she saw, things surely stranger than he. So, why him?

As she shuffled away from him, filling the forest with unnatural sounds, a figure materialized and bent to pick her up. The woman jerked when the figure touched her. Then she turned and saw a naked headless man, and closed the mouth she'd probably opened to scream. She grabbed the figure's ghostly white forearm.

"Please help me," she said. "I don't know where the animal came from."

Then the leopard opened his mouth, and laughed.

The woman's eyes widened and her hand fell away from the headless man, whose body also shook with silent laughter.

"So you're afraid of an animal, but not a spirit?"

Despite the confusion on her features, she snorted and crossed her arms. "Who said I was afraid of you? I was just surprised. I'm a hunter's daughter."

The leopard shook its head and prowled closer to her, baring his teeth. She didn't move, but swallowed. "And what is a hunter's daughter doing with magic? Magic she definitely doesn't know how to use?"

She uncrossed her arms and glared at him. "I've been using it for five years. Who told you I don't know what I'm doing?"

The leopard just looked at her until her lips began to tremble.

"Because if you did your body wouldn't look like two halves."

The woman inhaled sharply and marched to the pond. The leopard wondered if she would see what he did, the way one breast looked flatter, and one side of her face looked harder, more… boyish. And he sighed.

No one knew the curse of halves like the leopard. How could he not, when every night, he became a beast that was feared and hunted and skinned for glory, and every morning, he turned back into a man who had to remain nameless, upon pain of death.

The leopard walked to where the woman knelt. She kept touching her face. Then, like a dying wind, her body wilted, and she looked older, tired.

"I used to be…"

Her voice broke and she cleared her throat. Her eyes grew shiny and she shook her head.

So, the leopard sat beside her, placed a paw on her bare shoulder, and spoke. He wasn't sure why. Maybe it was a kindred spirit he sensed in her, a woman who was physically split in two, like him.

"I used to be human. My name was… They called me Nanlong." The surprise in her face was mild, which he supposed was fair. How many leopards could talk and laugh like a grown man?

"Ten years ago," he continued, "I used a spell to briefly turn myself into a leopard. I did it to impress someone."

As the words left him, they pulled at an old wound, one he hadn't realised still hurt.

"Unfortunately, I didn't know what I was doing, so the spell only worked halfway. I haven't... I haven't seen my family since that day."

Sometimes, he felt it was a punishment for something he hadn't even known was a crime. How was he supposed to understand as a child that the reason he wanted to impress Musa was because he wanted Musa's attention and playfully wandering fingers that he gave to the girls in their class, who giggled and swatted at his grabby fingers? How was he to realise there was a reason there were no men married to each other in the village, despite the number of naked men he'd seen touching each other under the cover of moonlight on the nights he'd sneak out to look at the stars?

Ten years, and he had become a nameless mysterious figure that disappeared when the sun set. He was still surprised no one had made a folk-song about him yet. The thought made him smile. There were no folk songs about men who loved other men, only horror stories, where deviants such as himself were ultimately erased from society.

The woman had stopped touching her face, her hands folded over her knees.

"I haven't seen my family either," she said.

The leopard nodded, and flicked his tail to pat her back. He understood. No one wanted to live where they weren't understood, where they would be treated not as what they were, but what they weren't.

"What about undoing it?" she asked in a small voice that felt to the leopard like it wasn't fully meant for him.

He smiled bitterly. "I've not been able to find a spell to undo the transformation, only to make it permanent."

Sometimes, he wondered what Musa was doing, whether he still thought of the boy who'd disappeared. Other times, he wondered what would happen if he sealed himself as a leopard. He'd seen what happened to men who were caught touching other men. The stonings, the burnings. They were feared and hunted. At least as a leopard, he would be feared and hunted, but as a predator, and not as prey.

The woman sighed and rubbed her eyes. The leopard said nothing, his tail flicking occasionally. In the silence, he dimly wondered why she hadn't yet complained about him knocking her spell items into the water, and scaring the rats from their baco bag prison into the bushes.

"I think I have a friend that can help," she said.

The leopard's heart stopped.

His skin tingled as he came back to himself, and his mind began to race. He didn't realise how much he was purring until the woman glanced at him sideways and shifted away.

"Why would you want to help me?"

She shrugged and stood, dusting off her wrapper. Moonlight gave her dark skin a bluish tint, and the leopard thought she looked magical.

"Maybe I just want to..." Her voice halted.

And with that, she left him there beside the pond, flicking his tail, wondering what it would be like to fully rejoin the world of the living. Would he finally be able to have his own moonlight trysts too?

* * *

"You never told me how you found that ritual."

Kyenpia shrugged, rolling her bony shoulders as she squeezed clothes and dropped them into her basket.

"One book I stole from our former school library. You'll be shocked what's in there. We'd probably have learned some of it if we hadn't run away."

She laughed, oblivious to the Muplang's pounding pulse, whose grip was painfully tight on her own basket.

"Do you know if there's a ritual that can undo transformations?"

The basket in Kyenpia's hands fell to the ground, undoing her afternoon of washing. Wrappers and shirts and underwear rolled over the grass and sand, but she paid them no mind as she dragged Muplang to the side of the dirt path, away from the other women.

"Are you mad? Why? You want to undo everything we've been doing for the past five years?"

Her anger, heaving bosom, and the use of the word 'we' snapped something in Muplang's chest.

"What do you mean 'we'? You that if you stopped doing the ritual nobody would care. Look around us. Nobody here knows anything about you, except that you and your husband like sleeping around."

Kyenpia's fingers were swift and sharp, her palm a mat of needles on Muplang's cheek. The other women nearby gaped and nudged each other. Muplang rubbed at her face to ease the sting of the slap.

Anger gave a glossy sheen to Kyenpia's eyes, and her fists were clenched.

But beneath that anger was fear, the same fear Muplang had seen the first time she'd visited her compound. Kyenpia had been seated in front of the huts in the commune, writing in her school notebook. The sounds around them made Muplang blush, as did the sight of the women sitting in front of the other huts in the compound, breasts barely hidden by threadbare wrappers. She hurried over to Kyenpia.

A small commotion from a hut opposite them drew their attention. Kyenpia's chest rose and fell rapidly, as she looked at a girl younger than their fifteen. She stumbled out of the hut, legs shaking, a white and blue bed sheet clutched tightly to her chest. A man with unbuckled trousers dashed out after her, shouting unintelligible words.

Before any of the women who'd stood could intervene, the man snatched the girl's hand from her chest, prying what looked like money notes from her fist. He stormed out of the compound, still cursing.

The woman closest to the girl – who underneath her purple eyeshadow and black lipstick resembled her enough to be her mother – drew her in for a hug. It took a moment of staring at the woman for Muplang to realise that her eyelids weren't purple, but bruised.

Was this all Kyenpia had to look forward to? A revolving door of men who would withhold their money but not their fists if their desires weren't satisfied no mater what? A lifetime of hearing market woman say 'see her now, just be sleeping with men anyhow, like mother like daughter'?

The woman eyed Muplang in a way that made her stomach twist, like she was fresh meat. Yet… the fact that she was being considered a potential worker in a women-only brothel was strangely validating, and sent a thrill through her body, one she had never felt before.

She hadn't had time to smile too long before Kyenpia dragged her out of the compound and to the forest for their ritual.

Now, Muplang stared at her friend. Changing her face, making her eyes smaller, fattening her cheeks, and thinning her lips hadn't erased that little girl's fear. She pulled her into a tight hug.

"You're not your mother," she whispered, rubbing her back. "Nobody can make you be that girl."

Kyenpia nodded against her back, and she sniffled, causing Muplang to laugh. Sniffle from now till tomorrow, Kyenpia will never let anyone see her cry.

"I'm just tired, Kyenpia," she said, and her voice broke. Her basket of clothes slipped from her hand. "I'm tired. Should it be this hard to just be who I am? Shouldn't it be easy?"

The tears falling from her eyes clogged her vision, so she did not see her best friend moving until strong arms wrapped around her heaving shoulders.

After a while, her tears stopped, and all that was left was a headache and so much tiredness. Kyenpia swiped her thumbs over her cheeks.

"I'll give you the ritual," she said in a low voice. "But when you're done, come and find me."

Muplang smiled, a small thing.

"Okay," she replied.

* * *

Nanlong frowned. "But why are there two sets of ingredients?"

"Nothing," Muplang replied. "Let's just do it before the sun goes down completely."

As she arranged the things and pounded the herbs, Muplang wondered where she would go to start a new life. Mangu was an option, miles away, enough to disappear from…Kyenpia. Her chest twisted and she shook her head. She needed a distraction.

"So who's the first person you'll go and see this evening? The girl you wanted to impress?" she asked in a teasing voice.

Nanlong's mood plummeted and he busied himself with grinding dried lizard bones to keep himself busy. The ritual would not undo the part of him that liked him. He would still be an outcast, half-leopard or not. Resentment rose hot and fierce, but he tamped it down. It wasn't Muplang's fault that she didn't know what he was.

As he ground the bones, his mind drifted to the first time he'd seen two men together, and what it had led to for him.

He'd been toying with the idea of returning home, explaining to his parents what happened and why. In his fantasies, his parents would laugh about it. His father would tell the story of how he met his wife. His mother would slap him upside the head, but gently, and say "boys".

And so, one evening, as the sun was setting, five years after running away from home, he stepped out of the forest. He'd timed it so he would turn just as the sun set, so his parents could see the truth of him faster. It'd been five years. He didn't want to wait any longer. Then a rustling sound nearby startled him into stopping. His breaths came out as barely-there mists in the rapidly cooling harmattan air.

"Who's there?" he called out.

The rustling came from his left again, followed by giggling and shushing. Then the sounds cut off abruptly, like a tap screwed shut. Nanlong smiled. Using the stealth he'd learned, he picked his way over stones and sticks and leaves towards the boulders at the edge of the mountain bordering the forest.

Then he saw the culprits. Two men in singlets and shorts, kissing in a feverish dance of teeth and tongue. A bolt of lust shot through Nanlong, so strong it crippled him and nearly brought him to his knees. The men's hands roamed over each other slowly, grasping, squeezing, and for every patch of skin touched, Nanlong's body burned.

After so many years, he was seeing others do what he now understood he had wanted to do with Musa those years ago. And he wept, joy bleeding through every pore and lightening him.

He stayed there for what seemed like an eternity, but from the setting of the sun, it was only a few minutes.

Then footsteps sounded, and he and the men froze. The steps were clumsy, snapping sticks and crunching dry leaves loudly. The men looked at each other, their eyes wide and terrified, and something ugly sliced through Nanlong. No one should ever look that afraid. They rushed to their feet and pulled their clothes on as quickly as they could.

Three men came round the other side of the mountain, hefting cutlasses and hoes, laughing and jostling each other. The other two men froze. So did the three men when they saw their state of undress. The laughter melted off their faces, leaving behind ugly disgust and cold fury. Nanlong's heart sank.

They descended on the men, whipping them mercilessly, blade tearing skin as they jeered and hemmed the men in. Nanlong's limbs vibrated so much his head ached, and he looked at the horizon, willing the sun to set faster.

For every moment that passed, his heart tore and his chest ached and it became harder to choke back his sobs. Until finally, the sun disappeared, and his bones began to rearrange themselves. For once he embraced the pain of the change, yelling his throat raw as fur grew and covered his extended limbs.

From then, everything was a blur of red in his vision. When he was done, he stood over fallen cutlasses and three flayed bodies. One of the two men huddled against the boulders, barely strong enough to stand. When he saw from Nanlong's inaction that he wasn't going to be harmed, he reached for his companion on the ground.

Even bloody, with shredded skin, their touches were still tender and loving.

Nanlong had turned and fled back into the forest, one thought hounding his steps.

What if his parents were like those men with the cutlasses?

A cool hand on his jerked him out of the memory.

He looked down into the mortar, which was now filled with fine bone dust. Muplang clutched her mortar tight and it shook in her hands. The pensiveness from the previous night was back, and Nanlong frowned.

Then it hit him, and he struggled to keep his face placid. Unless she thought they would probably mess up the ritual the first time, the second set of ingredients was for her. Which meant...

His heart raced and he said the first thing that came to his mind.

"What's the happiest you've ever been? The purest kind of joy you've ever felt?"

A smile so sad and pure and beatific creased her face. Nanlong began to smile too. Sometimes instinct was right.

"The first time," and she laughed, so much that the rest of her words stumbled out. "A...woman looked...at me like...like I had...potential to be...a...prostitute."

Nanlong burst into laughter, and tears rolled down his cheek from the force of it. "Why?!"

Muplang's laughs slowed and she adjusted the fallen sleeve of her blouse. Then she stopped altogether and twirled the end of her cornrows around her finger. "It was the first time someone acknowledged me as a woman. It made me feel like I wasn't mad."

Nanlong nodded. He understood that feeling, the depth of it that filled a hole so wide and seemingly never-ending. It was the same way he felt when he saw those two men and their fierce and tender love, both before and after their assault. He wanted that, or at least a chance at it.

"I don't know why you want to undo everything, but I do know that you'll miss that joy if you go through with this."

She smiled and chuckled. "You call it joy, I call it stress."

"It might be hard, but I think that's part of it. We have to keep choosing every time to be who we are, no matter how tough or stressful it may seem. Choose that joy."

Muplang was silent, absently mixing the herbs in the mortar. Her pensive expression was now on Nanlong's face and he couldn't help biting his lip. A few seconds passed where sunlit shadows on the trees above them passed over her face. Then the mortar in her arms tumbled to the ground, and tears fell from her eyes.

She stood, and took his outstretched arm. He rose to his feet and stripped off his shorts. As she painted his body, animals came out of the forest to join them. Pig-chickens, goat-lizards, rabbit-spiders. Rejects, all of them. Happy, every single one.

And then they danced. Until the moon shone and magic rained on them.

* * *

Now this man and this woman, the light of the moon turns his skin into glittering obsidian, and she is happy, and keeps choosing to be happy, even though sometimes she is tired and snaps at her best friend.

Danger from Wolves and Young Men

Aggie Novak

BOŽIDARKA STOOD over her twin brother's body. Killing him had been necessary – she'd spent all night convincing herself there was no other way. Besides, he'd deserved it.

Božidar and Božidarka. Her entire life she'd been nothing more than his female afterbirth. Not anymore. She grinned and wiped her blade on his white nightshirt. From around his neck, she removed a key tied with a thick cord. The only tragedy was that Božo wouldn't be here to see her steal his life.

She stripped out of her kotula, blouse, and underskirt, leaving them in a crumpled heap beside Božo. On his bed, smoothed over by their maid, Marta, lay his wedding outfit.

Loose black slacks paired with a white shirt. His vest had been embroidered specially for the occasion. An abstract pattern of gold and red danced around the hems, framing snarling wolves stitched in stark white. Božidarka pulled them on. They fit fairly well – she'd always been of a height with her twin, if a tad slimmer. The boots, wool embroidered to match the vest, were a little large, but she laced them tight and was confident she'd manage to dance in them without tripping.

Around her waist, she tied a bright red sash with a fringe of red, blue, and green threads. There was also a red felt crvenkapa, but Božidarka left it on the bed. She took the key instead. From a locked wooden chest, where her brother kept it safe from prying eyes, Božidarka pulled out the skin of a huge, grey wolf. It had been fashioned so the wolf's face, still complete with sharp canines, formed a mask, the rest of the skin falling in a cloak.

She hefted it high and settled the wolf's head over her own. The instant rush of power was more intoxicating than any drink. A wolf's strength fizzed through her veins and the magic of a vukodlak sparked under her skin.

Tonight was a new moon, and the strength of her power waxed with it. Like this, she could do anything. Anything Božo could have. More. With barely more effort than it would take to lift a newborn lamb, Božidarka picked up her brother's corpse and shoved it into the chest. She locked the lid over him.

The magic within Božidarka flexed like a new muscle, and she gasped. She wanted to run, and howl, and *eat*. Palm pressed flat against the door to Božo's – her – room, she took a slow breath. Later, she could roam the woods and hunt and howl, testing her new strength, but now it was time for her to be married.

When Božidarka arrived at the village square – festooned with red ribbon and loud with music – her wolf cloak garnered approving whoops from her cavorting cousins. Her Tata tugged her close for a brief hug.

"I'm proud of you, son."

Božidarka nodded, not trusting her voice. Tata had never once been proud of her.

The tamburicas quieted and a hush fell over the gathering. And there she was. A heavily embroidered red kotula fell to her ankles – paired to the design of Božidarka's vest. A rope of gold beads hung around her neck, and her hems jangled with silver coins. Unlike Božidarka, she had not eschewed her crvenkapa. A white habit was attached to the cap with golden hairpins. Jasenka.

Božidarka's chest tightened, and her magic flared with a painful heat. She clenched her fists, sharpening nails biting into her palms, and forced the feeling down. When she met Božidarka's wolfish gaze, Jasenka paled, skin stark next to the rich red of her clothes.

The strumming of the tamburicas picked back up, and the crowd grew lively and wild. Their families drank, danced, and joked. Jasenka's relatives taunted the bride with ritual song.

"There's danger for you, girl, from wolves and young men!"

"No more, no more!" Božidarka's family sang back. "For the wolf protects her this night."

It wasn't until they were wed, and Božidarka took Jasenka's hands in her own, that the edge of panic faded from her face.

"Božka," she whispered, her mouth by the wolf's ear, "it's really you."

In response, Božidarka wrapped her arms around Jasenka's waist and twirled her into a lively dance. "I promised, didn't I?"

They danced until Jasenka was flushed nearly as red as her skirt and Božidarka's shirt clung with sweat.

A chorus of frenzied howls filled the night. Fear clutched at her heart, thinking that somehow, wolves had come for her. Then Božidarka saw the men. Some were her cousins, who'd snuck off from the festivities. Others were boys and young men from the surrounding villages. All were dressed in their finest clothes, faces blackened with soot. The wealthier among them had wolf skins around their shoulders.

They circled Božidarka and Jasenka yipping and snarling – a feral pack she must protect her new wife from. She scooped Jasenka into her arms, and carried her away. Everyone followed, the men dancing and the women singing.

"Handsome Božo, mountain wolf, don't let Jasenka sleep tonight." The chant persisted til the door to Božo's – now Božidarka's – room slammed shut, bolt slid into place.

As soon as they were alone, Jasenka's lips were at her neck, gently biting, and her fingers at the sash about her waist.

"I was so worried," she said, breath tickling Božidarka's throat, "that you'd failed."

Božidarka tore the front of Jasenka's blouse open, with a nail turned dark and sharp as a blade. "I would never have let you marry him. Never." Her voice was a growl, low and menacing. The covetous looks he'd sent Jasenka's way had been hard enough to bear – allowing him to touch her, to marry her, was unthinkable.

"I want to kiss you." Jasenka ran her fingers across the snout of the wolf-mask, along the seam where fur turned to skin. She dug in, clearly intending to lift the skin from Božidarka, but found no purchase.

Božidarka nuzzled into Jasenka's collarbone, busy with the task of peeling off the layers of her wife's clothes. Her skin was soft and warm. Every caress sent her power soaring along with her lust.

"Please," Jasenka insisted. "I want to see you." She tugged again, to no avail.

"Let me." But Božidarka couldn't remove the wolf. It clung to her, tight as her own skin.

She yanked, and scratched at her neck, but the harder she tried, the more anxiety flooded her, the faster her heart beat. And the less control she felt, the less control she had. Everything surged. Wolf and magic, magic and wolf.

Pain bloomed as her shoulders broadened with a bony crack. Her feet lengthened, ripping through her boots. Her fingers were fully claws and thick fur, the same silver-grey as the wolfskin, sprouted down her arms. Hunger gnawed.

With her last shred of sane thought, Božidarka shoved Jasenka away. Her wife flew through the air like a straw doll, but Božidarka didn't pause to see how she landed. She pushed the door open and fled into the pitch-black night.

The woods swallowed her, welcomed her between its trees, at once unfamiliar and a homecoming. Prey – a rabbit maybe – darted through the undergrowth ahead, and Božidarka let go. Instinct took over.

She prowled the night, the faintest glimmer of the new moon enough to guide her when paired with her sensitive nose and sharp ears. She hunted and fed. She howled and ran, both alone and fleetingly with a pack that was happy enough to accept her presence for a while. Božidarka lived as a wolf, wild and free, until the pink kiss of dawn.

The coming of day wouldn't have stopped her, but instead of finding a suitable hollow to rest in, Božidarka stumbled into a clearing. And in that clearing, waited a god.

At least, that's how the figure appeared to her. A towering wolf-man, breaking from the shadows of the trees – almost as large as a tree himself. His fur was blacker than coal, and his eyes glowed with a reddish heat. Carved wooden figures hung from its neck. Discs engraved with unfamiliar patterns.

"You," it growled, spittle flying, "are not Božidar."

Božidarka fell to her knees, prostrating herself before the mighty wolf. Magic-stink and blood rolled off him in sickening waves.

"No, I am his sister, his twin."

"You have not paid the price, you have no claim to his wolf, nor to his power."

An invisible force like a fist of iron closed around her, pinning her arms to her sides, constricting her breaths.

"I claimed his life," Božidarka gasped, each word a sharp pain, "I took it for my own. What was his…is mine."

The wolf-man growled a growl that shook her bones. "You dare much, girl." The last word was spat like a curse. "The price cannot be shared. It must be paid."

The pressure released and Božidarka slumped. Dewy grass soaked through her trousers and wet her hands. She was insignificant.

"What price?" she asked. Her voice was stronger now. More like Božidar's.

"Blood," the being answered, "and sacrifice."

His luminescent eyes looked not at her, but beyond to the shadowed gaps between the pines. Božidarka turned. Jasenka.

She must have followed Božidarka's less-than-careful trail through the forest. Or perhaps magic had brought her here, for this moment.

"No, please." Božidarka's words were a whimper. Weak. "Don't hurt her."

"Your wife will not come to harm," the Wolf promised, "no matter that you took what was not yours to claim her."

"We claimed each other," said Jasenka, strong chin held high. "We acted as one."

The Wolf fixed Božidarka with red eyes. "Be that as it may, the blood price is yours to pay, the sacrifice yours to give." He licked his canines. "Or you can lay down the wolfskin and walk away as yourself. As you were."

As if in protest, a wave of magic pulsed through her, sparking at her fingertips.

"What is the sacrifice you would ask of me?" Blood was easy enough to give.

The Wolf grinned, all teeth. "Your old life. Your old life, and everyone in it. You would walk from this clearing alone, with no home to return to, without your wife."

Her choice was clear. She could be Božidarka again. Božidarka who was never as good as her brother, who her Tata had no use for. Božidarka who had no magic, no real strength of her own. Božidarka who loved Jasenka, and was loved by her.

But that woman was a murderer. She had killed her own twin and stuffed his still-bleeding body into a chest. Left him to rot while she married his betrothed. She couldn't return to that life. Going back home with Jasenka and no wolf-magic was a death sentence.

"You would have my life." Božidarka met his eyes as she said it. "Whatever I choose, you would have my life from me."

He let out a throaty growl not unlike a laugh. "Choices are not made to be easy. I never promised the price would be cheap."

Božidarka looked over her shoulder to Jasenka, hoping her face held the answers. But her face was hidden in the dimness, and Božidarka couldn't divine her thoughts. She could guess, of course. Jasenka would want her to stay. But Jasenka would also never ask her to give up her power, to cast aside all else she had wanted for her life.

"I would like to suggest a different price. A different price for a different life."

The Wolf snarled and lunged forward, quick in a way Božidarka wouldn't have believed possible. His teeth were at her throat, and his carnal breath, hot and rot-sweet, flooded her senses.

"You dare," he hissed, teeth scraping at her skin as he spoke, "you dare to bargain with me, girl-child?"

"I dare." Božidarka did not sound like her brother, but neither did she sound weak. "You gave me two choices that lead to death. One to the death of my human life, the death of my marriage. The other to my death for the crimes I have committed." The Wolf huffed and Božidarka gritted her teeth against the stench. "I will pay your price of blood, and so will Jasenka." A stick cracked behind her, soft footsteps moved closer. "We will pay in blood, and we will pay in sacrifice. I will lay this wolfskin at your feet, and I will surrender its power."

As she said the words, she felt the magic ebb, like an exhale she couldn't breathe back in. Božidarka lifted the wolfskin from her head, and it parted easily.

"And in return?" the Wolf asked.

"In return, we ask for your blessing – a ward to protect us from those that would hunt us down. We ask for safety from the life we leave behind. That will be the second part of our sacrifice. We will not return home again."

Božidarka lay the wolfskin on the grass. In the absence of its touch, her body changed, shrinking back to its original form. This time, there was no pain.

The Wolf stepped back from her, head at a tilt. "And what say you, wife of Božidarka? Will you pay the blood price and leave your past behind?"

Jasenka stood by Božidarka, put a trembling hand to her shoulder. "I will."

With one dagger-sharp claw, the wolf lashed out, slicing Božidarka in a fiery line down from her collarbone, over her sternum. In the next quick movement, he slashed Jasenka.

Blood ran down her front, to the soil. Beside her, she saw the red spreading, staining Jasenka's blouse.

"It is done," said the Wolf. "Leave me."

Arms wrapped around each other's waists, Božidarka and Jasenka stumbled from the clearing and into the forest.

They pushed on until they both swayed with dizziness and exhaustion. In the hollow of a mighty oak trunk, they stopped for rest.

"Let me," said Božidarka, carefully lifting Jasenka's sodden blouse from her injured chest.

"It doesn't hurt so badly," said Jasenka. "I thought it would be worse."

For all that it was done by the claw of a wolf, the cut was neat and clean. Božidarka tore a strip of fabric from the bottom of her own shirt, and used it to wipe away the blood. She went to tear another, but Jasenka stopped her with a gentle hand.

"Use my skirts," she said. "They're far too long for running through the woods anyway."

Božidarka obliged, carefully bandaging the wound.

"Now, let me see yours."

But a hint of magic must have lingered in her veins, for Božidarka's cut was already half-healed, scabbed over and tight with new pink skin.

"Thank you," said Jasenka, trailing a finger alongside the scar.

"For what?"

"For choosing me."

Božidarka caught Jasenka's hand in her own, lifted her fingertips to her lips, and kissed them gently. "I will always choose you."

Jasenka caressed Božidarka's cheek and pulled her in for a kiss. "We should keep going," she said after she broke away. "Find shelter. There's an old village, abandoned, not too far from here. My brother—" her voice broke on the words "—he said he saw some buildings still standing, when he was out shepherding last summer."

"Let's rest a while longer," said Božidarka, exhausted with both relief and sorrow.

They huddled in the oak's embrace and wept for the lives they left behind.

Starved

Rachel Nussbaum

I DON'T LET MYSELF have a lot of things. Relationships, friendships, it's all too big a risk. Human contact in general is off the table – I keep even my parents at arm's length (if my arms were two thousand miles long). It's just easier that way. Easier not to let yourself get attached to things that would be dangerous if they became a habit. It's the same with all aspects of my life. I work from home. Don't exercise. Don't eat red meat. I try to avoid going outside.

Except on the full moon.

Once I realized there was a huge patch of forest close by where camping wasn't permitted, I began driving out there to shift. The concrete of my reinforced basement had been giving me night terrors, so I thought, fine – let's let the beast tire herself out.

And something just snapped. Everything I bottle up, everything I keep inside, everything I deny myself. I can split out of my human skin and scream without vocal chords, as loud as I want. I can let everything out.

I tear through the trees, shaking off shreds of human skin, the wind pelting against my fur. I'm furious, I'm ravenous, and I'm so, so free.

I slash my claws against a tree, splintering wood apart just to destroy – just to feel powerful – and I charge through the brush. I want meat. The forest knows what I am is unnatural, and the animals know to stay away.

I'm faster than they are, though.

In this body, I can smell like a shark. I bend down on all fours and gallop – past the raccoons peering down at me (too puny to be satisfying), a river flowing in the distance (meat first, water after), and ah – there it is. A herd of deer, passed by not ten minutes ago. I swivel around, following the trail their scent marked for me. I'm so hungry that I don't question the sour stench of fear clinging to the path.

When the deer I'm chasing suddenly start running back towards me – one buck practically bashing into me – that's when I notice.

A new scent. One I've smelled on occasion, but never this close.

Ursus americanus.

The bear was already charging through the foliage, and as it sees me, it falters to a stop. But my beast is a dumb old girl, and she was already charging too. And she just keeps on going.

The human voice in the back of my mind finds this tragically hysterical – *Oh god, I'm going to start a fight with a bear. I'm going to get diced into ribbons by a bear and wake up with all kinds of scars and a clawed-out eye. Oh my god you stupid fucking—*

And just as the bear surges up on its hind legs to meet me, a massive blur tackles it to the ground.

I scramble to a stop, eyes wide. The two beasts thrash across the ground, their snarls echoing as they wrestle to the death. The scent of blood rises up around us. I swallow.

A loud crack of bone sounds out and the bear sags down – its assailant's fangs found the spinal cord. Breathing deeply, the victor turns and looks at me.

Rises up on two legs.

Even as a beast, I'm shocked.

I've never met another shifter – not since the one that bit me. I've known other humans who've met them, but they were all old and told me the same thing. How rare I was. I'd given up a decade ago.

Her fur is darker than mine, her mane shorter. She's not as tall as I am, but her form is more muscular. There's no questioning what she is.

And she's staring right at me.

I break out of my trance and automatically, my hackles raise. The human bit in the back of my mind winces. The shifter tilts her head, then lowers herself down to her kill. Her eyes are still pinned on me, but her nose twitches – and finally, she breaks eye contact with me to feed.

I stand still, watching her. Even in this body, it feels painfully awkward. I'm curious and afraid and excited and angry all at once – but something about watching her eat feels far too intrusive. Awkwardly, I finally lower myself and turn to leave.

A growl echoes behind me.

I snap my head back and she's glaring at me, blood staining her snout. She slides down the carcass, lifts an elongated arm, and pats at the bear's flank.

My fur prickles. I'm not used to complex thoughts in this body. I'm not used to social situations in *any* body. I take a step back.

You shouldn't do this.

But my beast is starving, and to be fair, I *did* distract the bear for her.

I join her and tear into the bear's hide. The meat is gamey, almost pungent. Across from me, the shifter's chest puffs up and she lowers her head back down. I can barely smell her over the strong scent of the carcass, but what I do smell – it's like me, but different. Less full of anger. Maybe just a little smug?

It smells nice. Like something I just met yet something I've known for a very long time.

* * *

After we feed, the shifter and I walk to the river. I drink deep and try not to look directly at her – though I can feel her glancing at me often.

The human part of me wonders if she's met many others.

A stone hits me in the side of my leg and I growl. She's hunched by the muddy bank, motioning for me to join her. I look down to see her drawing a symbol – it takes me a moment to recognize an arrow. I look up at her and she tilts her head to the starry night, reaching her clawed hand up and touching her chest.

Her sign. Sagittarius.

My chest flares warm and my cheeks burn (can I even blush in this body? I never wondered that before). Her tongue hangs from her mouth and she whines, pointing to me.

Now I know I'm blushing.

I bring my clawed finger to the mud, but I fumble – I know I'm a Cancer, but I can't remember the sign. Goddamnit. I draw an oval and give it legs, trying to get the point across. I look over to the shifter hopefully.

She stares at the crab and her chest spasms. Her mouth parts – a series of hiccuped yips fumble out, like a hyena.

She's fucking laughing at me.

I snarl at her on reflex, but she laughs harder. Flustered and angry, I reach out and shove her, hard enough that she falls onto her side. Beads of blood prickle up from where my claws punctured her.

My ears fall flat and I jerk back. *Shit.*

The shifter shakes her head, slowly rising. Her hackles raise and she stalks over to me. I stand still, waiting for her to make her move.

She reaches up and smears a handful of mud across my snout.

I growl and sputter and she runs. I take off after her, snarling and howling. She howls back and turns to look at me with a razor-sharp grin. Something tingles under my fur – the surge of anger that propelled me to chase her fizzles out, and now, something else is pushing me after her.

And the longer I chase her and we bark at each other, the more that fury that always burns inside me feels further and further away.

* * *

After hours of chasing, slashing at trees in a contest of strength, and hunting down another herd of deer (the hunger never stops), we finally rest. Wolves howl in the distance, and I answer them back. It seems to amuse my new shifter friend, and she joins me. Her howl is deeper than mine. Stronger.

When the wolves move on, she looks over at me. Slowly, she reaches down her arm and parts the wiry fur. A thick, angry scar stains her skin. Mismatched, jagged punctures.

She's showing me her bite.

Something tight coils in my chest. Part of me feels sad – sad to see proof of her curse, sad to know she has to see it every day.

But a bigger, more human part of me feels awed. That she'd show me this mark, this deeply personal thing. I think maybe, I'm the first one like us she's ever met too. And you'd think that would make me feel more lonely, but it doesn't.

This doesn't feel lonely at all.

I don't have the vocal cords to tell her this – what this means to me. So instead, I part the fur of my mane and turn.

She leans in, and I feel her breath on the back of my neck as she inspects my bite. It feels like it happened to another person now, like I was just watching from the sky as that massive beast wrapped his jaws around a young girl's neck. A bullet from a hunter saved her life a moment later, but it was a moment too late to prevent the curse from passing on.

I feel a wet lap across the back of my neck, and the past falls away. I freeze. It swipes across my scar again. My fur goes on end and my heart flutters.

Slowly, I turn to face her.

Our eyes meet, and hers drift closed. And I don't know how I even muster up the courage, but I lean in and nuzzle against her.

She lets out a deep sigh I had no idea she was holding, and her long arms circle around me tight. It takes me a while to realize how hard I'm shaking.

I didn't realize how much I missed this. How much I needed it.

I reach out and take her hand. It's funny how human yet monstrous it is – elongated, like her arms. Fingers dotted with deadly claws. A leathery palm. Just like mine.

I'm not alone, the human and beast in me say at the same time.

Not alone.

* * *

When I wake up in the morning I *am* alone, though. I shift in the grass, back in my human body. I sit up and look around.

But she's gone.

Of course she's gone.

I think about a lot as I trek through the woods. Really, I don't know what I expected to find in the morning. A warm body still curled up to me? A smiling face framed by sunshine? My heart thuds in my chest. I forgot how much wanting something makes you ache.

This is why you're not allowed to have things, damn it. It just hurts more when you realize nothing's yours to keep.

The buzzing in my brain is so loud, it follows me almost out to where I parked my car. Barely gives me a chance to notice there's another car next to it.

I dive behind a tree, but I already hear a door slam and a second later, the engine kicks on and the car drives off. I peer out behind the bark.

There's a torn scrap of paper under my windshield wipers. I yank it out as I dart into my car, hands practically shaking, words scrawled on the back of a ripped promotional flier.

> *Cancer,*
> *Figured this was your car. So sorry I had to leave you. Got an early shift to get to. Last night was amazing! Please meet me here again next month?*
> *– Sagittarius*

That tight thing that coiled in my chest last night tugs, hard and pulsing, and doesn't let go. I pull my coat on and drive home fast, climb into bed, and pull out my phone.

And look up everything I can about the zodiac.

* * *

You shouldn't let yourself want things, that nagging, worrying human voice in my brain whispers. *This is dangerous. You know you can't have relationships.*

That was before I found someone else like me, though.

Does that matter? There are checks and balances for a reason.

What's that supposed to mean? Letting myself have one goddamn scrap is gonna open a floodgate?

Exactly.

I put in my earbuds and listen to music. The thoughts stop after that, but the nervous uncertainty stays behind.

* * *

I look over her note a lot. It makes me feel better. The week's almost over – I just need to wait a bit longer.

But one part of it...

An early shift? How the hell did she time that?

It's not surprising though, considering what I saw of her. She was... smart. She attacked the bear when she knew it was distracted. She could use hand gestures.

She was in control.

She probably works a real job in the real world too, instead of locking herself up in a cage like a rabid animal.

I make my music louder.

***

I go outside for the first time in a while that isn't just a quick dart inside the gas station for a soda with my head down.

I walk the five blocks to the library. Head up. I go straight to the information directory. I check out two books on anxiety and one about zodiac signs.

On my way home, I feel elated – it was a small step, but it felt huge. I keep my head up high now, and I pay attention to all the colorful businesses I pass. A ballet studio. An Indian restaurant. An arts and crafts store. It's funny how something so mundane can feel so exciting. There's so much outside. So much to do. So much to see. To smell.

You know what smells the best too, don't you? That tender, delicious scent isn't coming from the restaurants.

I falter a little. I try not to let the thought ruin this. Just walk a little faster. I can do it.

Who's it coming from, do you think? Those high school students passing you by? That family coming out of the bodega?

That woman across the street with her baby?

I break into a run and breathe through my mouth the rest of the way home.

***

The books on anxiety help a little. Breathing exercises. Positive affirmations. Funnily enough, it's the stupid zodiac book that gets to me.

Cancers.

Selfish. Self-pitying. Mood swings. Manipulative.

Is that really what I am? I know the self-pity and mood swings fit. I haven't been around enough people to know if I'm selfish or manipulative.

It's pretty selfish to want something you know you shouldn't let yourself have. Risking the safety of everyone else around you for a stroll to the library. You'll risk her safety, too.

I close the book. What did I expect from a bunch of read-the-stars nonsense?

Because werewolves are so much more logical.

I roll over in bed and feel the guilt rise. It's not fair. Why can't I just have this one thing?

You know why.

***

I dream I'm chasing a girl down. She turns and I see a face, my own face staring back at me. I look younger, and even my beast can recognize that I'm chasing down my teenage self. I'm back at the beginning.

But my beast is too hungry to care. I tackle her to the ground, her screams muffled into the grass. My jaws are around my own neck – then in the next instant, they're around an arm.

It's *her*.

Her bones snap and splinter in my maw and she screams. I feel the blood and hot marrow drip down my throat and quench my thirst as she thrashes in agony. I fall out of the nightmare before I can see her face.

I breathe heavily. Wasn't real. Didn't happen. I *never* bit anyone.

You locked yourself up before you had the chance to.

No.

Because you knew you wanted to. Because you knew how delicious people smelled walking by you on the street, the closer to the full moon it got.

That's not—

Bullshit. You couldn't even let yourself run free until you were certain there were no campers in those woods.

…

Because you knew you couldn't help yourself. You're so goddamn hungry, and you know exactly what for. The animals you hunt down will never be enough.

And what, the moment you find someone willing to put up with you for a few hours, you'll throw it all away? Throw countless lives into danger?

It doesn't work that way. You don't fix something this broken with silly self-help books. You don't starve yourself of everything for years and just let your beast off the chain like you weren't holding her back for a reason.

You'll devour everything. Destroy everything.

Cancer.

* * *

When the full moon comes, I lock myself in the basement. Let the soundproof walls absorb my screams as my skin stretches and snaps apart. Let my beast cry out in misery when she realizes where we are.

It's for our own good. For everyone's good.

Especially *her*.

* * *

I scratched at the walls until my claws bled. When I finally curl up to whimper myself to sleep, it aches. My hands, the unending hunger, the unyielding loneliness. I wrap my long arms around myself and pretend it's her.

This is why you shouldn't want things. Because it hurts this bad when you have to let them go.

I didn't *need* to let her go.

You know you did.

I drift off, the human voice in the back of my head still buzzing and berating me. I dream of her, waiting for me, staring up at the moon. Howling for me.

My ears twitch and my eyes snap open. It's real. I can hear her.

That's impossible. This room is soundproof.

I lumber to my paws and stalk over to the window. It's closed (and barred) and somehow, I can hear her.

You're imagining what you want to—

Another howl sounds out, and I just know – it's her. Out there, miles away in the forest, calling out to the moon. Asking if I'm there.

I dig my bloody claws into the concrete. I'm sorry I didn't come. I'm sorry.

You know you couldn't—

Do I know that?

Of course you couldn't. You're not like her. You're not in control. You're feral. You're—

Why couldn't I have asked her for help? Ask how she did it? Why couldn't we have figured it out together?

There's no answer. Just silence as she cries out for me.

I grind my bony knuckles into concrete. *I'm so sorry*, I want to tell her. *I was scared. I'm scared of what I am. I'm scared of what I could do. I'm scared of what will happen if I let myself have anything. Even the things I want.*

I don't have the vocal cords to say this, though.

All I can do is howl.

* * *

I don't know if she could hear me in return. She kept howling long into the night, distant and sad until she faded away with the morning.

I sit in bed, drinking scalding tea and thumbing the note she left me. Will she come back next month? Would she wait that long? I read the words again and they tug at my chest. I turn the note over in my hand, absentmindedly scanning the torn flier.

And I freeze.

I didn't notice it before (it never even occurred to me) but the cut-off bold text is a logo. I bring the note to my face – there are only a few letters, but the smaller text below advertises a local event.

This is a flier for a business – one somewhere in town.

I yank my coat on over my pajamas and grab my keys as I run to the door.

* * *

It took me an hour of driving through town, holding up the little scrap of paper and comparing the logo corner to signs. After a while, I start narrowing it down. If she works morning shifts, it has to be something open early…

I can't believe it when I finally pull up to the fitness center. The loops of font that are still visible on the torn-off flier match up perfectly with the big sign on the roof.

The voices blare in my head – my human fears, my bestial rage.

I ignore every fucking one of them, and I run through the door.

The gym is loud, the sounds and scents overwhelming. The man at the counter greets me, but I pass him, eyes darting across the room.

There's a loud clatter as a pair of weights crash to the floor. I spin around, and halfway between a storage closet and the lobby, I see a woman.

It's her.

Her skin is darker than mine, her hair shorter. She's not as tall as I am, but her form is more muscular. There's no questioning who she is.

And she's staring right at me.

She brings her hand to her mouth and lets out a loud sob. I run to her, and she meets me in the middle, yanking me down into her arms.

"I was so scared I'd never find you again," she whispers.

I hold her as tight as I can.

"I'm sorry I kept you waiting," I tell her. My voice is shaking, but my words are strong. She beams, bright and beautiful.

A smiling face, framed by sunshine.

Loke's Wolf

From Norse Mythology

ALTHOUGH THE APPLES OF LIFE had been brought back, and although Loke appeared for some time very penitent and willing to obey the laws of the kind Odin, the gods had little faith in him. More than that, so much had they suffered, that now they were in constant fear of him. "We never know," plead Freyja and Sif and Idun, all of whom had good reason to fear him, "what mischief he may be planning."

And so it came about that Loke was driven forth from Asgard, as indeed he deserved to be.

Straight to the home of the giants Loke went – he always had been a giant at heart, the evil creature! – and was much more in harmony with them in their thoughts and acts, than ever he had been with the gods whom he claimed as his people.

But now that he was cast out from Asgard, and could no longer share its beauties and its joys, he had but one wish – that was, to be revenged upon the gods, to destroy them, and to ruin their golden city.

To do this he raised two dreadful creatures. Terrible monsters! Even the gods shuddered as they looked upon them.

"Loke! Loke!" thundered Odin, looking down upon him in wrath that he should dare such vengeance.

But Loke stood defiant. There was but one thing to be done, so the gods thought; and that was to take these terrible creatures from Loke's power.

"The serpent we will cast into the sea," said Thor. "But the wolf – what shall we do with the wolf? Certainly he cannot be left to wander up and down in Midgard. The sea would not hold him. Loke must not have him in Jotunheim. What shall be done with him?"

"Kill him," said some.

"No," answered Odin. "To him Loke has given the gift of everlasting life. He will not die as long as we the gods have life. There is but one way left open to us; and that is to bring the wolf into Asgard. Here we can watch him and keep him from much, if not all the evil he would do."

And so the wolf – the Fenris-wolf he was called – was brought into the home of the gods.

He was a dreadful creature to look upon. His eyes were like balls of fire; and his fangs were white, and sharp, and cruel.

Every day he grew more terrible. Fiercer and fiercer he grew, and larger and stronger and more dreadful to look upon.

"What is to be done with him?" asked Odin one day, his face white with despair, as he looked upon the wolf, and realized what sorrow by and by he would bring among them.

"Kill him!" cried one.

"Send him to Jotunheim," cried another.

"Chain him," thundered Thor. And indeed to chain him seemed really the only thing that could be done with him.

"We will make the chains this night," said Thor. And at once the great forge was set in motion. All night long Thor worked the forge, hammering with his mighty hammer the links that should make a chain to hold the Fenris-wolf.

Morning came. The gods were filled with hope as they saw the great heap of iron. "Now we shall be safe. Now we shall be free," they said; "for no creature living can break the irons that the god of Thunder forges."

The wolf growled and showed his wicked teeth as Thor approached and threw the chain about him. He knew the gods hated him and feared him. He knew, too, that, with his wondrous strength, even the chains of Thor were not too strong for him to break.

So, snarling and showing his fangs and lashing his tail, he allowed himself to be bound. "They are afraid of me," the cruel wolf grinned. "And well they may be; there is a power in me that even they do not yet dream of."

The chains were tightly fastened, and the gods waited eagerly for the wolf to test his strength with them.

Now, the wolf knew well enough that there were no chains that could hold him. "I will amuse myself," said he to himself, "by tormenting the gods." So he glared at the chains with his fiery eyes, sniffed here and there at them, lifted one paw and then the other, bit at them with his sharp teeth, and clawed at them with his strong claws; setting up now and then a howl that echoed, like the thunders of Thor, from cloud to cloud across the skies.

The faces of the gods grew brighter and brighter. They looked at each other and hope rose high in their hearts. "We are saved!" they whispered to each other. "Hear how he howls! He knows he cannot break chains forged in the smithy of the mighty Thor."

But Odin did not smile. He knew only too well that the wolf was amusing himself; and that when the gods were least expecting it, he would spring forth and shatter the links of the mighty chain, even as a mortal might shatter a chain of straw.

"Conquered at last, you cruel Fenris-wolf!" thundered Thor, lifting his hammer in scorn, to throw at the helpless wolf.

"The Fenris-wolf is never conquered," hissed the wolf; and with one bound he leaped across the walls of Asgard, down, down across the skies to Midgard, the links of the chains scattering like sparks of fire as he flew through the air.

"See! See!" cried the people of Midgard, as they saw the fiery eyes of Fenris gleam across the sky. "See! A star has fallen! A star has fallen into the sea!" For the people of Midgard cannot understand the wonders of the heavens and the mysteries of the gods.

The gods stood, wonder-struck. Their faces were pale with fright. The brow of Thor grew black and stern. Odin looked pityingly upon them all. "Lose not your courage," said he kindly. "The Fenris-wolf shall yet be bound; and there shall yet remain to us ages upon ages of happiness and freedom from his wicked power. Go now to the dwarfs who work their forges in the great mines beneath the mountains of Midgard. They shall make for you a magic chain that even Fenris cannot break."

Hardly were the words out of Odin's mouth when Thor set forth upon the wings of his own lightning, to the home of the dwarfs, to do the bidding of Odin the All-wise.

The Fenris Wolf

WITH WONDERFUL SPEED the chain was forged; and when the Sun-god lifted his head above the hills, to send forth his light again across the fields of Midgard, the first sight that greeted his return was Thor, a great mass of golden coil within his hand, speeding up the rainbow bridge to Asgard.

It was a tiny chain – hardly larger than a thread; but in it lay a magic strength.

Entering the great golden gate, Thor saw the Fenris wolf, again creeping stealthily up and down the streets.

Thor's hand shut tight upon the handle of his hammer. It was hard to believe that a blow from the hammer would not slay the wicked creature. For an instant Thor's face grew black. Then forcing a smile, and showing to the wolf the mass of gold, he said, "Come Fenris; come with me into the hall. There the gods are to meet and test our strength upon this magic coil. Whoever breaks it, and so proves himself the strongest, is to win a prize from the great All-father Odin."

The wolf stretched back his cruel lips, and showed his sharp fangs of teeth. He did not speak; but his wicked grin said, "You do not deceive the Fenris-wolf."

Together Thor and the Fenris-wolf entered the presence of Odin and the gods and goddesses.

"I have," said Thor, "a magic coil. It is very strong. The dwarfs made it for me; and Odin has promised a great prize to the one who shall be strong enough to break its links. Come, let us try."

Then the gods – for they all understood what Thor was about to do – sprang forward, seizing the coil, pulling and twisting it in every way and in every direction, coiling it about the pillars of the hall, and hanging by it from the arches; until at last, tired out and breathless, they sank exhausted upon the golden floors.

"Fenris," called Thor. "Now is your time to prove to us what you have so often said – that you are stronger than we. Try if you can break this golden thread which, small as it is, has proved too strong for the strength of the gods."

The wolf growled. He did not care to risk even his strength in a magic coil. He growled and slunk away.

"What! Fenris, are you a coward? After all your boasted strength, why is it that you shrink from a contest in which the gods have willingly taken part? Do you mean to say that, because the gods have been defeated, you fear that you, too, may be defeated?"

The wolf halted. He looked back at the gods and growled a long, low growl. The words of Thor had stung his pride.

Thor laughed. "O Fenris, Fenris! This is your boasted strength! Your boasted courage! To slink away in a contest with the gods – the gods at whose strength you have always sneered and scoffed."

"Fenris is a coward!" cried all the gods; and the heavens echoed with their laughter.

This was more than the wolf could bear. Back he sprang into the hall.

"I hear your sneers," he snarled. "I hear you call me coward. Give me the cord; bind me with it round and round; fasten me to the strongest pillar of this great hall. If the coil is an honest coil, Fenris can break it. There is no chain he cannot break. But if you are blinding me – if you have here a cord woven with magic such as no power can break – how am I to know? I put this test to you. Some one of you shall place your hand between my jaws. As long as that hand is there, you may coil and coil the thread about me. Then, if I find the cord a magic cord, Fenris shall set his teeth upon the hand and crush it."

The gods stared at one another. Surely, Thor must not lose his hand. Thor needed his hand with which to wield the magic hammer.

Then Tyre, the brave god Tyre, the god of courage and bravery and unselfishness stepped forth.

"Here is my hand, O Fenris-wolf. It shall be yours to destroy if you can not loose yourself when bound in the golden coil."

Again the Fenris-wolf showed his shining teeth. He seized the hand between his heavy jaws; Thor bound the cord about him. "Now free yourself," he thundered. "Free yourself, and prove to the gods the mighty power of the Fenris-wolf."

The wolf, his eyes blazing with wrath, and with fear as well, struggled with the coil. But alas for the wolf! And joy for the gods! The harder he struggled, the fiercer he battled, the tighter drew the cord. With a howl of rage that shook the city and echoed even to the base of the great Mt. Ida, he seized upon the hand of Tyre and tore it from his wrist. With another angry howl he sprang towards

Thor; but with a quick turn Thor seized one end of the coil, fastened it to a great rock, and before the wolf could set his fangs he hurled him, rock and all, over the walls of the city, down down into the mighty sea.

"And there, chained to his rocky island, he shall abide forever," cried the gods; "and now peace once more shall rest upon our city."

But Odin sighed, and to himself he said, "O happy children, there shall yet come a day when darkness shall fall upon us; the Fenris-wolf shall again be loosed; and even the gods shall be no more."

Solange, the Wolf-Girl

Antoinette Ogden, from the French of Marcel Prévost

ALL THAT AFTERNOON we had walked through the forest, stick in hand, our bags slung over our shoulders, through that magnificent forest of Tronsays, which covers one half the St. Amand country, and one half of Nevers. The little village of Ursay, squatting on the bank of the Cher, in the rent of the valley which cuts through the centre of the forest, was our last halting-place for the day. We dined with an old friend, the modest doctor of five or six neighboring communes; and after dinner we sat musing on the stoop, with our cherry pipes between our lips.

The shadows fell around us, over the dense blue mass of forest that encircled the horizon with all the solemn slowness of night in June. The sky was streaked with flights of swallows. The nine o'clock Angelus scattered its notes with intervals of silence from the height of a snuffer-like steeple which emerged from among the roofs. From distant farms came the barking of dogs calling and answering one another.

A woman, still young, in a red woollen skirt and a white linen shirt, came out of a house near by, and walked down toward the river. With her left arm she pressed a baby against her bosom. A little boy held her other hand, and gave his in turn to a still smaller brother. When they reached the bank of the Cher, the young woman sat upon a great stone; and while the two boys, hastily undressed, were paddling and splashing about like ducks in the stream, she nursed her last-born.

One of our party, who was a painter, said, "There is a picture that would be popular at the Salon. How splendidly built and well-lighted that woman is! And what a pretty bright spot that red skirt forms in the blue landscape!"

A voice behind us called out –

"The girl you see there, young men, is Solange, the wolf-girl." And our host, who had been detained by a consultation, came out to join us. As we asked him who was this wolf-girl, and how she had come by so strange a nickname, he told us this story –

"This Solange, the wolf-girl, whose real name is Solange Tournier, wife of Grillet, was the prettiest girl in the whole Tronsays country about ten years ago. Now, of course, working in the fields as she does, and having had five children, she looks hardened and worn. Still, considering her thirty years, she is handsome enough, as you see. At the time of the adventure whence she derived her strange nickname she was living with her parents, who were farmers of the Rein-du-Bois, some fifteen kilometres from here. Although very poor, she was much sought by all the boys, even by the well-to-do; but she accepted the addresses of only one – a certain Laurent Grillet, on whom she had set her heart when she was a wee bit of a girl, when the two kept the sheep together in the neighborhood of Rein-du-Bois.

"Laurent Grillet was a foundling, who had nothing in the world but his two arms for a fortune. Solange's parents felt no inclination to add poverty to poverty, especially as the girl had so many wealthy suitors.

"So Solange was forbidden to see her friend. Naturally, the girl never failed at a tryst. Living in the same commune, with the forest at hand, they never lost an opportunity of meeting there. When the father and mother Tournier realized that scoldings and blows were of no avail, they determined upon a radical step. Solange was accordingly sent out to work at Ursay, on the model farm of M. Roger Duflos, our deputy.

"Perhaps you think our two lovers ceased to see each other. Not in the least. They now met at night; they slept no more. After nightfall they both left the farms where they were employed and started toward each other; and then they remained together until nearly dawn in the maternal forest, the accomplice of their young love.

"This was in 1879. In this manner the summer and autumn went by. Then came the winter, and a fierce winter it was. The Cher carried ice-drifts, and finally froze from bank to bank. The Tronsays forests, covered with snow, were bent like the weak supports of an overladen roof. The roads were almost impassable. The forest, deserted by man, was gradually being reconquered by beasts. It was soon invaded by wolves, which had neither been seen nor heard of since the Terrible year.

"Yes, sir, wolves! They haunted the isolated farms around Lurcy-Lévy and Ursay. They even ventured into the streets of St. Bonnet le Désert – a little village in the heart of the forest on the banks of a pond. It reached such a point that men were organized into bands to beat the woods. A reward of fifty francs was offered for the head of a wolf.

"Neither winter nor wolves, however, daunted Solange and Laurent, or interfered with their nocturnal meetings. They continued their expeditions in the face of a thousand dangers. This was the dead season in the fields, the time when the land lies fallow. Every night Laurent left Lurcy-Lévy, a gun over his shoulder, and penetrated with a lively step into the black and white forest. Solange, on the other hand, started from Ursay at about nine o'clock, and they met near a glade some three kilometres from here, traversed by a road, and known as the Découverte.

"It so happened that one night, which, by the way, was Christmas Eve, Laurent Grillet, as he reached the rendezvous, slipped on the hardened snow and fell, breaking his right leg and spraining his right wrist. Solange tried to raise him, but could only drag him to a great elm, against which she propped him, after wrapping him in her own cloak.

"'Wait for me here, my poor Laurent,' said she; 'I will run to Ursay for the doctor, and get him to come for you in his carryall.'

"She started off, but had not reached the first turn in the road when she heard a report and the cry, 'Help!'

"She ran back and found her friend in an agony of pain and fear, his trembling hand on the gun which lay beside him. She said, 'What is it, Laurent? Was it you who fired?'

"He answered, 'It was I. I saw a beast about the size of a large dog, and with great red eyes. I believe, on my word, it was a wolf.'

"'Was it at him you fired?'

"'No. I cannot lift my gun on account of my arm. I fired on the ground to scare him. He has gone now.'

"Solange reflected for a moment. 'Will he come back?'

"'I am afraid he will,' answered the lad. 'Solange, you will have to stay, or that beast will eat me.'

"'Well,' she said, 'I will stay. Let me have the gun.'

"She took it, put in a fresh cartridge, and they both waited.

"An hour passed. The moon, as yet invisible, had risen, however, above the horizon, for the zenith reflected a confused light, which was gradually growing more intense. Laurent felt the fever coming upon him. He shivered and moaned. Solange, half frozen, as she stood leaning against the tree, was beginning to feel drowsy. Suddenly a bark – a sort of howl like that of a dog at night when it is tied – made her start. In the faint light she saw two red eyes fixed upon her. It was the wolf. Laurent tried to rise and take his gun, but the pain flung him back with a cry.

"'Load, Solange,' said he. 'Do not fire too soon, and aim between the eyes.'

"She shouldered, aimed, and fired, but the gun recoiled and missed aim. The beast was untouched. It ran off a short way down the road. Then it was heard howling at a distance, and other howls came in answer.

"The moon was climbing the sky. It suddenly passed the dark mass of the thickets and flooded the entire forest as the footlights illumine the scenery on the stage. Then Solange and Laurent saw this horrible sight: at a few feet from them five wolves were seated on their haunches, drawn in line across the road, while another, bolder than the rest, was walking slowly toward them.

"'Listen,' said Laurent. 'Aim at that one that is coming. If you bring him down, the others will eat him, and they will leave us in peace in the mean time.'

"The wolf continued to advance with short, cautious steps. They could now see his bloodshot eyeballs distinctly, the protruding rings of his spine, the sharp bones of his carcass, his dull hair and his open jaw, with the long tongue hanging out. 'Hold the butt-end well in the hollow of your shoulder. Now fire.'

"There was a report; the beast leaped to one side and fell dead without a groan. The whole band galloped off and disappeared in the copse.

"'Run, Solange!' cried Laurent, 'drag him as far as you can along the road. There is no danger; the others will not come back for a while yet.'

"She had started, when he called her back. 'It might be just as well to cut off that beast's head on account of the reward.'

"'Have you a knife?' asked Solange.

"'Yes; in my belt.'

"It was a short-handled, broad-bladed hunter's knife. She took it and ran to the dead wolf. She made a great effort and drove it in his throat, the warm blood trickling down her hands and along her skirt; she turned her knife around, cut deep, then hacked, and finally severed the head from the trunk, which she dragged by one leg over the slippery snow as far as she could. Then she returned to her lover with the bloody, bristly head of the beast in her hand.

"What Laurent had foreseen occurred. The wolves, at first frightened by the death of their leader, were soon brought back by the smell of the blood. In the white light of the moon, reflected by the snow like the fantastic light of a fairy scene, the two young people saw the group of lean, ravenous beasts rubbing their backs against one another, crowding around the fresh prey, tearing it limb from limb, growling and snarling over it, wrenching off the flesh, until nothing was left of it, not even a tuft of hair.

"Meanwhile the boy was suffering greatly from his injuries. Solange, whose nerves were beginning to relax, struggled vainly against exhaustion and sleep. Twice her gun fell from her hands. The wolves, having finished their meal, began to draw nearer. The girl fired twice in the lot, but her benumbed fingers trembled and she missed her aim. At each report the band turned tail, trotted about a hundred metres down the road, waited a moment and came back.

"Then the two poor children were convinced that it was all over with them, and that they must die. Solange dropped her gun. It never once occurred to her that she might save herself. She threw herself down beside her lover, clasped her arms around him, laid her cheek against his, and there under the same cloak they awaited death, half frozen with the cold, half burning with fever. Their confused brains conjured strange visions. Now they thought they had gone back to the balmy nights of June when the forest, clad in deep green, sheltered their peaceful meetings, then suddenly the wood was bare, lighted with a weird snowy light, peopled with shifting forms, eyes like burning embers, great open jaws that multiplied, and came nearer, ever nearer.

"But neither Solange nor Laurent was destined to die so horrible a death. Providence – yes, young men, I believe in a Providence – had decreed that I, on that Christmas morning, should find myself on that particular road on my way home in my carryall from St. Bonnet le Désert. I managed the lines; my man held the gun and inspected the road. No doubt our sleigh-bells frightened away the wolves, for we saw none. As we drove near the elm at the foot of which the lovers lay, my mare shied, and so drew our attention to them. I jumped down from the seat. My man and I settled them in the carryall as best as we could, covering them with what wraps we had along. They were unconscious and almost frozen. We took the bloody head of the wolf with us too.

"It was about seven o'clock in the morning when we reached Ursay. The day was breaking over a landscape of spun glass and white velvet. M. Roger Duflos' farmers and at least one half of the inhabitants of the borough, having heard of Solange's disappearance, came out to meet us; and in the very kitchen where we dined this evening, in front of a great fire of crackling heather, Laurent and his friend warmed themselves and told us the story of their terrible Christmas."

One of us said –

"And what followed, Doctor? Did they marry?"

"Yes; they were married," answered our host. "The will of Providence is sometimes so plainly indicated by events that the most obtuse cannot fail to perceive it. After the adventure with the wolves, Solange's parents consented to her marriage with Laurent Grillet. The marriage took place in the spring. The reward of fifty francs for the wolf's head paid for the wedding dress."

The doctor was silent. Night was full upon us. The sky, of a turquoise blue, reflected its first stars in the river. The mass of forest, dense and inky, shut off the horizon. We saw Solange, the wolf-girl, dress her two boys and start homeward with them, the youngest asleep on her shoulder. She passed very near us, and looking up, smiled at the doctor. The doctor said –

"Good-night, Solange!"

Wagner, the Wehr-Wolf
Chapters I-XII
George W.M. Reynolds

Part I
Prologue

IT WAS THE MONTH of January, 1516.

The night was dark and tempestuous; the thunder growled around; the lightning flashed at short intervals: and the wind swept furiously along in sudden and fitful gusts.

The streams of the great Black Forest of Germany babbled in playful melody no more, but rushed on with deafening din, mingling their torrent roar with the wild creaking of the huge oaks, the rustling of the firs, the howling of the affrighted wolves, and the hollow voices of the storm.

The dense black clouds were driving restlessly athwart the sky; and when the vivid lightning gleamed forth with rapid and eccentric glare, it seemed as if the dark jaws of some hideous monster, floating high above, opened to vomit flame.

And as the abrupt but furious gusts of wind swept through the forest, they raised strange echoes – as if the impervious mazes of that mighty wood were the abode of hideous fiends and evil spirits, who responded in shrieks, moans, and lamentations to the fearful din of the tempest.

It was, indeed, an appalling night!

An old – old man sat in his cottage on the verge of the Black Forest.

He had numbered ninety years; his head was completely bald – his mouth was toothless – his long beard was white as snow, and his limbs were feeble and trembling.

He was alone in the world; his wife, his children, his grandchildren, all his relations, in fine, save one, had preceded him on that long, last voyage, from which no traveler returns.

And that *one* was a grand-daughter, a beauteous girl of sixteen, who had hitherto been his solace and his comfort, but who had suddenly disappeared – he knew not how – a few days previously to the time when we discover him seated thus lonely in his poor cottage.

But perhaps she also was dead! An accident might have snatched her away from him, and sent her spirit to join those of her father and mother, her sisters and her brothers, whom a terrible pestilence – *the Black Death* – hurried to the tomb a few years before.

No: the old man could not believe that his darling granddaughter was no more – for he had sought her throughout the neighboring district of the Black Forest, and not a trace of her was to be seen. Had she fallen down a precipice, or perished by the ruthless murderer's hand, he would have discovered her mangled corpse: had she become the prey of the ravenous wolves, certain signs of her fate would have doubtless somewhere appeared.

The sad – the chilling conviction therefore, went to the old man's heart, that the only being left to solace him on earth, had deserted him; and his spirit was bowed down in despair.

Who now would prepare his food, while he tended his little flock? Who was there to collect the dry branches in the forest, for the winter's fuel, while the aged shepherd watched a few sheep that he possessed? Who would now spin him warm clothing to protect his weak and trembling limbs?

"Oh! Agnes," he murmured, in a tone indicative of a breaking heart, "why couldst thou have thus abandoned me? Didst thou quit the old man to follow some youthful lover, who will buoy thee up with bright hopes, and then deceive thee? O Agnes – my darling! Hast thou left me to perish without a soul to close my eyes?"

It was painful how that ancient shepherd wept.

Suddenly a loud knock at the door of the cottage aroused him from his painful reverie; and he hastened, as fast as his trembling limbs would permit him, to answer the summons.

He opened the door; and a tall man, apparently about forty years of age, entered the humble dwelling. His light hair would have been magnificent indeed, were it not sorely neglected; his blue eyes were naturally fine and intelligent, but fearful now to meet, so wild and wandering were their glances: his form was tall and admirably symmetrical, but prematurely bowed by the weight of sorrow, and his attire was of costly material, but indicative of inattention even more than it was travel-soiled.

The old man closed the door, and courteously drew a stool near the fire for the stranger who had sought in his cottage a refuge against the fury of the storm.

He also placed food before him; but the stranger touched it not – horror and dismay appearing to have taken possession of his soul.

Suddenly the thunder which had hitherto growled at a distance, burst above the humble abode; and the wind swept by with so violent a gust, that it shook the little tenement to its foundation, and filled the neighboring forest with strange, unearthly noises.

Then the countenance of the stranger expressed such ineffable horror, amounting to a fearful agony, that the old man was alarmed, and stretched out his hand to grasp a crucifix that hung over the chimney-piece; but his mysterious guest made a forbidding sign of so much earnestness mingled with such proud authority, that the aged shepherd sank back into his seat without touching the sacred symbol.

The roar of the thunder past – the shrieking, whistling, gushing wind became temporarily lulled into low moans and subdued lamentations, amid the mazes of the Black Forest; and the stranger grew more composed.

"Dost thou tremble at the storm?" inquired the old man.

"I am unhappy," was the evasive and somewhat impatient reply. "Seek not to know more of me – beware how you question me. But you, old man, are *not* happy! The traces of care seem to mingle with the wrinkles of age upon your brow!"

The shepherd narrated, in brief and touching terms, the unaccountable disappearance of his much-beloved granddaughter Agnes.

The stranger listened abstractedly at first; but afterward he appeared to reflect profoundly for several minutes.

"Your lot is wretched, old man," said he at length: "if you live a few years longer, that period must be passed in solitude and cheerlessness: – if you suddenly fall ill you must die the lingering death of famine, without a soul to place a morsel of food, or the cooling cup to your lips; and when you shall be no more, who will follow you to the grave? There are no habitations nigh; the nearest village is half-a-day's journey distant; and ere the peasants of that hamlet, or some passing traveler, might discover that the inmate of this hut had breathed his last, the wolves from the forest would have entered and mangled your corpse."

"Talk not thus!" cried the old man, with a visible shudder; then darting a half-terrified, half-curious glance at his guest, he said, "but who are you that speak in this awful strain – this warning voice?"

Again the thunder rolled, with crashing sound, above the cottage; and once more the wind swept by, laden, as it seemed, with the shrieks and groans of human beings in the agonies of death.

The stranger maintained a certain degree of composure only by means of a desperate effort, but he could not altogether subdue a wild flashing of the eyes and a ghastly change of the countenance – signs of a profoundly felt terror.

"Again I say, ask me not who I am!" he exclaimed, when the thunder and the gust had passed. "My soul recoils from the bare idea of pronouncing my own accursed name! But – unhappy as you see me – crushed, overwhelmed with deep affliction as you behold me – anxious, but unable to repent for the past as I am, and filled with appalling dread for the future as I now proclaim myself to be, still is my power far, far beyond that limit which hems mortal energies within so small a sphere. Speak, old man – wouldst thou change thy condition?

For to me – and to me alone of all human beings – belongs the means of giving thee new life – of bestowing upon thee the vigor of youth, of rendering that stooping form upright and strong, of restoring fire to those glazing eyes, and beauty to that wrinkled, sunken, withered countenance – of endowing thee, in a word, with a fresh tenure of existence and making that existence sweet by the aid of treasures so vast that no extravagance can dissipate them!"

A strong though indefinite dread assailed the old man as this astounding proffer was rapidly opened, in all its alluring details, to his mind; – and various images of terror presented themselves to his imagination; – but these feelings were almost immediately dominated by a wild and ardent hope, which became the more attractive and exciting in proportion as a rapid glance at his helpless, wretched, deserted condition led him to survey the contrast between what he then was, and what, if the stranger spoke truly, he might so soon become.

The stranger saw that he had made the desired impression; and he continued thus:

"Give but your assent, old man, and not only will I render thee young, handsome, and wealthy; but I will endow thy mind with an intelligence to match that proud position. Thou shalt go forth into the world to enjoy all those pleasures, those delights, and those luxuries, the names of which are even now scarcely known to thee!"

"And what is the price of this glorious boon?" asked the old man, trembling with mingled joy and terror through every limb.

"There are two conditions," answered the stranger, in a low, mysterious tone. "The first is, that you become the companion of my wanderings for one year and a half from the present time, until the hour of sunset, on the 30th of July, 1517, when we must part forever, you to go whithersoever your inclinations may guide you, and I— But of *that*, no matter!" he added, hastily, with a sudden motion as if of deep mental agony, and with wildly flashing eyes.

The old man shrank back in dismay from his mysterious guest: the thunder rolled again, the rude gust swept fiercely by, the dark forest rustled awfully, and the stranger's torturing feelings were evidently prolonged by the voices of the storm.

A pause ensued; and the silence was at length broken by the old man, who said, in a hollow and tremulous tone, "To the first condition I would willingly accede. But the second?"

"That you prey upon the human race, whom I hate; because of all the world I alone am so deeply, so terribly accurst!" was the ominously fearful yet only dimly significant reply.

The old man shook his head, scarcely comprehending the words of his guest, and yet daring not to ask to be more enlightened.

"Listen!" said the stranger, in a hasty but impressive voice: "I require a companion, one who has no human ties, and who still ministers to my caprices, – who will devote himself wholly and solely to watch me in my dark hours, and endeavor to recall me back to enjoyment and pleasure, who, when he shall be acquainted with my power, will devise new means in which to exercise it, for the purpose of conjuring up those scenes of enchantment and delight that may for a season win me away from thought. Such a companion do I need for a period of one year and a half; and you are, of all men, the best suited to my design. But the Spirit whom I must invoke to effect the promised change in thee, and by whose aid you can be given back to youth and comeliness, will demand some fearful sacrifice at your hands. And the nature of that sacrifice – the nature of the condition to be imposed – I can well divine!"

"Name the sacrifice – name the condition!" cried the old man, eagerly. "I am so miserable – so spirit-broken – so totally without hope in this world, that I greedily long to enter upon that new existence which you promised me! Say, then, what is the condition?"

"That you prey upon the human race, whom *he* hates as well as I," answered the stranger.

"Again these awful words!" ejaculated the old man, casting trembling glances around him.

"Yes – again those words," echoed the mysterious guest, looking with his fierce burning eyes into the glazed orbs of the aged shepherd. "And now learn their import!" he continued, in a solemn tone. "Knowest thou not that there is a belief in many parts of our native land that at particular seasons certain doomed men throw off the human shape and take that of ravenous wolves?"

"Oh, yes – yes – I have indeed heard of those strange legends in which the Wehr-Wolf is represented in such appalling colors!" exclaimed the old man, a terrible suspicion crossing his mind.

"'Tis said that at sunset on the last day of every month the mortal, to whom belongs the destiny of the Wehr-Wolf, must exchange his natural form for that of the savage animal; in which horrible shape he must remain until the moment when the morrow's sun dawns upon the earth."

"The legend that told thee this spoke truly," said the stranger. "And now dost thou comprehend the condition which must be imposed upon thee?"

"I do – I do!" murmured the old man with a fearful shudder. "But he who accepts that condition makes a compact with the evil one, and thereby endangers his immortal soul!"

"Not so," was the reply. "There is naught involved in this condition which— But hesitate not," added the stranger, hastily: "I have no time to waste in bandying words. Consider all I offer you: in another hour you shall be another man!"

"I accept the boon – and on the conditions stipulated!" exclaimed the shepherd.

"'Tis well, Wagner—"

"What! You know my name!" cried the old man. "And yet, meseems, I did not mention it to thee."

"Canst thou not already perceive that I am no common mortal?" demanded the stranger, bitterly. "And who I am, and whence I derive my power, all shall be revealed to thee so soon as the bond is formed that must link us for eighteen months together! In the meantime, await me here!"

And the mysterious stranger quitted the cottage abruptly, and plunged into the depths of the Black Forest.

One hour elapsed ere he returned – one mortal hour, during which Wagner sat bowed over his miserably scanty fire, dreaming of pleasure, youth, riches, and enjoyment; converting, in imagination, the myriad sparks which shone upon the extinguishing embers into piles of gold, and allowing his now uncurbed fancy to change the one single room of the wretched hovel into a splendid saloon, surrounded by resplendent mirrors and costly hangings, while the untasted fare for the stranger on the rude fir-table, became transformed, in his idea, into a magnificent banquet laid out, on a board glittering with plate, lustrous with innumerable lamps, and surrounded by an atmosphere fragrant with the most exquisite perfumes.

The return of the stranger awoke the old man from his charming dream, during which he had never once thought of the conditions whereby he was to purchase the complete realization of the vision.

"Oh! What a glorious reverie you have dissipated!" exclaimed Wagner. "Fulfill but one tenth part of that delightful dream—"

"I will fulfill it all!" interrupted the stranger: then, producing a small vial from the bosom of his doublet, he said, "Drink!"

The old man seized the bottle, and speedily drained it to the dregs.

He immediately fell back upon the seat, in a state of complete lethargy.

But it lasted not for many minutes; and when he awoke again, he experienced new and extraordinary sensations. His limbs were vigorous, his form was upright as an arrow; his eyes, for many years dim and failing, seemed gifted with the sight of an eagle, his head was warm with a natural covering; not a wrinkle remained upon his brow nor on his cheeks; and, as he smiled with mingled wonderment and delight, the parting lips revealed a set of brilliant teeth. And it seemed, too, as if by one magic touch the long fading tree of his intellect had suddenly burst into full foliage, and every cell of his brain was instantaneously stored with an amount of knowledge, the accumulation of which stunned him for an instant, and in the next appeared as familiar to him as if he had never been without it.

"Oh! Great and powerful being, whomsoever thou art," exclaimed Wagner, in the full, melodious voice of a young man of twenty-one, "how can I manifest to thee my deep, my boundless gratitude for this boon which thou hast conferred upon me!"

"By thinking no more of thy lost grand-child Agnes, but by preparing to follow me whither I shall now lead thee," replied the stranger.

"Command me: I am ready to obey in all things," cried Wagner. "But one word ere we set forth – who art thou, wondrous man?"

"Henceforth I have no secrets from thee, Wagner," was the answer, while the stranger's eyes gleamed with unearthly luster; then, bending forward, he whispered a few words in the other's ear.

Wagner started with a cold and fearful shudder as if at some appalling announcement; but he uttered not a word of reply – for his master beckoned him imperiously away from the humble cottage.

Chapter I
The Death-Bed – The Oath – The Last Injunctions

OUR TALE COMMENCES in the middle of the month of November, 1520, and at the hour of midnight.

In a magnificently furnished chamber, belonging to one of the largest mansions of Florence, a nobleman lay at the point of death.

The light of the lamp suspended to the ceiling played upon the ghastly countenance of the dying man, the stern expression of whose features was not even mitigated by the fears and uncertainties attendant on the hour of dissolution.

He was about forty-eight years of age, and had evidently been wondrously handsome in his youth: for though the frightful pallor of death was already upon his cheeks, and the fire of his large black eyes was dimmed with the ravages of a long-endured disease, still the faultless outlines of the aquiline profile remained unimpaired.

The most superficial observer might have read the aristocratic pride of his soul in the haughty curl of his short upper lip – the harshness of his domineering character in the lines that marked his forehead – and the cruel sternness of his disposition in the expression of his entire countenance.

Without absolutely scowling as he lay on that bed of death, his features were characterized by an inexorable severity which seemed to denote the predominant influence of some intense passion – some evil sentiment deeply rooted in his mind.

Two persons leant over the couch to which death was so rapidly approaching.

One was a lady of about twenty-five: the other was a youth of nineteen.

The former was eminently beautiful; but her countenance was marked with much of that severity – that determination – and even of that sternness, which characterized the dying nobleman. Indeed, a single glance was sufficient to show that they stood in the close relationship of father and daughter.

Her long, black, glossy hair now hung disheveled over the shoulders that were left partially bare by the hasty negligence with which she had thrown on a loose wrapper; and those shoulders were of the most dazzling whiteness.

The wrapper was confined by a broad band at the waist; and the slight drapery set off, rather than concealed, the rich contours of a form of mature but admirable symmetry.

Tall, graceful, and elegant, she united easy motion with fine proportion; thus possessing the lightness of the Sylph and the luxuriant fullness of the Hebe.

Her countenance was alike expressive of intellectuality and strong passions. Her large black eyes were full of fire, and their glances seemed to penetrate the soul. Her nose, of the finest aquiline development – her lips, narrow, but red and pouting, with the upper one short and slightly projecting over the lower – and her small, delicately rounded chin, indicated both decision and sensuality: but the insolent gaze of the libertine would have quailed beneath the look of sovereign hauteur which flashed from those brilliant eagle eyes.

In a word, she appeared to be a woman well adapted to command the admiration – receive the homage – excite the passions – and yet repel the insolence of the opposite sex.

But those appearances were to some degree deceitful; for never was homage offered to her – never was she courted nor flattered.

Ten years previously to the time of which we are writing – and when she was only fifteen – the death of her mother, under strange and mysterious circumstances, as it was generally reported, made such a terrible impression on her mind, that she hovered for months on the verge of dissolution; and when the physician who attended upon her communicated to her father the fact that her life was at length beyond danger, that assurance was followed by the sad and startling declaration, that she had forever lost the sense of hearing and the power of speech.

No wonder, then, that homage was never paid nor adulation offered to Nisida – the deaf and dumb daughter of the proud Count of Riverola!

Those who were intimate with this family ere the occurrence of that sad event – especially the physician, Dr. Duras, who had attended upon the mother in her last moments, and on the daughter during her illness – declared that, up to the period when the malady assailed her, Nisida was a sweet, amiable and retiring girl; but she had evidently been fearfully changed by the terrible affliction which that malady had left behind. For if she could no longer express herself in words, her eyes darted lightnings upon the unhappy menials who had the misfortune to incur her displeasure; and her lips would quiver with the violence of concentrated passion, at the most trifling neglect or error of which the female dependents immediately attached to her own person might happen to be guilty.

Toward her father she often manifested a strange ebullition of anger – bordering even on inveterate spite, when he offended her: and yet, singular though it were, the count was devotedly attached to his daughter. He frequently declared that, afflicted as she was, he was proud of her: for he was wont to behold in her flashing eyes – her curling lip – and her haughty air, the reflection of his own proud – his own inexorable spirit.

The youth of nineteen to whom we have alluded was Nisida's brother; and much as the father appeared to dote upon the daughter, was the son proportionately disliked by that stern and despotic man.

Perhaps this want of affection – or rather this complete aversion – on the part of the Count of Riverola toward the young Francisco, owed its origin to the total discrepancy of character existing between the father and son. Francisco was as amiable, generous-hearted, frank and agreeable as his sire was austere, stern, reserved and tyrannical. The youth was also unlike his father in personal appearance, his hair being of a rich brown, his eyes of a soft blue, and the general expression of his countenance indicating the fairest and most endearing qualities which can possibly characterize human nature.

We must, however, observe, before we pursue our narrative, that Nisida imitated not her father in her conduct toward Francisco; for she loved him – she loved him with the most ardent affection – such an affection as a sister seldom manifests toward a brother. It was rather the attachment of a mother for her child; inasmuch as Nisida studied all his comforts – watched over him, as it were, with the tenderest solicitude – was happy when he was present, melancholy when he was absent, and seemed to be constantly racking her imagination to devise new means to afford him pleasure.

To treat Francisco with the least neglect was to arouse the wrath of a fury in the breast of Nisida; and every unkind look which the count inflicted upon his son was sure, if perceived by his daughter, to evoke the terrible lightnings of her brilliant eyes.

Such were the three persons whom we have thus minutely described to our readers.

The count had been ill for some weeks at the time when this chapter opens; but on the night which marks that commencement, Dr. Duras had deemed it his duty to warn the nobleman that he had not many hours to live.

The dying man had accordingly desired that his children might be summoned; and when they entered the apartment, the physician and the priest were requested to withdraw.

Francisco now stood on one side of the bed, and Nisida on the other; while the count collected his remaining strength to address his last injunctions to his son.

"Francisco," he said, in a cold tone, "I have little inclination to speak at any great length; but the words I am about to utter are solemnly important. I believe you entertain the most sincere and earnest faith in that symbol which now lies beneath your hand."

"The crucifix!" ejaculated the young man. "Oh, yes, my dear father! – it is the emblem of that faith which teaches us how to live and die!"

"Then take it up – press it to your lips – and swear to obey the instructions which I am about to give you," said the count.

Francisco did as he was desired; and, although tears were streaming from his eyes, he exclaimed, in an emphatic manner, "I swear most solemnly to fulfill your commands, my dear father, so confident am I that you will enjoin nothing that involves aught dishonorable!"

"Spare your qualifications," cried the count, sternly; "and swear without reserve – or expect my dying curse, rather than my blessing."

"Oh! My dear father," ejaculated the youth, with intense anguish of soul; "talk not of so dreadful a thing as bequeathing me your dying curse! I swear to fulfill your injunctions – without reserve."

And he kissed the holy symbol.

"You act wisely," said the count, fixing his glaring eyes upon the handsome countenance of the young man, who now awaited, in breathless suspense, a communication thus solemnly prefaced. "This key," continued the nobleman, taking one from beneath his pillow as he spoke, "belongs to the door in yonder corner of the apartment."

"That door which is never opened!" exclaimed Francisco, casting an anxious glance in the direction indicated.

"Who told you that the door was never opened," demanded the count, sternly.

"I have heard the servants remark—" began the youth in a timid, but still frank and candid manner.

"Then, when I am no more, see that you put an end to such impertinent gossiping," said the nobleman, impatiently; "and you will be the better convinced of the propriety of thus acting, as soon as you have learned the nature of my injunctions. That door," he continued, "communicates with a small closet, which is accessible by no other means. Now my wish – my command is this: – Upon the day of your marriage, whenever such an event may occur – and I suppose you do not intend to remain unwedded all your life – I enjoin you to open the door of that closet. You must be accompanied by your bride – and by no other living soul. I also desire that this may be done with the least possible delay – the very morning – within the very hour after you quit the church. That closet contains the means of elucidating a mystery profoundly connected with me – with you – with the family – a mystery, the developments of which may prove of incalculable service alike to yourself and to her who may share your title and your wealth. But should you never marry, then must the closet remain unvisited by you; nor need you trouble yourself concerning the eventual discovery of the secret which it contains, by any person into whose hands the mansion may fall at your death. It is also my wish that your sister should remain in complete ignorance of the instructions which I am now giving you. Alas! poor girl – she cannot hear the words which fall from my lips! Neither shall you communicate their import to her by writing, nor by the language of the fingers. And remember that while I bestow upon you my blessing – my dying blessing – may that blessing become a withering curse – the curse of hell upon you – if in any way you violate one tittle of the injunctions which I have now given you."

"My dearest father," replied the weeping youth, who had listened with the most profound attention, to these extraordinary commands; "I would not for worlds act contrary to your wishes. Singular as they appear to me, they shall be fulfilled to the very letter."

He received from his father's hand the mysterious key, which he had secured about his person.

"You will find," resumed the count after a brief pause, "that I have left the whole of my property to you. At the same time my will specifies certain conditions relative to your sister Nisida, for whom I have made due provision only in the case – which is, alas! almost in defiance of every hope! – of her recovery from that dreadful affliction which renders her so completely dependent upon your kindness."

"Dearest father, you know how sincerely I am attached to my sister – how devoted she is to me—"

"Enough, enough!" cried the count; and overcome by the effort he had made to deliver his last injunction, he fell back insensible on his pillow.

Nisida, who had retained her face buried in her hands during the whole time occupied in the above conversation, happened to look up at that moment; and, perceiving the condition of her father, she made a hasty sign to Francisco to summon the physician and the priest from the room to which they had retired.

This commission was speedily executed, and in a few minutes the physician and the priest were once more by the side of the dying noble.

But the instant that Dr. Duras – who was a venerable looking man of about sixty years of age – approached the bed, he darted, unseen by Francisco, a glance of earnest inquiry toward Nisida, who responded by one of profound meaning, shaking her head gently, but in a manner expressive of deep melancholy, at the same time.

The physician appeared to be astonished at the negative thus conveyed by the beautiful mute; and he even manifested a sign of angry impatience.

But Nisida threw upon him a look of so imploring a nature, that his temporary vexation yielded to a feeling of immense commiseration for that afflicted creature: and he gave her to understand, by another rapid glance, that her prayer was accorded.

This interchange of signs of such deep mystery scarcely occupied a moment, and was altogether unobserved by Francisco.

Dr. Duras proceeded to administer restoratives to the dying nobleman – but in vain!

The count had fallen into a lethargic stupor, which lasted until four in the morning, when his spirit passed gently away.

The moment Francisco and Nisida became aware that they were orphans, they threw themselves into each other's arms, and renewed by that tender embrace the tacit compact of sincere affection which had ever existed between them.

Francisco's tears flowed freely; but Nisida did not weep!

A strange – an almost portentous light shone in her brilliant black eyes; and though that wild gleaming denoted powerful emotions, yet it shed no luster upon the depths of her soul – afforded no clew to the real nature of these agitated feelings.

Suddenly withdrawing himself from his sister's arms, Francisco conveyed to her by the language of the fingers the following tender sentiment: – You have lost a father, beloved Nisida, but you have a devoted and affectionate brother left to you!"

And Nisida replied through the same medium, "Your happiness, dearest brother, has ever been my only study, and shall continue so."

The physician and Father Marco, the priest, now advanced, and taking the brother and sister by the hands, led them from the chamber of death.

"Kind friends," said Francisco, now Count of Riverola, "I understand you. You would withdraw my sister and myself from a scene too mournful to contemplate. Alas! It is hard to lose a father; but especially so at my age, inexperienced as I am in the ways of the world!"

"The world is indeed made up of thorny paths and devious ways, my dear young friend," returned the physician; "but a stout heart and integrity of purpose will ever be found faithful guides. The more exalted and the wealthier the individual, the greater the temptations he will have to encounter. Reflect upon this, Francisco: it is advice which I, as an old – indeed, the oldest friend of your family – take the liberty to offer."

With these words, the venerable physician wrung the hands of the brother and sister, and hurried from the house, followed by the priest.

The orphans embraced each other, and retired to their respective apartments.

Chapter II
Nisida – The Mysterious Closet

THE ROOM TO which Nisida withdrew, between four and five o'clock on that mournful winter's morning, was one of a suit entirely appropriated to her own use.

This suit consisted of three apartments, communicating with each other, and all furnished in the elegant and tasteful manner of that age.

The innermost of the three rooms was used as her bed-chamber, and when she now entered it, a young girl of seventeen, beautiful as an angel, but dressed in the attire of a dependent, instantly arose from a seat near the fire that blazed on the hearth, and cast a respectful but inquiring glance toward her mistress.

Nisida gave her to understand, by a sign, that all was over.

The girl started, as if surprised that her lady indicated so little grief; but the latter motioned her, with an impatient gesture, to leave the room.

When Flora – such was the name of the dependent – had retired Nisida threw herself into a large arm-chair near the fire, and immediately became buried in a deep reverie. With her splendid hair flowing upon her white shoulders – her proud forehead supported on her delicate hand – her lips apart, and revealing the pearly teeth – her lids with their long black fringes half-closed over the brilliant eyes – and her fine form cast in voluptuous abandonment upon the soft cushions of the chair – she indeed seemed a magnificent creature!

But when, suddenly awaking from that profound meditation, she started from her seat with flashing eyes – heaving bosom – and an expression of countenance denoting a fixed determination to accomplish some deed from which her better feelings vainly bade her to abstain: – when she drew her tall – her even majestic form up to its full height, the drapery shadowing forth every contour of undulating bust and exquisitely modeled limb – while her haughty lip curled in contempt of any consideration save her own indomitable will – she appeared rather a heroine capable of leading an Amazonian army, than a woman to whom the sighing swain might venture to offer up the incense of love.

There was something awful in the aspect of this mysterious being – something ineffably grand and imposing in her demeanor – as she thus suddenly rose from her almost recumbent posture, and burst into the attitude of a resolute and energetic woman.

Drawing the wrapper around her form, she lighted a lamp, and was about to quit the chamber, when her eyes suddenly encountered the mild and benignant glance which the portrait of a lady appeared to cast upon her.

This portrait, which hung against the wall precisely opposite to the bed, represented a woman of about thirty years of age – a woman of a beauty much in the same style as that of Nisida, but not marred by anything approaching to a sternness of expression. On the contrary, if an angel had looked through those mild black eyes, their glances could not have been endowed with a holier kindness; the smiles of good spirits could not be more plaintively sweet than those which the artist had made to play upon the lips of that portrait.

Yet, in spite of this discrepancy between the expression of Nisida's countenance and that of the lady who had formed the subject of the picture, it was not difficult to perceive a certain physical likeness between the two; nor will the reader be surprised when we state that Nisida was gazing on the portrait of her deceased mother.

And that gaze – oh! How intent, how earnest, how enthusiastic it was! It manifested something more than love – something more impassioned and ardent than the affection which a daughter might exhibit toward even a living mother; it showed a complete devotion – an adoration – a worship!

Long and fixedly did Nisida gaze upon that portrait; till suddenly from her eyes, which shot forth such burning glances, gushed a torrent of tears.

Then – probably fearful lest this weakness on her part might impair the resolution necessary to execute the purpose which she had in view – Nisida dashed away the tears from her long lashes, hastily quitted the room.

Having traversed the other two apartments of her own suit, she cast a searching glance along the passage which she now entered; and, satisfied that none of the domestics were about, for it was not yet six o'clock on that winter's morning, she hastened to the end of the corridor.

The lamp flared with the speed at which she walked; and its uncertain light enhanced the pallor that now covered her countenance.

At the bottom of the passage she cautiously opened the door, and entered the room with which it communicated.

This was the sleeping apartment of her brother.

A single glance convinced her that he was wrapt in the arms of slumber.

He slept soundly too – for he was wearied with the vigil which he had passed by the death-bed of his father – worn out also by the thousand conflicting and unsatisfactory conjectures that the last instructions of his parent had naturally excited in his mind.

He had not, however, been asleep a quarter of an hour when Nisida stole, in the manner described, into his chamber.

A smile of mingled joy and triumph animated her countenance, and a carnation tinge flushed her cheeks when she found he was fast locked in the embrace of slumber.

Without a moment's hesitation, she examined his doublet, and clutched the key that his father had given to him scarcely six hours before.

Then, light as the fawn, she left the room.

Having retraced her steps half-way up the passage, she paused at the door of the chamber in which the corpse of her father lay.

For an instant – a single instant – she seemed to revolt from the prosecution of her design, then, with a stern contraction of the brows, and an imperious curl of the lip – as if she said within herself, "*Fool that I am to hesitate!*" – she entered the room.

Without fear – without compunction, she approached the bed. The body was laid out: stretched in its winding sheet, stiff and stark did it seem to repose on the mattress – the countenance rendered more ghastly than even death could make it, by the white band which tied up the under jaw.

The nurse who had thus disposed the corpse, had retired to snatch a few hours of rest; and there was consequently no spy upon Nisida's actions.

With a fearless step she advanced toward the closet – the mysterious closet relative to which such strange injunctions had been given.

Chapter III
The Manuscript – Flora Francatelli

NISIDA'S HAND TREMBLED not as she placed the key in the lock; but when it turned, and she knew that in another instant she might open that door if she chose, she compressed her lips firmly together – she called all her courage to her aid – for she seemed to imagine that it was necessary to prepare herself to behold something frightfully appalling.

And now again her cheeks were deadly pale; but the light that burned in her eyes was brilliant in the extreme.

White as was her countenance, her large black orbs appeared to shine – to glow – to burn, as if with a violent fever.

Advancing with her left hand, she half-opened the door of the closet with her right.

Then she plunged her glances with rapidity into the recess.

But, holy God! What a start that courageous, bold, and energetic woman gave – a start as if the cold hand of a corpse had been suddenly thrust forth to grasp her.

And oh! what horror convulsed her countenance – while her lips were compressed as tightly as if they were an iron vise.

Rapidly and instantly recoiling as that glance was, it had nevertheless revealed to her an object of interest as well as of horror; for with eyes now averted, she seized something within the closet, and thrust it into her bosom.

Then, hastily closing the door, she retraced her way to her brother's chamber.

He still slept soundly; Nisida returned the key to the pocket whence she had taken it, and hurried back to her own room, from which she had scarcely been absent five minutes.

And did she seek her couch? Did she repair to rest?

No; that energetic woman experienced no weariness – yielded to no lassitude.

Carefully bolting the door of her innermost chamber, she seated herself in the arm-chair and drew from her bosom the object which she had taken from the mysterious closet.

It was a manuscript, consisting of several small slips of paper, somewhat closely written upon.

The paper was doubtless familiar to her; for she paused not to consider its nature, but greedily addressed herself to the study of the meaning which it conveyed. And of terrible import seemed that manuscript to be; for while Nisida read, her countenance underwent many and awful changes – and her bosom heaved convulsively at one instant, while at another it remained motionless, as if respiration were suspended.

At length the perusal was completed; and grinding her teeth with demoniac rage, she threw the manuscript upon the floor. But at the same moment her eyes, which she cast wildly about her, caught the mild and benign countenance of her mother's portrait; and, as oil stills the fury of the boiling billows, did the influence of that picture calm in an instant the tremendous emotions of Nisida's soul.

Tears burst from her eyes, and she suddenly relapsed from the incarnate fiend into the subdued woman.

Then stooping down, she picked up the papers that lay scattered on the floor: but as she did so she averted her looks, with loathing and disgust, as much as possible from the pages that her hands collected almost at random.

And now another idea struck her – an idea the propriety of which evidently warred against her inclination.

She was not a woman of mere impulses – although she often acted speedily after a thought had entered her brain. But she was wondrously quick at weighing all reasons for or against the suggestions of her imagination; and thus, to any one who was not acquainted with her character, she might frequently appear to obey the first dictates of her impetuous passions.

Scarcely three minutes after the new idea had struck her, her resolution was fixed.

Once more concealing the papers in her bosom, she repaired with the lamp to her brother's room – purloined the key a second time – hastened to the chamber of death – opened the closet again – and again sustained the shock of a single glance at its horrors, as she returned the manuscript to the place whence she had originally taken it.

Then, having once more retraced her way to Francisco's chamber, she restored the key to the folds of his doublet – for he continued to sleep soundly; and Nisida succeeded in regaining her own apartments just in time to avoid the observation of the domestics, who were now beginning to move about.

Nisida sought her couch and slept until nearly ten o'clock, when she awoke with a start – doubtless caused by some unpleasant dream.

Having ascertained the hour by reference to a water-clock, or clepsydra, which stood on a marble pedestal near the head of the bed, she arose – unlocked the door of her apartment – rang a silver bell – and then returned to her bed.

In a few minutes Flora, who had been waiting in the adjoining room, entered the chamber.

Nisida, on regaining her couch, had turned her face toward the wall, and was therefore unable to perceive anything that took place in the apartment.

The mere mention of such a circumstance would be trivial in the extreme, were it not necessary to record it in consequence of an event which now occurred.

For, as Flora advanced into the room, her eyes fell on a written paper that lay immediately beneath the arm-chair; and conceiving from its appearance that it had not been thrown down on purpose, as it was in nowise crushed nor torn, she mechanically picked it up and placed it on the table.

She then proceeded to arrange the toilet table of her mistress, preparatory to that lady's rising; and while she is thus employed, we will endeavor to make our readers a little better acquainted with her than they can possibly yet be.

Flora Francatelli was the orphan daughter of parents who had suddenly been reduced from a state of affluence to a condition of extreme poverty. Signor Francatelli could not survive this blow:

he died of a broken heart; and his wife shortly afterward followed him to the tomb – also the victim of grief. They left two children behind them: Flora, who was then an infant, and a little boy, named Alessandro, who was five years old. The orphans were entirely dependent upon the kindness of a maiden aunt – their departed father's sister. This relative, whose name was, of course, also Francatelli, performed a mother's part toward the children: and deprived herself, not only of comforts, but at times even of necessaries, in order that they should not want. Father Marco, a priest belonging to one of the numerous monasteries of Florence, and who was a worthy man, took compassion upon this little family; and not only devoted his attention to teach the orphans to read and write – great accomplishments among the middle classes in those days – but also procured from a fund at the disposal of his abbot, certain pecuniary assistance for the aunt.

The care which this good relative took of the orphans, and the kindness of Father Marco, were well rewarded by the veneration and attachment which Alessandro and Flora manifested toward them. When Alessandro had numbered eighteen summers, he was fortunate enough to procure, through the interest of Father Marco, the situation of secretary to a Florentine noble, who was charged with a diplomatic mission to the Ottoman Porte; and the young man proceeded to Leghorn, whence he embarked for Constantinople, attended by the prayers, blessings, and hopes of the aunt and sister, and of the good priest, whom he left behind.

Two years after his departure, Father Marco obtained for Flora a situation about the person of the Lady Nisida; for the monk was confessor to the family of Riverola, and his influence was sufficient to secure that place for the young maiden.

We have already said that Flora was sweetly beautiful. Her large blue eyes were fringed with dark lashes, which gave them an expression of the most melting softness; her dark brown hair, arranged in the modest bands, seemed of even a darker hue when contrasted with the brilliant and transparent clearness of her complexion, and though her forehead was white and polished as alabaster, yet the rose-tint of health was upon her cheeks, and her lips had the rich redness of coral. Her nose was perfectly straight; her teeth were white and even, and the graceful arching of her swan-neck imparted something of nobility to her tall, sylph-like, and exquisitely proportioned figure.

Retiring and bashful in her manners, every look which fell from her eyes – every smile which wreathed her lips, denoted the chaste purity of her soul. With all her readiness to oblige – with all her anxiety to do her duty as she ought, she frequently incurred the anger of the irascible Nisida; but Flora supported those manifestations of wrath with the sweetest resignation, because the excellence of her disposition taught her to make every allowance for one so deeply afflicted as her mistress.

Such was the young maiden whom the nature of the present tale compels us thus particularly to introduce to our readers.

Having carefully arranged the boudoir, so that its strict neatness might be welcome to her mistress when that lady chose to rise from her couch, Flora seated herself near the table, and gave way to her reflections.

She thought of her aunt, who inhabited a neat little cottage on the banks of the Arno, and whom she was usually permitted to visit every Sabbath afternoon – she thought of her absent brother, who was still in the service of the Florentine Envoy to the Ottomon Porte, where that diplomatist was detained by the tardiness that marked the negotiations with which he was charged; and then she thought – thought too, with an involuntary sigh – of Francisco, Count of Riverola.

She perceived that she had sighed – and, without knowing precisely wherefore, she was angry with herself.

Anxious to turn the channel of her meditations in another direction, she rose from her seat to examine the clepsydra. That movement caused her eyes to fall upon the paper which she had picked up a quarter of an hour previously.

In spite of herself the image of Francisco was still uppermost in her thoughts; and, in the contemplative vein thus encouraged, her eyes lingered, unwittingly – and through no base motive of curiosity – upon the writing which that paper contained.

Thus she actually found herself reading the first four lines of the writing, before she recollected what she was doing.

The act was a purely mechanical one, which not the most rigid moralist could blame.

And had the contents of the paper been of no interest, she might even have continued to read more in that same abstracted mood; but those four first lines were of a nature which sent a thrilling sensation of horror through her entire frame; the feeling terminating with an icy coldness of the heart.

She shuddered without starting – shuddered as she stood; and not even a murmur escaped her lips.

The intenseness of that sudden pang of horror deprived her alike of speech and motion during the instant that it lasted.

And those lines, which produced so strange an impression upon the young maiden, ran thus: "merciless scalpel hacked and hewed away at the still almost palpitating flesh of the murdered man, in whose breast the dagger remained buried – a ferocious joy – a savage hyena-like triumph—"

Flora read no more; she could not – even if she had wished.

For a minute she remained rooted to the spot; then she threw herself into the chair, bewildered and dismayed at the terrible words which had met her eyes.

She thought that the handwriting was not unknown to her; but she could not recollect whose it was. One fact was, however, certain – it was not the writing of her mistress.

She was musing upon the horrible and mysterious contents of the paper, when Nisida rose from her couch.

Acknowledging with a slight nod of the head the respectful salutation of her attendant, she hastily slipped on a loose wrapper, and seated herself in the arm-chair which Flora had just abandoned.

The young girl then proceeded to comb out the long raven hair of her mistress.

But this occupation was most rudely interrupted: for Nisida's eyes suddenly fell upon the manuscript page on the table; and she started up in a paroxysm of mingled rage and alarm.

Having assured herself by a second glance that it was indeed a portion of the writings which had produced so strange an effect upon her a few hours previously, she turned abruptly toward Flora; and, imperiously confronting the young maiden, pointed to the paper in a significant manner.

Flora immediately indicated by a sign that she had found it on the floor, beneath the arm-chair.

"And you have read it!" was the accusation which, with wonderful rapidity, Nisida conveyed by means of her fingers – fixing her piercing, penetrating eyes on Flora's countenance at the same time.

The young maiden scorned the idea of a falsehood; although she perceived that her reply would prove far from agreeable to her mistress, she unhesitatingly admitted, by the language of the hands. "I read the first four lines, and no more."

A crimson glow instantly suffused the face, neck, shoulders, and bosom of Nisida; but instantly compressing her lips – as was her wont when under the influence of her boiling passions, she turned her flashing eyes once more upon the paper, to ascertain which leaf of the manuscript it was.

That rapid glance revealed to her the import, the dread, but profoundly mysterious import of the four first lines on that page; and, again darting her soul-searching looks upon the trembling Flora, she demanded, by the rapid play of her delicate taper fingers "Will you swear that you read no more?"

"As I hope for salvation!" was Flora's symbolic answer.

The penetrating, imperious glance of Nisida dwelt long upon the maiden's countenance; but no sinister expression – no suspicious change on that fair and candid face contradicted the assertion which she had made.

"I believe you; but beware how you breathe to a living soul a word of what you did read!"

Such was the injunction which Nisida now conveyed by her usual means of communication; and Flora signified implicit obedience.

Nisida then secured the page of writing in her jewel casket; and the details of the toilet were resumed.

Chapter IV
The Funeral – The Interruption of the Ceremony

EIGHT DAYS AFTER the death of the Count of Riverola, the funeral took place.

The obsequies were celebrated at night, with all the pomp observed amongst noble families on such occasions. The church in which the corpse was buried, was hung with black cloth; and even the innumerable wax tapers which burned upon the altar and around the coffin failed to diminish the lugubrious aspect of the scene.

At the head of the bier stood the youthful heir of Riverola; his pale countenance of even feminine beauty contrasting strangely with the mourning garments which he wore, and his eyes bent upon the dark chasm that formed the family vault into which the remains of his sire were about to be lowered.

Around the coffin stood Dr. Duras and other male friends of the deceased: for the females of the family were not permitted, by the custom of the age and the religion, to be present on occasions of this kind.

It was eleven o'clock at night: and the weather without was stormy and tempestuous.

The wind moaned through the long aisles, raising strange and ominous echoes, and making the vast folds of sable drapery wave slowly backward and forward, as if agitated by unseen hands. A few spectators, standing in the background, appeared like grim figures on a black tapestry; and the gleam of the wax tapers, oscillating on their countenances, made them seem death-like and ghastly.

From time to time the shrill wail of the shriek-owl, and the flapping of its wings against the diamond-paned windows of the church, added to the awful gloom of the funeral scene.

And now suddenly arose the chant of the priests – the parting hymn for the dead!

Francisco wept, for though his father had never manifested toward him an affection of the slightest endearing nature, yet the disposition of the young count was excellent; and, when he gazed upon the coffin, he remembered not the coldness with which its inmate in his lifetime had treated him – he thought only of a parent whom he had lost, and whose remains were there!

And truly, on the brink of the tomb no animosity should ever find a resting-place in the human heart. Though elsewhere men yield to the influence of their passions and their feelings, in pursuing each his separate interests – though, in the great world, we push and jostle each other, as if the earth were not large enough to allow us to follow our separate ways – yet, when we meet around the grave, to consign a fellow creature to his last resting-place, let peace and holy forgiveness occupy our souls. There let the clash of interests and the war of jealousies be forgotten; and let us endeavor to persuade ourselves that, as all the conflicting pursuits of life must terminate at this point at last, so should our feelings converge to the one focus of amenity and Christian love. And, after all, how many who have considered themselves to be antagonists must, during a moment of solemn reflection, become convinced that, when toiling in the great workshop of the world, they have been engaged, in unconscious fraternity, in building up the same fabric!

The priests were in the midst of their solemn chant – a deathlike silence and complete immovability prevailed among the mourners and the spectators – and the wind was moaning beneath the vaulted roofs, awaking those strange and tomb-like sounds which are only heard in large churches – when light but rushing footsteps were heard on the marble pavement; and in another minute a female, not clothed in a mourning garb, but splendidly as for a festival, precipitated herself toward the bier.

There her strength suddenly seemed to be exhausted; and, with a piercing scream, she sank senseless on the cold stones.

The chant of the priest was immediately stilled; and Francisco hurrying forward, raised the female in his arms, while Dr. Duras asked for water to sprinkle on her countenance.

Over her head the stranger wore a white veil of rich material, which was fastened above her brow by a single diamond of unusual size and brilliant luster. When the veil was drawn aside, shining auburn tresses were seen depending in wanton luxuriance over shoulders of alabaster whiteness: a beautiful but deadly pale countenance was revealed; and a splendid purple velvet dress delineated the soft and flowing outlines of a form modeled to the most perfect symmetry.

She seemed to be about twenty years of age – in the full splendor of loveliness, and endowed with charms which presented to the gaze of those around a very incarnation of the ideal beauty which forms the theme of raptured poets.

And now, as the vacillating and uncertain light of the wax-candles beamed upon her, as she lay senseless in the arms of the Count Riverola, her pale, placid face appeared that of a classic marble statue; but nothing could surpass the splendid effects which the funeral tapers produced on the rich redundancy of her hair, which seemed dark where the shadows rested on it, but glittering as with a bright glory where the luster played on its shining masses.

In spite of the solemnity of the place and the occasion, the mourners were struck by the dazzling beauty of that young female, who had thus appeared so strangely amongst them; but respect still retained at a distance those persons who were merely present from curiosity to witness the obsequies of one of the proudest nobles of Florence.

At length the lady opened her large hazel eyes, and glanced wildly around, a quick spasm passing like an electric shock over her frame at the same instant; for the funeral scene burst upon her view, and reminded her where she was, and why she was there.

Recovering herself almost as rapidly as she had succumbed beneath physical and mental exhaustion, she started from Francisco's arms; and turning upon him a beseeching, inquiring glance, exclaimed in a voice which ineffable anguish could not rob of its melody: "Is it true – oh, tell me is it true that the Count Riverola is no more?"

"It is, alas! Too true, lady," answered Francisco, in a tone of the deepest melancholy.

The heart of the fair stranger rebounded at the words which thus seemed to destroy a last hope that lingered in her soul; and a hysterical shriek burst from her lips as she threw her snow-white arms, bare to the shoulders, around the head of the pall-covered coffin.

"Oh! my much-loved – my noble Andrea!" she exclaimed, a torrent of tears now gushing from her eyes.

"That voice! – Is it possible?" cried one of the spectators who had been hitherto standing, as before said, at a respectful distance: and the speaker – a man of tall, commanding form, graceful demeanor, wondrously handsome countenance, and rich attire – immediately hurried toward the spot where the young female still clung to the coffin, no one having the heart to remove her.

The individual who had thus stepped forward, gave one rapid but searching glance at the lady's countenance; and, yielding to the surprise and joy which suddenly animated him, he exclaimed: "Yes – it is, indeed, the lost Agnes!"

The young female started when she heard her name thus pronounced in a place where she believed herself to be entirely unknown; and astonishment for an instant triumphed over the anguish of her heart.

Hastily withdrawing her snow-white arms from the head of the coffin, she turned toward the individual who had uttered her name, and he instantly clasped her in his arms, murmuring, "Dearest – dearest Agnes, art thou restored—"

But the lady shrieked, and struggled to escape from that tender embrace, exclaiming, "What means this insolence? Will no one protect me?"

"That will I," said Francisco, darting forward, and tearing her away from the stranger's arms. "But, in the name of Heaven! Let this misunderstanding be cleared up elsewhere. Lady – and you, signor – I call on you to remember where you are, and how solemn a ceremony you have both aided to interrupt."

"I know not that man!" ejaculated Agnes, indicating the stranger. "I come hither, because I heard – but an hour ago – that my noble Andrea was no more. And I would not believe those who told me. Oh! No – I could not think that Heaven had thus deprived me of all I loved on earth!"

"Lady, you are speaking of my father," said Francisco, in a somewhat severe tone.

"Your father!" cried Agnes, now surveying the young count with interest and curiosity. "Oh! Then, my lord, you can pity – you can feel for me, who in losing your father have lost all that could render existence sweet!"

"No – you have not lost all!" exclaimed the handsome stranger, advancing toward Agnes, and speaking in a profoundly impressive tone. "Have you not one single relative left in the world? Consider, lady – an old, old man – a shepherd in the Black Forest of Germany—"

"Speak not of him!" cried Agnes, wildly. "Did he know all, he would curse me – he would spurn me from him – he would discard me forever! Oh! When I think of that poor old man, with his venerable white hair – that aged, helpless man, who was so kind to me, who loved me so well, and whom I so cruelly abandoned. But tell me, signor," she exclaimed, in suddenly altered tone, while her breath came with the difficulty of acute suspense – "tell me, signor, does that old man still live?"

"He lives, Agnes," was the reply. "I know him well; at this moment he is in Florence!"

"In Florence!" repeated Agnes; and so unexpectedly came this announcement, that her limbs seemed to give way under her, and she would have fallen on the marble pavement, had not the stranger caught her in his arms.

"I will bear her away," he said; "she has a true friend in me."

And he was moving off with his senseless burden, when Francisco, struck by a sudden idea, caught him by the elegantly slashed sleeve of his doublet, and whispered thus, in a rapid tone: "From the few, but significant words which fell from that lady's lips, and from her still more impressive conduct, it would appear, alas! that my deceased father had wronged her. If so, signor, it will be my duty to make her all the reparation that can be afforded in such a case."

"'Tis well, my lord," answered the stranger, in a cold and haughty tone. "Tomorrow evening I will call upon you at your palace."

He then hurried on with the still senseless Agnes in his arms; and the Count of Riverola retraced his steps to the immediate vicinity of the coffin.

This scene, which so strangely interrupted the funeral ceremony, and which has taken so much space to describe, did not actually occupy ten minutes from the moment when the young lady first appeared in the church, until that when she was borne away by the handsome stranger. The funeral obsequies were completed; the coffin was lowered into the family vault; the spectators dispersed, and the mourners, headed by the young count, returned in procession to the Riverola mansion, which was situated at no great distance.

Chapter V
The Reading of the Will

WHEN THE MOURNERS reached the palace, Francisco led the way to an apartment where Nisida was awaiting their coming.

Francisco kissed her affectionately upon the forehead; and then took his seat at the head of the table, his sister placing herself on his right hand.

Dressed in deep mourning, and with her countenance unusually pale, Nisida's appearance inspired a feeling of profound interest in the minds of those who did not perceive that, beneath her calm and mournful demeanor, feelings of painful intensity agitated within her breast. But Dr. Duras, who knew her well – better, far better than even her own brother – noticed an occasional wild flashing of the eye, a nervous motion of the lips, and a degree of forced tranquillity of mien, which proved how acute was the suspense she in reality endured.

On Francisco's left hand the notary-general, who had acted as one of the chief mourners, took a seat. He was a short, thin, middle-aged man, with a pale complexion, twinkling gray eyes, and a sharp expression of countenance. Before him lay a sealed packet, on which the eyes of Nisida darted, at short intervals, looks, the burning impatience of which were comprehended by Dr. Duras alone; for next to Signor Vivaldi, the notary-general – and consequently opposite to Nisida – sat the physician.

The remainder of the company consisted of Father Marco and those most intimate friends of the family who had been invited to the funeral; but whom it is unnecessary to describe more particularly.

Father Marco having recited a short prayer, in obedience to the custom of the age, and the occasion, the notary-general proceeded to break the seals of the large packet which lay before him: then, in a precise and methodical manner, he drew forth a sheet of parchment, closely written on.

Nisida leaned her right arm upon the table, and half-buried her countenance in the snowy cambric handkerchief which she held.

The notary-general commenced the reading of the will.

After bestowing a few legacies, one of which was in favor of Dr. Duras, and another in that of Signor Vivaldi himself, the testamentary document ordained that the estates of the late Andrea, Count of Riverola, should be held in trust by the notary-general and the physician, for the benefit of Francisco, who was merely to enjoy the revenues produced by the same until the age of thirty, at which period the guardianship was to cease, and Francisco was then to enter into full and uncontrolled possession of those immense estates.

But to this clause there was an important condition attached; for the testamentary document ordained that should the Lady Nisida – either by medical skill, or the interposition of Heaven – recover the faculties of hearing and speaking at any time during the interval which was to elapse ere Francisco would attain the age of thirty, then the whole of the estates, with the exception of a very small one in the northern part of Tuscany, were to be immediately made over to her; but without the power of alienation on her part.

It must be observed that, in the middle ages many titles of nobility depended only on the feudal possession of a particular property. This was the case with the Riverola estates; and the title of Count of Riverola was conferred simply by the fact of the ownership of the landed property. Thus, supposing that Nisida became possessed of the estates, she would have enjoyed the title of countess, while her brother Francisco would have lost that of count.

We may also remind our readers that Francisco was now nineteen; and eleven years must consequently elapse ere he could become the lord and master of the vast territorial possessions of Riverola.

Great was the astonishment experienced by all who heard the provisions of this strange will – with the exception of the notary-general and Father Marco, the former of whom had drawn it up, and the latter of whom was privy to its contents (though under a vow of secrecy) in his capacity of father-confessor to the late count.

Francisco was himself surprised, and, in one sense, hurt; because the nature of the testamentary document seemed to imply that the property would have been inevitably left to his sister, with but a very small provision for himself, had she not been so sorely afflicted as she was; and this fact forced upon him the painful conviction that even when contemplating his departure to another world, his father had not softened toward his son!

But, on the other hand, Francisco was pleased that such consideration had been shown toward a sister whom he so devotedly loved; and he hastened, as soon as he could conquer his first emotions, to request the notary-general to permit Nisida to peruse the will, adding, in a mournful tone, "For all that your excellency has read has been, alas! unavailing in respect to her."

Signor Vivaldi handed the document to the young count, who gently touched his sister's shoulder and placed the parchment before her.

Nisida started as if convulsively, and raised from her handkerchief a countenance so pale, so deadly pale, that Francisco shrank back in alarm.

But instantly reflecting that the process of reading aloud a paper had been as it were a kind of mockery in respect to his afflicted sister, he pressed her hand tenderly, and made a sign for her to peruse the document.

She mechanically addressed herself to the task; but ere her eyes – now of burning, unearthly brilliancy – fell upon the parchment, they darted one rapid, electric glance of ineffable anguish toward Dr. Duras, adown whose cheeks large tears were trickling.

In a few minutes Nisida appeared to be absorbed in the perusal of the will; and the most solemn silence prevailed throughout the apartment!

At length she started violently, tossed the paper indignantly to the notary-general, and hastily wrote on a slip of paper these words:

"Should medical skill or the mercy of Heaven restore my speech and faculty of hearing, I will abandon all claim to the estates and title of Riverola to my dear brother Francisco."

She then handed the slip of paper to the notary-general, who read the contents aloud.

Francisco darted upon his sister a look of ineffable gratitude and love, but shook his head, as much as to imply that he could not accept the boon even if circumstances enabled her to confer it!

She returned the look with another, expressive of impatience at his refusal: and her eyes seemed to say, as eyes never yet spoke, "Oh, that I had the power to give verbal utterance to my feelings!"

Meantime the notary-general had written a few words beneath those penned by Nisida, to whom he had handed back the slip; and she hastened to read them, thus: "Your ladyship has no power to alienate the estates, should they come into your possession."

Nisida burst into an agony of tears and rushed from the room.

Her brother immediately followed to console her; and the company retired, each individual to his own abode.

But of all that company who had been present at the reading of the will, none experienced such painful emotions as Dr. Duras.

Chapter VI
The Pictures – Agnes and the Unknown – Mystery

WHEN AGNES AWOKE from the state of stupor in which she had been conveyed from the church, she found herself lying upon an ottoman, in a large and elegantly furnished apartment.

The room was lighted by two silver lamps suspended to the ceiling, and which, being fed with aromatic oil of the purest quality, imparted a delicious perfume to the atmosphere.

The walls were hung with paintings representing scenes of strange variety and interest, and connected with lands far – far away. Thus, one depicted a council of red men assembled around a blazing fire, on the border of one of the great forests of North America; another showed the interior of an Esquimaux hut amidst the eternal ice of the Pole; – a third delineated, with fearfully graphic truth, the writhing of a human victim in the folds of the terrific anaconda in the island of Ceylon; a fourth exhibited a pleasing contrast to the one previously cited, by having for its subject a family meeting of Chinese on the terraced roof of a high functionary's palace at Perkin; a fifth represented the splendid court of King Henry the Eighth in London; a sixth showed the interior of the harem of the Ottoman Sultan.

But there were two portraits amongst this beautiful and varied collection of pictures, all of which, we should observe, appeared to have been very recently executed – two portraits which we must pause to describe. One represented a tall man of about forty years of age, with magnificent light hair – fine blue eyes, but terrible in expression – a countenance indisputably handsome, though every lineament denoted horror and alarm – and a symmetrical form, bowed by the weight of sorrow. Beneath this portrait was the following inscription: –'*F., Count of A., terminated his career on the 1st of August, 1517.*'

The other portrait alluded to was that of an old – old man, who had apparently numbered ninety winters. He was represented as cowering over a few embers in a miserable hovel, while the most profound sorrow was depicted on his countenance. Beneath this picture was the ensuing inscription: – '*F. W., January 7th, 1516. His last day thus.*'

There was another feature in that apartment to which we must likewise direct our reader's attention, ere we pursue the thread of our narrative. This was an object hanging against the wall, next to the second portrait just now described. It also had the appearance of being a picture – or at all events a frame of the same dimensions as the others; but whether that frame contained a painting, or whether it were empty, it was impossible to say, so long as it remained concealed by the large black cloth which covered it, and which was carefully fastened by small silver nails at each corner.

This strange object gave a lugubrious and sinister appearance to a room in other respects cheerful, gay, and elegant.

But to resume our tale.

When Agnes awoke from her stupor, she found herself reclining on a soft ottoman of purple velvet, fringed with gold; and the handsome stranger, who had borne her from the church, was bathing her brow with water which he took from a crystal vase on a marble table.

As she slowly and languidly opened her large hazel eyes, her thoughts collected themselves in the gradient manner; and when her glance encountered that of her unknown friend, who was bending over her with an expression of deep interest on his features, there flashed upon her mind a recollection of all that had so recently taken place.

"Where am I?" she demanded, starting up, and casting her eyes wildly around her.

"In the abode of one who will not injure you," answered the stranger, in a kind and melodious tone.

"But who are you? And wherefore have you brought me hither?" exclaimed Agnes. "Oh! Remember – you spoke of that old man – my grandfather – the shepherd of the Black Forest—"

"You shall see him – you shall be restored to him," answered the stranger.

"But will he receive me – will he not spurn me from him?" asked Agnes, in a wildly impassioned – almost hysterical tone.

"The voice of pity cannot refuse to heave a sigh for thy fall," was the response. "If thou wast guilty in abandoning one who loved thee so tenderly, and whose earthly reliance was on thee, he, whom you did so abandon, has not the less need to ask pardon of thee. For he speedily forgot his darling Agnes – he traveled the world over, yet sought her not – her image was, as it were, effaced from his memory. But when accident—"

"Oh! Signor, you are mistaken – you know not the old man whom I deserted, and who was a shepherd on the verge of the Black Forest!" interrupted Agnes, in a tone expressive of bitter disappointment, "for he, who loved me so well, was old – very old, and could not possibly accomplish those long wanderings of which you speak. Indeed, if he be still alive – but that is scarcely possible—"

And she burst into tears.

"Agnes," cried the stranger, "the venerable shepherd of whom you speak accomplished those wanderings in spite of the ninety winters which marked his age. He is alive, too—"

"He is alive!" ejaculated the lady, with reviving hopes.

"He is alive – and at this moment in Florence!" was the emphatic answer. "Did I not ere now tell thee as much in the church?"

"Yes – I remember – but my brain is confused!" murmured Agnes, pressing her beautiful white hands upon her polished brow. "Oh, if he be indeed alive – and so near me as you say – delay not in conducting me to him; for he is now the only being on earth to whom I dare look for solace and sympathy."

"You are even now beneath the roof of your grandfather's dwelling," said the stranger, speaking slowly and anxiously watching the effect which this announcement was calculated to produce upon her to whom he addressed himself.

"Here! – This my grandsire's abode!" she exclaimed, clasping her hands together, and glancing upward, as if to express her gratitude to Heaven for this welcome intelligence. "But how can that old man, whom I left so poor, have become the owner of this lordly palace? Speak, signor! – all you have told me seems to involve some strange mystery," she added with breathless rapidity. "Those wanderings of which you ere now spoke – wanderings over the world, performed by a man bent down by age; and then this noble dwelling – the appearances of wealth which present themselves around – the splendor – the magnificence—"

"All – all are the old man's," answered the stranger, "and may some day become thine!"

"Holy Virgin!" exclaimed Agnes, sinking upon the ottoman from which she had ere now risen, "I thank thee that thou hast bestowed these blessings on my relative in his old age. And yet," she added, again overwhelmed by doubts, "it is scarcely possible – no, it is too romantic to be true! Signor, thou art of a surety mistaken in him whom thou supposes to be my grandsire?"

"Give me thine hand, Agnes – and I will convince thee," said the stranger.

The young lady complied mechanically; and her unknown friend led her toward the portrait of the old man of ninety.

Agnes recognized the countenance at a single glance, and would have fallen upon the floor had not her companion supported her in his arms.

Tears again came to her relief; but hastily wiping them away, she extended her arms passionately toward the portrait, exclaiming, "Oh! Now I comprehend you, signor! My grandsire lives in this dwelling indeed – beneath this roof; but lives only in that picture! Alas! Alas! It was thus, no doubt, that the poor old man seemed when he was abandoned by me – the lost, the guilty Agnes! It was thus that he sat in his lonely dwelling – crushed and overwhelmed by the black ingratitude of his granddaughter! Oh! That I had never seen this portrait – this perpetuation of so much loneliness and so much grief! Ah! Too faithful delineation of that sad scene which was wrought by me – vainly penitent that I am!"

And covering her face with her hands she threw herself on her knees before the portrait, and gave way to all the bitterness and all the wildness of her grief.

The stranger interrupted her not for some minutes: he allowed the flood of that anguish to have its full vent: but when it was partially subsiding he approached the kneeling penitent, raised her gently, and said, "Despair not! Your grandsire lives."

"He lives!" she repeated, her countenance once more expressing radiant hope, as the sudden gleam of sunshine bursts forth amidst the last drops of the April shower.

But, almost at the same instant that she uttered those words, her eyes caught sight of the inscription at the foot of the picture; and, bounding forward she read it aloud.

"Holy Virgin! I am deceived – basely, vilely deceived!" she continued, all the violence of her grief, which had begun to ebb so rapidly, now flowing back upon her soul; then turning abruptly round upon the stranger, she said in a hoarse hollow tone: "Signor, wherefore thus ungenerously trifle with my feelings – my best feelings? Who art thou? "hat would'st thou with me? And wherefore is that portrait here?"

"Agnes – Agnes!" exclaimed her companion, "compose yourself, I implore you! I do not trifle with you – I do not deceive you! Your grandsire, Fernand Wagner, is alive – and in this house. You shall see him presently; but in the meantime, listen to what I am about to say."

Agnes placed her finger impatiently upon the inscription at the bottom of the portrait, and exclaimed in a wild, hysterical tone, "Canst thou explain this, signor? 'January 7th, 1516,' – that was about a week after I abandoned him; and, oh! well indeed might those words be added—'His last day thus!'"

"You comprehend not the meaning of that inscription!" ejaculated the stranger, in an imploring tone, as if to beseech her to have patience to listen to him. "There is a dreadful mystery connected with Fernand Wagner – connected with me – connected with these two portraits – connected also with—"

He checked himself suddenly, and his whole form seemed convulsed with horror as he glanced toward the black cloth covering the neighboring frame.

"A mystery?" repeated Agnes. "Yes – all is mystery: and vague and undefinable terrors oppress my soul!"

"Thou shalt soon – too soon – be enlightened!" said the stranger, in a voice of profound melancholy; "at least, to a certain extent," he added, murmuringly. "But contemplate that other portrait for a few moments – that you may make yourself acquainted with the countenance of a wretch who, in conferring a fearful boon upon your grandsire, has plunged him into an abyss of unredeemable horror!"

Agnes cast her looks toward the portrait of the tall man with the magnificent hair, the flashing blue eyes, the wildly expressive countenance, and the symmetrical form bowed with affliction; and, having surveyed it for some time with repugnance strongly mingled with an invincible interest and curiosity, she suddenly pointed toward the inscription.

"Yes, yes; there is another terrible memorial!" cried the stranger. "But art thou now prepared to listen to a wondrous – an astonishing tale – such a tale as even nurses would scarcely dare narrate to lull children—"

"I am prepared," answered Agnes. "I perceive there is a dreadful mystery connected with my grandsire – with you, also – and perhaps with me; – and better learn at once the truth, than remain in this state of intolerable suspense."

Her unknown friend conducted her back to the ottoman, whereon she placed herself.

He took a seat by her side, and, after a few moments' profound meditation, addressed her in the following manner.

Chapter VII
Revelations

"YOU REMEMBER, AGNES, how happily the times passed when you were the darling of the old man in his poor cottage. All the other members of his once numerous family had been swept away by pestilence, malady, accident, or violence; and you only were left to him. When the trees of this great Black Forest were full of life and vegetable blood, in the genial warmth of summer, you gathered flowers which you arranged tastefully in the little hut; and those gifts of nature, so culled and so dispensed by your hands, gave the dwelling a more cheerful air than if it had been hung with tapestry richly fringed. Of an evening, with the setting sun, glowing gold, you were wont to kneel by the side of that old shepherd; and together ye chanted a hymn giving thanks for the mercies of the day, and imploring the renewal of them for the morrow. Then did the music of your sweet voice, as it flowed upon the old man's ears in its melting, silvery tones, possess a charm for his senses which taught him to rejoice and be grateful that, though the rest of his race was swept away, thou, Agnes, was left!

"When the winter came, and the trees were stripped of their verdure, the poor cottage had still its enjoyments; for though the cold was intense without, yet there were warm hearts within; and the cheerful fire of an evening, when the labors of the day were passed, seemed to make gay and joyous companionship."

"But suddenly you disappeared; and the old man found himself deserted. You left him, too, in the midst of winter m– at a time when his age and infirmities demanded additional attentions. For two or three days he sped wearily about, seeking you everywhere in the neighboring district of the Black Forest. His aching limbs were dragged up rude heights, that he might plunge his glances down into the hollow chasms; but still not a trace of Agnes! He roved along the precipices overlooking the rustling streams, and searched – diligently searched the mazes of the dark wood; but still not a trace of Agnes! At length the painful conviction broke upon him that he was deserted – abandoned; and he would sooner have found thee a mangled and disfigured corpse in the forest than have adopted that belief. Nay – weep not now; it is all past; and if I recapitulate these incidents, it is but to convince thee how wretched the old man was, and how great is the extenuation for the course which he was so soon persuaded to adopt."

"Then, who art thou that knowest all this?" exclaimed Agnes, casting looks of alarm upon her companion.

"Thou shalt soon learn who I am," was the reply.

Agnes still gazed upon him in mingled terror and wonder; for his words had gone to her heart, and she remembered how he had embraced her when she first encountered him in the church. His manners, too, were so mild, so kind, so paternal toward her; and yet he seemed but a few years older than herself.

"You have gazed upon the portrait of the old man," he continued, "as he appeared on that memorable evening which sealed his fate!"

Agnes started wildly.

"Yes, sealed his fate, but spared him his life!" said the unknown, emphatically. "As he is represented in that picture, so was he sitting mournfully over the sorry fire, for the morrow's renewal of which there was no wood! At that hour a man appeared – appeared in the midst of the dreadful storm which burst over the Black Forest. This man's countenance is now known to thee; it is perpetuated in the other portrait to which I directed thine attention."

"There is something of a wild and fearful interest in the aspect of that man," said Agnes, casting a shuddering glance behind her, and trembling lest the canvas had burst into life, and the countenance whose lineaments were depicted thereon was peering over her shoulder.

"Yes, and there was much of wild and fearful interest in his history," was the reply; "but of that I cannot speak – no, I dare not. Suffice it to say that he was a being possessed of superhuman powers, and that he proffered his services to the wretched – the abandoned – the deserted Wagner. He proposed to endow him with a new existence – to restore him to youth and manly beauty – to make him rich – to embellish his mind with wondrous attainments – to enable him to cast off the wrinkles of age—"

"Holy Virgin! Now I comprehend it all!" shrieked Agnes, throwing herself at the feet of her companion: "and you – you—"

"I am Fernand Wagner!" he exclaimed, folding her in his embrace.

"And can you pardon me, can you forgive my deep – deep ingratitude?" cried Agnes.

"Let us forgive each other!" said Wagner. "You can now understand the meaning of the inscription beneath my portrait. 'His last day thus' signifies that it was the last day on which I wore that aged, decrepit, and sinking form."

"But wherefore do you say, 'Let us forgive each other?'" demanded Agnes, scarcely knowing whether to rejoice or weep at the marvelous transformation of her grandsire.

"Did I not ere now inform thee that thou wast forgotten until accident threw thee in my way tonight?" exclaimed Fernand. "I have wandered about the earth and beheld all the scenes which are represented in those pictures – ay, and many others equally remarkable. For eighteen months I was the servant – and slave of him who conferred upon me this fatal boon—"

"At what price, then, have you purchased it?" asked Agnes, with a cold shudder.

"Seek not to learn my secret, girl!" cried Wagner, almost sternly; then, in a milder tone, he added, "By all you deem holy and sacred, I conjure you, Agnes, never again to question me on that head! I have told thee as much as it is necessary for thee to know—"

"One word – only one word!" exclaimed Agnes in an imploring voice. "Hast thou bartered thine immortal soul—"

"No – no!" responded Wagner, emphatically. "My fate is terrible indeed – but I am not beyond the pale of salvation. See! Agnes – I kiss the crucifix – the symbol of faith and hope!"

And, as he uttered these words, he pressed to his lips an ivory crucifix of exquisite workmanship, which he took from the table.

"The Virgin be thanked that my fearful suspicion should prove unfounded!" ejaculated Agnes.

"Yes – I am not altogether lost," answered Wagner. "But *he* – the unhappy man who made me what I am – and yet I dare not say more," he added, suddenly checking himself. "For one year and a half did I follow him as his servitor – profiting by his knowledge – gaining varied information from his experience – passing with the rapidity of thought from clime to clime – surveying scenes of ineffable bliss, and studying all the varieties of misery that fall to the lot of human nature. When he – my master – passed away—"

"On the 1st of August, 1517," observed Agnes, quoting from the inscription beneath the portrait of the individual alluded to.

"Yes; when he passed away," continued Wagner, "I continued my wanderings alone until the commencement of last year, when I settled myself in Florence. The mansion to which I have brought you is mine. It is in a somewhat secluded spot on the banks of the Arno, and is surrounded by gardens. My household consists of but few retainers; and they are elderly persons – docile and obedient. The moment that I entered this abode, I set to work to paint those portraits to which I have directed your attention – likewise these pictures," he added, glancing around, "and in which I have represented scenes that my own eyes have witnessed. Here, henceforth, Agnes, shalt thou dwell; and let the past be forgotten. But there are three conditions which I must impose upon thee."

"Name them," said Agnes; "I promise obedience beforehand."

"The first," returned Fernand, "is that you henceforth look upon me as your brother, and call me such when we are alone together or in the presence of strangers. The second is that you never seek to remove the black cloth which covers yon place—"

Agnes glanced toward the object alluded to and shuddered – as if the veil concealed some new mystery.

"And the third condition is that you revive not on any future occasion the subject of our present conversation, nor even question me in respect to those secrets which it may suit me to retain within my own breast."

Agnes promised obedience, and, embracing Wagner, said, "Heaven has been merciful to me, in my present affliction, in that it has given me *a brother*!"

"Thou speakest of thine afflictions, Agnes!" exclaimed Wagner; "this is the night of revelations and mutual confidences – and this night once passed, we will never again allude to the present topics, unless events should render their revival necessary. It now remains for thee to narrate to me all that has befallen thee since the winter of 1516."

Agnes hastened to comply with Fernand's request, and commenced her history in the following manner:

Chapter VIII
The History of Agnes

"WHEN YOU, DEAR brother – for so I shall henceforth call you – commenced your strange and wondrous revelations ere now, you painted in vivid colors the happiness which dwelt in our poor cottage on the borders of the Black Forest. You saw how deeply your words affected me – I could not restrain my tears. Let me not, however, dwell upon this subject; but rather hasten to explain those powerful causes which induced me to quit that happy home.

"It was about six weeks before my flight that I went into the forest to gather wood. I was in the midst of my occupation, gayly thrilling a native song, when the sound of a horse's feet upon the hard soil of the beaten path suddenly interrupted me. I turned around, seeing a cavalier of strikingly handsome countenance – though somewhat stern withal, and of noble mien. He was in reality forty-four years of age – as I afterward learnt; but he seemed scarcely forty, so light did time sit upon his brow. His dress was elegant, though of some strange fashion; for it was Italian costume that he wore. The moment he was close to the spot where I stood he considered me for a short while, till I felt my cheeks glowing beneath his ardent gaze. I cast down my eyes; and the next instant he had leapt from his horse and was by my side. He addressed me in gentle terms; and when again I looked at him his countenance no more seemed stern. It appeared that he was staying with the Baron von Nauemberg, with whom he had been out hunting in the Black Forest, and from whom and his suite he was separated in the ardor of the chase. Being a total stranger in those parts, he had lost his way. I immediately described to him the proper path for him to pursue; and he offered me gold as a recompense. I declined the guerdon; and he questioned me concerning my family and my position. I told him that I lived hard-by, with an only relative – a grandsire, to whom I was devotedly attached. He lingered long in conversation with me; and his manner was so kind, so condescending, and so respectful, that I thought not I was doing wrong to listen to him. At length he requested me to be on the same spot at the same hour on the morrow; and he departed.

"I was struck by his appearance – dazzled by the brilliancy of his discourse; for he spoke German fluently, although an Italian. He had made a deep impression on my mind; and I felt a secret longing to meet him again. Suddenly it occurred to me that I was acting with impropriety, and that you would be angry with me. I therefore resolved not to mention to you my accidental encounter with the handsome cavalier; but I determined at the same time not to repair to the forest next day. When the appointed hour drew near, my good genius deserted me; and I went. He was there, and he seemed pleased at my punctuality. I need not detail to you the nature of the discourse which he held toward me. Suffice it to say, that he declared how much he had been struck with my beauty, and how fondly he would love me; and he dazzled me still more by revealing his haughty name; and I found that I was beloved by the Count of Riverola.

"You can understand how a poor girl, who had hitherto dwelt in the seclusion of a cottage on the border of a vast wood, and who seldom saw any person of higher rank than herself, was likely to be dazzled by the fine things which that great nobleman breathed in her ear.

"And I was dazzled – flattered – excited – bewildered. I consented to meet him again: interview followed interview, until I no longer required any persuasion to induce me to keep the appointments thus given. But there were times when my conscience reproached me for conduct which I knew you would blame; and yet I dared not unburden my soul to you!

"Six weeks thus passed away; I was still innocent – but madly in love with the Count of Riverola. He was the subject of my thoughts by day – of my dreams by night; and I felt that I could make any sacrifice to retain his affection. That sacrifice was too soon demanded! At the expiration of the six weeks he informed me that on the following day he must return to Italy, whither important affairs called him sooner than he had anticipated. He urged me to accompany him; I was bewildered – maddened by the contemplation of my duty on the one hand, of my love on the other. My guardian saint deserted me; I yielded to the persuasion of the count – I became guilty – and there was now no alternative save to fly with him!

"Oh! Believe me when I declare that this decision cost me a dreadful pang; but the count would not leave me time for reflection. He bore me away on his fleet steed, and halted not until the tall towers of Nauemberg Castle appeared in the distance. Then he stopped at a poor peasant's cottage, where his gold insured me a welcome reception. Having communicated the plan which he proposed to adopt respecting our journey to Florence, he took an affectionate leave of me, with a promise to return on the ensuing morning. The remainder of the day was passed wretchedly enough by me; and I already began to repent of the step I had taken. The peasants who occupied the cottage vainly endeavored to cheer me; my heart was too full to admit of consolation. Night came at length, and I retired to rest; but my dreams were of so unpleasant a nature – so filled with frightful images – that never did I welcome the dawn with more enthusiastic joy. Shortly after daybreak the count appeared at the cottage, attended by one of his numerous suite – a faithful attendant on whom he could rely implicitly. They were mounted on good steeds; and Antonio – such was the name of the servitor – led a third by the bridle. This one the count had purchased at an adjacent hamlet, expressly for my use. He had also procured a page's attire; for in such disguise was it agreed that I should accompany the count to Italy.

"I should observe that the nobleman, in order to screen our amour as much as possible, had set out from Nauemberg Castle, attended by Antonio alone, alleging as an excuse that certain affairs compelled him to travel homeward with as much celerity as possible. The remainder of his suit were therefore ordered to follow at their leisure.

"Oh! With what agonizing emotion did my heart beat, as, in a private chamber of the cottage, I laid aside my peasant's garb and donned the doublet, hose, cap and cloak of a youthful page. I thought of you – of your helplessness – your age – and also of my native land, which I was about to quit – perhaps forever! Still I had gone too far to retreat, and regrets were useless. I must also confess that when I returned to the room where the count was waiting for me, and heard the flattering compliments which he paid me on my appearance in that disguise, I smiled – yes, I smiled, and much of my remorse vanished!

"We set out upon our journey toward the Alps; and the count exerted all his powers of conversation to chase away from my mind any regrets or repinings that might linger there. Though cold and stern – forbidding and reserved – haughty and austere in his bearing toward others, to me he was affectionate and tender. To be brief, yet with sorrow must I confess it, at the expiration of a few days I could bear to think, without weeping, of the fond relative whom I had left behind in the cottage of the Black Forest!

"We crossed the Alps in safety, but not without experiencing much peril; and in a short time glorious Italy spread itself out at our feet. The conversation of the count had already prepared me to admire—"

At this moment, Agnes' narrative was interrupted by a piercing shriek which burst from her lips; and extending her arms toward the window of the apartment, she screamed hysterically, "Again that countenance!" and fell back on the ottoman.

Chapter IX
Conclusion of the History of Agnes

IN ORDER THAT the reader may understand how Agnes could perceive any object outside the window, in the intense darkness of that tempestuous night – or rather morning, for it was now past one o'clock – we must observe that not only was the apartment in which Wagner and herself were seated brilliantly lighted by the silver lamps, but that, according to Florentine custom, there were also lamps suspended outside to the veranda, or large balcony belonging to the casements of the room above.

Agnes and Wagner were, moreover, placed near the window which looked into a large garden attached to the mansion; and thus it was easy for the lady, whose eyes happened to be fixed upon the casement in the earnest interest with which she was relating her narrative, to perceive the human countenance that appeared at one of the panes.

The moment her history was interrupted by the ejaculation of alarm that broke from her lips, Wagner started up and hastened to the window; but he could see nothing save the waving evergreens in his garden, and the light of a mansion which stood at a distance of about two hundred yards from his own abode.

He was about to open the casement and step into the garden, when Agnes caught him by the arm, exclaiming wildly, "Leave me not – I could not – I could not bear to remain alone!"

"No, I will not quit you, Agnes," replied Wagner, conducting her back to the sofa and resuming his seat by her side. "But wherefore that ejaculation of alarm? Whose countenance did you behold? Speak, dearest Agnes!"

"I will hasten to explain the cause of my terror," retorted Agnes, becoming more composed. "Ere now I was about to detail the particulars of my journey to Florence, in company with the Count of Riverola, and attended by Antonio; but as those particulars are of no material interest, I will at once pass on to the period when we arrived in this city."

"But the countenance at the window?" said Wagner, somewhat impatiently.

"Listen – and you will soon know all," replied Agnes. "It was in the evening when I entered Florence for the first time. Antonio had proceeded in advance to inform his mother – a widow who resided in a decent house, but in an obscure street near the cathedral – that she was speedily to receive a young lady as a guest. This young lady was myself; and accordingly, when the count assisted me to alight from my horse at the gate of Dame Margaretha's abode, the good widow had everything in readiness for my reception. The count conversed with her apart for a few minutes; and I observed that he also placed a heavy purse in her hand – doubtless to insure her secrecy relative to the *amour*, with the existence of which he was of course compelled to acquaint her. Having seen me comfortably installed in Dame Margaretha's best apartment, he quitted me, with a promise to return on the morrow."

Agnes paused for a few moments, sighed, and continued her narrative in the following manner:

"Fortunately for me, Dame Margaretha was a German woman, who had married an Italian, otherwise my condition would have been wretched in the extreme. She treated me with great kindness, mingled with respect; for though but a poor peasant girl, I was beloved and protected by one of the most powerful nobles of Florence. I retired early to rest: – sleep did not, however, immediately visit my eyes! Oh! No – I was in Florence, but my thoughts were far away in my native Germany, and on the borders of the Black Forest. At length I fell into an uneasy slumber, and when I awoke the sun was shining through the lattice. I arose and dressed myself, and to my ineffable delight found that I was no longer to wear the garb of a page. That disguise had been removed while I slept, and in its place were costly vestments, which I donned with a pleasure that triumphed over the gloom of my soul. In the course of the morning rich furniture was brought to the house, and in a few hours the apartments allotted to me were converted, in my estimation, into a little paradise. The count arrived soon afterward, and I now – pardon me the neglect and ingratitude which my words confess – I now felt very happy. The noble Andrea enjoined me to go abroad but seldom, and never without being accompanied by Dame Margaretha; he also besought me not to appear to recognize him should I chance to meet him in public at any time, nor to form acquaintances; in a word, to live retired and secluded as possible, alike for his sake and my own. I promised compliance with all he suggested, and he declared in return that he would never cease to love me."

"Dwell not upon details, Agnes," said Wagner; "for, although I am deeply interested in your narrative, my curiosity is strangely excited to learn the meaning of that terror which overcame you ere now."

"I will confine myself to material facts as much as possible," returned Agnes. "Time glided rapidly away; months flew by, and with sorrow and shame must I confess that the memories of the past, the memories of the bright, happy days of my innocence intruded but little on the life which I led. For, though he was so much older than I, yet I loved the Count of Riverola devotedly. Oh! Heaven knows how devotedly! His conversation delighted, fascinated me; and he seemed to experience a pleasure in imparting to me the extensive knowledge which he had acquired. To me he unbent as, doubtless, to human being he never unbent before; in my presence his sternness, his somber moods, his gloomy thoughts vanished. It was evident that he had much preying upon his mind; and perhaps he loved me thus fondly because – by some unaccountable whim or caprice, or strange influence – he found solace in my society. The presents which he heaped upon me, but which have been nearly all snatched from me, were of immense value; and when I remonstrated with him on account of a liberality so useless to one whom he allowed to want for nothing, he would reply, 'But remember, Agnes, when I shall be no more, riches will constitute your best friend, your safest protection; for such is the order of things in this world.' He generally spent two hours with me every day, and frequently visited me again in the evening. Thus did time pass; and at length I come to that incident which will explain the terror I ere now experienced."

Agnes cast a hasty glance toward the window, as if to assure herself that the object of her fears was no longer there; and, satisfied on this head, she proceeded in the following manner:

"It was about six months ago that I repaired as usual on the Sabbath morning to mass, accompanied by Dame Margaretha, when I found myself the object of some attention on the part of a lady, who was kneeling at a short distance from the place which I occupied in the church. The lady was enveloped in a dark, thick veil, the ample folds of which concealed her countenance, and meandered over her whole body's splendidly symmetrical length of limb in such a manner as to aid her rich attire in shaping, rather than hiding, the contours of that matchless form. I was struck by her fine proportions, which gave her, even in her kneeling attitude, a queen-like and majestic air; and I longed to obtain a glimpse of her countenance – the more so as I could perceive by her manner and the position of her head that from beneath her dark veil her eyes were intently fixed upon myself. At length the scrutiny to which I was thus subjected began to grow so irksome – nay, even alarming, that I hurriedly drew down my own veil, which I had raised through respect for the sacred altar whereat I was kneeling. Still I knew that the stranger lady was gazing on me; I *felt* that she was. A certain uneasy sensation – amounting almost to a superstitious awe – convinced me that I was the object of her undivided attention. Suddenly the priests, in procession, came down from the altar; and as they passed us, I instinctively raised my veil again, through motives of deferential respect. At the same instant I glanced toward the stranger lady; she also drew back the dark covering from her face. Oh! What a countenance was then revealed to me – a countenance of such sovereign beauty that, though of the same sex, I was struck with admiration; but, in the next moment, a thrill of terror shot through my heart – for the fascination of the basilisk could scarcely paralyze its victim with more appalling effect than did the eyes of that lady. It might be conscience qualms, excited by some unknown influence – it might even have been imagination; but it nevertheless appeared as if those large, black, burning orbs shot forth lightnings which seared and scorched my very soul! For that splendid countenance, of almost unearthly beauty, was suddenly marked by an expression of such vindictive rage, such ineffable hatred, such ferocious menace, that I should have screamed had I not been as it were stunned – stupefied!

"The procession of priests swept past. I averted my head from the stranger lady. In a few moments I again glanced hurriedly at the place which she had occupied – but she was gone. Then I felt relieved! On quitting the church, I frankly narrated to old Margaretha these particulars as I have now unfolded them to you; and methought that she was for a moment troubled as I spoke! But if she were, she speedily recovered her composure – endeavored to soothe me by attributing it all to my imagination, and earnestly advised me not to cause any uneasiness to the count by mentioning the subject to him. I readily promised compliance with this injunction; and in the course of a few days ceased to think upon the incident which has made so strange but evanescent an impression on my mind."

"Doubtless Dame Margaretha was right in her conjecture," said Wagner; "and your imagination—"

"Oh, no – no! It was not fancy!" interrupted Agnes, hastily. "But listen, and then judge for yourself. I informed you ere now that it was about six months ago when the event which I have just related took place. At that period, also, my noble lover – the ever-to be lamented Andrea – first experienced the symptoms of that internal disease which has, alas! carried him to the tomb."

Agnes paused, wiped away her tears, and continued thus:

"His visits to me consequently became less frequent; – I was more alone – for Margaretha was not always a companion who could solace me for the absence of one so dearly loved as my Andrea; and repeated fits of deep despondency seized upon my soul. At those times I felt as if some evil – vague and undefinable, but still terrible – were impending over me. Was it my lord's approaching death of which I had a presentiment? I know not! Weeks passed away; the count's visits occurred at intervals growing longer and longer – but his affection toward me had not abated. No: a malady that preyed upon his vitals retained him much at home; – and at last, about two months ago, I received through Antonio the afflicting intelligence that he was confined to his bed. My anguish now knew no bounds. I would fly to him – oh! I would fly to him: – who was more worthy to watch by his couch than I, who so dearly loved him! Dame Margaretha represented to me how painful it would be to his lordship were our *amour* to transpire through any rash proceeding on my part – the more so, as I knew that he had a daughter and a son! I accordingly restrained my impetuous longing to hasten to his bedside: – I could not so easily subdue my grief!

"One night I sat up late in my lonely chamber – pondering on the melancholy position in which I was placed – loving so tenderly, yet not daring to fly to him whom I loved – and giving way to all the mournful ideas which presented themselves to my imagination. At length my mind grew bewildered by those sad reflections; vague terrors gathered around me – multiplying in number and augmenting in intensity – until at length the very figures on the tapestry with which the room was hung appeared animated with power to scare and affright me. The wind moaned ominously without, and raised strange echoes within; oppressive feelings crowded on my soul. At length the gale swelled to a hurricane – a whirlwind, seldom experienced in this delicious clime. Howlings in a thousand tones appeared to flit through the air; and piercing lamentations seemed to sound down the black clouds that rolled their mighty volumes together, veiling the moon and stars in thickest gloom. Overcome with terror, I retired to rest – and I slept. But troubled dreams haunted me throughout the night, and I awoke at an early hour in the morning. But – holy angels protect me! – what did I behold? Bending over me, as I lay, was that same countenance which I had seen four months before in the church – and now, as it was *then*, darting upon me lightning from large black eyes that seemed to send shafts of flame and fire to the inmost recesses of my soul! Yet – distorted as it was with demoniac rage – that face was still endowed with the queen-like beauty – the majesty of loveliness, which had before struck me, and which even lent force to those looks of dreadful menace that were fixed upon me. There were the high forehead – the proud lip, curled in scorn – the brilliant teeth, glistening between the quivering vermilion – and the swan-like arching of the dazzling neck; there also was the dark glory of the luxuriant hair!

"For a few moments I was spell-bound – motionless – speechless. Clothed with terror and sublimity, yet in all the flush of the most perfect beauty, a strange – mysterious being stood over me: and I knew not whether she were a denizen of this world, or a spirit risen from another. Perhaps the transcendent loveliness of that countenance was but a mask and the wondrous symmetry of that form but a disguise, beneath which all the passions of hell were raging in the brain and in the heart of a fiend. Such were the ideas that flashed through my imagination; and I involuntarily closed my eyes, as if this action could avert the malignity that appeared to menace me. But dreadful thoughts still pursued me – enveloping me, as it were, in an oppressive mist wherein appalling though dimly seen images and forms were agitating; and I again opened my eyes. The lady – if an earthly being she really were – was gone. I rose from my couch and glanced nervously around – expecting almost to behold an apparition come forth from behind the tapestry, or the folds of the curtains. But my attention was suddenly arrested by a fact more germane to worldly occurrences. The casket wherein I kept the rich presents made to me at different times by my Andrea had been forced open and the most valuable portion of its contents were gone. On a closer investigation I observed that the articles which were left were those that were purchased new; whereas the jewels that had been abstracted were old ones, which, as the count had informed me, had belonged to his deceased wife.

"On discovering this robbery, I began to suspect that my mysterious visitress, who had caused me so much alarm, was the thief of my property; and I immediately summoned old Margaretha. She was of course astounded at the occurrence which I related; and, after some reflection, she suddenly remembered that she had forgotten to fasten the house-door ere she retired to rest on the preceding evening. I chided her for a neglect which had enabled some evil-disposed woman to penetrate into my chamber, and not only terrify but also plunder me. She implored my forgiveness, and besought me not to mention the incident to the count when next we met. Alas! My noble Andrea and I never met again.

"I was sorely perplexed by the event which I have just related. If the mysterious visitress were a common thief, why did she leave any of the jewels in the casket? And wherefore had she on two occasions contemplated me with looks of such dark rage and infernal menace? A thought struck me. Could the count's daughter have discovered our *amour*? And was it she who had come to gain possession of jewels belonging to the family? I hinted my suspicions to Margaretha; but she speedily convinced me that they were unfounded.

"'The Lady Nisida is deaf and dumb,' she said, 'and cannot possibly exercise such faculties of observation, nor adopt such means of obtaining information as would make her acquainted with all that has occurred between her father and yourself. Besides – she is constantly in attendance on her sire, who is very, very ill.'

"I now perceived the improbability of a deaf and dumb female discovering an *amour* so carefully concealed; but to assure myself more fully on that head, I desired Margaretha to describe the Lady Nisida. This she readily did, and I learnt from her that the count's daughter was of a beauty quite different from the lady whom I had seen in the church and in my own chamber. In a word, it appears that Nisida has light hair, blue eyes and a delicate form: whereas, the object of my interest, curiosity, and fear, is a woman of dark Italian loveliness.

"I have little more now to say. The loss of the jewels and the recollection of the mysterious lady were soon absorbed in the distressing thoughts which the serious illness of the count forced upon my mind. Weeks passed away, and he came not; but he sent repeated messages by Antonio, imploring me to console myself, as he should soon recover, and urging me not to take any step that might betray the existence of our *amour*. Need I say how religiously I obeyed him in the latter respect? Day after day did I hope to see him again, for I knew not that he was dying: and I used to dress myself in my gayest attire – even as now I am appareled – to welcome his expected visit. Alas! He never came; and his death was concealed from me, doubtless that the sad event might not be communicated until after the funeral, lest in the first frenzy of anguish I should rush to the Riverola palace to imprint a last kiss upon the cheek of the corpse. But a few hours ago, I learned the whole truth from two female friends of Dame Margaretha who called to visit her, and whom I had hastened to inform that she was temporarily absent. My noble Andrea was dead, and at that very moment his funeral obsequies were being celebrated in the neighboring church – the very church in which I had first beheld the mysterious lady! Frantic with grief – unmindful of the exposure that would ensue – reckless of the consequences, I left the house – I hastened to the church – I intruded my presence amidst the mourners. You know the rest, Fernand. It only remains for me to say that the countenance which I beheld ere now at the window – strongly delineated and darkly conspicuous amidst the blaze of light outside the casement – was that of the lady whom I have thus seen for the third time! But, tell me, Fernand, how could a stranger thus obtain admission to the gardens of your mansion?"

"You see yon lights, Agnes!" said Wagner, pointing toward the mansion which, as we stated at the commencement of that chapter, was situated at a distance of about two hundred yards from Fernand's dwelling, the backs of the two houses thus looking toward each other. "Those lights," he continued, "are shining in a mansion the gardens of which are separated from my own by a simple hedge of evergreens, that would not bar even the passage of a child. Should any inmate of that mansion possess curiosity sufficient to induce him or her to cross the boundary, traverse my gardens, and approach the casements of my residence, that curiosity may be easily gratified."

"And to whom does yon mansion belong?" asked Agnes.

"To Dr. Duras, an eminent physician," was the reply.

"Dr. Duras, the physician who attended my noble Andrea in his illness!" exclaimed Agnes. "Then the mysterious lady of whom I have spoken so much, and whose countenance ere now appeared at the casement, must be an inmate of the house of Dr. Duras; or at all events, a visitor there! Ah! Surely there is some connection between that lady and the family at Riverola?"

"Time will solve the mystery, dearest sister, for so I am henceforth to call you," said Fernand. "But beneath this roof, no harm can menace you. And now let me summon good Dame Paula, my housekeeper, to conduct you to the apartments which have been prepared for your reception. The morning is far advanced, and we both stand in need of rest."

Dame Paula, an elderly, good-tempered, kind-hearted matron, shortly made her appearance; and to her charge did Wagner consign his newly-found relative, whom he now represented to be his sister.

But as Agnes accompanied the worthy woman from the apartment, she shuddered involuntarily as she passed the frame which was covered with the black cloth, and which seemed ominous amidst the blaze of light that filled the room.

Chapter X
Francisco, Wagner and Nisida

ON THE ENSUING evening, Francisco, Count of Riverola, was seated in one of the splendid saloons of his palace, pondering upon the strange injunction which he had received from his deceased father, relative to the mysterious closet, when Wagner was announced.

Francisco rose to receive him, saying in a cordial though melancholy tone, "Signor, I expected you."

"And let me hasten to express the regret which I experienced at having addressed your lordship coldly and haughtily last night," exclaimed Wagner. "But, at the moment, I only beheld in you the son of him who had dishonored a being very dear to my heart."

"I can well understand your feelings on that occasion, signor," replied Francisco. "Alas! the sins of the fathers are too often visited upon the children in this world. But, in whatever direction our present conversation may turn, I implore you to spare as much as possible the memory of my sire."

"Think not, my lord," said Wagner, "that I should be so ungenerous as to reproach you for a deed in which you had no concern, and over which you exercised no control. Nor should I inflict so deep an injury upon you, as to speak in disrespectful terms of him who was the author of your being, but who is now no more."

"Your kind language has already made me your friend," exclaimed Francisco. "And now point out to me in what manner I can in any way repair – or mitigate – the wrong done to that fair creature in whom you express yourself interested."

"That young lady is my sister," said Wagner, emphatically.

"Your sister, signor! And yet, meseems, she recognized you not—"

"Long years have passed since we saw each other," interrupted Fernand; "for we were separated in our childhood."

"And did you not both speak of some relative – an old man who once dwelt on the confines of the Black Forest of Germany, but who is now in Florence?" asked Francisco.

"Alas! that old man is no more," returned Wagner. "I did but use his name to induce Agnes to place confidence in me, and allow me to withdraw her from a scene which her wild grief so unpleasantly interrupted; for I thought that were I then and there to announce myself as her brother, she might not believe me – she might suspect some treachery or snare in a city so notoriously profligate as Florence. But the subsequent explanations which took place between us cleared up all doubts on that subject."

"I am well pleased to hear that the poor girl has found so near a relative and so dear a friend, signor," said Francisco. "And now acquaint me, I pray thee, with the means whereby I may, to some extent, repair the injury your sister has sustained at the hands of him whose memory I implore you to spare!"

"Wealth I possess in abundance – oh! far greater abundance than is necessary to satisfy all my wants!" exclaimed Wagner, with something of bitterness and regret in his tone; "but, even were I poor, gold would not restore my sister's honor. No – let that subject, however, pass. I would only ask you, count, whether there be any scion of your family – any lady connected with you – who answers this description?"

And Wagner proceeded to delineate, in minute terms, the portraiture of the mysterious lady who had inspired Agnes on three occasions with so much terror, and whom Agnes herself had depicted in such glowing language.

"Signor! You are describing the Lady Nisida, my sister!" exclaimed Francisco, struck with astonishment at the fidelity of the portrait thus verbally drawn.

"Your sister, my lord!" cried Wagner. "Then has Dame Margaretha deceived Agnes in representing the Lady Nisida to be rather a beauty of the cold north than of the sunny south."

"Dame Margaretha!" said Francisco; "do you allude, signor, to the mother of my late father's confidential dependent, Antonio?"

"The same," was the answer. "It was at Dame Margaretha's house that your father placed my sister Agnes, who has resided there nearly four years."

"But wherefore have you made those inquiries relative to the Lady Nisida?" inquired Francisco.

"I will explain the motive with frankness," responded Wagner.

He then related to the young count all those particulars relative to the mysterious lady and Agnes, with which the reader is already acquainted.

"There must be some extraordinary mistake – some strange error, signor, in all this," observed Francisco. "My poor sister is, as you seem to be aware, so deeply afflicted that she possesses not faculties calculated to make her aware of that *amour* which even I, who possess those faculties in which she is deficient, never suspected, and concerning which no hint ever reached me, until the whole truth burst suddenly upon me last night at the funeral of my sire. Moreover, had accident revealed to Nisida the existence of the connection between my father and your sister, signor, she would have imparted the discovery to me, such is the confidence and so great is the love that exists between us. For habit has rendered us so skillful and quick in conversing with the language of the deaf and dumb, that no impediment ever exists to the free interchange of our thoughts."

"And yet, if the Lady Nisida *had* made such a discovery, her hatred of Agnes may be well understood," said Wagner; "for her ladyship must naturally look upon my sister as the partner of her father's weakness – the dishonored slave of his passions."

"Nisida has no secret from me," observed the young count, firmly.

"But wherefore did Dame Margaretha deceive my sister in respect to the personal appearance of the Lady Nisida?" inquired Wagner.

"I know not. At the same time—"

The door opened, and Nisida entered the apartment.

She was attired in deep black; her luxuriant raven hair, no longer depending in shining curls, was gathered up in massy bands at the sides, and a knot behind, whence hung a rich veil that meandered over her body's splendidly symmetrical length of limb in such a manner as to aid her attire in shaping rather than hiding the contours of that matchless form. The voluptuous development of her bust was shrouded, not concealed, by the stomacher of black velvet which she wore, and which set off in strong relief the dazzling whiteness of her neck.

The moment her lustrous dark eyes fell upon Fernand Wagner, she started slightly; but this movement was imperceptible alike to him whose presence caused it, and to her brother.

Francisco conveyed to her, by the rapid language of the fingers, the name of their visitor, and at the same time intimated to her that he was the brother of Agnes, the young and lovely female whose strange appearance at the funeral, and avowed connection with the late noble, had not been concealed from the haughty lady.

Nisida's eyes seemed to gleam with pleasure when she understood in what degree of relationship Wagner stood toward Agnes; and she bowed to him with a degree of courtesy seldom displayed by her to strangers.

Francisco then conveyed to her in the language of the dumb, all those details already related in respect to the "mysterious lady" who had so haunted the unfortunate Agnes.

A glow of indignation mounted to the cheeks of Nisida; and more than usually rapid was the reply she made through the medium of the alphabet of the fingers.

"My sister desires me to express to you, signor," said Francisco, turning toward Wagner, "that she is not the person whom the Lady Agnes has to complain against. My sister," he continued, "has never to her knowledge seen the Lady Agnes; much less has she ever penetrated into her chamber; and indignantly does she repel the accusation relative to the abstraction of the jewels. She also desires me to inform you that last night after reading of our father's last testament, she retired to her chamber, which she did not quit until this morning at the usual hour; and that therefore it was not her countenance which the Lady Agnes beheld at the casement of your saloon."

"I pray you, my lord, to let the subject drop now, and forever!" said Wagner, who was struck with profound admiration—almost amounting to love – for the Lady Nisida: "there is some strange mystery in all this, which time alone can clear up. Will your lordship express to your sister how grieved I am that any suspicion should have originated against her in respect to Agnes?"

Francisco signaled these remarks to Nisida; and the latter, rising from her seat, advanced toward Wagner, and presented him her hand in token of her readiness to forget the injurious imputations thrown out against her.

Fernand raised that fair hand to his lips, and respectfully kissed it; but the hand seemed to burn as he held it, and when he raised his eyes toward the lady's countenance, she darted on him a look so ardent and impassioned that it penetrated into his very soul.

That rapid interchange of glances seemed immediately to establish a kind of understanding – a species of intimacy between those extraordinary beings; for on the one side, Nisida read in the fine eyes of the handsome Fernand all the admiration expressed there, and he, on his part, instinctively understood that he was far from disagreeable to the proud sister of the young Count of Riverola. While he was ready to fall at her feet and do homage to her beauty, she experienced the kindling of all the fierce fires of sensuality in her breast.

But the unsophisticated and innocent-minded Francisco observed not the expression of these emotions on either side, for their manifestation occupied not a moment. The interchange of such feelings is ever too vivid and electric to attract the notice of the unsuspecting observer.

When Wagner was about to retire, Nisida made the following signal to her brother: – "Express to the signor that he will ever be a welcome guest at the palace of Riverola; for we owe kindness and friendship to the brother of her whom our father dishonored."

But, to the astonishment of both the count and the Lady Nisida, Wagner raised his hands, and displayed as perfect a knowledge of the language of the dumb as they themselves possessed.

"I thank your ladyship for this unexpected condescension," he signaled by the rapid play of his fingers; "and I shall not forget to avail myself of this most courteous invitation."

It were impossible to describe the sudden glow of pleasure and delight which animated Nisida's splendid countenance, when she thus discovered that Wagner was able to hold converse with her, and she hastened to reply thus: "We shall expect you to revisit us soon."

Wagner bowed low and took his departure, his mind full of the beautiful Nisida.

Chapter XI
Nisida and Wagner – Francisco and Flora – The Approach of Sunset

UPWARD OF TWO months had passed away since the occurrences related in the preceding chapter, and it was now the 31st of January, 1521.

The sun was verging toward the western hemisphere, but the rapid flight of the hours was unnoticed by Nisida and Fernand Wagner, as they were seated together in one of the splendid saloons of the Riverola mansion.

Their looks were fixed on each other's countenance; the eyes of Fernand expressing tenderness and admiration, those of Nisida beaming with all the passions of her ardent and sensual soul.

Suddenly the lady raised her hands, and by the rapid play of the fingers, asked, "Fernand, do you indeed love me as much as you would have me believe I am beloved?"

"Never in this world was woman so loved as you," he replied, by the aid of the same language.

"And yet I am an unfortunate being – deprived of those qualities which give the greatest charm to the companionship of those who love."

"But you are eminently beautiful, my Nisida; and I can fancy how sweet, how rich-toned would be your voice, could your lips frame the words, *I love thee!*"

A profound sigh agitated the breast of the lady; and at the same time her lips quivered strangely, as if she were essaying to speak.

Wagner caught her to his breast; and she wept long and plenteously. Those tears relieved her; and she returned his warm, impassioned kisses with an ardor that convinced him how dear he had become to that afflicted, but transcendently beautiful being. On her side, the blood in her veins appeared to circulate like molten lead; and her face, her neck, her bosom were suffused with burning blushes.

At length, raising her head, she conveyed this wish to her companion: "Thou hast given me an idea which may render me ridiculous in your estimation; but it is a whim, a fancy, a caprice, engendered only by the profound affection I entertain for thee. I would that thou shouldst say, in thy softest, tenderest tones, the words 'I love thee!' and, by the wreathing of thy lips, I shall see enough to enable my imagination to persuade itself that those words have really fallen upon my ears."

Fernand smiled assent; and, while Nisida's eyes were fixed upon him with the most enthusiastic interest, he said, "I love thee!"

The sovereign beauty of her countenance was suddenly lighted up with an expression of ineffable joy, of indescribable delight; and, signaling the assurance, "I love thee, dearest, dearest Fernand!" she threw herself into his arms.

But almost at the same moment voices were heard in the adjacent room: and Wagner, gently disengaging himself from Nisida's embrace, hastily conveyed to her an intimation of the vicinity of others.

The lady gave him to understand by a glance that she comprehended him; and they remained motionless, fondly gazing upon each other.

"I know not how it has occurred, Flora," said the voice of Francisco, speaking in a tender tone, in the adjoining room – "I know not how it has occurred that I should have addressed you in this manner – so soon, too, after the death of my lamented father, and while these mourning garments yet denote the loss which myself and sister have sustained—"

"Oh! My lord, suffer me to retire," exclaimed Flora Francatelli, in a tone of beseeching earnestness; "I should not have listened to your lordship so long in the gallery of pictures, much less have accompanied your lordship hither."

"I requested thee to come with me to this apartment, Flora, that I might declare, without fear of our interview being interrupted, how dear, how very dear, thou art to me, and how honorable is the passion with which thou hast inspired me. Oh, Flora," exclaimed the young count, "I could no longer conceal my love for thee! My heart was bursting to reveal its secret; and when I discovered thee alone, ere now, in the gallery of pictures, I could not resist the favorable opportunity accident seemed to have afforded for this avowal."

"Alas! My lord," murmured Flora, "I know not whether to rejoice or be sorrowful at the revelation which has this day met my ears."

"And yet you said ere now that you could love me, that you did love me in return," ejaculated Francisco.

"I spoke truly, my lord," answered the bashful maiden; "but, alas! How can the humble, obscure, portionless Flora become the wife of the rich, powerful and honored Count of Riverola? There is an inseparable gulf fixed between us, my lord."

"Am I not my own master? Can I not consult my own happiness in that most solemn and serious of the world's duties – marriage?" cried Francisco, with all the generous ardor of youth and his own noble disposition.

"Your lordship is free and independent in point of fact," said Flora, in a low, tender and yet impressive tone; "but your lordship has relations – friends."

"My relations will not thwart the wishes of him whom they love," answered Francisco; "and those who place obstacles in the way of my felicity cannot be denominated my friends."

"Oh! My lord – could I yield myself up to the hopes which your language inspires!" cried Flora.

"You can – you may, dearest girl!" exclaimed the young count. "And now I know that you love me! But many months must elapse ere I can call thee mine; and, indeed, a remorse smites my heart that I have dared to think of my own happiness, so soon after a mournful ceremony has consigned a parent to the tomb. Heaven knows that I do not the less deplore his loss – but wherefore art thou so pale, so trembling, Flora?"

"Meseems that a superstitious awe of evil omens has seized upon my soul," returned the maiden, in a tremulous tone. "Let us retire, my lord; the Lady Nisida may require my services elsewhere."

"Nisida!" repeated Francisco, as if the mention of his sister's name had suddenly awakened new ideas in his mind.

"Ah! My lord," said Flora, sorrowfully, "you now perceive that there is at least one who may not learn with satisfaction the alliance which your lordship would form with the poor and humble dependent."

"Nay, by my patron saint, thou hast misunderstood me!" exclaimed the young count warmly. "Nisida will not oppose her brother's happiness; and her strong mind will know how to despise those conventional usages which require that high birth should mate with high birth, and wealth ally itself to wealth. Yes; Nisida will consult my felicity alone; and when I ere now repeated her name as it fell from your lips, it was in a manner reproachful to myself, because I have retained my love for thee a secret from her. A secret from Nisida! Oh! I have been cruel, unjust, not to have confided in my sister long ago! And yet," he added more slowly, "she might reproach me for my selfishness in bestowing a thought on marriage soon, so very soon, after a funeral! Flora, dearest maiden, circumstances demand that the avowal which accident and opportunity have led me this day to make, should exist as a secret, known only unto yourself and me. But, in a few months I will explain all to my sister, and she will greet thee as her brother's chosen bride. Are thou content, Flora, that our mutual love should remain thus concealed until the proper time shall come for its revelation?"

"Yes, my lord, and for many reasons," was the answer.

"For many reasons, Flora!" exclaimed the young count.

"At least for more than one," rejoined the maiden. "In the first instance, it is expedient your lordship should have due leisure to reflect upon the important step which you propose to take – a step conferring so much honor on myself, but which may not insure your happiness."

"If this be a specimen of thy reasons, dear maiden," exclaimed Francisco, laughing, "I need hear no more. Be well assured," he added seriously, "that time will not impair the love I experience for you."

Flora murmured a reply which did not reach Wagner, and immediately afterward the sound of her light steps was heard retreating from the adjacent room. A profound silence of a few minutes occurred; and then Francisco also withdrew.

Wagner had been an unwilling listener to the preceding conversation; but while it was in progress, he from time to time threw looks of love and tenderness on his beautiful companion, who returned them with impassioned ardor.

Whether it were that her irritable temper was impatient of the restraint imposed upon herself and her lover by the vicinity of others, or whether she was annoyed at the fact of her brother and Flora being so long together (for Wagner had intimated to her who their neighbors were, the moment he had recognized their voices), we cannot say; but Nisida showed an occasional uneasiness of manner, which she, however, studied to subdue as much as possible, during the scene that took place in the adjoining apartment.

Fernand did not offer to convey to her any idea of the nature of the conversation which occupied her brother and Flora Francatelli; neither did she manifest the least curiosity to be enlightened on that head.

The moment the young lovers had quitted the next room Wagner intimated the fact to Nisida; but at the same instant, just as he was about to bestow upon her a tender caress, a dreadful, an appalling reminiscence burst upon him with such overwhelming force that he fell back stupefied on the sofa.

Nisida's countenance assumed an expression of the deepest solicitude, and her eloquent, sparkling eyes, implored him to intimate to her what ailed him.

But, starting wildly from his seat, and casting on her a look of such bitter, bitter anguish, that the appalling emotions thus expressed struck terror to her soul – Fernand rushed from the room.

Nisida sprung to the window; and, though the obscurity of the evening now announced the last flickerings of the setting sunbeams in the west, she could perceive her lover dashing furiously on through the spacious gardens that surrounded the Riverola Palace.

On – on he went toward the River Arno; and in a few minutes was out of sight.

Alas! Intoxicated with love, and giving himself up to the one delightful idea – that he was with the beauteous Nisida – then, absorbed in the interest of the conversation which he had overheard between Francisco and Flora – Wagner had forgotten until it was nearly too late, *that the sun was about to set on the last day of the month.*

Chapter XII
The Wehr-Wolf

'TWAS THE HOUR of sunset.

The eastern horizon, with its gloomy and somber twilight, offered a strange contrast to the glorious glowing hues of vermilion, and purple, and gold, that blended in long streaks athwart the western sky.

For even the winter sunset of Italy is accompanied with resplendent tints – as if an emperor, decked with a refulgent diadem, were repairing to his imperial couch.

The declining rays of the orb of light bathed in molten gold the pinnacles, steeples, and lofty palaces of proud Florence, and toyed with the limpid waves of the Arno, on whose banks innumerable villas and casinos already sent forth delicious strains of music, broken only by the mirth of joyous revelers.

And by degrees as the sun went down, the palaces of the superb city began to shed light from their lattices, set in rich sculptured masonry; and here and there, where festivity prevailed, grand illuminations sprung up with magical quickness, the reflection from each separate galaxy rendering it bright as day far, far around.

Vocal and instrumental melody floated through the still air; and the perfume of exotics, decorating the halls of the Florentine nobles, poured from the widely-opened portals, and rendered the air delicious.

For Florence was gay that evening – the last day of each month being the one which the wealthy lords and high-born ladies set apart for the reception of their friends.

The sun sank behind the western hills; and even the hothouse flowers closed up their buds – as if they were eyelids weighed down by slumber, and not to wake until the morning should arouse them again to welcome the return of their lover – that glorious sun!

Darkness seemed to dilate upon the sky like an image in the midst of a mirage, expanding into superhuman dimensions – then rapidly losing its shapeliness, and covering the vault above densely and confusedly.

But, by degrees, countless stars began to stud the colorless canopy of heaven, like gems of orient splendor; for the last – last flickering ray of the twilight in the west had expired in the increasing obscurity.

But, hark! What is that wild and fearful cry?

In the midst of a wood of evergreens on the banks of the Arno, a man – young, handsome, and splendidly attired – has thrown himself upon the ground, where he writhes like a stricken serpent, in horrible convulsions.

He is the prey of a demoniac excitement: an appalling consternation is on him – madness is in his brain – his mind is on fire.

Lightnings appear to gleam from his eyes, as if his soul were dismayed, and withering within his breast.

"Oh! No – no!" he cries with a piercing shriek, as if wrestling madly, furiously, but vainly against some unseen fiend that holds him in his grasp.

And the wood echoes to that terrible wail; and the startled bird flies fluttering from its bough.

But, lo! What awful change is taking place in the form of that doomed being? His handsome countenance elongates into one of savage and brute-like shape; the rich garments which he wears become a rough, shaggy, and wiry skin; his body loses its human contours, his arms and limbs take another form; and, with a frantic howl of misery, to which the woods give horribly faithful reverberations, and, with a rush like a hurling wind, the wretch starts wildly away, no longer a man, but a monstrous wolf!

On, on he goes: the wood is cleared – the open country is gained. Tree, hedge, and isolated cottage appear but dim points in the landscape – a moment seen, the next left behind; the very hills appear to leap after each other.

A cemetery stands in the monster's way, but he turns not aside – through the sacred inclosure – on, on he goes. There are situated many tombs, stretching up the slope of a gentle acclivity, from the dark soil of which the white monuments stand forth with white and ghastly gleaming, and on the summit of the hill is the church of St. Benedict the Blessed.

From the summit of the ivy-grown tower the very rooks, in the midst of their cawing, are scared away by the furious rush and the wild howl with which the Wehr-Wolf thunders over the hallowed ground.

At the same instant a train of monks appear round the angle of the church – for there is a funeral at that hour; and their torches flaring with the breeze that is now springing up, cast an awful and almost magical light on the dark gray walls of the edifice, the strange effect being enhanced by the prismatic reflection of the lurid blaze from the stained glass of the oriel window.

The solemn spectacle seemed to madden the Wehr-Wolf. His speed increased – he dashed through the funeral train – appalling cries of terror and alarm burst from the lips of the holy fathers – and the solemn procession was thrown into confusion. The coffin-bearers dropped their burden, and the corpse rolled out upon the ground, its decomposing countenance seeming horrible by the glare of the torch-light.

The monk who walked nearest the head of the coffin was thrown down by the violence with which the ferocious monster cleared its passage; and the venerable father – on whose brow sat the snow of eighty winters – fell with his head against a monument, and his brains were dashed out.

On, on fled the Wehr-Wolf, over mead and hill, through valley and dale. The very wind seemed to make way: he clove the air – he appeared to skim the ground – to fly.

Through the romantic glades and rural scenes of Etruria the monster sped – sounds, resembling shrieking howls, bursting ever and anon from his foaming mouth – his red eyes glaring in the dusk of the evening like ominous meteors – and his whole aspect so full of appalling ferocity, that never was seen so monstrous, so terrific a spectacle!

A village is gained; he turns not aside, but dashes madly through the little street formed by the huts and cottages of the Tuscan vine-dressers.

A little child is in his path – a sweet, blooming, ruddy, noble boy; with violet-colored eyes and flaxen hair – disporting merrily at a short distance from his parents, who are seated at the threshold of their dwelling.

Suddenly a strange and ominous rush – an unknown trampling of rapid feet falls upon their ears; then, with a savage cry, a monster sweeps past.

"My child! My child!" screams the affrighted mother; and simultaneously the shrill cry of an infant in the sudden agony of death carries desolation to the ear!

'Tis done – 'twas but the work of a moment; the wolf has swept by, the quick rustling of his feet is no longer heard in the village. But those sounds are succeeded by awful wails and heart-rending lamentations: for the child – the blooming, violet-eyed, flaxen-haired boy – the darling of his poor but tender parents, is weltering in his blood!

On, on speeds the destroyer, urged by an infernal influence which maddens the more intensely because its victim strives vainly to struggle against it: on, on, over the beaten road – over the fallow field – over the cottager's garden – over the grounds of the rich one's rural villa.

And now, to add to the horrors of the scene, a pack of dogs have started in pursuit of the wolf – dashing – hurrying – pushing – pressing upon one another in all the anxious ardor of the chase.

The silence and shade of the open country, in the mild starlight, seem eloquently to proclaim the peace and happiness of a rural life; but now that silence is broken by the mingled howling of the wolf, and the deep baying of the hounds – and this shade is crossed and darkened by the forms of the animals as they scour so fleetly – oh! with such whirlwind speed along.

But that Wehr-Wolf bears a charmed life; for though the hounds overtake him – fall upon him – and attack him with all the courage of their nature, yet does he hurl them from him, toss them aside, spurn them away, and at length free himself from their pursuit altogether!

And now the moon rises with unclouded splendor, like a maiden looking from her lattice screened with purple curtains; and still the monster hurries madly on with unrelaxing speed.

For hours has he pursued his way thus madly; and, on a sudden, as he passes the outskirts of a sleeping town, the church-bell is struck by the watcher's hand to proclaim midnight.

Over the town, over the neighboring fields – through the far-off forest, clanged that iron tongue: and the Wehr-Wolf sped all the faster, as if he were running a race with that Time whose voice had just spoken.

On, on went the Wehr-Wolf; but now his course began to deviate from the right line which he had hitherto pursued, and to assume a curved direction.

From a field a poor man was turning an ox into the main road, that he might drive the animal to his master's residence by daylight; the wolf swept by, and snapped furiously at the ox as he passed: and the beast, affrighted by the sudden appearance, gushing sound, and abrupt though evanescent attack of the infuriate monster, turned on the herdsman and gored him to death.

On went the terrific wolf, with wilder and more frequent howlings, which were answered in a thousand tones from the rocks and caverns overlooking the valley through whose bosom he was now careering with whirlwind speed along.

It was now two o'clock in the morning, and he had already described an immense circuit from the point where he had begun to deviate from a direct course.

At a turning of the road, as he emerged from the valley, the monster encountered a party of village girls repairing with the produce of their dairies, and of their poultry-yards, to some still far distant town, which they had hoped to reach shortly after daybreak.

Fair, gay, and smiling was the foremost maiden, as the bright moon and the silver starlight shone upon her countenance; but that sweet face, clad in the richest hues of health, was suddenly convulsed with horror, as the terrible Wehr-Wolf thundered by with appalling howls.

For a few moments the foremost village maiden stood rooted to the spot in speechless horror: then, uttering a wild cry, she fell backward, rolled down a steep bank, and was ingulfed in the rapid stream that chafed and fretted along the side of the path.

Her companions shrieked in agony of mind – the wail was echoed by a despairing cry from the drowning girl – a cry that swept frantically over the rippling waters; and, in another moment, she sank to rise no more!

The breeze had by this time increased to a sharp wind, icy and cold, as it usually is, even in southern climes, when the dawn is approaching; and the gale now whistled through the branches of the evergreen wood in the neighborhood of Florence – that vicinity to which the Wehr-Wolf was at length returning!

Still was his pace of arrow-like velocity – for some terrible power appeared to urge him on; and though his limbs failed not, though he staggered not in his lightning speed, yet did the foam at his mouth, the thick flakes of perspiration on his body, and the steam that enveloped him as in a dense vapor, denote how distressed the unhappy being in reality was.

At last – at last a faint tinge was visible above the eastern horizon; gradually the light increased and put to flight the stars.

But now the Oriental sky was to some extent obscured with clouds; and the Wehr-Wolf gnashed his teeth with rage, and uttered a savage howl, as if impatient of the delay of dawn.

His speed began to relax; the infernal influence which had governed him for so many hours already grew less stern, less powerful, and as the twilight shone forth more plainly in proportion did the Wehr-Wolf's velocity diminish.

Suddenly a piercing chill darted through his frame, and he fell in strong convulsions upon the ground, in the midst of the same wood where his transformation had taken place on the preceding evening.

The sun rose angrily, imparting a lurid, reddened hue to the dark clouds that hung upon the Oriental heaven, as if the mantling curtains of a night's pavilion strove to repel the wooing kisses of the morn; and the cold chill breeze made the branches swing to and fro with ominous flapping, like the wings of the fabulous Simoorg.

But in the midst of the appalling spasmodic convulsions, with direful writhings on the soil, and with cries of bitter anguish, the Wehr-Wolf gradually threw off his monster-shape; and at the very moment when the first sunbeam penetrated the wood and glinted on his face he rose a handsome, young, and perfect man once more!

The complete and unabridged text is available online, from *flametreepublishing.com/extras*

The She-Wolf

Saki

LEONARD BILSITER was one of those people who have failed to find this world attractive or interesting, and who have sought compensation in an 'unseen world' of their own experience or imagination – or invention. Children do that sort of thing successfully, but children are content to convince themselves, and do not vulgarise their beliefs by trying to convince other people. Leonard Bilsiter's beliefs were for 'the few', that is to say, anyone who would listen to him.

His dabblings in the unseen might not have carried him beyond the customary platitudes of the drawing-room visionary if accident had not reinforced his stock-in-trade of mystical lore. In company with a friend, who was interested in a Ural mining concern, he had made a trip across Eastern Europe at a moment when the great Russian railway strike was developing from a threat to a reality; its outbreak caught him on the return journey, somewhere on the further side of Perm, and it was while waiting for a couple of days at a wayside station in a state of suspended locomotion that he made the acquaintance of a dealer in harness and metalware, who profitably whiled away the tedium of the long halt by initiating his English travelling companion in a fragmentary system of folk-lore that he had picked up from Trans-Baikal traders and natives. Leonard returned to his home circle garrulous about his Russian strike experiences, but oppressively reticent about certain dark mysteries, which he alluded to under the resounding title of Siberian Magic. The reticence wore off in a week or two under the influence of an entire lack of general curiosity, and Leonard began to make more detailed allusions to the enormous powers which this new esoteric force, to use his own description of it, conferred on the initiated few who knew how to wield it. His aunt, Cecilia Hoops, who loved sensation perhaps rather better than she loved the truth, gave him as clamorous an advertisement as anyone could wish for by retailing an account of how he had turned a vegetable marrow into a wood pigeon before her very eyes. As a manifestation of the possession of supernatural powers, the story was discounted in some quarters by the respect accorded to Mrs. Hoops' powers of imagination.

However divided opinion might be on the question of Leonard's status as a wonderworker or a charlatan, he certainly arrived at Mary Hampton's house-party with a reputation for pre-eminence in one or other of those professions, and he was not disposed to shun such publicity as might fall to his share. Esoteric forces and unusual powers figured largely in whatever conversation he or his aunt had a share in, and his own performances, past and potential, were the subject of mysterious hints and dark avowals.

"I wish you would turn me into a wolf, Mr. Bilsiter," said his hostess at luncheon the day after his arrival.

"My dear Mary," said Colonel Hampton, "I never knew you had a craving in that direction."

"A she-wolf, of course," continued Mrs. Hampton; "it would be too confusing to change one's sex as well as one's species at a moment's notice."

357

"I don't think one should jest on these subjects," said Leonard.

"I'm not jesting, I'm quite serious, I assure you. Only don't do it today; we have only eight available bridge players, and it would break up one of our tables. Tomorrow we shall be a larger party. Tomorrow night, after dinner—"

"In our present imperfect understanding of these hidden forces I think one should approach them with humbleness rather than mockery," observed Leonard, with such severity that the subject was forthwith dropped.

Clovis Sangrail had sat unusually silent during the discussion on the possibilities of Siberian Magic; after lunch he side-tracked Lord Pabham into the comparative seclusion of the billiard-room and delivered himself of a searching question.

"Have you such a thing as a she-wolf in your collection of wild animals? A she-wolf of moderately good temper?"

Lord Pabham considered. "There is Louisa," he said, "a rather fine specimen of the timber-wolf. I got her two years ago in exchange for some Arctic foxes. Most of my animals get to be fairly tame before they've been with me very long; I think I can say Louisa has an angelic temper, as she-wolves go. Why do you ask?"

"I was wondering whether you would lend her to me for tomorrow night," said Clovis, with the careless solicitude of one who borrows a collar stud or a tennis racquet.

"Tomorrow night?"

"Yes, wolves are nocturnal animals, so the late hours won't hurt her," said Clovis, with the air of one who has taken everything into consideration; "one of your men could bring her over from Pabham Park after dusk, and with a little help he ought to be able to smuggle her into the conservatory at the same moment that Mary Hampton makes an unobtrusive exit."

Lord Pabham stared at Clovis for a moment in pardonable bewilderment; then his face broke into a wrinkled network of laughter.

"Oh, that's your game, is it? You are going to do a little Siberian Magic on your own account. And is Mrs. Hampton willing to be a fellow-conspirator?"

"Mary is pledged to see me through with it, if you will guarantee Louisa's temper."

"I'll answer for Louisa," said Lord Pabham.

By the following day the house-party had swollen to larger proportions, and Bilsiter's instinct for self-advertisement expanded duly under the stimulant of an increased audience. At dinner that evening he held forth at length on the subject of unseen forces and untested powers, and his flow of impressive eloquence continued unabated while coffee was being served in the drawing-room preparatory to a general migration to the card-room.

His aunt ensured a respectful hearing for his utterances, but her sensation-loving soul hankered after something more dramatic than mere vocal demonstration.

"Won't you do something to *convince* them of your powers, Leonard?" she pleaded; "change something into another shape. He can, you know, if he only chooses to," she informed the company.

"Oh, do," said Mavis Pellington earnestly, and her request was echoed by nearly everyone present. Even those who were not open to conviction were perfectly willing to be entertained by an exhibition of amateur conjuring.

Leonard felt that something tangible was expected of him.

"Has anyone present," he asked, "got a three-penny bit or some small object of no particular value – ?"

"You're surely not going to make coins disappear, or something primitive of that sort?" said Clovis contemptuously.

"I think it very unkind of you not to carry out my suggestion of turning me into a wolf," said Mary Hampton, as she crossed over to the conservatory to give her macaws their usual tribute from the dessert dishes.

"I have already warned you of the danger of treating these powers in a mocking spirit," said Leonard solemnly.

"I don't believe you can do it," laughed Mary provocatively from the conservatory; "I dare you to do it if you can. I defy you to turn me into a wolf."

As she said this she was lost to view behind a clump of azaleas.

"Mrs. Hampton—" began Leonard with increased solemnity, but he got no further. A breath of chill air seemed to rush across the room, and at the same time the macaws broke forth into ear-splitting screams.

"What on earth is the matter with those confounded birds, Mary?" exclaimed Colonel Hampton; at the same moment an even more piercing scream from Mavis Pellington stampeded the entire company from their seats. In various attitudes of helpless horror or instinctive defence they confronted the evil-looking grey beast that was peering at them from amid a setting of fern and azalea.

Mrs. Hoops was the first to recover from the general chaos of fright and bewilderment.

"Leonard!" she screamed shrilly to her nephew, "turn it back into Mrs. Hampton at once! It may fly at us at any moment. Turn it back!"

"I – I don't know how to," faltered Leonard, who looked more scared and horrified than anyone.

"What!" shouted Colonel Hampton, "you've taken the abominable liberty of turning my wife into a wolf, and now you stand there calmly and say you can't turn her back again!"

To do strict justice to Leonard, calmness was not a distinguishing feature of his attitude at the moment.

"I assure you I didn't turn Mrs. Hampton into a wolf; nothing was farther from my intentions," he protested.

"Then where is she, and how came that animal into the conservatory?" demanded the Colonel.

"Of course we must accept your assurance that you didn't turn Mrs. Hampton into a wolf," said Clovis politely, "but you will agree that appearances are against you."

"Are we to have all these recriminations with that beast standing there ready to tear us to pieces?" wailed Mavis indignantly.

"Lord Pabham, you know a good deal about wild beasts—" suggested Colonel Hampton.

"The wild beasts that I have been accustomed to," said Lord Pabham, "have come with proper credentials from well-known dealers, or have been bred in my own menagerie. I've never before been confronted with an animal that walks unconcernedly out of an azalea bush, leaving a charming and popular hostess unaccounted for. As far as one can judge from *outward* characteristics," he continued, "it has the appearance of a well-grown female of the North American timber-wolf, a variety of the common species *canis lupus*."

"Oh, never mind its Latin name," screamed Mavis, as the beast came a step or two further into the room; "can't you entice it away with food, and shut it up where it can't do any harm?"

"If it is really Mrs. Hampton, who has just had a very good dinner, I don't suppose food will appeal to it very strongly," said Clovis.

"Leonard," beseeched Mrs. Hoops tearfully, "even if this is none of your doing can't you use your great powers to turn this dreadful beast into something harmless before it bites us all – a rabbit or something?"

"I don't suppose Colonel Hampton would care to have his wife turned into a succession of fancy animals as though we were playing a round game with her," interposed Clovis.

"I absolutely forbid it," thundered the Colonel.

"Most wolves that I've had anything to do with have been inordinately fond of sugar," said Lord Pabham; "if you like I'll try the effect on this one."

He took a piece of sugar from the saucer of his coffee cup and flung it to the expectant Louisa, who snapped it in mid-air. There was a sigh of relief from the company; a wolf that ate sugar when it might at the least have been employed in tearing macaws to pieces had already shed some of its terrors. The sigh deepened to a gasp of thanks-giving when Lord Pabham decoyed the animal out of the room by a pretended largesse of further sugar. There was an instant rush to the vacated conservatory. There was no trace of Mrs. Hampton except the plate containing the macaws' supper.

"The door is locked on the inside!" exclaimed Clovis, who had deftly turned the key as he affected to test it.

Everyone turned towards Bilsiter.

"If you haven't turned my wife into a wolf," said Colonel Hampton, "will you kindly explain where she has disappeared to, since she obviously could not have gone through a locked door? I will not press you for an explanation of how a North American timber-wolf suddenly appeared in the conservatory, but I think I have some right to inquire what has become of Mrs. Hampton."

Bilsiter's reiterated disclaimer was met with a general murmur of impatient disbelief.

"I refuse to stay another hour under this roof," declared Mavis Pellington.

"If our hostess has really vanished out of human form," said Mrs. Hoops, "none of the ladies of the party can very well remain. I absolutely decline to be chaperoned by a wolf!"

"It's a she-wolf," said Clovis soothingly.

The correct etiquette to be observed under the unusual circumstances received no further elucidation. The sudden entry of Mary Hampton deprived the discussion of its immediate interest.

"Someone has mesmerised me," she exclaimed crossly; "I found myself in the game larder, of all places, being fed with sugar by Lord Pabham. I hate being mesmerised, and the doctor has forbidden me to touch sugar."

The situation was explained to her, as far as it permitted of anything that could be called explanation.

"Then you *really* did turn me into a wolf, Mr. Bilsiter?" she exclaimed excitedly.

But Leonard had burned the boat in which he might now have embarked on a sea of glory. He could only shake his head feebly.

"It was I who took that liberty," said Clovis; "you see, I happen to have lived for a couple of years in North-Eastern Russia, and I have more than a tourist's acquaintance with the magic craft of that region. One does not care to speak about these strange powers, but once in a way, when one hears a lot of nonsense being talked about them, one is tempted to show what Siberian magic can accomplish in the hands of someone who really understands it. I yielded to that temptation. May I have some brandy? The effort has left me rather faint."

If Leonard Bilsiter could at that moment have transformed Clovis into a cockroach and then have stepped on him he would gladly have performed both operations.

Curse of the Bayou

Natalie Shea

CECILE SETTLED into the rocking chair on her cabin's wide, front porch and looked out over the bayou. She was a pretty girl of almost twenty with shoulder-length dark hair that she usually kept pulled back. Blue eyes framed with dark lashes peered out over a pointy nose and pouty lips. Cecille's pale, slender frame was covered in a faded, cotton dress in her favorite color of blue. She relished sitting on the front porch in the evenings watching the day turn into night. The bayou was home to her. She couldn't imagine living anywhere else. The cabin that she was born and raised in, was almost surrounded by swamp. The closest neighbor was a half mile by boat. Cypress trees covered in thick Spanish moss, reached for the sky. The moss was impenetrable on the branches, blocking the view of the stagnant water further down the bayou. Mangrove trees with twisted roots bordered the swamp, the roots reminded Cecile of human brains. The water was still despite the coming storm. Wind rustled the trees, making the Spanish moss swing. The swamp was alive. She heard a splash as a fish jumped from the water and landed again. A snake slithered into the water. Cecile wasn't afraid of the wildlife although she respected it.

Cecile hummed to herself as she rocked, watching the sun set. The sky was dark purple, adding to the mystery of the bayou. The breeze was picking up and it played with Cecile's hair. She tried to tuck the loose strands back into her ponytail. Bullfrogs bellowed loudly and cicadas chirped from the trees. The thick humidity made the spring night feel warmer than it was. A lightning bug lit up, followed by two more. It would be dark soon and Cecile shivered, but not from cold. Tonight, the moon would be full. The rocking chair made a creaking sound as it moved back and forth on the worn, wooden slats of the porch. The phone ringing from inside startled her out of her reverie. Cecile jumped out of the chair and opened the squeaky, screen door.

"Hello," she said into the receiver, twisting the cord around her finger.

"Cecile?" It was the familiar voice of her grandmother. "How are you, Cher?"

"Oh, Mawmaw." Cecile let out the breath she didn't realize she had been holding. "I'm okay. Is anything wrong?"

"No, I was just calling to check on you and let you know that there's a storm coming. You better stay inside. It's liable to be a bad one."

"I was fixin' to come in when you called, Mawmaw," Cecile said. She glanced at the crucifix that hung on the wall and crossed herself out of habit.

"Good, good," her grandmother said. "I worry about you being by yourself. Call me if you need anything."

Cecile wrapped up the call and placed the phone back in the cradle where it hung by the door. She stared at it for a moment, blue eyes wide, then, shaking her head, she turned to shut and lock the front door. Cecile knew that night was coming and she wanted to be ready. The kitchen was cozy with a hint of the smoky boudin she had simmering on the stove. An antiquated refrigerator took up a large portion of the room. There was a single table with two chairs under the window just left of the door. Cecile no longer needed the second chair; her mother was gone now. Mama had disappeared into the swamp and thought to have drowned several months ago. She had never known her father. He had been killed in an accident at the plant where he had worked before she was born.

A flash lit up the sky, followed by a low rumble of thunder. Cecile shivered again. She reached for the oil lamp. A peal of thunder sounded, this time rattling the windows in the small house. Darkness settled over the bayou. Cecile tried not to panic, but her heartbeat was getting faster. She heard the scrape of something on the front porch. Reaching for the door, she checked to see that it was locked, even though she knew it was. She sank down onto a chair at the kitchen table. The scraping sound reached her again and she covered her ears with pale hands.

"There's nothing on the porch," she said to herself.

The rain started then, pelting the tin roof of Cecile's little home. The rain came down in sheets, knocking the power out. Taking a deep breath, Cecile lit the lamp. Shadows flickered onto the wall, making the room seem strange. Over the sound of the rain, she heard scratching.

No, there's nothing there. It's only my imagination, she thought, but the idea didn't calm her any. Her heart raced. Lightning lit up the sky outside the window, casting light into the kitchen. Thunder rumbled, but Cecile didn't notice. She was straining to hear something out of the ordinary, but the bayou was eerily quiet aside from the storm.

I'm okay, she thought. *It's just your mind playing tricks on you. There's no such thing as Rougarou. Humans can't become animals!* She shook her head as if to dispel the silly notion.

The storm continued to rage as Cecile sat, her head cocked to one side, listening. Only the sounds of the storm could be heard. She let out her breath as she placed her hands palms down onto the table and raised herself from the chair.

Suddenly, there was an unmistakable howl coming from beyond the front door, causing Cecile to freeze. She felt cold. Her heart seemed to skip a beat and her breathing came in short gasps. Her feet didn't want to move. The sound seemed to last for several minutes instead of seconds. Should she dare peek out the window? As she was deciding, she heard scratching, this time closer to the door. She gently lifted the curtain with a shaking hand and looked out. She could barely make out the silhouette of the rocking chair in the darkness, but she couldn't see anything else.

"There's nothing out there." She spoke the words out loud, hoping she would believe them. Forgetting the now cold boudin, she grabbed the lamp and retreated to the bedroom glancing at the rifle in the corner of the room and praying she wouldn't need to use it. The springs of the bed groaned in protest when she sat. The room was small, with room for an oak dresser and double bed made of metal. A single window was covered by a white, lace curtain. Cecile kicked off her shoes and lay down, drawing the quilt over her head as if she was a little girl again. She willed herself to fall asleep, but her racing thoughts kept her from feeling tired. She could barely breathe under the worn blanket, but she was too frightened to remove the cover. The ticking of the clock could be heard along with the storm and Cecile hoped the night would pass quickly.

There was the mysterious scratching, as if something was clawing at her door. She swallowed. The loud howl began again, emanating from the porch. Cecile curled into a ball. A rumble of thunder signaled that the storm was moving away. The clouds were dissipating, allowing the moonlight to filter through the curtain. Cecile lay trembling beneath the quilt. She squeezed her eyes shut, praying that whatever was out there couldn't get into the cabin. Another noise. It sounded as if something was trying to turn the handle to the front door. Cecile's blood ran cold. *This can't be happening*, she thought. *Thank God I locked the door!*

The howling continued for hours before Cecile could fall asleep. When she finally did, she slept fitfully. She woke to sunlight poking through the holes in the lace of the curtain. She ran out of the bedroom and threw open the front door. There on the porch stood her mama, barefoot and in a filthy, tattered dress. Cecile threw her arms around the woman's bony shoulders and drew her into the cabin.

"Mama, where have you been?" Cecile guided her dazed mother into a kitchen chair. The woman shook her head back and forth making her matted hair bounce. She was mumbling incoherently. Cecile put her ear close to her mama's mouth, trying to understand what the woman was saying, but she couldn't make out the words. Her mother was a petite woman. Her blue eyes stared vacantly. Cecile wrinkled her nose in displeasure at the smell of wet dog that seemed to be coming from her mother.

"Mama, you're hurt," Cecile motioned to her mama's bruised arms. "Let me help you."

Cecile was near tears. Her mama's arms were covered with dark marks. The woman's wrists were the worst. It looked as though her mama had been held against her will. The thought terrified Cecile. She glanced back out the front door to make sure there was no one else out there. Cecile had always felt safe in the bayou until recently. The wildlife was dangerous, but she understood that she should respect it, not fear it. The murky water took many lives but that didn't frighten Cecile either. Whatever had happened to her mama wasn't natural.

"Here, Mama, drink some water." Cecile pushed a glass at her mother, but her mother turned away from it. Cecile didn't know what to do. She was finally able to get her mother into the bedroom and onto the bed. The springs groaned as the woman lay down. Cecile pulled the quilt over her mother's battered body and adjusted the lace curtain to try to darken the room. Her mother was shivering violently, and Cecile reached for the extra blanket draped over the metal rail at the foot of the bed. She pulled the faded blanket over her mother and left the room.

Cecile grabbed the telephone receiver and tried clumsily to tap in her grandmother's number. It took her a few attempts. Her grandmother answered on the first ring.

"Cecile, I was just about to call you. How did you fare during the storm, Cher?"

"Mama's home!" Cecile interjected.

"What?" her grandmother gasped.

"Mama's home," Cecile repeated.

"Oh, thank God!"

"Something's wrong," Cecile continued. "She looks like she's been beaten. She keeps trying to say something but I…"

"Where is she, Cher?" Her grandmother cut in.

"She's in the bed, but I…"

"I'll be right over." The line went dead. Cecile replaced the phone on the wall, and legs trembling, sank down into the kitchen chair. Glancing at the crucifix, she crossed herself, praying that everything would be okay. She took a few deep breaths and then laid her head on the table on her folded arms. She stayed like that until she heard the porch boards creak, signaling her grandmother's arrival. Cecile swung open the creaky screen door and her grandmother rushed in, gathering Cecile into her arms.

"Mawmaw," Cecile said as she dissolved into tears. Her grandmother shushed her.

"Cher." She held Cecile at arm's length and looked at her with deep, brown eyes. She had gray hair that stuck out like a broom. Cecile's grandmother was a small, wiry woman wearing tall, rubber boots. Her bosom rose and fell as she tried to catch her breath. "We need to shut your mama up in that room, make sure she can't get out."

Cecile stared at her grandmother, horrified.

"Cecile," her grandmother said. "Did you hear the Rougarou last night?"

"The Rougarou," Cecile shook her head. "It's not real. I don't…"

"Cecile, listen to me. We don't have time to waste. Did you hear it last night?"

"I heard something, I don't know." Cecile was becoming frantic. She didn't understand what her grandmother was asking her. She watched as her grandmother hurried around the cabin shutting the door to the bedroom as she went.

"We've got to find some way to bar this door, Cher." Her grandmother surveyed the closed door and then looked around furtively for something to use to keep it closed.

"Mawmaw, please!" Cecile begged.

"There's no time, Cecile. We've got to work fast. Your mother has been compromised. If we don't hurry, she'll kill us all!" Her grandmother began trying to maneuver the heavy refrigerator, but it wouldn't budge. Cecile moved to help her and together they were able to slide the large appliance in front of the bedroom door. Cecile felt like she was about to collapse when they finished. She wasn't sure if it was because of the strenuous work or if it was from fear. She walked out onto the porch and collapsed into her rocker. Her grandmother joined her and sat down on the top step of the porch. It was still early but the humidity was especially thick because of the rain the night before. The sun shone brilliantly, adding heat to the already stuffy day. Cecile could hear the birds chirping and the buzzing of insects from all around the bayou. A slight breeze ruffled her hair and she reached to secure the loose strands in her ponytail.

"Mawmaw, what is going on?" Cecile asked. She moved the rocking chair forward to look at Mawmaw as her grandmother sat on the porch step.

Her grandmother took a deep breath and looked straight into Cecile's eyes.

"The Rougarou has gotten your Mama, I'm afraid, Cher." Her grandmother crossed herself as she said it.

Her grandmother proceeded to tell Cecile about how the Rougarou had been terrorizing the bayou for many years. Cecile couldn't wrap her mind around it. She had always thought the stories of Rougarou, humans shapeshifting into wolves, had been made up to frighten children. She had lived in the bayou her entire life and had never seen anything to lend credence to the tales. *That is, until last night*, she thought, a shiver of fear traveling up her spine. If what her grandmother was telling her was true, Mama was cursed. She listened to her grandmother, hoping that the woman was wrong. When her grandmother finished explaining, Cecile rose slowly. She wasn't sure what to do now.

Cecile let herself into the house, the screen door banging shut behind her. She poured out the boudin that she had made the night before and tried to focus on making something for them to eat. She felt it was necessary to keep her hands busy. The kitchen looked strange with the refrigerator moved from its place and her once comfortable home seemed surreal to Cecile.

Cecile was wiping up the counters after their meal when she heard her mother stirring in the bedroom. The bedroom door banged into the refrigerator and her mother made a whimpering sound. Both Cecile and her grandmother froze, eyes locked on the large appliance that barred the door. The door banged again and again as if her mother was trying to force her way out. Cecile looked at her grandmother with wide blue eyes. Her heart was beating wildly, and she felt like she might be sick. Mawmaw met Cecile's gaze and motioned for her to keep quiet.

"Lisette?" Mawmaw questioned, but there was no answer, only the repeated banging of the bedroom door as Cecile's mother tried to get out of the room.

"Lisette!" Grandmother snapped. "You have to stay in there for your safety and for ours."

The sound of the banging was causing Cecile to panic. Her breath was coming in gasps. Her grandmother placed a hand on Cecile's arm to calm her. Cecile was grateful for the comforting gesture although it didn't help to alleviate the fear she felt. Tears were forming behind Cecile's eyes, and she blinked to keep them at bay. She looked to the crucifix hanging on the wall, mouthing a prayer for strength.

"Cecile, you need to sit down, Cher," Mawmaw said, drawing Cecile over to a kitchen chair. Cecile dropped into the chair. The room became eerily quiet when Cecile's mother stopped pushing the bedroom door against the refrigerator. Cecile looked at her grandmother questioningly. The older woman met Cecile's gaze with steady, unflinching eyes. Neither of them knew what to make of this change. Suddenly, a loud shriek pierced the silence. It emanated from the bedroom, but Cecile couldn't believe the sound had come from her mother. It was inhuman. Cecile's heart seemed to stop beating and the hair on the back of her neck stood up. Mawmaw's face twisted in terror.

The room was covered in shadows as the sun sank lower over the bayou. The sky was a deep orange tinged with pink as the light slowly faded from the day. Cecile could see lightning bugs blinking through the screen door. The crickets chirped and the bullfrogs bellowed. It seemed like a peaceful night in the bayou until another screech tore through the cabin. Cecile could feel the scream down to her bones. She was visibly shaking. Cecile's mother began banging the door into the refrigerator that was blocking it again. To Cecile's horror, the large appliance moved some from the force of her mother's pushing. Mawmaw lunged toward the refrigerator. She positioned her small frame in front of the barricade, but Mawmaw was no match for Lisette's superhuman strength. The refrigerator lurched and almost toppled over.

"Run, Cher," Mawmaw instructed Cecile, but Cecile was frozen in terror. She stayed rooted to her spot until the door was open about six inches, then she turned and ran out of the cabin. She could hear her grandmother struggling to keep her mother from escaping and Cecile vacillated between saving herself and returning to help her grandmother. Another shove and Lisette was out of the bedroom. Cecile's mother bounded out of the cabin on all fours and was swallowed up into the darkness of the bayou. The screen door slammed behind her with a thwack.

"Mawmaw?" Cecile cried, hoping that her grandmother was unhurt. Cecile's grandmother pushed open the screen door and stepped out onto the porch. Mawmaw's wiry, gray hair was sticking up all over her head, but she appeared unscathed.

"Come in, Cher," Mawmaw said to Cecile. "We need to get inside the cabin and lock the door."

Cecile nodded absently and followed her grandmother back inside. Once the door was locked, Cecile dropped into a chair. She didn't know how much more she would be able to stand. Resting her elbows on the table, Cecile held her head in her shaking hands. Her grandmother collapsed into the other chair breathing heavily. Mawmaw reached for Cecile and their eyes met.

"We're safe for now," Mawmaw told Cecile, but Cecile didn't feel safe. She was more frightened than she had ever been.

"What about Mama?" Cecile asked.

Mawmaw let out a sigh before answering.

"Only the good Lord knows," Mawmaw said. Cecile could read the exhaustion on her grandmother's face.

After returning the refrigerator to its original spot, the two women retired to the bedroom. Cecile straightened the quilt on the bed and lay down on top of the cover. She didn't figure she would get much sleep tonight, but after spending the previous night awake, she dozed off within minutes. She awoke to the scratching sound at the door. The room was pitch dark, but Cecile could hear the steady, rhythmic breathing of her grandmother beside her. The scratching sound had not woken Mawmaw. Cecile held her breath and listened to the Rougarou pawing and scratching around the door of the cabin.

No, not the Rougarou, thought Cecile. *Mama!*

Cecile heard the creaking of the porch boards as the monster tried to find a way through the front door. Lisette let out a deep, guttural howl that turned Cecile's blood cold and Cecile could feel her grandmother stirring beside her.

"Where's your gun, Cher?" Mawmaw asked, referring to the rifle Cecile used to kill wild animals that became a threat. Cecile couldn't answer. She was horrified at the thought of having to shoot her mother.

"Cecile?" Mawmaw tried again.

"I can't shoot Mama," Cecile argued, but her grandmother shushed her.

"Hopefully it won't come to that," Mawmaw said. "But we need to protect ourselves."

Cecile sat up and reached for the light. She dutifully made her way over to the heavy gun in the corner of the room and picked it up to check that it was loaded. Another howl rang out and Cecile backed up to the bed, easing herself down onto the groaning springs as she carefully handled the rifle. Mawmaw came around and sat beside Cecile on the bed. The two women sat stoically facing the outer door in the other room. Cecile could feel the cool metal of the gun's barrel on her palm. She kept her finger ready to find the trigger if the need arose. The Rougarou continued scratching at the door and howling intermittently. The clock ticked, marking time, but the two women didn't move from their post. At one time, Cecile felt sure that her mother was going to make it into the house and her heart dropped at the thought of having to defend herself. She brushed tears away from her eyes as the gravity of the situation hit her.

The scratching sound became louder and more insistent, the howls more terrifying. The Rougarou was pacing on the front porch. The women could hear the monster's bray echo through the bayou. Cecile's shoulders were beginning to droop from sitting for so long when she heard the unmistakable sound of the screen door opening. She stiffened, fear causing her heart to race. *The front door is locked. It will keep us safe*, she thought, trying to convince herself that it was true.

"Do you want me to take the gun?" Mawmaw asked, but Cecile shook her head.

The sounds coming from the porch were constant now and it was obvious the Rougarou was trying to get to Cecile and her grandmother. Cecile held her breath, hoping to calm the beating of her heart.

"If it makes it inside, you'll have to shoot," Mawmaw said. Cecile grasped the gun firmly and nodded.

The door sounded as if it was being ripped off the hinges. Howls resounded, ringing Cecile's ears. She tried to steady her breathing. Suddenly there was a crash as the front window was broken out. Cecile watched in horror as a wolf-like creature poked its head in past the fluttering curtain. It let out a terrible scream and with one leap, the Rougarou burst through the front door. It paused when it saw the two women. Cecile licked her lips and raised the gun. She placed her finger on the trigger and started to count.

It's just like a wild animal, she told herself. Cecile inhaled, holding her breath for a moment. As she exhaled, she squeezed the trigger. The gun was loud in the small cabin. The Rougarou let out a blood-curdling scream and fell to the ground. Cecile blinked back tears and could see that her grandmother was trying hard to keep herself from sobbing as well. Lowering the gun, Cecile walked slowly toward her mother. Only, it wasn't Cecile's mother that was laying on the floor in a pool of blood. It was a man that was a stranger to Cecile. Mawmaw sucked in her breath and crossed herself when she saw that it wasn't Lisette.

"Thank God," Mawmaw said.

Cecile was looking at her grandmother, puzzled.

"I don't understand," Cecile said.

"Don't you see, Cher? Your mama is not the Rougarou. This is J.W. Landry," Mawmaw said, nudging the body with the toe of her rubber boot.

The creaking of the porch steps signaled someone coming and Cecile looked up. There in the doorway stood her mother. She was still very much human. Lisette's eyes were clear, and she had control of her faculties.

"It's over," Lisette said. "You've killed the Rougarou and broken the curse." Lisette moved toward Cecile, arms outstretched.

Cecile set the rifle down on the table as she went to her mother.

The White Dog

Fyodor Sologub

EVERYTHING GREW IRKSOME for Alexandra Ivanovna in the workshop of this out-of-the-way town – the patterns, the clatter of machines, the complaints of the customers; it was the shop in which she had served as apprentice and now for several years as cutter. Everything irritated Alexandra Ivanovna; she quarrelled with everyone and abused the innocent apprentice. Among others to suffer from her outbursts of temper was Tanechka, the youngest of the seamstresses, who only lately had been an apprentice. In the beginning Tanechka submitted to her abuse in silence. In the end she revolted, and, addressing herself to her assailant, said, quite calmly and affably, so that everyone laughed:

"Alexandra Ivanovna, you are a downright dog!"

Alexandra Ivanovna felt humiliated.

"You are a dog yourself!" she exclaimed.

Tanechka sat there sewing. She paused now and then from her work and said in a calm, deliberate manner:

"You always whine… Certainly, you are a dog… You have a dog's snout… And a dog's ears… And a wagging tail… The mistress will soon drive you out of doors, because you are the most detestable of dogs, a poodle."

Tanechka was a young, plump, rosy-cheeked girl with an innocent, good-natured face, which revealed, however, a trace of cunning. She sat there so demure, barefooted, still dressed in her apprentice clothes; her eyes were clear, and her brows were highly arched on her fine curved white forehead, framed by straight, dark chestnut hair, which in the distance looked black. Tanechka's voice was clear, even, sweet, insinuating, and if one could have heard its sound only, and not given heed to the words, it would have given the impression that she was paying Alexandra Ivanovna compliments.

The other seamstresses laughed, the apprentices chuckled, they covered their faces with their black aprons and cast side glances at Alexandra Ivanovna. As for Alexandra Ivanovna, she was livid with rage.

"Wretch!" she exclaimed. "I will pull your ears for you! I won't leave a hair on your head."

Tanechka replied in a gentle voice:

"The paws are a trifle short… The poodle bites as well as barks… It may be necessary to buy a muzzle."

Alexandra Ivanovna made a movement toward Tanechka. But before Tanechka had time to lay aside her work and get up, the mistress of the establishment, a large, serious-looking woman, entered, rustling her dress.

She said sternly: "Alexandra Ivanovna, what do you mean by making such a fuss?"

Alexandra Ivanovna, much agitated, replied: "Irina Petrovna, I wish you would forbid her to call me a dog!"

Tanechka in her turn complained: "She is always snarling at something or other. Always quibbling at the smallest trifles."

But the mistress looked at her sternly and said: "Tanechka, I can see through you. Are you sure you didn't begin? You needn't think that because you are a seamstress now you are an important person. If it weren't for your mother's sake—"

Tanechka grew red, but preserved her innocent and affable manner. She addressed her mistress in a subdued voice: "Forgive me, Irina Petrovna, I will not do it again. But it wasn't altogether my fault…"

* * *

Alexandra Ivanovna returned home almost ill with rage. Tanechka had guessed her weakness.

"A dog! Well, then I am a dog," thought Alexandra Ivanovna, "but it is none of her affair! Have I looked to see whether she is a serpent or a fox? It is easy to find one out, but why make a fuss about it? Is a dog worse than any other animal?"

The clear summer night languished and sighed, a soft breeze from the adjacent fields occasionally blew down the peaceful streets. The moon rose clear and full, that very same moon which rose long ago at another place, over the broad desolate steppe, the home of the wild, of those who ran free, and whined in their ancient earthly travail. The very same, as then and in that region.

And now, as then, glowed eyes sick with longing; and her heart, still wild, not forgetting in town the great spaciousness of the steppe felt oppressed; her throat was troubled with a tormenting desire to howl like a wild thing.

She was about to undress, but what was the use? She could not sleep, anyway.

She went into the passage. The warm planks of the floor bent and creaked under her, and small shavings and sand which covered them tickled her feet not unpleasantly.

She went out on the doorstep. There sat the *babushka* Stepanida, a black figure in her black shawl, gaunt and shrivelled. She sat with her head bent, and it seemed as though she were warming herself in the rays of the cold moon.

Alexandra Ivanovna sat down beside her. She kept looking at the old woman sideways. The large curved nose of her companion seemed to her like the beak of an old bird.

"A crow?" Alexandra Ivanovna asked herself.

She smiled, forgetting for the moment her longing and her fears. Shrewd as the eyes of a dog her own lighted up with the joy of her discovery. In the pale green light of the moon the wrinkles of her faded face became altogether invisible, and she seemed once more young and merry and light-hearted, just as she was ten years ago, when the moon had not yet called upon her to bark and bay of nights before the windows of the dark bathhouse.

She moved closer to the old woman, and said affably: "*Babushka* Stepanida, there is something I have been wanting to ask you."

The old woman turned to her, her dark face furrowed with wrinkles, and asked in a sharp, oldish voice that sounded like a caw:

"Well, my dear? Go ahead and ask."

Alexandra Ivanovna gave a repressed laugh; her thin shoulders suddenly trembled from a chill that ran down her spine.

She spoke very quietly: "*Babushka* Stepanida, it seems to me – tell me is it true? – I don't know exactly how to put it – but you, *babushka*, please don't take offence – it is not from malice that I—"

"Go on, my dear, never fear, say it," said the old woman.

She looked at Alexandra Ivanovna with glowing, penetrating eyes.

"It seems to me, *babushka* – please, now, don't take offence – as though you, *babushka* were a crow."

The old woman turned away. She was silent and merely nodded her head. She had the appearance of one who had recalled something. Her head, with its sharply outlined nose, bowed and nodded, and at last it seemed to Alexandra Ivanovna that the old woman was dozing. Dozing, and mumbling something under her nose. Nodding her head and mumbling some old forgotten words – old magic words.

An intense quiet reigned out of doors. It was neither light nor dark, and everything seemed bewitched with the inarticulate mumbling of old forgotten words. Everything languished and seemed lost in apathy. Again a longing oppressed her heart. And it was neither a dream nor an illusion. A thousand perfumes, imperceptible by day, became subtly distinguishable, and they recalled something ancient and primitive, something forgotten in the long ages.

In a barely audible voice the old woman mumbled: "Yes, I am a crow. Only I have no wings. But there are times when I caw, and I caw, and tell of woe. And I am given to forebodings, my dear; each time I have one I simply must caw. People are not particularly anxious to hear me. And when I see a doomed person I have such a strong desire to caw."

The old woman suddenly made a sweeping movement with her arms, and in a shrill voice cried out twice: "Kar-r, Kar-r!"

Alexandra Ivanovna shuddered, and asked: "*Babushka*, at whom are you cawing?"

The old woman answered: "At you, my dear – at you."

It had become too painful to sit with the old woman any longer. Alexandra Ivanovna went to her own room. She sat down before the open window and listened to two voices at the gate.

"It simply won't stop whining!" said a low and harsh voice.

"And uncle, did you see—?" asked an agreeable young tenor.

Alexandra Ivanovna recognized in this last the voice of the curly-headed, somewhat red, freckled-faced lad who lived in the same court.

A brief and depressing silence followed. Then she heard a hoarse and harsh voice say suddenly: "Yes, I saw. It's very large – and white. Lies near the bathhouse, and bays at the moon."

The voice gave her an image of the man, of his shovel-shaped beard, his low, furrowed forehead, his small, piggish eyes, and his spread-out fat legs.

"And why does it bay, uncle?" asked the agreeable voice.

And again the hoarse voice did not reply at once.

"Certainly to no good purpose – and where it came from is more than I can say."

"Do you think, uncle, it may be a were-wolf?" asked the agreeable voice.

"I should not advise you to investigate," replied the hoarse voice.

She could not quite understand what these words implied, nor did she wish to think of them. She did not feel inclined to listen further. What was the sound and significance of human words to *her*?

The moon looked straight into her face, and persistently called her and tormented her. Her heart was restless with a dark longing, and she could not sit still.

Alexandra Ivanovna quickly undressed herself. Naked, all white, she silently stole through the passage; she then opened the outer door – there was no one on the step or outside – and ran quickly across the court and the vegetable garden, and reached the bathhouse. The sharp contact of her body with the cold air and her feet with the cold ground gave her pleasure. But soon her body was warm.

She lay down in the grass, on her stomach. Then, raising herself on her elbows, she lifted her face toward the pale, brooding moon, and gave a long-drawn-out whine.

"Listen, uncle, it is whining," said the curly-haired lad at the gate.

The agreeable tenor voice trembled perceptibly.

"Whining again, the accursed one," said the hoarse, harsh voice slowly.

They rose from the bench. The gate latch clicked.

They went silently across the courtyard and the vegetable garden, the two of them. The older man, black-bearded and powerful, walked in front, a gun in his hand. The curly-headed lad followed tremblingly, and looked constantly behind.

Near the bathhouse, in the grass, lay a huge white dog, whining piteously. Its head, black on the crown, was raised to the moon, which pursued its way in the cold sky; its hind legs were strangely thrown backward, while the front ones, firm and straight, pressed hard against the ground.

In the pale green and unreal light of the moon it seemed enormous, so huge a dog was surely never seen on earth. It was thick and fat. The black spot, which began at the head and stretched in uneven strands down the entire spine, seemed like a woman's loosened hair. No tail was visible, presumably it was turned under. The fur on the body was so short that in the distance the dog seemed wholly naked, and its hide shone dimly in the moonlight, so that altogether it resembled the body of a nude woman, who lay in the grass and bayed at the moon.

The man with the black beard took aim. The curly-haired lad crossed himself and mumbled something.

The discharge of a rifle sounded in the night air. The dog gave a groan, jumped up on its hind legs, became a naked woman, who, her body covered with blood, started to run, all the while groaning, weeping and raising cries of distress.

The black-bearded one and the curly-haired one threw themselves in the grass, and began to moan in wild terror.

The Other Side
A Breton Legend
Eric Stenbock

"**NOT THAT I LIKE IT**, but one does feel so much better after it – oh, thank you, Mère Yvonne, yes just a little drop more." So the old crones fell to drinking their hot brandy and water (although of course they only took it medicinally, as a remedy for their rheumatics), all seated round the big fire and Mère Pinquèle continued her story.

"Oh, yes, then when they get to the top of the hill, there is an altar with six candles quite black and a sort of something in between, that nobody sees quite clearly, and the old black ram with the man's face and long horns begins to say Mass in a sort of gibberish nobody understands, and two black strange things like monkeys glide about with the book and the cruets – and there's music too, such music. There are things the top half like black cats, and the bottom part like men only their legs are all covered with close black hair, and they play on the bag-pipes, and when they come to the elevation, then—" Amid the old crones there was lying on the hearth-rug, before the fire, a boy whose large lovely eyes dilated and whose limbs quivered in the very ecstacy of terror.

"Is that all true, Mère Pinquèle?" he said.

"Oh, quite true, and not only that, the best part is yet to come; for they take a child and—" Here Mère Pinquèle showed her fang-like teeth.

"Oh! Mère Pinquèle, are you a witch too?"

"Silence, Gabriel," said Mère Yvonne, "how can you say anything so wicked? Why, bless me, the boy ought to have been in bed ages ago."

Just then all shuddered, and all made the sign of the cross except Mère Pinquèle, for they heard that most dreadful of dreadful sounds – the howl of a wolf, which begins with three sharp barks and then lifts itself up in a long protracted wail of commingled cruelty and despair, and at last subsides into a whispered growl fraught with eternal malice.

There was a forest and a village and a brook, the village was on one side of the brook, none had dared to cross to the other side. Where the village was, all was green and glad and fertile and fruitful; on the other side the trees never put forth green leaves, and a dark shadow hung over it even at noon-day, and in the night-time one could hear the wolves howling – the were-wolves and the wolf-men and the men-wolves, and those very wicked men who for nine days in every year are turned into wolves; but on the green side no wolf was ever seen, and only one little running brook like a silver streak flowed between.

It was spring now and the old crones sat no longer by the fire but before their cottages sunning themselves, and everyone felt so happy that they ceased to tell stories of the 'other side'. But Gabriel wandered by the brook as he was wont to wander, drawn thither by some strange attraction mingled with intense horror.

His schoolfellows did not like Gabriel; all laughed and jeered at him, because he was less cruel and more gentle of nature than the rest, and even as a rare and beautiful bird escaped from a cage is hacked to death by the common sparrows, so was Gabriel among his fellows. Everyone wondered how Mère Yvonne, that buxom and worthy matron, could have produced a son like this, with strange dreamy eyes, who was as they said *"pas comme les autres gamins"*. His only friends were the Abbé Félicien whose Mass he served each morning, and one little girl called Carmeille, who loved him, no one could make out why.

The sun had already set, Gabriel still wandered by the brook, filled with vague terror and irresistible fascination. The sun set and the moon rose, the full moon, very large and very clear, and the moonlight flooded the forest both this side and 'the other side', and just on the 'other side' of the brook, hanging over, Gabriel saw a large deep blue flower, whose strange intoxicating perfume reached him and fascinated him even where he stood.

"If I could only make one step across," he thought, "nothing could harm me if I only plucked that one flower, and nobody would know I had been over at all," for the villagers looked with hatred and suspicion on anyone who was said to have crossed to the 'other side', so summing up courage he leapt lightly to the other side of the brook. Then the moon breaking from a cloud shone with unusual brilliance, and he saw, stretching before him, long reaches of the same strange blue flowers each one lovelier than the last, till, not being able to make up his mind which one flower to take or whether to take several, he went on and on, and the moon shone very brightly and a strange unseen bird, somewhat like a nightingale, but louder and lovelier, sang, and his heart was filled with longing for he knew not what, and the moon shone and the nightingale sang. But on a sudden a black cloud covered the moon entirely, and all was black, utter darkness, and through the darkness he heard wolves howling and shrieking in the hideous ardour of the chase, and there passed before him a horrible procession of wolves (black wolves with red fiery eyes), and with them men that had the heads of wolves and wolves that had the heads of men, and above them flew owls (black owls with red fiery eyes), and bats and long serpentine black things, and last of all seated on an enormous black ram with hideous human face the wolf-keeper on whose face was eternal shadow; but they continued their horrid chase and passed him by, and when they had passed the moon shone out more beautiful than ever, and the strange nightingale sang again, and the strange intense blue flowers were in long reaches in front to the right and to the left. But one thing was there which had not been before, among the deep blue flowers walked one with long gleaming golden hair, and she turned once round and her eyes were of the same colour as the strange blue flowers, and she walked on and Gabriel could not choose but follow. But when a cloud passed over the moon he saw no beautiful woman but a wolf, so in utter terror he turned and fled, plucking one of the strange blue flowers on the way, and leapt again over the brook and ran home.

When he got home Gabriel could not resist showing his treasure to his mother, though he knew she would not appreciate it; but when she saw the strange blue flower, Mère Yvonne turned pale and said, "Why child, where hast thou been? sure it is the witch flower"; and so saying she snatched it from him and cast it into the corner, and immediately all its beauty and strange fragrance faded from it and it looked charred as though it had been burnt. So Gabriel sat down silently and rather sulkily, and having eaten no supper went up to bed, but he did got sleep but waited and waited till all was quiet within the house. Then he crept downstairs in his long white night-shirt and bare feet on the square cold stones and picked hurriedly up the charred and faded flower and put it in his warm bosom next his heart, and immediately the flower bloomed again lovelier than ever, and he fell into a deep sleep, but through his sleep he seemed to hear a soft low voice singing underneath his window in a strange language (in which the subtle sounds melted into one another), but he could distinguish no word except his own name.

When he went forth in the morning to serve Mass, he still kept the flower with him next his heart. Now when the priest began Mass and said *"Intriobo ad altare Dei,"* then said Gabriel *"Qui nequiquam laetificavit juventutem meam."* And the Abbé Félicien turned round on hearing this strange response, and he saw the boy's face deadly pale, his eyes fixed and his limbs rigid, and as the priest looked on him Gabriel fell fainting to the floor, so the sacristan had to carry him home and seek another acolyte for the Abbé Félicien.

Now when the Abbé Félicien came to see after him, Gabriel felt strangely reluctant to say anything about the blue flower and for the first time he deceived the priest.

In the afternoon as sunset drew nigh he felt better and Carmeille came to see him and begged him to go out with her into the fresh air. So they went out hand in hand, the dark haired, gazelle-eyed boy, and the fair wavy haired girl, and something, he knew not what, led his steps (half knowingly and yet not so, for he could not but walk thither) to the brook, and they sat down together on the bank.

Gabriel thought at least he might tell his secret to Carmeille, so he took out the flower from his bosom and said, "Look here, Carmeille, hast thou seen ever so lovely a flower as this?" but Carmeille turned pale and faint and said, "Oh, Gabriel what is this flower? I but touched it and I felt something strange come over me. No, no, I don't like its perfume, no there's something not quite right about it, oh, dear Gabriel, do let me throw it away," and before he had time to answer, she cast it from her, and again all its beauty and fragrance went from it and it looked charred as though it had been burnt. But suddenly where the flower had been thrown on this side of the brook, there appeared a wolf, which stood and looked at the children.

Carmeille said, "What shall we do," and clung to Gabriel, but the wolf looked at them very steadfastly and Gabriel recognized in the eyes of the wolf the strange deep intense blue eyes of the wolf-woman he had seen on the 'other side', so he said, "Stay here, dear Carmeille, see she is looking gently at us and will not hurt us."

"But it is a wolf," said Carmeille, and quivered all over with fear, but again Gabriel said languidly, "She will not hurt us." Then Carmeille seized Gabriel's hand in an agony of terror and dragged him along with her till they reached the village, where she gave the alarm and all the lads of the village gathered together. They had never seen a wolf on this side of the brook, so they excited themselves greatly and arranged a grand wolf hunt for the morrow, but Gabriel sat silently apart and said no word.

That night Gabriel could not sleep at all nor could he bring himself to say his prayers; but he sat in his little room by the window with his shirt open at the throat and the strange blue flower at his heart and again this night he heard a voice singing beneath his window in the same soft, subtle, liquid language as before –

Ma zála liral va jé Cwamûlo zhajéla je Cárma urádi el javé Járma, symai – carmé – Zhála javály thra je al vú al vlaûle va azré Safralje vairálje va já? Cárma seraja Lâja lâja Luzhà!

And as he looked he could see the silvern shadows slide on the glimmering light of golden hair, and the strange eyes gleaming dark blue through the night and it seemed to him that he could not but follow; so he walked half clad and bare foot as he was with eyes fixed as in a dream silently down the stairs and out into the night.

And ever and again she turned to look on him with her strange blue eyes full of tenderness and passion and sadness beyond the sadness of things human – and as he foreknew his steps led him to the brink of the brook. Then she, taking his hand, familiarly said, "Won't you help me over Gabriel?"

Then it seemed to him as though he had known her all his life – so he went with her to the 'other side' but he saw no one by him; and looking again beside him there were two wolves. In a frenzy of terror, he (who had never thought to kill any living thing before) seized a log of wood lying by and smote one of the wolves on the head.

Immediately he saw the wolf-woman again at his side with blood streaming from her forehead, staining her wonderful golden hair, and with eyes looking at him with infinite reproach, she said – "Who did this?"

Then she whispered a few words to the other wolf, which leapt over the brook and made its way towards the village, and turning again towards him she said, "Oh Gabriel, how could you strike me, who would have loved you so long and so well." Then it seemed to him again as though he had known her all his life but he felt dazed and said nothing – but she gathered a dark green strangely shaped leaf and holding it to her forehead, she said – "Gabriel, kiss the place all will be well again." So he kissed as she had bidden him and he felt the salt taste of blood in his mouth and then he knew no more.

Again he saw the wolf-keeper with his horrible troupe around him, but this time not engaged in the chase but sitting in strange conclave in a circle and the black owls sat in the trees and the black bats hung downwards from the branches. Gabriel stood alone in the middle with a hundred wicked eyes fixed on him. They seemed to deliberate about what should be done with him, speaking in that same strange tongue which he had heard in the songs beneath his window. Suddenly he felt a hand pressing in his and saw the mysterious wolf-woman by his side. Then began what seemed a kind of incantation where human or half human creatures seemed to howl, and beasts to speak with human speech but in the unknown tongue. Then the wolf-keeper whose face was ever veiled in shadow spake some words in a voice that seemed to come from afar off, but all he could distinguish was his own name Gabriel and her name Lilith. Then he felt arms enlacing him.

Gabriel awoke – in his own room – so it was a dream after all – but what a dreadful dream. Yes, but was it his own room? Of course there was his coat hanging over the chair – yes but – the Crucifix – where was the Crucifix and the benetier and the consecrated palm branch and the antique image of Our Lady perpetuae salutis, with the little ever-burning lamp before it, before which he placed every day the flowers he had gathered, yet had not dared to place the blue flower.

Every morning he lifted his still dream-laden eyes to it and said Ave Maria and made the sign of the cross, which bringeth peace to the soul – but how horrible, how maddening, it was not there, not at all. No surely he could not be awake, at least not quite awake, he would make the benedictive sign and he would be freed from this fearful illusion – yes but the sign, he would make the sign – oh, but what was the sign? Had he forgotten? Or was his arm paralyzed? No he could not move. Then he had forgotten – and the prayer – he must remember that. *A-vae-nunc-mortis-fructus*. No surely it did not run thus – but something like it surely – yes, he was awake he could move at any rate – he would reassure himself – he would get up – he would see the grey old church with the exquisitely pointed gables bathed in the light of dawn, and presently the deep solemn bell would toll and he would run down and don his red cassock and lace-worked cotta and light the tall candles on the altar and wait reverently to vest the good and gracious Abbé Félicien, kissing each vestment as he lifted it with reverent hands.

But surely this was not the light of dawn; it was like sunset! He leapt from his small white bed, and a vague terror came over him, he trembled and had to hold on to the chair before he reached the window. No, the solemn spires of the grey church were not to be seen – he was in the depths of the forest; but in a part he had never seen before – but surely he had explored every part, it must be the 'other side'. To terror succeeded a languor and lassitude not without charm – passivity, acquiescence, indulgence – he felt, as it were, the strong caress of another will flowing over him like water and clothing him with invisible hands in an impalpable garment; so he dressed himself almost mechanically and walked downstairs, the same stairs it seemed to him down which it was his wont to run and spring. The broad square stones seemed singularly beautiful and iridescent with many strange colours – how was it he had never noticed this before – but he was gradually losing the power of wondering – he entered the room below – the wonted coffee and bread-rolls were on the table.

"Why Gabriel, how late you are today." The voice was very sweet but the intonation strange – and there sat Lilith, the mysterious wolf-woman, her glittering gold hair tied in a loose knot and an embroidery whereon she was tracing strange serpentine patterns, lay over the lap of her maize coloured garment – and she looked at Gabriel steadfastly with her wonderful dark blue eyes and said, "Why, Gabriel, you are late today," and Gabriel answered, "I was tired yesterday, give me some coffee."

A dream within a dream – yes, he had known her all his life, and they dwelt together; had they not always done so? And she would take him through the glades of the forest and gather for him flowers, such as he had never seen before, and tell him stories in her strange, low deep voice, which seemed ever to be accompanied by the faint vibration of strings, looking at him fixedly the while with her marvellous blue eyes.

Little by little the flame of vitality which burned within him seemed to grow fainter and fainter, and his lithe lissom limbs waxed languorous and luxurious – yet was he ever filled with a languid content and a will not his own perpetually overshadowed him.

One day in their wanderings he saw a strange dark blue flower like unto the eyes of Lilith, and a sudden half remembrance flashed through his mind.

"What is this blue flower?" he said, and Lilith shuddered and said nothing; but as they went a little further there was a brook – the brook he thought, and felt his fetters falling off him, and he prepared to spring over the brook; but Lilith seized him by the arm and held him back with all her strength, and trembling all over she said, "Promise me Gabriel that you will not cross over." But he said, "Tell me what is this blue flower, and why you will not tell me?" And she said, "Look Gabriel at the brook." And he looked and saw that though it was just like the brook of separation it was not the same, the waters did not flow.

As Gabriel looked steadfastly into the still waters it seemed to him as though he saw voices – some impression of the Vespers for the Dead. "*Hei mihi quia incolatus sum*," and again "*De profundis clamavi ad te*" – oh, that veil, that overshadowing veil! Why could he not hear properly and see, and why did he only remember as one looking through a threefold semi-transparent curtain. Yes they were praying for him – but who were they? He heard again the voice of Lilith in whispered anguish, "Come away!"

Then he said, this time in monotone, "What is this blue flower, and what is its use?"

And the low thrilling voice answered, "It is called *lûli uzhûri*, two drops pressed upon the face of the sleeper and he will sleep."

He was as a child in her hand and suffered himself to be led from thence, nevertheless he plucked listlessly one of the blue flowers, holding it downwards in his hand. What did she mean? Would the sleeper wake? Would the blue flower leave any stain? Could that stain be wiped off?

But as he lay asleep at early dawn he heard voices from afar off praying for him – the Abbé Félicien, Carmeille, his mother too, then some familiar words struck his ear: "*Libera mea porta inferi*." Mass was being said for the repose of his soul, he knew this. No, he could not stay, he would leap over the brook, he knew the way – he had forgotten that the brook did not flow. Ah, but Lilith would know – what should he do? The blue flower – there it lay close by his bedside – he understood now; so he crept very silently to where Lilith lay asleep, her long hair glistening gold, shining like a glory round about her. He pressed two drops on her forehead, she sighed once, and a shade of praeternatural anguish passed over her beautiful face. He fled – terror, remorse, and hope tearing his soul and making fleet his feet. He came to the brook – he did not see that the water did not flow – of course it was the brook for separation; one bound, he should be with things human again. He leapt over and—

A change had come over him – what was it? He could not tell – did he walk on all fours? Yes surely. He looked into the brook, whose still waters were fixed as a mirror, and there, horror, he beheld himself; or was it himself? His head and face, yes; but his body transformed to that of a wolf. Even as he looked he heard a sound of hideous mocking laughter behind him. He turned round – there, in a gleam of red lurid light, he saw one whose body was human, but whose head was that of a wolf, with eyes of infinite malice; and, while this hideous being laughed with a loud human laugh, he, essaying to speak, could only utter the prolonged howl of a wolf.

But we will transfer our thoughts from the alien things on the 'other side' to the simple human village where Gabriel used to dwell. Mère Yvonne was not much surprised when Gabriel did not turn up to breakfast – he often did not, so absent-minded was he; this time she said, "I suppose he has gone with the others to the wolf hunt." Not that Gabriel was given to hunting, but, as she sagely said, "There was no knowing what he might do next." The boys said, "Of course that muff Gabriel is skulking and hiding himself, he's afraid to join the wolf hunt; why, he wouldn't even kill a cat," for their one notion of excellence was slaughter – so the greater the game the greater the glory. They were chiefly now confined to cats and sparrows, but they all hoped in after time to become generals of armies.

Yet these children had been taught all their life through with the gentle words of Christ – but alas, nearly all the seed falls by the wayside, where it could not bear flower or fruit; how little these know the suffering and bitter anguish or realize the full meaning of the words to those, of whom it is written 'Some fell among thorns'.

The wolf hunt was so far a success that they did actually see a wolf, but not a success, as they did not kill it before it leapt over the brook to the 'other side', where, of course, they were afraid to pursue it. No emotion is more inrooted and intense in the minds of common people than hatred and fear of anything 'strange'.

Days passed by but Gabriel was nowhere seen – and Mère Yvonne began to see clearly at last how deeply she loved her only son, who was so unlike her that she had thought herself an object of pity to other mothers – the goose and the swan's egg. People searched and pretended to search, they even went to the length of dragging the ponds, which the boys thought very amusing, as it enabled them to kill a great number of water rats, and Carmeille sat in a corner and cried all day long. Mère Pinquèle also sat in a corner and chuckled and said that she had always said Gabriel would come to no good. The Abbé Félicien looked pale and anxious, but said very little, save to God and those that dwelt with God.

At last, as Gabriel was not there, they supposed he must be nowhere – that is dead. (Their knowledge of other localities being so limited, that it did not even occur to them to suppose he might be living elsewhere than in the village.) So it was agreed that an empty catafalque should be put up in the church with tall candles round it, and Mère Yvonne said all the prayers that were in her prayer book, beginning at the beginning and ending at the end, regardless of their appropriateness – not even omitting the instructions of the rubrics. And Carmeille sat in the corner of the little side chapel and cried, and cried. And the Abbé Félicien caused the boys to sing the Vespers for the Dead (this did not amuse them so much as dragging the pond), and on the following morning, in the silence of early dawn, said the Dirge and the Requiem – and this Gabriel heard.

Then the Abbé Félicien received a message to bring the Holy Viaticum to one sick. So they set forth in solemn procession with great torches, and their way lay along the brook of separation.

Essaying to speak he could only utter the prolonged howl of a wolf – the most fearful of all bestial sounds. He howled and howled again – perhaps Lilith would hear him! Perhaps she could rescue him? Then he remembered the blue flower – the beginning and end of all his woe. His cries aroused all the denizens of the forest – the wolves, the wolf-men, and the men-wolves. He fled before them in an agony of terror – behind him, seated on the black ram with human face, was the wolf-keeper, whose face was veiled in eternal shadow. Only once he turned to look behind – for among the shrieks and howls of bestial chase he heard one thrilling voice moan with pain. And there among them he beheld Lilith, her body too was that of a wolf, almost hidden in the masses of her glittering golden hair, on her forehead was a stain of blue, like in colour to her mysterious eyes, now veiled with tears she could not shed.

The way of the Most Holy Viaticum lay along the brook of separation. They heard the fearful howlings afar off, the torch bearers turned pale and trembled – but the Abbé Félicien, holding aloft the Ciborium, said, "They cannot harm us."

Suddenly the whole horrid chase came in sight. Gabriel sprang over the brook, the Abbé Félicien held the most Blessed Sacrament before him, and his shape was restored to him and he fell down prostrate in adoration. But the Abbé Félicien still held aloft the Sacred Ciborium, and the people fell on their knees in the agony of fear, but the face of the priest seemed to shine with divine effulgence. Then the wolf-keeper held up in his hands the shape of something horrible and inconceivable – a monstrance to the Sacrament of Hell, and three times he raised it, in mockery of the blessed rite of Benediction. And on the third time streams of fire went forth from his fingers, and all the 'other side' of the forest took fire, and great darkness was over all.

All who were there and saw and heard it have kept the impress thereof for the rest of their lives – nor till in their death hour was the remembrance thereof absent from their minds. Shrieks, horrible beyond conception, were heard till nightfall – then the rain rained.

The 'other side' is harmless now – charred ashes only; but none dares to cross but Gabriel alone – for once a year for nine days a strange madness comes over him.

The Werewolf

Swedish Fairy Tale

ONCE UPON A TIME there was a king, who reigned over a great kingdom. He had a queen, but only a single daughter, a girl. In consequence the little girl was the apple of her parents' eyes; they loved her above everything else in the world, and their dearest thought was the pleasure they would take in her when she was older. But the unexpected often happens; for before the king's daughter began to grow up, the queen her mother fell ill and died. It is not hard to imagine the grief that reigned, not alone in the royal castle, but throughout the land; for the queen had been beloved of all. The king grieved so that he would not marry again, and his one joy was the little princess.

A long time passed, and with each succeeding day the king's daughter grew taller and more beautiful, and her father granted her every wish. Now there were a number of women who had nothing to do but wait on the princess and carry out her commands. Among them was a woman who had formerly married and had two daughters. She had an engaging appearance, a smooth tongue and a winning way of talking, and she was as soft and pliable as silk; but at heart she was full of machinations and falseness. Now when the queen died, she at once began to plan how she might marry the king, so that her daughters might be kept like royal princesses. With this end in view, she drew the young princess to her, paid her the most fulsome compliments on everything she said and did, and was forever bringing the conversation around to how happy she would be were the king to take another wife. There was much said on this head, early and late, and before very long the princess came to believe that the woman knew all there was to know about everything. So she asked her what sort of a woman the king ought to choose for a wife. The woman answered as sweet as honey: "It is not my affair to give advice in this matter; yet he should choose for queen someone who is kind to the little princess. For one thing I know, and that is, were I fortunate enough to be chosen, my one thought would be to do all I could for the little princess, and if she wished to wash her hands, one of my daughters would have to hold the wash-bowl and the other hand her the towel." This and much more she told the king's daughter, and the princess believed it, as children will.

From that day forward the princess gave her father no peace, and begged him again and again to marry the good court lady. Yet he did not want to marry her. But the king's daughter gave him no rest; but urged him again and again, as the false court lady had persuaded her to do. Finally, one day, when she again brought up the matter, the king cried: "I can see you will end by having your own way about this, even though it be entirely against my will. But I will do so only on one condition." "What is the condition?" asked the princess. "If I marry again," said the king, "it is only because of your ceaseless pleading. Therefore you must promise that, if in the future you are not satisfied with your step-mother or your step-sisters, not a single lament or complaint on your part reaches my ears." This she promised the king, and it was agreed that he should marry the court lady and make her queen of the whole country.

As time passed on, the king's daughter had grown to be the most beautiful maiden to be found far and wide; the queen's daughters, on the other hand, were homely, evil of disposition, and no one knew any good of them. Hence it was not surprising that many youths came from East and West to sue for the princess's hand; but that none of them took any interest in the queen's daughters. This made the step-mother very angry; but she concealed her rage, and was as sweet and friendly as ever. Among the wooers was a king's son from another country. He was young and brave, and since he loved the princess dearly, she accepted his proposal and they plighted their troth. The queen observed this with an angry eye, for it would have pleased her had the prince chosen one of her own daughters. She therefore made up her mind that the young pair should never be happy together, and from that time on thought only of how she might part them from each other.

An opportunity soon offered itself. News came that the enemy had entered the land, and the king was compelled to go to war. Now the princess began to find out the kind of step-mother she had. For no sooner had the king departed than the queen showed her true nature, and was just as harsh and unkind as she formerly had pretended to be friendly and obliging. Not a day went by without her scolding and threatening the princess; and the queen's daughters were every bit as malicious as their mother. But the king's son, the lover of the princess, found himself in even worse position. He had gone hunting one day, had lost his way, and could not find his people. Then the queen used her black arts and turned him into a werewolf, to wander through the forest for the remainder of his life in that shape. When evening came and there was no sign of the prince, his people returned home, and one can imagine what sorrow they caused when the princess learned how the hunt had ended. She grieved, wept day and night, and was not to be consoled. But the queen laughed at her grief, and her heart was filled with joy to think that all had turned out exactly as she wished.

Now it chanced one day, as the king's daughter was sitting alone in her room, that she thought she would go herself into the forest where the prince had disappeared. She went to her step-mother and begged permission to go out into the forest, in order to forget her surpassing grief. The queen did not want to grant her request, for she always preferred saying no to yes. But the princess begged her so winningly that at last she was unable to say no, and she ordered one of her daughters to go along with her and watch her. That caused a great deal of discussion, for neither of the step-daughters wanted to go with her; each made all sorts of excuses, and asked what pleasures were there in going with the king's daughter, who did nothing but cry. But the queen had the last word in the end, and ordered that one of her daughters must accompany the princess, even though it be against her will. So the girls wandered out of the castle into the forest. The king's daughter walked among the trees, and listened to the song of the birds, and thought of her lover, for whom she longed, and who was now no longer there. And the queen's daughter followed her, vexed, in her malice, with the king's daughter and her sorrow.

After they had walked a while, they came to a little hut, lying deep in the dark forest. By then the king's daughter was very thirsty, and wanted to go into the little hut with her step-sister, in order to get a drink of water. But the queen's daughter was much annoyed and said: "Is it not enough for me to be running around here in the wilderness with you? Now you even want me, who am a princess, to enter that wretched little hut. No, I will not step a foot over the threshold! If you want to go in, why go in alone!" The king's daughter lost no time; but did as her step-sister advised, and stepped into the little hut. When she entered she saw an old woman sitting there on a bench, so enfeebled by age that her head shook. The princess spoke to her in her usual friendly way: "Good evening, motherkin. May I ask you for a drink of water?" "You are heartily welcome to it," said the old woman. "Who may you be, that step beneath my lowly roof and greet me in so winning a way?" The king's daughter told her who she was, and that she had gone out to relieve her heart, in order to forget her great grief. "And what may your great grief be?" asked the old woman. "No doubt it is my fate to grieve," said the princess, "and I can never be happy again. I have lost my only love, and God alone knows whether I shall ever see him again." And she also told her why it was, and the tears ran down her cheeks in streams, so that any one would have felt sorry for her. When she had ended the old woman said: "You did well in confiding your sorrow to me. I have lived long and may be able to give you a bit of good advice. When you leave here you will see a lily growing from the ground. This lily is not like other lilies, however, but has many strange virtues. Run quickly over to it, and pick it. If you can do that then you need not worry, for then one will appear who will tell you what to do." Then they parted and the king's daughter thanked her and went her way; while the old woman sat on the bench and wagged her head. But the queen's daughter had been standing without the hut the entire time, vexing herself, and grumbling because the king's daughter had taken so long.

So when the latter stepped out, she had to listen to all sorts of abuse from her step-sister, as was to be expected. Yet she paid no attention to her, and thought only of how she might find the flower of which the old woman had spoken. They went through the forest, and suddenly she saw a beautiful white lily growing in their very path. She was much pleased and ran up at once to pick it; but that very moment it disappeared and reappeared somewhat further away.

The king's daughter was now filled with eagerness, no longer listened to her step-sister's calls, and kept right on running; yet each time when she stooped to pick the lily, it suddenly disappeared and reappeared somewhat further away. Thus it went for some time, and the princess was drawn further and further into the deep forest. But the lily continued to stand, and disappear and move further away, and each time the flower seemed larger and more beautiful than before. At length the princess came to a high hill, and as she looked toward its summit, there stood the lily high on the naked rock, glittering as white and radiant as the brightest star. The king's daughter now began to climb the hill, and in her eagerness she paid no attention to stones nor steepness. And when at last she reached the summit of the hill, lo and behold! the lily no longer evaded her grasp; but remained where it was, and the princess stooped and picked it and hid it in her bosom, and so heartfelt was her happiness that she forgot her step-sisters and everything else in the world.

For a long time she did not tire of looking at the beautiful flower. Then she suddenly began to wonder what her step-mother would say when she came home after having remained out so long. And she looked around, in order to find the way back to the castle. But as she looked around, behold, the sun had set and no more than a little strip of daylight rested on the summit of the hill. Below her lay the forest, so dark and shadowed that she had no faith in her ability to find the homeward path. And now she grew very sad, for she could think of nothing better to do than to spend the night on the hill-top. She seated herself on the rock, put her hand to her cheek, cried, and thought of her unkind step-mother and step-sisters, and of all the harsh words she would have to endure when she returned. And she thought of her father, the king, who was away at war, and of the love of her heart, whom she would never see again; and she grieved so bitterly that she did not even know she wept. Night came and darkness, and the stars rose, and still the princess sat in the same spot and wept. And while she sat there, lost in her thoughts, she heard a voice say: "Good evening, lovely maiden! Why do you sit here so sad and lonely?" She stood up hastily, and felt much embarrassed, which was not surprising. When she looked around there was nothing to be seen but a tiny old man, who nodded to her and seemed to be very humble. She answered: "Yes, it is no doubt my fate to grieve, and never be happy again. I have lost my dearest love, and now I have lost my way in the forest, and am afraid of being devoured by wild beasts." "As to that," said the old man, "you need have no fear. If you will do exactly as I say, I will help you." This made the princess happy; for she felt that all the rest of the world had abandoned her. Then the old man drew out flint and steel and said: "Lovely maiden, you must first build a fire." She did as he told her, gathered moss, brush and dry sticks, struck sparks and lit such a fire on the hill-top that the flame blazed up to the skies. That done the old man said: "Go on a bit and you will find a kettle of tar, and bring the kettle to me." This the king's daughter did. The old man continued: "Now put the kettle on the fire." And the princess did that as well. When the tar began to boil, the old man said: "Now throw your white lily into the kettle." The princess thought this a harsh command, and earnestly begged to be allowed to keep the lily. But the old man said: "Did you not promise to obey my every command? Do as I tell you or you will regret it." The king's daughter turned away her eyes, and threw the lily into the boiling tar; but it was altogether against her will, so fond had she grown of the beautiful flower.

The moment she did so a hollow roar, like that of some wild beast, sounded from the forest. It came nearer, and turned into such a terrible howling that all the surrounding hills echoed it. Finally there was a cracking and breaking among the trees, the bushes were thrust aside, and the princess saw a great grey wolf come running out of the forest and straight up the hill. She was much frightened and would gladly have run away, had she been able. But the old man said: "Make haste, run to the edge of the hill and the moment the wolf comes along, upset the kettle on him!" The princess was terrified, and hardly knew what she was about; yet she did as the old man said, took the kettle, ran to the edge of the hill, and poured its contents over the wolf just as he was about to run up. And then a strange thing happened: no sooner had she done so, than the wolf was transformed, cast off his thick grey pelt, and in place of the horrible wild beast, there stood a handsome young man, looking up to the hill. And when the king's daughter collected herself and looked at him, she saw that it was really and truly her lover, who had been turned into a werewolf.

It is easy to imagine how the princess felt. She opened her arms, and could neither ask questions nor reply to them, so moved and delighted was she. But the prince ran hastily up the hill, embraced her tenderly, and thanked her for delivering him. Nor did he forget the little old man, but thanked him with many civil expressions for his powerful aid. Then they sat down together on the hill-top, and had a pleasant talk. The prince told how he had been turned into a wolf, and of all he had suffered while running about in the forest; and the princess told of her grief, and the many tears she had shed while he had been gone. So they sat the whole night through, and never noticed it until the stars grew pale and it was light enough to see. When the sun rose, they saw that a broad path led from the hill-top straight to the royal castle; for they had a view of the whole surrounding country from the hill-top. Then the old man said: "Lovely maiden, turn around! Do you see anything out yonder?" "Yes," said the princess, "I see a horseman on a foaming horse, riding as fast as he can." Then the old man said: "He is a messenger sent on ahead by the king your father. And your father with all his army is following him." That pleased the princess above all things, and she wanted to descend the hill at once to meet her father. But the old man detained her and said: "Wait a while, it is too early yet. Let us wait and see how everything turns out."

Time passed and the sun was shining brightly, and its rays fell straight on the royal castle down below. Then the old man said: "Lovely maiden, turn around! Do you see anything down below?" "Yes," replied the princess, "I see a number of people coming out of my father's castle, and some are going along the road, and others into the forest." The old man said: "Those are your step-mother's servants. She has sent some to meet the king and welcome him; but she has sent others to the forest to look for you." At these words the princess grew uneasy, and wished to go down to the queen's servants. But the old man withheld her and said: "Wait a while, and let us first see how everything turns out."

More time passed, and the king's daughter was still looking down the road from which the king would appear, when the old man said: "Lovely maiden, turn around! Do you see anything down below?" "Yes," answered the princess, "there is a great commotion in my father's castle, and they are hanging it with black." The old man said: "That is your step-mother and her people. They will assure your father that you are dead." Then the king's daughter felt bitter anguish, and she implored from the depths of her heart: "Let me go, let me go, so that I may spare my father this anguish!" But the old man detained her and said: "No, wait, it is still too early. Let us first see how everything turns out."

Again time passed, the sun lay high above the fields, and the warm air blew over meadow and forest. The royal maid and youth still sat on the hill-top with the old man, where we had left them. Then they saw a little cloud rise against the horizon, far away in the distance, and the little cloud grew larger and larger, and came nearer and nearer along the road, and as it moved one could see it was agleam with weapons, and nodding helmets, and waving flags, one could hear the rattle of swords, and the neighing of horses, and finally recognize the banner of the king. It is not hard to imagine how pleased the king's daughter was, and how she insisted on going down and greeting her father. But the old man held her back and said: "Lovely maiden, turn around! Do you see anything happening at the castle?" "Yes," answered the princess, "I can see my step-mother and step-sisters coming out, dressed in mourning, holding white kerchiefs to their faces, and weeping bitterly." The old man answered: "Now they are pretending to weep because of your death. Wait just a little while longer. We have not yet seen how everything will turn out."

After a time the old man said again: "Lovely maiden, turn around! Do you see anything down below?" "Yes," said the princess, "I see people bringing a black coffin – now my father is having it opened. Look, the queen and her daughters are down on their knees, and my father is threatening them with his sword!" Then the old man said: "Your father wished to see your body, and so your evil step-mother had to confess the truth." When the princess heard that she said earnestly: "Let me go, let me go, so that I may comfort my father in his great sorrow!" But the old man held her back and said: "Take my advice and stay here a little while longer. We have not yet seen how everything will turn out."

Again time went by, and the king's daughter and the prince and the old man were still sitting on the hill-top. Then the old man said: "Lovely maiden, turn around! Do you see anything down below?" "Yes," answered the princess, "I see my father and my step-sisters and my step-mother with all their following moving this way." The old man said: "Now they have started out to look for you. Go down and bring up the wolf's pelt in the gorge." The king's daughter did as he told her. The old man continued: "Now stand at the edge of the hill." And the princess did that, too. Now one could see the queen and her daughters coming along the way, and stopping just below the hill. Then the old man said: "Now throw down the wolf's pelt!" The princess obeyed him, and threw down the wolf's pelt according to his command. It fell directly on the evil queen and her daughters. And then a most wonderful thing happened: no sooner had the pelt touched the three evil women than they immediately changed shape, and turning into three horrible werewolves, they ran away as fast as they could into the forest, howling dreadfully.

No more had this happened than the king himself arrived at the foot of the hill with his whole retinue. When he looked up and recognized the princess, he could not at first believe his eyes; but stood motionless, thinking her a vision. Then the old man cried: "Lovely maiden, now hasten, run down and make your father happy!" There was no need to tell the princess twice. She took her lover by the hand and they ran down the hill. When they came to the king, the princess ran on ahead, fell on her father's neck, and wept with joy. And the young prince wept as well, and the king himself wept; and their meeting was a pleasant sight for everyone. There was great joy and many embraces, and the princess told of her evil step-mother and step-sisters and of her lover, and all that she had suffered, and of the old man who had helped them in such a wonderful way. But when the king turned around to thank the old man he had completely vanished, and from that day on no one could say who he had been or what had become of him.

The king and his whole retinue now returned to the castle, where the king had a splendid banquet prepared, to which he invited all the able and distinguished people throughout the kingdom, and bestowed his daughter on the young prince. And the wedding was celebrated with gladness and music and amusements of every kind for many days. I was there, too, and when I rode through the forest I met a wolf with two young wolves, and they showed me their teeth and seemed very angry. And I was told they were none other than the evil step-mother and her two daughters.

The Eyes of Sebastien

Allan Sullivan

THIS IS A TALE of the big timber that grows in league-long patches where the headwaters of the Saguenay find their birth amongst tumbled foothills of the Laurentian range. Thence flows the Saguenay, a chill and formidable stream, gathering volume as it moves southward with countless tributaries from unknown lakes and moose-trampled marshes, loitering on its way through stretches of cedar-bordered solitude, flinging itself headlong over cataracts where the tawny water rages thunderously day and night, ever more deep, forbidding and austere, till at last it merges majestically with the great St. Lawrence, the mother of many rivers, and spends itself between the thousand-foot crags of Capes Trinity and Eternity.

All along the Saguenay it is a French country, as French as when two hundred years ago the peasants of Brittany and Normandy first fared northward into the unexplored wilderness. Amid the big timber and beside untamed waters they raised their log-hewn walls, with the mud-chinked joints, the tiny deep set windows and the massive roofs that must bear the weight of winter snows. Out of the forest they carved their farms, planting grain between the unconquerable roots, drawing sustenance from wood and stream, beating off marauding Indians, gathering in the long winter evenings round pine-heaped hearths, utterly alone save when in summer the yellow bows of a canoe glided round a point, and a missionary Jesuit Father landed from Quebec; or when in winter the man of God tramped, solitary, through endless miles of big timber on his errand of mercy and peace.

But always there was talk of France, with lingering, poignant pictures of the land they had left, of the red roofs of Quiberon that look across the bay at Croise and the cobbled streets of Rennes that lead to the swift waters of the Vilaine.

In one of the patches of timber on Lac St. Luc there is a lumber-camp, a nest of long buildings, ten feet high, that occupy a roughly cleared space close to the water's edge. From the camp there radiates a maze of winter roads traversed by a hundred lumberjacks in gaudy woollen capotes, with axes and saws over their shoulders, and down these roads, which slope gently to the lake, great logs are drawn, to be dumped, rumbling, on the ice. All through the day one can hear, near and far, the crash of big timber toppling earthward, the creak of straining harness, the crack of whips, the stroke of axes and the whine of distant saws. At night there is talk beside great cast-iron stoves stuffed with fuel, much smoke, the drone of winter winds and the plaintive hoot of the great white owl.

It fell on a day when the sun shone bright and the snow was like a sparkling blanket, that a man emerged from the Saguenay trail and struck across Lac St. Luc. He walked with a long, easy swing, bending a little forward beneath the weight of his pack. Threading his way between the piles of logs, he halted at the door of the main building, twisted his feet free of snowshoes and entered.

"Hallo!" he said with a smile. "I have again arrived."

The cook looked round, and straightway forgot his cooking, for the new-comer was none other than Antoine Carnot the peddler – the bringer of news – the teller of tales – the confidential go-between in the wilderness – the human link with the outside world. Antoine was all of these, and more. A bit of a doctor, a bit more of a lawyer, a shrewd trader, and withal possessed of unfailing humour and a heart of gold. No wonder that Pierre Colange forgot his cooking and hurried forward, hands outstretched.

"Ten thousand welcomes, mon vieux. No, you shall not talk till you have eaten. Behold, a partridge which was for the boss, but eat and say nothing. The wind makes a chill in the stomach, but you have an hour before the men come in. Fill thyself, and say nothing till afterwards."

Antoine nodded and obeyed, while Pierre watched him admiringly. Then there was news, much news from a dozen villages, while the pack was unrolled and its contents spread on a table in the corner. Knives and neckties, shirts and razors and mouth-organs, jimcracks and cheap jewellery, studs and celluloid collars – the result of Antoine's annual trip to Quebec. A great man was Antoine; had he not once sent a telegram to Montreal and got an answer the very next day, and he right there in Quebec all the time! Presently his wares were displayed to his satisfaction, and he sent Pierre a swift glance.

"Jean Deslormes, he is still here?"

Pierre nodded. "He makes good money, forty dollars a month – and spends nothing save for tobacco."

"I was at Villeneuve this day two weeks ago," said Antoine thoughtfully, "and saw the girl Marie Fisette. They are betrothed."

Pierre laughed at this. "Does not the whole camp know it, and how many times has Jean not told us! Every morning he goes along the road making verses to that girl with his mouth. It is well that he cannot write – but perhaps I do not understand such things. I made no verses to my Henriette."

Antoine looked a little grave, "Sebastien was also at Villeneuve, and full of anger when he heard of the betrothal. Marie told me that he said strange and threatening things, that she should never marry Jean. Then he barked something like a wolf, and she did not see him again."

"Loup Garou!" whispered Pierre under his breath. It was a word of awe through the outlying French country. The story of the Loup Garou, that strange and malign combination of man and wolf, had come across with them from the hills of Brittany. The belief still held north of the Laurentians. It was always an old dog wolf, tenanted by some evil and human spirit, endowed with wild powers of murder and revenge, a lean grey beast that patrolled the winter hills and sent his savage note drifting down into solitary villages where simple folk gathered closer round the fire and glanced apprehensively at the window-fastenings. Sometimes it was a man who took the form of a wolf to serve his dread purpose, and became again human when his deadly part was played.

This had been whispered of Sebastien behind his back. Where the man came from none knew, only that calamity came with him. He was small, dark and very active, with hollow cheeks and burning eyes, and moved about through the French country, seldom doing any work, but living apparently without effort. He was disliked and feared, but the folk made no protest – at least to Sebastien. There was the case of Georges Famieux who threw Sebastien out of his barn one evening, and next morning found his prize cow with her throat torn. One remembered that sort of thing in a district where cows were scarce. So now the good Antoine pushed out his lips and nodded gravely.

"Yes," he said thoughtfully, "it can be nothing else."

A little silence fell in the cook's camp, and both men had a vision of Marie Fisette of the parish of Villeneuve, Marie the prettiest girl north of Cape Trinity, with her flaxen hair and white skin like milk and a smile that was remembered and treasured enviously in every lumber-camp on the Saguenay. They said that she chose Jean Deslormes when she saw him driving logs through the chute at Les Arables. And what Jean did then ought to be enough for any girl.

"They will be married this summer – yes?" asked Pierre.

And just at this moment the door opened without sound, and Sebastien himself strolled in. He rubbed his long hands to set the blood going, glanced shrewdly at the two men and stared meaningly toward the heaped platters on the stove. Pierre gave him food, this being the law of the wilderness, while Antoine began to re-arrange his stock. Both were a little breathless. Presently Sebastien pushed away his plate.

"Without doubt, Pierre, you are the best cook in the Saguenay camps. I will tell them so in Villeneuve." He lit his pipe and began to smoke contentedly.

"You go then to Villeneuve?" hazarded Antoine.

"Yes, I start at once, this very day."

"By the Saguenay trail?"

Sebastien sent him an inscrutable smile. "My trail is my own, Antoine," then, meaningly, "let him follow who can."

"It is ninety miles to Villeneuve as the goose flies. What takes you there in mid-winter?"

"The thing that takes all men to all places no matter what the season. The face of a woman."

Pierre lifted a kettle from the stove, and the lid rattled. "Is it then that Sebastien marries at his age?"

"What is age to the man who desires? In five days I shall have what has been desired by many."

He announced this in a voice that lifted as he spoke, and surveyed the others with burning, insolent eyes as though daring them to protest. There was in his manner something suggesting that he had at his disposal powers of which they knew nothing. He leaned a little forward, every line of his sinewy body resembling an animal crouched to spring, and there was but one animal in the minds of the others. He was known to travel swiftly, and always alone, but no man had ever found his tracks. And though he could not marry till after he had been in Villeneuve for at least three days, he now stated he would marry in five. That left two days to cover ninety miles, measured as the goose flies. There was but one beast in the big timber that could travel like this. Antoine glanced furtively at Pierre, and the latter gave the faintest nod. 'Loup Garou,' their lips signalled.

Sebastien got up, stretched himself, gave a short laugh and strode to the door. "For a good dinner, bien merci, mon vieux. It is I who shall feed you when the logs come down past Villeneuve in the spring. Every woman of the family of Fisette is an incomparable cook. We shall be ready, Marie and I."

For a moment after he disappeared there was silence in the camp, till both men stepped quickly to the window. Sebastien had reached the ice, and putting on his snowshoes already struck southward across Lac St. Luc. He walked swiftly, dwindling as they watched to a dark speck that vanished round a nearby point. Then Antoine looked at his friend and swore a great oath.

"Jean – where is Jean?"

"He comes with the sawyers in ten minutes. But wait, will call them now."

Pierre went out and smote with a poker on a large steel triangle that hung close to the door. Straightway the woods throbbed with a clear singing note that lifted through the green tops and caused a dropping of axes and cessation of droning saws, till down the winter roads trooped the lumberjacks, hungry as bears and chanting musically of Alluette and La Claire Fontaine. At their head came Jean Delormes, a young, tawny-haired giant, straight as a hemlock and shouldered like a bull moose. He caught sight of Antoine outside the camp, and, running forward, flung round him a pair of gigantic arms.

"Ah, c'est le vieux Papa Carnot. When didst thou arrive, and hast thou perchance been at a place called Villeneuve?"

Antoine struggled for breath, "I would first that some young fools learn their strength – and use it less," he gasped – then, in a whisper, "No, I have not visited Villeneuve since a fortnight past, but—"

"A fortnight! That is but a moment, while I have not been there for two months. Is there nothing then, to tell me, no message?"

"Shout not thy love to the whole camp, my son. There was one here a moment ago who even now is on his way to Villeneuve."

"Have you then sold all your stock to the good Pierre, and send out for more?"

Antoine shook his head. "The name of the traveller is Sebastien, and he goes fast."

"Le Loup Garou," said Jean grimly. "But why to Villeneuve?"

"In search of one Marie Fisette, who he swears will be his in the space of five days. My son will need all his strength, and must act very quickly. Let go, Jean, you break my arm!"

"He took what trail – quick!" Jean swayed a little, with such a tremor as runs through the brown column of a pine when the saw eats at its heart.

"He said that his trail was his own, and that any might follow who could, then struck south around the point. Shut up thy Marie in thy breast, my son, and hasten; but" – and here Antoine sent him an eloquent glance – "search not always for the form of a man as you travel."

Jean hurled himself into the sleeping-camp.

In ten minutes he was out on the ice, and, clearing the strewn logs, swung forward toward the first southerly point of Lac St. Luc. Thus led Sebastien's trail – long, narrow tracks with the points of the shoes turned up a little more than was usual in a bush country and the tail of one with an outward twist. He would remember that. They took him round that point, straight as an arrow-flight past the next one and on to a glassy patch where the water had come up and turned a mile of Lac St. Luc into a looking-glass. Here he slipped off his shoes, trotted across and cast about close to the shore line. There was no more trail. He stood for a moment, shaking his head like a great puzzled dog. This was the trail that any might follow who could! His lips became dry as he doubled back, and, picking up his own tracks, traversed the edge of the patch till he came to them again. "By Gar!" he whispered. "By Gar!"

Eighty miles due south was Villeneuve, with Marie and tinkling sleigh-bells and pearl-grey smoke climbing from heaped roofs. Somewhere to the south was something nosing swiftly through the big timber. "Search not always for the form of a man," Antoine had said. Jean jerked out a tense petition to St. Joseph, patron and guardian of the family Fisette, then put on his shoes.

There was moonlight by seven. It turned the snow to a pale purple, on which blue-black shadows of big timber lay in wide and parallel bars. He tramped across these, bar to bar, leaning forward with massive arms swinging, his legs working like pistons; a vast engine of a man moving in a white flurry and spouting deep-drawn jets of vapour. There was no sound save the creak of shoes, and a muffled thud as some overburdened cedar doffed its load of snow and straightened its tender branches in the stinging air. Presently he came to a frozen swamp.

On the other side of this, where the shadows began again, stood a lone wolf.

It vanished as he stared, merging like one shadow into another. Jean paused for a moment while a new thought dawned, and struck off sharp to the right. Two hundred yards away he found it – a wolf track – the triangular pad with the long sharp projecting toe and narrow trailing heel. He followed this back a quarter-mile, noting that it paralleled his own, curving where his curved and holding south for Villeneuve. And then Jean knew.

At four in the morning the moon went down in a bank of cloud. Came a whine of wind and a few drifting flakes. The woods grew dark. By this time Jean was very hungry, and therefore felt cold, for in these latitudes the body, like a boiler, demands fuel. He shoveled aside the snow, made fire and tea, searching the gloom with quick and furtive glances, crossing himself between gulps. In ten minutes he heard a rabbit squeal. That meant death in the ground hemlock near by. Something else was feeding there, and resting – resting.

As the goose flies it is ninety miles from the camp on St. Luc to Villeneuve, but as man travels not less than a hundred. As a wolf might go it is perhaps ninety-five. At sunrise Jean knew it was the same this time for man and wolf. There was not so much concealment now. He saw the gaunt, grey form flitting, wraith-like, between brown trunks, a malign beast with deep, lean shoulders and bony, arrow-shaped head. It rested when he rested, ate when he ate – and kept always a little in advance.

By mid-afternoon it became difficult to think of anything else and he grew very sleepy. It was only the vision of Marie with her flaxen hair, her smiling mouth and white arms that held him awake. At sundown he knew that he must sleep if only for half an hour, or he would lose his way. There were no stars this time, and no moon. He made two fires of green birch-logs, laid spruce-boughs between them, pulled the hood of his capote over his nose and stretched out.

Instantly, it seemed he began to dream. There was no loup garou now, but only love and the whiteness of his girl's shoulder. At this unction his body yielded, his great muscles relaxed; till, smiling, he plunged into an abyss of slumber, lulled by tiny, crepitant voices from the surrounding forest. Then, horribly, the dream became distorted. Marie's face, so close to his own, changed to a grinning mask with black lifted lips, fat, sleek skull and malevolent yellow eyes. The yellow gave place to black. They were the eyes of Sebastien. Simultaneously came a strange warmth on his cheeks. He blinked. Something was staring at him, something so near that it shut out the rest of the world. He gave a cry and sprang to his feet. There was a scramble in the snow by the spruce-boughs. Jean Deslornes was alone again.

"Que le bon Dieu nous sauvasit!" he whispered, trembling.

From a southward ridge came answer, not by le bon Dieu, but the wild and haunting voice of the grey wolf. Through the big timber it drifted, savage, remote, but inescapable, the note of terror that in a season of the year carries its own message to fur and hide on the foothills of the Laurentians. To Jean it also carried a message, and he flung himself forward. It could not now be more than thirty miles to Villeneuve. He swung on, summoning his vast reserve of strength, plunging through underbrush where once he would have gone round, himself now a thing of the woods in the manner of his going – this giant with the mind of a child. He stayed not to rest or eat; he looked not again for the grey shape. Then a remembered hilltop – a winter road for drawing wood – an outlying pasture – the bark of a distant dog – and below, in the valley, revealed in the half-light of dawn, the spire of a church and the forty farms they called Villeneuve. Into the crisping air climbed forty pencils of pearl smoke, like the exhalations of those who slumbered yet a while ere facing the rigour of the day.

Jean tore downhill to the house of Marthe Fisette, the mother of Marie. It seemed that all was safe here. He paused at the door, heard inside the crackling of a fire, and knocked. At sight of him the old woman dropped an armful of wood.

"Jean!" she stammered, "how came you here?"

"As flies the goose from Lac St. Luc," he said, breathing hard; "and Marie?"

Marthe did not answer that, but stared at him wonderingly and with a touch of awe. "It is undoubtedly the good God who has sent you, but how did you know?"

"Antoine Carnot told me; and, hearing it, I waited for nothing—" He broke off, staring back. "Then it is true?"

"Sebastien?" Her lips framed the name.

He nodded. "Le Loup Garou! Together we have come from the camp on Lac St. Luc, and this morning he also is in Villeneuve, but in what form I know not. Last night when for a moment I closed my eyes he came and crouched beside me, breathing in my face, and would have torn my throat had I not suddenly awakened. I brought no gun, for one cannot kill a loup garou except with a bullet that has been blessed, and there was no priest on Lac St. Luc."

Marthe crossed herself fervently. "That is true – always it has been so."

"And the friends here – what do they say?"

"They shrug their shoulders – and say nothing. It is not well to quarrel with Sebastien. There is that affair of the good Famieux – a thing all remember."

"And Marie?" he demanded.

Marthe sent him a wintry smile. "Look over your shoulder, my son."

She was halfway down the ladder-stair from the room above; Marie with thick, yellow, knitted strands down her back, great, slumbrous roses in her smooth cheeks and drowsy love in her blue eyes. Jean gave a huge, gusty sigh of delight, put out his mighty arms and lifted her as one picks up an acorn. She hid her face in his capote.

"My little one," he said softly, "my little partridge; thou art safe here, very safe."

Presently they put food before him, and he ate ravenously, telling in snatches of the trip from Lac St. Luc – "ninety-five miles in forty-two hours, by Gar!" while Marie clucked over him as though she were indeed a hen partridge, and Marthe busied herself without words between stove and table. Then Jean got up.

"I go now to Pere Leduc, for we shall be married in three days. Also there is the matter of blessing some bullets." He paused, and waved a hand at the encircling bush. "It is there I shall use them."

"I also shall go," said Marie, divided between love and fear.

He shook his great head. "Such talk is not for my little bird, but thou shalt go so far as the store, and wait there. In three days my soul shall go everywhere with me. Be content, my swallow."

They went off down the packed road, where the snowplough had left four-foot ridges on either side, down to the store which was diagonally opposite the church and the house of the good Father. Here Jean left her clasped to the expansive bosom of Madame Famieux, crossed the road, kicked his shoe-packs clean and found Pere Leduc in his book-lined study. And books were precious north of the Laurentians. He spoke first of his heart's desire.

The Father nodded, smiling. He loved this young Anak, this son of the wilderness, with his great thews and child-like heart. Wise and tender was Pere Leduc, a pure flame that glowed constantly, healing both minds and souls with a wide spiritual paternity.

"It is well for you both – and the good Marthe agrees?"

Jean nodded.

"Then I will call your names at vespers this very night, so that it may take place in three days. A good girl, your Marie. You go yourself back to Lac St. Luc?"

No, Jean would not do that. He had saved eight hundred dollars for a farm – and the farm of Georges Laurier was it not in the market? He paused a moment.

"There is another matter. *Mon pere* – that of these bullets." He held out a dozen, cupped in a gigantic palm. "May it please you to bless them?"

Pere Leduc shook his head gently. Had he not been very wise he would have laughed. He knew – knew all about it. Individually he knew more than the entire village put together. Part of his strength was that he only revealed a fraction of his knowledge. And now he wanted to hear what this enormous child had to say – all of it.

"Tell me, my son."

Jean told him, from the very start, touching not on the physical marvel of the trip – for to Jean it was no marvel – but only on its terror. How did Sebastien leave the flooded patch on Lac St. Luc? What became of his shoes when he turned into a wolf. What did he mean by breathing in Jean's face? Why did he lead the way to Villeneuve? And most of all, what was the import of his boast about Marie? There must be an end to this – the end brought by a bullet that had been blessed. All Villeneuve was waiting for that.

Pere Leduc put his hand on the young giant's shoulder, and spoke of tradition and legends and the powers of evil. "No, my son, you yourself are about to give answer to Sebastien – a final answer. You and this dear daughter of the parish will have my blessing, and not these bullets. When in three days you leave the church with Marie on your arm and joy in your heart you will have replied to Sebastien. He will have written himself down as a loud-speaking fool at whom not only the village of Villeneuve will laugh. That laugh will run up and down the

Saguenay, till he will wish to walk into the stream itself to escape it. As for what you saw and searched for, but did not find on your way here, when the mind of a man be distraught with weariness, and perhaps fear, there is not much of which he can be very sure. You have had an evil dream, but it is past. Go now, my son, and take peace and happiness with you. Le bon Dieu is not forgetful of his children on the Saguenay."

Jean went out, cheered but not convinced. It was all very well to talk like that. But he knew, while the good Father had not been on the trail from St. Luc. He rubbed the bullets together in his pocket, stalked across to the store and gathered in Marie.

"Behold my wife in three days – this little spruce partridge," he said to the fat Madame Famieux. "*Viens donc, cherie*; there is much to talk of."

Up the shining road, arms linked, they walked, while Jean told her the words of Pere Leduc. Nor was Marie convinced. The good Father had never felt Sebastien's burning eyes, nor could he understand what it meant to a girl to shrink and quiver beneath that insolent stare till she became weak and helpless like a bird in a net.

"It is but one thing we shall do, Jean."

"What is that, my dove?"

"You shall meet Sebastien and take his promise, or make it, that there is an end to all this."

"Of what value then is the word of a wolf, could he speak it?" grunted Jean. Then, looking up, his heart leaped. Sebastien had rounded a bend in the road and came straight toward them. Marie saw him, shivered and clung the closer.

"Jean," she whispered, "not now!"

Drawing nearer he walked more slowly, staring first at the giant with strange, inscrutable gaze, then at Marie with a wild, unhuman hunger. His cheeks were hollow, but he moved lightly on his feet. They were not the feet of a man who had travelled ninety miles in forty-two hours – or less. He came level with them. Marie found herself pushed gently forward and past him. Jean stood motionless, every sinew in him turned to fire.

"Loup Garou," he said thickly, "Loup Garou, what seek you now?"

Sebastien did not speak, but lowered his lids, and from hot, half-veiled eyes sent the big man a look of contemptuous pity. So keen was it, so utterly penetrating, that Jean felt as though a hand were fumbling in his breast and groping for secrets. Then, as Sebastien was about to pass on, a mighty arm shot out and took him by the throat. He was shaken as a wolverine shakes a rabbit, shaken till his teeth chattered and flung headlong into the crusted snow. Jean turned on his heel and followed Marie.

"It is done, my turtle – and the wolf did not bark."

Late that night, after Jean had gone to sleep at the farm of Christophe Famieux, Marie talked long with her mother and told her the words of Pere Leduc. Marthe could make no answer to these words, but found them nevertheless devoid of comfort. Presently she climbed the stair ladder, returning with a small image of St. Joseph, patron saint to every good Fisette.

"It is lead," she murmured, "and from Ste. Anne de Beaupre it came, where it was blessed by his Eminence from Quebec. Is it not that the head of the holy man is of the size of a bullet?"

Marie nodded, her eyes brightening.

"Then the rest of it I leave to thee, my pigeon. When thy mountain of a husband shall take thee from me in a sleigh to Beaulieu on the third day from this, see that the short gun of Christophe be thus loaded, and near at hand under the robes. It is in my mind that there will be need of that gun."

So on the third day, Gaston Roubidoux, sacristan, sent a rocking peal from the wooden church, and those of Villeneuve came in box-like sleighs stuffed with straw, and drawn by short-legged, round-bodied Percheron horses, to see the union of Jean and Marie – doubly intriguing because it spelled the humiliation of Le Loup Garou. Marie was all in white, with everlastings in her hair; Jean in a new, tight and very bright blue suit into which he just wedged his great body, celluloid collar anchored by a large rolled-gold stud, yellow tie and patent-leather shoes that hurt abominably. Then Pere Leduc spoke words of peace and love, after which they all went to the house of Christophe, the largest in the village, where was given the marriage feast, with riotous quadrilles and great good feeling. And Sebastien had not been seen by anyone since three days – which added not a little to the general hilarity.

Beaulieu lay thirty miles away – or was it only three? Jean, being dizzy with happiness and pride, was not quite sure when at sunset he tucked his girl into the sleigh, wrapping the robes closely round her feet. There was plenty of straw underneath. Marthe had seen to that. The horses, pet team of Christophe, arching their glossy necks, dashed off with a jangle of bells amid laughter and cheers. The good Father nodded contentedly and turned homeward. These children of his – how gay and handsome they were!

Halfway to Beaulieu – the horses going like playful kittens – Marie pressing to his side – frosty roses in her cheeks – the blue eyes like stars – with all this Jean could hardly believe his own good fortune. What a noble day it had been, and how many others, even more wonderful, lay ahead!

His feet were now very sore – that being from the dancing-his collar-stud was boring a hole in his gullet, but he was bursting with joy.

"My love," he breathed, "my soul – my little ptarmigan!"

Just at this moment there came from a belt of cedar hard by the pulsing howl of a timber wolf. Marie heard and shivered. Jean heard, and his heart stopped, then began to race. The Percherons heard, whinnied their alarm and plunged forward. Jean, gripping the reins, lashed out till the woods streamed past in a blur. If the road only held open he could make Beaulieu in an hour.

They swung into a clearing where the wind had got at the snow and the road was drifted level. Knee-deep toiled the Percherons, heads down, backs rippled with straining muscles. Jean stood up. Something shot across just ahead, turned, doubled back and made a ripping, darting stroke at the throat of the nearest horse.

"Quick, Jean, under the straw at my feet – the gun of Christophe with the head of St. Joseph!" panted Marie.

He wondered what St. Joseph had to do with it, but a gun was a gun, and, burrowing swiftly, he recognised the short, single-barrelled muzzle-loader with half-inch bore. Pushing the reins into the girl's hands, he cuddled his cheek against the brown stock – and waited. The near Percheron was bleeding at the throat. Again that lean, darting form, ears flattened back on the sleek skull, again the curving attack rapid as light.

The wolf was in mid-air when the foresight covered a grey shoulder for a fraction of time. Jean crooked his finger – saw horses rearing in a tangle of harness – heard Marie cry out in a jangle of bells. Then a lank, hairy body seemed to have been thrust away, and stretched, twitching, just ahead of the driving hoofs.

He snatched back the reins, forced on the Percherons and fetched them up, quivering, on top of the thing on the road. Here for a deadly second the steel-shod, dancing feet hammered down – down, till what lay beneath was a shapeless lump of bloody hide. Marie covered her eyes, but Jean, soothing his team, stared at it hard before he bent over and kissed the roses back to her cheeks. It was in his mind that the eyes of this wolf, instead of being long and yellow, had been large and dark and burning. They did not burn now. But he said nothing of this.

"My little weasel spoke of the gun of Christophe with the head of the good St. Joseph," he smiled. "And what did she mean by that?"

Marie told him, and for months after that there was little talk of Sebastien. Then summer arrived. The logs from St. Luc began to come down the Saguenay, and Jean was persuaded to help the drive through the chute of Les Arables. Marie went with him, and so it happened that Pierre Colange on a certain day did indeed sit at the table of an incomparable cook. The shanty that Jean knocked together stood close to the river, and the table was outside. They were talking of Sebastien when Pierre got up, shaded his eyes and stared hard at the tawny water.

"It has been in my mind, *mon vieux*, that we should meet him yet once again. What is that between the two hemlocks?"

He had come down with the logs – come from the unknown – and circled slowly in a great eddy. The smooth face was still unscarred. One sodden arm rested on the ribbed bark. The eddy brought him toward shore, bobbing as though something were twitching at his heels. The three gazed at each other, till Jean, remembering the prophecy of Pere Leduc, lifted his brows and signalled.

"Go inside a moment, my little beaver. It is not for thee to see."

There is a cross underneath a jack-pine just below that eddy. Jean hewed it. On a flat stone at the foot is a small leaden image without a head. That was the thought of Marie. On the cross Pierre Colange, with some misgivings, put the name – one word. He could not decide what else, under the circumstances, one might safely say. It stood there after the drive went on and the following sweep had cleared every stranded log. Squirrels perched on it, rabbits hopped about it, red-headed woodpeckers sometimes tried their strength on its tough fibre. But nothing happened till Antoine Carnot passed in the autumn.

He saw it, read the one word and exactly appreciated the difficulty. So, smiling, he lit his pipe, squatted close, and began to carve with firm, deep strokes.

"Sebastien. Le Loup Garou," read the next lumberjack who came that way.

No Eye-Witnesses

Henry S. Whitehead

THERE WERE BLOOD stains on Everard Simon's shoes... Simon's father had given up his country house in Rye when his wife died, and moved into an apartment in Flatbush among the rising apartment houses which were steadily replacing the original rural atmosphere of that residential section of swelling Brooklyn.

Blood stains – and forest mold – on his shoes!

The younger Simon – he was thirty-seven, his father getting on toward seventy – always spent his winters in the West Indies, returning in the spring, going back again in October. He was a popular writer of informative magazine articles. As soon as his various visits for weekends and odd days were concluded, he would move his trunks into the Flatbush apartment and spend a week or two, sometimes longer, with his father. There was a room for him in the apartment, and this he would occupy until it was time for him to leave for his summer camp in the Adirondacks. Early in September he would repeat the process, always ending his autumn stay in the United States with his father until it was time to sail back to St. Thomas or Martinique or wherever he imagined he could write best for that particular winter.

There was only one drawback in this arrangement. This was the long ride in the subway necessitated by his dropping in to his New York club every day. The club was his real American headquarters. There he received his mail. There he usually lunched and often dined as well. It was at the club that he received his visitors and his telephone calls. The club was on Forty-Fourth Street, and to get there from the apartment he walked to the Church Avenue subway station, changed at De Kalb Avenue, and then took a Times Square express train over the Manhattan Bridge. The time consumed between the door of the apartment and the door of the club was exactly three-quarters of an hour, barring delays. For the older man the arrangement was ideal. He could be in his office, he boasted, in twenty minutes.

To avoid the annoyances of rush hours in the subway, Mr. Simon senior commonly left home quite early in the morning, about seven o'clock. He was a methodical person, always leaving before seven in the morning, and getting his breakfast in a downtown restaurant near the office. Everard Simon rarely left the apartment until after nine, thus avoiding the morning rush-hour at its other end. During the five or six weeks every year that they lived together the two men really saw little of each other, although strong bonds of understanding, affection, and respect bound them together. Sometimes the older man would awaken his son early in the morning for a brief conversation. Occasionally the two would have a meal together, evenings, or on Sundays; now and then an evening would be spent in each other's company. They had little to converse about. During the day they would sometimes call each other up and speak together briefly on the telephone from club to office or office to club. On the day when Everard Simon sailed south, his father and he always took a farewell luncheon together somewhere downtown. On the day of his return seven months later, his father always made it a point to meet him at the dock. These arrangements had prevailed for eleven years. He must get that blood wiped off. Blood! How—?

During that period, the neighborhood of the apartment had changed out of all recognition. Open lots, community tennis-courts, and many of the older one-family houses had disappeared, to be replaced by the ubiquitous apartment houses. In 1928 the neighborhood which had been almost rural when the older Simon had taken up his abode 'twenty minutes from his Wall Street office' was solidly built up except for an occasional, and now incongruous, frame house standing lonely and dwarfed in its own grounds among the towering apartment houses, like a lost child in a preoccupied crowd of adults whose business caused them to look over the child's head.

* * *

One evening, not long before the end of his autumn sojourn in Flatbush, Everard Simon, having dined alone in his club, started for the Times Square subway station about a quarter before nine. Doubled together lengthwise, and pressing the pocket of his coat out of shape, was a magazine, out that day, which contained one of his articles. He stepped on board a waiting Sea Beach express train, in the rearmost car, sat down, and opened the magazine, looking down the table of contents to find his article. The train started after the ringing of the warning bell and the automatic closing of the side doors, while he was putting on his reading-spectacles. He began on the article.

He was dimly conscious of the slight bustle of incoming passengers at Broadway and Canal Street, and again when the train ran out on the Manhattan Bridge because of the change in the light, but his closing of the magazine with a page-corner turned down, and the replacing of the spectacles in his inside pocket when the train drew in to De Kalb Avenue, were almost entirely mechanical. He could make that change almost without thought. He had to cross the platform here at De Kalb Avenue, get into a Brighton Beach local train. The Brighton Beach expresses ran only in rush hours and he almost never travelled during those periods.

He got into his train, found a seat, and resumed his reading. He paid no attention to the stations – Atlantic and Seventh Avenues. The next stop after that, Prospect Park, would give him one of his mechanical signals, like coming out on the bridge. The train emerged from its tunnel at Prospect Park, only to re-enter it again at Parkside Avenue, the next following station. After that came Church Avenue, where he got out every evening.

As the train drew in to that station, he repeated the mechanics of turning down a page in the magazine, replacing his spectacles in their case, and putting the case in his inside pocket. His mind entirely on the article, he got up, left the train, walked back toward the Caton Avenue exit, started to mount the stairs.

A few moments later he was walking, his mind still entirely occupied with his article, in the long-familiar direction of his father's apartment.

The first matter which reminded him of his surroundings was the contrast in his breathing after the somewhat stuffy air of the subway train. Consciously he drew in a deep breath of the fresh, sweet outdoor air. There was a spicy odor of wet leaves about it somehow. It seemed, as he noticed his environment with the edge of his mind, darker than usual. The crossing of Church and Caton Avenues was a brightly lighted corner. Possibly something was temporarily wrong with the lighting system. He looked up. Great trees nodded above his head. He could see the stars twinkling above their lofty tops. The sickle edge of a moon cut sharply against black branches moving gently in a fresh wind from the sea.

He walked on several steps before he paused, slackened his gait, then stopped dead, his mind responding in a note of quiet wonderment.

Great trees stood all about him. From some distance ahead a joyous song in a manly bass, slightly muffled by the wood of the thick trees, came to his ears. It was a song new to him. He found himself listening to it eagerly. The song was entirely strange to him, the words unfamiliar. He listened intently. The singer came nearer. He caught various words, English words. He distinguished "merry", and "heart", and "repine".

It seemed entirely natural to be here, and yet, as he glanced down at his brown clothes, his highly polished shoes, felt the magazine bulging his pocket, the edge of his mind caught a note of incongruity. He remembered with a smile that strange drawing of Aubrey Beardsley's, of a lady playing an upright cottage pianoforte in the midst of a field of daisies! He stood, he perceived, in a kind of rough path worn by long usage. The ground was damp underfoot. Already his polished shoes were soiled with mold.

The singer came nearer and nearer. Obviously, as the fresh voice indicated, it was a young man. Just as the voice presaged that before many seconds the singer must come out of the screening array of tree boles, Everard Simon was startled by a crashing, quite near by, at his right. The singer paused in the middle of a note, and for an instant there was a primeval silence undisturbed by the rustle of a single leaf.

Then a huge timber wolf burst through the underbrush to the right, paused, crouched, and sprang, in a direction diagonal to that in which Everard Simon was facing, toward the singer.

* * *

Startled into a frigid immobility, Simon stood as though petrified. He heard an exclamation, in the singer's voice, a quick "heh"; then the sound of a struggle. The great wolf, apparently, had failed to knock down his quarry. Then without warning, the two figures, man and wolf, came into plain sight; the singer, for so Simon thought of him, a tall, robust fellow, in fringed deerskin, slashing desperately with a hunting-knife, the beast crouching now, snapping with a tearing motion of a great punishing jaw. Short-breathed "heh's" came from the man, as he parried dexterously the lashing snaps of the wicked jaws.

The two, revolving about each other, came very close. Everard Simon watched the struggle, fascinated, motionless. Suddenly the animal shifted its tactics. It backed away stealthily, preparing for another spring. The young woodsman abruptly dropped his knife, reached for the great pistol which depended from his belt in a rough leather holster. There was a blinding flash, and the wolf slithered down, its legs giving under it. A great cloud of acrid smoke drifted about Everard Simon, cutting off his vision; choking smoke which made him cough.

But through it, he saw the look of horrified wonderment on the face of the young woodsman; saw the pistol drop on the damp ground as the knife had dropped; followed with his eyes, through the dimming medium of the hanging smoke, the fascinated, round-eyed stare of the man who had fired the pistol.

There, a few feet away from him, he saw an eldritch change passing over the beast, shivering now in its death-struggle. He saw the hair of the great paws dissolve, the jaws shorten and shrink, the lithe body buckle and heave strangely. He closed his eyes, and when he opened them, he saw the figure in deerskins standing mutely over the body of a man, lying prone across tree-roots, a pool of blood spreading, spreading, from the concealed face, mingling with the damp earth under the tree-roots.

Then the strange spell of quiescence which had held him in its weird thrall was dissolved, and, moved by a nameless terror, he ran, wildly, straight down the narrow path between the trees…

* * *

It seemed to him that he had been running only a short distance when something, the moon above the trees, perhaps, began to increase in size, to give a more brilliant light. He slackened his pace. The ground now felt firm underfoot, no longer damp, slippery. Other lights joined that of the moon. Things became brighter all about him, and as this brilliance increased, the great trees all about him turned dim and pale. The ground was now quite hard underfoot. He looked up. A brick wall faced him. It was pierced with windows. He looked down. He stood on pavement. Overhead a streetlight swung lightly in the late September breeze. A faint smell of wet leaves was in the air, mingled now with the fresh wind from the sea. The magazine was clutched tightly in his left hand. He had, it appeared, drawn it from his pocket. He looked at it curiously, put it back into the pocket.

He stepped along over familiar pavement, past well-known facades. The entrance to his father's apartment loomed before him. Mechanically he thrust his left hand into his trousers pocket. He took out his key, opened the door, traversed the familiar hallway with its rugs and marble walls and bracket side-wall light-clusters. He mounted the stairs, one flight, turned the corner, reached the door of the apartment, let himself in with his key.

It was half-past nine and his father had already retired. They talked through the old man's bedroom door, monosyllabically. The conversation ended with the request from his father that he close the bedroom door. He did so, after wishing the old man good-night.

He sat down in an armchair in the living-room, passed a hand over his forehead, bemused. He sat for fifteen minutes. Then he reached into his pocket for a cigarette. They were all gone. Then he remembered that he had meant to buy a fresh supply on his way to the apartment. He had meant to get the cigarettes from the drug-store between the Church Avenue subway station and the apartment! He looked about the room for one. His father's supply, too, seemed depleted.

He rose, walked into the entry, put on his hat, stepped out again into the hallway, descended the one flight, went out into the street. He walked into an unwonted atmosphere of excitement. People were conversing as they passed, in excited tones; about the drug-store entrance a crowd was gathered. Slightly puzzled, he walked toward it, paused, blocked, on the outer edge.

"What's happened?" he inquired of a young man whom he found standing just beside him, a little to the fore.

"It's a shooting of some kind," the young man explained. "I only just got here myself. The fellow that got bumped off is inside the drug-store, bathroom and prepared for his morning – what's left of him. Some gang-war stuff, I guess."

He walked away, skirting the rounded edge of the clustering crowd of curiosity mongers, proceeded down the street, procured the cigarettes elsewhere. He passed the now enlarged crowd on the other side of the street on his way back, returned to the apartment, where he sat, smoking and thinking, until eleven, when he retired. Curious – a man shot; just at the time, or about the time, he had let that imagination of his get the better of him – those trees!

* * *

His father awakened him about five minutes before seven. The old man held a newspaper in his hand. He pointed to a scare-head on the front page.

"This must have happened about the time you came in," remarked Mr. Simon.

"Yes – the crowd was around the drugstore when I went out to get some cigarettes," replied Everard Simon, stretching and yawning.

When his father was gone and he had finished with his bath, he sat down, in a bathrobe, to glance over the newspaper account. A phrase arrested him:

"…the body was identified as that of 'Jerry the Wolf', a notorious gangster with a long prison record." Then, lower down, when he had resumed his reading:

"…a large-caliber bullet which, entering the lower jaw, penetrated the base of the brain… no eye-witnesses…"

Everard Simon sat for a long time after he had finished the account, the newspaper on the floor by his chair. "No eyewitnesses!" He must, really, keep that imagination of his within bounds, within his control.

Slowly and reflectively, this good resolution uppermost, he went back to the bathroom and prepared for his morning shave.

Putting on his shoes, in his room, he observed something amiss. He picked up a shoe, examined it carefully. The soles of the shoes were caked with black mold, precisely like the mold from the woodpaths about his Adirondack camp. Little withered leaves and dried pine-needles clung to the mold. And on the side of the right shoe were brownish stains, exactly like freshly dried bloodstains. He shuddered as he carried the shoes into the bathroom, wiped them clean with a damp towel, then rinsed out the towel. He put them on, and shortly afterward, before he entered the subway to go over to the club for the day, he had them polished.

The bootblack spoke of the killing on that corner the night before. The bootblack noticed nothing amiss with the shoes, and when he had finished, there was no trace of any stains.

* * *

Simon did not change at De Kalb Avenue that morning. An idea had occurred to him between Church Avenue and De Kalb, and he stayed on the Brighton local, secured a seat after the emptying process which took place at De Kalb, and went on through the East River tunnel.

He sent in his name to Forrest, a college acquaintance, now in the district attorney's office, and Forrest received him after a brief delay.

"I wanted to ask a detail about this gangster who was killed in Flatbush last night," said Simon. "I suppose you have his record, haven't you?"

"Yes, we know pretty well all about him. What particular thing did you want to know?"

"About his name," replied Simon. "Why was he called 'Jerry the Wolf', that is, why 'The Wolf' particularly?"

"That's a very queer thing, Simon. Such a name is not, really, uncommon. There was that fellow, Goddard, you remember. They called him 'The Wolf of Wall Street'. There was the fiction criminal known as 'The Lone Wolf'. There have been plenty of 'wolves' among criminal 'monikers'. But this fellow, Jerry Goraffsky, was a Hungarian, really. He was called 'The Wolf' queerly enough, because there were those in his gang who believed he was one of those birds who could change himself into a wolf! It's a queer combination, isn't it? – For a New York gangster?"

"Yes," said Everard Simon, "it is, very queer, when you come to think of it. I'm much obliged to you for telling me. I was curious about it somehow."

"That isn't the only queer aspect of this case, however," resumed Forrest, a light frown suddenly showing on his keen face. "In fact that wolf-thing isn't a part of the case – doesn't concern us, of course, here in the district attorney's office. That's nothing but blah. Gangsters are as superstitious as sailors; more so, in fact!"

"No. The real mystery in this affair is – the bullet, Simon. Want to see it?"

"Why – yes; of course – if you like, Forrest. What's wrong with the bullet?"

Forrest stepped out of the room, returned at once, laid a large, round ball on his desk. Both men bent over it curiously.

"Notice that diameter, Simon," said Forrest. "It's a hand-molded round ball – belongs in a collection of curios, not in any gangster's gat! Why, man, it's like the slugs they used to hunt the bison before the old Sharps rifle was invented. It's the kind of a ball Fenimore Cooper's people used – 'Deerslayer!' It would take a young cannon to throw that thing. Smashed in the whole front of Jerry's ugly mug. The inside works of his head were spilled all over the sidewalk! It's what the newspapers always call a 'clue'. Who do you suppose resurrected the horse-pistol – or the ship's blunderbuss to do that job on Jerry? Clever, in a way. Hooked it out of some dime museum, perhaps. There are still a few of those old 'pitches' still operating, you know, at the old stand – along East Fourteenth Street."

"A flintlock, single-shot horse-pistol, I'd imagine," said Everard Simon, laying the ounce lead ball back on the mahogany desk. He knew something of weapons, new and old. As a writer of informational articles that was part of his permanent equipment.

"Very likely," mused the assistant district attorney. "Glad you came in, old man."

And Everard Simon went on uptown to his club.

He Who Would Chase the Sun

M.M. Williams

LONG AGO, far above the line of winter darkness, under the light of the longest day, a child took her first breath.

For most, the day was beautiful. Columns of smoke swirled above midsummer bonfires, and underneath, the people sang songs of gratitude as they danced, drank, made love, laughed. They told stories of battle and bloodshed, of wisdom and honor, loud enough for me to hear their words in the pauses between screams.

The midwives had long since rinsed the blood from their arms and departed. Sunlight streamed hot through our doorway as Mor's hand grew cold in my grasp. Within the hearth, the dying embers of our morning fire released their last breath of smoke. I had not been tending to it. I had forsaken all my chores to weep.

Yestermorn, I had dreamt of the day when the babe would be strong enough to venture outdoors, and I would proudly parade it in front of our friends and kin.

I could no longer dream. The future had become clear now, and it was bitter. Today, sadness in the form of salt would stream down our cheeks. Tomorrow, a new burial mound would take shape on the hill of the dead.

And for all days to come, I would have no sister, for I knew what was to happen.

She sat swaddled in my arms now, crying weakly for the nourishment an elder brother could not offer, as I read the lines of her face.

Even in his highest grief, Far knelt and spoke to me with kindness. "No other will take her to nurse. That is no life for a little one. Let us spare her the suffering of starvation and allow her to die with honor."

She was such a small thing, scrunched and pink, her fingers tucked against her chin. Had fate chosen differently, I knew that she would have been fair as the stars. As fierce as fire.

"I will do it," I said through a burning throat. "I will take her."

I looked over the bedcushion, the pale skin and sweat-sodden ropes of flaxen hair and eyes of darkest brown. I wondered if the babe would have resembled her, or if, like me, she would have taken after Far, with hair nearly black.

Miniature fingers curled around my thumb, gripping hard.

"Shall we give her a name?" I asked.

Far's dark eyes welled with tears. "To name her is to murder her."

A sob of my own began to grow. "No one shall know but us. She fought to enter this realm. She ought to receive at least one gift from it before they carry her away."

He placed her upon his knee, welcoming her – however briefly – to our family line. "A midsummer's child." He pressed one kiss to her brow, his shaking hand a cap over her fuzz-strewn head. "Sol."

It was a fine name. A worthy name for a child of the longest day, and one who had so valiantly endured a breech birth. He kissed her twice more and released her to my charge. I tucked Sol against my chest, muttering to soothe her distress, and left.

Once outside, I stopped briefly to look over the goats. The labor had stolen our eyes and ears too long for us to notice that one of the kids had died sometime in the night – at the hands of a hound, it seemed, though she had not been devoured.

I bent my head and continued toward the mountain, toward the trail of the lost. The dances and poems halted as I passed. If the midwives had not yet informed them, then my presence with the babe was announcement enough. All heads bowed as I made my procession to the trees, up the hillside, to the altar where the troll-wives collected their offerings.

It was a mere slab, nestled in the belly of a stone circle. Here, we lay all new life we could not care for. Here, our elders came to sit in a final act of valor when they grew close to death. Most years, these rituals were enough to satisfy the creatures' lust for living blood.

In our darkest years, another soul had to be chosen, offered as sacrifice, lest they descend upon us all.

I had seen one, once, as a child. In a fit of curiosity, I had hidden in a nearby tree, disguising my scent with ashes and herbs, and watched every moment as they came under the safety of night, driven blackened teeth into a grey-haired fisherman, slurped and slobbered and slinked back into the dark with bulging bellies. In mere minutes, my sister would join those dead. Though the sun would not fully rest today, the rock pillars of the mountain would provide shadow enough for them to reach the altar and take her back to their wretched caves.

She held tight to me, unaware of all danger, and inside my chest, my heart twisted to rope. My breath quickened. My eyes burned.

No. *No.*

I could not abandon my helpless sister to this circle of stone.

I held her closely once more, turning to run, and found myself trapped by fur and teeth. Endless eyes stared at me, deep as the sky. When I searched for the pupil within, I tumbled forward into a dark ocean. Through the black water, a woman ran, yellow hair streaming behind her like the tail of a fallen star, and behind her, an ink-coat wolf.

As fast as the vision had come, it fell away, and I stood once again in the woods, facing the beast. Whether the wolf was this one, I could not say, but I knew in my very soul that I had just seen little Sol, grown into womanhood.

"What do you want?" I asked the wolf.

It said nothing.

On my hip, I had only a filleting knife, but bravery could make swords of needles. I raised the blade. "You are no ordinary hill-hound, child of Loki. Tell me your business or let me pass."

He then bowed his head to address me, speaking as a man. "Mani, son of Gotr, born under full moon on the ninth hour of midwinter. You must not allow the life-drinkers to taste the blood of a midsummer's child, lest you give them power to feed when they please."

In shock, I lifted the babe and looked over her. "Her blood will allow them to walk in the sunlight?"

But no answer came, and when I turned to face him, the wolf was gone. I did not dare linger. I ran as only the wind could, to give Sol safety within the walls of our home, far from this cursed mountain.

When I burst through the doorway, I saw Mor first, shrouded and ready for burial. Far shot upward, standing straight as a pole, cold as stone.

"Tell me my eyes lie," he said, the words weak. "Tell me you have not done this."

"I will care for her."

Fury took him in an instant. "No! You have allowed your soft heart to grow so large that it blinds you! You walk to their mountain and then deny them their crimson mead? You will bring their wrath to us!"

"There is a guardian spirit, a black wolf, and she has received his blessing." I clutched Sol tightly, my arm a shield around her. "But spirits or not, I will not lose her on the same day I have lost my mother. The midnight sun will keep them back from the village."

"And how do you propose to feed her with your flat chest?" he demanded in anger, in fear, in despair. "Will she drink blood like the troll-wives? Will you offer her ale? Seawater?"

For that, I had no answer until a mournful bleat sounded. Together, we walked to our pen, to see the she-goat who had lost her kid, and I knew why the goatling had died. The wolf had cleared this trail for me, for her.

I looked to the sun and thanked it for the light that would serve as our armor for several weeks more. In that time, there would be milk enough for Sol. I held her beneath the goat, guided her toward the teat, and she drank.

"I am your brother, little dawn-blood, and I shall keep you safe," I promised her. "You shall never run alone."

* * *

Only moments after the Long Day first turned to dark, I heard the screams and shouts.

Far rushed to Sol's cradle, to hide her, as I exited into the night.

Moonlight shone strong. On the road stood not one troll-wife, but ten, each one tall and thin as a growing birch, draped in blue hair and cloaks of spider's webs. Underneath bulbous white eyes, their mouths bubbled over with yellowed fangs. Other men and women of the village had drawn their weapons, but the troll-wives had not yet attacked.

"What do you want?" I called.

The tallest lifted her nose to the sky, her cheeks twitching as she caught and recognized my scent. When she spoke to me, spittle flowed and dripped from her lips. "Where is the child of midsummer?"

"Dead from a harsh birth and lack of milk," I told them with ease, for I had already practiced the falsehood a hundred times. "It happened as I walked toward the altar. This is why I kept her back. She would have been a spoiled sacrifice, her blood dead and undrinkable."

"You lie!" the creature hissed.

I held my shoulders firm and repeated myself. "She was dead then and is dead now, already reclaimed by the soil. If you must drink today, take from me instead."

They approached. I bowed my head and waited for my end. Instead, she dragged a claw against her own skin, revealing blood as thick and dark as pitch.

The others descended fast, driving me to my knees, holding my head to the sky. No matter how I struggled, I could not break free, and the leader held her wound above me. Drops of black fell against my lips. With their gnarled hands at my jaw, I could not prevent it from entering my mouth and staining my tongue. My throat rejected it. Bitter, acrid venom.

"For your defiance," she snarled, "you will live as we do. The sun's rays will be as a sword through your breast. And you will watch now as we drain your kin."

After the words were said, Far suddenly left our home. "Begone, creatures of the corrupted mountain!" he thundered, holding forward Sol in her swaddled bundle. "Take the child and leave us!"

The troll-wives flicked out their tongues in bloodlust and abandoned me.

"No!" I cried, but they ran as birds, too fast to chase. They grabbed her from him and tore back up the mountainside, crawling over the trees and rock faces like dashing spiders.

Anger flared in my middle, and I turned to my father with hatred. "You've murdered her. You've murdered all of us!"

He did not cower, nor did he speak. Silently, he bade me follow him into our home. I did and was stunned at what awaited me. Safe with the stone walls was our little Sol, still resting in her cradle, asleep despite the commotion.

"I wrapped one of the young pigs," he explained. "The troll-wives cannot see as we can, and the babe's scent is on the cloth. They will not realize the deception until after they reach their home and drink."

The rotten taste of their blood lingered still on my tongue. "What will happen when they do?"

"Run, Mani." He grabbed a sack and began to fill it with what little food we had stored. "Tell the others, take as many as the boats will carry. You must run to the sea and venture down the coast."

Before tonight, I had not known that they would be aware of the gift within Sol's blood. Now, I understood their wrath would not die. After slaughtering whoever remained here, they would hunt all of us who ran, and we would not be able to go far. We had no vessels worthy of the open sea.

"You must come," I whispered, feeling quite young despite my sixteen years. "I cannot do this without you, not with their poison inside me."

"If even a few gain the power to walk in the sun, Norway will be lost to their hunt," he said, hands on my shoulders. "My fate is here, to hold them back and die with your mother. Your fate is elsewhere. Pray to the black wolf. He offered you his protection once before. Ask him to heed your call now."

I had no time to grieve. Fast as I could, I placed Sol in a basket and gathered all neighbors willing to come. We ran toward the coast, toward a lone howl. When we reached the docks, the wolf was there, and the sounds of battle began to ring upon the hills.

"Please," I begged him. "You must take them – take her – far from here. I will die when the morning comes. I cannot protect her."

"Cut some hair from my back," he ordered, "and then from your head, and bleed upon it."

I placed Sol in the arms of a friend and obeyed, shaving fur away from him and taking locks of my own, and I placed them upon the sand. I cut my arm and let the red rain fall.

Carefully, his great paws wove together his hair and mine, rinsing them with blood and seawater, and the form of a wolf took shape. Once his weaving was complete, he pressed his nose against the fur and breathed life into the new garment. He ordered me to lift and don it. I pulled the head of the Skin over my shoulders

My body bent forward, too far for normal man, and my spine cracked. Screams shook inside my changing throat, my lengthening mouth. Agony. Agony of broken bones, of torn muscles and cords and tissue. Like fire in my bloodways, it surged forward until it had reached every part of me.

At length, the anguish faded, as all things did. Strength from the moonlight filled my blood, and I stood from my rebirth on four legs.

Though animal in shape, I could still speak as man. "What am I to do?"

"When worn, you shall run as I do, hardened against their bite," he told me. "In the days, it shall shield your skin from the sunlight."

"Name the price," I said. "No gift as valuable as this is given freely."

"You will know when the time comes. For now, you must run, son of the moon."

Gently, I gathered Sol's basket in my jaw, and I did as he asked.

* * *

Fjord by fjord, for fifteen years, our people traveled south and north and south again, running from the vengeance of the troll-wives. Though we had learned rituals to hide our scent from them, they hunted so viciously that we could make no permanent home.

Someday, I wished for Sol to know a life within true walls, but for now, I knew that movement was all that could save her. In the days, I slept as a wolf. In the nights, I walked freely as a man, watching over my people with my weapon drawn.

One peaceful night, as we sat beside our fire, my sister collapsed to the earth, and I knew fear like I never had before.

"It burns!" she gasped, clawing at her neck, her arms with fervor enough to break the skin.

I rushed to her, gathering her up and taking her to her bedroll. In the safety of our tent, she did not writhe or weep.

Unease filled me. "When did this begin?"

Her voice was weak. "When I ate."

My alarm grew. All around us, people began to shout in pain, and I ordered them all into their shelters, out of the moon's glow. I ran to the water stream, fetched a bucket, and brought it back to our camp. I dipped my hand inside and found truth. The water had been tainted black.

In horror, I realized what had happened. A clever troll-wife had sent their poison from afar, and now all were cursed as I had been, but against the moon rather than the sunlight.

I put on my Skin and released a loud howl, calling the great wolf to listen. He arrived fast, listening to my prayer.

"The Long Night approaches, but Sol has been cursed and cannot bear the moon's light," I said. "Give her a Skin, and I shall do anything you ask of me."

He gave her the instructions he had once given me, but once again, he did not state his price. He ran, leaving me to watch her torment. Soon enough, the moonlight's burn ceased, and Sol stood in front of me as a white wolf.

"This gift must be shared," she told me. "They all carry the black poison. We cannot abandon them."

My heart grew heavy with sadness. "The wolf will not make so many Skins for us. He has already fled."

"Twice now you have watched him weave. Take my fur and do as he did."

Whether I could do such a thing, I did not know, but I would not abandon my people to painful nights. For hours, I cut hair from Sol's back and the heads of my kin, wove, and breathed upon the fur until my fingers cracked and bled with effort. Until nearly all the newly cursed were cloaked in pelt and fang.

They were lesser Skins, not as powerful as our own, but hearty enough to shield and strengthen. Only the smallest children remained uncloaked, their small bones yet unable to embrace the power of the change. When they grew, I would weave them Skins. Until then, we would shelter them carefully with wood and stone.

Together as wolves, we left behind our tents and began to build home.

* * *

Seven years passed before the Red Morning.

A cloud of great ash spread across the sky, coming steadily from the north until it had consumed every drop of sky blue. There was no moon, or starlight, or sun. Only crimson shadow and burnt snow falling from above, choking all who dared to breathe it.

It was too dangerous for any guards to stand near the walls, and while we sheltered from the toxic air, the troll-wives finally had freedom to march upon us. They came in a horde, not only those of my childhood, but all who had ever walked the mountains of Norway.

When they were close, I donned my Skin and walked into the ashen rain. At the front of their line stood the very same one who had poisoned me in my youth, her great yellow teeth bared.

"Tainted-bloods, all of you," she said. "You have made mockery of both man and wolf."

"To be insulted by such empty creatures is an honor," I laughed. "Call me Skoll, the mocker. Call my sister Hati, full of hate. No matter what words you choose, they shall not make us weaker any more than calling you beautiful shall make you easier to behold."

She shrieked and ran, and I bared my teeth to howl. Every capable man and woman donned their Skin to join the battle upon the ash fields, and they fought valiantly, tearing at the troll-wives with tooth and claw until the ground was red as the sky.

Our victory was inevitable until I turned and saw a pile of white. Upon the earth was my sister, her leg broken and bent. Without my knowledge, she had come to fight.

"Sol!" I cried.

For only a second, my heart had broken through my armor, and they spied the opening. The leader soared toward me and plunged her claws into my chest, tearing at my insides. Sol reached but could not touch me before the same was done to her.

The troll-wives did not rush to drink. They only crowded together and cried in glee, hands to the sky in praise of our downfall and pained screams.

As I watched my blood spill, black as a winter's sky, it caught and held the moonlight. It was then that I knew the purpose for which the wolf had spared our lives.

Today, we paid for our Skins.

"You will never taste her blood," I announced, "nor the blood of any other here. The children of the night are under my protection."

Sol lifted her head. "And mine."

I arose despite my wounds and faced the blood-spillers. With shaking knees, I delivered my final message. "Hear me now: no matter how you poison them, they will run freely as wolves, protected by the skins we've woven. Day or night, even the weakest of our kin will best yours."

With the last word, I saw the ash cloud begin to part, releasing the hidden dawn. And upon hearing the hiss of their skin turning to stone, I released myself into the steady arms of the Valkyries.

* * *

I awoke upon a branch. Sol lay at my side, her eyes already open, her shoulders covered in a dress of gold that stood in contrast to my tunic of blue. The wolf was near, his paws crossed as he watched us.

"I know you now," I said to him. "Fenrir, breaker of bonds. And I know the task you wish us to take."

He rose and shook out his coat. "Since my birth, I have chased the sun in the days. Soon, my attention must go elsewhere."

"And I was fated to take it from you," Sol realized aloud.

"We were wrong," I told her. "The troll-wives did not wish to drink your blood, only to spill it. They, too, had seen your destiny and wished to kill you before you grew capable of it, ensuring an eternal night for themselves."

She grabbed my hand, just as she had on her first day. "Thank you, brother, for saving me."

"Your fate is also here, Mani, as shepherd of the moon." With his great snout, Fenrir dragged my Skin to my feet. "No longer will sunlight kill you, but the stain of their poison will linger. From now until Ragnarok, when the sun glows, you will still feel agony and only find respite under your fur." He turned to Sol and lay her own Skin over her shoulder. "And you, daughter of the sun, will need to do the same under the reign of the moon."

In younger years, the knowledge of the persistent curse may have tasted bitter, but I found peace in the thought our kin still in Midgard would not bear their suffering alone.

"The tasks are yours now," said Fenrir as he walked down the branch of the world tree. "They were chosen for you from birth."

Sol placed her palms upon my cheeks, offering a kind smile. "My dearest brother. My fiercest friend. Run the journey beside me in the days, and I will run with you in the nights. And on the nights when the moon does not shine, we can sit together and watch the dancing colors."

Pride filled my chest. I had done what I was meant to do, and for the first time since before her birth, I breathed without weight. No longer would the great wolf hunt the lights across the sky. As brother and sister, as both human and wolf, we would carry the light.

Sol released her hair from its binds, grabbed the daylight in her arms, and ran forward into the darkness, laughing all the while.

I could not keep from grinning. I folded myself within my Skin, breathing in the spirit of the wolf, and began to chase her.

Mouths

Zez Wyatt

AT ROUGHLY FOUR in the morning on a wild, wooded cliffside a few miles out from the city, the woman, wife and mother turns into a multitude of wild, vicious wolves. She does not consider why she was so far from her house at such an hour; it no longer feels important. She runs all the way home, because now her many wolf-legs are tense with energy, and the smells of the world are sharp and intoxicating. There is the warm drumbeat of blood in the air. One of her breaks from the pack to chase down a rabbit, strayed too far from its warren. She crunches its ribcage between her teeth and her mouth fills with the taste of its wriggling heart.

She reaches the boundary between the city and the woods with the moon still low and heavy in the sky. She leaps over the threshold in a single many-legged bound and lands softly on the asphalt of the other side. It is late, and the streets are mostly empty. A lone car swerves and nearly careens off the road as she lopes down the center of the street, far too large and many to fit on a sidewalk. Someone in a bright fuchsia puffer vest backs into someone's porch as she passes. She growls at them with every one of her mouths.

Dawn has broken over the tiled roofs of the city by the time she reaches her house. The smell of it is different now: rotting leaves, window cleaner. She steps cautiously on the lawn her husband mowed just a few days ago, already somehow thick with clover and dandelion and other weeds, then makes her way onto the porch. Movement catches one of her eyes, and she turns in unison towards the living room window. Her many shadowed silhouettes, gleaming in the faint glow of the porch light, stare back at her.

She pushes over the terracotta camellia pot with one of her noses for the spare key but is barely able to pick it up in her mouth, and of course lacks the hands to use it. One of her begins to whine, and soon the rest of her join in. She paws at the door. Her claws leave long gashes in the yellow paint.

Soon her husband appears, wrapped hastily in his checkered robe.

"What happened to you?" he asks, rubbing his eyes. "Where have you been?"

She howls. It is difficult to explain, after all.

"It's nearly five in the morning," he says.

One of her moves to rub against his leg. He smells soft, like linens and shampoo, but there is something underneath it: a wet smell, an animal smell. She had never noticed any of this before. She nuzzles him with one of her snouts.

"Alright, come back to bed," he says, and turns around, yawning. "We'll talk tomorrow. I have to get to the office early. I'll drop the kids off on the way."

She follows him into the house, her paws sinking into the carpeted stairs. He falls into their bed, their too-large king bed that now only a few of her fit upon. Some of her curl up under the covers; others sleep in a pile. One of her nestles up against her husband and he puts his arm around her neck, fingers twisted gently into her fur.

She does not sleep. Her minds are sharp and vibrant in the moonlight, and the taste of the rabbit's blood still lingers, somehow, in every one of her mouths.

*　*　*

She must have dozed off at some point, because when she wakes light is streaming through the half-shuttered window. She stretches, the warmth of the sun luxurious in her thick fur. One of her eyes finds the clock – it is almost eleven already. It has been a long time since she has slept in this late. She hopes her husband managed to get their children up and off to school on time. She hopes he remembered to pack their lunches and fill up their water bottles and make them brush their teeth after breakfast.

She jumps from the bed and one of her nearly lands on something lying on the floor. It is her husband's favorite photo of her, that usually lives on the tall bookshelf beside their bed. The glass of it is cracked, and the frame broken in two. She stares at it, unable to call up any particular emotion, and leaves it where it lies.

She paces around the house, exploring every one of its new smells and tastes. The basement is heavy with dust and sweat and the juicy bodies of spiders. She catches a cobweb in the corner of the garage with a probing tongue and revels in its strange tastelessness. Her children's bedroom smells of scented markers and spilled juice; she makes a mental note to track down the source of the spill and clean it up.

She is hungry, she realizes, that single rabbit from the night before barely enough to satiate one of her mouths, and so she returns to the kitchen. There may not be prey to catch and crunch between her teeth, but there is always low-fat yogurt, and cereal bars, and sometimes trail mix. She selects an apple from the kitchen counter and holds it delicately in her jaws as she carries it to the kitchen table. When she takes a bite, carefully, it feels as soft as a baked potato. Another of her pulls open the door to the pantry and removes a slice of gluten-free zucchini bread, the kind that the pantry is always full of because she told her husband that she loved it. It is on one of the higher shelves, but at her full height even one of her is taller than she ever was before. She places the bread gingerly upon the table. Another of her grabs the container of almond butter, and an attempt to open the lid punctures the hard plastic with one of her canines. She places it on the counter, ashamed, and all of her split the slice of bread and the apple. It is good to have breakfast. She casts her mind back to her lunch yesterday, a sandwich of the same bread with spinach and hummus, and reminds herself to be more careful of her carbohydrate consumption at lunch.

Afterwards, she splits up; there is work to do, and now she has many bodies to do it with. One of her picks up her children's toys, left strewn around the room; another gathers her husband's dirty clothing and runs a load of laundry. Three of her form a team to vacuum the living room together. She is not very effective at any of this. Her teeth slice into her daughter's soft dolls and snap apart her son's Lego creations. She splits two laundry pods, one bursting in her mouth and one sliced open by her claws, before successfully navigating one into the washing machine. The vacuum is too loud. It takes all of her power to suppress her instinct to pounce upon it as it roars to life, and she whines all the way through using it. She will just have to adapt, she supposes.

But her legs itch, itch, itch, and so she goes down to the basement and tries to take turns on her husband's treadmill, but it is too small for even a single bound of her wolf-legs. She tries anyways and tumbles to the ground, one after another, until finally giving up. Frustrated, she returns upstairs, trying to remember what it is she used to do when she felt like this. She selects an avocado hair mask from the collection of lotions and treatments in the drawer of her bedside table. She turns the shower on hot, and one of her gingerly bites down on the tube to squirt cream on another's back, until the container is empty and the bathroom is heavy with the scent of tea-tree oil. Out of habit one of her wipes her forehead against the foggy bathroom mirror, and she sees that the mint-green cream hangs in globs from her thick fur, and a pile of it sits in between her ears. She looks ridiculous. One of her turns the shower temperature up as hot as it will go and tries to scrub herself clean. When she finally exits the bathroom, her fur is soft and silken but a cloying stickiness clings to her paws.

* * *

"Are you going to be able to make dinner?" her husband asks, when he comes home from work. The kids are still at an after-school program and won't be home for another hour. There is clear tape over the wound in the almond butter jar.

Of course, she growls, and makes her way back into the kitchen. She may be less dexterous than before, but there are more than enough of her to make up for it.

Her husband pauses. "I'm glad you're feeling better, then," he says, and drops a kiss on one of her heads before turning around and disappearing upstairs. "Just let me know if you want help, alright?" he calls.

She decides to make pasta with meat sauce and broccoli. It is harder than she anticipated to fill a pot with water and move it to the stove with her wolf-mouths, or to open a jar of pasta sauce, or to wield a knife to chop the vegetables. The refrigerator door is clumsy to both her claws and teeth, but she manages to get it open, navigating one of her mouths around its handle and wrenching with all of her strength. She ends up breaking the glass of the marinara jar and runs the remaining sauce through a fine sifter to remove any pieces of glass. One of her washes her mouth thoroughly before carefully, furtively, splitting the broccoli with her teeth. Her teeth are less effective, however, at removing the sizzling pan from the oven, and so the broccoli chars while she attempts to fit a dish towel into her mouth to protect her from the heat. Part of her lips burn, still, while she navigates the pan onto the counter.

When she drops the pot of pasta on the ground with a crash, barely missing one of her feet, her husband appears from upstairs. "I'm sorry. I should have helped," he says, bending down and scratching behind the ears of one of her bodies, the way he used to ruffle her hair. "I'll go get the kids, and pick up a pizza on the way home?"

She stares at the burnt broccoli, the spilled pasta, the broken glass on the counter.

"I can help you clean," he says, but it is meaningless, because the kids are still at their after-school program and must be picked up. She flicks her ears and begins herding the fallen pasta into a pile.

When he returns home, she sits at the table and tries to bark soft answers as her children pepper her with questions about her new bodies.

"Which one of you is you?" her daughter asks, swinging her legs.

"Can you do the wolf howl, like on TV?" her son demands. She obliges, throwing her heads back and howling, but it is far too loud for their small kitchen, and her son begins to cry. She stops, guilty. Two of her get up from the table and lay their heads in her children's laps, and the novelty of this makes them giggle, the howl forgotten.

"Does this mean you're gonna start playing with us again?" her son asks.

She nuzzles him. Of course, she barks softly. Everything will be different now. Her son feeds her a slice of ham pizza under the table while her husband pretends not to notice and her daughter launches a campaign of distraction, and soon they are all laughing. She eats two more slices of pizza and bites through three sponges cleaning up.

* * *

That night, her husband begins running his hand up and down the length of one of her stomachs. "What?" he asks, when she pulls back to look at him. "The kids are asleep. And you're still my wife."

I am your wife, she grunts in bemused confirmation. Why is she so surprised by this? She looks at his bare skin in the soft moonlight. He still smells like soap. She leans one of her snouts closer, trying to smell the heat of him beneath it. He grins.

"We haven't in so long," he says. "And you've been walking around the house all day, completely naked…"

She supposes that she is naked, technically.

"I've actually been thinking about this all day," he says in a conspiratorial whisper.

Oh, is all she can think. She is not sure what to make of this. He presses her against him and buries his face into her neck.

* * *

The next morning, she gets up along with her husband. He gives her a quick kiss on her nearest head and she flinches from it; he does not seem to notice. The sour scent of sweat and heat hangs sticky in the room.

She rouses her children, nudging them with her noses and whining until they wake up. Another of her fetches the cereal from the top shelf on the pantry and brings it to the kitchen table. Some of the honey flakes spill onto the linoleum floor; she devours them quickly, before anyone can notice.

"I can keep dropping the kids off until you figure out if you can drive again," her husband says, mouth full of cinnamon toast. She opens her mouths to respond and he cuts her off. "Don't worry about it. Let's just say you owe me one." A growl escapes her mouth before she can stop it.

When her husband and children leave, she cleans up the kitchen after them, and then makes herself a bowl of granola. It is difficult to chew granola with wolf-teeth, and so the clusters of oats with coconut sugar scrape her throats on the way down. She salivates, thinking of the rabbit she ate on the journey back from the woods. Again, her legs itch. She wants to run. Her tails jerk back and forth in the air. One of her breaks free of the pack and bounds up the carpeted stairs and back down again. Surely it cannot be too bad to go for a quick jog. She has never been one for jogging before, but then again, many of her friends and neighbors had suddenly, overnight, become people who jog. It is a good plan.

She cannot open the front door herself, her paws slipping uselessly against the round doorknob. She splits up, weaving amongst the furniture in a search for a window left open; there are none. The sun still filters warmly through the curtains. She begins to whine. One of her begins gnawing on the edge of their Chesterfield sofa. The ache of hunger rears its head inside her bellies, and she forces it down. She has already eaten breakfast. She checks the windows again, in case she missed any the first time. There are twenty-four windows in her house. She checks again, and there are twenty-five: she had forgotten to check the window in her children's bathroom. It is also closed, and locked, and she could likely not fit through it if it were open.

When her husband arrives with the children there is too much to do to consider going for a run, and so she puts it out of her mind. That night she knocks over the pot of chicken stock while trying to add a mouthful of diced onion. The boiling water scalds one of her mouths and splashes onto her haunches. Her husband applies a bag of frozen peas, and tells her that he will finish preparing dinner. Both of her children complain that the soup is not very good. Her husband tells them to be grateful, and that their mother will be back to cooking dinners soon, and then looks at her guiltily and tells her he didn't mean it that way. Her lips and chest throb. There are blisters forming underneath her fur.

* * *

She wakes before her husband does. First she fetches the cereal from the top shelf of the pantry, and then gathers her children's backpacks from where they had been strewn around the house. In each of them she places an apple, which she holds carefully in her teeth so she does not break the skin.

Her husband stumbles downstairs, tired, and puts some cinnamon bread in the toaster. One of her follows him as he goes through the rituals of the morning, her eyes tracking him across the room. He smells sticky with sweat and chicken soup.

Then her children come down and complain that there isn't the right kind of cereal anymore. She ignores them, and her son pulls on one of her tails to get her attention. It is hardly enough to hurt, but she still whirls around and barely restrains herself from growling. He giggles. She guides her children through brushing their teeth and put their cereal back on the top shelf.

When all of this is done and her husband is almost out the door, because he is already late and if he is much later the children will be marked as tardy, she tries to ask if he could leave the door unlocked, or open up a window. But he is not listening, or he does not understand her. He plants a quick kiss on the top of her head and slams the door shut. She snarls.

She runs up and down and up and down the stairs. She is so hungry. The hollowness of her stomachs feels like it is stretching up, up, up throughout her bodies, filling every crevice of her with a horrible gaping emptiness. She fears she will collapse in on herself like a black hole. It is too much. She is too empty. She races back to the kitchen. She paws open the pantry and makes quick work of the dried apricots she would put in her children's lunch bags every morning, and the granola mix she once purchased in bulk during one of her periodic attempts to make her husband eat healthier. The top shelf, higher than her children can reach, has the cookies. She stands on hind legs and knocks them to the floor with her head.

She wrenches open the refrigerator door and a new wave of smells assails her noses. She salivates. Her teeth slice through the plastic packaging around lunch meats and puncture tubs of pre-sliced cheese. She gorges herself on whole onions and halved avocados and a carton of fresh whipping cream. On the third shelf from the floor is a flank steak. She rips it free of its packaging and all of her descend upon it, ripping off jagged chunks of red flesh. Soon there is no food left in the kitchen and she leaves, the door of the refrigerator still open. It is not enough. She has so many mouths and they are all still so very, very hungry. She continues to stalk around the house, desperate for any sign of more food.

She catches sight of herself in the full-length mirror that hangs inside their bedroom. Her muzzles are smeared with red and brown and flecks of yogurt. She remembers how she used to look: soft and pink-fleshed, like a cut of uncooked chicken. She tilts all of her heads, confused. All of her mouths begin to growl. Then one of her breaks from the pack, dashes down the hallways, hurls herself at the reflection. The glass shatters. Shards of it jut out of her fur.

One of her carefully pulls out as many as she can with her teeth. Another nudges the glass into piles; it is important that her children do not step on it by accident.

* * *

When her husband returns home, he is surprised, and confused, and angry. Food scraps litter the kitchen floor, and the steak they were supposed to have for dinner is gone. The house is littered with bloody pawprints and neatly arranged piles of broken glass.

She is everywhere in the house at this point, pacing back and forth, her legs tense with energy. Her husband yells but only briefly, and then apologizes. He says that they can order another pizza for dinner and have the leftovers for breakfast, and then they can talk about plans for grocery shopping tomorrow. The promise of a meal draws all of her to the ransacked kitchen, where her children make jokes about food fights and giggle at her stained fur. They do not know what stains are blood. They do not know how hungry she is.

It is like it never happened. The kitchen is cleaned, the glass disposed of. The house is the same as it always was. When the pizza arrives she forces herself to sit down around the table.

"We learned about triangles in class today!" her son announces. She peels her many lips back in what she hopes resembles a smile. She does not want to hear about triangles. She wants to eat. With all of the cabinets and drawers closed it is like there still could be food in the kitchen, and only she can smell its absence. She eats four slices of pizza, because the rest must be saved for leftovers. She wants to howl. She is still so hungry.

* * *

"What are you going to wear to dinner with the Perrys tomorrow?" her husband calls from the bathroom.

I am a pack of wolves, she howls back desperately. *I have tails and ears and paws and a hundred sharp, jagged teeth. I will not fit in any of my clothes.*

He opens the door, toweling his hair with one hand. He is wearing nothing but boxers, and his skin radiates warmth from the shower. She wrinkles her noses at the smell of him. "We could have some new clothes made, if you want. Poke earholes in your favorite hats," he says.

She knows that she loves having dinner with the Perrys; she had made the plans herself two weeks ago, in an attempt to return things to normal. But it would all feel so hollow now: the drinks, the cooking, the stories. The clothes. Her lips pull back into a snarl.

"Alright, alright." He backs away, smiling, his hands up in mocking surrender. "Probably would cost a fortune anyways. And you don't have to go to the Perrys, don't worry. I'm sure they'll understand if we reschedule." He turns around, his back to her. Still the smell.

She forces herself to stop pacing and lie down in the bed while her husband lays out his clothes for the following day. He hums as he moves; some of her bury her heads in the blankets in an attempt to drown out the sound.

"So... about the mirror," her husband says, finally sliding underneath the comforter. She looks at him, but before she can respond he says, "I guess it must be hard, seeing yourself like this."

She peels back her lips and growls. *I wish I had broken every mirror I ever looked into,* she snarls. *I wish I had ripped out the eyes of everyone who ever saw me.*

Her husband reaches out to stroke the fur around her neck. His smile is so caring. He loves her so very much. He smells like soap and linens and blood and heat and the rabbit she devoured in the woods.

"You know, I really do still think you're beautiful like this," he says.

Oh, she thinks, and while she thinks, her mouths open wide and clamp down on his soft, pale body. Blood splatters their white linen sheets. He makes a sound of shock, and his mouth moves as if to form words, but one of her has already torn out his throat. She snaps his bones between her teeth. His stringy meat is hot on her tongues.

One of her children comes inside, drawn by the noise, and screams. There is not much left of her husband at this point. She turns towards him, her son, with all of her many heads, in order to tell him that it will all be okay. That she will take care of him. This is what she means to say, but she cannot. The words become a growl, low and threatening. Her son flees. She returns to her feast.

When all of the flesh has been licked from her husband's bones and his blood has soaked so deeply through the bed that it drips from the bottom of the mattress to the carpeted floor in slow red globs, she rises. There is the beginning of a fullness in her stomachs that she has not felt in years.

She pads down the hallway, pushing open the door to her children's room with her nose. Both of her children are in the same bed, curled up against each other. She must have frightened them. Their breathing is shallow and uneven; they are awake. Perhaps they are hiding from her. She steps closer.

"I'm scared, mama," her daughter whispers.

Her son begins to wail. The sound of it is pitiful. She feels the need to comfort them rising in her chest like a sickness, and she hates it, because she is so, so hungry, and she does not want to lie down and become their mother again. They are so full of need. They cannot reach the top shelf where the cereals are kept. She wants to scream. She wants to howl. The children continue to cry. She must stop it. She lunges. The crying becomes screaming, and she must stop that as well. She cannot stand by and do nothing while her children scream. She bites down hard on their tiny little heads and splits them open like cherry tomatoes. Now they will not need her anymore.

There, she thinks, sucking the last scraps of sinew from her children's bones. Now there is nobody left who needs her, nobody left who knows what she used to be. She will run. She will run back to the woods and never return. She will feast on rabbit every night and terrorize hikers and campers and joggers and owe nothing to no one. She will be nobody's wife and nobody's mother.

She skids down the stairs. The house is still locked. She hurls one of her bodies at the window beside it and bounces off, her shoulder blade throbbing from the collision. The window remains uncracked. She tries again, this time backing up the carpeted stairs and leaping from the final step with the power of a cannonball. Her body *thunks* uselessly against the glass. Another of her tries, and another, until all of her are leaping at the window and landing in a tangle of limbs on the carpet. One of her slams her jaw against the glass, over and over. Her teeth crack. Blood fills her mouth.

I am a wild animal, she begs to the stains of the night sky still visible through the bloodstained window. I do not belong here. I have never belonged here.

The world outside does not respond.

She realizes that she can see herself framed in the reflection of the window. Her many eyes flash in the moonlight as she stares into the glass. She can see the faint pink of her underbellies. In the smudged glass it almost looks like skin again.

No, she howls desperately. I have eaten my husband and children. I have feasted on everything that ever held me here. I am free.

But they are inside of me, she realizes. They will always be inside of me. I will always be inside of me. She stares at the hollow eyes of her reflections, and her mouths twist into a growl. She is not free. There is still someone left holding her here, who knows her as a woman and a wife and a mother. She feels the flesh of what was once her family coil and turn inside of her many stomachs and she can almost hear them reaching for her, begging for her, and then she is hungry again, hungrier than she has ever been before—

One of her bites down hard on another's bloodied shoulder, and pain wrenches through her as she feels the flesh ripped away from one body into another. She gags as it slides down her throat, but then the taste of blood hits her mouth, hot and pulsing. She salivates. Her meat is richer than anything she has ever tasted before. Her rage becomes a terrible, violent pleasure. Her bodies leap at each other, and it is a frenzy of howls and teeth and sinew. She devours herself whole, ripping chunks of ragged flesh from her bodies and choking them down. Her many hearts contract with grief and wrath and ecstasy. Soon there is no meat remaining. There are only mouths, twitching, snapping, empty.

Worse than a Wolf

Wen Wen Yang

THE SOUND OF THE METAL grinding against the whetstone reverberated up my arms. My father was sharpening his ax, preparing for the day's work. "I invited Mu to dinner tonight," he said.

I shuddered.

Mu was a woodsman whose family came from a neighboring village in China and had settled in the same rural town in Oregon a decade before my family. How happy my family was to hear our dialect! It almost made this foreign country feel safe.

"Why?" I stirred the pot on the wood stove and inhaled the smell of comfort: ginger and garlic. I was cooking the wonton soup my grandmother liked. My cousins and I had often fought over who made better-looking wontons and always lost to our grandmother. "He visited just last week for the Mid-Autumn Festival."

"He brought those double-yolk mooncakes," my grandmother recalled as she folded a clean shirt into a crisp square in the far corner of the room. She was a short woman and every year seemed to lose another inch.

When my parents first arrived, Mu had persuaded his boss to hire my father to clear the trails and the smaller brush. It paid better than the fish processing plants and you didn't need to speak the language to trim overgrown hedges. My mother had been glad my father no longer reeked of fish.

Mu had found a small cottage at the outskirts of town large enough for my grandmother, my parents and me. We no longer had to squeeze into a space meant for one family with my aunt, uncle and three cousins.

Not long after we moved into the cottage I first noticed the paw prints in the morning dew, and the feeling of being watched when I hung the laundry to dry. My aunt warned me to leave an offering in the woods, because we were the ones entering the wolf's territory. I did not tell her that I understood the local wolf, that she seemed more afraid of us than we were of her. Appeasing a wolf's temper seemed easier than easing her husband's.

After I saw the mother wolf with her cubs one night, I left her a cut of fat from a pork belly. She had three cubs. The next morning, I heard her scolding them.

"Don't eat that!" she snapped. "Humans will poison you."

"It's safe to eat," I whispered out my window. The mother wolf's ears pricked, but she led her cubs into the undergrowth. The pork fat was gone the next night. We didn't have much to spare after that first offering.

In the kitchen, my father asked, "What's wrong with you? You used to like Mu."

It was true. Mu had congratulated my father on his industrious daughter with the neat stacks of clean laundry that pleased our customers. Even my cautious mother had trusted him. He had brought flaky egg tarts, still warm from the bakery.

I cannot eat them anymore.

My eldest cousin was unquestionably more charming, more talented. She could make the guzheng sing. And yet Mu had made me feel beautiful, despite my inheritance of my father's wide nose and my mother's crooked teeth. He had complimented my thick black hair while his hair was thinning at the crown.

Then he made me feel broken and dirty.

There was a drawer of his gifts that I could not bear to look at. I left them with my cousins.

"He makes a good living," my father continued, turning his ax. "Winter is coming. Don't you want a warm hearth, a full belly?"

Being hungry was preferable to Mu's company. He had large hands that I could not swat away like a biting fly. Now my father was offering to put Mu's hands around my throat.

"If I'd had a choice," my grandmother interrupted as she tied together the bundle of fresh shirts. "I would have picked a man who could read and write."

I curse the person who taught my grandfather how to gamble instead of how to read. Two years before my family crossed the ocean, he lost the money we had been saving for the voyage. The next summer, a tiger mauled him to death. My grandmother found his body, his blood staining the rice field.

"In English and Mandarin," I agreed, dividing the wontons among the three bowls.

"It's a struggle to live with an ignorant man." Grandma sucked her teeth. "My mother told me that it's better to be with a smart man who beats you than a foolish man. As if those were my only choices."

How many generations of women have endured a life instead of enjoyed it?

"This brings in some money." I gestured at the clean laundry. "You couldn't take care of Grandma alone." He could not deny filial piety, not when it was cooked into my marrow.

My father grimaced. I had hurt his pride.

"I will find work like my biao jie." My oldest cousin was a bookkeeper at the tailor's shop. Better than washing and ironing for pennies.

"You don't have the head for numbers like she does." My father sucked his teeth.

Embarrassment stung my cheeks.

"Besides, she'll marry the tailor's son soon enough. You wouldn't attract a man as wealthy as the tailor before the end of the season."

My father thought the monster chasing me was winter's cold and hunger, when it was actually the man he had allowed into our home. I could not bear to tell my father that he had trusted the wrong man. I was afraid of what he would do with his ax, of what this country's justice would do with a murderous foreigner.

"Don't rush your daughter," my grandmother scolded. "What family wouldn't want an obedient daughter-in-law?" Her words burned through me. *Obedient.* Like a dog. Told to stay quiet, to not tell anyone.

I could feel my tears coming, my bile rising, and retreated outside to harvest the spinach from the garden. The breeze tore at my hot cheeks. Tears gathered in my throat. I would rather go hungry and scavenge in the woods, I wanted to scream. I would rather my clothes smell of rotten fish than Mu's sweat. Some nights, I woke from nightmares of Mu's stubble scratching my cheek, his breath in my ear. I would lie awake, refusing to return to my dreams, until I heard my father shuffle into the kitchen.

I slashed at the weeds, pretending the knife was a claw, until my eyes were clear, my chest heaving. If I only ate weeds, would I still need to marry Mu?

I knelt on the ground where we had buried my mother. When the fever took her, I felt so angry that she had left me behind. Did she know now what I couldn't find the words to say?

When I came back inside, my father was rubbing camphor oil into his shoulders.

"I had two children by the time *I* was nineteen." My grandmother washed the greens I harvested. "But they do things differently in this country."

"Where are your glasses?" my father asked.

She sucked her teeth. "I can't find them because I can't see!" Her glasses cost nearly a month of laundry work plus two weeks of my father's wages.

I went into her room and found the glasses between her mattress and the wall. They had fallen back there last month too. The lenses were scratched but my grandmother had insisted they were still fine. If I married Mu, could I buy my grandmother new glasses?

"They grow legs when you aren't looking," she exclaimed when I presented them to her. She blinked up at me with her magnified eyes and called me by my mother's name. I didn't correct her. My father never said my mother's name anymore.

"There's some taro in the woods, ready for harvest," my father said abruptly, washing his hands. "Over by the river."

"Taro, here?" my grandmother asked. I had missed the starchy sweetness.

"I'd recognize those leaves anywhere." My father nodded toward the nearly empty pantry. "Harvest it all. That could be dinner for everyone." With Mu joining us, we had to stretch our food with what the woods could offer.

We ate breakfast carefully, maneuvering around the bundles of customers' clothes. My father retrieved his ax just as the morning sunlight touched the curtains. "Take care of your grandmother. Beware of the wolves," he called over his shoulder as he left.

I brushed my grandmother's hair. Her fine white hair was almost transparent. Perhaps next week I would need to trim it before it hung over her hooded eyes. While living all together, my family had decided my hands were steadiest and I had become the family haircutter. When I shaved my uncle, I had often thought of pressing the razor a touch too deep along his throat.

"Grandma, your ears are so large." I untangled the ends of her hair.

"Big ears are very lucky. Like the Buddha's. I could hear the cows asking to be milked, the chickens shouting 'good morning!'" While my aunt and I could hear animals like my grandmother, it seemed to have skipped my father.

For the rest of the morning, Grandma and I cleaned, shoulder to shoulder, to prepare to receive Mu. Did she already imagine me married to Mu, depending on his money as long as I was obedient? How else could I fill the pantry, buy my grandmother new glasses?

"I'll look for that taro." I pulled on the coat my mother had made for me, desperate to escape the impending dinner.

I'd started to outgrow my previous coat, a hand-me-down from my eldest cousin, two winters ago. The sleeves had crept up my arm and the wind stole the warmth from my belly. My mother had started sewing a new coat for me. Then she became too sick to help with laundry. Then she was too exhausted to work the sewing machine. When she died, the red coat lay unfinished across her lap, needle and thread still in her hand.

My grandmother had finished the buttons and topstitching, but it was my mother's care I remembered when I wore it.

"Be careful of the wolves," Grandma called after me. I heard her lock the door.

I balanced the empty basket on my hip and trekked through the woods. Dry leaves crunched under my boots and swirled around me. The birdsong that had sounded so strange when we first arrived had now lost its novelty. Dark, loud crows had replaced cranes.

I searched for red berries. If I could find a large, mature ginseng root, I could sell it to the herbalist. Perhaps that would be enough to keep me out of marriage for another six months.

Up the side of one tree was a dark crop of wood ear fungus. I trimmed off pieces, careful to keep them intact. My grandmother had taught me how to search for it, how to cut it from the tree. When I first harvested them, I had whispered my secrets into those dark misshapen ears. Perhaps, when my family ate them, they would know what Mu did. But my grandmother only said that I had to wash them more carefully next time, there was still dirt in hers.

Clusters of mushrooms grew along the fallen trees. Some were pristine white bulbs with rings along the stems. If they were dangerous, how could I keep a morsel from my father or grandmother's bowls? My grandmother had not taught me how to spot poisonous mushrooms or dangerous men.

At the bottom of the hill, I found the taro. Large spearhead leaves hung over the river. I dug and scraped the roots from the corms with my spade.

The basket was nearly full when I heard another set of footsteps. Had Mu tracked me? My breathing became ragged, my palms sweaty. I grasped the dirty spade.

Then the wind changed direction, and I recognized the scent of a wolf: decaying crops and black pepper.

I turned, my body burning with fear under the red coat. If they could wash the blood out of it, perhaps my middle cousin could wear it next.

The wolf approached, shoulder blades sharp under the skin. Her belly was gaunt, empty of food for her and her pups. There were spots where her fur had fallen out, exposing her pink skin. Her tail was as thin as a whip.

"So small." Her voice was reedy, disapproving. She sounded like my aunt when browsing the fruit stalls too late in the day. The wolf sat in front of me, one front paw lifted in consideration. "Can you even run, little one? Do you not fear wolves, girl?"

"Of course I do, Madam Wolf. Everyone can see your true nature from your fangs to your claws. Every villager warns their children to come in before dark. We shutter our windows and bolt our doors."

The wolf's head rose, elegant and haughty. "Have you met anyone more terrifying?" she asked. "Don't I wear this wolfskin well?"

Wear? I peered into her eyes. They were brown, like mine. She was human underneath that fur.

"Could I wear it too?" I asked, tears lapping over my voice.

"And why would you want to live in the forest instead of inside your four walls?" Her breath clouded around her muzzle. "I will not give you my fur."

"There are sneakier creatures," I answered. "There was a man who was invited into my home. I set a place for him at the table. He smiled with bright white teeth in a mouth that knew how to charm everyone. His hands had clean trimmed nails. But when no one was looking, he unleashed something worse than a wolf."

Her lips pulled back, exposing her fangs. "I would like to see this man who is worse than a wolf."

Was that why she was now a wolf? Was she betrayed, or did she run into the forest to arm herself with fangs and claws?

"He hid it so well," I whispered. "You wouldn't know until it was too late." I wiped my eyes with the coat sleeve. "He is large, and boasts of killing moose."

"He has taken my prey." Her ears perked. She licked her lips. "Have you taken my prey, girl?"

"No, Madam Wolf." I pointed at the basket. "I have only dug up the taro. But this man, he will be your dinner."

Her dark eyes focused on me. "And what will you give me in return, girl, for taking down this formidable man?"

I wore no jewelry and carried no coins. What would a wolf want with those things anyway?

"Perhaps I'll have one of your family," she suggested impatiently.

"My grandmother, my father, they are old and frail," I pleaded, wondering what I could offer that would save their lives.

I could count the wolf's ribs under her patchy fur. Her skin rippled; she was shivering.

"Will you take my coat?"

Surely, my mother would gift warmth to a mother wolf, to trade her dying efforts for protection. What good was warmth without safety? I would endure winter's bite instead.

I removed my keys from the coat pocket and dropped them into the basket. Shrugging off the coat, I breathed in its scent one more time. It no longer smelled like my mother, my own sweat having seeped into the fabric. I draped it over the wolf's shoulders, double-knotting the arms across her neck. The coat will soon smell like her.

"It's very warm," she sighed with half-closed eyes. The wolf sniffed. Her breath was wet and musty.

Tonight, I will bring a wolf to dinner.

* * *

On the way home with the wolf, my eyes did not stray from the path, not even to look for ginseng's red berries. Without my coat, I was no longer sweating.

When we reached my home, she circled it, sniffing. Could she smell Mu from his last visit?

As Madam Wolf disappeared behind the cottage, I heard someone on the path. My stomach dropped.

I turned. It was Mu. The woodsman carried his ax as easily as if it was a part of his arm. His shirt was sweat-stained, covered in splinters. When he smiled, his wrinkles looked like gashes. I wanted to run, to claw his eyes out for even looking at me. Why was he here so early?

As he approached, his shadow engulfed mine, engulfed my body.

"It is so good to see you." He took my hand from my side and pressed his lips to my knuckles. He had taken on the manners of this new country, where this closeness was expected. "You shouldn't go into the woods alone. There are wolves in there."

I pulled my hand back.

"I was safe there." I did not reach for my keys, refusing him entry.

My eyes traveled up the length of his ax. What if he hurt Madam Wolf?

"My, what a big ax." I extended a dainty finger to the head of the ax. "May I try to hold it?"

He chuckled. "Of course you may."

I set down my basket. He placed the ax in my hands and grinned as I feigned weakness. The ax was lighter than the basket I had hauled through the woods. It was lighter than my youngest cousin, who had squirmed the whole night while my aunt searched for her drunk husband.

"It is so heavy." I gripped it, my knuckles taut.

Mu flexed his arms and shoulders. "They don't make them for young ladies."

"My, how sharp this ax is," I said in a breathless voice that didn't sound familiar. "How many trees have you cut down?"

"Hundreds!" He swelled, roaring, "Not just trees, but deer and bears." I imagined the bloody bodies around him, a wasted feast.

He glanced behind him. "I was hoping we could speak before your father came home."

The hair on the back of my neck rose. I lowered my eyes.

"Why?" I asked through clenched teeth.

"I think we should be married. To make it alright between us. I have already asked your father and he agrees." He coughed, shrugged. "Well, he agreed yesterday. But today he said I should ask you first. But we agreed you shouldn't marry a foreigner."

I gave a derisive laugh at his calling this country's people foreigners when they used the same words against us. We were all foreigners to the wolves.

"Why not?" My voice dipped lower. "My biao jie may marry that tailor's son." Even this country of possibilities could not abide a lone woman.

"They can't take any more of our women," Mu spat. Were my cousins like a tea set that belonged together? Did he see me like his ax, his shirt? Heat rose from my chest to my face.

If my uncle had been a foreigner, would my father have defended my aunt? Or was there no other option for a woman and her three children?

"Can you imagine it?" he asked. "You won't have to wash these foreigners' clothes anymore. We'll spend the rest of our lives together."

The blood rushed in my ears. Every night, his sweat. Every morning, his breath.

No. Not another night, not another morning.

Mu turned at the sound of the leaves rustling behind him. He groped for the ax but I retreated out of reach. I stepped out of his shadow.

He hissed at me, confused, angry. "Give me the ax, you stupid—"

Madam Wolf landed on him, jaws around his neck. He fell, those large hands stretching toward me. She pinned him to the ground, muzzle darkening with blood. Madam Wolf struck his throat, his shoulders, his hands. Blood pooled under him, soaking into his clothes.

When he stopped moving, she panted. Her warm metallic breath clouded, catching the last rays of sunlight. It sounded human, soft and shallow.

She darted back into the safety of the woods.

The front door opened. I spun, hefting the dripping ax.

My grandmother gasped, terror in her wide eyes.

On the bloody ground, there was no other shadow. The widening puddle of blood covered the bloody paw prints.

My grandmother hobbled toward me.

"There was a wolf." I pointed into the trees. "It had fearsome teeth, and claws sharper than an ax. It attacked Mu." My voice cracked.

She nodded.

"It stole my coat."

She laid her tender hands over my splattered knuckles.

"He fought bravely, didn't he?" she asked as she pried the ax from my hands and laid it by Mu's body.

I nodded, my hands shaking in hers.

"He saved you from the wolf."

I shivered, suddenly cold without my coat.

She pulled a handkerchief from her pocket and started to wipe my blood-speckled face. Her voice was steady as she stared into my eyes.

"The wolves here are as dangerous as the tigers back home, aren't they, granddaughter?"

I nodded, remembering my grandfather's blood staining the hems of her pants, her hands. What was under the tiger's stripes?

My grandmother repeated the story of Mu's bravery to my father, to the police. After every retelling, I almost believed her too.

Biographies & Sources

R. Nisbet Bain
The Iron Wolf
(Originally Published in *Cossack Fairy Tales and Folk Tales*, 1916)
A distinguished historian, with a special interest in the Scandinavian and Slavic nations, London-born Bain (1854–1909) spent many years attached to the British Museum. He contributed biographies of important historical figures to *Encyclopaedia Britannica*. He mastered twenty languages, translating texts from Russian, Danish, Finnish and Hungarian into English. His linguistic facility was of course a boon in his historical investigations and in his literary interests (he translated tales by Leo Tolstoy and Maxim Gorky). His great passion, though, was for European folklore.

Clifford Ball
The Werewolf Howls
(Originally Published in *Weird Tales*, Volume 36, Issue 2, 1941)
Though born in New York City, Clifford Ball (1908–47) was brought up by his mother in Millerstown, PA, his parents having separated when he was small. After leaving school, he did a wide variety of low-grade jobs, from factory work and bartending to labouring, but channelled most of his energies into his imaginative life. His voracious reading of *Weird Tales* plunged him into the world of fantasy fiction – and, more specifically, the 'sword and sorcery' of Robert E. Howard.

Richard Beauchamp
The Cull
(First Publication)
Richard Beauchamp hails from the hills and hollers of Ozark country. It is from these ancient, verdant hills that he often finds inspiration and uses as settings in his stories. His fiction has appeared in several esteemed anthologies and literary magazines, including Cohesion Press's award winning *SNAFU* anthologies, and Dark Peninsula Press's *Cellar Door* series. His debut fiction collection *Black Tongue and Other Anomalies* was a 2022 Splatterpunk Awards nominee, and his story 'Sons of Luna' was a 2018 Pushcart Prize finalist. Richard is an avid outdoorsman, and lives in Missouri with his wife and many animals.

Algernon Blackwood
The Camp of the Dog
(Originally Published in *John Silence, Physician Extraordinary*, 1908)
Algernon Henry Blackwood (1869–1951) was a writer who crafted his tales with extraordinary vision. Born in Kent but working at numerous careers in America and Canada in his youth, he eventually settled back in England in his thirties. He wrote many novels and short stories including 'The Willows', which was rated by Lovecraft as one of his favourite stories, and he is credited by many scholars as a real master of imagery who wrote at a consistently high standard.

Charlotte Bond
Moonskin
(First Publication)

Charlotte is an author of horror and dark fantasy. She is also a freelance editor, ghostwriter, and podcaster, co-hosting the award-winning podcast, Breaking the Glass Slipper. Her micro collection *The Watcher in the Woods* won the British Fantasy Society's award for Best Collection in 2021. Her dragon novellas *The Fireborne Blade* and *The Bloodless Princes* were published by Tordotcom in 2024. Werewolf stories have fascinated her since childhood, and she's collected as many anthologies about them as she can – and now she's in one!

B.A. Booher
The Claws Come Out
(First Publication)
Bret Booher lives in Indiana with his wife, two children, a dog, and two cats. He began writing horror in college but spent years exploring fantasy and science fiction before returning to his first love with this piece. When he's not writing, Bret creates videos about Moodle and English Language Arts on his YouTube channel, *The Hoosier Moodler*. You can also find him at the Gored Ox Pub nearly every Tuesday, Thursday, and Saturday from 8:15 p.m. to 11 p.m. ET.

Gilbert Edward Campbell
The White Wolf of Kostopchin
(Originally Published in *Wild and Weird: Tales of Imagination and Mystery*, 1889)
Sir Gilbert Edward Campbell (1838–96) was the son of a baronet. After Harrow, he joined the Army, and took part in the suppression of the Indian Rebellion of 1857. Whilst he inherited his father's title in 1870, his life became less and less respectable. His ventures as a writer of sensational short stories and translator of French crime fiction placed him at the very lowest end of the literary hierarchy, but a succession of fraudulent schemes led to his trial and disgrace in 1892.

Ramsey Campbell
The Change
(Originally Published in *Dark Companions*, 1982 © Ramsey Campbell 1982)
Ramsey Campbell has been given more awards than any other writer in the field, including the Grand Master Award of the World Horror Convention, the Lifetime Achievement Award of the Horror Writers Association, the Living Legend Award of the International Horror Guild and the World Fantasy Lifetime Achievement Award. In 2015 he was made an Honorary Fellow of Liverpool John Moores University for outstanding services to literature. Among his novels available from Flame Tree Press are *Thirteen Days by Sunset Beach*, *The Wise Friend*, *Somebody's Voice*, *Fellstones*, *The Lonely Lands*, *The Incubations* and his *Three Births of Daoloth* trilogy: *The Searching Dead*, *Born to the Dark* and *The Way of the Worm*.

Bernard Capes
The Thing in the Forest
(Originally Published in *The Fabulists*, 1915)
Bernard Capes (1854–1918) was born in London, England, and was one of eleven children. He was a very prolific writer and published over forty books, including romances, ghost stories, poetry, and history. He won a prize offered by the Chicago Record in 1898 for his story *The Lake of Wine*. He died in 1918 during the Spanish flu epidemic and a memorial plaque was placed in Winchester Cathedral (where he lived for his last years).

Catherine Cavendish
Dance, Mephisto
(First Publication)
Cat is the author of supernatural, ghostly and Gothic suspense novels and short story collections, including: *The Stones of Landane, Those Who Dwell in Mordenhyrst Hall, The After-Death of Caroline Rand, Dark Observation, In Darkness, Shadows Breathe, The Garden of Bewitchment, The Haunting of Henderson Close* and much more. She finds inspiration in haunted places and wandering around prehistoric stone circles and historic houses. Her home is in Southport, England with her longsuffering husband and black cat (who remembers that her species used to be worshipped in ancient Egypt and sees no reason why that practice should not continue).

Marie de France
The Lay of the Were-Wolf
(Originally Published in *French Mediaeval Romances from the Lays of Marie de France*, translated by Eugene Mason, 1911)
Little is known of Marie de France (c. 1150–c. 1215) except that she does appear to have been French by birth but to have spent much of her adult life in England at the court of Henry II. She won renown for her 'lays' – narrative poems of courtly love. 'The Lay of the Were-Wolf' is one of these, the knight's magical transformation a plot device in a tale of romance which exhibits little interest in the preoccupations of modern horror. If anything, even less is known of Eugene Mason except that he was a translator of medieval French literature, active in the early twentieth century.

E.C. Dorgan
Rougarou Moon
(Originally Published in *Pulp Literature*, December 2023 (Issue No. 41, Winter 2024), under the title 'Moon Eater')
E.C. Dorgan writes weird fiction and horror stories on Treaty 6 territory near Edmonton, Canada. Her short fiction appears in anthologies such as *Northern Nights* (Undertow Publications) and *Afterlives: The Year's Best Death Fiction* (Psychopomp), and in magazines such as *Gamut, Augur*, and *Reckoning*. In 2024, Writer's Trust Canada named her a 'Rising Star'. She is a member of the Métis Nation of Alberta and she is currently working on her first novel.

Arthur Conan Doyle
A Pastoral Horror
(Originally Published in *The People*, 1890)
Arthur Conan Doyle (1859–1930) was born in Edinburgh, Scotland. As a medical student Doyle was so impressed by his professor's powers of deduction that he was inspired to create the much-loved figure Sherlock Holmes. However, he became increasingly interested in spiritualism and the supernatural, leaving him keen to explore fantastical elements in his stories.

Eugene Field
The Werewolf
(Originally Published in *Second Book of Tales*, 1896)
Born in St Louis, Missouri, then after his mother's death brought up by an aunt in Massachusetts, Eugene Field (1850–95) failed to settle as a student – or, subsequently, as an actor or a lawyer. His maverick mind finally found its place as a humorous columnist with the *Chicago Daily*

News, and he had found wide recognition as a wit before he published his first book of children's poems in 1879 and became known as the 'Poet of Childhood'. He remained wide-ranging in his interests, though, and also wrote works with a gothic sensibility.

Roy Graham
We Are Not the Wolf
(First Publication)
Roy Graham is a writer from New York and graduate of the Rutgers-Camden MFA program and the Viable Paradise class of 2022. His nonfiction has been featured in *Rolling Stone*, *Playboy*, and *Motherboard*. He is currently a story lead at Wizards of the Coast. He is represented by Arley Sorg, at KT literary.

Maria Haskins
Margaery the Wolf
(Originally Published in *See the Elephant Magazine #4*, 2018)
Maria Haskins is a Swedish-Canadian writer of speculative fiction. Currently, she's located just outside Vancouver with two kids, a husband, a snake, several noisy birds, and a very large black dog. Her work is available in the short story collections *Wolves & Girls* (2023, Brain Jar Press) and *Six Dreams About the Train* (2021, Trepidatio Publishing). She is an Aurora Awards nominee and an Ignyte Awards nominee. Maria's work has appeared in several publications and anthologies, including *Best Horror of the Year*, *Nightmare*, *Lightspeed*, *The Deadlands*, *Black Static*, *Shimmer*, *Beneath Ceaseless Skies*, and elsewhere.

Clemence Housman
The Were-Wolf
(Originally Published in *Atalanta*, December 1890; later published as a standalone novel in 1896)
Sister of scholar-poet A.E. Housman and the writer and illustrator Laurence Housman, Clemence Housman (1861–1955) was born in Bromsgrove, Worcestershire. Like Laurence, she had an artistic bent and trained as a wood-engraver. She also shared his commitment to the cause of Votes for Women: together they founded the 'Suffrage Atelier', which made banners and designed leaflets for the movement. The first of three novels – all works of fantasy, with an underlying Christian theme – was *The Were-Wolf*, praised by H.P. Lovecraft.

Robert E. Howard
In the Forest of Villefére
(Originally Published in *Weird Tales*, August 1925)
Robert Ervin Howard (1906–36) was born in Peaster, Texas. He is responsible for forming the subgenre within fantasy known as 'Sword and Sorcery', establishing him as a pulp fiction writer. Being a very intellectual and athletic man, Howard wrote within the genres of westerns, boxing, historical and horror fiction as well. Howard will perhaps always be known best for his association with the pulp magazine *Weird Tales*, in which he published many tales of a horror and fantasy nature. As well as Conan the Barbarian, Howard also created the character Kull of Atlantis, whose first appearance in a published story was in 'The Shadow Kingdom'.

Joseph Jacobs
Morraha
(Originally Published in *More Celtic Fairy Tales*, 1895)

Born to a British-Jewish family in Sydney, New South Wales, Joseph Jacobs (1854–1916) became a distinguished scholar of Jewish history and culture. But his first love was folklore: inspired by the achievements of the German Brothers Grimm, he wrote up some of the best-known English tales ('Jack and the Beanstalk', 'The Three Little Pigs', 'Goldilocks'...) as well as assembling important collections of Celtic stories (like 'The Sea-Maiden') and other myths from Europe, India and elsewhere.

Rebecca Jones-Howe
When It Happens
(Originally Published in *Dark Moon Digest Issue #41*, October 2020)
Rebecca Jones-Howe is the Filipino-Canadian author of *Ending in Ashes* and *Vile Men*. Her stories explore human sexuality, feminism, and social economics by blending elements of erotica, horror, transgression and satire into stories that evoke both dread and catharsis. She has published stories in *PANK*, *Dark Moon Digest*, *The New Black* and *Human Monsters*. Rebecca lives in Kamloops, British Columbia, with her husband and two children. She enjoys short walks through the thrift store, Danny McBride shows, and uses public transit. V.C. Andrews books are her guilty pleasure.

Dr. Ignácz Kúnos
Boy Beautiful, the Golden Apples, and the Were-Wolf
(Originally Published in *Turkish Fairy Tales and Folk Tales*, translated by Robert Nisbet Bain, 1901)
Born in eastern Hungary, Ignacz Kúnos (1860–1945) studied in Debrecen and then subsequently Budapest University to become one of the leading linguistics scholars of his day. His interest in the Turkish language expanded into a wider fascination with the ethnography and folk literature of Turkey. His skillset was of course very much like that of R. Nisbet Bain, whose translations of his Hungarian translations helped bring his work – and an appreciation of Turkish folklore more generally – to English readers.

Andrew Lang and Mrs. Lang
How William of Palermo Was Carried off by the Werwolf
(Originally Published in *The Red Romance Book*, 1921)
The White Wolf
(Originally Published in *The Grey Fairy Book*, 1900)
The Son of the Wolf Chief
(Originally Published in *The Strange Story Book by Mrs. Lang*, edited by Andrew Lang, 1913)
Scottish writer and critic Andrew Lang (1844–1912) was born and raised in Selkirk. In 1875 he married Leonora 'Nora' Blanche Alleyne (1851–1933), who would become his collaborator on many works. Although Lang worked variously as a historian, journalist, poet, and anthropologist, his greatest legacy has been his works on folklore, mythology, and religion. Among these are the *Fairy Books*, 25 volumes of folk and fairy tales published Lang published with his wife, including *The Arabian Nights Entertainments* (1898), their adaptation of the One Thousand Nights and a Night folk tales. While many volumes in the series list Lang alone as the editor, it was in fact Nora who translated and adapted these works. Lang later acknowledged his wife's significant contribution in the preface to *The Lilac Fairy Book* (1910), crediting almost all of the series to 'the work of Mrs. Lang', and later volumes also listed her as an author.

Andrew Lyall
The Feelings of Sheep
(Originally Published in *Lurking in the Dark: A HorrorTube Anthology*, 2022)

Andrew Lyall lives in the south of England with his wife and dog. He is a lifelong fan of horror, and while his body may be sitting at a desk in a 9–5 office job, his heart and mind belong to the works of Dario Argento and Edgar Allan Poe. He has written a horror short story collection, *17 Stories of Death and Desire*, a post-apocalyptic fairy tale novella, *The Well at the End of the World*, and is currently working on a horror novella inspired by Grimms' fairy tales and the life and crimes of Ed Gein.

Mark Patrick Lynch
When Sleeping Wolves Lie
(First Publication)
Mark Patrick Lynch was born and raised in West Yorkshire, England. His short stories, mainstream and genre, have appeared in various publications across the world, from Alfred Hitchcock's *Mystery Magazine* to *Zahir*. His latest novel is *Walking Horatio* and his latest collection is *Cardinal Points*. Say hi to him on Blue Sky if you like: @markpatricklynch.bsky.social, where he promises not to do the "I used to be a werewolf but I'm all right now – ooooh!" joke.

George MacDonald
The Gray Wolf
(Originally Published in *The Portent and Other Stories*, 1924)
George MacDonald (1824–1905) was a Scottish writer of non-fiction, poetry and general and fantasy fiction. His first novel, *David Elginbrod*, was published in 1863. He is best known for the fantasy novels *Phantastes* (1858), *The Princess and the Goblin* (1872), *At the Back of the North Wind* (1871), and *Lilith* (1895), as well as the fairy tales 'The Light Princess', 'The Golden Key', and 'The Wise Woman'. After a very successful career, which included a tour in the USA where he performed to great numbers for the time, MacDonald served as a mentor to Lewis Carroll. His influence over many modern fantasy writers, including C.S. Lewis who featured him as a character in his novel *The Great Divorce* (1945), led him to become very highly regarded. He is often referred to as the founding father of fantasy.

Clara MacGauffin
Skin Traders
(First Publication)
Clara MacGauffin lives in a big, old house in the middle of a Scandinavian forest, where deep snow blankets the winters, and summers blaze with heat. She is the author of 'Skin Traders', a dark tale of werewolves and humanity's primal nature. Her writing blends her background in historical fiction and academia with her passion for folklore and myth, creating haunting, atmospheric stories inspired by her surroundings and the ancient lore of her homeland.

Dr. Karen E. Macfarlane
Foreword
Karen E. Macfarlane is a Professor in the Department of English at Mount Saint Vincent University, Halifax, Canada. She is past president of the International Gothic Association and organised the association's 17th Biennial conference in 2024. She has published widely in Gothic studies, with a specific interest in monsters at the turns of centuries. Her recent publications include 'Where Have all the Monsters Gone?' (*Australasian Journal of Popular Culture*) and 'Creepy Little Girl' (*Gothic Studies*). She is has also published on zombies, post-humanism and technology, on reanimated mummies, and on haunted real estate.

Natasha Marshall
Madame Bisclavret
(First Publication)
Natasha Marshall is a writer born and raised just outside of New York City in northern New Jersey. A recent graduate of Rutgers University, she studied English, Spanish, and Creative Writing, and completed her honors thesis in Creative Writing. Her work typically centers around women's stories, environmental topics, and fantastical worlds. She also loves to find inspiration in fairy tales and historical works, particularly medieval literature. When she isn't writing, Natasha enjoys participating in theatre, adventuring outdoors, and spending time with her friends, family, and pets.

Sutherland Menzies
Hugues the Wer-Wolf
(Originally Published in *Victorian Ghost Stories*, 1933)
For such a prolific author of popular history and fantasy fiction, Sutherland Menzies remains remarkably unknown. There's a possibility this name was actually Elizabeth Stone (1803–81), who may have found the nom de plume convenient in keeping such sensationalist writings clearly separate from the more serious works of social history, feminist polemic and political fiction she published under own name.

F.A. Milne
Arthur and Gorlagon
(Originally Published in *Folk-Lore: A Quarterly Review from the Folklore Society, Volume 15*, 1904)
Francis ('Frank') Alexander Milne (1854–1930) was born in Barnet, northwest London. A lawyer, he shared the widespread interest of his late-Victorian age in Arthurian legend, and in folklore more widely. His work in this area brought him into contact with Alfred Nutt, who provided the notes when this story was published in the *Folk-Lore* journal. An eminent scholar of Arthurian Romance, Nutt had a special interest in its roots in Celtic myth. Though English by birth and background, he played a role in Ireland's Celtic Revival, helping to establish the Irish Texts Society in 1898.

William Morris & Eiríkur Magnússon
Sigmund, Sinfjotli and the Wolf Pelts from *The Story of the Volsungs*
(Originally Published in *The Story of the Volsungs*, 1888)
A love of all things medieval famously underpinned William Morris' (1834–96) vision – in arts and crafts, in politics and poetry. Less well known is the breadth of his interest in the Middle Ages and – for example – the passion with which he pursued his studies in (and translations from) Old Norse. He did so with the help of the Icelandic scholar Eiríkur Magnússon (1833–1913), who from 1862 was at the University of Cambridge. They worked together on this version of the Volsungs Saga, a text originally written in Icelandic (Old Norse) in the thirteenth century A.D.

Jim Moss
The Cage in the Forest
(First Publication)
Jim Moss is a playwright who dabbles in short stories. His work has been produced in London, Off-Broadway in New York, and all over the US. His short stories and plays have appeared in numerous anthologies including *Diabolical Plots, Smith and Kraus Best Monologues and Plays*, and Palm Circle Press. In 2018 his play *Tagged* won three awards: First place in Theatre

Odyssey's One-Act Play Festival in Sarasota, Best Lab Works Production at the Pittsburgh New Works Festival, and the British Theatre Challenge in London. He is a regular contributor to *Werewolf Magazine Reborn*.

James Musgrave
Fangs Fur Love
(First Publication)
James recently placed third in the 2024 Line of Advance Colonel Darren L. Wright Fiction Award for 'The Secret Garden', written by US Military Veterans. He also had his story 'Mulo' featured in a Bram Stoker Finalist anthology, and has two science fiction novels: *Life in 2050* has been completed and *Auschwitz Dancer* is looking for a publisher. Formerly an English and Literature professor for 25 years, James also served as Supervisor of Management Development at Caltech/JPL for five years. His work is influenced by J.K. Rowling, Stephen King, and Ramsey Campbell.

Jane Pentzer Myers
Bran, the Wolf-Dog
(Originally Published in *Stories of Enchantment*, 1901))
Ohio-born Myers (1852–1917) haunts the fantasy literature of her age, a tantalizing presence. Her stories, though widely taken up by magazines, have since been lost. A collection, *Stories of Enchantment*, came out in 1904. Though well-received, it remains her only published book. Like so many middle-class women of her age, Myers seems to have disappeared into her familial role: such creative time as she could carve out for herself was devoted to music. She turned to writing only when forced to stop playing by rheumatism in her forties.

Plangdi Neple
Happy Dancing Rejects
(First Publication)
Plangdi Neple is a Nigerian writer whose dark and fantastical tales have appeared in magazines such as *Anathema*, *Omenana*, and *FIYAH*. A lover of the weird and unnatural, his works draw inspiration from Nigerian myth, folklore and tradition. He is a co-recipient of the Milford 2024 Bursary, and a Voodoonauts 2024 Fellow. Find him at @plangdi_neple on Twitter (X) and @plangdineple.bsky.social on bluesky.

Aggie Novak
Danger from Wolves and Young Men
(First Publication)
Aggie lives with her wife by the beach in Australia, where she spends most of her time hiding from the sun and heat. She writes around studying for her pharmacy degree and entertaining her two dogs. She loves all kinds of speculative fiction and often draws inspiration from Slavic folklore and mythology. When not writing she can be found drinking tea and reading everything in sight. Her published works can be found in Hexagon, Flash Fiction Online and more! For the full list see aggienovak.com.

Rachel Nussbaum
Starved
(Originally Published in *More than a Monster*, Grendel Press, 2023)

Rachel Nussbaum is an author and artist from The Big Island of Hawaii. Her stories and poetry have been featured in many anthologies, including her novelette *Tunnel Vision*, published in *The Mammoth Book of Dieselpunk*, and short stories such as 'Adrift' (*Cosmic Horror Monthly* Issue #28) and 'You're Mine Now' (*Welcome to the Splatter Club III*). Her first novella, *We Rotted in the Bitterlands*, is available now from Mannison Press. Rachel currently resides in the Bay Area, where she enjoys drinking too much coffee, combing beaches and thrift stores for treasure, and exploring new places with her friends. She hopes to one day write and illustrate her own novels and comics.

Mara L. Pratt
Loke's Wolf
(Originally Published in *Legends of Norseland*, 1894)
US writer Mara Louise Pratt-Chadwick (1857–1921) was best known in her own day for her children's treatments of American history. Though at pains to distinguish between a clear-sighted and fair-minded love of country and an unreflecting bigotry, she came to be seen as her country's patriotic chronicler. Her eagerness to acknowledge the worth of other cultures comes out in the collections she made of myths and folktales from around the world.

Antoinette Ogden, from the French of Marcel Prévost
Solange, the Wolf-Girl
(Originally Published in *Christmas Stories from the French and Spanish*, 1892)
Along with a string of successful novels and plays, Parisian writer Marcel Prévost (1862–1941) produced reactionary polemics on girls' education, which he saw as essentially corruptive. It is no surprise, then, that this story sees a certain kinship connection between Solange and the Wolf – more so, perhaps, that she shows such humanity and courage. This story is only known in this translation by the American writer Antoinette Ogden, who included it in her collection of *Christmas Stories from the French and Spanish*.

George W.M. Reynolds
Wagner, the Wehr-Wolf
(Originally Published in 1848)
George W.M. Reynolds was born in 1814 in Sandwich, Kent. Although his guardian enrolled him in the Royal Military College, Reynolds rebelled and left England for France with his younger brother Edward in tow. In France, Reynolds worked in a Paris bookstore, and composed his first novel, *The Youthful Imposter* (1835). Reynolds was a prolific writer, publishing novels, short stories, and nonfiction articles. Reynolds would go on to write over twenty serialized novels, including *Wagner, the Wehr-Wolf* (1846–47), *The Coral Island* (1848–49) and *The Rye House Plot* (1853-54). His oeuvre included historical and gothic fiction, along with tales of adventure that frequently featured violence, gore, and licentious female characters.

Saki
The She-Wolf
(Originally Published in *Beasts and Super-Beats*, 1914)
Saki was the pen-name for Hector Hugh Munro (1870–1916). Born in British Burma, the son of an Inspector General of the Imperial Indian Police, Munro lost his mother early and was brought up by grandparents in England. He signed up for the Imperial Police himself, but was quickly

invalided home. At a loose end in London, he wrote for newspapers and magazines. The theory always was that his witty, but frequently macabre, short stories were just a way of supporting him as he worked on serious studies of Russian history and politics. In practice, they were to become the basis of both his contemporary and his enduring fame.

Natalie Shea
Curse of the Bayou
(First Publication)
Natalie Shea is a Master of English and creative writing and received her degree from Southern New Hampshire University. She is also an artist and holds a bachelor's degree in art education from Columbus State University. Natalie enjoys expressing herself through art and writing. Gothic horror, Southern folklore, and fairy tales fascinate and inspire her work. She resides in Cataula, Georgia, USA with her partner Jeffrey and daughter Bo Taylor.

Fyodor Sologub
The White Dog
(Originally Published in *The Old House and Other Tales*, translated from the Russian by John Cournos, 1916)
A tailor's son from St Petersburg, Sologub (1863–1927) is best known now as a Symbolist novelist. Peredonov, protagonist of his *The Petty Demon* (1907), a sadistic schoolmaster, struggling to stay afloat in a sea of his own pessimism, emblematized the mood of Russia in the years before the Revolution. Though a supporter of reform, Sologub fell foul of the Bolshevik censors. He sought permission for himself and his wife Anastasia Chebotarevskaya to leave the Soviet Union. After two years he secured it, but on the eve of their departure, in 1921, Anastasia committed suicide. He himself died six years later, in what was now Leningrad.

Eric Stenbock
The Other Side
(Originally Published in *The Spirit Lamp, Vol IV, No 2.*, 1893)
Though by birth a Swedish aristocrat, with estates both in southern Sweden and across the Baltic on Estonia's northern coast, Eric Stenbock (1860–95) was brought up an English gentleman. Only to become, on his arrival in Oxford, an aesthete, a convert first to Catholicism, then to Buddhism and ultimately to a decadent paganism which was clearly designed to shock. In the Wildean spirit of the time, his literary works were an extension of his self-presentation, which was self-consciously eccentric and macabre.

Clara Stroebe
The Werewolf
(Originally Published in *The Swedish Fairy Book*, translated by Frederick H. Martens, 1921)
Clara or Klara Stroebe (1887–1932) was a German author, born in Freiburg im Breisgau. She attended Heidelberg University in 1907, followed by Ludwig Maximillian University of Munich from 1909 to 1910. Stroebe gathered and edited a number of fairy tale collections, including *The Swedish Fairy Book* (1921) and *The Norwegian Fairy Book* (1922), among several others. These books were published as part of The Fairy Book series produced by the Frederick A. Stokes Company. Frederick H. Martens (1874–1932) was an American translator and music journalist. His translation work mainly consisted of books for children, and he worked several times with Clara to translate her collections of stories and fairy tales into English.

Alan Sullivan
The Eyes of Sebastien
(Originally Published in *The Popular Magazine*, January 20, 1925)
Best known for his 1935 novel *The Great Divide*, an epic account of the construction of the Canadian Pacific Railway, Alan Sullivan (1868–1947) started life in Montreal. Before he was two, however, he was taken to Chicago when his father, an Episcopal clergyman, was transferred there. After some years at school in Scotland, he trained in Toronto as a mining engineer: writing (poems, short stories, articles) began as a hobby but eventually took over.

Henry S. Whitehead
No Eye-Witnesses
(Originally Published in *Weird Tales*, August 1932)
Born in Elizabeth, New Jersey, into the upper middle class, Henry S. Whitehead (1882–1932) grew up to go to Harvard, and then take orders as an Episcopalian clergyman. By no means a conventional one, however. 'He has nothing of the musty cleric about him,' wrote an approving H.P. Lovecraft, who became a great friend and encouraged Whitehead's other vocation as a writer of fantasy and horror fiction – even collaborating with him in the writing of the short story 'Bothon'.

M.M. Williams
He Who Would Chase the Sun
(First Publication)
M.M. Williams is an author of Norse-inspired Fantasy novels and speculative short fiction. A native of the Pacific Northwest, she currently lives in Northern Utah with her spouse, toddler, and tyrannical tortoiseshell cat. She began writing fiction in 2018 while at university studying International Relations and Scandinavian Studies – and, to her keyboard's dismay, she hasn't been able to stop. When not writing or parenting, she can be found studying folklore and history, experimenting in the kitchen, or translating old handwritten documents.

Zez Wyatt
Mouths
(First Publication)
Zez (any pronouns) is a queer writer from San Francisco who takes himself altogether too seriously. They were a member of the 2023 Clarion Writers' Workshop, have degrees in linguistics and creative writing from the University of Chicago, and their work has previously appeared in *Augur Magazine*. When not writing upsetting little short stories, she likes to practice martial arts and keep elaborate lists of all the birds she's seen. He thinks fun is overrated and wants to be dropped into the ocean to become whalefall if he ever dies.

Wen Wen Yang
Worse than a Wolf
(Originally Published in *Cast of Wonders*, November 2024)
Wen Wen Yang is a Chinese American from the Bronx, New York. She graduated from Barnard College of Columbia University with a degree in English and creative writing. You can find her short fiction in *Fantasy Magazine*, *Apex*, *Cast of Wonders* and more. An up-to-date bibliography is on WenWenWrites.com.

FLAME TREE PUBLISHING
Epic, Dark, Thrilling & Gothic
New & Classic Writing

Flame Tree's Gothic Fantasy books offer a carefully curated series of new titles, each with combinations of original and classic writing:

A Dying Planet • African Ghost • Agents & Spies • Alien Invasion • Alternate History
American Gothic • Asian Ghost • Black Sci-Fi • Bodies in the Library • Chilling Crime
Chilling Ghost • Chilling Horror • Christmas Gothic • Compelling Science Fiction • Cosy Crime
Crime & Mystery • Detective Mysteries • Detective Thrillers • Dystopia Utopia • Endless Apocalypse
Epic Fantasy • First Peoples Shared Stories • Footsteps in the Dark • Haunted House
Heroic Fantasy • Hidden Realms • Immigrant Sci-Fi • Learning to be Human
Lost Atlantis • Lost Souls • Lost Worlds • Lovecraft Mythos • Moon Falling • Murder Mayhem
Pirates & Ghosts • Robots & AI • Science Fiction • Shadows on the Water • Spirits & Ghouls
Strange Lands • Sun Rising • Supernatural Horror • Swords & Steam
Terrifying Ghosts • Time Travel • Urban Crime • Weird Horror • Were Wolf

Also, new companion titles offer rich collections of classic fiction, myths and tales in the gothic fantasy tradition:

Charles Dickens Supernatural • George Orwell Visions of Dystopia • H.G. Wells • Lovecraft
Sherlock Holmes • Edgar Allan Poe • Bram Stoker Horror • Mary Shelley Horror
M.R. James Ghost Stories • Algernon Blackwood Horror Stories • Arthur Machen Horror Stories
William Hope Hodgson Horror Stories • Robert Louis Stevenson Collection • The Divine Comedy
The Age of Queen Victoria • Brothers Grimm Fairy Tales • Hans Christian Andersen Fairy Tales
Moby Dick • Alice's Adventures in Wonderland • King Arthur & The Knights of the Round Table
The Wonderful Wizard of Oz • Ramayana • The Odyssey and the Iliad • The Aeneid
Paradise Lost • The Decameron • Don Quixote • One Thousand and One Arabian Nights
Babylon & Sumer Myths & Tales • Persian Myths & Tales • African Myths & Tales
Celtic Myths & Tales • Greek Myths & Tales • Norse Myths & Tales • Chinese Myths & Tales
Japanese Myths & Tales • Native American Myths & Tales • Aztec Myths & Tales
Egyptian Myths & Tales • Irish Fairy Tales • Scottish Folk & Fairy Tales • Viking Folk & Fairy Tales
Heroes & Heroines Myths & Tales • Quests & Journeys Myths & Tales
Gods & Monsters Myths & Tales • Titans & Giants Myths & Tales
Beasts & Creatures Myths & Tales • Witches, Wizards, Seers & Healers Myths & Tales

Available from all good bookstores, worldwide, and online at
flametreepublishing.com

See our new fiction imprint
FLAME TREE PRESS | FICTION WITHOUT FRONTIERS
New and original writing in Horror, Crime, SF and Fantasy

And join our monthly newsletter with offers and more stories:
FLAME TREE FICTION NEWSLETTER
flametreepress.com

For our books, calendars, blog
and latest special offers please see:
flametreepublishing.com